# MAYHEM IN MARYLAND

# MAYHEM IN MARYLAND

THREE ROMANCE MYSTERIES

## CANDICE SPEARE

BARBOUR
PUBLISHING

Cover thumbnails:
Design by Kirk DouPonce, DogEared Design
Illustration by Jody Williams

Published by Barbour Publishing, Inc., P.O. Box 719, Uhrichsville, OH 44683, www. barbourbooks.com

*Our mission is to publish and distribute inspirational products offering exceptional value and biblical encouragement to the masses.*

ecpa Member of the
Evangelical Christian
Publishers Association

Printed in the United States of America.

# MURDER IN THE MILK CASE

# 1

Death wasn't normally on my mind in the grocery store parking lot. Today, however, my thoughts lingered on the untimely demise of our pet hamster. Not due to excessive amounts of grief but because I didn't have to remember to buy hamster food. Now I could concentrate on more important things—like milk.

After parking in front of the Shopper's Super Saver, I climbed from my SUV. A strong spring breeze whipped through my hair as I searched in vain for my grocery list. As usual, I had misplaced it. I tried to assemble another one in my head, but the sound of loud male voices distracted me.

I squinted in their direction. Next to a side entrance to the store, I saw Daryl Boyd, the assistant manager and an old high school acquaintance, in an intense conversation with a balding man in a blue sports jacket. Well, perhaps intense conversation wasn't an apt description. Both men's fists were balled at their sides. Daryl took a swipe at the other man, who ducked, just missing what would have been a whopping black eye. The last time I'd witnessed so much machismo had been between two fathers on the sidelines during a high school football game.

I shifted, trying to see more clearly. The men noticed me and stopped yelling. My own temper flared when I realized the identity of the man in the sports coat: Jim Bob Jenkins, the pharmacist. Today was supposed to be his day off, which was one reason I'd picked this morning to shop. He stared at me, hands on hips, then marched back inside, followed closely by Daryl, who had started yelling again.

I leaned against the SUV, asking God to help me fight my warring emotions. The good Trish against the bad Trish. Truthfully, there's nothing I like better than a fight—something I'd been known to participate in myself when I was young, much to my parents' chagrin. I was a true rough-and-ready redneck tomboy. Underneath, I guess I still am. And I especially like fights when the bad guy gets what's coming to him. That's what made my conflict of conscience so hard today. And why I needed to pray. As far as I was concerned, Jim Bob deserved to be decked. I wanted to do it myself when, during a quarrel over a prescription, he'd hissed a threat in my ear about something in the past. I didn't believe he'd meant it—until he'd come by the office the next Friday and reminded me. I got mad and yelled at him. I told him he was wrong. He smirked and said he'd be back after I had time to reconsider what he'd said.

Right now, I wanted to go home, but I needed to shop because today was my day off. With one more glance at the door where the men had disappeared, I headed for the store. At least customers were sparse on a Monday morning, which made shopping easier. I grabbed my cart, passing through the Easter displays, trying to ignore the dread in my stomach that I might see Jim Bob. After putting a couple of impulsive candy purchases in my cart, I headed for the deli to get some coffee, one of my favorite parts of shopping.

Unfortunately, when I got there, the self-serve pump thermoses that normally held my favorite beverage were nowhere in sight. And no one was in the deli. I tapped my fingers on the glass counter, wondering why they didn't have a little bell I could bang in frustration. Meats, cheeses, and salads were still covered. Opaque plastic covered the huge slicing machines, and several knives lay next to the sink.

"Hello?" I yelled.

"Trish?"

I turned around and saw Daryl there in his red jacket, holding a hammer. His brown hair was slightly askew, probably from his run-in with Jim Bob.

"Hi, Daryl. I need coffee bad."

"We had two deli employees call in sick. Stomach bug. They're working on getting someone else in here." He sighed. "This hasn't been a good morning."

"No, I guess not," I said. "I saw you in the parking lot."

His face darkened. "No one has had any peace since that man—"

"Daryl? Oh, hey, Trish."

We both turned. Lee Ann Snyder stood in the doorway between the back room and the deli, her black hair pulled back in a ponytail. She was younger than me by two years. Back when we'd both been in 4-H, I'd taken her under my wing. "We gonna get some work done today?" she asked. "Frank is hyperventilating."

"Isn't that normal for Frank?" I'd known the store manager for years.

Daryl smirked and glanced at me. "Well, I can't disagree, but anyway, I'm sorry about the deli. We'll have somebody here as soon as possible to get things up and running."

He said good-bye and went into the back of the store, followed by Lee Ann, who gave me a backward wave. With time marching on, I decided not to wait. Problem was, I had no grocery list. And without caffeine, I had no brain with which to think. That meant I'd have to guess what I needed. I mulled over the produce, finally settling on bananas, apples, potatoes, and a selection of salad fixings. Then I wheeled up and down the aisles, tossing in boxes and cans of stuff. Distracted only once by the books and magazines, I selected several. I love magazines with recipes in them.

At that point, I had to use the ladies' room. I didn't want to. Unlike some stores that have official customer restrooms, these are in the bowels of the building, reached only by going through two thick, swinging doors next to the meat case, then into a back room. I parked my cart and proceeded to the back, following a winding path between towering piles of cartons and cases. I didn't like being back there even when it was well lit, but today the lights were dim.

As I hurried along, clicks from my shoe heels echoed in the cavernous space, and I had visions of scary monsters from B movies slipping out from behind boxes and stealthily dogging my steps. Monsters are the only things that frighten me, and that was my fault. When I was a teenager, I'd watched every horror flick known to man—unbeknownst to my poor parents who struggled to keep me in line. Every frame of those films was etched in my memory, ready to leap to the forefront at the slightest opportunity. Like right now. Only the distant sound of human voices kept my palms from sweating.

The beige-, brown-, and white-tiled bathroom was too warm and smelled of bleach and heavy-duty floral room deodorizer. While I was in the stall, the bathroom door opened, but no one came in. When I was done, I quickly washed my hands and rushed out the door, back into the storeroom. I heard a bang behind me, jumped, and turned, half expecting to see a slavering beast straight from my movie-fed imagination. But all I saw was a glimpse of red, followed by a whisper of a sound I couldn't identify. Then nothing. I whirled around and hurried on, ignoring the bristling of hair on my neck and the feeling that I was being watched.

When I reached the double doors, they were moving on their hinges as if someone else had just passed through them. With relief, I pushed them open and saw a red-jacketed man hurrying up a store aisle. I'd recognize that Jack Sprat body anywhere. Frank Gaines, the store manager, otherwise known as "Dudley Do-It-All-Right," so named in grade school after the Canadian Mounties cartoon character Dudley Do-Right. Seeing him made everything feel okay again. Frank was annoying and obnoxious, but he wasn't a monster.

I grabbed my cart and hurried to finish shopping, hoping I wouldn't run into Jim Bob. Meat was next. As I stood pondering hamburger, I glanced through the glass windows into the meat-cutting room. A door to the room opened, and Lee Ann walked in. She looked up, saw me, and gave me a tepid wave. This year, we'd seen more of each other. Her daughter, Julie, was my stepdaughter's best friend. I smiled and proceeded to choose meat that I hoped I didn't have at home in the freezer. Then I hurried on to the milk case. There I opened the glass door, grabbed three gallons, and turned to leave, but the hand behind the milk had already caught my eye. It just took a minute to move along my optic nerves to my brain.

*No way*, I told myself as I peered back into the dairy case. There couldn't possibly be a hand behind the 2 percent milk. Surely this was a hallucination. I blinked. Twice.

Nope. Not a hallucination. A hand lay in the back of the same slot from which I'd pulled the milk. It had to be a joke. Maybe some kids had put it there.

I felt the hand and knew right away it wasn't rubber. I don't know how I knew. Reaching out and touching someone has a whole new meaning for me now. The closest I've come to dead people is reading mystery books and viewing a weekly forensic show while I fold laundry.

I felt nauseated but pulled out a few gallons of regular milk that obscured my view. I stuck my head in the dairy case for a closer look, and the cold metal racks bit into my chest. Chilly air assailed my face, temporarily removing the nausea. A little voice in the recesses of my mind screamed that a normal woman would immediately call for help. Not me. I had to investigate.

Sure enough. The hand was attached to an arm.

It made sense in a macabre way. There was no blood on the hand, which there would have been had it been separated from its arm. At least if it were fresh. I guess.

I squinted to see into the cold room behind the dairy case. In my peripheral vision, I thought I saw a flash of red, but the realization that the arm was attached to a man's body distracted me. He was sprawled over a six-wheeled cart, positioned in a way that would be terribly uncomfortable for someone alive. A familiar bald head dangled, facing away from me, and a large knife protruded from his white-shirt-clad stomach.

I had run into Jim Bob, all right. But I doubted I'd ever run into him again.

I averted my eyes, feeling a sense of unreality. The nausea returned with a vengeance. About that time, I sensed a presence behind me—mostly from all the noise he made clearing his throat. I guess I did look pretty strange with my upper body stuffed in the dairy case and my derriere sticking out in the aisle.

"Ma'am, may I help you?"

I jerked my head out so quickly I hit it on the rack. When I turned, Frank Gaines was staring at me with a puzzled look on his face.

"Trish. I didn't recognize you. What in the world are you doing?"

"Hi, Dud—Frank." I swallowed hard, grateful that I hadn't had coffee at the deli. "Did you know Jim Bob Jenkins is in the milk case?" I glanced back where I'd seen the pharmacist, and then once again faced Frank.

"Excuse me?" Frank managed to look gallant and disbelieving at the same time.

"Jim Bob is in the milk case," I repeated.

"I'm sorry," he said in the same calm tone that annoyed me when we were in school together. "I must have misunderstood you." He smiled and nodded, as though we shared a joke. "I thought you said that Jim Bob Jenkins is in the milk case."

"I did."

"You did?"

"I did." I turned to peer into the case one more time on the off chance that I was delirious. I wasn't.

"That's really not funny, Trish. You shouldn't joke about things like that." He shook his head as if I were a wayward child.

I turned back to him, wanting to slap him. "I am not joking. Jim Bob is in the milk case. With a knife in his stomach." I said the words very slowly, as I do with my younger stepson, Charlie.

It was as if someone pushed a button and turned Frank on. His perfect, plastic manager look disappeared, and a series of expressions crossed his face, the likes of which I'd never seen there before. Each muscle in his face twitched. He pushed me out of the way to look and stuck his head in the racks, messing up his perfect hair. Then he promptly fell to the floor in a dead faint.

---

An hour later, I sat on an orange plastic chair in the employee lunchroom, twisting my hands in my lap. The police left me alone for a moment, no doubt to gear up for more questions. I'd called Max, my husband, who was in the midst of a meeting two hours away. He said he would leave as soon as possible. He reminded me that he played baseball with the detective who was questioning me and expected I'd be treated well. I'd seen the detective around myself, but never in a situation like this. Max sounded slightly annoyed with me. At least I wasn't calling from the emergency room—a place I ended up more times than I like to admit, after doing things that a woman my age probably shouldn't—like skateboarding.

The pungent odor of old coffee baking in a carafe in a little kitchenlike corner of the room mixed with the more pleasant smell of popcorn. I glanced around the blue-walled room for what seemed like the millionth time. A pile of certificate frames lay stacked on the gray counter, along with an open toolbox, one with molded indentations for each tool. I loved tools and wanted to see exactly what was there, but several deputies in uniforms, plus the detective, whose last name was Scott, had ordered me to sit and stay. They had isolated a number of people in different locations, and I was sure they meant every word they said.

I crossed my legs and wondered how long it would take for word to get out to the general population of Four Oaks that Trish Cunningham, aka, the woman who is always in trouble, had found a body. And not just any body. Jim Bob Jenkins, the pharmacist. Murdered. With a knife in his gut.

My stomach turned over. In an effort to forget the dead man, I turned my attention again to the tools. The hammer was missing. I wondered if that was the one that Daryl had been carrying. I paused midthought and planted both feet on the floor. Had I told the detective about the hammer? I wasn't sure. Did it matter? And then there were the knives next to the sink in the deli. Had I mentioned those? The events of the morning had taken on a dreamlike quality, melting together in a collage of scenes that had no particular order. Was there anything else I hadn't told him?

I heard footsteps outside the door. A deputy stepped into the room. He resembled Santa Claus, minus the beard, but I knew from speaking with him earlier that he was a hostile alien impersonating the merry Christmas elf.

"Mrs. Cunningham, Detective Scott wants to talk to you again. He'll be here in a moment."

"Okay." I bit my lip. I wasn't feeling well. I was tired. I just wanted to go home.

He stood by the door, arms clasped in front of him, studying me as if I were a splotch of something unpleasant on a microscope slide.

After two seconds, the silence was unbearable.

I met his gaze head-on. "So, are you guys done yet?"

He averted his eyes. "No, ma'am."

I frowned at him. "Well, what all do you have to do? I mean, how long does this take, anyway? Is it like hours or all day or what? I want to go home. Sammie, my daughter, is in kindergarten. She'll be home at lunchtime."

His bushy eyebrows edged up his forehead as his glance swept over me. "Um, well, I understand, ma'am, but we have to investigate 'til we're satisfied. You can go home when Detective Scott says you can."

"Well, I should call my car pool partner. I don't want Sammie dropped off if I'm not there." I crossed my legs again. "Is this like one of those forensic shows where crime-scene cops crawl all over the place with chemicals and cameras and stuff? Using tweezers and tape? And what about Jim Bob, er, the body, uh, the corpse. Who takes care of him? Is there a morgue van that carries him—the body—away?"

"Everything's under control, ma'am," the deputy mumbled.

"What does that mean?" I asked.

He shook his head slightly. "Just what I said."

"Oh." I sighed. "I get it. You can't tell me anything. Like on television. Everyone's a suspect until proven innocent. I found the murdered man. I'm at the top of the list. Hey, I've watched reruns of *Columbo* and *Murder She Wrote*. I know how it is."

His mouth opened and closed a few times, but he was spared answering by the entrance of Detective Eric Scott, who wore a suit. While he wasn't an alien, the detective had lost any sense of humor he might have had, and I had yet to see him smile.

After glancing at me, the detective turned to Santa Cop. "Fletcher? Everything okay here?"

Did he think I was going to threaten the deputy with bodily harm? All one hundred pounds of me? Or did he think I had suddenly confessed to murdering Jim Bob? I eyed Santa Cop who eyed me.

"Things are fine, Sarge," he said.

"Good." Detective Scott turned his enigmatic gaze on me. "Mrs. Cunningham, I'd like to go over your statement again, if you don't mind."

And if I did mind, would I be hauled off to jail? Feeling irritable, I wondered if imprisonment would be a better alternative than answering a million questions. I decided *No* and nodded. "Fine. Go ahead."

"Please tell me again what you did from the time you arrived in the parking lot."

I proceeded to do so. They were checking their notes. When I got to the part about having to use the bathroom, both men jerked their heads up and stared at me.

Detective Scott's lips narrowed. "Mrs. Cunningham, you said nothing about this earlier."

"I didn't?" I tried to remember. "Well, it's all very confusing. I mean, I had no list and I didn't have any coffee."

"What?" the detective asked.

I shook my head and stared at the ceiling, trying to think. "Well, I really don't know what to say. There were the knives in the deli. And Daryl's hammer." Was there anything else I'd forgotten? I met both their gazes. "Did I tell you about those things?"

I had never experienced stares and vibes quite like those emanating from the two officers who stood across the room from me. I felt much worse than something icky on a microscope slide—more like a butterfly pinned alive on a display board.

Detective Scott slapped his notebook shut. "Mrs. Cunningham, we need to continue this interview at the sheriff's office."

My mouth fell open. The sheriff's office? I shivered, feeling like I'd been dropped into a play where all the cast members knew their parts but me.

Detective Scott noticed. His expression softened a fraction. "This is just normal procedure, ma'am. We'll drive you. And while you're there, I'll see to it that you speak to a victim advocate."

Before I could ask who that was, he had turned to the deputy.

"Fletcher, get her ready to go downtown. You can take her. Get her whatever she needs."

"You got it, Sarge."

Detective Scott left the room. Fletcher and I exchanged glances. For just a second, I thought maybe I saw a glimpse of compassion in his eyes. Then he motioned at the table.

"Grab your purse, Mrs. Cunningham. I'll show you to my car."

I snatched up my purse and hung on to it like it was a life preserver.

At the sheriff's office, Fletcher escorted me into a room barren of anything but a table and chairs for my first-ever police interview. He seemed resigned to my chatter, which is always worse when I'm nervous. He got me a cold bottle of water, and while I yammered on, he kept eyeing me when he thought I wasn't looking at him. That encouraged me to keep on talking, although after I called him Deputy Fletcher several times, he informed me that he was a corporal, not a deputy. When I asked his permission to make a phone call to arrange for Sammie to be taken care of, he agreed with alacrity, probably relieved that I'd be babbling at someone else.

That was the extent of our conversation because while I was on my cell phone, a well-dressed, proper young woman walked into the room. I hung up, and Corporal Fletcher introduced her as the victim advocate; then he left. For some reason, I found myself wanting the big man to stay. Maybe it was one of those captor/captive brainwashing things that happens to kidnapping victims. He'd been nice to me, so I felt pathetically grateful.

The advocate seemed very concerned about my well-being, asking me about my distressing experience and assuring me that she would do whatever she could to help me through this difficult time. "After all," she said, "finding a body is very, very disturbing."

No joke. I nodded and smiled as she spoke, only responding with yep or nope when I had to. Call me suspicious, but I didn't believe that she was on my side. In fact, I wanted Corporal Fletcher to come back. At least he was obvious about how he felt.

When she left, Detective Scott joined me. He greeted me with a polite, professional smile, inquiring after my well-being. I didn't bother to tell him that my well-being would be better if I never saw him or another law-enforcement officer again the rest of my life. He informed me that our interview would be taped. Then, question by question, he grilled me. Not a moment of my time at the store was left out. He even wanted to know what I'd done in the bathroom. I laughed. My first good chuckle of the day. He wasn't amused.

When we were finished and I had signed my official statement, Detective Scott wanted someone to drive me straight home. I assured him I was going to be okay. I just wanted someone to take me back to my SUV, which was still in the grocery-store parking lot. He frowned at me. I wasn't sure why. Worry? Or maybe

14

suspicion because I wasn't collapsed in an emotional heap? Now that I thought about it, when I made that unfortunate run to the ladies' room, I could have stabbed Jim Bob. And I suppose that my own reaction, or lack thereof, when I found Jim Bob could be a sign of guilt. I hadn't fainted like Frank. Did Detective Scott think an innocent woman would have overreacted and at least screamed? The thing he didn't know was that I'd been raised on a farm. Though finding a dead person is distressing, death doesn't surprise me like it might someone who's never dragged a dead cow from a field on a chain behind a tractor.

A young, clean-cut deputy drove me back to the store. He waited until I unlocked my van before he took off. While I fumbled with my key in the ignition, I heard a tap on my window and looked up. Frank Gaines stood there. I hadn't realized he'd returned. He'd been taken to the sheriff's office for an interview, too, and crime-scene people closed the store pending collection of evidence.

I rolled down the window. His crisp, red jacket, complete with a bright yellow store logo, looked garish in the sunlight.

"What did you tell them?" he demanded, not wasting a breath on civilities.

"Hello, Frank," I said. "How are you?"

He snorted. "How do you think I'm doing? What a stupid question. Anyway, what did they ask you?"

Frank and I had had some confrontations when we were kids because of his obnoxious personality. So I decided if he was going to be unpleasant right now, I would be, too. Not the godly response, but I was past irritable and into serious grumpiness. I wanted to annoy someone. I stared at him with a purposefully vacuous, dumb-blond look. "They who?"

The muscles in his jaw worked, and a red flush crawled from his neck to his cheeks like a rash. That concerned me. I didn't want him to die of a coronary. All we needed was another body at the Shopper's Super Saver.

"Oh, you must mean the cops?" I asked innocently.

He glared down at me. "Who else?"

Even if I were going to tell him, which I wasn't, my brain had shut down. I'd be lucky to find my way home, let alone speak coherently.

"Well?" he asked impatiently, glancing at the squad cars still parked in the lot. "I don't know."

"What?" He stared at me, looking ready to explode. "How can you not know?"

Would it be possible to carry on a whole conversation with one-syllable words?

Tiredness enveloped me like the proverbial shroud. I didn't have the energy to continue messing with his head, so I dropped my stupid act. "Look, Frank, I'm tired and crabby. I can't think. I'm liable to say something I don't want to if I continue talking. I'm positive they didn't ask me anything they didn't ask you." I turned the key in the ignition.

He gripped my windowsill. "Can't you just—"

"No, I can't," I snapped. I wished he would go away. Would I be hauled to the sheriff's office again if I ran over his toes?

He didn't move. I looked up at his face. The redness had subsided, and his expression was smirky, a look that I recognized from years of attending school with him—starting with kindergarten. I call it his tattletale face. His biggest claim to fame had been telling on people. Mostly for purposes of payback. A lot of people outgrow their juvenile behavior. Not Frank.

He leaned down, and I could see the hairs in his nose. "You had a huge fight with Jim Bob last week, remember?"

I glared at him. "I wouldn't call it huge."

Frank laughed, but not pleasantly. "You threatened to get his license as a pharmacist taken away. Everyone heard you within a mile radius."

"Yeah? And so what, anyway?" Oh, that sounded adult. I guess in terms of outgrowing juvenile behavior, I couldn't throw stones. Still, he had a point. I had argued with Jim Bob. And I hadn't told Detective Scott about it.

"Didn't Jim Bob see you again after that?"

I blinked. How did Frank know that? Then I wanted to kick myself. His smirk grew. He knew he'd scored a hit. "The cops need to know everything you know. For purposes of finding motivation for the killing. That's what they told me."

I doubted the cops told Frank anything. I shrugged, refusing to wilt under his implied threat even though I was close to hyperventilating. Motivation was a word that scared me. Mostly because I had plenty of it.

He smirked again and backed up, giving me a tiny little wave before he turned around and walked away. I asked the Lord to forgive me even while I thought how nice it would be to plant a foot hard on Frank's behind. As I pulled from the parking lot, I knew I hadn't heard the last of my unfortunate encounters with Jim Bob.

---

I slouched on the overstuffed, denim-covered couch in the family room. Max had called. I whined about how I'd wasted all that time shopping and didn't even get to bring my groceries home. He listened sympathetically and promised to pick up some milk.

I shivered and yanked a crocheted afghan from the back of the couch and wrapped myself up in it. Sammie was in her bedroom with enough soda, potato chips, and chocolate chip cookies to put a healthy person in a diabetic coma. I'd done that out of desperation to be alone. Poor kid would be bouncing off the walls in an hour.

When I'd picked her up from my car pool partner's house on the way home, the woman handed me Sammie's backpack and said in a stage whisper, "I didn't tell her about what's happening, but I'm going to tell my kids tonight. I'm sure it'll be all over the kindergarten class and the school tomorrow." No doubt. I was sure that my latest misfortune would be all over Four Oaks by dinnertime.

My Bible and the cordless phone sat on the end table, along with my latest mystery from the library. I glanced at them but didn't think I'd be able to concentrate because my mind was running amok. I thought about calling Abbie, my best friend, but I didn't want to talk. I had some serious thinking to do. Finding a murdered man was bad. But worse, I had known him and disliked him. In fact, if I were honest with myself and God, I felt a sense of relief that Jim Bob wouldn't be around to threaten me anymore. Now how could I reconcile that feeling with what should be grief that a man had died?

I reached for my Bible, running my fingers over the worn leather cover. It was my lifeline. At my most helpless times, just holding it gave me comfort. But that didn't happen today. The guilt was too strong. I was thinking hateful thoughts, reduced to quibbling with Frank, and I hadn't told Detective Scott about my argument with Jim Bob. That alone would give me enough motivation to be at the top of his suspect list. Even Max didn't know, because I needed to find out if what Jim Bob had said was true.

The phone rang. Unfortunately, the caller was my mother. I love my mother, but I like to be prepared for the conversational assaults that often occur when we talk.

"Hi, Ma." My voice was tense, and I tried to relax.

"Well, I would have thought you would call me first," she said. "I had to hear all the gory details from Gail's sister's neighbor. After all I've been through with you, and this is how you repay me? By not telling me things?"

"Sorry." I stared at the ceiling. I tend to avoid telling my mother most anything because it's just too hard to deal with the aftermath. Questions, sarcasm, accusations. Still, I could tell she was worried about me. "I'm fine. I'm just not thinking clearly." And that wasn't the half of it.

"Well, I guess you have good reason to not think—for once. If I'd found a murdered person, I wouldn't think, either. I mean, the pictures left in your mind would—"

"Yep, I'm just fine," I said. "Sitting here on the couch."

"Where is Samantha?" she asked.

"In her room eating cookies and potato chips." My stomach growled, and I sat up quickly, an action I regretted. Spots in my vision made it difficult to hear my mother, an oddity for which I had no explanation.

"Cookies and potato chips? At the same time? In her room?"

I glanced at the clock. Three. "Yes."

"Well, I never! Do you do that all the time? Land sakes! That child will have clogged arteries before she's twenty if you keep that up."

This coming from a woman who sells doughnuts for a living. I braced myself for the onslaught of lecture number one thousand, three hundred, and fifty about How to Care for Children. While waiting for the tirade to end, I slowly made my way to the kitchen and heated up some coffee. Then I went to the pantry and reached behind the cans of baked beans where I'd hidden my emergency stash of chocolate. Finally, armed with a large dark-chocolate bar and a strong cup of coffee, I sat at my round, oak kitchen table with the phone resting between my head and shoulder, still listening to her with only partial attention. When my mother is on a rant, I only need to grunt now and then to keep up my end of the conversation.

". . .although I suppose the children are fine so far." She took a deep breath. "Was it really Jim Bob?"

For anyone who isn't used to her, my mother's machine-gun conversational techniques can cause mental whiplash. I've just learned to anticipate the rapid shifts in topic.

"Yep, it was Jim Bob." I stared at my coffee, trying not to remember the knife in his stomach.

"Brutally murdered?" she asked.

"Um. . .yes." *Is there any other way to be murdered?*

She clucked her tongue. "Well, I'm not surprised."

I wasn't, either, but I wondered just what my mother knew about him. I was sure that she didn't know he'd threatened me.

"Your name will be in the paper tomorrow, you know," she informed me.

I grunted. Relieved by the change of topic, I jammed another huge piece of chocolate in my mouth, followed by a gulp of coffee.

"Were you wearing nice clothes?"

"Why?" I asked with my mouth full. Isn't it enough that I always wear clean underwear because of her constant, dire warnings that I might be in a tragic accident and the rescue workers will see my underclothes?

"Why?" My mother's tone indicated I had lost my mind. "You can't be serious. Didn't someone take your picture?"

I licked my fingers. "Not that I know of." In my stomach, coffee met chocolate in what could only be called a pitched battle. "Look, Mom, I don't want to talk about it anymore. It's too gruesome. My stomach feels queasy."

"Of course it does. I'd be worried if it didn't. Finding someone you know like that would be enough to make a normal person throw up."

I swallowed hard and ignored the implication that I wasn't normal.

"But you know what they say. This, too, shall pass. Besides, it could be worse, you know. It could have been—"

"I have to go," I said, before she explained in great detail what was worse

18

than finding Jim Bob Jenkins with a knife in him. Something like being arrested for his murder, for instance? "I'll talk to you tomorrow, okay?"

I hung up but didn't move. The last of the uneaten chocolate sat in the torn wrapper in front of me. I couldn't finish it while the rest laughed viciously at me from my stomach. That was an unexpected reaction to my favorite bad habit.

My new side-by-side, stainless steel refrigerator kicked on, and I looked toward it. The metal gleamed. I swallowed, reminded of the steel doors of the refrigerated units in morgues that I'd seen on television. I never paid close attention to the details when the shows aired. I wished I had. Where was the body from the dairy case right now? Had it begun to decay already? Was it stretched out on some cold, metal examining table with a masked and goggled doctor standing over it with a whirring—

"Mommy, how long before dead bodies smell?"

I choked on a mouthful of coffee and almost wrenched my neck turning around. Had Sammie already heard about her mother's megaexploits at the grocery store before I could tell her myself? Relief flooded through me when I saw that my precious youngest daughter held an elaborately decorated shoe box with our deceased hamster's name spelled out in glitter on the top.

"We can wait to bury Hammie tomorrow, but he might smell by then. Charlie says that soon the body will puff all up and turn black. Then beetles and flies—"

"We'll do it tonight after Daddy gets home," I said quickly, trying not to think about her description, which was all too real for me. "Did you wash your hands?"

"Uh-huh." She met my gaze. "It's okay if we wait."

I studied her face suspiciously. Was that hope in her eyes? Did she want to see the body puffed up and, well. . . Using all my self-control, I smiled. "We'll have the funeral tonight." I pulled her close to me while I avoided the box. I didn't feel like touching another dead body, even through cardboard.

"Okay." She sighed.

"Charlie can be a little gruesome," I said.

She nodded, her little mouth pursed, brows drawn into a frown. "Yeah, Charlie sees dead people."

I know from expert opinion—mine—that the challenge of following childhood conversational twists is the leading cause of brain-cell loss in mothers. Not to mention dealing with the issues said conversations reveal.

"Charlie—sees—what?" The slowness of my speech was an outward indication of the sluggishness of my mind. Had I just heard my sweet, Christian-school-educated daughter say what I thought she said about her Christian-school-educated brother?

Sam pulled away and put her empty hand on her mouth. "Oops. I shouldn't have told you."

Charlie has yet to learn that telling his younger sister anything is tantamount to sending a taped advertisement to the local radio station. Or telling his grandmother.

He had arrived home a couple of minutes ago. I glanced toward the doorway that led to the family room where he was watching television, his favorite activity after arguing. Dead people? I had to do something about this, but before I could try to think, the kitchen door flew open, banging against the yellow wall. Tommy, my seventeen-year-old stepson breezed in, followed by my stepdaughter, Karen.

Tommy grinned with a look so reminiscent of his father that I automatically smiled. "Way cool, Mom! You're a celebrity!"

Karen crossed her arms and stared at me, saying nothing. That wasn't surprising, given she was a moody fifteen-year-old, using up her daily store of friendly conversation on the telephone with Julie Snyder, Lee Ann's daughter.

Sam watched everyone with bright eyes, distracted from planning Hammie's funeral. I was sure her active mind was already mulling over all the possible reasons for her mother's sudden notoriety. She slipped a chubby hand into mine and put her mouth next to my ear. "Mommy, what is he talking about?"

Before I could answer, the back door opened again and in walked Max. His black hair, graying slightly at his temples, ruffled from the wind, gave him the casual appearance of a wealthy man just in from yachting—something his snooty mother claimed he'd do on a regular basis if it weren't for me. As far as she was concerned, I was too much of a redneck and too young to be a good wife for Max.

He put a small plastic bag on the counter.

Sammie ran to him. "Daddy! We're going to have a funeral!"

"Dad, did you hear the cool news about Mom and the body?" Tommy said.

Karen just stared at all of us in turn with her mouth quirked in a slight sneer.

Max fielded the questions and a physical assault on his knees by Sammie with his usual aplomb.

"That's why I'm home early." He picked Sammie up and hugged her.

"Dad, did you hear—" Tommy began.

"I heard." Max looked at me. "Did you start dinner yet, honey?"

"You mean you want to eat tonight?" I joked while I tried to remember what was in the freezer.

Tommy's body vibrated with the energy only teenage boys emanate. "Yeah, but did you—"

"Why don't all of you decide what kind of pizza you'd like, call in the order, and go pick it up?" Over Sammie's head, Max put his finger to his lips. Tommy's eyes widened, and he nodded. Max wanted to wait to tell Sammie about her mother's misadventures. He kissed Sam's cheek and put her down. Then he pulled out his wallet and handed Tommy some twenties. "Let's talk about everything when you get home. Oh, and grab Charlie, too. He's probably watching television."

"I don't want to go," Karen grumbled.

Max fixed her with a level stare. "Go anyway."

As the kids trooped from the kitchen, I met Max's gaze. He closed the distance between us before I could blink, reached out for my hands, and lifted me to my feet, enclosing me in a hug. The lingering crisp scent of the aftershave he'd put on that morning smelled good. For a moment, I tried to forget everything but the feel of his body against mine and his arms wrapped tightly around me.

"There is something to be said for the old days when a man could lock his wife away for safekeeping," he murmured in my hair.

"Very funny," I said into his shirt.

"I brought you something." He backed up, smiled, and went back to the counter for the bag, pulled out a little box, and handed it to me with a kiss. "I was saving this for Easter, but I know this was a hard day, so I want you to have it now."

I opened the box and found a tiny gold cross on a braided, gold chain. "Oh, Max, it's beautiful." I blinked back tears.

"It's to remind you of our first date."

We had our first date alone after church on Easter Sunday.

"Thank you, honey," I whispered. I pulled the delicate necklace from the box, thinking how much I didn't deserve the gift.

He helped me put it on. I turned around so he could see it. Then I looked up at him.

Worry creased his brow above his green eyes. "I sent all the kids away so we could talk. Are you sure you're okay?"

"Yes." I tried to ignore the feeling of apprehension in my stomach. Now that Jim Bob was dead, did I really have to say anything? Perhaps the past could stay in the past. I wrapped my arms around Max again and lifted my face. He kissed me, an activity that I usually enjoy more than just about anything else in the world. I almost succeeded in forgetting my day until I heard a gagging sound.

"Eeeww. Come on, you guys. Stop it."

Max and I reluctantly parted lips and turned. Charlie stood framed in the kitchen doorway, red hair stuck out at odd angles, and he had a fierce scowl on his face.

He stalked over to stand in front of us. "Why didn't you tell me about the grocery store? Mike just told me on the phone. This is important."

Max knelt in front of Charlie. "We're not going to talk about it right now. Go with your brother and sisters and pick up the pizza. We'll discuss it later."

"But, Dad."

Max stood. "Please."

Charlie's cheeks puffed up with all the words he wanted to say. Then he whirled on his heels and left the room.

My husband watched the doorway until he heard the front door slam. "Good. They're gone." He turned to me and studied my face. "You want to tell me about today?"

"Not really. I don't feel like talking about it." I had a feeling Max wanted to do more than listen. He probably had a few things he wanted to say, as well. I braced myself for his comments, which would be something along the line of "Why can't you stay out of trouble for one week?"

He shook his head. "You're sure? It's not like you not to talk."

How well he knew me—but I kept my lips zipped and nodded.

He sighed. "Of all the people in Four Oaks, why were you the one to find a body? In the milk case of all places?"

I'd been right. I stuck my chin in the air. "I didn't do it on purpose. And don't remind me of the milk case. I'll never be able to look at dairy products the same again."

"I'm sorry," he said.

I crossed my arms. "Well, at least I didn't get hurt. It's not as bad as when I tried to hog-tie that calf to prove I could, and then it kicked me. Or when I sprained my wrist skateboarding with Charlie, or the time I went rock climbing with Tommy and got stuck. Or. . ."

"Trish, honey," Max said softly.

"Yeah?"

"Please don't remind me. I worry about you as much as I worry about the kids."

I sighed in exasperation. "This isn't the same. It was someone else who got hurt." I paused. "Well, killed."

"You found him," he said.

"So you keep reminding me. Don't worry. It's over." I hoped.

He rubbed his temple. "Well, at least your part in this should be over, except that you might have to eventually go to trial or something to testify about what you saw. You should like that." He grinned slightly. He knows how much I enjoy drama and yelling.

But this time, I wasn't excited. I glanced at the floor. "Well, a trial could be fun." As long as I was a witness and not the accused.

He put his hands on my arms. "Baby, are you okay? You're not acting right."

"Yes." I wasn't quite truthful. Even the use of my pet name wasn't enough to make me feel better.

"Trish?" His concern was so evident in his furrowed forehead that I hugged him.

"Don't worry," I whispered in his ear. "It'll be okay. All's well that ends well. That's what my mother says."

"I hope so." He pulled me close. "I really, really hope so."

I did, too.

3

I woke to light shining brightly through the miniblinds on the windows. Max's side of the bed was empty. I looked at the clock. Eight in the morning. I never sleep that late.

I flung myself from the bed and ran to the bathroom. My stomach felt queasy. I hoped it was nerves and not the stomach bug from the store employees. I brushed my teeth and jerked on my fuzzy purple robe and matching slippers. Then I yanked the bedroom door open and hurled myself down the hallway— straight into Max.

He grabbed my shoulders to keep me from bouncing backward. "Hey! Take it easy."

"Why did you let me oversleep?" I gasped, frantically trying to get loose. "What about the children?"

"All taken care of," he said.

"Breakfast?" I stopped struggling, breathing heavily.

Max loosened his grip. "Fixed and finished."

"Car pool?" My heartbeat slowed.

"Took care of it. Honey, relax. Everything's under control. You needed the sleep."

I took a deep breath and tried to think of all the things I knew I had to remember. "Four Oaks Self-Storage?"

"We both took the morning off. I told you, everything's under control." He rubbed his hands up and down my arms. "You want something to eat?" He linked my arm in his and walked me downstairs to the kitchen.

"Okay." I wouldn't argue, although I didn't feel like eating. But I did want to read the paper. I wanted to see if my picture was in there and to make sure nothing had been said to incriminate me.

He went to the refrigerator. "Eggs?"

"No, thanks." I looked around for the newspaper. "My stomach feels weird this morning. How about toast and jelly?"

A note lay on the table next to the cordless phone. *Abbie and George called* and *Grandmom got a letter from Uncle Russ* were written in different scrawls.

I held it up. "What's all this?"

"Phone calls. Russ wrote his first letter from boot camp."

My little brother, in the Navy now. And inaccessible for weeks.

24

Max grabbed the bread from the bread box. "Abbie said she's coming over this afternoon. She's bringing coffee cake from your mother's shop."

My mother's coffee cake was famous, just like her doughnuts, and for good reason. And my heart warmed with pleasure at the thought of visiting with my best friend.

Max put bread in the toaster. "You sure this is all you want?"

"Yep." The morning paper lay folded on the chair where Max had been sitting. I reached over, grabbed it, and shook it open.

"I wish you wouldn't read that right now." Max was getting jelly from the refrigerator.

"I want to see if my name's in the paper," I mumbled.

The paper didn't have a picture of me, but there was a lengthy article about Jim Bob's murder. I had just begun to scan that when Max snatched it out from under me and placed my food on the table. I hadn't even seen him coming.

"Hey, you pushy man." I tried to grab it back.

"Pushy and overprotective. That's me." He grinned as he folded it and tucked it under his arm. "Maybe I am, but would you mind eating first? And would you consider reining in your inquisitive mind and just leaving the whole mess behind you?"

If only he knew that I couldn't. But before I could accuse him of chronic bossiness, as well as chauvinism, the phone rang.

I grabbed it. "Hello?"

"Mrs. C? This is Shirl."

Shirl managed the office at Four Oaks Self-Storage. She's so good at her job she never calls us at home unless something has happened.

"What's wrong?" I asked.

"That gate program isn't working again. People can't use their codes to get in. That kid Kevin who works on the weekends was having trouble, too."

I glanced at my husband who still held the paper under his arm. "You need to talk to Max."

Smiling inwardly, I shoved the phone into Max's hand. "It's Shirl." Then I snatched the paper from him.

As I smoothed it on the table, his voice rumbled in the background. I heard him say, "Just leave the gate open for now. I need to buy a new program anyway. Thank you for calling. Listen, I've got another call beeping in."

The article didn't say any more than I already knew. That was good as far as I was concerned.

The sound of Max's voice stopped. He put the phone on the table. I looked up. He was staring at me with a frown.

"What?" I asked.

"That was Eric Scott. He needs to talk to you."

I felt my heart sink to my toes, but I couldn't avoid Max's gaze. "What does he want?"

"For you to go to the sheriff's office for an interview." Max crossed his arms. "In an hour."

I glanced at the clock, feeling the weight of shame press in on me. I might not be guilty of anything as heinous as murder, but I was certainly guilty of keeping secrets.

"I have a bad feeling about this," Max murmured as he rubbed the bridge of his nose.

Me, too, and guilt made me irritable. I folded the paper and slapped it on the table. "I didn't find Jim Bob in the milk case on purpose."

"I know that, honey," Max said.

"And I didn't do it to embarrass your mother." Her kind didn't shop at the Shopper's Super Saver. Fortunately, my hoity-toity in-laws had just come back from a cruise the night before. Now they were in Florida and weren't likely to hear by phone about how their hayseed daughter-in-law was in trouble again, until at least after brunch when their equally hoity-toity friends would have finished the morning paper—I hoped.

He took a couple of deep breaths. "I could care less what my mother thinks. I'm worried about you. You're so impetuous I don't know what you're going to do next."

Technically that was true, but I didn't want to admit it. "So then, it's not a big problem, right?"

"Your impulsiveness or the murder?" he asked.

"The murder," I grumbled. "I understand exactly how you feel about the other issue."

He walked over and kissed my forehead. "No, you don't. One of the reasons I love you so much is your impulsive nature. For a control freak like me, it's a breath of fresh air. However, it can be frightening, too, especially when there's a dead body involved."

"But finding Jim Bob Jenkins wasn't anything impulsive on my part," I said. "I didn't put him there."

"I know, I know. I just wish you weren't involved in all this." Max sighed again. "Your toast is cold. I'll make you more while you get ready to go. Then I'll drive you down there. You can eat on the way. I hope this is the last we hear about Jim Bob's murder except in the news."

Me, too. But, as my mother would say, "If wishes were horses, beggars would ride."

⌐

Once again I was shown to an interview room, but Corporal Fletcher was nowhere in sight. As I sat down, Detective Scott arrived, alone. He sat near me, at the corner of my side of the table.

"Thank you for coming, Mrs. Cunningham." He pulled a pen and notebook from his pocket.

"You can call me Trish," I said.

He nodded and met my gaze with a slight smile. "Okay, Trish. How are you today?"

"Fine." I resisted the urge to twist my hands together in my lap.

"Can I get you anything?" he asked. "A drink?"

"No, thank you." I just wanted to get this over with.

"I'd like to ask you a few more questions, if I may." He tapped his pen on the table. "How well did you know Jim Bob Jenkins?"

I shrugged, glancing at the detective, then away. "He was the pharmacist at the store. His deceased wife used to be in the garden club with my mother."

*Tap, tap, tap, tap.*

"So, how well did you know him?" Detective Scott's body was taut.

I shrugged again. "Like I said, he was the pharmacist at the store. I mean, how well do you get to know someone like that? Of course I did hear things from my mother about his wife. She died suddenly."

He nodded and leaned toward me. "Did you have contact with him recently?"

I ground my teeth for just a second, knowing Frank had told on me. Perhaps avoidance would work. "I know what's going on. You're wondering if I've forgotten to tell you anything else."

*Tap, tap, tap, tap.*

"Yes. Like, did you have any contact with Jim Bob recently?" Detective Scott's eyes bore into mine.

He wasn't going to let this go. I finally heaved a sigh. "Oh, all right. Obviously, Dudley Do-It-All-Right already talked to you. He's the biggest pain in the whole world. I thought maybe he had changed, but no. Not at all." I put my elbows on the table. "I went to school with him, you know."

The detective's eyes had widened. "Dudley Do-It-All-Right?"

"Yes. Frank Gaines. We called him that in school after that perfect Canadian Mountie guy. Frank always thought he was so above everyone, and he's a tattletale of the worst kind. I beat him up in first grade. And then in third and sixth. He's had it in for me ever since."

"I see." Detective Scott coughed and shifted in his chair. "Let's get back to my question. Did you have contact with Jim Bob Jenkins lately?"

I glanced down at the table. The detective wasn't going to let me out of this. "Yes," I mumbled, rubbing my fingers on my knees.

"Where?" he asked.

"At the pharmacy." I met Detective Scott's gaze. "Jim Bob messed up Sammie's prescription. When I discovered the mistake, I was furious. He could kill her by being careless like that."

"And what did you say to him?" The detective's tone was mild, but his eyes were sharp, watching me like a bird of prey.

"I told him I was going to report him and get his license taken away."

"Mmm." He kept staring at me. "And then what happened?"

"We had a fight." I absolutely did not want to tell Detective Scott about my deep, dark secret.

"Can you tell me about that fight?" he asked.

I glanced at the table again. "Well, we sort of worked it all out after that."

"Worked it out?"

"He, uh, stopped arguing."

"He stopped arguing," Detective Scott repeated, his eyes narrowed.

"Yes. And Frank butted in and offered me a discount on my purchases. It was like he was protecting Jim Bob or something." I met Detective Scott's eyes defiantly. I refused to say anything about Jim Bob's threats until I knew if they had basis in fact.

"Is that all?" the detective asked.

"Well, I don't remember what I bought that day or anything." I crossed my arms. "Except that I should own stock in the store because I'm there so much. However, after this, I—"

"Anything else you remember? Anything you want to tell me?"

I shook my head.

Detective Scott stared at me for a moment more, then shut his notebook, tucked it in his pocket, and stood.

"Well, that will be all today. Thank you, Trish."

I felt off balance because he'd given up too easily. As I picked up my purse, I wondered why. He opened the door for me. As I walked out to the hall, I felt his eyes on my back.

"Trish?" he said behind me.

I turned. "Yes?"

"Is this yours?" He held my cell phone in his hand.

I glanced into my purse. No phone. "Yes."

As I took it from him, he met my eyes with a slight smile and assessing gaze. "I'll be in touch."

I involuntarily shivered. That sounded a great deal like a threat.

—

Max and I were standing at the front door in the process of a very nice good-bye.

He looked devastatingly handsome in a navy pinstripe suit that always distracted me. I ran his lapel through my fingers and wished for one whole day alone together without disruptions or the guilt I now carried.

After he thoroughly kissed me, he leaned down and picked up his briefcase. "Dad'll be home in a few days. Today I'm going to finalize plans with the architect for the new facility outside Baltimore."

Max and his father had big plans for a self-storage empire, although that was only one of their many business ventures. The fact that my in-laws were returning soon wasn't good news.

"Honey?"

I glanced up.

He brushed hair from my face. "What are you doing this afternoon?"

Was he checking up on my activities? "Well, I don't intend to find another body, if that's what you're worried about."

He inhaled. "That's not what I meant."

I relented. Inner turmoil was making me snappy. "I'm sorry. Abbie's coming over, remember? Then I'll do some bookkeeping since I didn't get to work today."

Sammie arrived as he was leaving, and they had a little powwow, apparently discussing the possible addition of another hamster to our family. She and I ate lunch together; then I got her settled in the family room, feeling guilty that I was entertaining my child with television. I could only imagine what my mother would say about that. Seemed lately that my life was one huge guilt trip.

As I made coffee in preparation for Abbie's visit, her shadow appeared at the back door, and I waved her in.

"Hey, thanks for taking a break from your writing."

"Hi, hon. No problem." She kissed my cheek and put a bag on the table. "Your mother says she never sees you anymore."

"She always says that." I pulled two mugs from the cupboard and placed them on the table.

Abbie laughed and slipped fluidly onto a chair, crossing her long legs at the ankles. The pink of her sweater shouldn't have looked good with her red hair, but on her, the effect was stunning. In her black jeans, she looked like one of the heroines in the novels she wrote. If I hadn't known her since kindergarten and loved her so much, I'd be rabidly jealous of her good looks.

"How is the book coming along?" I pulled the bag off the coffee cake. It smelled wonderful, as do all my mother's baked goods.

She laughed. "I'm at the point where my brain is fried. I needed a break."

"I can't wait to read it." I leaned against the counter. "Are you sure working at the health fair this Saturday won't be a problem for you?"

She shook her head. "Not at all. Another mental health respite. Besides, how could I break our yearly tradition?"

As I poured coffee, she watched me closely. "You okay? You look a little pale."

"Finding a body will do that." I put the carafe back on the coffeemaker and grabbed a knife from the drawer. The blade glittered in the sunlight that streamed through the kitchen windows. My mind flashed to Jim Bob's body. I put the knife on the table and shoved it toward Abbie. "How about you cut?"

She nodded and glanced at me with narrowed eyes. "Sit, Trish. You look like you're going to fall over."

I sat down and put my chin in my hands. She served both of us and then settled back in her chair. "Okay, tell me about what happened at the store."

I shook my head. I couldn't start there. I had to start earlier. "Do you remember that rash of road-sign thefts eight years ago?"

She raised her eyebrows. I jabbed my fork in the coffee cake, breaking it into pieces.

"What does that have to do with anything, especially Jim Bob's murder?" she asked.

Unwanted tears sprang into my eyes. I dropped my fork and picked up a napkin. "He was threatening me, Abbie. He said that Russ was involved in those thefts, and he was going to tell Max and his family. That gives me motive to murder Jim Bob."

She put her fork down, too. "Why in the world?"

"Because Max's wife was killed at an intersection where a stop sign had been removed."

4

O h, Trish." Abbie stared at me with wide eyes.

"Remember that big fight I had with Jim Bob at the pharmacy a couple weeks ago?" I asked.

She nodded.

"I threatened to report him to whatever board supervises pharmacists. Frank intervened, but Jim Bob told me I shouldn't throw stones." I continued to poke at my coffee cake. "I figured he was just referring to my tendency for mishaps. Well, last Friday before Shirl got in the office, Jim Bob came by Four Oaks Self-Storage. That's when he told me about the stop sign. He said if I didn't give him free storage units he was going to tell Max and his family, plus get Russ kicked out of the Navy. Involuntary manslaughter or something like that." I glanced at Abbie. "I haven't told Max yet. I need to know for sure."

She frowned. "Why can't you ask Russ?"

"Boot camp, remember?"

"Oh, yeah." She sighed. "Okay, well, do you think Russ was involved?"

"I have no idea. But I do remember when I was watching him pack I saw what could have been sheet-covered road signs in his closet." I bunched up my napkin. "You know this makes me look guilty in the cops' eyes."

She tucked her hair behind her ears. "Perhaps."

"I have a feeling that Detective Eric Scott suspects something."

She sat up straight. "So he's the lead investigator?"

I nodded. "Yeah. And this morning, I was down in the interview room for the second time. I think he knows."

Her gaze met mine. "You didn't tell him?"

I took a sip of coffee then set the cup down hard. "I sort of hoped that with Jim Bob dead no one would ever have to know."

She gazed at me with one delicate eyebrow raised. "So you're saying if they find Jim Bob's murderer today you're going to keep this a secret the rest of your life? Even from Max, and even if it's true?" She paused and tapped a finger on the table. "And if they don't find his murderer right away and you're somehow implicated in all of this, then the secret's out. Russ could be yanked out of the Navy, charged with Lindsey's death, and Max will feel like you betrayed him."

Put that way, it all sounded horrible. Was that what I was saying? Could I not tell Max the rest of my life? And if he did find out before I told him. . .I

31

mashed a piece of coffee cake into my plate with my fingertip. "I guess I'm just scared. Sometimes it's hard enough living with what feels like the ghost of a first wife and the kids' real mother. But you're right. I'm not thinking clearly at all. I don't know what to do."

She leaned across the table. "Come on, Trish, it's not like you to be so helpless and obtuse."

Her words felt like a slap. I glared at her. "What exactly does that mean?"

She smiled serenely and leaned back in her chair. I could see cogs turning in her brain. "Seems to me you'd want to find out what you can yourself. And remember, if Jim Bob knew, then he had to have heard it from someone else. Besides, Eric isn't going to let up."

I hadn't thought about it all quite like that. Then I realized she'd used the detective's first name. "You know Detective Scott?"

"Know him?" She shrugged. "I'm not sure he's knowable. With his impenetrable stares, he's so self-contained it's annoying. He just happens to be the person I ended up with as a writing consultant. The other guy who was helping me retired and sent me Eric's way. Ironically, he doesn't seem to like my books."

Who could not like Abbie's books? "Maybe he just doesn't like to read."

"Who knows? But he's nothing if not persistent." She nibbled on a piece of coffee cake and then put her fork down, meeting my gaze with a grin. "Do you remember when we were in sixth grade and decided we were going to be the Hardy Boys—only we were girls?"

I nodded. We'd called ourselves the Hardier Girls and ordered fingerprint powder and other detective stuff from mail-order places. We spent that summer following people around, looking for crimes. My mother finally banned the two of us from using the powder in the house because it was so messy.

I frowned. "So you're saying I need to investigate?"

"You have to tell Max, Trish—sooner than later. But it would be nice if you knew the facts. We need to look into this further. Find some answers."

"You know what?" I sat up straight. "Maybe I could find out who killed Jim Bob. Then Detective Scott would leave me and my family alone."

One corner of her mouth turned up. "That's my girl. Tell you what. I'll go to the library, look through old newspapers, and see what the articles said about Lindsey's accident. I have to go there anyway."

I nodded. Abbie took another bite of coffee cake. I didn't feel well, so I left mine uneaten.

"I'm on a deadline, so I can't help much, but this is a good plan. It'll take your mind off things and give me satisfaction."

"Satisfaction?" I asked.

"Yes." She smiled but didn't explain.

I had a feeling she wanted to one-up Detective Scott. That was fine with me, for two reasons. First, he annoyed me, too. Second, turnabout was fair play. She helped me. I could help her. My mind was already formulating ideas. "Thank you."

"What are friends for?" She held out her index finger.

I held out mine, and we touched the tips.

Our old sign of friendship. When we were little, we'd pricked our fingers, made them bleed, and held them together. Blood sisters.

"Here's to crime solving," she said.

"Yes." I felt a stirring inside me. "Here's to crime solving."

---

After Abbie left, my three oldest children came home, leaving me no time to think.

Charlie grunted at me as he ran through the kitchen to the family room.

Tommy kissed my cheek as he passed through. "Hey, Mom. I'm working this evening, so I won't be here for dinner. Dad knows."

"Okay." I looked at Karen. "How was school?"

"Fine." She opened the refrigerator. "I'm going over to Julie's in a while. Tommy's taking me on his way to work."

She was spending a lot of time at the Snyders' house. Thin, sad-eyed Julie was Lee Ann's only daughter. The girls' relationship benefited my shopping. Lee Ann always clued me in to the meat sales at the Shopper's Super Saver, and she didn't mind doing special cuts for me. But I was concerned about Karen. As she and Julie got closer, there was a distinct deterioration in Karen's behavior. She'd recently dropped all of her extracurricular activities, which disturbed us because she needed them to get into college. Max and I were praying for wisdom about how to handle the situation.

A long silence ensued while she rummaged through the shelves.

"I'm going to eat dinner there," she finally said.

"That's fine. Does your father know?"

She snatched a diet soda from the refrigerator, slammed the door, and turned to face me. "I'm sure you'll tell him."

Whoops. Worse than normal. Maybe she had PMS. "No doubt I will." I eyed her. "You want some chocolate?"

She put her hands on her hips. "Is that a joke?"

"Do you want it to be?"

She grabbed her pants and shook the fabric. "I don't need any more calories. I'm too tall. I'm getting fat. And I hate my hair."

Was that a slam against mine, which looked very much like hers? Long, blond, and very, very curly.

"You're lucky to be short and skinny," she said as she stomped from the kitchen.

Well, that didn't go too badly considering how things had been recently.

Strains of discordant, eerie music drifted from the family room. I peeked in. Sammie sat on the couch. Charlie was hunched two feet in front of the wide-screen television. Over his spiky hair, I saw a man dressed in a white suit, walking from the shadows, slowly filling the screen. The spooky music subsided slightly as he droned in a grim, melodramatic voice. "The accounts you will see today are real, although some of the drama is represented by actors." He paused, staring intently into the camera, which closed in on his face. Aided by makeup and lighting, his facial bones protruded, making him appear almost skeletal. "My name is Perry Mitchell. Welcome to"—he paused dramatically—"*Mysterious Disappearances*."

No wonder Charlie saw dead people. Max and I had to talk about this. "Charlie, please turn that off."

"But, Mom, I watch this over at Mike's. It's great! You wouldn't believe how many people disappear all the time. I mean, even you or Dad could be faking everything and really be serial killers."

I gazed at Charlie, disturbed and amazed at the way his brain worked. It didn't seem right for an eight-year-old kid. Besides, Sammie's rapt, openmouthed attention to Charlie's words and subsequent quizzical glance in my direction told me I'd better stop this serial-killer rumor right here; otherwise, I'd be hearing about it from my mother.

"Don't be silly, Charlie," I said. "You know Dad and I are who we say we are—you know our parents. Now turn it off."

"But I—"

The ringing phone interrupted him.

"Maybe that's Mike." Charlie galloped to the kitchen to grab the cordless. He probably hoped that Mike would invite him over so he could watch the show there.

I heard the sound of his murmuring voice; then he bounced back into the family room. "It's Grandmom—your mother. She wants to take me and Sammie out for ice cream tonight."

Sammie squealed and clapped her hands. "Please say yes, Mommy."

"Okay." I took the phone from Charlie, turned off the television, and the two scampered out of the room. I took a deep breath and put the receiver to my ear. "Hi, Ma. That's nice of you to offer. They're excited."

"Well, I don't see any of you often enough, so I had to take things into my own hands. I love Max's children like they were my own grandchildren, you know."

I did know. About taking things into her own hands and loving Max's kids.

I dropped onto the sofa. Perhaps I could distract her. "How is Daddy doing at that sale. . . ? Where is it? Pennsylvania?"

"Yes. He bought two cows. Why we need them is beyond me. But he's worried about you. He'll be back in time for Sunday dinner. So did you work today?"

"No. I went to talk to Detective Scott. I—"

"Did you remember that Jim Bob's wife was one of my dearest, deceased friends?"

"Yes." I accepted the fact that I wouldn't get a word in edgewise, which was just as well. Then I wouldn't have to hear her interpretation of my words months later.

"It's terrible," she droned. "Horrible."

"Yes, it is." I wondered if she realized how horrible it was for the person who found Jim Bob. "When did his wife die?"

"Not long enough for him to have remarried last year, but he did anyway." The indignant tone in her voice indicated there was much more to the story. "Don't you remember that? I told you all about it."

"Well, now that you mention it," I murmured.

She sighed. "After five years—can you believe it? He had the nerve to marry again."

"Five years," I repeated. "I would think five years would be plenty of—"

"Well, that shows how much you know." She snorted. "As far as I'm concerned, he should have waited forever. What in the world does a man his age want with a woman thirty years his junior?"

Well, I could think of at least one thing.

"And not only that, he let her redecorate the house. I'm sure Estelle turned over in her grave. It's indecent. And now this. I tell you, what goes around comes around."

I chewed on my fingernail as I tried to figure out what had gone around and come back again. Then I realized I was missing a valuable opportunity to gather clues. "So Jim Bob's widow is young. . . ."

"Didn't I say that? You need to listen to me. Oops, I have a customer. Gail had to leave early for a doctor's appointment. It's been a busy day. I'll talk to you later."

The phone clicked in my ear. I sat staring at the receiver in my hand. The plot thickened, so to speak. After becoming a recluse, Jim Bob's first wife died unexpectedly. He married someone much younger. I'd think the mystery was solved. That he killed his wife in order to marry a greedy younger woman, and she, in turn, killed him for his money. Problem was, Jim Bob waited five years before he remarried.

—

After dinner, Abbie called. She'd made copies of articles for me but hadn't learned anything that we didn't already know. She had to get back to her writing but promised to keep checking around for more information. She encouraged me to check for motivations and suggested that perhaps someone else was guilty of the road-sign thefts but pointed the finger at Russ.

I debated writing a letter to Russ at boot camp to ask him about the stop sign. That would clear things up right away, but I couldn't. Boot camp was hard enough without the added pressure of this problem. If he wasn't guilty, then he'd just sit there and worry. I glanced at the four- and five-year-old Sunday school curriculum laid out on the kitchen table. I was supposed to be preparing for Sunday's lesson. The practical part of the lesson was about a little girl who lied to her parents. I ignored the niggling of my conscience that I hadn't yet told Max about Jim Bob's threat. But I did have to figure things out first. At least that's what I kept telling myself.

Was my brother really guilty? And who had killed Jim Bob? What exactly had my mother said? I pulled a blank piece of paper from my notebook and began to doodle. Then I wrote down *Jim Bob* and *young wife*. I followed those words with MOTIVATION written in large block letters. What exactly gave someone motivation to murder? Strong emotion, like love gone wrong, or hate, or fear. . .

"Hey, baby." Max walked in the room behind me. I shoved my notes under the Sunday school lesson. If Max knew what I was doing, he'd want to know why.

He rubbed my shoulders. I leaned back and looked up at him.

"Can you take a break and come sit with me?" he asked. "We're alone."

I hadn't even thought about that, which was unusual since alone time for us was so rare, and I love spending time with him. But now that Max mentioned it, the house was quiet. Sammie and Charlie wouldn't be home for another hour. Karen was over at Julie's house, and Tommy was working.

On the couch in the family room, I nestled against Max with my head on his shoulder, trying valiantly to clear my mind.

"Isn't it nice to have all the kids in school now?" He stroked my hair. "That little kid thing is just about over."

I nodded. "Yeah, I guess. But the issues we deal with are bigger. Like, Karen and her moodiness, and Charlie. He sees dead people."

Max laughed. "Charlie has an imagination that's almost as big as yours."

I pulled away from him. "Come on. Be serious. It worries me. I mean, we take him to Sunday school and church. He goes to Christian school. He knows there aren't any such things as ghosts. What will his teachers think? We need to talk to him."

"I don't think he really sees things." Max pulled me tight. "Now let's enjoy being alone and not talk about the kids or anything important."

I saw the gleam in his eye. "Just what did you have in mind?"

He leaned down and kissed me.

I willed myself to stop thinking. I almost succeeded, but the secret I held wouldn't be still and wiggled in the back of my brain. After a very pleasant couple of minutes, I could no longer contain my thoughts. I pulled away from him.

He frowned at me. "What's wrong?"

I glanced at his face. I'd memorized every inch of it, from his green eyes and the skin that crinkled around them when he smiled, to the scar on his cheek that he'd gotten when he was just a kid and fell off the swing set. My heart ached keeping what I knew from him, and I had to tell him.

"Max, I wanted to talk to you—"

He cupped his hand under my chin. "I don't really feel like talking."

"But—"

He kissed me again, successfully shutting me up; then the front door burst open, banging against the wall. We had barely separated lips when Karen whirled into the room.

"Dad."

I brushed hair out of my eyes, and Max adjusted his collar.

"Oh—my—stars! I can't believe you guys." She put her hands on her hips. "What if I had company?"

She didn't, but I decided not to point that out.

"What's wrong?" Max asked.

Tears welled up in her eyes. "I had to leave Julie's. Her mother kicked her father out. Julie can't stop crying, and her mother is acting all weird. There's this guy. . ." She heaved a sigh. "It's horrible. I mean, I remember when Mommy. . ." Her voice broke.

My breath caught in my throat.

Max patted the sofa next to him. "Why don't you come sit down and talk?"

Karen shook her head. "No. Especially not after what I just saw." She whirled on her heel and left the room.

I was not going to survive this. If my brother were guilty in any way of Lindsey's death, my relationship with my stepchildren—in particular, Karen—might be ruined forever.

Max leaned back on the couch.

I felt sick but needed to encourage him. "She's still insecure about losing her mother. That, on top of being a teenage girl."

He took a deep breath and stared at his hands; then he twirled his wedding ring around and around. "Maybe." He glanced at me. "Well, since we were interrupted anyway, what did you want to talk about?"

I wanted to tell him about Russ so badly, but the timing wasn't right. Besides, even though I might feel better for the confession, all I had was supposition. An accusation that may or may not be true. I had to know for certain.

"It can wait." I sat up straight. "You should go talk to Karen."

He frowned. "Are you sure?"

I nodded.

"I guess you're right." He kissed my cheek. "I'm really sorry, Trish."

"It's okay."

I watched him leave the room; then I followed more slowly, heading to our bedroom. It wasn't okay. I wondered if things would be okay ever again.

My mind whirled with the murder and accompanying complications.

Detective Scott hadn't given me any indication about the direction of the investigation, not that he would. I turned over all the possible suspects. Frank? His reaction at the scene didn't appear to be that of a guilty person, but what would I know about how guilty people acted? Though I had gone to school with him, I really didn't know Frank at all. His Dudley Do-It-All-Right reputation stood in place to this day. But that didn't mean Frank was a murderer. To the contrary, one could assume the opposite was the case.

Much of the staff of the store was sick that morning, at least according to Daryl. Besides the people at the registers up front, I'd only seen Lee Ann, Daryl, Frank, and a few customers. Who had the most to gain from Jim Bob's death? Besides me?

5

On Wednesday morning, I rushed through the front door of Four Oaks Self-Storage fifteen minutes late. I'd been sick that morning. I had to find out what was going on sooner rather than later so things could calm down, including my stomach.

Shirl peered over the high, gray Formica counter that surrounded her desk and held out some mail. "Hey, Mrs. C."

"Hi." I took the envelopes from her then went to my office where I fired up my computer and got to work. Max needed me to run through some figures for the new phase of construction across the street, as well as those for the new facility.

I heard the hum of cars arriving and leaving as customers came in to rent units or take care of bills. I paid no attention to anything until I heard the rumbling of Max's voice. He strolled into my office and shut the door. With his blue work shirt and jeans, he looked like every woman's dream of a hunky construction worker, with muscles in all the right places.

"Hi, honey." His gaze made me feel warm.

I leaned back in my chair. "Karen seemed okay this morning."

"Last night she accused me of acting like a teenage boy when I'm around you." He grinned, and his eyes sparkled, which made him look a lot like a teenager.

That could explain some of her hostile behavior. Not only was she jealous of me, she was also going through the stage where she didn't want to acknowledge that her father was a normal, healthy male. "You okay with that?" I asked.

He flashed me a wide smile. "What do you think?"

I motioned toward a chair. "You wanna sit?"

He shook his head. "Nope. I just came by to say hello. George is across the street at the site, checking out the work. Seeing him reminded me of you. He sends his regards."

I smiled at the mention of George's name. He'd introduced me to Max. "Tell him I said hi."

"Okay," Max said. "You remember the baseball game tonight, right?"

I nodded. The ball game might be a good place to look for clues.

He walked around the desk and kissed me; then he headed for the front office. "I'll try to be home a bit early," he said over his shoulder. "That way we have time to eat dinner."

He left, banging the front door behind him. I went to the window to watch him cross the parking lot. The mention of George made me feel nostalgic. Even after six years, I still couldn't believe that I'd landed Max Cunningham. I clamped my fists tightly at my side. I would make sure that nothing happened to ruin what we had.

Time to gather clues. I walked out to the front office and leaned against the counter. Shirl was thumbing through a catalog.

"Can I talk to you?" I asked.

"Sure." She marked her place and faced me.

"What do you know about Jim Bob Jenkins?"

She crossed her arms. "Only that no one will miss the louse."

Well, that was straightforward and not a nice thing to say about a dead man. "Why is that?"

She shook her head. "He always acted like he was everyone's friend, but he was mean as a snake. Turn on a body faster than a rabid dog."

I nodded, and that encouraged her to continue.

"Then the old coot up and married that hussy. Nothin' good could come from that, I'll tell you what."

Louse, snake, mean dog, old coot—not a very flattering picture of the dearly departed. As for his wife, this was the second time I'd heard not-so-good things about her.

"Did you hear anything about suspects? Like Frank Gaines or Daryl Boyd?" I asked.

Shirl laughed. "Don't know much about Frank, but Daryl? That big weenie? Only way he'd kill someone is if he ran over 'em trying to get away from his wife when she's on a rampage."

I knew Daryl's wife and wouldn't blame anyone for running away from her.

"That's the thing, you know," Shirl said. "He married the woman for her money. She makes him work, so there he is at Shopper's Super Saver. He's too afraid of her to do anything. At least in front of her face." Shirl paused and tapped her finger on her forehead. "But you know what? Maybe Daryl is sneaky. You know how men can be when they want something."

I could only imagine what she meant by that comment, but she brought up a really good point. Sneakiness was an interesting character trait. Maybe it was just a short slide from being sneaky to slaughtering someone.

—◦—

When I arrived home at noon, I saw a strange car parked out front on the road. An equally strange man stood on the sidewalk, looking at our house. I pulled my SUV into the driveway, and he turned around to peer at me.

I didn't get out, and I made sure I'd locked my doors. Finding Jim Bob's body had made me wary, more conscious of possible danger. Though we live in the country suburbs, we're near enough to larger towns to get the occasional roaming bad guy. The tall, skinny man, dressed in baggy chinos and a white knit shirt, ambled over to my car. I cracked the window and left my engine running, in case I had to make a quick getaway.

He said something to me, but I could barely hear him for staring at the massive gray and brown mop of hair that covered his head and his upper lip that sported the largest mustache I'd seen outside of Civil War movies.

"Mrs. Cunningham?"

"Who wants to know?" I demanded.

He flashed a smarmy, big-toothed smile. "I'm a reporter from the *Four Oaks Times Gazette*. Can you tell me about the body you found in the dairy case?"

I didn't want any more publicity over this whole thing. I didn't think Max or his parents would be happy, either.

"Look, Mr. . . ."

"Call me Carey." He paused. "Carey Snook." He reached out a hand, but I didn't roll down my window. He put his hand down. "Can you just tell me about the body you found in the dairy case?"

I shook my head. "No."

He shoved his hands in his pockets. "Is there another time I could come back, then?"

"No."

He stuck his face in my window. "You know, I want this story. Lots of people could be guilty of his murder. Everyone has secrets. That's what I'm looking for."

I couldn't speak. Was he implying something? What did he already know? He smiled and then turned, walked to his car, and hopped inside. I waited until he was out of sight before I parked my vehicle in the garage.

My legs felt shaky. All I needed was a newspaper person hounding me, looking for secrets. One more good reason to find my answers—fast.

I walked into the kitchen and flung my purse on the table as the phone rang. I snatched the handset off the wall. "Hello?"

"Hello. Is Maxwell there?" A woman's voice, dripping a honeyed southern accent, came from the receiver.

"Maxwell?" Only Max's mother called him Maxwell. "Who's calling?"

"This is the Cunningham residence, isn't it?" For each syllable, she added another.

"Yes, but he's not available," I said. "Who is this?"

"He's not at work. I can't find him anywhere. Well, I guess I'll call him later then. Thank you."

She hung up without answering my question. I stood in the hall, holding my phone.

I'll be the first to admit I suffer from jealousy. Not because of anything Max has done. The way women respond to him isn't his fault. I just have a bit of a self-esteem problem. And right then, I felt even worse because I had this huge secret I was keeping from him.

So it was logical that I would wonder why a woman who wouldn't leave a message was looking all over the place for my husband. I wanted to ask him, but I couldn't reach him. I tried his cell phone, but he'd turned it off, which he sometimes does when he's in a meeting. Then I called the office only to have Shirl tell me that he was out and she didn't know where.

What to do? I paced the ceramic-tile floor in my kitchen waiting for Sammie to get home and trying to decide on my course of action. Knowing that Detective Scott was on the case made me edgy. I suspected I didn't have much time before he would discover that my altercation with Jim Bob was more than just what happened at the store. Now a hairy-faced reporter was sniffing around.

I had to think. Logically. This was no time to become unhinged. My first order of business was Russ. Had I really seen road signs in his closet? I took a deep breath and ticked off thoughts in my head. First, road signs. Second, find out who was talking to Jim Bob about Russ. One of Russ's old friends perhaps? For that I needed a list of who he'd known, and I knew just where to find one.

While my mother was at work and my father was away, Sammie and I could make a foray to the old family homestead and see if I could find a stop sign.

------

"Mommy, what do you have to find here?" Sammie asked, as I pulled up to my parents'. The white Victorian farmhouse with its large, airy rooms and nooks and crannies had been my home from the time I was born until I moved into my own apartment. I missed living in an old house.

"I'm just getting something that Grandmom stored." I parked my vehicle next to the back porch. I'd told my mother that I needed to look for an old book. Not technically a lie, since I was going to get my brother's yearbooks, but I was disturbed that my half-truths were adding up. I undid Sammie's seat belt and mine, and we climbed out. Two white chickens scurried past us. Sammie laughed and began to chase them. "I'll be right back out," I yelled after her. "Stay in the yard."

I went in the back door, passed through a mudroom, and rushed into the kitchen. The smell of floor polish, lemon wax, and baking enveloped me, reminding me of coming home after school when I was little, grabbing a handful of cookies, and running outside to play. My biggest problem back then was escaping my mother's tongue. But now I was no longer a child. I was an adult with adult-sized problems.

I heard a dog bark and glanced out the window over the kitchen sink.

Sammie was playing with Buddy, my father's border collie. Good. The dog was like a third parent. I hurried through the kitchen, down the hall to the staircase. I ran my hands over the smooth walnut handrail, thinking of all the times I'd slid down its length. The stairs, polished and worn from age, creaked under my feet as I jogged up them.

Russ's room was first on the right. Like all the other rooms, it was spacious, with dark wood trim and large, rectangular windows that reached almost from floor to ceiling. I went straight to his closet where I remembered seeing something covered with a sheet. Besides his clothes and shoes, there was very little. Russ was fanatically neat, a trait that would serve him well in the military. Had I imagined the sign?

I left his room and went down the hall to a door that led to the attic stairs. I scurried up those. At the top, I switched on a light and glanced around. Among my mother's many traits, good and bad, was compulsive organization. She labeled everything. I would have no problem finding his yearbooks. Each of us had plastic bins containing years of school paraphernalia.

I did a quick perimeter search, checking for road signs, as well. I was beginning to feel a sense of relief. Perhaps I hadn't a sign at all, and there was nothing to the threat. Maybe Jim Bob had made up the whole thing based on rumor, which I had to squelch.

"Mommy!" Sammie's voice came from the bottom of the stairs. "Can I come up?"

"No, honey. I'm coming down." I took another quick glance around with a lighter heart, opened Russ's high school box, and grabbed his yearbooks. Then I turned off the light and went down the stairs.

Sammie waited for me at the back door. "Buddy showed me where the new kittens are," she said. "In that old shed next to the garage. You wanna see?"

No, I didn't want to see. I'm not keen about cats even though I was raised with them, but I couldn't ignore Sammie's shining eyes.

"Okay, sweetie, show me."

My father built the small, clapboard lean-to next to the garage when I was Sammie's age. Years of white paint, lumpy in spots, covered the wood. He'd replaced the door recently with one that had a real handle instead of just a hook and eye. Sammie pointed to the corner where a tabby cat had made a bed with what looked to be an old insulated shirt of my dad's. Multicolored kittens, eyes barely opened, crawled over her.

I had to admit that the kittens were cute, but I wasn't looking at them. I was looking at the large, sheet-covered object behind them, feeling my heart fall to my toes.

# 6

My ride to the ball game with Max was subdued. Charlie and Sammie were home with Karen. Tommy was working. All I could think about was the stop sign I'd found in my father's shed.

Max didn't notice my preoccupation. He was telling me all about the meetings he'd had regarding the new self-storage facility. His typical male denseness was to my benefit tonight.

He parked the SUV at the community ball field. Another car whipped into the spot next to us. I grabbed my purse. Then I watched as a tall blond got out of the vehicle. She sashayed to the front of her car wearing a lime green skirt just this side of too short. A green-and-white-striped tank top showed off her other attributes, which the matching green sweater she had tied around her shoulders only partially covered. White, strappy, high-heeled sandals, not at all appropriate for a ball game, adorned her delicate feet.

When she saw us—in particular, Max—her eyes grew wide in her beautiful, oval face. Then she smiled and waved as if greeting an old friend.

I surmised from the woman's reaction that she knew my husband. When I turned on Max, I had only one question. "Who is that?"

"Stefanie Jenkins," Max said, undoing his seat belt.

"Who?" The name sounded familiar.

"Jim Bob's wife, er, widow," he said.

The widow sidled over to my husband's window. He opened it.

"Maxwell?" I heard her southern accent and knew I'd spoken with her earlier that day. "May I speak with you?"

"Shouldn't she be grieving at home?" I whispered in Max's ear, as suspicion niggled in my brain.

He smiled at her. "I'll be out in just a moment." He put the window up and turned to face me. "Trish, be nice. She just lost her husband."

"Exactly my point." I jammed my index finger into his shoulder for emphasis. "Shouldn't she be grieving at home?"

"Let's go, baby." He kissed me thoroughly. "I've got to get our team settled."

He was out of the car first and joined Stefanie, who leaned too close to him for my liking. I joined them quickly, and she greeted me with a white, toothy smile.

"You must be Trish. Maxwell speaks so highly of you." She looked down at me with those wide baby blues. "I'm Stefanie with an *F.* You can call me Steffie."

"Steffie." I nodded. It sounded so collegiate. I looked closer at the widow. No wrinkles. No mustache hairs. She even looked collegiate. Now I understood why my mother had oozed disapproval over Jim Bob's marriage, and why, if such a thing were possible, Estelle would have turned over in her grave.

"I'm so sorry for your loss," I said, watching her and wondering why she was here.

As if she read my thoughts, tears welled up in her eyes. "Thank you. And I want to express my sympathy that you were the unfortunate one to. . .find. . .my husband."

I'd seen better acting on Saturday-morning cartoons. Something about her wasn't right, which explained why I said what I said next.

"I'm really surprised that you're out and about so soon. Especially to a ball game."

Max looked down at me in surprise; then he put his arm around my shoulders and squeezed. I put my arm around his waist and pinched him in return as I smiled sweetly at Stefanie.

Tears hung on her eyelashes. She blinked rapidly, and I couldn't tell if she was fluttering her eyelids or getting rid of tears. "I just couldn't sit at home by myself. I heard about the game and decided it would be a distraction for me."

"It's a good idea," Max the Dense said.

She turned to him and batted her eyes.

An older couple I knew from church arrived and offered their sympathies to her. Max took my hand and led me to the other side of my SUV. Concern wrinkled his forehead. "Trish, I can't remember your ever being so unkind. Well, except around my mother, which is understandable. What's wrong?"

I stared up at him while I tried to figure out just exactly what was bothering me besides a raging attack of jealousy. "Stefanie called you today at our house, but she wouldn't leave a message. She said she'd been looking all over for you and couldn't find you."

"What?" He frowned at me.

"I know it was her. Who can miss that accent?"

"Honey. . ."

"There's something not right with her, Max. I mean, her husband just died. She's never come to a ball game before—I would have noticed. And as far as I know, she doesn't know any of the players. Besides, I don't like the way she looks at you."

"People sometimes do strange things when someone they know dies," he said.

45

"Not her. She's up to no good." I meant that in more ways than one.

"Are you jealous?" he asked.

I put my hands on my hips. "Should I be?"

He laughed. "I'm flattered, but you've got a really suspicious mind. You should work with Eric Scott."

That gave me pause.

Max must have seen my expression. "Hey, I'm not serious. I want you to leave all that behind you." He grabbed my hand and squeezed it. "You have nothing to worry about, by the way. I adore you."

He didn't understand at all.

An hour later, I sat at the top of the hard, metal bleachers. A cool breeze blew, and I was glad I'd worn long sleeves. I glanced around at the crowd and noticed Stefanie seated at ground level next to the same couple who had spoken with her earlier.

As I considered the widow's pert nose and perfect hair, I realized that Max hadn't told me how he knew her. That aggravated me, so I went to the soda machine to get something to drink. While I stood there deciding, April May Winters, one of my mother's employees, wandered up.

"Hey, Trish." The chubby redhead contemplated sodas over my shoulder.

"Hi, April."

"I see Miss Priss Stefanie Jenkins is here."

Ah, perhaps here would be a source of information. I hastily picked a Diet Coke, pushed the button, and then pulled out more quarters. "You want a soda?"

"Well, sure," she said enthusiastically. "Grape."

I put more money into the machine and out popped the soda, which I handed to her. I watched her open it and take a huge gulp.

"Stefanie told me and Max that she's so sad and lonely she's come here for company," I said.

April May choked. I thought I might have to do the Heimlich maneuver, but she recovered. "She said that? I can't believe it. She must think you guys are stupid or something."

That's not exactly what I wanted to hear. My mouth must have been hanging open because April immediately backtracked.

"Oh, sorry. That sounded really bad. I didn't mean it. I don't think you and Max are dumb."

"It's okay. We might be a little stupid when it comes to Stefanie." I said *we* when I really meant *he*, but April didn't have to know that. "So Stefanie's not grieving?" I asked.

April snorted about ten times, which is the way she laughs, and I worried that she would choke again. When she regained control, she shook her head. "She married the man for his money. Unfortunately, Jim Bob was as sneaky as he was ugly and mean, er. . .God rest his soul."

Now I had two sneaky men for my list. And April was the third person I'd spoken to who had nothing good to say about Jim Bob. "He had money? Why was he a pharmacist?"

"Dunno." She shrugged. "I just heard he had it, but he didn't act like it, nasty tightwad. He made your mother deliver a box of free doughnuts to the pharmacy once a week."

That was news to me, but I didn't have time to think about it because April was on a roll.

"Him and Miss Fancy-Pants met out there on one of them Cayman Islands. You know, like what you hear about? Where people swim buck naked and all. I mean, imagine." She paused, possibly to do just that.

I didn't know anything about the Caymans or swimming nude and didn't care, but I nodded anyway. She took my attention very seriously. I doubted she had much opportunity to talk when she worked with my mother.

"Well, next thing you know, here he comes back to Four Oaks married to her. Everyone knew what she was up to. I mean, her and him? The old goat." Snort. "He must have been really stupid. Of course, he is a man." She snorted three more times.

I'm not a man basher, but tonight I was irritated enough with my husband's lack of astuteness about Stefanie to agree. I smiled widely and nodded again to encourage April to continue.

"Well, they lived in unhappiness. Can't figure out why they stayed together."

"Hey, April!" someone shouted from the bleachers.

"Gotta go," she said. "It's been good to talk. You know, I don't always agree with your mother."

Neither do I, but I wondered which of my mother's opinions about me April referred to. She walked away, and my head spun. Too much information in too short a time. With April May's comments, my temper had subsided, and I felt compelled to go back to the game and support Max. On rare occasions, he stopped thinking about the team's performance long enough to look for me in the bleachers for a thumbs-up. I needed to be there just in case. Besides, watching him play is a pleasure all its own.

Max's team won, which didn't surprise me. The intrepid Detective Scott played almost as well as Max. I wandered around, shooting the breeze with people, watching Stefanie out of the corner of my eye. She had a lot of hair. A long, bleached-blond, curly pouf, resembling what I'd seen on beauty contestants. She met my eye and tottered over to me on her high heels. Without being rude, there was no way I could avoid her.

"Oh, Trish. The game was wonderful. Max is so talented. He plays like a pro."

"Thanks," I murmured. I hoped his game was his only quality she'd been watching.

I was so busy fighting my bad feelings that I didn't see Detective Eric Scott until he was standing next to me.

He smiled. I thought I would fall over.

"Hello, Trish." He turned his gaze on Steffie. "Mrs. Jenkins. How are you tonight?"

She focused her big baby blues on him. "Oh, Detective Scott. You are such a good ball player."

"Thank you." He continued to smile, but I saw past that to his eyes. Shrewd and assessing. I was relieved that he wasn't looking at me for once. "It's a team effort, of course," he said. "No one person is responsible for our game."

She blinked several times and continued to smile brightly. "Oh, that is so true." She turned to me. "Maxwell is so good."

If she said one more thing about how good Max was, I was going to hit her.

"Must be hard to be out so soon after the death of Jim Bob," Detective Scott said.

I coughed trying to cover a laugh. I was thinking better and better of him.

"This is such a good distraction for me." Tears filled her eyes again. "Detective Scott, I'm so impressed by your dedication to finding the person who did this."

As far as I was concerned, she was laying it on a little thick.

"Have no fear, Mrs. Jenkins; I'll solve this crime." He jauntily saluted us. "Ladies. I have to get a move on. Crime fighting never ends." He jogged away. As I watched him go, I noticed a bald man disappear behind the cement building that held the bathrooms. I didn't recognize him.

Stefanie sighed. I turned back to her.

"Seeing the police brings back my loss," she said in a breathy voice. "I need to go home."

She walked in the direction of the parking lot. I wandered around the grounds, greeting people. Peggy Nichols, the principal of Charlie and Sammie's school, stopped me. "Trish, will you still be able to man your booth this Saturday?" She squinted at me through thick glasses.

"Sure. I'm fine."

She shook her head. "I wouldn't be if I were you. I can't believe all the things happening in our little town. It's like a bacteria eating from the inside out."

That was certainly descriptive. Unfortunately, it sounded a little like what was happening to me. I was being eaten up inside by guilt. We chatted a bit more; then I left to find Max and noticed Stefanie coming from the bathroom. That was strange. I thought she'd been in a hurry to leave.

## 7

When Max and I returned home, Karen was passing through the foyer on her way to her room with the cordless. In the past, when I'd suggested she have one permanently implanted, she wasn't amused. But then what did I expect? When she turned fifteen, she lost her sense of humor and ceased to be amused by anything I said.

Max motioned for her to wait.

She sighed hugely and put her hand over the receiver. "What, Dad? This is really important. Julie is afraid her mother has a boyfriend. He's a loser who works at some school. Julie's crying. She wants her dad."

Lee Ann dating someone else? She and Norm had been together since high school—inseparable. He'd rescued her from an abusive home situation. I still couldn't imagine their breaking up.

"Were there any phone calls for us?" Max asked.

She shook her head. "Nah. No phone calls except Grandmom. Oh, and Abbie called to say she'd pick up doughnuts for the health fair."

Those weren't considered real phone calls, since they weren't for Karen.

She tapped her fingers on the railing. "Sammie's in bed and wants you to come up and hug her good night. Charlie's in his room. He keeps talking about dead people." She sighed and rolled her eyes toward the ceiling. "Why do I have to have such a weird brother? Why do I have such a weird family?" She put the phone back to her mouth and tromped up the stairs.

Max and I exchanged glances.

"I think I'll talk to Charlie tonight about the dead people after I tuck Sammie in and pray with her."

"Okay," he said. "But I don't think it's any big deal. He's probably just teasing the girls. You know how he is."

I did, perhaps better than Max. Charlie and I are like soul mates. We feel deeply, have great imaginations, and we're both scrappers.

I went upstairs to say good night to Sammie, but I was too late. She was already asleep. I stood next to her canopy bed and watched as hair that had fallen over her face rose and fell with her breaths. My baby. I was praying for her when Max joined me. He stood quietly next to me until I was done.

When we were back in the hall, he headed for the stairs. "I'll be in my office," he said over his shoulder. "I have to call George. Remember, he'll be in tomorrow morning to talk about the figures you put together. Since you know all the details, you can explain them to him."

"Okay." I watched him go downstairs and wished we could have one day with no one around and nothing between us.

I peeked into Charlie's room. His wiry, pajama-clad body was huddled in a chair at his desk where he intently studied an open book.

"You ready for bed?" I asked.

He jumped as if I'd set off a firecracker. "Uh, yeah." He slammed the book shut and shoved it under his schoolbooks.

Nothing says guilty like a child hiding something from his parent's view. "What is that, Charlie?"

He stared at me defiantly. "It's just a book."

"What book?" I walked over to his desk.

He heaved a sigh and pulled it back out from under the pile with exaggerated motions. "Here."

*Mysterious Disappearances—The Facts, Plain and Simple.*

Okay, well, at least it wasn't a book of naked women. Still, the way he hid it told me he knew what I'd say about it.

"So they put out a book?" I fingered the cover, illustrated by superimposed, graphic, black-and-white crime images. "Whose is this?"

"Mike's."

I didn't know how to handle this situation. "I told you I don't like that show."

He stared at the floor. "I know."

I ruffled his hair. "Sweetie, is this what makes you see ghosts?"

His head shot up. "What are you talking about?"

"You don't see ghosts?"

His disapproving frown was similar to Max's. "Mom, I don't believe in stuff like that."

"But Karen said something about it," I said.

Charlie snorted. "Karen. She's a girl."

"And that means?"

"Well, all she does is talk on the phone with Julie. She needs a life. She needs to stop listening to other people and make up her own mind about things."

Okay, then. I guess that settled that. Perhaps Max was right, and Charlie was just teasing his sisters. "Well, why don't you return the book to Mike tomorrow? We'll just drop the whole thing."

Charlie stared at me. I could tell he was trying to find a loophole, but he finally nodded. "Okay."

I wanted to smile, but I didn't. He was so much like me he could have been my biological son.

After we prayed together, I tucked Charlie into bed; then I sat down in front of the television and flipped to the local news.

The perky news anchor read a teaser about the local landfill, which was temporarily closing. That's where Norm, Lee Ann's husband, worked.

The newscaster moved on to the murder at the grocery store. "The local Shopper's Super Saver is now open after the body of pharmacist Jim Bob Jenkins, a local resident, was discovered murdered in the refrigerated room behind the dairy case. Police report that the investigation is ongoing. A source close to the situation has indicated that store finances might be involved. Store manager Frank Gaines spoke with us earlier."

They cut to a clip of an interview with poor Frank. His charming, Dudley Do-It-All-Right persona had lost quite a bit of its shine. His hair was flat, and his tie was crooked.

The newsperson shoved the mike closer into Frank's face. "Can you tell us what you know about the murder investigation?"

If I were a betting person, I would wager that Frank's scowl indicated more than minor irritation. "I'm not privy to the investigation," he snarled. "I have nothing to say."

Yep. I was right.

The news cut back to the studio. Ms. Perky beamed into the camera, as though she'd just covered a cheery piece of Americana. Then she babbled on about an investigation at the landfill—something about hauling in medical waste from New Jersey.

I turned off the television. The phone rang. Why would someone call this late? Shortly after, I heard Tommy tromping down the stairs.

"Where's Dad? He's got a call." He waved the phone in the air.

"In his study," I said. "Who is it?"

He covered the receiver. "It's Mrs. Jenkins."

Dear Steffie. Now why was she calling Max? I jumped up from the couch. "Give me the phone. I'll take it to your father." I snatched it from Tommy's hand.

He stared at me with an open mouth. "Mom, Dad has a phone in his office, you know."

"Yes, I know."

I trotted down the hall, pushed open the study door, and marched inside.

"Come on in," Max said, staring at me over reading glasses, with a slight grin on his lips. His desk was littered with bluish architectural plans.

I made sure my hand was over the receiver. "The phone's for you. It's Steffie." I said it as if it were a four-letter word.

Max took off his glasses, pinched the bridge of his nose, and then picked up the phone on his desk.

Okay, so I have no pride. I listened in on the headset I held.

"Maxwell, hello." At least six syllables.

"Hello, Stefanie." He glanced at me.

"I'm so sorry to call you so late. I hope I didn't wake your wife." Did Steffie want to talk to Max without my knowing? My grip on the phone got tighter.

"No, it's fine," Max said. "What can I do for you?"

I sat in a chair opposite his desk. He looked up at me with a slight grin and winked.

Stefanie began to talk. "Sugar, I need to get into Jim Bob's unit as soon as possible. There are things in there I absolutely must have."

*Sugar?* I raised my eyebrows and watched Max.

"I told you that I need a court order." He spoke in a low, even tone and tapped his fingers on the desk.

My mind processed the information. Jim Bob must have had a storage unit contract on which Steffie's name wasn't listed.

"But surely you can understand given my delicate state that I can't wait for those old judges to make a decision. Please, sugar, make this teeny little exception for me."

I stuck my finger into my mouth and pretended to gag.

Max ignored me. He also ignored her pleas. "I'm sorry. I can't make any exceptions."

I stared at him in admiration. There is something terribly attractive about a man who can say something like that and still sound nice. In the silence that followed, I heard her breathing. I wondered if she was going to offer a bribe of the intimate sort to get the unit open, in which case I would be obligated to find her and rip out her hair.

"Please, Maxwell. Just take me into the unit. You can stand there. I only need a couple teeny little papers. Nothing big. I'll make it worth your while."

*"Worth your while"* was open to interpretation. Unfortunately, it wasn't blatant enough to excuse any ripping or tearing. Max met my gaze and tapped his fingers harder on the desk. "I'm sorry, Stefanie. I have to obey the law."

The Widow Jenkins's sweetness slipped. "This is an inconvenience, you know."

Max stayed right on the party line. "I understand you're inconvenienced. I want to open it for you and will as soon as I can."

She sniffed. "I guess that will have to do."

"I'm sorry," Max said. "If there's anything else we can do for you, please let us know."

I hung up after he did and put my phone on the floor. He stared at me with a smirk on his lips.

I hopped up, walked over to him with exaggerated swings of my hips, and leaned against the edge of his desk in my best imitation of a femme fatale. "Sugar, just do what I want, and I'll make it worth your while." My imitation sounded surprisingly like her.

Max grinned and pulled me close. "You really dislike Steffie."

I ran my finger over his lips. "Dislike? No. It's nothing personal. I just don't like her going on and on about how good you are. Besides, I have a bad feeling about her."

He had the nerve to laugh. "You're adorable."

"Chauvinist," I said.

"Guilty as charged." Max pulled me into his lap. "You have nothing to worry about. And I guess you figured out what's going on. She's even been by the office a couple of times. She needs to get into a storage unit that Jim Bob rented a year ago, but her name isn't on the contract."

"I guess we can't, either, can we?" I glanced at him hopefully, wishing we could take one little look.

Max kissed me lightly. "Curious, aren't you? But you're right. I won't touch it at this point until everything is settled. It's just too bad people don't think about things like emergency access in case of injury or death when they rent units."

Of all the negative character traits I'd heard about Jim Bob, stupidity wasn't one of them. I wondered if he'd left Stefanie off the contract on purpose.

8

"You're going to call the doctor today, right?" Max asked as he buttoned his shirt in the mirror.

"I'll be fine, Max." I had spent the first few minutes out of bed that morning being sick. Now I was trying to figure out what to wear.

He turned around to face me and gave me a once-over. "Trish, you haven't been feeling well for days."

I finally decided on nice jeans and a pink shirt. "I'm just overwrought. It's got to be nerves. Stop worrying." Of course, that's what happens when you keep secrets and guilt eats you from the inside out. I yanked on the shirt.

He blinked, and his mouth twitched. "Touchy, aren't you?"

"Well, I'm just tired of everyone telling me that I don't look well. It makes me feel flabby and white, like my mother's doughnut dough." I adjusted my blouse collar and glared at him. "So stop thinking that."

He grinned. "I wasn't thinking that."

I put my hands on my hips. "Well, then, what were you thinking?"

He walked around the bed. "Actually, I was reflecting on how good you look."

"What?"

His eyes had that little gleam in them.

"Max, we have a meeting and—"

I can't talk and kiss. And once again, my guilty conscience was bugging me, which was distressing because kissing Max is one of the joys of my life. However, pounding at our bedroom door distracted both of us.

"Mom!" Charlie shouted. "I can't find my math book."

Interruption by child. Morning had begun.

———

Doughnuts were in my blood. Hopefully the fat wasn't. My mother began perfecting her doughnut recipes when I was too little to eat them. Now she owned Doris's Doughnuts. The store was in a tiny strip mall near Four Oaks Self-Storage, so I decided to stop by and pick up a dozen to take for the guys in the meeting. George, the contractor who would be in the office this morning, loved my mother's doughnuts.

Since she now offers a lunch menu as well as baked goods and coffee that rival the chains, the store is a favorite spot for everyone from construction workers to cops. I sincerely hoped there would be no cops there today.

The bell above my head rang as I walked into the bright red and white room. The scent of coffee and fresh doughnuts made my mouth water. Ma looked up from behind the cash register. From the glance she gave me, I knew I was in for it.

"Well, it's about time." No one's voice is louder than my mother's, especially when she's trying to make a point. Everyone in the place looked up. "People have been asking about my daughter. I say, what daughter?"

"Oh, sure. I never talk to you. I'm surprised you even recognize me." I headed for the self-serve coffee, recalling what the pastor had told me in premarital counseling about one of the sources of my self-esteem issues—my mother.

"Just like kids, isn't it?" Gail, my mother's best friend and longtime help, nodded like a bobblehead doll. "Ungrateful. All of them. We give birth, go through all that agony, and then what?"

As if I hadn't gone through labor myself. I ignored them and poured some fresh Colombian into a Styrofoam cup at the counter. Then I scoped out the fresh, doughy, fattening circles.

"One day you'll wish you had visited me every day," Ma said as she handed a customer a bag stuffed with pastry. "When I'm dead and gone, buried next to your father."

"Yeah, yeah, whatever," I said under my breath. She was on a roll. The white tables and chairs were mostly filled, which meant she had an audience for her comments—something she reveled in. I tried not to take her seriously, but dealing with her barbs was hard.

"Are you here to buy?" she asked.

I took a huge sip of coffee. "Yeah. I need a dozen to take to work. You choose. Oh, and a bear claw, too. That's my breakfast."

"Something going on?" She deftly picked up the doughnuts and boxed them.

"A meeting with George about the expansion." The coffee wasn't settling well in my stomach.

"I'm surprised you can eat anything after finding poor Jim Bob stabbed to death, sprawled over a grocery cart, guts in all directions," Gail said as she turned on the espresso machine. "It's only been four days."

Well, there went my appetite.

"I mean, really, imagine the blood," she continued as steam hissed from the machine and brown liquid squirted into a tiny cup.

Ma sadly shook her head in total agreement. "What a mess. I wonder if they hired someone to clean up the floor."

My stomach twisted.

April May came from the back with flour on her hands. "I heard there was gore from one end of that place to another."

Ma looked at April and back at Gail. "Now, do you suppose there are companies that do that sort of thing? Clean up murder scenes? Can you imagine? What happens to all the parts?"

The memory of Jim Bob came back with a vengeance. The coffee in my stomach curdled. "Back in a minute," I managed to gasp as I slapped my hand over my mouth. I made it to the bathroom just in time. When I'd finished, I pulled a cleaning wipe from a plastic pouch in my purse and wiped my mouth. I stood for a few minutes in the bathroom, waiting for my stomach to settle. After I stuck a piece of gum in my mouth, I went back to the counter.

"Are you sick?" Ma asked.

"I think I have a bug or something." I was beginning to suspect I was allergic to caffeine or had an ulcer. I paid for my coffee and the doughnuts, although it would be awhile before I could ingest either.

"I hope you're not pregnant," she said in a loud voice.

From the sudden silence and surreptitious looks from the people sitting at tables, everyone in the room heard her. Great. Now rumors would fly. I felt heat crawl up my face. There was no way I could be pregnant. The doctors said so. Sammie had been a miracle.

"That's all you need—more kids. Four is plenty," she said as the bobbleheads Gail and April nodded rapidly in the background. "You don't want to be like all them Perrys havin' all those kids out in their shantytown near the landfill." She took a deep breath.

"I can't imagine how they do it," Gail chimed in. "I mean Cheryl Perry must have one every nine months."

I considered explaining exactly how it was done, but I refrained.

"Landfill germs," my mother said. "They breathe 'em in every day, especially now."

April May wrapped a breakfast sandwich in foil for a customer. "Think of the hospital bills."

"That's probably why doctors cost so much," Gail said. "I mean, even with insurance we're robbed blind. Look at all I just paid when I was there the other day."

"I spent years paying off my three children," my mother said, eyeing me as if I were responsible for me and my brothers.

"Nowadays, people like the Perrys don't have to pay for nothing." Gail slapped a coffee-filter basket against the edge of a trash can, and the used filter slid into its depths. "The government pays for everything out of our pockets. Bunch of thieves."

"Well, some people just don't have good insurance," April said, the voice of reason.

"Then they should get jobs," Gail pontificated. "I mean, even Shopper's Super Saver has good insurance. I overheard what Daryl's co-pay was that day I went. And he had stitches and a smashed finger."

Before the conversation digressed further, I decided to leave. I waved at my mother, but before I stepped out the door, I heard Dudley Do-It-All-Right's name and halted midstep.

"And what's going to happen to Shopper's Super Saver now after all that stuff about Frank is out in the open?" Gail clucked her tongue.

I turned back around to listen.

"You can't be too careful these days. The best people can be living double lives," April May intoned.

"Isn't that the truth?" Gail looked up at me as if I were hiding the very worst of secrets, which I was.

Ma nodded. "Just look at Frank. He's always been perfect. His wife, kids, and house are perfect. Those two youngest of his are cute as bugs. They go to Sammie and Charlie's school, you know."

"That just goes to show you," Gail said.

I waited to find out what it goes to show, but no one said anything.

"What do you think he did with the money?" Ma asked.

Gail put on a new pot of coffee. "Gold. I'm sure he bought gold." She's convinced that the world is headed for a financial collapse and gold is the only safe investment. She also believes that NASA faked the moonwalk.

They busied themselves behind the counter. I waited. My mother finally looked at me, hands on her hips.

"You need something else? You should sit down if you don't feel well. You certainly look like it. Something about your face. Pasty and a little swollen like you're holding water maybe? Is your blood pressure okay?"

I reached up to feel my face, expecting it to feel spongy, like a balloon. If I hadn't felt bad before, I did now. "I should go," I said.

"Well, don't let me stop you. At least I'll see you again on Sunday."

My mind was whirling, but not because of Sunday dinner. "Before I go, I want to know about Frank," I said.

Gail almost dropped the mug she held. "You mean you don't know?"

April stared at me openmouthed. "I would have thought you'd know everything seeing as how you're in the loop and so close to the police and all."

"Rumors 'R Us" had been busy. Of course, this was their company headquarters. But why did April think I was in the know with Detective Eric Scott?

"Where in the world did you get that idea?" I asked.

"Your mother's been telling everyone about it," April May said. "You've been called in for meetings a couple of times."

I stared at my mother in disbelief. She'd always done that. Made me feel like a loser in private but bragged to everyone about all my accomplishments—even those I hadn't done. She lived in a different reality. I was a suspect, for crying out loud. But there was no sense in trying to convince the bobbleheads. They'd believe what she wanted them to believe. "Just tell me about Frank, please."

Gail, April, and Ma exchanged glances.

She sighed. "Frank has been stealing money from the store."

Frank? Dudley Do-It-All-Right? Stealing from the store? "Embezzling?" I asked.

"See," Ma said triumphantly. "You knew. You just wanted to see if we knew."

I headed for the door once again. "See you later, Ma."

She waved her hand in the air, and I left. In my SUV, I placed the box of doughnuts on the passenger seat, musing how easy it was to think you really knew someone when, in reality, you didn't know them at all. Of all the people in town, I would never, ever have thought Frank capable of embezzling.

This was an interesting turn of events. Did Frank's crime have anything to do with Jim Bob's death? I pulled a pen from my purse and turned over the receipt my mother had given me to jot some notes. Using the dashboard like a desk, I started to write. *Embezzling. Frank a murderer?*

Gail had said something. . .something that was important. I was so engrossed in my thoughts I didn't see Detective Eric Scott until he tapped on my window. I jumped and stuffed the paper and pen into my purse. He motioned for me to roll down the glass. As I did, Corporal Nick Fletcher, otherwise known as Santa Cop, nodded at me from an unmarked car. Stupid me. I'd stayed too long.

I looked up at the tall, blond detective. "Are you harassing me?"

"I hope not," he said in a mild tone.

"Then why won't you leave me alone? I see you all the time now." I glanced at the window of my mother's store. She, Gail, and April were watching us. That was maddening, and I turned on him. "Do you realize that everyone thinks I'm in some sort of inner circle with you? My mother is convinced that I'm like your confidante or something because you've hauled me in to the sheriff's office twice now. They won't believe I'm just another suspect. And this is not going to help. Not at all."

He glanced at the store then back at me. "I'm sorry. No one is accusing you of anything."

There was that mild, even tone again. "Detective Scott, are you trained to sound nice even when you don't want to? Is it how you get people to talk to you?"

The left side of his mouth lifted. A half smile that told me everything I needed to know.

I sighed. "I have to go to work. What do you want?"

"I was going to suggest that perhaps we need to have another talk."

My heart pounded. "Why?"

"Just to see if you remember anything else." He shifted. The gold circle–enclosed star glittered on his belt in the early morning sun; then I noticed a serious-looking black gun nestled in a brown leather holster at his side.

I glanced up and met his gaze. "Do I have to?"

He leaned his upper arm on the hood of my SUV and stared down at me. "Might be a good thing."

I felt claustrophobic with him hovering over me like that. "Well—"

"How about this afternoon? Say around two?"

"I have to find someone to watch Sammie." I mentally went through a list in my head. Then I looked up at him. "If I come in to talk to you, will you do me a favor?"

He straightened and narrowed his eyes. "I don't work like that."

"Please. It's nothing bad." I glanced at the store where Gail had her face pressed against the glass. Her mouth was moving rapidly. I could only imagine what she was saying. "Could you tell my mother that you and I aren't working together? Maybe she'll believe you."

He glanced from me to the store and back to me. Then he laughed. "I come here almost every morning, and I have for years. I know your mother well enough to say with confidence that no one can deter her from anything she thinks."

There we had it from a police detective—what I'd known my whole life.

After watching the three aforementioned women watch Detective Scott and Corporal Fletcher enter the store, I slumped in my seat. Another interview. And I hadn't had time to find out what I needed to know. If I could just come up with an idea before I met with the detective, then maybe I could distract him. What had Gail said? Something about the murder scene? Now that my stomach had gone back to normal, I could picture everything in my mind without throwing up. What was it that bugged me? There was Jim Bob on a cart and a nasty-looking knife in his stomach and. . .no blood. That's what was wrong. How could Jim Bob have been stabbed to death without blood going all over? Perhaps I missed it all. A trick of my mind to protect me. Still, I wasn't sure, and that bothered me.

———

George and I were sitting in my office after the meeting, eating doughnuts while Max ran a few errands. Years ago, when I worked for George as his office manager, we got doughnuts once a week and sat together just like this. In fact, it was over doughnuts when he'd first introduced me to Max, who had been inquiring about George's contracting business.

I swallowed a bite of my bear claw. "Did you know Jim Bob Jenkins?"

He frowned and wiped his mouth on a napkin. "Enough to know he was

a. . . Well, I don't want to use that kind of language in front of you, Trish."

"Can't you tell me without cussing?" I took another bite.

He shook his head. "Not sure I can, and I hate to speak ill of the dead."

"No one else hesitates," I said through crumbs on my lips.

He smiled. "I'm sure they don't. He didn't exactly inspire good feelings in folks."

I waited.

George eyed me. "You got a reason for asking?"

"Curiosity. I found the body."

"Yes, well, that was too bad. No woman should see something like that. Max is worried about you. Says the whole thing might have given you an ulcer."

"Max worries too much." I sniffed and wiped my fingers.

George grinned at me. "For good reason, besides which he's nuts over you. Was from the first time he saw you."

I grinned back, happy with the thought that Max was nuts for me; then I remembered that maybe the only reason I had Max was because my brother killed Lindsey.

George misinterpreted my change of expression. "Okay, I'll tell you. You don't need to get upset." The chair squeaked under his weight as he crossed his legs. "Jim Bob was always trying to find people's weak spots. He'd make like he was so nice. Then idiots would confide stuff, or somebody would tell him something about somebody else, and he'd use it to get things from them. He tried it with me. I told him to. . .er, stop it."

That sounded suspiciously like what Jim Bob had done to me. "You mean blackmail?"

"You could call it that," George said.

"Doesn't sound like he was a nice guy at all." I frowned at him. "If he was blackmailing people, why didn't someone tell the police?"

George shook his head. "Lack of proof, for one thing. And the other reason was that people probably didn't want their dirty little secrets to get out."

I stared at the napkin in my lap. Dirty little secrets. That added a real dimension to motivation for his death. Apparently I was only one of many who had motivation to kill Jim Bob. I wondered if Steffie knew about her husband's activities. I looked up at George. "What do you think of Stefanie?"

"Her?" His guttural tone made the pronoun sound like a bad word. "All's I can say is they deserved each other."

"So you don't think she's attractive?" I couldn't help it. I had to know.

He snorted. "Please, Trish. I'm too old to have my head turned by a pretty face. Yeah, she's got some obvious, er, attributes, but there's different kinds of pretty. You got what'll last. You're a fine-looking, nice, interesting young woman."

Max sauntered into the office with his arms behind his back. "Are you flirting with my wife, George?"

He laughed. "I'm too old, buddy. Couldn't keep up with her if I had to. That kind of spunk needs someone who can handle it. Like you."

I blushed.

Max regarded me with a smoky glance that made my blood warm. Then he took his hands from behind his back. He held a bouquet of flowers. Roses.

"For you, baby," he said and smiled. "Having George around is bringing back lots of good memories."

George grinned. "See? He's nuts over you."

I stood and took the flowers from Max, blinking back tears. He leaned over and kissed my forehead. "I love you," he whispered. "George is right."

"Thank you, honey." I buried my face in the blooms so he wouldn't see just how upset I was. I didn't deserve flowers. Not at all.

Max slipped into a chair, stretching his legs out, crossing them at the ankles. "Honey, you remember that self-storage convention in Chicago?"

I nodded, glad for the change of topic. After I put the flowers on my desk, I took a deep breath and sat down. The family had gone a few years ago when Max and his dad first started planning their self-storage empire.

"It's coming up in a couple of days," he said.

I nodded again.

He watched me. "Getting the kids taken care of, like their car pools and things, is hard with short notice."

"That's true," I murmured. Still, the thought of time away from here was wonderful. We'd have time alone together. We could really talk, and then, far away from the familiar, I could tell Max everything. I began making a mental list of phone calls I would make if we went.

"You should go," George said. "You gotta get things settled. With plans in the works for the new facility, you gotta get some good programs. Nothin' chases the renters away like not being able to get into their units or keeping their stuff in a facility that isn't secured."

Our gate program still wasn't working right, and we had to leave the gate open twenty-four hours—something that we had to take care of soon.

I glanced at my watch. Time had gotten away from me. I jumped to my feet. "I have to go. I have to find someone to watch Sammie. I, ah, have to go see Detective Scott this afternoon."

"Again?" Max frowned. "This is the third time. Why?"

I shrugged. "He has a few more questions. It's just standard procedure."

"I wouldn't think so. . .unless you're a suspect." He frowned. "Are you? Eric didn't say anything last night, but you were at the store, and you did find the body." He paused. "Honey, is there something you're not telling me?"

I tried not to choke.

George cleared his throat and stood. "I think it's time for me to head out."

Max was distracted for a moment, saying good-bye to George. That meant I had just a second's reprieve. My husband might be dense to certain subtleties of mood, but once he latched on to something, his mind was like lightning—and he didn't let go until he had answers. I needed to figure things out quickly. Perhaps Max would pick up Sammie, and I'd have time for a quick visit to Abbie's.

I turned to my desk and picked up my flowers as the guys said their good-byes. Maybe I could distract him.

"Trish?"

I stuck my nose in the flowers. "Where did you get these? They're lovely."

"Glad you like them." I felt his eyes boring into the back of my head.

I reached for my purse. "Would you pick up Sammie for me, honey? I might like to visit Abbie before I go to the sheriff's office."

"No problem," he said softly.

I made sure my phone was in my purse. "I'll pick up something from the deli for dinner, okay? How about subs? And a movie? We can watch a movie tonight."

He cleared his throat.

I slowly turned around. Max had his arms crossed.

"I should go now," I said.

"I think you should tell me what's going on first." The only part of him that moved was his mouth. His eyes were slightly narrowed, and he looked a bit like a panther ready to pounce. I rarely saw Max's aggressive side. A hard-nosed businessman who had learned at the feet of his harder-nosed father. I didn't like it.

I clasped the handle of my purse until my knuckles turned white. "Detective Scott says that by talking to me over and over again, things I've seen but don't remember might come back to me." As much as the detective had annoyed me, I couldn't believe I was defending him.

Max studied me very much like the cops had. Then he took a deep breath and glanced at his watch. "Something's not right here, but I need to go pick up Sammie. This is the last time I'll allow you to go to the sheriff's office without a lawyer. I want you to tell Eric that, okay?"

Great. All I needed was a lawyer friend of the Cunninghams picking my brain. He'd be like all Max's family—Harvard educated and smart as a whip. That would be worse than talking to Detective Scott. And despite lawyer/client privilege, I'd wonder what the lawyer was telling the family.

"Okay." I didn't meet Max's eyes, just studied his very firm chin. He had a nice chin, with a tiny, little cleft right in the middle.

"Is there anything else you need to tell me?" he asked.

My gaze snapped up to his. "Like did I murder him? Is that what you mean?"

He closed his eyes for a second, rubbing the bridge of his nose. Then he crossed the room in three steps and pulled me into his arms. "No, honey. I know you didn't kill him. I just love you so much. The thought of something happening to you makes me crazy. I'm sorry."

Well, I'd succeeded in distracting him, but now I felt worse. With his words, he heaped red coals of shame upon my head. How much more could I take? I had to find my answers and fast.

9

With my arms full of yearbooks, a bag from the drugstore, and my purse, I brushed past a surprised Abbie at her front door. I was out of breath from running up the stairs. She lived above an antique shop in the middle of town.

I dumped everything on her taupe leather sofa, whirled around, and faced her. "I have another interview with Detective Scott today." I glanced at my watch. "In exactly ninety minutes. I need you to help me prepare. I hope you have some time. If you'd answer your phone or get a cell phone, I'd be able to get in touch with you."

She shut her front door and faced me. "I was in the shower, so I didn't hear the answering machine. And I hate cell phones."

"I brought bribes." I pointed at the stuff I'd dropped. "I also brought a notebook to make notes in. And I have all of Russ's yearbooks. I need to make a list of things to distract the police so I have more time to check into Russ's past and see who was blabbing to Jim Bob."

"Have you talked to Max yet?" she asked.

"No." I met her gaze. "I tried. Then Karen walked in and started talking about her mother. I couldn't do it after that."

She studied my face a moment more; then she glided to the couch and fished through the plastic bag, pulling out two plain stenographer's pads and six Cadbury eggs. She grinned and bounced an egg on her palm. "My very favorite. You're serious about bribery, I see. Are they all for me?"

I nodded.

She waved a pad in the air. "Couldn't you have gotten notebooks that were a little more decorative?"

I took it from her. "This is serious business. I didn't want to show up at Detective Scott's office with something that had pink and purple fairies on the cover."

She continued to bounce the egg in her hand. "Okay. Here's the deal. I'll help you if you promise to talk to Max within the next week."

"I want to. I'm trying." I crossed my arms. "Why are you so insistent about this?"

"I don't want anything to happen to you guys. Remember my short marriage? My ex was keeping secrets."

"Yeah, but his secret was two women on the side. He betrayed you."

"Don't you think Max will feel betrayed by something like this?"

I raked my fingers through my hair. "Yes. Yes, he will. I know that. That's what makes this hard. But if Russ is guilty, then my stepkids are going to hate me. And. . .I don't know how Max will feel. I mean. . ." My throat closed up, and tears filled my eyes.

"Oh, hon, I'm sorry." Abbie hugged me. "I don't think you're giving everyone enough credit, but I don't know for sure."

I sniffled into her shoulder for a minute until I got hold of myself.

"Let's get to work." She motioned to the dining room table. "But I have my doubts that you'll be able to distract Eric."

Once again, I sensed the edge in her voice when she mentioned his name. Abbie's ex-husband had been a police officer. As we sat down, a thought occurred to me. I glanced at her. "Is the reason you don't like Detective Scott because he reminds you of your ex-husband?"

Abbie raised her chin, and her eyes looked like flint. "Eric went to the academy with him. They were friends. He has a lot of nerve judging me when he and his wife split up, too." She huffed. "I don't want to discuss it, okay?"

"Okay." I knew better than to ask anything else. She'd tell me in her own good time.

I opened a notebook and pulled a pen from my purse. "I think Jim Bob was a blackmailer. He was trying to blackmail me. And he tried to pull something on George."

"Well, most everyone agrees he wasn't a nice guy." The corner of Abbie's mouth twitched. "Which could explain why Stefanie did what she did."

I eyed Abbie. "What did she do?"

"Well, at the hairdresser yesterday, I heard whispers about her and Daryl."

I remembered Shirl's comment about sneaky men. "You're not saying that Daryl and Stefanie. . ."

Abbie raised an eyebrow. "The Bible calls it adultery."

"That's hard to believe." I shuddered. "I mean, we're talking about Daryl."

She shrugged. "If you didn't know him like you do, you'd think he was quite good-looking."

The Dweeb? Good-looking? I couldn't get past the gross little boy I'd known in grade school.

"Right there are some mighty good motivations." Abbie crossed her legs. "You've got lust and anger and greed."

"I get the lust and anger part, but greed?"

"Sure. Maybe Stefanie thought Daryl could get a piece of his wife's fortune."

If I'd been a cartoon character, there would be a lightbulb over my head. "Of course. She was looking for her next well-to-do guy. Or at least one with the potential." There weren't many in our area, really. Daryl, Max, although his family didn't have as much as Daryl's wife's. . .oh. . .Max.

I clenched my fists. "She's been flirting with Max, trying to get into Jim Bob's storage unit. Do you suppose she wants more than that?"

"From what I've heard, I'd say that if Max succumbed she'd jump in with both feet."

I couldn't speak.

Abbie looked at me with a tiny grin. "Trish, close your mouth. You'll catch flies."

I snapped my jaw shut and said nothing. Though some of my suspicions about Steffie were vindicated, Abbie's words triggered my latent insecurity. I, Trish Cunningham, redneck and the daughter of a struggling farmer, had married Maxwell Cunningham the Third, third child and only son of a wealthy family. No one could have predicted such a match. He was way out of my league. Something his mother had hinted at on more than one occasion, making it difficult for me to forget. Now, if my brother had been responsible for Max's first wife's death. . . well, I would never live that down.

I forced my mind from the Cunninghams and back to the problem at hand. "Okay, so Daryl and the not-so-grieving widow could have been in cahoots. I know she wasn't at the store that morning—at least not as far as I know—but Daryl was. And Gail says that Daryl was at the doctor's that afternoon. He needed stitches."

Abbie nodded. "Make a note of that. And what about Frank?"

"You heard about the embezzling?" I asked.

"Yes, but he hasn't been charged yet."

"He's still a tattletale like he was in school. He told Detective Scott about me and Jim Bob. I also wonder if he's the one who said something to Jim Bob about Russ."

She scooted next to me. "Let's check out Russ's friends."

We opened the yearbook for his senior year. The front flap had a dedication to Daryl's little brother Tim, who had drowned in a lake.

"That was so sad," I said. "Russ and Tim were good friends, you know. Tim was a bad influence. He always got away with stuff because his folks and Daryl doted on him."

She glanced at me. "Then put his name on your list."

I did. Then feeling a little like a voyeur, I glanced at all the inscriptions that Russ's friends had written. I tapped a finger on one. "I had forgotten this. Russ dated Peggy Nichols."

"Really?"

"Yep. He broke her heart."

"We'll ask her some questions on Saturday, then." Abbie flipped through more pages. "I had forgotten that Lee Ann's husband, Norm, had hung out with Russ."

"Me, too."

Abbie glanced at her watch. "You need to go. Cops don't like to be kept waiting." She grinned ever so slightly. "However, they do like to keep you waiting. Be prepared to sit in the lobby. It's a tactic to keep you off guard."

—

Abbie's warning served me well. I arrived fifteen minutes early. Fifteen minutes after my scheduled appointment, Corporal Fletcher walked through the door into the lobby.

"Sorry to keep you waiting, Mrs. C."

I narrowed my eyes. How many people called me Mrs. C.? Shirley? The people who worked for me and Max?

"Come on in." He held open the door to the inner sanctum of the sheriff's office as though inviting me into his home. "You want something to drink? A Coke? Some water?"

"No, thank you, Corporal Fletcher," I said through stiff lips.

He had the nerve to smile at me as he directed me toward some stairs and motioned for me to go up ahead of him. "Detective Scott is waiting for you."

"Is he now?" My irritation level rivaled my nervousness.

The corporal said nothing else, just directed me to the same interview room where I'd been questioned before. Detective Scott was already there and stood as I entered. I noticed several files on the table, as well as a notepad and a pen.

"Hello, Mrs. Cunningham. Please have a seat. Did Corporal Fletcher offer you something to drink?"

"Yes. I don't want anything, thank you."

He nodded at the corporal, who shut the door, leaving me alone with the detective. He motioned for me to sit in a chair. As he sat opposite me, I pulled my notebook from my bag. "I have some thoughts for you." I flipped to the first page and ran my finger down my list. "I've been investigating."

"What?" he demanded.

I glanced up at him, meeting his frowning gaze. "I said I've been investigating. I've gathered some information for you."

His silence told me a lot. I'd startled him. That was good. I wanted to keep him off balance for a change.

"Well, I've jotted down some things that I've heard. Like, did you know that Jim Bob Jenkins was a blackmailer? He tried to blackmail George." I put the steno pad on the table and tapped it with my index finger. "And Daryl Boyd was supposedly sleeping with Stefanie. She was out for money, you know. At least that's the theory."

Detective Scott leaned toward me. "Mrs. Cunningham, you can't investigate this—"

I waved a hand in the air. "Call me Trish, please. And I'm only collecting information to give to you. You're the detective."

His lips narrowed. "This is a murder investigation."

"Yes. I know. I'm the one who found Jim Bob, which makes me a suspect, too. I don't want to be a suspect, so I'm collecting information."

"No one is accusing you of anything," he pronounced. Again.

I snorted. "This is the third time I've been here, Detective. Max is worried. He wants to get me a lawyer." I picked up my pad of paper and brandished it like a fan. "As I see it, there aren't too many people who could be the killers." I frowned. "Except if a perfect stranger came in through the side door. Do you think that Jim Bob and Daryl left the side door open?"

I glanced at Detective Scott out of the corner of my eyes.

He leaned back in his chair and tapped his pen on the table slowly. It sounded like a second hand on a clock. "Trish, when did you last speak to Jim Bob Jenkins?"

I dropped the notebook on the table. "Well, I talked to him at the Shopper's Super Saver. And you know what? As far as I can tell, there are three main suspects. Besides me, of course—"

"Was that the last time you spoke to him?" Detective Scott's voice was low and insistent. *Tap, tap, tap, tap.*

The sound of his pen was worse than water torture. A suspect would talk just to get him to stop doing that.

I flipped the paper in my notebook. "Well, I told you that I saw him in the parking lot at the grocery store and—"

*Tap, tap, tap, tap.*

"Trish, where did you last speak to Jim Bob Jenkins?"

Abbie was right. Detective Scott was not distractible. I finally met his gaze. He knew. The fact that Corporal Fletcher called me Mrs. C. was my first clue. He'd probably done it on purpose to let me know they'd been to Four Oaks Self-Storage to investigate. We had cameras that recorded the office and grounds twenty-four hours a day. Not sound, just pictures. The police could have easily viewed those. If I lied, things would be much worse for me than they already were.

I bowed my head and felt tears prickling in my eyes. "Last Friday," I whispered.

I heard his breath escape in a tiny sigh as though he'd been holding it, waiting for me to tell him the truth. He put the pen down. "Can you tell me about that?"

His voice was gentle, and that was worse than anything else. Tears spilled over my lower eyelids. I swiped hard at them. I hate crying. I'd rather fight.

"Do I have to?" I sniveled and fought for control.

"It would be best if you did," he said.

———

"Confession is good for the soul" is a platitude that my mother used when I was young to make me tell her all the things I'd done wrong. It lost its meaning early in my life because I realized that she would use my confessions against me at some point in the future. However, in the case of me and Detective Scott, the saying held true to a degree. After spilling my guts to him, I felt a small sense of relief. Maybe that was simply because I no longer feared that deputies would show up at my door to arrest me. At least not right now. I was sure I was still on the suspect list, but telling the truth goes a long way.

So, it was with a semilighter heart that I rushed into the school auditorium on Saturday morning, trailed by Max and Tommy, who carried my stuff in boxes. That I would be in charge of a healthy-heart booth at a health fair was a little ironic, considering my mother made a living selling heart attacks. That's probably why I allowed myself to be coerced into doing it. To be fair, people needed to be warned of the dangers of consuming too much fat. Then, fairly warned, they could eat doughnuts, and I wouldn't have to feel vicariously guilty.

Max and Tommy left everything at my table and took off. Abbie was already there, dressed in an ivory pantsuit, talking with the principal of the school, Peggy Nichols, my brother's onetime girlfriend. They both turned when we arrived and greeted us. Then a bald custodian walked by. He looked like the man I'd seen at the baseball game.

"Who is that?" I asked, pointing in his direction.

"Peter Ramsey, the custodian," Peggy said. "Will you excuse me, please? I need to speak with him."

Maybe that explained his attendance at the game. Sometimes school custodians hired out to help at other functions.

"Hi, Abs," I said as I placed a box on a battered particleboard table.

"Hi, hon."

I covered the table with a pretty cloth; then Abbie and I quickly set up everything else. I glanced around the room. During the week, it served as a cafeteria. Beige-painted, cinder-block walls were the backdrop for the event. More tables filled the room this year, but I couldn't figure out which were the new ones. Although the event was called a health fair, it had evolved into much more than that. Now, in addition to the local dentist, doctor, and hospital, the sheriff's department had a table, as well as other community organizations.

As people began to arrive, Abbie sat on one stool, while I perched on the other. We surreptitiously ate doughnuts, which she'd picked up from Ma's.

"Detective Scott knows about Jim Bob, me, and Russ," I said through a mouthful of glazed doughnut. "He knew before I told him."

Abbie nodded. "That doesn't surprise me."

"He promised he would look into Lindsey's death for me. Maybe it was solved or something and Jim Bob was just using it to try to get free storage. Then he told me I have to talk to Max."

"Good. So when are you going to talk to Max?"

I bit my lip and sighed. "Well, today is shot. He's going shopping with Sammie and Charlie tonight. Sammie's getting a new hamster. I want the timing to be perfect. No chance for interruptions. Tomorrow we're eating dinner at my folks,' so I'm thinking that I'll leave the little kids there, and Max and I can go out tomorrow night."

"That sounds like a good plan," she said. Then she frowned. "Frank is here. With his kids."

I followed her gaze. He was at one of the other tables. "His kids go to school here. I guess he decided not to hide out in shame. Maybe he's not guilty."

"Well, his wife kicked him out, and he's living with his parents. He's no longer employed at Shopper's Super Saver. He probably doesn't have anything else to do."

I felt a tug of sympathy for Frank. "How do you know all this stuff, Abs? You're like a walking encyclopedia of Four Oaks."

She winked. "I make it my business to know things. And I suspect Jim Bob was also hassling Peggy Nichols."

"Why?"

"Because earlier I expressed my concern that we had a murderer loose in Four Oaks. She snarled and said lots of people had reason to see Jim Bob dead, and then she clammed up."

Abbie's gaze lifted over my head, and her face grew tight. I turned and saw Detective Scott approaching the table.

"Why are you here?" I asked rudely. I'd never seen him in a uniform. Usually he wore a suit, and I found the change a bit intimidating.

"I'm taking my turn at the Sheriff's Department table." He didn't seem to take offense at my tone. "We're fingerprinting little kids." His eyes flickered over Abbie.

"Eric," she said coolly.

He nodded slightly then looked at me. "Trish, may I have a word with you for just a moment?"

I felt my stomach lurch.

"Go ahead," Abbie said. "I'll man the table."

"Thanks a lot," I mouthed to her.

Detective Scott walked me out of the auditorium and into the hallway. I imagined how this would play out later with Rumors 'R Us. We stopped in front of the school office. An appropriate location, since it's where the principal's office was, and the way he took me out of the auditorium reminded me of all the times I'd been yanked out of class when I was young and in trouble.

I looked up at him. "Are you going to arrest me now?"

He shook his head. "If I were going to arrest you, I wouldn't politely walk you from the room." He paused. "I looked into Lindsey's death. The case is still open."

I felt like throwing up. "What does that mean?"

He took a deep breath. "Whoever took that sign is probably guilty of involuntary manslaughter. There's no statute of limitations on that, I'm afraid."

I swallowed. "So Russ could be arrested?"

Detective Scott shrugged. "If he's guilty. But we don't know that. Yet. I'm looking into anything that has to do with Jim Bob Jenkins and his murder." The detective paused and gazed down at me. I thought I saw some concern there. "Trish, you need to tell Max about your brother. And just as important, stay away from the murder investigation. Someone is playing for keeps."

"Does that mean I'm not a suspect?"

His expression turned blank. "I told you, you're not accused of anything. You'll know if I change my mind."

⁓

Tommy came to help clean up; then he would take me home. He, Abbie, and I carted stuff back and forth until everything was packed in the car. A group of deputies walked by, along with Detective Scott. He saluted me.

"You ready to go, Mom?" Tommy asked.

"Just about. I need to run to the bathroom real fast." I glanced at Abbie. "Thanks for helping, Abs."

"I had a good time, as usual," she said.

After she hugged me, she walked to her red Mustang, passing right by Detective Scott. She acknowledged him with a slight dip of her head and kept walking with a stiff back. He watched until she climbed into her car.

"Mom?" My son's voice pulled me from my observations. "You going to the ladies room?"

I turned and smiled at him. "Yeah. I'll be right back."

The halls were empty when I ran into the bathroom. I used the facilities and freshened my lipstick. Then I charged back out into the hallway.

"Looking for more bodies?"

I skidded to a stop and turned around. Frank stood there, hands in his pockets and a scowl on his face.

71

I crossed my arms and glared at him. "That's a horrible thing to say. Why are you here?"

"To talk to you." He stared down at me, jingling change in his pocket. "Did you tell the cops about the knife?"

"What? You mean the one in Jim Bob? Of course." I stared at him. Why was he asking this?

"Did it look like a meat cutter's knife?" he asked.

"Come on, Frank. I have no idea what a meat cutter's knife looks like. Now, I'm tired of talking." I turned to leave.

"You talk enough to the cops." He said the words softly, but I sensed terrible anger in the tone.

I whirled around to face him again. "Can I help it if they keep asking me questions?"

Briefly, I felt like we were kids in grade school again, fighting on the playground. The lights flickered and went off. I heard voices in the distance; then they stopped. The only illumination came from windows in the classrooms. The twilightlike atmosphere heightened my senses. I smelled chalk and floor wax. The dim hallway loomed in both directions like an endless tunnel going nowhere. Frank's rapid breathing and the beating of my heart matched paces. I no longer felt like a kid.

I heard the sound of footsteps behind me. Frank stood at attention and backed up. I turned around. My stepson was trotting down the hall.

"Mom? Is everything okay?" he asked.

My breath whooshed out in relief. "Yes. Everything is fine." Now.

Frank said nothing, just walked past us and hurried away. I linked my arm in Tommy's as we walked down the hall. Frank had made me feel cold. I needed the comfort of human touch.

Tommy glanced down at me. "I was worried because Dad said you haven't been feeling well."

"Thank you. I'm glad you came."

We reached the foyer, and I welcomed the sunlight.

"That was Frank, right?" Tommy asked.

I nodded.

He opened the door and waited for me to pass by. "He was putting off some seriously bad vibes, Mom."

That had occurred to me, too. "I think he blames me for his problems. He's just looking for a scapegoat."

Tommy glanced at me. "If he thinks that, he's an idiot."

I'd always thought so, despite trying hard not to. I'd just never seen his creepy side.

10

Sunday mornings had always been one of my favorite times of the week, especially since they reminded me of my courtship with Max. But not this morning. My relief after confessing to Detective Scott had faded, and now I was in the throes of abject misery, feeling sick with worry about talking to Max tonight.

To make matters worse, I taught the five- and six-year-olds the lesson about the dangers of lying. Then the pastor added to my wretched state by continuing a series about family that was leading up to Easter Sunday. Today's was about marriage.

Max grabbed my hand, and the two of us followed Charlie and Sammie to my SUV. Our two oldest had taken off right after church.

"Karen and Tommy will meet us at your folks', right?" Max asked.

"Yep. Tommy has a big exam tomorrow, so he's not staying long after lunch. And Karen is going to see Julie."

After the kids were settled in the vehicle, Max opened my door. As I climbed in, my steno pad slipped out from under the seat where I'd put it.

Max grabbed it. After a quick glance, he frowned and held it up. "What is this?"

"Nothing much." I tried to snatch it from his hand, my heart pounding.

He held it out of my reach and flipped it open. "This looks suspiciously like—"

"Nothing," I said. "It's not important. It's old. I was just sort of downloading thoughts last week." I held my hand out.

He narrowed his eyes and didn't give me the notebook. "You're not still involved in all this, are you? You told me Eric Scott said you weren't a suspect."

I lowered my hand and shrugged. "What do you mean by *involved*?"

I got a glittery-eyed glance. "You're avoiding the question. A simple yes or no would do. Frankly, I want you to leave the whole thing behind."

How could I leave it all behind? "You're being overprotective and maybe even a little bossy."

"What?" He ran his other hand through his hair. "I'm not. . ." He glanced at the children.

I turned to look at them, too. Two pairs of bright eyes stared at us. I'm always amazed at how children listen when they aren't supposed to and ignore the things they're supposed to listen to.

Max said nothing else, just handed me the notebook and helped me into the SUV, shut my door, and climbed into the driver's side. We didn't speak as he drove from the parking lot. I had a feeling the topic would come up again.

When we'd gotten premarital counseling, the pastor had given us tests, so he could determine our strengths and weaknesses. Max rated pretty high in bossiness, although they called it something else that didn't sound quite so negative. He tried his best to watch his attitude with me, but he wasn't always successful.

A couple of minutes later, he reached over and squeezed my hand. "Remember we talked about that convention in Chicago?"

I nodded.

"I've decided I have to go. I need to see the programs and try them before we buy. It starts on Monday afternoon."

I bit my lip. That didn't give me much time to get ready, but a trip would give me more time alone with Max than just this evening. It was perfect. "Okay, I can be packed by tonight. I'm sure Mom and Dad will watch the kids."

He glanced at me, surprise on his face. "What are you talking about?"

"I'm thinking out loud." I smiled at him, but he wasn't smiling back.

His attention went to the road while he turned a corner; then he turned back to me. "Why would you think that you're going with me?"

Panic gripped my chest. "You're joking, right?"

"No, I'm not." His hands tightened on the steering wheel. "I thought we agreed yesterday that you couldn't leave right now."

Yesterday? Had I said that? Had we agreed? I couldn't remember. And I couldn't believe he was going without me. When was I going to talk to him?

"I know this isn't a good time to leave you, but with the expansion, I need to shop programs and other things now." His words came out in a rush.

"Max, I thought we were both going."

He ran a hand through his hair. "I've already booked my flight. I'm sorry. I thought we agreed."

I wanted to stomp my feet on the floor. "We didn't agree at all. Why are you leaving me?"

The vehicle had become deathly quiet. Max glanced in the rearview mirror. I could feel the children leaning forward in their seats, waiting to see who said what next.

"Let's discuss it later," I said quietly, although I was screaming on the inside.

He nodded. "Good idea."

My agenda for the evening was shot. As my mother would say, "The best-laid plans of mice and men. . ."

When we walked into her kitchen, the steamy air was fragrant with the smell of potatoes and roast. My father was leaning against the counter. I met his wide smile with one of my own. Besides Max, my father is the most important man in my life. He crossed the room in three steps to hug me. I clung to him for a beat longer than I usually did. He looked down at me with narrowed eyes but said nothing. He had always been able to read me—sometimes too well. If we'd been alone, he would have probed to find out what was wrong.

The huge dining room table was loaded with food. Ma served roast beef with all the trimmings. The only sounds I heard for the first few minutes were forks clinking against plates as we all ate. Everyone except Karen, who had been moping all morning. That didn't go unnoticed by my mother.

"What's ailin' you, Karen?" she finally asked.

Karen twirled her fork in her mashed potatoes and sighed dramatically. "Nothing."

"Hah!" Charlie said. "She's upset 'cause her best friend wants to run away."

That sounded serious. I wondered if Lee Ann knew.

"You shut up," Karen said to Charlie. "At least I'm not a freak who sees ghosts."

"Karen. . . ," Max warned.

"What are you talking about?" Charlie yelled.

"All your talk about dead people," she said.

"What do you know anyway, so busy talking on the phone and—"

"That's enough," Max said sternly. His order, combined with his frown, made an impression. The kids quieted—for a moment.

My mother and father, along with Sammie, watched Charlie and Karen with wide eyes.

Tommy, who was so busy stuffing his face that I didn't think he'd noticed anything, waved his fork in the air. "Sometimes I think Charlie knows more than we all give him credit for."

"What?" Karen yelped. "You're crazy. So is he. My whole family is crazy. A total embarrassment. I should just leave with Julie."

"I said, that's enough." Max's angry tone and glittering eyes left no question in anyone's mind that he meant what he said.

"More gravy, Tommy? Mashed potatoes?" My mother asked brightly, as if gravy and potatoes would fix everything.

"Daddy's going, too, like Julie," Sammie piped up. "He's leaving Mommy."

The silence that followed her statement was louder than Karen yelling. I can safely say that children hear everything, but important facts get lost in the translation.

"What she means is, Max is going out of town," I said, trying to keep my voice neutral.

My mother dropped her fork to her plate. "Out of town? Without you?"

"Yes, without me." I couldn't help the way my voice wavered.

"Well, I never. I thought the two of you were attached at the hip." She glanced from me to Max. "If you ask me, it'll be good for you. Too much togetherness is unhealthy."

I hadn't asked her. And it wasn't like Max and I had time to really be together. I'd married a man with three children. We'd hardly had a honeymoon to speak of because Charlie had been so little at the time and we didn't want to leave him for long. Automatic family. Now, with four kids and a growing business, not to mention our church activities, running the kids around, and things like ball games, we had very little time alone together. I opened my mouth to express my thoughts, but Daddy must have seen the anger in my eyes.

He cleared his throat. "So, Max, where are you going?"

"Chicago. To a self-storage convention." Max went on to explain in great detail why he was going and what he needed to accomplish.

He probably wanted me to listen so I'd understand, but I didn't. Instead, I twirled my mashed potatoes like Karen. Now when would I get a chance to talk to him? Tonight he'd want to spend time with the family. Plus, he was leaving me stuck at home alone with quarreling children. I felt his gaze on me but didn't look up. I was not a happy camper.

———

Monday night, after the kids were in bed, I pulled on one of Max's sweatshirts instead of pajamas and retrieved my steno pad. While I waited for him to call me, I'd organize all my clues. Maybe while he was gone, I could come up with some answers. I'd been right about having no time to talk to him the night before. Besides, telling him that my brother had possibly killed his first wife wasn't something I wanted to drop on him before a business trip.

I reviewed the notes I'd taken at Abbie's, starting with Russ's friends. I didn't remember much about my brother's life back then. I was ten years older. Tim, Peggy Nichols, Norm. I bit the end of my pen. Was it possible that Tim had stolen the stop sign and Daryl told Jim Bob that Russ did it just to protect his dead brother? And maybe Peggy still had sour grapes over Russ dumping her. She'd never married. Was it possible to carry a torch that long? Then there was Norm. He was a bit older than Russ, but they used to hang out together during the summer. That's all I knew, which frustrated me, so I flipped a page. I'd work on Jim Bob's murder instead.

As soon as I'd written MOTIVATIONS in big letters, the phone rang. I snatched it from the bedside table, dropping my steno pad on the floor in my hurry.

"Hello? Max?"

"Hi, baby." His voice on the phone is even better than in person. Low and intimate. Just hearing it through the receiver makes my insides feel like warm syrup. "I miss you. I hate sleeping alone."

"Me, too. So. . .are you. . .having a good time?" I hoped not.

"*Good time* isn't the right word. I'm getting things done. I think I've found a new computer program, but I wanted to talk it over with you before I buy it."

"Tell me," I said, settling back against the headboard.

He talked for about thirty minutes. We discussed the pros and cons.

"What do you think?" he asked.

I agreed with his choice.

Silence fell between us. I was afraid to speak because I might cry.

"Trish, what's wrong?" Max asked. "Has Eric been in touch with you again?"

"No, but. . .Max, we need to talk." I picked at the sheet.

He paused. "I thought we were talking."

"No, I have something we need to talk about. In person. That's why I wanted to go to Chicago with you."

I heard him breathing; then he inhaled. "Are you okay? Did you go to the doctor?"

I almost laughed, realizing where his mind was going. He thought I was ill. "I'm fine. It's nothing like that."

He took a deep breath. "I want you to go to the doctor, okay?"

I didn't answer, because I didn't intend to go. But I did feel bad for Max. He's so self-assured that I sometimes forget he's got vulnerabilities.

"I'm serious, Trish."

"Okay, okay," I grumbled.

He sighed. "Are you sure you don't want to discuss whatever it is right now?"

"Yes. I'm sure."

He sighed again. "All right. Get some sleep. I'll call you tomorrow."

I slept fitfully, thrashing around in bed. At around two in the morning, I woke with my covers and legs twisted together like a pretzel. I untangled myself and rolled over on my back. Something banged against the side of the house. I sat up. Then I heard another sound, like scratching. Was the wind blowing? My heart pounded. I held my breath and listened.

Nothing. I waited. Still nothing.

But now I was wide awake and would most likely toss and turn with guilt if I tried to sleep. Maybe I should eat a peanut butter and jelly sandwich. Nothing says comfort like peanut butter and jelly.

I pulled on a pair of jeans to wear with Max's sweatshirt, slid into my favorite old bunny slippers, and crept down the stairs. All the kids were asleep. Everything was dark except for a tiny night-light next to the front door. I walked down the hallway, scuffing my slippers on the wood floor. Then I heard scratching again.

*It's the wind*, I told myself. But it continued, sounding like dog nails on the front door. Our front door is massive. One of those solid metal doors with tiny little windows at the top. It also has a really nice doorknob. Brass. And it was jiggling.

**11**

I'm calling the police right now, so you'd better back off," I yelled as I jerked on the lights to the hall and the porch. Praying under my breath, I backed down the hallway, hands on the wall, feeling my way to the kitchen. After almost falling over the doorjamb, I turned and fumbled for the light switch and turned it on. Then I snatched the cordless phone from its bed on the wall and dialed 9-1-1.

Even while dispatch answered, I crept back up the hallway. I had to protect my children from whoever was trying to break in. But the doorknob had stopped moving.

After I explained what was going on, the dispatcher cautioned me not to open the door. Like I'm that stupid.

I assured her I was staying put; then I got a beep telling me I had another call. I ignored it and sat on the bottom step, watching the doorknob. Still no movement.

She kept me on the phone until squad cars with flashing lights filled my driveway and deputies were at the door.

I flung it open. Detective Eric Scott stood there, face scruffy with beard growth, dressed in jeans and a dark blue sweatshirt. He would have looked almost human except for the gun on his waist and his eyes, which were squinting at me.

"I didn't do anything," I said automatically.

"What?" He rubbed his face then shook his head. "I know that. We need to come in and check things out. Are you okay?"

Mad, scared, heart still pounding, but. . . "Yes." I stood back.

The detective came in, followed by Corporal Fletcher and a younger deputy.

"We'll check things out, Sarge," the corporal said.

"Good." Detective Scott nodded.

"My kids are asleep," I said.

"Not all of them." Corporal Fletcher motioned behind me.

I turned; Tommy, clad only in jeans, was tromping down the stairs, followed by Karen in a bathrobe.

"What's going on, Mom?" Tommy asked.

"Someone tried to break in," I said. "Are Charlie and Sammie still in bed?"

Karen nodded.

Detective Scott glanced at the corporal. "Fletcher, I want you outside to supervise, okay?"

"Yes, sir." Corporal Fletcher turned and walked off the porch.

"Is there somewhere we can sit?" the detective asked.

I nodded and led the way to the kitchen where I slumped into a chair, placing the phone on the table. I felt Tommy's presence at my back. Karen was leaning against the counter, twirling her hair in her fingers.

I rubbed my eyes and explained everything.

When I was done, Detective Scott took a deep breath. "Are you aware that someone tried to break into the offices of Four Oaks Self-Storage tonight?"

"What?" Tommy barked behind me. "Mom, we gotta call Dad."

"In a minute, Tommy." I didn't want to talk to Max until I'd totally calmed down. I wondered if the beep I'd ignored had been the alarm company trying to call me about the attempt at the storage offices.

"Did they get in?" Tommy asked, sounding very much like his father.

"No," the detective said.

About that time, I heard Charlie's voice. "Mom! Where are you?" He stormed into the kitchen, face squished up with fear. "What is going on around here? There are cops upstairs and cop cars outside."

"Someone tried to break in the house, but it's okay." I attempted to sound reassuring, feeling anything but. Things weren't okay. My fear was dissipating, leaving behind only anger. I needed to talk to the detective. I turned to the children. "Would you three mind giving me a few minutes alone with Detective Scott? Karen, go check on Sammie. Charlie, if she wakes up, don't you dare scare her with this. I mean it."

Karen nodded and left the room.

Charlie bounced next to me. "Mom, can I—"

"Charlie," I snapped. "Just go away, okay?"

He ran from the room. I had a feeling he was going outside to watch the activity. I didn't try to stop him.

Tommy didn't move. I turned and looked up at him.

His jaw was set. "Mom, I'd really like to stay. Dad sort of left me in charge."

I didn't want any of the kids in here in case Detective Scott said something about Russ. "I appreciate your concern for me, but I think perhaps the other kids could use your strength right now."

"I think I should stay," he said, crossing his arms.

I met his gaze and shook my head. We had a silent battle of wills, a stare down of sorts. He finally looked away. Then he put his shoulders back and gave the detective a steely glance. "All right. But if you need me for anything, call."

Detective Scott watched him leave. "Tommy really watches out for you."

"Just what I need—another keeper," I grumbled as I waved at a chair. "Why don't you sit down?"

He did.

"Would you like coffee, Detective?"

"Yes, please," he said. "Black."

I busied myself fixing it, my anger growing by the second. When the liquid started to drip into the carafe, I whirled around. I guess the anger showed on my face or in my gaze because his eyes widened.

With as much dignity as I could muster, given that I was wearing fuzzy pink bunny slippers with crossed eyes and Max's sweatshirt, which hung to my knees, I decided to tell the detective what I thought. "It was Stefanie Jenkins."

"What?" He fastened his sharp gaze on my face. "Did you see her?"

"Well, no."

"Why do you think that?"

I crossed my arms. "Because she wants to get into Jim Bob's storage unit and will use any method possible, including offering to do anything for Max. We're both adults, and I'm sure you understand like I do what that means. She tries to act nice, but I don't believe her. Do you think a little locked door is going to keep her from trying to steal a key? Not to mention, she was probably hoping Max would be here alone or something."

The detective's mouth twitched as though he wanted to laugh. I wasn't amused. I filled a mug with black coffee and clunked it down in front of him. Then I got some for me and sat at the table.

"So how could she have been in two places at once?" He lifted his coffee to his lips, watching me over the rim of the cup.

"How should I know? But I'm sure if she could offer favors to Max, she's capable of offering the same thing to someone else to help her." I leaned forward. "What's in that unit that she wants so bad?"

Detective Scott watched me.

"You know, she married him for his money. That's the only thing that makes sense because he wasn't exactly the studly kind of guy that a looker like Stefanie would be attracted to. Everyone says he was ugly. Of course, ugly is as ugly does, as my mother would say. Steffie probably killed him." I paused, took a sip of coffee, and put the cup down. "Then there's Frank. Maybe Jim Bob knew about the embezzling and threatened Frank. He is a creep. I didn't know that before, but now I do. I guess if he could embezzle and be creepy then murder wouldn't be out of the question." I frowned at the detective. "I have trouble imagining the Dweeb guilty of murder."

Detective Scott set his mug down hard. "The Dweeb?"

"Daryl. He's been the Dweeb since kindergarten." I tapped a finger on my mug. "I heard he was having an affair with Stefanie. That surprised me because I know his wife."

"Sarge!" Corporal Nick "Santa Cop" Fletcher burst into the kitchen. "We got signs of attempted entry in a number of places, including windows. Looks like whoever it was tried to use a credit card to open the front door.

I took a huge swig of coffee, nearly half the cup, and suddenly had a brilliant thought. "Hey, I know how it happened."

Both men stared at me.

"Well, Stefanie did one, and Daryl did the other. He's so used to his wife pushing him around that he could be talked into anything."

Silence filled the room as both men stared at me.

Detective Scott nodded slowly and took another sip of coffee. Then he put his cup down. "You think you'll be okay now?"

I realized he'd been tolerating my blabbering until he was sure I was okay. He wasn't taking me seriously at all. "No, I'm not okay, Detective Scott. All these people have a motive for the murder, just like me. Even my mother. She delivered a free box of doughnuts to Jim Bob every week. The world as I knew it no longer exists. Shopper's Super Saver is not safe. I can't drink milk. I'm sick to my stomach. I don't know the people I thought I did. And Max is in Chicago without me." I blinked back sudden tears.

"You oughta call him, Mrs. C.," Corporal Fletcher said. "I'd want my wife to call me."

"He's in Chicago," I repeated. My stomach gurgled.

"We know." Detective Scott pushed the phone toward me. "Please call him."

I frowned and swiped at my nose with the sweatshirt sleeve. "How did you know where he was?"

"He asked me to make sure you were okay while he was gone." The detective sighed. "After he threatened to get you a lawyer if I interviewed you again. Have you told him about Russ?"

"No," I murmured as my stomach clenched.

"You need to tell him." Detective Scott rubbed his forehead; then he picked up the phone and held it out to me. "Call him now and tell him you're okay."

"I will, but first. . ." I ran to the bathroom and threw up.

---

When I'd informed Max of the latest mishap, he'd let loose a spate of words that weren't clear through the receiver. He'd catch an early morning flight home, probably through a friend of his father's or something.

I'm not sure I'd ever heard him quite so upset.

I tried to sleep after everyone left but lay awake, stiff and furious that someone dared try to break into my house. Then I went to work despite total exhaustion but got little done. I couldn't focus on anything except my mystery and Max.

After falling asleep at my desk with my chin in my hand and waking up with a palm wet from drool, I went home to wait for him. I'd promised Detective Scott I would tell Max about Russ today. That made me edgy. To distract myself, I retrieved my steno pad and pen and then sat cross-legged on the couch in the family room. I turned to the page I'd started last night.

MOTIVATIONS. Though anyone at the store could have been guilty, I only knew three for sure, although Stefanie could have been behind her husband's murder.

Frank was embezzling. Jim Bob blackmailed people. He could have been blackmailing Frank, and Frank got tired of it.

I made a note. *Frank—embezzling; Jim Bob—blackmailing?*

If the rumors were true about Daryl and he was sleeping with Stefanie, he had motivation. I wrote, *Daryl sleeping with Stefanie? Blackmail? Did she have him do it?* Then I thought about the storage unit. *What does she want so badly?*

What about Lee Ann? I paused and chewed the pen. Maybe she had a boyfriend, and that's what made Norm leave. Jim Bob found out and blackmailed her. I jotted down, *Lee Ann? Boyfriend? Blackmail?*

The roar of a car engine and subsequent screeching brakes distracted me from my list. Max was home. Based on his earlier reaction, I wasn't sure what to expect. The kitchen door opened and slammed.

"Trish?"

"I'm in the family room." I shoved the notebook under a pillow on the couch and stood.

He rushed into the room and grabbed me up in his arms, mumbling a stream of incoherent words. Wrinkles etched his forehead and the skin around his mouth. He looked as scruffy as Detective Scott had the night before.

I buried my head in his chest, smelling the scent of airplanes and hotel in his shirt.

"The kids in school?" he murmured into my hair.

"Yep."

"Are they okay?"

"Yes. Tommy's mad that someone tried something while he was in charge. Sammie didn't even wake up during the whole thing, so she's only heard a modified version of what happened. Charlie spent a couple hours regaling the deputies with his theories about which fugitives from justice on *Mysterious Disappearances* tried to hack their way into our house. And Karen wasn't speaking when she left, so everything's the same with her."

He let go of me and stepped back.

I brushed his scratchy cheek with my finger. "Would you like some lunch?"

"No. Let's go sit down."

In the family room, he dropped onto the couch and pulled me next to him, but I couldn't enjoy his touch. I knew I had to talk to him about Russ.

"This has been a bad couple of weeks." He tightened his arm around me. "Tell me what happened."

I explained how I'd discovered the moving doorknob and the ensuing events. When I was done, I twisted my hands in my lap. "Have you talked to Detective Scott?"

"Ye–e–s." He drew the vowel out, extending the length of the word. "Why?"

"Did he tell you. . .everything?" My voice faltered.

Max sat very still. "What do you mean by *everything*?"

I didn't look at him. "Like. . .everything?"

He took my chin and lifted, forcing me to meet his gaze. "Do you mean everything as in what you wanted to talk to me about?"

I nodded, swallowed, and blinked back tears.

He brushed hair from my face. "Trish, what is it?"

I gulped and couldn't seem to catch my breath. "Give me a second, okay?"

He shifted so that he could see me. That was when I knew he'd caught sight of my mystery-list notebook. He grabbed it.

"You're still making notes?" he asked, after an interminable silence. "Why?"

"Because I have to figure it all out. That's what I want to talk to you about."

"Solving Jim Bob's murder is Detective Eric Scott's job, not yours." Max enunciated each word. "He's the one with the badge and the gun."

"Yes, but. . .I have to solve this. Jim Bob was trying to blackmail me."

Max's head jerked, and his eyes widened. "What?"

"I'm involved in this up to my eyeteeth. I have to figure things out for me and for our family. I don't want to go to jail. I don't want to lose you." Once I started, the words tumbled out before I could think.

"What are you talking about?" He stared at me like I had the proverbial two heads.

The rapid thumping of my heart and a loud roar in my skull made it hard to talk. Max's face wavered in front of me, but I wasn't sure if it was from tears or if I was about to pass out.

"Trish?"

"Russ might have stolen the stop sign where Lindsey was killed," I whispered.

His mouth hung open for just a moment; then he blinked. "What did you say?"

I cleared my throat and tried to speak louder. "Russ used to steal road signs. You know how the kids are around here. He. . .he might have taken the one where Lindsey was killed. That's what Jim Bob was trying to blackmail me about."

Max stared at me and didn't move. "And you didn't see fit to tell me this before? Trish, what were you thinking?"

His gaze felt like a knife slicing through me. That question was one my mother asked me incessantly when I was young. According to her, I never thought anything through. But before I could speak, the phone rang. I wanted to throw it across the room.

"Let me check and see who that is." He grabbed the receiver from the end table.

"The high school," he said staring at me as he pushed the button to answer. "Hello." His eyes lost their focus. "No, we weren't aware of that." He took a deep breath. "She did what?" He listened awhile longer, lips narrowing and nostrils flaring. "Yes, I understand. Thank you."

When he hung up, his cheeks were drawn. "That was Karen's principal. She skipped school today. Apparently, she called the attendance office this morning pretending to be you and told them she wouldn't be there. Someone saw her and Julie out in the woods near the high school and the library and reported them. I have to go pick her up." He got to his feet and looked down at me. "This really hasn't been a good couple of weeks."

That was an understatement.

12

Breakfast on Wednesday morning was tense. Max and I were treading around each other like two wary dogs. He was angry that I hadn't told him right away about Russ, the stop sign, and Jim Bob's threats. He asked me for time to digest what I'd told him before we discussed it at length again. I had to respect that, but I felt like I was dying inside.

He had also grounded Karen from outside social activities for two weeks, and she let us know how unhappy she was by a variety of methods, including screaming and yelling. She should have been grateful to me. I managed to talk her father into allowing her phone privileges, as well as study time at the library.

She never gave him a reasonable explanation for why she skipped school. It might have been nothing more than teenage rebellion, just like Julie's talk of running away might have been the outward expression of a girl angry that her parents had split up, but I had my doubts.

"Trish, did you remember I have meetings in Baltimore today?" Max asked over his shoulder as he opened the door to the garage to leave.

"Yes," I said, staring at his back.

He turned around. "Can you pick up my suit from the cleaners?"

"Yes."

Even though he had hugged me and kissed me good-bye, I still felt bereft. I didn't realize I was twisting my hands in front of me until he glanced down.

He put his briefcase on the floor, came over to stand in front of me, and put his hands on my shoulders. "Honey, what you told me hasn't changed the fact that I love you. Forever and always. But I have some things to work through, plus there's a whole lot to consider. First, we need to know if it's true."

I stared up at him. He had dark circles under his eyes. He hadn't slept any better than I had.

He pushed a piece of hair from my face. "Listen, I hate to ask you this, given everything that's going on, but could you talk to Julie's mom? See if she has any idea what's going on with the girls?"

I nodded. Right now I'd do anything he asked me, just to make him happy again.

"Thank you," he said. "Maybe it'll help us."

I realized he felt as ineffectual in dealing with Karen as I did, but for different reasons. He was a guy and didn't understand. I had once been a fifteen-year-old girl. I did understand. I was also her stepmother, and that, I suspected, had become a problem for her. Of course, now there was the potential for things to get even worse.

Before I left to take the little kids to school and go to work, I called Lee Ann again and finally reached her. She sounded out of breath. She agreed to meet me that night at Bo's Burger Barn.

———

"Hi, Mrs. C.," Shirl said when I arrived at work. "You okay?"

"Yeah," I fibbed.

"I made coffee."

"I'm trying to quit." I sifted through yesterday's mail, pulling out bills to pay.

"What?" She stared at me. "You quit drinking coffee? I can't believe that."

"Believe it," I muttered. "My head does." Caffeine withdrawal wasn't pleasant, but after serious consideration, I had come to the conclusion that coffee, in addition to Jim Bob's murder, contributed to my stomach ailment.

"Say, did you know that Peggy Nichols has been dragged down to the sheriff's office almost as many times as you have?" Shirl asked.

I gazed at her in surprise. "Why?"

She shrugged. "No clue. I just heard it from someone who was here this morning." She glanced at her desk where she kept her notepad. "Listen, some guy from the paper called. Said he's coming by to interview you."

I gritted my teeth. "Was his name Carey Snook?"

She nodded.

"I don't want to talk to him." I started for my office. I was in no mood to deal with anybody today, especially a nosy reporter.

"I'm sorry. He hung up before I could get a number to call him back. Caller ID said it was unlisted."

"Not a problem," I hollered from my desk. "I'll take care of it."

I would do so by calling Carey at the newspaper office and telling him to quit bugging me, but when I asked for Carey Snook, I was informed that he didn't work there. He'd never worked there.

Why in the world would someone set up an appointment with me and lie about who he was? I could reach only one conclusion—I was about to have a meeting with a fake.

While I waited for him to arrive, I got a phone call from my mother-in-law. She began by inquiring about my health, sounding solicitous, but in reality she just wanted to let me know she'd heard about my latest escapades and didn't think my behavior was suitable for the wife of someone like Max. For an insane moment, I considered informing her about everything going on. However, the satisfaction of listening to her shriek now wouldn't be worth the price I'd have to pay later.

I paced my office and tried to pray but felt, as my mother would say, the heavens were brass. By the time I saw Mr. Counterfeit Reporter pull into the parking lot, I was in a state.

"Send Mr. Snook into the conference room when he gets inside," I growled as I stomped through the front office.

Standing at the copier, Shirl watched me with raised brows. "Guess I shouldn't offer him anything to drink?"

"No." I must have gestured wildly because she took a step away from me. I didn't apologize, just went on into the conference room to wait.

Shortly after, she brought Carey Snook to the door. "Here he is," she announced and went back to her desk where she plopped in her chair and rolled it to a place where she could see and hear everything.

"Mr. Snook, is it?" I said in greeting.

"Yes, ma'am. Thank you for meeting with me." His smile was oily, like a bad used-car salesman. I really disliked his hair. Today he wore big, black glasses.

His eyes narrowed slightly. "I want to talk about Jim Bob. Like I said the other day, everyone's got secrets. I rather thought you might want to talk to me."

That's when it hit me. Carey Snook somehow knew about me and Jim Bob. I wondered how.

Exhaustion and the conversation with my mother-in-law were to blame for my reaction. I walked over to the door and edged it shut so Shirl couldn't see us. I turned back to him. "Snook. Is that German?"

Carey frowned. I'd caught him off guard.

I smiled. "It's quite unusual. I suppose it's your real name?"

"Of course," he said.

I shook my head. "Those silly people at the paper. I called them. They've never heard of you."

He raised his chin. "I'm a freelancer."

"No, you're not." I put my hands on my hips. "You're lying."

The corners of his mouth turned up. "I'm lying?"

The bell over the front door rang. I studied the man who was studying me, too angry to be afraid. He scratched his head, and I noticed that his hair looked a little off-kilter.

I pointed at it. "Is that a hairpiece?" I moved closer to him. "It is. You don't even have your own hair. That's a good thing for you because it's very ugly." My voice grew louder. "Who are you, anyway?"

Shirl peered around the conference room door. "You okay, Mrs. C.?"

"Yes, but Carey Snook is leaving right now." I was itching to grab at the mop on his head just to see if it came off.

After the briefest pause, he grinned. "You have a good day, Mrs. Cunningham." He lowered his voice so only I could hear him. "I'm sure you'll reconsider talking to me before I talk to your husband's family. I'd rather hear the whole story from you." He brushed past me, knocking me off balance. I grasped the door frame and watched him saunter out the front door.

Shirl's gaze followed him until he disappeared; then she turned to me. "You okay, Mrs. C.?"

"Yeah, I'm okay." I went out to where she stood and saw Hank, one of our longtime customers, leaning against the counter. When I was in high school, he'd been one of my teachers. I made his life rough for a year. Now he was retired from that and had become a dispatcher for the sheriff's office. Seems like a dispatcher would be the harder job. Then again, dealing with students like me for years might make anything else seem like a piece of cake.

Shirl dropped into her chair. "What was that all about?"

I forced a laugh. "I really couldn't tell you. I'm not sure. He calls himself Carey Snook, and he says he's a reporter. But he doesn't work at the paper, and he wears a hairpiece."

Hank stared at me in amazement. "You haven't tried to attack a fellow like that since you've grown up."

"Oh, for crying out loud," I said impatiently, knowing how this would play out with the rumor mill. "I didn't attack him."

Hank was shaking his head. "You know what they say—'Still waters run deep.' You can't change Mother Nature." Had Hank been to platitude school with my mother?

"Whatever." I walked past the two of them and into my office where I plopped in a chair and put my head in my hands. Shirl was talking loud enough for me to hear her.

"You know," she said, "it seems like things around here are just going to you-know-where."

I had to agree.

---

"I'll be just a minute," I told the kids as I pulled up at the dry cleaner's. "I have to get your father's suit."

Sammie and Charlie babbled at each other in the back. Karen was next to me in the passenger seat, but she might as well have been in the next state. She had ignored me when she got in the car, turning her body so she couldn't see me. I snatched up my purse and dug around for my wallet.

"Mom," Charlie said. "I don't like the way she's looking at us."

"Karen, don't stare at the little kids," I said as I put my purse on the floor.

"Oh, good grief," she mumbled.

"Not Karen," Charlie yelped. "Her. On the sidewalk."

I glanced out the windshield and met the gaze of my nemesis over whose arm draped several dry cleaning bags. I wondered if the dry cleaners gave Stefanie Jenkins a discount because there was so little of her clothes to clean.

"Mom, do we know her?" Charlie asked. "I'm sure—"

"Yes, we know her. It's Mrs. Jenkins. I'll be back in a minute."

Charlie was mumbling as I shut the door to the van.

"Trish!" Stefanie greeted me like an old friend. She wore tight, black pants with a tight, cropped, fluorescent orange knit shirt that showed a great deal of belly. No one should look good in a color like that, but she managed to. Her nails were a darker shade of the same color and matched her lipstick. How did she coordinate everything?

"Hello, Stefanie." I was still shaken up from my run-in with the hairpiece-wearing liar and really didn't feel like dealing with Miss Fancy-Pants.

"Oh, please call me Steffie," she gushed. "I just know we can be good friends."

Not in a million years. "What can I do for you?" I asked.

She gave me a bright smile. "I'm hoping you can convince Maxwell to let me into my storage unit."

I was astounded by her audacity. "I can't do that. It's not yours."

"I just thought you'd have some"—she winked—"powers of persuasion. Your husband is obviously crazy about you."

I was glad that was obvious. "I'm sorry, Steffie. What you're asking is illegal."

I watched anger flash in her eyes; then she forced a smile. "No one has to know; just leave me the key somewhere. It'll be our secret."

I gave her my own forced smile. "I'm sorry. I can't help you."

Her charm had run its course. The gloves were off, and her body vibrated with anger. "I don't believe this. My belongings are in that storage unit, and I'm going to get them out."

I gave her my most withering stare. "You'll do it without my help."

I turned my back to her and went inside to pick up my dry cleaning. After I gave the clerk my ticket, I glanced out the window and saw Stephanie get into a car driven by a man. I squinted at them. Was he the same guy I'd seen at the ball game? The custodian at the school? His profile looked familiar.

"Ma'am?" the clerk said, interrupting my thoughts.

I turned around and paid for Max's suit. By the time I got outside, Stefanie was gone.

## 13

I met Lee Ann in front of Bo's Burger Barn. She didn't say much, just walked ahead of me. A heavyset greeter seated us, slapping menus on the yellow table and informing us that a server would be with us shortly.

"My treat," I said to Lee Ann as I slid into the chartreuse booth. "Get whatever you want."

She narrowed her eyes. "You don't need to do that. I can buy myself a cup of coffee."

"Sorry," I said. "I wasn't trying to insult you."

She sighed. "I just need to feel like I can do something myself."

Lee Ann had always been moody. Back when we had been in 4-H together, I'd managed to offend her at least once every couple of months. Still, we had some good times together. She'd been a bit like a little sister, something I'd never had.

Our server—Gail's granddaughter, Glenda—bounced up to the booth.

"Hey, Trish." She plunked two glasses of water on the table; then she pulled her ticket book from an apron pocket, along with a pen. "You guys hungry? We got a fried catfish special tonight."

I glanced at Lee Ann who shook her head.

"No, we're not getting much," I said. "Hope that's okay. I just want some onion rings and a Diet Coke." I hoped the soda would give me relief from my headache.

"That's fine." She winked. "Don't matter. You're a celebrity around here anyway. My granny says you're in cahoots with the cops. I've been telling everybody."

Oh, that was just great. "Listen, I'm not in cahoots—"

"Can you give me the scoop about who they suspect? Granny says you're in the sheriff's office, like, every day."

"No," I said. "I—"

"It must be just so thrilling to be in on things like that. I saw a picture of the detective from the sheriff's office on television. He's to die for." She fanned herself with her ticket book and heaved a dramatic sigh. "Good thing you have a hot man at home, huh? Otherwise, it'd be hard to keep your mind on the right things." She rolled her eyes toward the ceiling in an expression of ecstasy. "I just love men in uniforms who carry guns."

Not me. I'd be happier if I never saw another cop uniform in my life. And

Detective Scott? To die for? Wouldn't Abbie snort about that?

Glenda finished her flight of rapture and looked at me. "Well, it's good you're closemouthed. They wouldn't trust you otherwise." She turned to Lee Ann. "Whaddaya want?"

Eyeing Glenda with distaste, Lee Ann ordered coffee.

"Okay. I'll be back."

"So what's all that about?" Lee Ann asked.

I shook my head. "My mother has been telling everyone I'm some sort of police informant. I wish she'd stop because I'm not, although it's true I've been at the sheriff's office a lot. They seem to think I saw something that day, and they're determined to get it out of me." I took a sip of water and met Lee Ann's gaze. "But that's not what I called you to talk about."

Her lips were pursed. "Did Karen say that the girls' skipping school was Julie's fault?"

That explained Lee Ann's attitude. "No, not at all. In fact, she won't talk about it. But Charlie overheard Karen say something about Julie running away. I thought you should know."

Lee Ann's expression relaxed. "I know about that. It's because of her father."

I took a big sip of water. "Well, Karen's got issues, too. Maybe you and I could work together somehow to help them."

Lee Ann nodded. "I think Karen's going through that teenage thing where she's mad because her father remarried. Girls are really emotional like that."

She got it in one.

Glenda brought the drinks. "Yours is on the house," she said to me.

Her remark made me feel bad, especially when Lee Ann glared at Glenda's back as she walked away. After she poured sugar and cream into her coffee, Lee Ann took a deep breath and looked at me. "So what have you heard about me and Norm?"

I shrugged. "Not much, really. Just that Norm left for a while."

"Left? That's not quite what happened." She scowled. "I kicked him out. Did you know he started drinking? He drank at work. During lunch. During his break. Packed straight whiskey in his thermos. Used to sit out there under the trees near the landfill and get drunk. Only problem is, by the time he got home, he was coming down. After all these years, he was turning into my old man."

Ouch. That was bad news. "I'm sorry. I remember how your dad was. Norm always seemed to be the stable one."

"Yeah, he was." Lee Ann said nothing else, just sipped her coffee.

"Well, Karen says you have a boyfriend. That might be a good thing."

Her head jerked up. "A boyfriend? Are you joking?"

"I guess you don't?" I asked.

"Definitely not. I don't ever want to deal with another man again." She stared at me. "You're so lucky."

She'd said that more than once when we were young. In fact, we'd had some competitive moments, with jealousy on both sides. Compared to her home life, mine had been good. At least I wasn't beaten on a regular basis, but still, life hadn't been easy living with someone like my mother.

I decided to change the subject, perhaps dig up some clues for my list. "Hey, has some reporter guy been following you around, asking questions?"

Lee Ann frowned and shook her head.

"He's not a real reporter," I said.

"That's weird. How do you know?"

"I called the paper and asked. He came by the office, and I confronted him. I think he wears a hairpiece."

She sat back in her seat. "Well, what does he want to know?"

I wondered how much to tell her. "All he'll say is that he's trying to dig up people's secrets. I'd like to know who he really is. The police should probably talk to him."

"Yeah, sounds like it." She took another sip of coffee and then searched through her purse. "Thank you for thinking about Julie. I'll be watching out for her. Everything's going to be okay."

"Do you have to go?" I wanted to ask her more questions.

She nodded and put a couple of bills on the table. "I need to check on her."

I paid our bill and left. Although I'd succeeded in my original goal of warning Lee Ann about Julie's threats, I wasn't able to learn anything to further my quest to solve Jim Bob's murder or to find out if Russ was guilty of Lindsey's death.

I walked out to my SUV, got inside, leaned back, and thought. My thoughts were running over one another in my head. I needed someone to help me sort things out. Abbie. I started my vehicle and headed over to her apartment. I wondered how her book was coming and whether Detective Scott was still helping her with law-enforcement questions. I chuckled as I thought about Glenda's comments. Then bright headlights in my rearview mirror interrupted my woolgathering. After several blocks of this, I wondered if the car was following me. When I pulled over in front of the now closed antique store, I didn't turn my SUV off, in case the other vehicle stopped behind me. It didn't. Instead, it just kept going and made a right turn several streets up from where I was. My imagination was as bad as Charlie's.

The front windows of Abbie's apartment were dark. I should have called first, but she so rarely went out at night that I just expected her to be home. Once again, I wished she had a cell phone. Maybe she was in the back, in her bedroom. I hopped from my vehicle and went to the side of the building where I pulled at a metal door. It scraped open, hinges squealing. I ran up one narrow flight of stairs, turned a corner, and ran up another. Carrying groceries this far had to be a royal pain.

At the top, I went through another metal door to the landing where the entrance to her apartment was. I knocked. No one answered. I dug out my cell phone, which was where it was supposed to be for once. I dialed Abbie's number and heard her phone ringing inside. Then the answering machine kicked on. I leaned against the wall, wanting to growl in frustration. The ceiling lamp above me cast a harsh light on the tan walls. I heard nothing inside her apartment and knocked again. Silence swallowed the sound. I felt a prickle of uneasiness on my neck. A car without a muffler passed by on the street. Then a motorcycle. Then nothing. I suddenly felt very alone and punched my cell phone to dial home.

"Trish?" Max answered. "Are you done talking to Lee Ann?"

Hearing his voice made me feel braver, and I walked down the stairs, through the heavy outside door, and into the night.

"Yeah," I said.

"So are you on your way home?" he asked. "I put the little kids to bed. I want to hear how it went with Lee Ann. And you and I need to talk."

"Okay. Be there in a few." Maybe Max and I could get back on solid ground.

When I got home, he was in his office. Tommy's car was gone. I assumed Karen was hiding in her room, talking on the phone. I peered in at Max.

He looked up, took off his glasses, and put them on the desk. "Hi."

He leaned back. "How did it go?" He sounded hopeful, like my talk with Lee Ann would somehow help us solve the Karen problem.

I shrugged. "She didn't really have anything to say about the situation, only confirming what I suspected. That Karen resents me."

I settled in a brown leather chair, curling my legs underneath me.

He sighed, green eyes dark with worry. "Why, exactly, does she resent you?"

"I'm not her real mother."

We stared at each other. I knew he was thinking what I was thinking. If Russ were to blame in any way for Lindsey's death, then Karen's resentment would deepen. I wasn't sure my relationship with her would ever be the same.

Tension creased his forehead. A black cloud had descended over our house, and I wasn't sure how to counteract it. I was about to suggest we pray and then discuss Russ and the stop sign when I heard Karen's rushed footsteps on the stairs.

The back of my chair faced the door, so when Karen stormed in, she didn't see me. "Dad, you wouldn't believe what Mom did—"

I turned and gazed around the chair. She stopped, put her hands on her hips, and glared at me.

Max sat still, glancing rapidly from me to Karen and back again. "What were you saying, Karen?" His words were mild, but I wasn't fooled. His jaw tightened in anger.

"Well, she blabbed to Mrs. Snyder that Julie was talking about running away. That wasn't any of her business to tell. Julie got yelled at and everything." Karen scowled through blond bangs. "Then Mrs. Snyder grounded her and left."

And that, of course, was my fault.

Max's eyes flashed with anger. "Karen, I don't like your tone or your accusations. I was the one who asked your mother to talk to Mrs. Snyder."

Karen's body vibrated with anger. "Quit calling her that," she shouted. "She's not my mother. And I don't like the way you always take her side." She whirled around and ran from the room, her footsteps on the stairs echoing down the hall.

Max jumped up from his desk to follow her, but I stood and grabbed his arm. "Let her go. Talking to her when she's this upset won't help at all. Give her a couple minutes."

He didn't meet my eyes, and I could tell he didn't want to listen to me.

"Trust me, Max. Just a couple of minutes. While we wait, let's sit in the family room. It's more comfortable."

His breath was rapid, and his eyes still shone bright green, a sure sign he was upset. He didn't say anything, just followed me.

"Rub your shoulders?" I asked before he sat on the couch, knowing that we would be unable to discuss the Russ situation until he had a chance to talk to Karen.

"Please," he said and settled cross-legged at my feet.

I dug my fingers into his shoulders. He took a deep breath and relaxed. That was a good sign. I needed to talk to him about Carey Snook. Maybe Max would help me figure out what Carey was up to.

I told him first about the fake reporter showing up at the house. Max's muscles tensed. Then I mentioned Carey's hair and mustache, describing them in great detail. Max's body became so rigid that his shoulders felt like granite. He pulled away from me, turned his head, and faced me with green eyes that shot sparks.

"Did you tell Detective Scott about this Carey fellow?" he demanded in a loud voice.

The thought hadn't occurred to me. It should have. The fact that I'd neglected something so obvious hurt my pride and made me want to point the finger elsewhere. "I don't want to talk to Detective Scott. He makes me sick."

"What?" Max stared at me.

"He does. My stomach has been upset since I met him." I knew it wasn't the detective. Since I'd cut back on coffee, my stomach felt a lot better. "When I don't see him, I don't get sick."

"That's ridiculous," Max snapped. "You really don't understand why I'm upset, do you?"

I did, but I was having trouble thinking because he'd never spoken to me like that before. Maybe it's unusual, but in six years of marriage, Max had never yelled at me. "I guess you're going to tell me?" I squeaked. I blinked back tears.

"Yes, I am." He jumped to his feet, and his voice bounced off the walls. "Did it ever occur to you that you could be in danger?"

"Well, not really. . ." Then I remembered how I'd felt tonight at Abbie's. "Maybe. Why?"

He pinched the bridge of his nose. "I can't believe you have to ask that."

My breath caught in my chest. I grabbed a pillow and hugged it. "I can't believe you're hollering at me."

"I've never been so worried before." He ran a hand through his hair and paced the room, breathing hard. Then he stopped and gazed down at me. "I'm sorry. I shouldn't have yelled."

No, he shouldn't have. I stood and tossed the pillow on the couch. "I'm going upstairs."

I tried to make a dramatic, dignified exit, but Max caught my arm.

"Trish, please."

"Let go." I yanked, but he held tight.

"Honey, listen to me."

I stopped but didn't look at him. "I'm listening."

"We don't know why someone tried to break into the house. Jim Bob's murderer is still on the loose. And we have the situation with your brother hanging over us. I don't know how it all fits together."

"So? I told you guys that was Stefanie. She wants in Jim Bob's storage unit."

"You don't know that." He dropped my arm. "Eric told me I needed to keep a close eye on you. It's harder than holding a cat in water. Sometimes—"

"I know exactly what you mean," I yelled and whirled around. All my insecurities rushed in, battering my mind like an emotional hailstorm. "Sometimes you wish you hadn't married me. I'm just a troublesome redneck and out of your league."

"What?" He put his hands on my shoulders. "Why would you say such a thing?"

"It's true, isn't it? I'm not good enough for you. Your mother always insinuates it. And now my brother. . ." I couldn't continue. I felt my lower lip quiver.

"My mother. . ." Max pulled me close. "Honey, please listen to me. I worry about you—a whole lot. I'm worried about everything that's going on right now, but I have never, ever wished that I hadn't married you."

I didn't feel better.

"I'm sorry," he said. "This has been a bad time. I'm not handling it well. Forgive me, please."

"Okay," I said because I had to, not because I was ready to.

We eyed each other with wariness.

Max sighed. "It doesn't feel okay."

I allowed him to hug me; then I left the room. As I passed the foot of the stairs, I saw movement upstairs. Karen was in the hallway. She had a smile on her face.

## 14

Thursday morning was gray, raining the proverbial cats and dogs. Max had already gotten up. We still hadn't talked much. He'd spent a great deal of time the night before talking to Karen; then he'd stayed in his office until after midnight.

I sat on the edge of the bed in jeans and T-shirt wondering sleepily which of my five pairs of slippers to wear. Along with my purple fuzzies and pink, cross-eyed rabbits, I also had brown leather moccasins, black-and-white cows, and a simple pair of white slip-ons. I was debating between the moccasins and the bunny slippers when the bedroom door burst open, and Max rushed in.

"Trish? Are you awake?"

Obviously. I was sitting up. I frowned at him. His body language didn't bode well. After last night, I still felt on guard around him. "What's wrong?"

"Eric is here, and he needs to talk with you." Max stood in front of me with his hands on his hips. "Trish, did you come straight home last night after you met Lee Ann?"

I felt his anxiety, and my heart thumped. "Yes. . .no. Well, I stopped at Abbie's first, but she wasn't home."

He groaned. "Come on. Get dressed. He's waiting."

"Okay, but first I have to brush my teeth." I went to the bathroom, shut the door, and stood at the sink, staring in the mirror. My hair looked like someone had turned me upside down and used me to mop a floor. My brown eyes were red-rimmed. Not an attractive sight.

"Dad!" I heard Charlie yell. "Did you know there's cop cars outside again?"

"Yes, son, I know. Go eat breakfast."

I looked briefly at the bathroom window, wondering how long it would take to remove the screen and climb down the side of the house. Would Detective Scott chase me, lights flashing and siren blaring? And what would my hoity-toity mother-in-law say when word got around that her crass daughter-in-law was running down the road in her nightgown? I briefly considered that. It might actually be worth the effort.

"Hey, Dad," Tommy's deeper, booming voice came through the door. "What are the cops doing here? Is Mom in trouble again?"

"Would you please see that the little kids eat breakfast?" Max said. "And that everyone gets ready for school?" His voice sounded stressed. "Trish, come on. Eric's waiting."

"Oh, all right, I'm coming." I brushed my teeth then stumbled out of the bathroom. "What does he want?"

"He wants to know where you were last night."

"Why?" I chose my moccasin slippers, which were a whole lot more dignified than the cross-eyed bunnies.

"He didn't say, but I don't imagine it's good."

Max hadn't smiled at me once since bursting into the bedroom, and he had a hard edge that reminded me of our discussion the night before.

As we walked down the stairs, I heard the sound of Charlie's voice. When we drew closer to the living room, I could finally understand him.

". . .out from *Mysterious Disappearances* that a lot of people aren't who we think they are."

Detective Scott stood in the living room, along with Corporal Fletcher. Both men were watching Charlie with raised brows.

"Even you could really be someone else, Mr. Detective. That's important to know when you're a cop."

"Charlie, go eat breakfast," Max said.

"But Dad, they need to look into these people—"

"Son, didn't your mother tell you we don't want you watching *Mysterious Disappearances* anymore?"

"But, Dad. . .," he wailed.

My heart went out to him. He was so frustrated. I knew just how he felt.

Max took Charlie's hand to lead him from the room.

"Why are you still so grumpy, Dad?" Charlie asked. He kept jabbering as they walked down the hall. The sound of his voice faded as they went into the kitchen.

"Charlie reminds me of someone," Detective Scott said thoughtfully, staring after Max and Charlie. Then he squinted in my direction. "You."

An astute observation.

"Why do you need to know where I was last night?" I asked.

The detective glanced at Corporal Fletcher then back at me. "Tell me where you were, please."

Their grim expressions scared me. I sat on the edge of the couch and swallowed hard. "I met Lee Ann at Bo's Burger Barn. We talked for about a half an hour, maybe forty-five minutes. Then I went over to see my friend, Abbie."

"Lee Ann Snyder?" Detective Scott asked.

"Yes," I said.

Corporal Fletcher made a note.

"Abbie Grenville," the detective told the corporal.

He made another note.

"What time did you leave Bo's?" the detective asked.

"I have no idea." The way the two men loomed over me made me feel ganged up on and vulnerable.

"What time did you get to Abbie's?" Corporal Fletcher asked.

"I don't know. I called Max from there. It'll be on our cell phones."

Max came back into the room, forehead wrinkled, cheeks drawn.

"What time did you get home?" Detective Scott asked.

"About ten after nine," Max answered for me.

I waited for the corporal to write that down, which he did. "What is this about?" I asked again.

"We need you to come with us," Detective Scott said. "We have some questions to ask you." He glanced at Max.

He had paled. "Is she being accused of anything?"

The detective shook his head. "I'm not accusing anyone."

Max ran a hand over his head, disheveling his already tousled hair. "I'd better call a lawyer."

"That's your prerogative," Detective Scott said.

I stood, and my legs felt shaky. "Do I really need a lawyer? I mean, is the situation that serious?"

"I can't advise you either way," the detective said. "That's your and Max's decision." He motioned to Corporal Fletcher. "He'll take you to the sheriff's office. I'll meet you there." Detective Scott strode from the room, followed by Max.

I swallowed and glanced at the corporal. "Can I put on some decent clothes?"

"Yeah, Mrs. C., you go on and do that." He was tucking his notepad into his pocket and eyed me. "But don't be long."

⸺

Corporal Fletcher showed me into the interview room. The low ceilings and white walls were just as oppressive as they were before.

"I should bring plants to decorate since this appears to be my second home," I grumbled.

"Mrs. C., you need anything?" he asked. "Water?"

I shook my head. "No. I just want to back my life up two weeks and never go shopping at Shopper's Super Saver again." I felt his eyes on me, and I turned to face him. "Corporal Fletcher, this has been the worst two weeks of my life."

He might have had sympathy in his eyes, but Detective Scott walked in, so I didn't have time to find out for sure.

"Mrs. Cunningham, please have a seat." He motioned to my regular chair.

I obeyed. Max had told me to wait for a lawyer, but I just wanted to get the questions over with. Surely nothing could be so bad that I needed legal representation.

Detective Scott sat in his regular chair and placed his arms on the table. Corporal Fletcher remained standing behind him, but he pulled a notebook and pen from his pocket.

Nobody mentioned a lawyer. I had a feeling the cops didn't want me to have one any more than I wanted one.

The detective leaned toward me. "Tell me what you know about Peter Ramsey."

The name sounded familiar. I rubbed my cheeks with my hands. "I don't know. . . . I don't remember."

Detective Scott stared at me. Corporal Fletcher's raised eyebrows indicated that he thought I'd just lied, which wasn't good because, of the two of them, I thought he liked me better.

"You don't know Peter Ramsey?" Detective Scott asked.

"Should I?" I looked at him and frowned. "I know I've heard the name, but I don't remember where. I'm too tired, and I haven't been sleeping well and—"

"We have evidence that you do."

I leaned toward him. "How could you have evidence that I know someone I don't know?"

"Your name and the address of Four Oaks Self-Storage were in his pocket." Detective Scott leaned toward me. "You were seen in an altercation with him."

The light dawned. I recalled why the profile of the man with Stefanie at the dry cleaners had looked so familiar. "Carey Snook. Carey Snook is Peter Ramsey. I knew there was something screwy about him. I mean, that hair said it all, really."

"Carey Snook?" Corporal Fletcher's pen-filled hand was in the air above his notebook.

"Trish, what are you talking about?" Detective Scott asked.

I tapped my fingers on the table. "He told me his name was Carey Snook, and he lied to me about being a reporter at the paper. He's no reporter."

While the two law officers exchanged glances, I wondered how they'd found out about my argument.

The detective turned to me again. "Tell me about Carey Snook."

"Well, besides being an obnoxious liar, he's about your height, big mustache, fake hair. That was the ugliest-looking mess I've ever seen. Sort of like a raccoon. He had funny-looking glasses. Big and black."

"Hmm," the detective said.

I got mad. "*Hmm*, what? I hate it when people *hmm*. Especially you. Don't do that to me."

"Tell me more about Carey Snook," Detective Scott said.

"He's sneaky," I said. "I wanted to yank off his ugly hairpiece."

Corporal Fletcher's pen flew over his notebook.

"And?" Detective Scott stared at me with his blank expression. He began to tap his pen on the table.

"And what?" I snapped.

*Tap, tap, tap, tap.*

I wanted to break his pen.

The detective scowled. "And what happened then?"

I couldn't imagine why all this was so important. "He stomped out. Hank, one of our customers. . ." I paused in realization. "That's how you found out about the fight: Hank. He never did like me when he was my teacher. Did you know that he gave me a D in history? I think it was to get even for the time I glued the pages of his teacher's book together. I've never seen anybody—"

"Trish, please answer my question."

*Tap, tap, tap, tap.*

"Well, Hank accused me of trying to beat Carey up, after which Shirl said it seemed like everything around here was going to you-know-where."

"You-know-where. . . ? Oh." The detective sighed. "Did you threaten him?"

"What? Threaten him? Sure, Detective Scott. I always threaten everyone who irritates me." I jumped to my feet. "If you don't tell me what this is all about, I'm going to leave." I crossed my arms and tightened my lips. "And I won't talk to you again, either."

Before he could answer or argue with me, the door to the interview room opened and a clean-shaven, portly man carrying a very expensive briefcase strolled in. I could tell the gray suit he wore had been made for him. Six years of contact with Max's family had taught me at least that much. And he was so stereotypical of all of Max's father's acquaintances that I knew who he was before he introduced himself.

He placed his briefcase deliberately on the table and gazed at all of us in turn. "I am Calvin Schiller." His smooth, polished voice made me think of a politician. "I'm here to represent Mrs. Cunningham. She will not answer any further questions without my counsel and until I know if you're going to charge her."

I turned around and exchanged glances with Corporal Fletcher. Then I rolled my eyes. I saw the twitch of a smile pass over his lips.

"Mr. Schiller, I don't mind answering their questions." I dropped back into a chair.

He looked down his nose at me, with an expression amazingly like my mother-in-law's. The one that said, *Did I give you permission to speak, redneck peon?* "Mrs. Cunningham, your husband hired me to give you legal advice. At this point in time, I advise you say nothing else."

"But it's no big deal," I said. "All I—"

"Why is she here?" The lawyer stepped between me and the officers, effectively cutting me off.

Detective Scott stood. "Peter Ramsey was found murdered early this morning. It appears that Mrs. Cunningham was one of the last people to be seen with him. Unfortunately, they had an altercation yesterday."

*Altercation* sounded copish and made me irritable. I jumped to my feet, scooted around Calvin Schiller, and stared at the detective. "So Peter was Carey."

"That might very well be the case," Detective Scott said.

---

I was mad. Carey Snook had had the nerve to die with my name and number on a piece of paper in his pocket, putting me on another murder-suspect list. I'd also humiliated myself by getting sick in the hallway of the sheriff's office. Then there was my uppity lawyer who treated me like I was a grease stain on his tie. I wanted a lawyer like Andy Griffith's Matlock character. A down-home, country person who ate hot dogs and sang folk songs.

"I don't like Calvin Schiller," I grumbled at my husband while I sat at the kitchen table, contemplating the toast and jelly on my plate that he'd shoved in front of me. "He's a snob. He probably went to Harvard."

"Well, so did I." Max stood across the table from me. "Calvin is the best lawyer I know. From now on, you don't set foot in the sheriff's office without him."

"I don't want a—"

"I also took the liberty of calling Dr. Starling. You have an appointment with him in two days, right after work. I'll stay with Sammie while you're there."

"You did what?" I clenched my fists. "Does Harvard have classes to teach the students how to be autocratic? So what's next? Are you going to start telling me when to breathe?"

His nostrils flared. "If I feel like I have to, I will."

"Your bossiness is out of control, Max. Besides, I'm feeling better now."

"I'm out of control?" He snorted and crossed his arms.

I glared at him. He glared back. We were in danger of having another fight. Two in as many days would be two too many. I backed off, stuck my finger in the jelly, and then smeared it on the plate like Sammie does.

"We need to talk," Max said.

"Can't talk." I refused to look at him. "I have to eat. That's what you ordered me to do. And we have to go to work, you know."

He ignored what I said. "I'll go get ready while you finish your toast. I'll be back, and then we're going to talk."

He left the room. Reduced to childishness after spending the morning with pushy men, I stuck my tongue out after him. Then I shoved another piece of toast in my mouth. With the interruption of Mr. Harvard Law School at the sheriff's office, I hadn't had the chance to say anything to Detective Scott about Stefanie possibly knowing Peter-Carey, nor had I mentioned that I thought the liar was trying to take over Jim Bob's blackmail business. To me, that meant the two murders might be related. Did I dare call the detective without first contacting my cultured counsel? I was, as my mother would say, between a rock and a hard place. Help Detective Scott or obey my husband? What I really wanted to do was look at my mystery list, but I didn't dare do it right now with Max in this mood.

I washed the crust down with my last gulp of orange juice and wondered who would have killed Peter-Carey and why. Stefanie?

Max appeared in the doorway wearing jeans and a work shirt. I wasn't ready to forgive him enough to enjoy how he looked.

"You done?" he asked.

My plate was empty. My glass of orange juice was empty. My stomach felt okay.

"No," I said.

He walked into the kitchen and glanced pointedly at the table. "Are you planning to eat the plate?"

"I might get something else." I didn't look at him.

He ignored my words and sat opposite me at the table.

"Detective Scott isn't going to like you anymore," I said. "And you're not winning any popularity contests with me."

Max shrugged. "I'm not trying to be popular. And Eric understands I'm protecting you. He told me to watch out for you when all of this started. And frankly, even if he didn't like me, he isn't my concern. You're all I care about."

I was glad Max cared for me, but I didn't like the way he was showing it. I'd never seen him this controlling. Then again, I'd never before been interviewed by the police about two different murders.

"I didn't kill him, just like I didn't kill Jim Bob. Why do all these people die and point the finger at me?" I looked up at him. "If I'm a suspect, do you think this means I won't be able to teach Sunday school anymore? I love my Sunday school class."

Max shrugged and shook his head. "I don't know why that would happen unless a parent complains or something. I'm going to call the pastor anyway in the next few days. I'll talk to him about it. The problem is, I don't know exactly how you fit into all of this. I think Peter's death was set up to look like you did it."

I tapped my fingers on the table. "That makes no sense at all. Like I'm that important?"

Max's jaw tensed. "Trish, you're the one who said that you're involved in all of this up to your eyeteeth. I agree. Do you recall the conversation we had last night?"

I stared at my plate. "The one where you yelled at me?"

He reached for my hand, and I reluctantly let him take it. "I'm sorry for that, but yes, that one. Listen, Trish, from what Calvin said, the sheriff's office thinks the two murders are related."

My suspicions were confirmed. I opened my mouth and took a breath to ask for details.

Max held up his hand. "Calvin doesn't know anything for sure. That's just his gut feeling. He also doesn't think you're top on the list of suspects."

I shifted in my chair. If Stefanie did indeed know Peter-Carey, then maybe she did it. I had to get my notebook out and study my clues. I also needed to investigate more.

"Honey?" Max leaned forward, eyes full of concern. "Listen to me. You found Jim Bob. For some reason, Peter wanted to talk with you. Then someone attempted to break into our house. Peter came to see you again, after which he was found dead with your name and phone number in his pocket. Not to mention this thing with Russ and the road sign. There are too many unanswered questions in which you are an active participant."

I stared at Max but didn't see him. Spelled out like that, it sounded really bad for me.

15

My mind whirled with thoughts I itched to write down on my list, but I had no time. Things at Four Oaks Self-Storage were crazy. And that afternoon after work, I was doing chauffeur duties, picking up Karen from the library and Charlie from Mike's.

I guided my SUV up the drive between the library and the woods that bordered the other side. Picnic tables under the tall trees of the lawn reminded me of summers past when I would bring the kids here for reading hour. After that, we'd eat lunch in the shade. I felt a rush of nostalgia that too quickly my kids were growing up. When I was young, I'd dreamed of having a huge family, but then I found out I couldn't. I was grateful I married a man who already had children. Sammie had been my only baby.

Charlie was two when I married Max. Karen had been nine, and Tommy eleven. They weren't too young to feel grief over the loss of their mother. I'm convinced that the loss of a parent, especially at such a young age, leaves lifelong scars that only God can mend.

From age ten to fourteen, Karen had been happier. Although she'd never been cheery like Sammie, she'd been quietly content with her head stuck in a book or listening to music. Our best times were when we read together. That's why I couldn't let Max take her library privileges away, even though I suspected she used the time to meet Julie.

Karen walked from the building, climbed into the car, and said nothing, just slouched in her seat and stared out the window.

I faced her. "Did you have a good time?"

She turned and glared at me. "Why would you care?"

Her tone and words burned me like fire. Perhaps the time had come to prod her and give her an avenue to vent her hostilities. That was the only way I knew to really find out what was wrong.

"Why do I care?" I murmured. "Well now, there's a good question. Probably because I love you. And whether you like it or not, I'm your stepmother and will remain so."

I'd said the stepmother thing on purpose, knowing she would explode. I braced for the blow, asking God to help me.

Her eyes turned to slits, and a red flush crawled up her cheeks. "You're not my real mother," she screamed. "I hate you. The day Dad married you was the second worst day of my life."

I turned away quickly to hide the tears that filled my eyes. She'd aimed to wound me, and it worked.

After I regained control, I faced her. "I'm not your real mother, but I've always loved you as though I were."

She clenched her fists. "Well, you embarrass me. Always hanging all over Dad. Kissing him and stuff. Is that all you guys think about?"

Hurt and anger threatened to choke me. "No. But you need to remember that your father is my husband. That's what married people do." I paused for a breath. "Is that all that's bothering you?"

She slammed her fist on a book in her lap. "No." Her chin quivered. "You're always doing something to get Dad's attention. Like this morning. All those police there. It's so embarrassing. And now you're a suspect. Isn't that just great? My stepmother, the killer. The woman who smashes people to death. How am I going to live that down?" Tears rolled down her cheeks.

I was right. She was jealous. I understood to a degree, but I'd never lost a mother. I also knew that I couldn't deal with this problem myself, nor would it be taken care of by simple conversation. It was bigger than me or Max. God needed to intervene, and perhaps we needed to get some help.

I wished I could cry or scream back at her. Her words cut me as deeply as she'd intended. I felt as though someone had just taken a knife to my heart and sliced it into tiny slivers. But one of us had to be an adult, and since I was older and supposedly more mature, that would be me. I breathed a quick prayer for wisdom.

"Do you think I'm a killer?" I asked softly.

Her anger must have run its course because her body sort of folded in on itself. "No." Then she jerked around to face me. "I suppose you're gonna tell Dad about this?"

"I don't know," I said.

Her hostile silence remained as I picked up Charlie, but letting off steam had helped some. He hopped into the backseat, mouth already in gear. "Mom, you wouldn't believe what Mike has." He picked up a bungee cord from the floor and held it in his hands, stretching it in the air.

"Put your seat belt on," I ordered.

"Mike doesn't have to wear his in the backseat," Charlie said, bouncing up and down.

"Tough. It's the law," I said.

He wiggled around then snapped the buckle. "Mike has a snake. A pine snake. It's not as cool as a boa, but it's still cool." He wiggled the cord, aiming for Karen's head, and hissed.

She swiped his hand away. "Stop it, you moron."

"Karen, don't call him a moron. Charlie, don't tease your sister." I glanced at him in the rearview mirror.

I fought a bone-deep weariness unlike anything I could remember. I took the back way home, deciding no traffic lights were better than the four through town. A mile into our trip, I noticed a beige car behind us. It sped up and then slowed down, moving closer and backing off. A kid, I thought, as I deliberately lowered my speed so whoever it was would pass me.

That didn't work. The vehicle slowed and began to keep steady with my pace. I looked more carefully in the rearview mirror, remembering how I'd been tailgated the night before. I shook my head. Not possible. I was just paranoid.

The car stayed behind me for a mile. My uneasiness mounted. Then, on a long, straight stretch of road, it leaped forward. My heart pounded. I was afraid I was going to be rammed from the rear, but that didn't happen. It passed me. Too close, and I swerved aside, so it wouldn't sideswipe me. I was too busy controlling my SUV to try to see the driver, but the car was one of those big, old station wagons with fake wood trim on the side. As it roared on down the road, gravel flew from its tires, leaving a pockmark on my windshield.

When we got home, Karen stomped into the house, followed by Charlie, who was still babbling about snakes. I stayed out in the garage and examined my windshield. The hole was large enough that I'd have to get it repaired or cracks would spiderweb all over the glass.

The door opened behind me. I glanced over my shoulder. Max was standing in the doorway, wearing worn blue jeans, a faded blue T-shirt, and a dark scowl. "Karen said you nearly ran off the road?"

She appeared to have a new strategy—trying to make Max think badly of me. Not that that would be hard at this point. "No, I didn't almost run off the road," I stated calmly, ignoring my desire to yell. "Some car passed me too close, and I swerved to get away from it. The tires spit gravel up and left this hole in my windshield. Stupid people. That's the second time I've been tailgated." I poked at the hole with my finger. "I'll call those windshield-repair people tomorrow and see when they can come out."

"What did you just say?" he asked very softly and forcefully.

I glanced around at him in surprise. "I said I would call the windshield-repair people to come out—"

"That's not what I mean." He padded on bare feet over to me, looking tall and formidable. "What did you say about the tailgating?"

I looked up at him. "Tailgating?"

"Yes." He was breathing hard.

I frowned. "Just that I've been tailgated twice."

He ran his fingers through his hair, closed his eyes, and slowed his breathing. "Why didn't you tell me about this right away?"

"Because. . ." I hesitated. "You think it was something to do with the murders, don't you?"

"You don't?" he snapped. "You're the one with lists of clues and suspects. Why wouldn't this occur to you?"

I crossed my arms. "Well, maybe because Karen had just finished telling me that she hated me. She also said the day I married you was the second worst day of her life."

Max slumped like I'd hit him. "Oh, baby. I'm sorry."

I turned away from him, put my head in my hands, and cried.

---

Karen pitched a fit worthy of a two-year-old on Friday morning. That was because Max had grounded her from the phone and the library for two weeks, in addition to her other grounding. She was angry with me, of course, because I'd told him what she said.

I was extremely tired, having slept only fitfully. Karen's words kept racing through my mind, as did the fact that I could be in danger, in turn endangering my children. I was also worried about Max. He wasn't coping well. I'd never seen him like this. He might be bossy and a bit arrogant, but he had always been steady. The night before, he'd stayed in his office until the wee hours of the morning. The only good thing was that I'd noticed his Bible open on his desk.

We'd never had this kind of distance between us, and I felt like I was missing a vital organ. I kept praying, hoping for inspiration. I even got up extra early to make waffles because Max loves them, but they had no effect on him. He ate quickly, excused himself, and went into his home office to use the phone. Afterward, he kissed me good-bye and left earlier than normal.

Then Corporal Fletcher came to the door as Sammie and Charlie ran up the stairs to get ready for school.

"Mrs. C., you mind stepping outside?"

I obeyed, too tired to do otherwise. "What did I do now? Are you going to escort me to the sheriff's office again?"

The corporal smiled. "Nope. Sarge told me to come by and talk to you about some car."

"You mean the one tailgating me?" Max must have called Detective Scott.

Corporal Fletcher nodded and pulled his pen and notebook from his pocket. "Tell me everything."

I did, and I gave him the best description I could, given that I hadn't seen much.

When I was done, he put his pen and notebook in his pocket and took a deep breath. "I gotta tell you, I don't like this. I want you to be careful, okay?"

"You sound like Max," I said.

The corporal looked down at me, frowning. "Sarge says you been investigating."

I nodded. "I have to find out what happened." I looked over my shoulder to make sure one of my kids hadn't opened the door. Then I lowered my voice. "Maybe you don't understand, Corporal, but there's a lot at stake here. If my brother is guilty of causing Lindsey's death, my stepkids might never forgive me or Russ. So, I'm asking questions, but only from people I know. It's not like I'm out there with the scum of the earth."

He shook his head. "Mrs. C., you need to stop. Scum doesn't always look like scum. Sometimes they look just like us."

I stared up at him.

He tipped his hat at me, turned, and walked down the stairs. As I watched him go to his car, I shivered.

At Four Oaks Self-Storage, Max's car wasn't in the parking lot. I asked Shirl where he was, but she didn't know. She kept to herself, but her little furtive glances in my direction told me she felt my tension.

I didn't bother calling Max's cell phone. I was too tired. He'd come in when he was good and ready. Bleary-eyed, I put my chin in my hand and stared at my computer screen, but I couldn't focus. The clacking of Shirl's keyboard was punctuated by the occasional ringing of the phone. I closed my eyes and must have drifted to sleep because the sound of Max's voice made me jump.

"Trish?"

I jerked my head up and saw him standing in the doorway.

"Are you sleeping, honey?" He walked in and shut the door behind him.

"Probably." Max had a different air about him. The furrows in his forehead weren't as deep.

He came over and kissed my forehead. "Mind if I sit? I need to talk to you."

"Sure." I waved at a chair, hoping I wasn't in for another lecture.

He pulled it to the front of my desk and sat down, leaning his elbows on the wood top. "I've been to see the pastor."

I sat up straight. "Why?" Was my biggest fear about to come true? Was Max thinking about leaving me? Tears of panic filled my eyes.

He saw my reaction and grabbed both my hands. "Hey, it's okay. I just needed to talk to him."

"What about?" I sought assurance in Max's gaze and found it. He wasn't upset.

"The pastor helped us so much during premarital counseling. I thought maybe he could give me guidance now." Max took a deep breath. "Especially about the Russ thing. I have to tell you, that bothers me a lot."

"I'm sorry," I whispered. "If you only knew how guilty I feel about it. What if the only reason I have you is. . ." My voice broke, and I started to cry.

He stood, walked around the desk, and pulled me to my feet. "I might still be struggling with that, but it has nothing to do with you. And I'll work through it. What's important is that you're my wife and I love you."

I hiccupped.

He rubbed my back. "The other thing that bothers me is that you didn't trust me enough to tell me. Why?"

"I don't know," I said. "I guess I was afraid of your reaction, and I wanted to find out if Russ really did it before I said anything."

He stroked my cheek. "I might be overbearing sometimes, but have I ever treated you badly? Well, except for the other night?"

"Noo, but. . ." A wisp of a thought hit me.

"Honey, this was serious. A man was blackmailing you. I'm your husband. You should have told me."

My thought gelled. "I think it was because of my mother."

Max let go of me and backed up. "What?"

"I avoid confiding in her because she always uses it against me. I guess when this came up, I automatically treated you the same way as I do her."

Max nodded. "I can see that, but I'm not like your mother."

"I know. I'm sorry." I looked up at him. "What did the pastor say?"

"Lots of things," Max said. "Including that you, Karen, and I need to make an appointment to see him together. But that wasn't what we talked most about. He pointed out that I still have an issue with control, which is harder because you're unalterably curious, spontaneous, stubborn, and seem destined for trouble." He gave me a quirky little grin. "I did know that when I married you, by the way. Your father warned me many times."

"He did?"

Max nodded. "For some crazy reason, it's all part of your charm. I wouldn't change any of it. I just need to learn to. . . Well, I can't change you. I can change me. I'm my biggest problem."

I couldn't imagine what he was talking about. "Max, none of what's been happening is your fault. Well, except when you yelled at me and hired that lawyer."

Max laughed. "I know it's not my fault." He squeezed my fingers. "But the way I handle my reaction to everything is my responsibility, and I'm not doing a good job." He sighed. "See, my parents taught me that anything can be taken care of with money or sheer force of will. That eliminates faith from the equation."

"But you're so strong. . . ." I stroked his hand with my thumb.

"Exactly. In myself. And what happens when I'm no longer able to keep a tight handle on things? Am I going to yell at everyone around me? Or am I going to turn to God?" He smiled. "Another thing I've realized is that you and I need time alone. Really alone. Yes, the kids are older, and we've got more freedom, for which I'm glad, but we need to go somewhere. Just you and me."

God had answered my pleas, and so quickly. I stared into Max's eyes, anticipation waking me up. That sounded like an excellent plan. Then I remembered that either Russ or I, possibly even both, might be arrested. I didn't want anything to interfere with time alone with Max. I had to solve this mystery as quickly as possible.

—

I smacked Daryl with a door in my hurry to get into the building to make my doctor's appointment on time.

"Oh. Sorry. Hi." I looked up at him. I'd have to be late. I didn't want to miss a chance to ask some questions. I thought about Corporal Fletcher's comment about scum, but I just couldn't see Daryl as a bad guy.

"Hey, Trish." He met my gaze.

"Is your thumb okay?" I asked.

"Uh, yeah." He shifted from foot to foot.

"Listen, Daryl, do you remember that our brothers were friends?"

His lips tightened, and he didn't meet my eyes. "I don't remember a lot. Too painful. Always living in the shadow of a dead younger brother. My mom never recovered."

"I'm sorry." I shifted my purse. "Have you gone to the sheriff's office a lot to be questioned?"

He glanced down at me. "Maybe a couple of times. Like everyone else. Listen, I gotta run. I'm, uh, temporary manager."

"That's great," I said.

He smiled briefly. Then he turned and left.

Well, that didn't get me anywhere but more frustrated. I took a deep breath and went inside.

A couple of minutes later, I was sitting on an examining table.

White coat flapping, Dr. Bill Starling walked through the door of the examining room, holding my folder in his hand. "Trish, how is that stomach?"

"It's okay. Better, in fact. It was just coffee and stress." I wanted to get my appointment out of the way and move on. I had a lot to think about.

He pulled out his stethoscope. "Well, we can take care of you. Let's see what's going on."

Twenty minutes later, minus several vials of blood and other bodily fluids and holding a referral to a gastric specialist, I paid my bill and left the clinic. Bill promised to call me if the blood tests indicated anything that he could help with.

Max had phoned me on my cell to say that he'd returned to the office. George was coming by. Tommy and Karen were home with the little kids.

I decided, spur of the moment, to surprise Max with a picnic dinner. We needed some time to talk. I called Tommy to ask if he'd continue to watch the kids. He grumbled but agreed. I didn't dare ask Karen right now.

I picked up some food and drove back to Four Oaks Self-Storage. Two vehicles were parked in the lot. One was Max's. The other looked familiar, but it wasn't George's. Odd because office hours were over.

I went inside carrying two bags. "Max? I brought dinner."

"Hi, baby. I'm in my office."

He sounded too perky and bright.

"Is something wrong?" I walked into the room. That's when I remembered why I'd recognized the car parked outside.

Stefanie was perched on the edge of Max's desk, swinging her shapely legs. Sandals with impossibly high heels dangled from her toes. She looked at me rather like the cat that swallowed the canary. The teeny, black skirt and turquoise shirt she wore left very little to the imagination.

Max was in his chair, leaning back, legs stretched out in front of him, arms behind his head. His lips were turned up in a tiny little smile as if he knew exactly what I was thinking.

"Hi, honey," he said.

"Anyone hungry?" I used my iciest tone.

"I'm starving," Max said as if nothing were wrong.

I tossed my purse on the floor, ignoring everything that fell out. I proceeded to place the food and drinks on a file cabinet, laying everything out neatly, giving myself a chance to collect my thoughts. Then I turned around to survey the scene. Max looked disheveled. That was normal and didn't really mean anything. By the end of the day, when he was working on the new part of the facility, he was always tousled.

But the lipstick on the shoulder of his shirt wasn't normal. It wasn't my shade.

I knew that Max wasn't guilty of anything, but Stefanie's motivations. . . Her big, blue eyes took in every move I made, including my reaction when I'd seen the lipstick. I clenched my fists. Her smug expression almost pushed me over the edge. I eyed her precarious position. Just a little shove was all it would take. I could make it appear like an accident, perhaps falling over an imaginary lump in the carpet and bumping into her. Oops. Sorry, Miss Fancy-Pants. Hope you're not hurt—too bad.

"I guess you're wondering why I'm here," she said in her breathy tone.

"No, not really." I met her gaze with a slight smile and can only assume that my thoughts showed in my eyes. For the first time since I'd arrived, she looked worried. "I know exactly why you're here." I didn't look at Max, just kept my gaze focused on her. "You want to get into your dearly departed's storage unit. Did you bring your court order?" I moved closer to her.

"Trish, honey." Max could probably read my mind, and it scared him. "Stefanie is about to leave."

"Yes, she is," I said firmly. I smiled again and moved closer still. Steffie wasn't dense. She hopped from the desk in an unladylike hurry.

"Yes, I'm leaving. And no, I don't have a court order. I—I—" She pouted, and tears welled up in her eyes. "You just don't know how painful this is."

If she thought her tears would move me, she was greatly mistaken. "Oh, I see how it is, all right. Those mean ole court people. Jim Bob has been dead for, what? A little over a week now? Having the right priorities is, after all, a matter of great pain."

Steffie's tears dried up quicker than a drop of water on a hot griddle. She picked up her purse, flung it over her shoulder, and turned to Max.

"Thank you for your sympathy, Maxwell. We'll talk again soon, I hope."

When she turned back to me, I stepped aside for her to leave, motioning toward the front door. "There will be no more talking until you have your court order. Good-bye, Stefanie."

She stomped from the room and the building, slamming the front door behind her. I followed and waited until she pulled from the lot. Then I locked the door and returned to Max's office.

He had his feet up, leaning back in his chair, looking too composed and self-satisfied. That was so like him, I had to try hard not to smile.

"Trish," he said with a little grin.

"Max."

"Baby."

"Don't 'Baby' me." I walked to his desk, placed my palms on the fine wood finish, and leaned over it. "After our nice little talk this morning, I bring you a picnic dinner and interrupt some sort of rendezvous—"

"It wasn't a rendezvous." Max didn't look the least bit repentant.

I stood up straight and crossed my arms. "Then explain the lipstick on your shoulder."

"What lipstick?" He sat up and pulled out the fabric of his shirt so he could see it. The dumb male expression on his face was funny, and I had trouble not laughing. "Well, I'll be," he said in amazement.

"I'll tell you what you'll be—sorry—if you don't explain really fast." I pretended to glare at him.

Max looked at me with a grin. "I love it when you get possessive."

"Don't flatter me. Explain," I ordered.

"Stefanie arrived a little bit ago, right after George left. I was outside doing some last-minute things when she drove up. I managed to call Tommy as she waltzed from her car and begged him to find you and tell you to drive over here. He said you were already on your way. I didn't want to take any chances, which was obviously a wise move. She flung herself at me presumably for a comfort hug."

I wanted to spit nails at the thought of her in my husband's arms. "Comfort?"

He had the nerve to laugh. "After I pried myself loose, I invited her into my office to talk, positioning myself behind my desk and in full view of the security camera." He motioned toward said camera with his head. "I thought about pushing the alarm button under my desk, but I figured I wouldn't do that unless she jumped me. When she heard you come in, she hopped on the desk, posed to give you the full effect of her, ah, assets. I'm not stupid."

I didn't like the fact that he'd even noticed her assets. "All men are stupid," I snapped. "At least when it comes to women's wiles."

He stood and stretched. "Maybe. But, Trish, I love you. I would never do anything like that. If for no other reason than I wouldn't want to be on the receiving end of your temper." He paused. "Is it safe for me to move now?"

"Is that the only reason you wouldn't do anything? You're afraid of my temper?"

"Oh, I think you know better than that." Max walked around the desk.

I pointed at his shirt. "Take that off."

He laughed again and began to undo the buttons. "This is just an excuse to see me in my undershirt."

"You're pretty full of yourself, mister," I said. "I wouldn't push me too far if I were you."

"Oh, don't worry. I remember you used to help neuter your father's cattle."

"I haven't forgotten how," I said.

Max tossed his shirt on the desk. He looked good in his undershirt. All things considered, I felt sorrier for Stefanie than angry. After all, Max was mine.

"You know what?" He reached out for my hand.

"What?"

"I think we should pack up the picnic dinner, put it in the refrigerator here for Shirl and Kevin, and go out. That little French place you love. Just you and me. Alone."

"The one with candlelight and servers in tuxes?" I asked.

He smiled. "Yep."

"And we can hold hands under the table and stare into each other's eyes over the table?" I was getting excited.

He grinned and nodded.

"Then we can share a dessert and you can feed me from your fork?" I could barely contain myself.

"If that's what you want."

I thought the idea was brilliant.

On Saturday morning, the house was quiet. My spur-of-the-moment date with Max the night before had been as romantic as I'd hoped, more than making up for the days I felt so guilty and bereft. He knew how to sweep me off my feet, and he'd done it with abandon, leaving me feeling breathless. The only rough moment had been when he informed me he was going to hire a PI to help solve the question of Russ. I was mildly offended that he didn't think I was capable of discovering the truth, but more than that, I was afraid where the truth might lead.

However, I was so happy to have our relationship back on an even keel I let the topic go. Today, Tommy was out with friends. Max took the other kids to the mall and then to lunch at Bo's before the playoff game. I had suggested the outing and stayed home in an effort to give the children time alone with him. I hoped Karen would come around and realize that she was as important to him as I was. Perhaps doing this on a regular basis would alleviate possible future problems with our younger kids.

They would be heading to the game immediately after lunch. I was going to eat with Abbie and then join my family at the ball field.

I made lasagna for Sunday. Then, while I waited to leave, I settled in the family room, holding my steno pad. Several things besides Stefanie's visit to Max spurred me on to think about my mystery. Knowing I was in danger, for one, and in turn, so were my children. But now I had the additional challenge of beating a PI to an answer, if I could.

I flipped the pad open and added the fact that Peggy Nichols had been dragged to the sheriff's office for questioning. Then I reviewed the notes I'd already written down.

*Stefanie. Why did she want in Jim Bob's storage unit?* I bit my lip, and a thought occurred to me. If Jim Bob was blackmailing everyone else, maybe he held something over Stefanie's head, too. Why else would she stay with him? I jotted down: *Was Jim Bob blackmailing Stefanie? What's in the unit that she wants so bad?*

I looked at my next note. *Frank—embezzling; Jim Bob—blackmailing?* Why was Frank so hostile? I scribbled: *Frank is weird and creepy. Makes me scared.*

Now, what about Daryl? I'd already written, *Daryl sleeping with Stefanie?* What else did I know about him? I tapped the pen against my head. Then I wrote: *Did his brother take the road sign?* I also added: *smashed thumb and stitches,* although I couldn't figure out how that fit in.

Then there was Lee Ann. I knew she was upset about Norm. But how could that have led to her killing Jim Bob? Besides, she was a woman. Jim Bob might have been middle-aged, but he was still a man and wouldn't have lain down and let her stab him. That had to have taken strength.

And that led me to the question I'd forgotten about. Why wasn't there blood all over the milk case? Unless Jim Bob had been stabbed somewhere else and moved. That was possible given he was on the cart.

As I wrote that down, the phone rang. I took my notebook to the kitchen and yanked the receiver off the wall.

"Hello?"

"Trish? This is Bill—Dr. Starling."

"Hi, Bill."

"Tried to reach the cell phone number you gave me, but no one answered."

I stuffed my notebook into the kitchen junk drawer to hide it and grabbed my purse to see if I'd lost my phone again.

"What can I do for you?" I asked as I dumped the contents on the kitchen table. I couldn't imagine why he'd call me at home on a Saturday.

Bill cleared his throat. "Well, last minute I decided to do an additional test. I was in the office for an emergency this morning and noticed the results. If you made that appointment with the specialist, you can cancel it."

"Why?" I still couldn't find my phone and headed for the garage to look in the SUV.

"Remember when you were pregnant with Sammie? How coffee made you sick? I took the liberty of doing a pregnancy test just to eliminate that possibility. I'm glad I did. You're pregnant. Congratulations."

I stopped midstep, feeling as though I'd been hit in the stomach. All my thoughts crashed and jumbled into a useless wad of incoherence.

"Trish? Are you there?"

"Yeah," I managed to say. How could I be pregnant?

"You should make an appointment with an obstetrician as soon as possible, given your background. You'll be able to get help with the nausea if it's still a problem. And then you'll find out how far along you are."

"Bill, I can't be pregnant. You know that. All the doctors said I couldn't conceive again. Besides, I'm thirty-two."

"Still a perfect age to have a baby. And you did have Sammie despite the odds. Sometimes miracles happen. You really need to stay out of trouble now. You've got a baby to think about."

"I've had coffee to drink and two painkillers." Like that was my biggest concern.

"Not to worry. Just stop. Call me if I can do anything else for you." He hung up.

I held the receiver in my hand. *Pregnant?* Worry overran a tiny quiver of happiness. Max and I had tried for two years to have another baby after Sammie, but the doctors said it was highly unlikely unless we sought very expensive procedures. Neither of us felt right about that and agreed that four children were enough. I knew Max didn't really want any more kids at his age. I still did but had to agree that four were plenty. How many times recently had he insinuated that he was glad they were all getting older? Last night at the restaurant, he'd mentioned how happy he was that we were going to have more time together because the kids were growing up. How would I tell him this news? Especially on top of everything else.

I glanced at the clock. I was due over at Abbie's. The way things were planned, I could avoid telling Max until after the game. If he saw me beforehand, he'd know something was up. Even though he'd come to terms with things recently, I didn't want to add to his burden, especially right before a game. He might be upset, play horribly, lose, and I'd feel doubly guilty. Besides, I needed some time to sort this out. With Abbie.

My cell phone was nowhere to be found. As I dressed to go out, I tried to recall where I'd put it. The last time I'd used it was to call Tommy and tell him I was going to see Max. It had been in my purse then, and. . .it must have fallen out in Max's office.

I called Four Oaks Self-Storage and asked Kevin to look for it. As I suspected, it lay under one of Max's chairs. I asked Kevin to put it on Max's desk and said I'd be there to get it in a couple of hours.

Abbie met me at her door with a hug. "Come on into the kitchen. I'm finishing our lunch." I followed her and sat at the breakfast bar. She went back to the counter where she was working. "You going to the game after we eat?"

I nodded. "First I have to go get my phone from the self-storage. It fell out of my purse in Max's office."

She glanced over her shoulder at me and laughed. "You and your phone. You should attach it to your purse with rope. Hey, you want coffee? I can make some."

"I can't. It makes me sick when I'm pregnant."

"What?" She turned around, bread in one hand, knife in another. "How far along?"

"I don't know. Bill told me an hour ago."

"Wow." She grinned. "Well, given the past and the fact that all the doctors said this wasn't likely to happen, I guess it's a miracle."

That was what Bill had said. Would Max see it the same way?

"I guess you're right." I rubbed my fingers over the beige countertop.

"You haven't told Max yet, I take it?" she asked.

"No. I don't want to tell him until after the game." I paused. "Truthfully, I don't want to tell him at all. Lately he's been talking a lot about how glad he is that the kids are getting older."

She smiled. "I think he'll be happy."

"I don't know." I shifted on my stool.

"Let's eat in the living room," she said. "It'll be more comfortable."

She handed me two plates to carry. I hopped off the stool and ambled into the living room to wait for her, relaxing in her eclectic taste. Framed modern art accented the red wall above the sofa. The rest of the walls were off-white. Her desk was in an alcove on one side of the room. Shelves, where she kept all her reference books, covered the three walls. I'd never really taken an in-depth interest in her research before, but now, as I looked over the bindings, I realized I'd been stupid. Given that many of the books were about cops and forensics, Abbie could probably answer my question about Jim Bob's lack of blood.

Distracted from my immediate concern over the pregnancy, I put the plates on the glass coffee table and went over to the shelves. I pulled out a book called *Crime Scene Investigation* and riffled through the pages.

Ice tinkled behind me as Abbie walked into the room. "What are you looking at, hon?"

I turned with the book in my hand. "Jim Bob was stabbed, but there wasn't any blood splattered anywhere. Why? Besides the fact that maybe he'd been moved?"

Abbie put the glasses on the coffee table. She then came over to where I stood. "Two reasons as far as I know." She took the book from me, flipped through the pages, and pointed. "One is that he was on his back and was stabbed in the liver. That would result in internal bleeding."

I glanced at the page. That was possible given Jim Bob's position and where the knife had been located. I looked up at her. "What's the other reason?"

"He was already dead when he was stabbed."

———

When I arrived at Four Oaks Self-Storage, the door was unlocked, but Kevin wasn't at the front desk. His car was in the parking lot, along with another that I didn't recognize. I wondered if he'd gone out to show someone a unit.

I ran into Max's office, but my phone wasn't on the desk. I heard a step behind me.

"Kevin?" I asked, looking under some papers. "Where is my phone?"

No one answered. I turned around to see the muzzle of a gun in my face. My breath caught in my throat like a choke hold.

"Lose this?" Stefanie Jenkins asked, grinning widely and holding my phone in her hand.

After I started breathing again, I realized my phone wasn't the only thing that had been lost. She no longer had an accent. And for once, she'd dressed like a normal person in blue jeans and a cotton shirt that covered everything.

"It's so convenient that you're here," she said.

"Where is Kevin?" I hoped maybe he'd been out of the building when she arrived and he'd come in and rescue me.

"He's, shall we say, indisposed in the back room closet." She smiled slowly. "It's amazing what most men will do when a pretty girl offers them favors. He was so easily overcome."

She tossed my phone on the floor and pressed the gun into my stomach, making me wince. Then she pulled two keys from her pocket and dangled them from perfectly manicured fingers. "I'm quite convincing. Kevin confessed to me that the unit was double locked. He also gave me the code to get into the building. I don't need you, but you're coming with me anyway."

"What happened to your accent?" I asked.

"I'm not from the South at all." She jabbed the gun harder. "Come on."

I really had no choice seeing as how she had a weapon pointed at me. Then I remembered the alarm button and sidled toward Max's desk.

"You must really think I'm a moron, Trish. Touch that alarm, and your guts are going to be splattered all over this office."

I did what she asked. Guts all over the place proved too vivid a description to ignore.

With her gun in my back, we walked to the climate-controlled building that housed Jim Bob's unit. I wished that one of our customers would pull in right now, but no one did. Saturday afternoons could be very slow. I punched the code into the keypad to get inside. The twenty-minute light came on, illuminating the hallway and the insides of the units. She handed me the keys. I undid the padlocks and pulled up the door.

People often keep weird things in their storage units, from cookies to trash, but I'd never seen the likes of Jim Bob's. It looked like a home office, complete with a desk, swivel chair, battery-operated light, and three large file cabinets.

Stefanie shoved me inside. I fell to my knees and bashed my head on the corner of the desk. Blood began to dribble down my face. I tried to stop the bleeding with pressure while I watched her, just wishing for one chance to pull her hair out by the roots. Why hadn't I knocked her off Max's desk when I had the chance?

She shut the unit door and turned. "Do you know what my biggest regret is?"

I shook my head.

She closed her eyes and sighed. "That I didn't get a piece of that husband of yours. I certainly tried hard enough and on many different occasions."

Pulling her hair out by the roots wasn't going to be enough.

Her eyes shot open. "I should kill you just because he was faithful. Most men eventually succumb, even if it's just once. Maxwell never did."

My husband had never mentioned the other times she'd tried to seduce him. That made me so mad I stood up and took two steps toward her without thinking.

"Stop right there. Don't do that again. I'll pull this trigger in a second." She waved the gun at me. "Sit down against the wall and put your hands on top of your head."

I did what she said and looked around the unit. File cabinets, a desk. . . I knew what it all was. "I guess this was Jim Bob's headquarters?"

She nodded. "Yes. My dear husband's second job."

"So," I said, "he was probably blackmailing half of the town."

"Quite a few. He never asked for much from anyone. Just a little money or other things here and there. Didn't seem like much, taken one at a time, but altogether it was quite lucrative." She pulled a drawer from the desk.

"Did you kill him?"

"Oh my, no." She'd turned on her southern accent again. "Stabbing someone? Sugar, I'd get my nails dirty. If I ever wanted to kill someone, I'd make sure it wasn't messy." On her knees, she reached into the empty hole where the drawer had been and pulled out some keys.

"Do you know who did?" I asked.

"Nope." She got to her feet, smiling. "Lots of people had reason to, including you." She glanced up at me slyly. "Isn't it ironic that you've been hauled down to the sheriff's office on a regular basis?"

"Did you have an affair with Daryl?" I asked.

"Until I found out who held the purse strings at his house." She walked over to a file cabinet.

"Why'd you stay with Jim Bob?"

"Everyone has things to hide. Unfortunately, he made me pay for my secrets by staying with him. Besides, there were other things I wanted." She waved the gun at me again. "Now, shut up, will you?"

She unlocked a file cabinet and yanked open a drawer. Her breath hissed through her teeth. She unlocked another and opened it. Then another. In a frenzy, she jerked every drawer open. One of the cabinets leaned forward. I wished it would fall on top of her and break her legs. She whirled around and faced me.

"Who took everything out of here?" She moved closer, pointing the gun at me. "Did you?"

I shook my head mutely, wondering if I was about to die.

"Did Maxwell?"

"I don't know."

If she shot a bullet at close range, would it travel through my body into the next unit? I remembered the baby. I couldn't die here.

She stomped her feet, cursed, and spun around, wiping the desktop clean with her arm. Everything crashed to the floor. The light broke into two pieces. "It was the police. I'm sure it was."

She stood silently; then she turned to face me again, this time with slow deliberation that was far scarier than her frenzy. "All that time your husband was leading me on, making me think the stuff was still in here."

She moved closer to me and stood very still. I knew in that moment that she wanted nothing more than to get even with Max by killing me. I closed my eyes and prayed. Tension crackled in the silence. Neither of us moved, though I felt her gaze on me like heat.

The thought of Max finding me dead was more than I could stand. Poor man. He'd be a widower twice. And my baby would die. I wanted to cry, but I was too afraid. Instead, I involuntarily reached up and grabbed the cross necklace Max had given me, thinking about how much he meant to me and how badly I wanted to live and spend the rest of my life with him. She said she wouldn't kill someone in a messy way. *Please, God. Please let her remember that.*

Her breathing changed, and I felt the air shift as she moved. I opened my eyes, expecting to see the barrel of the gun pointed at my head. Instead, she'd walked over to the unit's closed door.

"I'm leaving you locked in here. Everyone is at the baseball game. They'll only start missing you in a couple hours. That'll give me time to get away. I hope they find you before you die of thirst."

With that, she turned her back, walked out of the unit, and pulled the door down, wheels grating in their tracks. Then I heard the snaps of the padlocks shutting. The outside door slammed as she left, sending a *whoosh* of air down the hall that vibrated the building's metal walls. The lights went out, leaving me in total blackness.

## 17

The building creaked and settled around me. I stood up and wondered when Max would notice I wasn't at the game. My legs started to shake. I groped around until I found Jim Bob's desk chair and dropped into it. Max and Detective Scott were going to kill me if I didn't die in this unit first. I'd done exactly what they told me not to do. Put myself in danger, although I really couldn't have anticipated this.

I heard voices in the distance. They could belong to anyone, so I didn't get my hopes up. Where was Stefanie? She must have gotten a new car, because I didn't recognize the one in the lot as hers.

I thought about how she'd tried to seduce Max over and over again. My shaking stopped. I got mad. How dare Miss Fancy-Pants lock me in a storage unit? I hopped out of the chair and shuffled over to the wall, feeling my way to the door. There had to be a way to break out of here. I'd do it, even if I had to dismantle the door with my bare hands. I'd just begun to investigate the mechanism with my fingers when I heard the building door open. The lights came on.

I held my breath. Had Stefanie changed her mind and returned to shoot me? I reached down and grabbed the body of the broken desk light to hit her with.

"Trish? Are you in there?"

Max. I was so relieved to hear him that I didn't care if he was mad, as long as he hugged me first. I dropped the piece of lamp I held.

"Yes," I said.

The locks jiggled, and then the door slid open revealing Max, Detective Scott, and Corporal Fletcher.

"Thank God." Max rushed in, yanked me into his arms, and held me tight. Very tight. Too tight.

"Max," I gasped.

"What, baby?"

"I can't breathe."

"Oh, sorry." He loosened his grip. Then he noticed the blood and examined my head with his fingers. "Are you hurt bad?"

Corporal Fletcher moved closer to us. "Mrs. C., you need to go to the doctor and get that checked out."

"I'll be okay." I tried to push Max's hand away. All the tall men hovering nearby were making me irritable.

"I'm glad to see you alive," Detective Scott said. "We got Stefanie."

"How did you know I was here?" I asked. "Why didn't I hear sirens?" I wished Max would stop messing with my head.

"Abbie," he said. "I called her when you didn't show up. She told us where you'd gone."

Detective Scott nodded. "We didn't use the sirens because we didn't want to broadcast the fact that we were coming."

Max's arm was securely around my shoulders as we walked from the climate-controlled building. Cop cars with flashing lights surrounded the office, and five or six uniformed deputies stood around. Too many cops.

"Kevin's in the storage closet," I said. "I imagine he'll think twice before kissing another woman again."

Detective Scott glanced at me. "We found him."

I thought about Stefanie trying to seduce Max. My anger grew. "Where is Steffie?"

"In a cruiser," the detective answered.

"I want to see." I pulled away from Max and headed toward the cop cars.

Max hurried to keep up with me. "Trish, I don't think that's a good idea." He realized my true intention. The other men didn't know me so well.

I marched to the car where she was held. I hoped she wasn't handcuffed—that she would jump out and attack me, because I was ready to take her down.

I yanked the door open.

Across the parking lot, one of the deputies who was jaw jacking with another, noticed me. "Ma'am, you can't do that," he yelled.

I heard footsteps running toward me. Stefanie didn't look up.

"Not too brave when you don't have a gun, are you?" I snarled at her. "And who's going to do your nails in jail, anyway? Too bad, because that orange color you wear might match your prison jumpsuit."

She shifted until her back faced me.

"Mrs. C.," Corporal Fletcher said behind me, "you need to get away from the car."

I ignored him, clenching my fists. "I should have shoved you off Max's desk when I had a chance."

The corporal appeared in my field of vision and grasped my arm. I felt Max's hands on my shoulders and realized that as much as I wanted to rip Stefanie's hair out, the loss of dignity wasn't worth it. Not to mention a possible lawsuit, another trip to the sheriff's office, and possible time in jail for assault.

I slammed the car door and turned to face Max. "I want to go home." Then I glared at the detective and Corporal Fletcher. "I absolutely do not want to talk to that advocate person. She's too nice."

The men glanced at each other.

"Fletcher can take a statement right now," Detective Scott said.

For the second time that week, I sat on the edge of an examining table. This time at the hospital emergency room. Max sat in a chair in a corner.

After bandaging my head, the emergency room doctor began to scribble on his pad. "I'm going to write you a prescription for pain medication."

If he did, Max would make me take it, and I couldn't because of the baby. This wasn't exactly the place I wanted to tell him.

"Make sure it's safe for pregnant women," I whispered, hoping Max wouldn't hear me.

The doctor glanced up at me. "Did you say you're expecting?"

Max's head jerked up, and his eyes widened. "Expecting?"

The doctor glanced from me to Max. "Okay, that changes things a little." He tore up the paper he'd already written and started a new one.

"You're pregnant?" Max said, sitting very still.

The doctor eyed Max as he handed me a slip of paper. "Ah, let me know if there's anything else I can do." He hurried from the room.

"You're pregnant?" Max demanded.

"Yes." I didn't look at his eyes, just gazed at his chin.

He stood. "Let's go."

He helped me off the table and pulled the curtain aside to let me pass. I finally glanced at him, but now he wasn't looking at me. I felt the prickle of tears in my eyes but kept them at bay. He guided me out of the building to the car. There, he opened the door for me, holding my arm as I got in. Then he got into his side.

I didn't speak. Max's breathing was irregular, and he tapped a finger on the steering wheel.

"How long have you known?" he asked quietly.

"Since this afternoon." I couldn't think of anything else to say.

—

We lay silently in bed. We hadn't really talked yet, but that wasn't Max's fault. He'd tried, but I hadn't given him a chance. I felt unreasonably cranky, out of sorts, and mad that he hadn't been ecstatic when he learned about the baby, even though I knew perfectly well that his reaction was predictable given the circumstances. When we got home, I immediately took a shower and went to bed, leaving him to talk to the kids, call my parents, and even call his folks if he wanted to. Someone had to explain my latest mishap, and I wasn't in the mood.

I tossed and turned, and slumber evaded me. When he got into bed, I pretended to be asleep.

Soft light from the street filtered through the blinds. A dog barked in the distance.

Max rolled over. "I know you're awake."

"How?" I asked.

"The way you're breathing. Plus, your fists are clenched."

Stupid fists. They were clenched on top of the covers. I immediately relaxed them and shoved my hands under the blanket, keeping my eyes closed. "Okay, I'm asleep now."

"Come on, Trish. Neither one of us will get any rest if we don't talk."

"Are you going to fuss at me?" I asked with my eyes still shut.

"No."

"Promise?" I peeked at him.

"Yes." He was on his back with his hands under his head and his ankles crossed. "I'm sorry. I know my reaction wasn't what you expected."

"Actually, it was precisely what I expected," I grumbled.

He sat up and turned on the light. Then he stuffed a pillow behind him and leaned against the headboard. "I'll admit, I was upset."

"Duh," I said, sitting up and shoving my pillow behind my head.

He glanced at me. "Not because you're pregnant, but because you hadn't told me, especially after our recent issues. That wasn't exactly a great way to find out."

"It wasn't exactly how I'd planned to tell you," I said, meeting his gaze.

He frowned. "Well, that brings us to the crux of the matter. When were you planning to tell me?"

"After the game," I said.

He looked away from me, focusing on his toes. "I thought we agreed that we would tell each other everything." He paused. "So did you tell Abbie?"

"Yes," I said.

His expression was bland, but his right cheek muscle was twitching. "I'm your husband, Trish. Why didn't you call me and tell me first?"

I sat up and pushed some of his hair back, feeling like the most horrible wife in the world. I'd hurt him. "Oh, honey. I'm sorry. I wasn't thinking, I guess. As usual. I was worried about your reaction. I didn't want you to lose the game, which happened anyway because you guys had to come and rescue me."

"We've rescheduled." He adjusted the pillow under his neck and stared at the wall. "Is that the only reason?"

"I figured you'd think I did it on purpose and be mad. I knew you didn't want more kids. I talked to Abbie first so I could figure out a way to tell you."

He took my hand. "That makes no sense. How could you have done it on purpose? It takes two, doesn't it?"

That was just like Max to say such a logical thing. I faced him. "You're right. I was wrong. What can I do to make up for this?"

He smiled slowly. "First, come here and let me hold you. Second, don't get locked in any more storage units. Third, don't keep anything else from me."

I scooted next to him and put my lips to his ear. "I didn't get locked in that unit on purpose."

"I know." He kissed me. "I love you. And. . .well, your pregnancy is unexpected and not exactly what we'd planned, but sometimes things happen for a reason. In fact, given all the odds, this baby has to be a gift from God."

"Really?" I wrapped my arm around him.

"Yes, really." He kissed me again.

A bit later, I wasn't sleeping yet, but I was content. We'd discussed baby names and decided to tell the kids the next day. Max was already breathing evenly like he does right before he falls asleep. I was happy to be next to him. I wasn't dead or shivering in Jim Bob's storage unit.

Old Jim Bob, the man everyone hated. So much so that someone killed him. Stefanie denied it, but she was certainly interested in something that he kept in his secret office in one of the file cabinets. . .empty file cabinets. . . I'd forgotten to ask Max about them.

I sat up and turned the light on.

Max jumped up as if on a spring. "Are you okay?" He stared at me with wide eyes.

"Yes, I'm fine. When did the police get the stuff out of Jim Bob's unit, and why didn't you say anything? You had to have let them in. Did they have a search warrant? Did they need one? Furthermore, what was in there that Stefanie wanted so badly? Do you know?"

Max groaned and lay back down, pulling the pillow over his head.

I yanked it off his face. "No sleeping until you tell me."

He kept his eyes shut. "I guess there's no chance this can wait until tomorrow morning?"

"I won't be able to sleep for wondering."

Max sighed, rolled on his side to face me, and rested on his elbow. "Okay. Yes, Eric searched Jim Bob's unit not too long after the murder. Yes, they had a warrant. Yes, I let them in. I don't know exactly what he found, but it must have implicated Stefanie in some way because he was keeping an eye on her. However, he let everyone, including her, think that the unit was intact."

"You knew and didn't tell me?" I demanded.

He sighed. "Yes, I knew. And I didn't tell you."

"And you're mad at me for not telling you things?" I huffed.

He shook his head. "I think the situations are just a little different."

That was beside the point. "So why didn't you tell me?"

"Because Eric asked me not to."

I sat up and crossed my legs. "Is there something wrong with me? Am I untrustworthy? Did neither of you think I could keep a secret?"

"It wasn't my decision. And I assume he wanted as few people to know as possible. Police business and all. Besides, he was treating you as a suspect."

Max's words didn't pacify me.

"Can I go to sleep now?" he asked.

"No. I'm not done." I crossed my arms. "I know Jim Bob was blackmailing people. What exactly did they find inside? Copies of blackmail letters? And what did Stefanie want in there?"

Max shook his head. "I don't know."

"She's tricky enough to commit murder, but I didn't see her in the grocery store that morning. At least I don't think so. Unless she was in disguise. Do you think she killed him?"

He shrugged one shoulder.

"Who is Stefanie, anyway?" I asked. "You know her southern accent was fake, don't you?"

He said nothing, just kept staring at me.

"Do you know what she told me?" I clenched my fists. "She was sorry she didn't get a piece of you."

Max raised his eyebrow. "And that bothers you?"

I frowned. "Well, yeah, because she said she tried more than once."

He laughed. "You have absolutely nothing to worry about."

I scowled at him. "Besides having the morals of an alley cat, who was she really?"

He groaned. "I don't know. I don't care. I want to sleep."

I shifted positions and bounced. "How can you sleep knowing that you don't know who she really is?"

"Easy. Watch." He reached over me, turned out the light, and flopped back on the bed.

"But—"

"Hush," he said. "Go to sleep."

## 18

"I—am—so—humiliated!" Karen pushed her chair from the table and jumped up. "I can't believe it, Dad. You're too old to have babies." She ran from the room.

We'd made the big announcement to the kids during a special Italian-themed Sunday lunch. Karen's reaction didn't surprise me at all.

Max put his fork down. "I'll go talk to her."

"No," I said. "Leave her alone. Don't let her ruin the meal for the rest of us."

He took a deep breath, debating his decision. "Okay," he finally said.

Sammie kept eating tiny bites of lasagna noodles and watching everyone. Charlie's mouth was stuffed full of Italian bread.

Tommy grabbed another piece of lasagna. "Don't mind her. Julie is a wreck, so Karen is a wreck. Girls can be so dramatic."

I agreed, although I'd seen my share of melodramatic men. When Karen became human again, I'd encourage her to join the drama club.

Sammie put her fork down and eyed first her father, then me. "Why?" she asked.

"Why what, sweetie?" I took a bite of salad.

"Why is Daddy too old? What happens with babies?"

Tommy snorted and covered his mouth. Max's lips twitched. I blinked and for a moment couldn't figure out what she meant. Then I got it and blushed. Max and Tommy looked at me as though answering the question was my responsibility.

Was there any way I could deflect this until she was older? "Well, uh, Sammie. . ."

Charlie interrupted me with a wave of his hand. "It's no big deal. In Sunday school this morning, we read about how that Abraham guy had kids when he was really ancient. That means Dad can have them, too."

"Oh," Sammie said. "Okay."

And that took care of that.

*Old man*, I mouthed at Max.

He winked at me and grabbed my hand.

After lunch, I rewarded Charlie for his quick thinking by agreeing to sit down and watch *Mysterious Disappearances* with him. I had to admit that by the time the show was half over, I was hooked.

During a commercial break, he turned to me with a wide grin. "This is how I knew that Mrs. Jenkins was a bad lady."

"Huh?" I'd missed something.

"I saw a show about a lady who rips off rich men. She marries them and disappears with all their money."

I gaped at him.

Apparently that was enough encouragement because he began to talk faster. "I tried to tell you, Mom. First I saw a picture of that guy who worked at my school on the show. Then I saw a really bad picture of her. He was her husband, but he was supposed to be dead."

That's why Charlie saw dead people. And everyone thought he was imagining things. Poor kid. "I'm sorry we didn't listen." Things began to fall into place in my mind. I ruffled his hair. Charlie would be getting his own *Mysterious Disappearances* book for his birthday.

I needed to review all my clues. If what Charlie said was true, then Steffie had plenty of motivation to murder Jim Bob. But she wasn't there that day, was she? And where did Peter-Carey fit in? Was he the accomplice? The supposed dead man who was now really dead? She had denied any part of the murders. As much as she'd been bragging, it seemed to me that she would have bragged about that, too.

~

I'd spread the contents of my kitchen junk drawer on the counter to look for my mystery notebook. It was gone. Perhaps I wasn't remembering right where I'd put it.

Max had taken all the kids out for ice cream, leaving me home to rest. His orders. My short confinement in the storage unit caught up with me after lunch. My head hurt, as did my body, and of course I didn't want to take anything for the pain because of the baby. So I was going to rest as ordered. With my clues. But now I couldn't find the steno pad. As I stuffed everything back into the drawer, the doorbell rang. I slammed the drawer shut and made my way to the front door, aching muscles protesting against my attempt to hurry.

Through the peephole, I saw Detective Scott. I flung the door open. "Why are you here? I didn't do anything."

He smiled. "I know you didn't. I just need to talk to you for a moment."

I stepped back to let him in. "We can go into the family room. Max and the kids are out getting ice cream. I'm supposed to be napping."

Detective Scott followed me. He was dressed casually, in dress pants and shirt, not in a uniform or a suit, but he still made me nervous. I hoped I wouldn't have to call my erstwhile lawyer.

"Have a seat." I motioned to one of the white, overstuffed, slipcovered chairs, and watched him with suspicion.

"I'd like to review your statement from last night." He sat, holding some papers on a clipboard.

I relaxed and dropped onto the sofa. "That's fine."

He talked me through my confrontation with Stefanie, helping me remember things that I'd forgotten about. Because so much had happened in such a short time, I felt as if I was in some emotional netherworld, one step removed from everything.

When we were done, he had me sign the form. Then he sat back down and studied me. His eyes were different than they had been the times he'd interviewed me. Not so pinpointed and hard. "Trish, are you feeling okay?"

"I guess I'm a little numb, at least emotionally. My body aches, and my head hurts. Probably from when Steffie pushed me across the storage unit." As if to confirm my statement, a muscle spasm in my shoulder made me wince.

He leaned forward. "You need to take care of yourself now. You've got a baby to worry about."

"Yeah." I was rubbing my shoulder. But then I stopped. I hadn't told him I was pregnant. "How did you know?"

His face twitched. "Abbie Grenville. She, ah, informed me at church. Then she told me to leave you alone."

I hadn't realized they went to the same church. I wanted to laugh at his expression. Like he'd been chastened. "She looks out for me."

"Obviously," he said.

I folded my legs under me. "We've been best friends since kindergarten."

"That explains a lot," he muttered.

I decided to let that comment go, although I was certain it wasn't complimentary. "I have something to tell you that might be important."

He sat up straight, eyes fastened on my face, becoming a cop once again.

I told him about Charlie and *Mysterious Disappearances*.

"Yes. I checked into that. Your stepson is observant." The detective tapped his finger on his leg. "A good cop follows every lead, even those from a kid."

A lesson I would do well to learn.

I decided to take advantage of Detective Scott's regard for my son's brilliance and tell him what I thought. "I don't believe Stefanie killed two men."

His body tensed, and he squinted at me. "I want you to forget about the whole thing. You don't have to be involved in this anymore."

"Then I guess I'm not a suspect?" I asked.

"I never said you were."

*But you sure acted like it.* I put my hands on my legs and went back to my original topic as though he hadn't spoken. "I was there with her in that storage unit. She could have killed me. If she were a murderer, she would have. What did she have to lose? I don't think I'm reading this situation wrong."

"You need to stop thinking about it," he said.

"But—" I started to argue; then I saw the expression on his face and understood. He didn't believe the murderer was Stefanie, either. That meant that Jim Bob and Peter-Carey's killer was still on the loose. But why wasn't I still a suspect?

Silence filled the air between us. I met his gaze and ignored his order to stop thinking. "Here's my biggest question. Why wasn't there blood from Jim Bob's body squirted all over the place in the cold room? Was it because he was on his back and got stabbed in the liver or because he was already dead?"

Detective Scott's breath hissed through his teeth. Poor man. I'd caught him off guard. "Trish, I told you to. . . You're not going to stop thinking about all this, are you?"

I shook my head. "I can't. I also have to figure out about Russ and the stop sign."

"I heard Max hired a PI," Detective Scott said.

"Yes," I grumbled. "Probably some highfalutin, educated, Cunningham-type guy who's too big for his britches. Like that lawyer."

Detective Scott laughed.

I joined him; then I sobered. "I have to know."

"I'm sure it's only a matter of time until the truth comes out," he said. "Now, you need to promise me something."

"What?"

"If you must think about all of this, do it, but don't go out and ask questions." He paused and eyed me. "And stay home as much as possible. I don't want to have to worry about you."

For the first time since that horrible day when I found Jim Bob, I felt a few warm fuzzies for the detective. And his attitude toward me had mellowed. Perhaps I could use this to my advantage. I crossed my arms. "Let's make a deal."

He snorted and shook his head. "Cops don't make deals. Lawyers make deals."

I folded my hands under my chin in proper begging fashion. "Please? All I want you to do is answer some questions for me."

He blinked a couple of times; then he laughed again. "Fine. All right. Ask. But no guarantees."

I grinned. "Okay. Who is Stefanie, really?"

He thought for a moment. "That is a matter of public record, so I can answer. Sybil Lefebvre Ramsey from Poughkeepsie, New York. She's wanted by the FBI."

"Sybil?" I giggled. "Are you for real?"

"Why is that funny?" he asked.

"There's this movie about this woman named Sybil with multiple personalities, and it's just ironic that. . ." I stopped when I realized what he'd said. "Her last name was Ramsey?"

He nodded.

"So Carey, or Peter, or whoever he was, was her husband?"

He nodded again. "Yep. Got it in one."

"She wasn't legally married to Jim Bob?"

"Nope," Detective Scott said.

*Alley cat* did not begin to describe Stefanie. "Was she a true blond?"

He stared at me as if I was crazy. "I have no idea, although her hair was different in each place she lived."

She was as bad as her husband, disguising herself. "Well, did she murder Peter?"

He shrugged. "Can't answer that."

"Can't or won't?" I asked.

"I can't, and I won't," he said.

That probably meant she hadn't. "Okay, was it true that Peter Ramsey was supposedly dead?"

He nodded. "That's what the public thought, yes. But the FBI didn't believe it. Sybil and Peter's last scam didn't go so well. Their victim figured it out before they could leave, and Peter accosted him. After the two disappeared with thousands, the man died, thus making Peter wanted for murder. But a month later, his belongings were found neatly piled on the railing of a very high bridge with a suicide note. His body was never found. Of course, there was no body to find."

I made a mental note to watch *Mysterious Disappearances* every day. Who knew what I'd learn? "Did you find proof of all of Jim Bob's blackmailing victims in that unit?"

"That's possible," he said.

"And he had the unit to keep Stefanie from getting into his stuff, right? I mean, the timing of his rental coincides with his marriage."

Detective Scott shrugged. "Probably, but we'll never know for sure."

I frowned. "What, exactly, was she looking for in there? Seems to me, she'd have taken his money and run after he died. . . ." I met Detective Scott's gaze while my mind raced.

Jim Bob had met Stefanie in the Cayman Islands. From what I had heard about Jim Bob, he didn't strike me as a Cayman Island kind of guy. But I knew from movies that those kinds of places had banks where people hid their money.

I grinned. "Never mind. I think I get it. He probably had an offshore bank account and hid the information in his unit."

Detective Scott stood. "I think I've more than fulfilled my side of the bargain. Now promise me you'll stay out of trouble."

"Okay." I got up from the sofa, my muscles protesting mightily. Then I walked him to the front door. Truthfully, I would have agreed even if he hadn't answered any of my questions. He was right. I had a baby inside me to think about. A miracle.

After Detective Scott left, I went nuts trying to find my steno pad. I had to add the information I'd found out. I'd ransacked my bedroom and the kitchen drawers; then I pulled the cushions off the couch. Now I was looking underneath a stack of magazines. I began to pick through them one at a time when I heard steps behind me. I turned.

"Are you looking for this?" Max stood in the doorway, holding my notebook. "Karen found it last night and gave it to me."

She was still trying to get me in trouble. He leaned against the door frame. His black jeans and red shirt made him look breathtakingly handsome, but I didn't let that deter me from my quest.

"Good. I didn't want to have to start over—" I stopped. My mouth opened and shut like a bass. I had just confessed that I was still looking into the mystery.

"You're supposed to be resting," he said softly. "You're incorrigible."

"Yes." I looked at the floor.

"Stubborn."

"Yes." I looked at his feet.

"Persistent."

"That, too." I peeked up at him. He wasn't frowning.

"Detective Scott told me some stuff I want to add to it."

Max cocked his head and frowned. "When?"

"He came by while you were gone and—"

"You talked to him without a lawyer?" Max demanded.

"Well, it wasn't a big deal. He just wanted me to sign my statement. Then he told me to stay out of trouble and take care of my baby."

Max relaxed a fraction. "What was on the statement?"

"Just my observations from last night." I took a step toward him. "It's okay. I didn't need my snooty lawyer."

"I just don't know. . . ," he said.

I was salivating to write down everything I'd learned. I walked over to him and held my hand out for my list. "Give that to me, Max." I stood on my tiptoes and tried to grab it from him.

With little effort, he kept it out of my reach. "First, I have a surprise for you."

A surprise? I put my arm down and stared at him. I loved surprises, especially from my husband. "What is it?"

"How about a deal, and then I give it to you?"

"A deal?" The second one of the day.

He nodded.

"Okay, what is it?" I was enjoying myself immensely.

He grinned. "The surprise and the notebook in exchange for your promise not to run around and ask questions."

I narrowed my eyes and pretended to consider his request, although doing that wouldn't be hard since I'd already promised Detective Scott the same thing. Then it occurred to me that Max must know what I suspected. "So you don't believe the killer has been found, either?"

He now held the notebook at his side. I could easily have snatched it, but I didn't. The fear and concern that tightened his face and filled his eyes made me want to hug him and tell him everything would be okay.

He shook his head. "Figures you'd figure that out. Eric never came out and said as much, but he did caution me to watch out for you."

"Okay, then." I crossed my arms. "I'll play your game, Mr. Tough Negotiator. But I won't agree to anything without knowing what my surprise is."

He pulled a sheaf of folded papers from his back pocket and handed it to me, along with the notebook.

I dropped that on the sofa and glanced through the papers. Itineraries for cruises.

I looked up at him. "For us? Just you and me?"

"Yes." The sparkling eagerness in his eyes made him look like a little boy. "These are the trips the travel agent said were available in the next few months. I discussed them with the kids today. Karen wouldn't join in, of course, but the rest did. You'll notice stars on some of the pages—those are the ones they thought were the best. Honey, I want us to go away together alone for a week. Soon. I've already talked to our parents and made arrangements for the kids. Now all that's left is for you to choose one."

A week alone with Max on a ship. I could think of nothing more fun. I had two concerns. The first was Karen's reaction. This would only fuel her jealousy. I had to think of a way to counteract that. Maybe Max could take her for the day to her favorite amusement park. The second was my brother. I still had no idea if he was guilty of causing Lindsey's death.

"Don't worry about that," Max said softly.

"What?" I looked up at him.

"The thing with Russ won't affect our trip either way, okay?"

He'd read my mind. "Okay. You have a deal." I put my hand out.

He shook it, even while he narrowed his eyes. "That was too easy. What are you up to?"

"Nothing, Max. Absolutely nothing. I'm going to be good. I'm going to cook, clean, work, and take care of my family. That's all."

And I meant it. I was going to do everything in my power to keep my part of the deal. I had a baby to think about. Besides, I wanted to be alone with Max more than anything in the world.

19

Gail worked behind the counter as I walked through the door of Doris's Doughnuts. My mother was nowhere in sight. The scent of coffee permeated the air. I inhaled it, thinking resignedly that I had at least a year before I could drink it again. I slowly made my way to the counter, nervous about being here. I'd talked to Daddy earlier, and he'd encouraged me to come here to tell my mother about the baby. He said she'd be happy to find out with her friends. Yeah, she'd be happy to have some drama in front of her friends. I was going to do what he asked, but after her comment about my having plenty of kids already, I wasn't sure how she would react.

"Well, if it isn't the local champion of justice." Gail banged a dish.

I wasn't sure if she meant it or not.

"Doris!" she yelled. "Your daughter has arrived."

Ma came bustling from the back, followed by April May.

"Well, I guess your stomach is feeling better now"—Ma sniffed—"since you finally saw fit to come and see me."

I leaned against the counter. "It's not a problem. The nausea is nothing that the obstetrician can't take care of."

"Kids. Well, you know what I say. . ." She stopped midsentence. Very slowly, she and the two bobbleheads turned to stare at me.

"Obstetrician?" my mother whispered.

She and Gail exchanged glances.

"My, my, you've certainly been busy," Gail announced as though she were a loudspeaker. "Solving crimes and getting knocked up."

My face turned bright red. I knew I should have waited until my mother was at home to tell her.

"Wow!" April May clapped her hands together. "Well, you know, if I had a husband who looked like Max, I'd be pregnant all the time."

Better yet, I should have sent a telegram announcing the news.

My mother slapped April May's arm, but I could tell she was pleased. "This calls for a celebration. Free coffee for everyone." She looked pointedly at me. "Except you, missy. You'll have a decaf mocha latte with whole milk."

She beamed as she worked and said nothing. I'd have to mark this down on my calendar as the day my mother was momentarily speechless and pleased with me at the same time.

"Guess it's all solved, then," Gail said, eyeing me. "You cornered that strumpet and got her arrested."

Funny how things got exaggerated in the telling. "I didn't exactly corner her. It was more like she cornered—"

"Now Four Oaks will once again be safe," she said. "We can sleep tight knowing we won't be murdered in our beds. What with fingerprints on that knife that was stuck in Jim Bob, they should be able to nail her."

I wasn't even going to try to dissuade her from her opinion that all was well, even though I knew it wasn't.

Ma handed me my latte, still beaming. "Well, I'm sure that police detective is grateful for my daughter's help. Why, just yesterday I was at Shopper's Super Saver getting some sirloin ground when Daryl walked by. I told him he was lucky Trish was on the case. What with his physical injuries and all, I'm sure they were ready to blame him. I mean, what about all those stitches? I'll tell you what. I always knew one day Trish's stubbornness would pay off."

That was news to me, or maybe I had amnesia. I only remembered the times she'd told me my persistence would be the death of her.

Ma put her hands on her hips and stared at me. "Why don't all of you come over to dinner tonight? We can celebrate. You have to eat well now. You're too thin."

I guess too thin is better than holding water and looking puffy. "Thanks, Ma, but I'll have to check with Max. He's with his dad, looking over the new storage facility site outside of Baltimore. Then they were going to meet with some people at the county offices. I don't know when he'll be home."

"Well, you and the kids come on without him," she said, as if I'd already replied in the affirmative. "We'll send dinner home for him."

At least we'd eat well. I headed to a table to sit down. I really wished she'd stop talking about me to people. Daryl might still be guilty. In fact, knowing that Sybil-Stefanie had been married to Peter-Carey would certainly give Daryl some motivation. Jealousy.

I sipped my drink and watched April May wipe tables. When she got to me, she stopped and sat down. "I'm happy for you."

"Thanks," I said.

"I'm glad some people's marriages are working out. So many around here aren't. Besides Stefanie and Jim Bob, I mean. That was doomed from the start because they were both bad people."

April had a succinct way of putting things. I nodded in agreement, although I knew Jim Bob and Stefanie hadn't really been married.

"I have a new boyfriend." She smiled at me shyly with shiny eyes. "I think maybe he's the one."

"That's wonderful," I said.

"He worked at the landfill under Norm." She leaned toward me. "But he began to suspect things weren't right there. You know, the bad trash being hauled in."

I nodded.

"He went over to work at the Shopper's Super Saver. He's a night manager and might be offered the assistant-manager position."

She looked proud, and though I was pleased, I wondered what that meant for Daryl. He was the assistant manager. Had he been arrested or something?

She shook her head. "Isn't it amazing? I mean, this is a small town and all this stuff is happening. Can you believe Frank?"

"He always seemed so good," I murmured, still thinking about Daryl.

"Yes. He was in here the other day. Your mother thinks he's guilty as sin." April waved her sponge in the air. "Your mother reminded him that you were helping the police. Then Gail said her granddaughter talked to you and told her all about it."

I wanted to groan.

"I'm sure you know this, but the cops have been all over him like a June bug on a porch light. He's living with his parents, but pretty soon, I reckon he'll be living in jail for stealing. It's only a matter of time. His poor kids." She stood. "Not only did he lose his wife, but he lost his fancy car, and he doesn't have a job." She smiled at me. "You're really lucky, Trish. Your mother keeps telling all of us how she's so glad her kids never did nothing really bad."

As usual, my mother was representing things to people the way she wanted them to be. For all our sakes, I hoped that Russ wasn't guilty. My mother would definitely suffer. She might have to close her store from the humiliation.

⸺

That afternoon, Karen didn't come home from school, and she didn't answer her cell phone. I called Tommy at work.

"Hey, Mom, what's up?" he asked.

"Why didn't you bring Karen home?"

He breathed hard into the phone. "She told me you were picking her up."

That wasn't good news. "She isn't here. Did you talk to her any other time today?"

"I saw her between classes. She was upset because Julie left or something like that."

"Tommy, when we ask you to do something, we expect you to do it." Even as I snapped at him, I knew I was overreacting.

"I'm sorry, Mom." He spoke so fast I knew he felt guilty. "I'll ask around, okay?"

I tried to reach Lee Ann. She wasn't at work or at home. Then I called Max.

Fortunately, he had his phone turned on.

"Hi, baby." He sounded so relaxed and happy I hated to tell him that his elder daughter was missing.

"Have you heard from Karen?" I asked.

"No." His voice tightened. "Is something wrong?"

"She didn't come home from school. Tommy said Julie was absent and that upset Karen."

Max inhaled. "I hope they haven't run away together. Listen, I'll call the police; then I'll extricate myself from things here. I'll be home in about an hour and a half, if I don't get caught in traffic. Rush hour starts around this time. Let me know if you hear from her."

Five horrible minutes later, during which I prayed out loud as I paced the hall, the family room, the kitchen, the living room, and Max's office, the phone rang. Karen's cell phone number appeared on caller ID.

I was furious, yanking the receiver up like I was going to choke it. "Karen?"

"I need a ride home." Her voice sounded belligerent.

I didn't understand how she could be so disaffected. I'd be scared if I knew I'd be facing Max after something like this. "Why didn't you get a ride with Tommy? We've been looking all over for you. Your father is calling the police. Why didn't you come home?"

"Why did he call the police?" She sighed. "I know he's really mad. I'm sorry. Can you pick me up at the library?"

"Yes. I'll be there in twenty minutes. Be waiting for me."

I phoned Max. "Karen's at the library. You can cancel the cops. Sammie and I will run over and get her. We'll be here when you get home."

"Yes. Good." He sounded as mad as I felt.

Vehicles filled the library parking lot. I drove around several times and didn't see Karen, nor did I find a space in which to park. Finally, I left the SUV along the side of the road that ran between the library and the woods.

"Come on," I said to Sammie. "Let's go inside."

I didn't find Karen there, either. Over in the children's section, a gray-haired woman read to a group of children gathered on the floor around her feet, her soothing voice a direct contrast to my racing heart.

"Mommy, can I listen?" Sammie whispered.

Having her entertained would help me a lot. "Yes. I have to find Karen. You stay here. I'll be right back, okay?"

She settled on the floor with the other kids.

Karen was nowhere in the building. I even peered into the men's room. At the desk, I got the immediate attention of a librarian, even though there was a line. Pounding on the counter has that effect on people.

"I'm looking for my daughter. She's supposed to be here." My voice sounded high-pitched and tight. "She's taller than you, with long, blond, curly hair."

The woman nodded. "Yes, she was here awhile ago. She used the bathroom and then left."

I ran outside, scanning the parking lot, trying to control my panic. No sign of her. Maybe she'd seen my SUV and was waiting for us next to it. I ran over to where I'd parked and noticed a big, wood-trimmed station wagon parked in front of my vehicle, but Karen wasn't there. Something wasn't right.

"Mom?"

At the sound of her voice, my breath gushed out in relief. "Karen?" I turned. She stood on the edge of the woods.

"Where have you been?" I snapped as I walked toward her. "You are so grounded. You might not ever have a life. I can't believe—"

"Mom. . ." Her voice squeaked. "I'm sorry. I didn't know."

"What?" I asked, as I got closer.

That's when I noticed someone standing behind her. Lee Ann. She reached around Karen and held a knife to her throat.

"Don't do anything stupid," she said.

I reached into my purse for my cell phone and miraculously found it.

"Drop your purse and the phone," Lee Ann growled, "or I'll kill her right now."

I did what she said.

20

Lee Ann dragged Karen farther back into the woods. I followed. Soon the shrubby growth under the trees and my SUV hid us from sight. Anyone driving by would have to stop and focus to see what was really happening.

"Where's Julie?" I asked softly.

"With her father," Lee Ann said.

Karen's chest heaved with ragged breaths that hissed through her clenched teeth. Tears filled her wide eyes. My body shook, but I locked my knees and squeezed my hands shut to control the movement. I had to stay focused.

"What are you doing, Lee Ann?" I hated the way my voice quavered. "You can't possibly get away with this."

"Maybe. Maybe not. Doesn't matter at this point. That stupid detective is sniffing around my door. Because of you."

The knife shifted at Karen's neck. She whimpered as it nicked the skin on her throat. I saw red, as my mother would say, and not just blood. A red haze of fury.

"Why is that because of me?" I asked through stiff lips.

"You've been talking to the cops. Your mouthy mother brags about it, even at the grocery store. And Karen here has been keeping me up on everything you're doing. She's so gullible. She hates you, you know." Lee Ann shrugged.

"I don't, Mom," Karen whispered. "I didn't mean it." Large tears rolled down her face.

I wanted to tackle Lee Ann so badly that my body shook. "Is this because of Norm drinking? Are you mad because your marriage is failing and mine isn't?"

She snorted. "Norm isn't drinking. That's just what I told people."

Voices drifted from the library. Little kids and their parents began to spill into the parking lot. Then my cell phone rang on the ground behind me.

"Don't pick that up." Lee Ann grabbed Karen's arm, yanking her behind a tree and out of view.

If I screamed, Karen might die. Rushing Lee Ann was too risky. Not with the knife at Karen's throat.

I shifted my position so I could see them, taking deep breaths, trying to calm my mind. The rings of the phone made me want to scream in frustration and fear, but hysteria wouldn't get us out of this. Karen's eyes watched every nuance of my behavior. I couldn't act afraid. I had to keep Lee Ann talking. Then I could figure out a way to disarm her.

The ringing finally stopped.

"Where did you get that knife?" I asked. "It looks like the one that killed Jim Bob."

She laughed. "Jim Bob didn't die from stabbing. That's just what everybody thinks."

"Mommy? Where are you?" Sammie's shout came from the library.

Karen gasped. I trembled as I peered through the trees and the windows of my SUV. Sammie stood on the library's front stoop, looking for me. I was still, hoping she wouldn't see me. She hopped onto the pavement and headed for my vehicle.

My fingernails dug holes in my palms. Lee Ann swore softly behind me. Then a woman rushed out of the library. I heard the low hum of her voice and the high squeak of Sammie's.

"Don't make a sound," Lee Ann hissed.

Sammie hesitated, then trudged back to take the woman's hand. They disappeared into the library. I breathed a prayer of thanks. Now, to get me and Karen out of this.

"We're leaving," Lee Ann said.

I turned around.

Fury had twisted her face into an unrecognizable mask. "It won't be long before they call the cops."

"Let Karen go," I begged. "Take me."

"Shut up, Trish. You're driving." She glanced around to make sure no one was looking and pushed Karen from behind the tree to where I stood.

I knew if we got in the car with her we were as good as dead. My mind raced. "Where are we going?"

Lee Ann grinned. "Norm's favorite place. Very lucrative."

It didn't take much imagination to know she meant the landfill.

Lee Ann took the knife from Karen's throat and held it to her back. She motioned for me to get in the passenger door. I stood where I was.

"Get a move on, Trish."

I met Karen's gaze. She nodded ever so slightly, and I tried to figure out what she meant. Next thing I knew, she fell to her hands and knees.

"Get up." Lee Ann kicked her.

Kicking my daughter was Lee Ann's last mistake. I roared and leaped at her. She shrieked and lifted the knife. It glinted as it arced toward me.

"No!" Karen screamed and grabbed Lee Ann's leg.

The knife missed my arm by an inch. I tackled her, slamming her into a tree. The knife fell from her hand, landing on the dirt with a dull thud. Karen scrabbled for it, but Lee Ann kicked wildly, hitting Karen's hip, knocking her off balance. I grabbed a handful of Lee Ann's hair. She screamed and clawed at my face. Her nail caught my nose.

Sirens blared in the distance, but I ignored them. I'd had enough. Perhaps Lee Ann didn't remember my temper in school or the kids I'd beat up. What she really didn't understand was my desperation to save Karen and my unborn baby.

I twisted a hank of her hair in my hands and hooked my foot on her leg. She fell to her knees. I held her hair tight, wrapped around my fingers, but she kept fighting me, so I punched her in the gut. She groaned and slithered to the ground. I rolled her over onto her stomach. Then I kicked the knife away and knelt, with my knees in her back.

"Karen, get a couple of those bungee hook things from the car."

She scrambled to the SUV. The sirens came closer, and I prayed they were coming for us. Lee Ann struggled under me, trying to knock me off balance, but I jerked her hair and stayed put.

"I thought we were friends," I said.

She swore at me, calling me horrible things that I couldn't hear clearly over the din in the parking lot.

I glared down at her. "I have a feeling you're guilty of a lot of things, but as far as I'm concerned, the very worst thing you did was threaten to kill my daughter."

Karen handed me two bungee cords. I took them from her and wrapped Lee Ann's hands and feet together.

Red and blue reflections of police-car lights glared on my SUV windows and those of the library.

"Wow, Mom." Karen stared at me like I was a superhero. I smiled at her, and for the first time in months, she smiled in return.

I heard shouts and more sirens.

"Go tell them where we are," I ordered, standing guard over Lee Ann.

The next person I saw was Corporal Nick Fletcher.

He reached my side and looked down at Lee Ann. He took his hat off and scratched his head. "Well now, that's got to be the finest example of hog-tying I've ever seen. Too bad we gotta undo it."

He nodded at two other deputies, who took off my bungee cords and hauled Lee Ann to her feet, efficiently handcuffing her. They walked her away with more gentleness than I thought necessary.

I saw Karen in the parking lot talking with Detective Scott, while a deputy put a blanket around her and bundled her into the front seat of a squad car. She was safe.

That's when my knees gave way.

Corporal Fletcher grabbed me under my arms. "Whoa there, Mrs. C. We gotta get you outta here."

Detective Scott ran toward us shouting, but I couldn't hear him clearly, given that I had those annoying little spots in my vision.

"Fletcher. . . Trish. . . Oh, man." He turned around and yelled for a paramedic.

"Just let me sit," I muttered.

Corporal Fletcher lowered me gently to the ground. I leaned against my SUV.

Then he stood and put his hands on his hips, a wide smile on his lips. "Sarge, I never seen anything like this. She's a little firecracker."

Funny, but I kinda liked the guy despite his profession.

The detective knelt next to me and examined my face. "Are you hurt? You're shaking. Your nose is bleeding."

"I'm fine. Just shook up." I met his gaze, trying to hold my hands still. "Her nail got my nose. I'll probably get cooties."

He took a deep breath. "I'm glad that's all."

I felt the concern in his gaze. "You know what?"

"What?" he asked.

"That car that tailgated me was hers. Max was right as usual. I should have told you about it the first time."

He patted my arm.

"I don't want to go to the hospital," I grumbled. "They're going to start charging me rent."

He shrugged. "They won't take you if you don't need to go, but I do want you and Karen checked out."

"Well, I have to call Max. He's going to kill me anyway, so maybe we should wait until then."

Detective Scott smiled. "We can't wait. I just talked to him. He's stuck in Baltimore rush hour traffic."

I swallowed. "I guess he's not very happy."

He shook his head. "That's putting it mildly, but he does know you're both alive."

The paramedics arrived. The detective stood. He and Corporal Fletcher moved out of their way.

"Detective Scott," I called as they arranged me on the stretcher.

"Yes?"

"This wasn't something I did on purpose. I didn't break my promise."

"I know."

Max stopped in the doorway of the family room, tie undone, hair mussed, staring at me and Karen as if seeing a vision. His chest moved with short, uneven breaths. Then he crossed the room, holding out his arms. "Both of you come here."

We did. He grabbed our shoulders and kissed the tops of our heads. "When I couldn't reach either of you, I almost lost my mind," he whispered. "I was so worried. All I could do was pray. I didn't know what I'd do if. . ."

I stood on my toes and put my lips on his cheek. It felt wet and tasted salty. Maxwell Cunningham the Third, my husband, the love of my life, was crying.

I looked over his shoulder where my mother and father stood, watching. They had come to pick up Charlie and Sammie. For the second time this week, my mother didn't say a word.

Detective Scott arrived shortly after, and Max brought him into the family room.

Karen and I were huddled under blankets on the couch. I'd tried to tell Max that I was hot and didn't need to be covered, but he ignored me.

"I'm sorry," the detective said. "I wish I could have acted faster. I had a feeling Lee Ann was getting ready to leave town, especially when she sent Julie away to meet Norm. I was working with the DA to put together an arrest warrant."

Max sat next to me and put his arm around my shoulders. As much as I loved being near him, I was sweating from the combination of the blanket and his body heat.

"I need a statement from you tonight," Detective Scott said.

Karen spoke first. Lee Ann had called and begged Karen for a meeting. Julie had supposedly run away, and Lee Ann wanted Karen's opinions about where Julie had gone.

I managed to wriggle the blanket off while Karen talked, but I couldn't escape Max's arm—not that I wanted to.

"We talked in her car in the parking lot," Karen said. "Then she told me I should call Mom to come and get me. She'd wait with me and explain." Karen swallowed. "After I called, I went to the bathroom and came back outside to wait with her. That's when I started to realize something was wrong."

Max's arm had tightened on my shoulders as Karen spoke.

"Mrs. Snyder had already said something about Mom smashing Peter's head in, but I thought she was sort of joking." Karen glanced at me. "She did say that Mom had been a violent maniac in school and had everyone fooled that she'd changed."

Sounded to me like Lee Ann took advantage of an already angry child. I still couldn't comprehend that she could pretend to be my friend and hate me that much.

I wiggled in Max's too-tight grasp as he looked at Karen. He loosened his hold. "What do you think now?"

Karen wouldn't look at us. "I. . .don't believe it. Mom told Mrs. Snyder to take her and leave me. She was going to die for me." Her voice broke.

I put my arms around her. We had a lot to work out, but this was a start.

Detective Scott asked me to explain what happened at the library, which I did. Then I asked Karen to go upstairs and take a hot bath. I had a couple of things to ask the detective that I didn't want her to hear.

After she was gone, I met his gaze. "I know Jim Bob wasn't killed with the knife. I think he was already dead when he was stabbed, probably by Frank, since he was so terribly concerned about the knife and acted like he wanted to point the finger at a meat cutter. Big, fat tattletale. I think Lee Ann killed Jim Bob. Maybe with that hammer I told you about. Remember what Lee Ann told Karen about me smashing in Peter-Carey's head?"

Detective Scott said nothing. Neither did Max.

"Well?" I asked.

The detective stood. "I'm not at liberty to discuss any of that."

The statement was so like him that I laughed.

21

That evening would be forever etched in my mind, as I'm sure it would be in Karen's. God had used a bad situation for good. Since that night, Karen and I had reached an understanding of sorts. She finally understood how much I loved her, but the emotions that had been driving her hadn't totally disappeared. During our first emergency counseling session with the pastor, I realized the anger she directed at me was misplaced. She was really angry that God had allowed her real mother to die, and for some reason, it had taken this long to surface.

Max's PI hadn't discovered anything about Russ, Lindsey, or the stop sign. I had to admit a certain feeling of satisfaction, although I really wanted to know.

I picked out my cruise. Almost a month later, when the time drew near, I began to make lists, which I promptly lost. I had to buy clothes. That wasn't one of my favorite things to do. Especially dressy ones. I'm a jeans and sweatshirt kind of girl. But when I saw the red evening gown at the mall, I knew it was perfect. Given the cut and how it fell just right, I was pretty sure Max would get that gleam in his eyes when he saw it, so I'd keep it a secret until I wore it on the ship.

I had two errands to do on my way home. The first was a visit to the sheriff's office to see Detective Scott. He'd called and requested that I come by. Being back in the building made me sweat. I felt immediately guilty, even though I'd done nothing. I told the guy behind a glass window that I was there to see Detective Scott. He told me to be seated, but it wasn't long before the detective himself came to get me. After he greeted me, he led me back into the inner sanctum and up the stairs and surprised me when he didn't lead me to the interview room. Instead, he took me to his office.

"Have a seat, please," he said.

I settled into a chair and put my purse on the floor. On the credenza behind him was a picture of a girl who looked to be high school age. I saw no picture of a wife. I guessed he hadn't remarried.

I turned my gaze on him and saw a smile on his face.

He tapped a folder on his desk. "I have some good news for you."

Was it possible? I leaned forward. "Russ?"

Detective Scott nodded. "Yes. I don't think he did it."

I began to cry, something I'd been more prone to since I'd gotten pregnant.

Detective Scott handed me a tissue.

"Who did it?" I sniveled.

"We suspect Tim, Daryl's brother. But my first lead came from an interesting source."

"Who?" I asked as I wiped my nose.

"You. Then your parents."

That dried up my tears. "What?"

He grinned. "You'd mentioned that box of doughnuts your mother delivered to Jim Bob. I had to follow up on that, although I didn't suspect her, so I went to your parents' house to chat. Your father was there. When she broke down and confessed, he got upset and asked her why she never told him. She said, like you, she'd seen the stop sign and thought Russ had done it. Your father informed both of us that Tim Boyd had given the sign to Russ. After several meetings with Daryl, where I tried to, er, convince him to tell me the truth, he finally admitted that he suspected his brother, too."

Poor Daryl probably confessed because he had been tortured by the tapping of Detective Scott's pen, just like I had been. And I found it just a little disturbing that my mother and I had both been threatened by the same person and kept it a secret from our husbands. I did not want to be like my mother. I looked at Detective Scott. "So what happens now?"

He sighed. "Case closed. Tim is dead. I told Max this morning and asked him to let me tell you. He's going to tell Lindsey's parents. He doesn't think they'll want any publicity."

I was sure, too. Lindsey's parents were friends of the Cunninghams and, like them, despised bad publicity. My heart ached for them. And for Max.

"Thank you," I said.

"You're welcome."

I shifted in my chair. "Can you answer some questions for me while I'm here?"

He briefly tapped his pen on the desk then put it down. "I still can't answer everything, but I'll tell you what I can."

"That'll do," I said. "What's going on with Frank?"

"He's been charged with embezzlement. Since he stabbed a dead guy, we can't charge him with murder. And since he thought Jim Bob was alive, he can't be charged with messing with a corpse or a crime scene."

"I'll bet lawyers said that. It's full of loopholes." I thought about Calvin Schiller.

Detective Scott laughed. "Yep."

"What about Lee Ann?" I bit my lip. I'd begun to feel guilty that I hadn't seen the whole thing coming and somehow prevented it. Despite what she'd done, I couldn't forget all the time we'd spent together.

Eric shook his head. "We have enough evidence to prove that she killed two men. She's been arrested, as has Norm, for the landfill fiasco."

"Ah," I said. "Jim Bob was blackmailing her about the landfill, wasn't he? I'll bet he found out somehow from April's boyfriend. Lee Ann smashed Jim Bob with that hammer, didn't she?"

Detective Scott shook his head. "I'm listening."

"And she and Norm were running away, weren't they? I think he made money in paybacks at the landfill for accepting out-of-state trash." I laid my arms on his desk. "Then Peter-Carey started threatening her like he did me, so she killed him, right?" I paused.

"I'm still listening," the detective said.

Would he answer any of my questions? I'd try something else. "How did Jim Bob's body get behind the milk?"

"Well, it's still a matter of some speculation on my part." He eyed me. "And please don't talk about this with anyone, okay?"

At least he finally trusted me to keep my word.

"We think Lee Ann lost her temper with Jim Bob and whacked him with the hammer that she was taking to Daryl. She didn't think she'd killed him at first." He squinted at me. "She must have left Jim Bob somewhere in a back room. When she checked on him again, he was dead. That's where Frank comes in.

"Frank was on a rampage about knives. He was adamant about keeping things in their proper place, so perhaps he was taking one back to where it belonged in the meat department. He saw Jim Bob, thought he was unconscious, and stabbed him. Then he put him on that cart and wheeled him somewhere to keep him hidden."

"Didn't either one of them think they'd be caught?" I asked. "Sounds stupid."

Detective Scott grinned. "That's what makes my job easier. If crooks were smart, we wouldn't be able to catch them. Besides, much of the staff was absent that morning with the flu. That made hiding Jim Bob a lot easier."

"Well, how did Jim Bob end up behind the milk?"

"We think Lee Ann looked for him and finally found the cart. When she saw that he'd been stabbed, she shoved the cart into the cold room where he could be found easily. She hoped the police would think he'd been stabbed to death and that his head had been bashed as he fell."

I thought about Lee Ann and the possible things that had driven her to the point of murder. I looked at my finger and bit at my nail. "I feel bad about all this. I keep wondering if there was anything I could have done differently. Maybe if I'd been closer to Lee Ann in recent years, she would have talked instead of killing. And poor Frank. He's annoying and all, but when I beat him up in school, do you think I messed up his mind?"

Detective Scott shook his head. "One thing I can say without any hesitation. This was not your fault. I've seen a lot in my job, more bad than good, I'm afraid. Maybe you weren't the kindest person when you were young. Maybe you've made some mistakes, but I can say without a doubt that you're one of the good people." He grinned. "Maybe a little stubborn and impetuous, but still very nice."

I blinked. Had he just said something sweet to me?

He stood. "Don't look so surprised. I can be nice, too."

"Thank you." I grabbed my purse and jumped to my feet. "I have to finish packing. Max is taking me on a cruise for a whole week."

"I heard. Please have fun. You deserve it after all this. Now you can leave it all behind. When you come back, your life can return to normal."

I wasn't sure I wanted my life to return to normal. I didn't like my kids being threatened, or even me, but I did like making mystery lists and thinking about them.

He walked around his desk and picked up something from the floor. "You might want this."

I took my phone from his hand. He walked me out the door and stood there as I walked down the hall. I had a thought and turned around. "Next time, I'll let you see my notebook," I said. "It was quite thorough, if I do say so myself."

His mouth fell open. "Next time?"

I didn't answer, just turned around and chuckled all the way to my car.

My visit with Eric left me in a good frame of mind to deal with the next thing I needed to face. Before I could truly leave things behind, I had to beat my foe. The milk case at the Shopper's Super Saver. I hadn't been back since the murder.

I hurried to the back of the store to get it over with. As I stood in front of the glass doors, looking at gallons of milk, I remembered that horrible morning. Poor Jim Bob. He had been a very nasty man, but no one deserved to die like that.

"Trish?"

I whirled around. "Daryl."

He wore the red Shopper's Super Saver manager's jacket. He'd gotten a promotion. Dweeb that he'd been, I suddenly saw what Abbie meant. He wasn't bad as men went, although he wasn't Maxwell Cunningham by any stretch of the imagination. Strangely, Daryl's new position fit him. I found myself hoping that maybe some new self-respect would help him be more confident in his marriage.

"Hi," I said and glanced behind me at the milk. "This is the first time I've been back since. . .you know."

He nodded. "Why don't you take three gallons of milk free for your pain. And. . ." He sighed. "As an apology for the road sign thing. I'm sorry. I was trying to protect my brother's reputation."

Who was I to throw stones, as my mother would say. I had done the same.

"It's over now, Daryl. And I'm sorry, too."

"Listen, Trish—" He moved closer to me. "I owe you big time, and not just for that."

"For what?"

He glanced around. "Well, I know that without your help, I might have been arrested for Jim Bob's murder. My fingerprints were on that hammer. I was hanging certificates in my office that morning. I managed to break some glass while I was at it, as well as smash my thumb."

Another answer to a question. That's why he'd been at the doctor's office. "You know, Daryl, I didn't help with the investigation. I was a suspect, too. I mean—"

"Don't be modest. Your mother has been telling everyone what you did." He smiled at me. "You're a real sleuth."

———

Moonlight over the ocean is one of the most romantic sights in the world, especially wrapped in the arms of a man like Max. I leaned back against his chest, and his arms tightened around my shoulders.

I loved our cozy little deck. Although we'd attended a fancy dinner with the captain tonight, we'd eaten most of our meals out here alone, watching the water, discussing topics as mundane as our favorite cheeses and as complicated as world politics. We explored our faith, grateful to God for what we had and for each other. I had my wish—time alone with Max. Without guilt.

This was better than a honeymoon. No newlywed nerves to get over or awkwardness to work through. In the familiarity, we'd discovered things about each other that we'd never known before.

"Baby, are you happy?" Max nibbled my neck.

"Mmm."

"Your dress makes me crazy." He kissed my ear.

I smiled to myself. The red gown did exactly what I'd hoped.

He laid a hand on my stomach. "You haven't been sick since we left."

"No coffee. I feel really good." Content. Peaceful.

"I'm happy, too," he said. "Having another baby seems right, somehow. Like confirmation of how much I love you. Of our love for each other and God's love for us."

He couldn't have said anything nicer. I extricated myself from his arms and turned around to face him. His black tuxedo and my dress added a dash of sophistication and mysteriousness to the night, like we were the hero and heroine in one of Abbie's novels. I ran his lapels between my fingers. Talk about making someone crazy. Nobody looks better in a suit than Max. I glanced up at his face.

He smiled and touched my cross necklace. "You're still wearing it."

"It means as much to me as my wedding ring," I said, thinking how much Max meant to me and how grateful I was to God for him and my family.

He ran a finger over my lips. "I'm glad it's all over." His eyes looked fathomless in the moonlight.

"What's over?" I murmured as I kissed his neck.

"Murder and mayhem. Police investigations."

"Oh. That." I didn't want to admit to Max that I missed writing down clues.

He pulled me closer. I leaned my head against his chest, listening to the solid thump of his heart and sighed with pleasure. No interruptions. No children knocking at the door. No ringing phones. Just me and Max.

"And no more mystery lists." He stepped back, looked me up and down, and his eyes gleamed. "How about let's go inside."

I smiled. All of Max's attention was on me. As single-minded as he was, that made for lots of fun. I, however, was more easily distracted, even from him for once. As we stepped back into our cabin, I told myself that when I got home, I was going to buy more steno pads, which were easy to use and transport. Maybe something would come up. I sort of liked solving mysteries.

# BAND ROOM
# BASH

1

*This is developing into a very bad habit!*
*I don't know if I can explain it to you.*
*It's not only against the law, it's wrong.*
—Mortimer Brewster
in *Arsenic and Old Lace*

No matter how old I get, when I stand in front of the doors of Four Oaks High School, I have flashbacks. Like today, the crisp fall air reminded me of playing in the marching band during halftime. Of course, the good memories are interspersed with memories of rampaging insecurities—something I still struggle with.

I yanked open the doors and turned my focus to my reason for being here—a committee meeting about *Arsenic and Old Lace*, a play in which Tommy, my teenage stepson, had a role. Somehow, I'd been coerced into collecting advertising from local merchants for the play program. Not that I resented doing things for my kids, but I was eight months pregnant and feeling slightly irritable because I'd originally taken off the afternoon to prepare for a romantic evening alone with my husband.

I headed down the locker-lined hall toward the end of the building where I was supposed to meet the other committee members in the band room. When I rounded a corner, I saw Carla Bickford, the school principal, walking toward me. She held a clipboard stacked with papers in one hand and a Styrofoam coffee cup in the other.

"Trish, I'm glad I caught you." Her chest moved with rapid breaths. "The play meeting has just been canceled. Marvin is feeling poorly and has to go home. We need him for this meeting. I've rescheduled for Wednesday, same time."

"That works for me." Things were looking up. Even though I'd have to take time off work again to attend the next meeting, the extra time this afternoon was a gift. I glanced at my watch. I could make it home in plenty of time to make a special dinner for my husband, sans kids.

Carla cleared her throat. "I've tried to get the message to everyone, but I could only find Marvin. He was down in the teacher's lounge getting a Coke." Her lips tightened. "I told him that was foolish. He's had indigestion for weeks.

He probably has an ulcer because he's so high-strung. You never know what he's going to do next."

Her comment surprised me. Marvin was the best band director the school ever had, leading the band to honors at prestigious contests. A miracle for a small town high school. And though he'd impressed me as an intense musician, he never seemed flaky.

"I hope he's feeling better soon." I turned to go, my mind already focused on the cute black maternity dress I'd bought to entice my husband.

"Wait," Carla said. "We can't put the play program advertising on hold for two days."

I turned back around to face her. "No problem." I already had several potential contributors in mind, including our family-owned self-storage business.

"Good. Come to my office for a moment. I have some forms that I was going to give to you today. You can take them now."

I stared at Carla. "Forms?"

"Yes." She walked past me toward the front of the building. "I'd like you to get people to fill them out when they agree to advertise."

I wondered why we had to go to the extreme of having people fill out official forms, but I said nothing, just followed her. Her gray suit fit her like a military uniform. Her broad shoulders didn't need the shoulder pads in her jacket. Everything about her was boxy, including her brown hair, which reminded me of a helmet.

In her office, Carla put the cup on a credenza. On her desk, piles of papers lay in neat rows, their edges perpendicular with the edges of the desktop. Without hesitation, she picked up one of the stacks.

"Here. You can ask one of my secretaries to make copies for you if you need more." She stretched out her arm to give them to me, and I saw a delicate gold watch on her desk.

"That's pretty." I took the papers from her hand.

She snatched it up. "It needs some work."

"Is it broken?" I asked.

"Yes." She opened her middle desk drawer and dropped the watch into it.

She frowned and opened the drawer wider. I noticed scattered pens and mechanical pencils, along with a tube of lipstick, a compact, and a couple of prescription bottles. She slammed the drawer shut.

"That's too bad. It's a very nice watch." I glanced at the forms in my hand and thumbed through the top one, thinking that a two-page agreement for a simple advertisement in a school play program was overkill.

"It's from my fiancé," she said as she picked up her phone and punched in a number.

I glanced up at her. She didn't bother with niceties when someone answered. "Have you been in my desk again?" she demanded.

I heard murmurs from the receiver in her hand.

A red flush worked up Carla's cheeks. "I know I was away. That's no excuse."

More murmurs came through the receiver.

Carla glanced at me and took a deep breath. "Well, I'll let it slide this time because you're a new employee, but I don't like anyone in my desk. It's mine."

I thought it likely Carla had never lived with children. If she had, she'd be used to having her desk and everything else in her life ransacked.

After slapping the phone down, she looked at me. "I don't understand why people can't comprehend the idea of personal property." She sniffed and pointed at the stack of forms in my hand. "I want those filled out completely."

I nodded.

Her gaze fell to my stomach. "When, exactly, are you due?"

"In—"

"Soon," she interrupted me. "I can tell by your size." Her eyes met mine. "Are you sure you can handle the advertising?"

"Well, I—"

"A birth in the middle of planning would be detrimental, you know. This has—"

"I'm fine." Interrupting her in return was the only way I'd be able to stop her. "I have one more month. The advertising will be taken care of before the baby comes."

She raised her brows. "Well, if you're sure."

"I'm absolutely sure."

Like the job of getting advertising for a small town high school play program was the equivalent of being an ad exec for a huge corporation. I stared at the wrinkles on Carla's forehead. She'd been principal for two years. She had always been pushy, but lately her behavior reminded me of a big-wheeled monster truck at the fair, running over everything in its path.

I stood to go.

"Wait one more minute, please," she said. "I haven't been able to find Connie Gilbert to notify her about the meeting cancellation. My new secretary informed me that she was here with some sample costumes for us to look at, but I was on the phone and couldn't catch her. My secretary also said that Connie was searching for Georgia Winters. Apparently, they are quarreling."

She made a note on the top paper on her clipboard. "I don't have time to continue the search, and I don't want to get involved in their personal issues. Will you please try to find Connie for me?" She pointed at another stack of forms on her desk. "These are for her. I'd like her to pick them up today. They're forms for each of the play participants to fill out with their measurements."

The phone on her desk rang.

"I don't—"

"Thank you, Trish. Oh, and perhaps you can find Georgia, as well. Tell her to meet me in my office. We have a dinner engagement." Carla snatched up the receiver. "Yes?"

I had been dismissed. After being given orders. Well, I'd search while I looked for Tommy. Besides, as tense as Carla seemed to be, maybe this would ease some of her pressure.

Ten minutes later, after a fruitless visit to the teacher's lounge, I found Connie Gilbert in Georgia Winters's English classroom. Connie had her back to the door. There was no sign of Georgia.

"Hey, Connie."

She whirled around, body stiff, mouth in an O. Then she met my gaze and relaxed. "Trish." She held a folded piece of paper in her hand and slipped it into the pocket of her blue linen jacket.

As I walked into the room, I smelled a strong floral perfume. I wondered if it was Connie's or Georgia's. Georgia's desk was covered with papers, but unlike Carla's, everything here was a mess. A white coffee mug sat there with lipstick on the rim. A black grade book was partially covered by a paper plate on which sat a half-eaten powdered sugar doughnut. Pens and pencils overflowed a long, flowered dish.

I met Connie's gaze. "I'm on assignment to tell you that the meeting has been canceled, and Carla has some forms on her desk for you to pick up."

"Yes, Marvin told me awhile ago." She brushed a stray piece of wispy blond hair from her pale face. Her nose was pink at the end and her eyes slightly puffy. I wondered if she had a cold. Though she was on the wiry side, she had shape in the right places and was very pretty in a soft, unfocused way. Just the kind of woman men fall over themselves to help because she comes across as defenseless. I'd never been able to accomplish that and was jealous of women who could.

"Are you okay?" I asked.

She nodded and bowed her head.

"So you're doing the costumes for the play?"

"Yes." She took a wool costume jacket from a box on the floor and brushed off the lapels. "I just got a bunch from someone I know who does off-Broadway," she said in her soft voice. "I think I'm going to need another storage unit. Do you guys have any available?"

I thought about the occupancy chart I'd looked at before I left Four Oaks Self-Storage that afternoon. "Yeah, I think we do have a vacancy in the building where your other units are. Just call Shirl and tell her I said to hold it for you. If you can come by tomorrow morning, we'll get you set up."

"Thank you," Connie said. "Oh, I saw Tommy earlier. He's gotten quite tall this last year. I might have to let out hems on the costumes for him."

"A seventeen-year growth spurt," I said. "How long ago did you see him? I need to give him a message."

She shrugged. "Probably about thirty minutes ago, heading for the band room."

"What about Georgia? Have you seen her?"

"No." Connie carefully folded the costume jacket and added it to a neat stack on a student desk, patting it into place. "In fact, Carla's secretary told me Carla was looking for Georgia. So was Tommy."

I frowned at her. "Why was Tommy looking for her?"

Connie picked up a shirt and folded it. "Something about a test."

I sighed, resigned that I was going to spend the next hour tracking people down. I'd start in the band room.

The band room door was closed. I grabbed the handle and pushed, expecting it to swing open. It didn't. I pushed again and met the same resistance. Something was holding the door shut.

"Hello?" I yelled. "Marvin? Are you there?"

I leaned on the door, pushing harder, and it gave enough that I could stick my hand through the crack and try to figure out what was blocking my entrance. I felt the top of a chair and tried to scoot it out of the way, but it wouldn't move. I removed my hand and jammed my face against the door, peering inside with one eye. The distinctive smell of the band room wafted out through the crack, strong in the stuffy silence. Cork grease, spit from the instruments, teenagers—I wasn't sure what created the odor, but it hadn't changed since I was a kid. Light from the afternoon sunshine coming through the windows, along with the glare of fluorescent lights on the ceiling, clearly illuminated two overturned music stands, along with scattered music next to a bassoon on the floor.

Had there been some sort of struggle? I backed up, not sure what to do. That's when I realized how alone I was. Hairs on the back of my neck prickled. I'd been so focused on finding Tommy and Georgia that I hadn't noticed the emptiness of the halls. I fumbled in my purse for my cell phone. Then I heard the thud of footsteps coming down the hall. I whirled around.

Tommy.

I let out a whoosh of air and didn't realize until that moment that I'd been holding my breath. "I was looking for you. I'm glad you're here. I can't get the band room door open."

Tommy frowned. "That's weird. Let me try."

I stepped aside. He pressed his body against the door. It didn't budge. He backed up a step for momentum then slammed into the door with all his weight. It opened enough to allow us entrance. He stepped inside and scanned the room then peered behind the door.

"Whoa."

"Whoa what?" I rushed inside, nearly tripping on the bassoon. Then I skidded to a stop.

We'd found Georgia. She was lying in the space behind the door next to the chair and a fallen music stand. The weight of her prone body must have been what held the door shut.

I swallowed hard then shook the strap of my purse off my shoulder and dropped it to the floor. "Tommy, call 911."

"Mom, you gotta be careful. Dad said to watch out for you and—"

"Thank you, but please, just call." I knelt clumsily next to Georgia, ignoring the murmurs of Tommy's voice. Blood oozed through her thick, black, shoulder-length hair, gathering in a puddle on the floor, which was drying around the edges. She had been sick—I saw remnants of that, too. Her eyes were open and sightless. I was raised on a farm. I'd seen the eyes of enough dead animals to recognize no life when I saw it. Still, I felt for a pulse.

Tommy was breathing heavily. "It's Ms. Winters," he said into the phone. "Uh, that would be, uh, Georgia Winters." He put his finger over the mouthpiece. "Mom, the 911 people want to know what's wrong."

"Tell them she's dead."

irens wailed nearby, making my ears ring and my nerves twitch. Help was arriving quickly, because the fire department was just down the road from the high school. The 911 dispatcher told Tommy and me to stay put, so after I'd done a visual sweep of the room, I sat on a chair next to Marvin's desk in the front of the band room, biting one of my fingernails. Tommy slouched against the wall, hands in his pockets, and stared at the floor.

Despite my best efforts, my gaze kept wandering to the spot where Georgia lay.

Six months ago I had found the stabbed body of Jim Bob Jenkins in the milk case of the local supermarket. That image was forever imprinted in my mind, and I'd only lately reached the point that memories of his lifeless body didn't crop up at weird times. And while I love solving mysteries, death disturbed me, no matter whose it was. I always wondered if the deceased was ready to meet God.

I deliberately turned my gaze to Tommy. "We need to call and let your father know what's going on." I wasn't sure I wanted to talk to Max right now. He hadn't reacted well to Jim Bob's murder and the ensuing investigation. I wanted to get ahold of my own emotions before I talked to him. I clasped my hands together. "Would you mind calling him?"

I closed my eyes to breathe a quick prayer as Tommy reached for his cell, but we were both interrupted by the entrance of Carla Bickford who stood, hands planted on her hips, glaring at me. "What's happening here? Someone told me an ambulance is on its way. Why didn't you call me first?"

"I was a little distracted." I pointed in the general direction of the body. "Georgia Winters is dead behind the door."

Carla whirled around and stared at Georgia, standing motionless, as if she'd been cast in plaster.

The sirens stopped their hideous shrieks. Moments later paramedics rushed into the room. They ordered Carla out of the way. She exploded to life and walked purposefully from the room, calling Marvin Slade's name.

I wondered where Marvin had been all this time. Music and instrument catalogs covered the surface of his desk, along with a travel mug, two Styrofoam coffee cups, and some other papers. I scooted my chair closer so I could study what was there without disturbing anything.

As the sound of different sirens, probably police, pierced the air, I glimpsed what looked like a receipt sticking out from under a grade book. The top bore the name of a business, but I could only partially read "op" at the end of the name. A distinctive fleur-de-lis decorated the top corner of the paper. I was about to reach over and pull the receipt out to look more closely when two deputies rushed into the room. One made a beeline for Georgia. The other stared at me.

"Are you the one who found her?" he asked, body tense.

"Yes."

"Did you touch anything?"

"Um, well, we probably moved her when we pushed the door open." I wondered if we were in big trouble.

"Who's—"

Someone began barking orders from the hallway, and the deputy raised his hand. "Just a moment, ma'am."

A familiar male voice inquired, "Who was first at the scene?"

Both deputies turned toward the doorway as if yanked by invisible leashes. Detective Eric Scott walked into the band room. I couldn't imagine how he'd gotten here so quickly from the sheriff's office.

The three men spoke briefly, in hushed tones, one deputy motioning toward the body. The other must have said something about me, because Detective Scott's gaze sliced the room until it met mine.

He turned back to the deputies and pointed at a door behind me that led to the instrument storage room. "There's another entrance we can use in the storage area. I've been informed it's kept locked. Get access to that. Work with Fletcher. Make a perimeter, and make sure nobody leaves. Set up places to interview people."

"Yes, sir," they both replied and left the room.

"You." The tall, blond detective motioned at me. "Don't move. Wait for Fletcher." Then he motioned at Tommy. "Go out into the hall and wait." He turned and watched the paramedics.

I didn't bother to say anything. It would do no good. The detective and I were well acquainted from close contact during the investigation into Jim Bob's murder. I knew he could be unbearably bossy when he had a mind to be, especially when I was involved in his investigation.

One of the paramedics turned to him. "She's dead, sir."

I could have told them that. But had she been murdered? And if so, was the weapon the bassoon? I had seen no blood on the instrument, but that didn't mean anything. I hadn't examined it, fearful of messing up evidence.

The sudden sound of yelling filtered through the door from the storage room, and Carla burst back into the room with a deputy on her heels.

Detective Scott whirled around.

"Sorry, sir," the deputy said. "She unlocked the door and ran right past us." He tried to grab her arm.

She evaded his grasp and marched across the room. "Detective."

"Stop right there." His irritation was obvious in his scowl.

She obeyed, but her lips were pursed in displeasure. "I want to know what is going on."

"You need to leave the room right now," he said. "Talk to my corporal."

As if on cue, Corporal Fletcher strode into the room. Both he and the deputy stood behind Carla. Corporal Fletcher's Santa Claus–like appearance probably fooled some people into thinking he was a jovial softie. That impression would be a mistake.

"This is my school," Carla snapped, totally ignoring the corporal. "You know that. And that woman was one of my employees. She was also my friend. . . ." Her voice broke then she took a deep breath and grew angry again. "I have a right to know what's happening. Was this an accident?"

"You need to leave like everyone else," Detective Scott said, ignoring her question and her emotions.

I leaned forward, watching the exchange with interest. If anyone could halt a seemingly unstoppable principal, Detective Scott could. Unfortunately, there's nothing I like better than a good fight, a remnant from my past and something I constantly remind the Lord is not appropriate for a churchgoing mommy. As if He didn't know that already.

"I insist on staying here until I get some answers," she said. "The school board will want a full report. I have a right to know."

Detective Scott's stiff spine was body language I understood. "You'll leave the room on your own or with our help. I don't care. But you'll leave the room."

I had experienced the detective's cold civility, but I'd never heard him on the verge of losing his temper.

Carla squared her shoulders more, which I wouldn't have thought physically possible and stood nose to nose with Detective Scott. "I'm the principal."

"And I'm the detective in charge of this scene." He nodded almost imperceptibly at Corporal Fletcher and the deputy, who closed in on either side of her.

She finally deigned to glance at them and crossed her arms, as if daring them to touch her.

This was more fun than watching parents squabble with referees at the high school football games.

Detective Scott sucked in a deep breath. "I understand you're the principal and you're concerned about your school. I'm sorry, but it's sheriff's office procedure to clear everyone from a scene like this. I assure you that I'll keep you notified of everything you need to know."

A couple seconds ticked by; then Carla heaved a sigh. No doubt she realized she was in the presence of someone whose word and will were backed by his badge and the authority given to him by the sheriff's office. I was impressed. He'd caught his temper before he lost it, but he'd still won. Impressive. That took skill. What Carla probably didn't understand was that "need to know" meant she'd find out very little. Experience had taught me how the detective worked.

I couldn't blame her for listening and obeying. The detective appeared totally intimidating, even to me. Most of the time he wore a suit, but today he had on his uniform, and his black belt bristled with attachments—a telephone, a gun in a holster, and other dangerous looking things I didn't recognize, although I was sure he had handcuffs somewhere.

Before she left the room, Carla pointed at me. "What about *her*?"

Oh, now *that* was mature.

Detective Scott glanced from me to Carla and back again. "I'm questioning *her*." Then he looked at the corporal. "Fletcher. Interviews. Trish first."

"Yes, sir," Fletcher replied.

By the time Carla had walked out of the room, head held high, Detective Scott was standing over the body. I didn't notice Corporal Fletcher was back in the room until he appeared at my elbow.

"Mrs. C.?" He called me by my nickname as he waggled his finger at me, indicating I should follow him. I snatched up my purse and obeyed.

Members of the crime scene unit arrived as I left the room. Detective Scott greeted them. I heard him say, "The medical examiner is on the way. I want to know time of death. I don't think it's been long."

We walked through the storage room and into the hallway. There several deputies were herding people around. I caught a glimpse of Tommy, as well as Marvin Slade, whose deep-set, dark eyes looked like black marbles in his narrow, blanched face. If a person ever lived up to the platitude "He looked like he'd seen a ghost," it was Marvin.

Corporal Fletcher led me up the hallway, away from everyone, then pulled out a notebook.

"We didn't move the body on purpose, and I have a good reason to be here," I said before he could ask me anything. I crossed my arms. "It's because of the school play. I'm on the committee. I'm helping with the advertising for the play program. We were supposed to have a meeting today. They're doing *Arsenic and Old Lace*. You know the one. About Mortimer Brewster who finds out his aunts kill off their boarders. Tommy's in the play and. . ." I paused for a breath.

"It's okay, Mrs. C. Just relax." The expression in Corporal Fletcher's eyes was kind under his bushy eyebrows.

"How did you guys get here so fast, anyway?" I asked.

"Sarge and I were on our way here for a meeting with the principal," he said. "The parents are pushing to up the security at the school, and the school board wanted her to talk to law enforcement. The sheriff sent us since Sarge's daughter attends this school."

"Well, they should be concerned—if Georgia was murdered." My thoughts raced. "Do you think she was? Like bashed in the head with the bassoon?"

"We don't know anything right now." He pulled a pen from his pocket. "Just tell me who you were going to meet with."

I dropped my arms to my side. "I was supposed to be meeting with Carla, Marvin Slade, the band director, Connie Gilbert, and. . .Georgia, and a few other people."

"So no one was here when you found the victim except for you and Tommy?" he asked.

"Right. The meeting had been canceled."

"And why was the meeting canceled?"

While I told him, I leaned against the wall to support my suddenly shaky legs. I guessed it was a delayed reaction to finding Georgia. He frowned. "Let's get you somewhere to sit down." He tucked his notebook and pen into his pocket. "Wait here."

As he walked away, I noticed that the crowd in the hallway was considerably smaller. Carla had disappeared. Marvin was gone, too. One deputy was talking to a football player and Kent Smith, the football coach. Kent reminded me of one of my father's favorite bulls, a short and stocky animal with a massive chest and head.

Tommy's face was dark with an emotion I couldn't identify. Maybe fear, which I didn't understand. I wanted to go hug him, but I knew that wouldn't be cool. When I finally caught his gaze, I tried to reassure him with a smile, but he didn't return the gesture. He just looked away and stared at the floor. That disturbed me more than anything else. Tommy had always been the steadiest of our children. No problems at all, unlike his siblings.

I was distracted by a tall teenage girl rushing down the hall past me. Her face looked familiar, but I couldn't place it at the moment. Tommy's expression softened into a smile as she approached. When she stopped in front of him, he bent his head to talk to her in quiet tones.

*Uh-oh*. I recognized the look. Tommy was smitten.

A few minutes later, a deputy appeared to direct me to the school library. As I walked into the room, I saw Corporal Fletcher attempting to clear the library of the one person who hadn't run down the hall to gawk at the band room door. If the clam-faced librarian ever had a curious bone in her body, she'd shelved it in the reference room's prehistoric section. I had to look closely to make sure she wasn't the mummy of the same librarian who had manned the desk when I attended high school here.

She sniffed and looked askance at the corporal's uniform and gun. "I told the other police officer that I don't think the library is an appropriate place for a police investigation. *Someone* needs to man the front desk."

Corporal Fletcher shrugged and smiled at her as she stood, hands on her hips, glaring at him. "Sorry, ma'am. We're appropriating the library for sheriff's office use with the permission of the principal. You're going to have to leave."

The librarian swiped a stack of books off the desk and held them to her bosom defensively. "This library is the place where our students come to study. We shouldn't have to close the doors. This is absolutely the last straw. There have been far too many others in here today disturbing our peace. Arguing. Now we have you *police officers.*"

His eyes sharpened with interest. "We're deputies. Now, what other people have been in here arguing?"

She sniffed. "People who should know better."

"Who?" The big man balanced on his toes, reminding me of the first time I met him—right after I found Jim Bob Jenkins's body.

She frowned. "What people do in a library is protected. I don't have to tell you."

"Uh-huh." The corporal pulled out a notepad. "What's your name?"

She wouldn't give him her name and adamantly refused to leave the library. It wasn't until he threatened her with arrest that she finally told him who she was. After that, she turned her back to him and grabbed her square, black pocketbook from her office. "I won't be intimidated." She tilted her chin as she walked out from behind the desk in a huff.

"Oh yeah, I got your number," Corporal Fletcher murmured just loud enough for me to hear. "Liberty for all, and no cops." He winked at me, cleared his throat, and followed her to the door. "I'm sorry. You can take up your complaints with my boss, Sergeant Eric Scott. I'm sure he'd love to discuss proper police procedure with you." The irony in his voice made me smile, especially since I knew Detective Scott and his method of dealing with annoying people.

She didn't catch on. "I *will* speak to him. This is highly inappropriate. The unmitigated gall. . ." She snatched at the handle and yanked open the door. "And to think that a crime has occurred here, on school property. That's because we open our doors to you people. I just don't know. . . ." The door closed, effectively shutting her up.

"Fruitcake," Corporal Fletcher mumbled. "Probably reads too many of those commie books by weirdo political professor types. Sergeant'll slice her to bits."

"Yeah. He's good at slicing. I've experienced a bit of that myself." I felt keyed up and crabby. Probably a result of finding Georgia, hunger, and pregnancy hormones, topped off by bad library memories.

The librarian clone who had just walked out was like the one who had banished me from the hallowed book cloister when I was in school. That was because I hit a classmate with a sacred *National Geographic* and inadvertently ripped the cover. When strange things started happening to the librarian, like the day she discovered a formaldehyde-preserved frog in place of the meat in her sandwich, I was briefly expelled. That was the first and last time my daddy ever tanned my hide. But then, my parents never knew half the stuff I did when I was young.

"Say, Mrs. C., don't you worry about Sarge." Corporal Fletcher must have seen the scowl on my face, but he misinterpreted it. "You'll be fine."

I stiffened my shoulders and stared out the window. How long would I be stuck here? "He's not acting real nice today." I was dreading talking to the sergeant, especially since Tommy and I had moved the body.

"Umm. . .yeah, well, probably," the corporal said behind me. "To be expected."

I faced him. "Why?"

From his narrowed eyes, I could tell he was thinking, but I wasn't sure what about. "Well, a possible crime in a school is bad news. Real political. We got a couple of new county commissioners who are being a real pain right now. That and the citizen advisory board. Now this."

"That's no excuse for grumpiness." Even as I said it, I realized it was the proverbial pot calling the kettle black. I wasn't little Miss Sunshine today, myself.

Corporal Fletcher glanced over his shoulder then sidled up closer to me. "You gotta give people leeway, Mrs. C. Things happen. I'm sure you're aware of that. You have good. . .sources. You hear things. Now, why don't you sit down?" He pulled a chair out from under a table.

I opened my mouth to ask what he was talking about, but he avoided my gaze.

"I'm going to get you a bottle of water," he said. "We can't have you fainting or something."

That was sweet of him. He probably recalled the time I sort of fell into his arms after I had been threatened by a murderer.

"I need to call Max."

"You do that. I'll be right back."

I pulled out my cell phone and reluctantly speed-dialed Max's cell. He was overly protective on a good day, but with me being pregnant. . .

I braced myself for a lecture, but Max didn't pick up. Perversely, I felt annoyed with him, and I left a message that probably let him know how I felt.

After I snapped my phone closed, Corporal Fletcher's words ran through my mind. He'd implied that I might know something by way of gossip. Too antsy to sit, I began pacing the library. What did he mean? Had I missed something important?

I was sorely tempted to make notes. During the investigation into Jim Bob's murder, I'd discovered I liked making mystery lists and solving crimes. Afterward,

I bought a stack of steno pads, just in case—steno pads being small enough to tuck into my purse but large enough to keep decent notes. My mind began a mental debate. Georgia's death intrigued me as much as it chilled me, and somehow, being that interested didn't seem quite proper.

By the time Corporal Fletcher returned and gave me a bottle of water and package of crackers, intrigue had won over propriety. I was jotting down my thoughts on an old grocery receipt I found in my purse. I told myself that my motives were noble. I knew the detective would want to know in detail what I had observed, so this would be handy.

I hated packaged crackers, but I ate them because Corporal Fletcher had been nice enough to buy them. Besides, they would stave off my hunger pains. He disappeared again, leaving me alone with my thoughts.

As I swallowed the last dry crumbs, Detective Scott burst into the room, followed closely by the corporal. "I'm going to interview Tommy," the detective said when I looked up.

"That's fine."

"Fletcher, send someone to find my daughter. Then get Tommy. The medical examiner said that. . ." His voice trailed off as he glanced at me; then he motioned toward the hallway with his head. Corporal Fletcher followed him out the door. Well, that was a pointed and not very nice way to let me know I wasn't in the loop.

When he walked back into the library, I glanced up. "We didn't move the body on purpose."

"I know that," he said.

"So I'm not in trouble?"

"Not as far as I can tell right now." He yanked a chair from under a table and dragged it in front of me.

Since trouble and Trish are synonymous, that wouldn't last. I stared back down at my list.

"What are you writing?" he asked me irritably.

"Notes." I chewed on the pen.

"I knew it." Detective Scott sat down hard on the chair with an exaggerated sigh. "Trish."

I looked up at him. "Yes?"

"Why are you making notes?" His expression hadn't changed from earlier in the band room.

"Well, it helps me remember everything, and then I can help you better." Unfortunately, he knew about my mystery lists. Me and my big mouth. I'd told him during the investigation into Jim Bob's murder.

"Listen to me," he said. "I just need your statement. I don't need your help."

"There's a difference?" I asked.

"You know exactly what I mean." His right eye twitched. "I don't want to have to worry about you. Especially now that you're expecting. Last time was plenty for me. I'm sure Max would agree."

"Oh, I get it." I gripped my pen tighter. "You're threatening to tell Max that I was sitting here making notes. And you hope he will keep me under control and make me stop."

"Got it in one." Detective Scott pulled a notebook from his pocket.

His attitude was reminiscent of the way he'd acted in the past. So was my immediate annoyance with him.

"Your reaction must mean that this was a murder," I said.

He eyed me. "We don't know anything yet."

"Right. As usual. And you really won't *know* anything until the case is solved, at which time you'll tell me everything I *need* to know." I looked at my list, fighting a growing sense of irritation.

His breath hissed through his teeth. "Trish, would you please pay attention and answer my questions?"

"Of course." I laid the pen and paper on my knees and folded my hands on my stomach. "I'm listening."

The nerve at the corner of his eye continued to twitch. "Why do I feel like you're just tolerating me?"

I shrugged.

He tapped his pen on his notebook. "Were you alone when you found Georgia?"

"No. Tommy was with me."

He jotted a note. "Did you and Tommy arrive together?"

I frowned. "No, he was already here."

The detective's eyes narrowed, and he bounced his pen on his leg. *Tap, tap, tap.* "Was he with you when you discovered Georgia?"

"Yes. . .well." I met his gaze. "He got to the band room right after I did, but he noticed her first."

"I want to know everything you saw from the moment you pulled into the school parking lot."

I took a deep breath, pointedly picked up my pen, lifted the paper, and shook it for emphasis. I heard him sigh as I began to read. He interrupted me when I mentioned Connie.

"Connie who?" he asked.

"Gilbert. She does the costumes for the play. I spoke to her in Georgia's classroom before I went to the band room."

He made a note. "All right. Proceed."

He didn't interrupt me again, and when I finished, I put the paper down and stared at him.

"Thank you," he said as he jotted down notes. He glanced up at me. "Now, tell me again exactly what you saw when you were walking up to the victim," he said. "You skipped that part."

I swallowed. I didn't want to talk about that. I didn't want to remember Georgia Winters's dead body.

"I'm sorry, Trish," he said in a softer tone. "This is very difficult for you, I know. I can arrange for you to talk to a victim advocate if you'd like."

That made me get ahold of myself. I'd met his victim advocate. She was very sweet, with one of those soft voices pitched just right to be soothing. Anyone who acted like that couldn't possibly be real, and that made me suspicious.

"No, thanks. I'm fine." I told him exactly what I'd seen. "My biggest question is how whoever murdered her—if she was murdered—got out of the band room. There was a chair behind the door to the room, you know."

He asked me to describe that to him again, which I did.

"I didn't even look at the door in the instrument storage room," I said, "but you said it was locked, right?"

"Is that all?" Of course he didn't answer me, just tapped his pen hard on his leg.

"Yes," I said.

"Are you sure?"

"Aren't I always sure?" I slapped the paper on my lap, irritated at him again.

"Unfortunately."

But before I could ask him what, exactly, *that* meant, I heard the library door open. I turned and saw Tommy holding it for the pretty teenage girl he'd been talking to in the hall. Now I remembered where I'd seen her face. From a photo in Detective Scott's office.

"Hey, Daddy," she said. "You remember my car is in the shop?"

Tommy looked at me then at Detective Scott, who wasn't smiling.

"I remember," he said to his daughter.

"Well, Tommy was supposed to drive me home so we could practice a little more. I'll wait until you're done talking to him."

The detective's gaze had fallen on my son, like a scientist studying a germ under a microscope. Finally, he looked back at his daughter. "I'll have one of the deputies drive you home. I'm going to talk to Tommy next. We could be here for a while."

A flash of anger lit her eyes. "I don't want to ride home with one of your people. Can't I just wait for Tommy?"

Detective Scott glanced from her to my stepson, frowning. "Uh, no. I want you to go home. Why don't you call your aunt Elissa?"

The anger remained in his daughter's eyes. "I know what's going on. It's all over the school. Ms. Winters got bashed in the head. A lot of people were mad at her. But Tommy and I still need to practice."

What the detective's daughter had said just dawned on me. "You're in the play, too?"

She and Tommy exchanged chummy grins.

"Yeah, isn't it great?" she said.

"Sherry's got the part of Elaine," Tommy said. "I've got the part of Mortimer Brewster."

I met Detective Scott's startled gaze. For one of the very first times, I could precisely read his thoughts. Dismay. Our teenagers were in the same play. Their parts involved romance. With each other.

# 3

Detective Scott cleared his throat. Tommy and Sherry severed their glances.

"I'd like to speak with you in the hall," the detective said to his daughter.

She whirled on her heel without a word and headed for the library door. He followed her with a stiff back.

This wasn't good. Neither was Tommy's expression. Worry creased his brow.

"Detective Scott wants to talk to you," I said. "I do, too."

"Yeah," Tommy said. "But I gotta get to work after he talks to me, and I still have to get my algebra book from my locker."

I glanced at my watch. "I'll go get the book and then wait for you. Why don't you give me the combination?"

"Okay, but can't we talk later?" he asked.

Was he avoiding me? "No, I'll wait," I said. "I'll go get the book right now; then I'll be back. We can talk on the way to your car."

Tommy told me how to get into his locker. Then, as I reached for the library door handle, Detective Scott opened the doors and passed me with a frown on his face.

Out in the hall, Sherry stood with her face twisted in a scowl, watching her father shut the doors. She noticed me and made an effort to smile, then turned to leave. She was heading the same way I was.

I stepped up and walked next to her. "I'm going to Tommy's locker to get a book."

"I'm going there, too. My locker is in the same hall. Corporal Fletcher is meeting me." Her words were chopped and tense.

"He's a nice man," I said by way of trying to soothe her.

"Yeah, maybe, but he's my dad's friend."

She said "dad's friend" as if it were a bad word. Things were definitely not good at the Scott house-hold. Maybe I could distract her by asking her some questions.

"So, how long have you and Tommy known each other?" I thought it odd that he hadn't mentioned her before. The school wasn't that large.

"Only this year," she said. "We met the first day of school. He helped me settle in. I was in a private school before." She glanced at me. "I lived with my mom until this year."

"Where was that?" I asked.

"Virginia Beach," she said. "My stepdad is in the military. He just got transferred overseas."

"It must be rough to switch schools so close to graduation."

She shrugged. "I'm used to moving around. I wanted to go with them."

"And you couldn't?"

She shook her head, brows lowered. "All the adults got together and made the decision. Nobody asked me what I wanted." The tone of her voice was too bitter for a girl her age.

"Your dad mentioned your aunt. Is that his sister?"

Sherry nodded. "Yeah, Aunt Elissa. She's moved in with me and dad for this year." She glanced at me. "They say it's because she's on leave right now and needs to rethink her life. I know it's because they're worried about me and think someone has to watch out for me."

I glanced at her and realized there was far more to her than met the eye. "Any particular reason they think that?"

She stared straight ahead. "I don't always do what I'm told."

I wondered what, exactly, that meant. She didn't look like she used drugs, but one couldn't always tell by physical appearance.

She peeked at me and read my thoughts correctly. "It's nothing like you're thinking. I just have definite ideas about how things should be. I didn't want to move in with my dad, and I threatened to run away."

That made me smile. "I threatened to run away a lot when I was in high school."

"You did?" She seemed surprised.

"Sure."

"Well, what did your parents do?"

"My mother offered to help me pack."

Sherry stared at me in disbelief; then she laughed, a contagious sound that made me join in. "Wow. That's reverse psychology, isn't it?"

"Yeah, but it turned out okay. Nobody got that upset, which really helped calm me down."

"I wish my dad was calm." The expression on her face became gloomy.

"He's worried, I'm sure. If you haven't lived with him before this, he's probably feeling overwhelmed."

"Yeah, that's what Aunt Elissa says."

By that time, we'd reached the hall where the lockers were located. I stopped short. I saw Corporal Fletcher and another deputy poking around in a locker, while a third looked on.

I charged up to them. "What are you doing? Is that Tommy's?"

"No need to get excited, Mrs. C.," the corporal said. "We're just doing a routine investigation."

"Yes, but why Tommy's locker?" I wondered if this had to do with Detective Scott questioning him. Was my son a suspect?

The corporal gently took my elbow. I allowed him to pull me away, mostly because I knew I wouldn't have any choice in the matter. Sherry's cold and distant expression as she watched the other deputy work reminded me of her father.

When the corporal and I had walked a ways down the hall, he let go of my arm. "Everything is fine. We just need to eliminate Tommy."

"Eliminate him? From what? Is he. . ." My voice trailed off. Tommy had been in the right place at the right time to commit murder. This was not good. Not at all.

———

I got back to the library just in time for Tommy to open the door.

"I have to get to work," he said.

"I know. I'll walk with you to your car."

"Did you get my algebra book?" he asked.

"Yes." I glanced at him. "*After* I convinced the deputies searching your locker to give it to me."

Tommy's nostrils flared. "They were searching my locker? Why?"

"To eliminate you," I said.

He took a deep breath. "I just talked to Dad."

"You reached him?"

"Yeah. I caught him just when he was leaving a meeting."

"And?" I asked.

"I told him everything is fine. He was really worried about you, but I told him that you're okay. He told me to tell you to call him when you get home. He'll keep his phone on vibrate, so even if he's in a meeting, he can get it."

I felt like Tommy was trying to distract me, so I gave him my mother eye. "Is everything really fine?"

"Yes."

The mother eye didn't work. He wouldn't look at me. "What did Detective Scott ask you?"

Tommy stared straight ahead. "Probably the same things he asked you."

"And that would be?"

"Just why I was here and what I was doing. I told him I was practicing."

We reached the door that led to the parking lot. "So, what's with you and Sherry?"

He shrugged. "She's really cool. We're in the play together."

I suspected she was more than cool, but he wasn't going to tell me. Besides, his legs were so long, and he was walking so fast, I was having trouble keeping up with him.

"Someone told me you were looking for Georgia?"

We'd reached his car, and he unlocked the door. "Yeah, I had to talk to her. Listen, I have to get to work." He leaned down and kissed my forehead, an action so like his father that I couldn't speak. "It'll all be okay; you just wait and see."

---

I considered Tommy's words as I stopped by the local Dairy Delite for a chocolate milk shake. I needed something in my stomach besides packaged crackers. My nerves felt ragged, like they'd been scraped raw on a cement sidewalk. I hoped that something sweet and chocolaty would soothe me.

When a picture of Georgia's body flickered through my mind, I deliberately turned my thoughts to other things. The problem was, everything that came to mind right now was disturbing. I wasn't well enough acquainted with Georgia to know whether she had known the Lord. And then there was Tommy. The fact that he'd made so much effort to assure me not to worry made me worried. What was so significant that Detective Scott had reason to search Tommy's locker? How big a suspect was he?

As I pulled around to the drive-through, I finally hit on a good memory. All the nights I'd come here with my best friend, Abbie, when we were in high school. That made me realize I hadn't spoken to her in a couple of days. I really needed to talk to her now.

At the drive-up window, I looked inside and saw the manager. I waved at her out of politeness, and she hustled over to the window, pushing aside the teenager who had just taken my order.

"Trish! Oh my! I heard about what happened at the school. How horrible for you!"

"It wasn't pleasant." She had a habit of speaking in exclamation points.

She leaned out the window, her chest smashed on the sill. I wondered if it hurt.

"I can just imagine!" She tried to wiggle closer to me, and I was afraid she was going to cut herself in half. "What was it like?"

"What was what like?" I asked.

"You know," she said in a stage whisper. She glanced over her shoulder, which put her at risk for losing her balance and falling out the window. "Finding her. I can't even imagine that."

"Um. . .it was unpleasant?" Her relish for details about Georgia's death was going to ruin my appetite for a milk shake.

She nodded as though I'd said something terribly profound. "I understand, I really do."

I doubted that. Not unless she'd ever found a dead body.

"You know," she said. "She was the kind of person who was easy to be mad at."

Her comment rang a bell, and I remembered that Sherry Scott had said something similar.

"How come?" I asked.

"Oh! I went to school with her, you know. She was overbearing, but lately!"

"Lately?" I asked.

"Well, she's gotten a real attitude. Especially with her family. I'm sure there are a few people who will be happy she's dead."

Happy? What a dreadful thing to say. Someone called her name at the same time my milk shake arrived. I watched with relief as she pulled herself back inside the window.

As I drove away, I passed the strip mall where my mother had her doughnut shop, Doris's Doughnuts. I thought about stopping, but I didn't want to face the grilling I'd get there. I'd wait until I got home to call her.

The milk shake had the desired effect. In just a few miles, my stomach wasn't churning anymore. I had managed to tamp down all my screaming worries and enjoy the scenery. Only two minutes out of town in any direction and everything turns to farm fields. I could tell fall was coming. The lush fields were no longer green with growth. The trees would start changing colors soon.

The serene landscape made me feel peaceful. I took a deep breath, relaxed my shoulders, and began to look forward to my evening with Max. When my cell phone rang again, I eagerly dug it out of my purse, but when I glanced at the little screen, my heart plummeted. It was my mother.

# 4

I debated answering my cell phone at all. I love my mother, but I don't always like talking to her. That's because of the conversational arrows I have to evade. Still, she'd probably heard about the murder, and I didn't want her to worry.

I pushed the button and jammed the phone against my ear. "Hi, Ma. Did Daddy pick up Charlie and Sammie after school?"

"Of course he did," she said. "When we say we'll babysit, we always do it. We don't ignore things like some people do. I saw you drive right by the shop. I can't believe you didn't stop, and you haven't called me. Once again, I'm the last to know that my daughter is involved in a crime."

I sighed. "I'm not involved in a crime. I don't even know if it really *was* a crime. Maybe it was an accident. Besides, I haven't even talked to Max yet, so you aren't left out."

"Well, I'm your mother. And it was a crime. I heard it was murder. I nearly had a heart attack. One day you're going to kill me. It's just hard to believe that I actually carried you for nine months and you could be so insensitive. And the labor was the worst pain of my life. . . ."

I tuned her out and stared at the road ahead of me while she finished telling me in detail the agony she went through to have me and why I should feel guilty. I'd heard it all so many times I could have lectured myself.

". . .as if your ignoring me isn't enough, I also heard that someone is planning to bring a large housing development into Four Oaks. Can you imagine that? I mean—"

I nearly ran off the road. "What?"

"I knew you weren't listening to me." She clucked her tongue.

I hoped I wasn't in for another lengthy discourse about how grateful I should be that I was born before she explained what she'd just said. To my relief, she was eager to share the little she knew.

"I found out today at the shop that someone is planning to bring a housing development to our town."

Doris's Doughnuts was the source of anything newsworthy in Four Oaks and the surrounding vicinity. Well, *newsworthy* was a misnomer. *Gossip* was a better word. Still, chances were that anything coming from my mother had at least a grain of truth in it. I was horrified.

"Can you imagine?" she asked. "After housing developments come shopping centers. Big ones. With hardware stores and fast-food places and. . .doughnut shops." Her voice cracked, and I felt bad for her. She'd worked hard to build up her business.

I doubted anyone could really compete with my mother, but I wouldn't bother to try to assure her. She'd just argue. "So you don't know anything else? Like who would think of doing such a thing?" An influx of new people and the traffic and noise would destroy everything I loved about country living. Slowly the countryside would be eaten up by "progress."

"We've seen it happening in counties closer to the city," Ma said. "Why, the next thing you know, we could be the gambling capital of the East Coast. Look at what they tried to do in Gettysburg. A casino and slot machines. What were they thinking? Why, I wouldn't be a bit surprised if Georgia Winters was killed by some mob stranger coming in and scouting out the land."

I tried to picture guys in black suits crawling around Four Oaks looking for people to murder. "Come on, Ma. That's a little bit dramatic."

"You think so? April said that Georgia wanted to sell off her granny's farm, and there you go. She lived there, you know. The perfect place for a casino. It's all about commerce. Greed. Avarice."

Avarice? My mother was developing quite a vocabulary, even if her word choices were redundant.

"What purpose would be served by the mob killing Georgia?"

"Why, to get the farm, of course."

"Oh." I wasn't going to pursue it further right now. I'd reached my house, which is in a very small rural development. The only one in Four Oaks and the only one I wanted to see here—ever. I pulled into the driveway and punched the button on the garage door opener. "Well, we'll see, I guess."

"You mark my words," my mother said. "It's all about greediness. Selfishness."

"Okay. Well, I'm home now. I need to go. I have to call Max."

"Well, I hope you learned a lesson. I mean—"

"I did," I agreed, even though I wasn't exactly sure what lesson I was supposed to have learned except not to answer my cell phone when my mother called.

"Well, good."

"I'll talk to you later. Tell Daddy hello."

"This will just kill him," she said.

Whatever "this" was. And I doubted that anything would shake him up. My daddy was an unflappable kind of guy. He had to be to live with my mother. I hung up and then dialed Max as I pulled into the garage. I hoped he was already on his way home. I could get things ready quickly.

"Trish?" He answered on the third ring. "Baby, I'm so glad to hear from you. Are you okay?"

"Yeah." His use of my favorite pet name always made me a little weak in the knees. A dangerous thing for someone in my condition. "How are you?" I got out of the SUV and went inside.

"Hectic," he said. "Worried about you. Tommy told me everything. I'm sorry I couldn't get the phone when you called. I was stuck in meetings."

"I'm fine. Really." In the kitchen, I tossed my purse on the table.

He sighed. "I can't say I'm surprised this happened."

My poor husband. He says living with me is like riding a roller coaster. He never knows what to expect next.

"Well, at least I didn't sprain or break anything." In the past, my habit of joining my kids in activities like Rollerblading had landed me in the hospital more than once.

He inhaled. "Don't even say that. You've managed to stay out of the hospital for almost nine months. The next time you go there, I want it to be when the baby is born."

"That shouldn't be a problem," I said. "I'm being really good. Are you on your way home?"

"Not yet."

Well, that gave me a little more time to take a bath and put on my dress.

"So, Tommy told you everything, right?" I wondered if he'd told his father that Detective Scott had questioned him like a suspect.

"Everything?" Max asked quickly. "Like what?"

"Well, about us finding Georgia and all," I said.

"Yes. Well, he said you two found Georgia behind the door. That must have been pretty traumatic for you. Are you sure you're all right?"

"Yes, although it was a little bloodier than when I found Jim Bob." I thought I heard Max groan. "Then Detective Scott questioned us. Both of us. Separately."

"And a lot of other people," Max said. "Tommy said just about everyone was pulled aside."

"So that's not unusual?" I asked.

"Not at all. You should remember that from last time you were. . .uh, involved in a murder."

"I wasn't *involved*. I just found the body."

"Isn't finding the body being involved?" he asked.

"Well, not like that. Like I committed a crime or something. But, whatever. This time was different. . .there were just more of us, including Tommy." I opened the refrigerator to take out the steaks so I could marinate them.

"Well, he found the body with you. I wouldn't expect anything different."

Perhaps I was overreacting to Detective Scott's attitude. Maybe he was just a protective father who wasn't thrilled about his daughter liking a boy, and that's what accounted for the hard looks he gave Tommy.

"When will you be home?" I asked. "I'm just about to start dinner."

His pause was long enough to tell me he wasn't sure. "I've got one more meeting." He paused again. "I don't want to be insensitive. You said you're okay, but you've been through a lot today. I could leave if you need me to."

I slammed the refrigerator door shut on the steaks. As usual, he was being fair, but I could read between the lines. This meeting was important. Besides, I'd already told him I was fine. I couldn't reverse myself and be traumatized. Yes, I wanted him to come home right now, but I didn't "need" him to.

I decided to try a different tact. Whining. "The meeting is that important?"

"Yes, otherwise I would be home already. I worry about you."

I felt guilty for making him feel bad, but that didn't stop me from continuing. "Well, I had a nice dinner planned—"

"Do you think it can wait until tomorrow?" he asked. "Maybe you and the kids can go out."

"The kids are with my mother," I said. "And speaking of my mother, she told me that someone is planning to build a huge housing development in Four Oaks."

Through the receiver, I heard voices in the background. "Hang on a second," Max said.

I waited and felt sorry for myself. Not only had I found a dead woman, but Four Oaks was threatened with a housing development. And to top it off, I wanted time alone with my husband, but—

"Trish?"

"Is the meeting canceled?" I could always hope.

"Uh, no. In fact, I need to go right now. Are you sure you're okay?"

I sighed. "Yes, I guess so."

"I'm sorry. Thank you for understanding."

"You're welcome," I murmured.

"I'll be home as soon as possible. I love you."

"I love you, too." I put the phone down and rested my chin in my hand.

The last month or so, Max seemed to be drifting away from me, spending more time at work and less time at home. Granted, we'd been married for almost seven years, but up until now, the romantic part of our marriage was perfect. At least as perfect as it could be with so many kids around and my pregnancy, which, I reminded myself, was a miracle. I'd been told I couldn't have any more children.

But miracle pregnancy or not, this one was tougher on me than when I was carrying Sammie. I had pains where I hadn't had pains before, and I fought exhaustion daily.

I shifted on the hard chair and glanced around my yellow and white kitchen. I needed a distraction from my self-pity, which was stupid and selfish. Things could be worse. Much worse. At least I was alive, unlike poor Georgia. She'd never have the opportunity to feel sorry for herself again.

Why would somebody kill her? What could a high school English teacher have done to bring out that kind of passion in someone? What motive could somebody possibly have to murder her?

I was becoming curious. And Detective Scott's insistence that I not get involved egged me on. One of my biggest faults was wanting to do the things I shouldn't do. Maybe I was a bit like Sherry that way.

I glanced at the drawer where I'd stored the steno pads I'd bought months ago; then my gaze slid up to the counter above the drawer, where I'd left my Bible and the booklet from my women's Bible study. That's what I *should* be doing. We were studying the fruit of the Spirit: love, joy, peace, patience, kindness, goodness, faithfulness, gentleness, and self-control. Definitely a Bible study I needed.

I walked to the counter and glanced at the Bible study. This week's lesson was on love. The first item of discussion was *Love is action, not always feeling.* I bit a fingernail in indecision. Bible study or clue notebook? I decided I was too keyed up to study. I'd feel better after I wrote down all my clues.

I whispered a quick "I'm sorry" to the Lord, yanked a steno pad from the drawer, and picked up my Bible study booklet. I returned to the table where I dug in my purse and pulled out a pen and the receipt on which I'd written my clues earlier. Then I stuffed the booklet into my purse. I'd read through it at work tomorrow.

I opened the notebook to the first blank page and bit the end of my pen. Although Georgia's death could have been an accident, I doubted it. Not the way Detective Scott had spoken about the medical examiner to Corporal Fletcher.

From previous experience, I knew that clues are only as good as a sleuth's observations. Things that didn't seem important at first could gain great significance later. With that in mind, I set my pen to paper.

*Section I. The Scene: Georgia dead in the band room behind the door. Wound on her head. Bassoon lying on the floor near her. Chairs knocked over. Music on the floor.*

Who should be on my initial suspect list? Realistically, every person at the school at the time Georgia was killed—which was the reason Detective Scott had to follow up on everyone, including my son.

One thing I knew from past experience was that everything hinged around the victim.

On the same page I wrote, *The Victim: Georgia Winters.*

What had I heard about her today? *Developed an attitude lately with her family. Lives with her granny. Might want to sell off the farm.*

And when, exactly, *was* she killed? I wasn't sure about that, but I figured from what the detective said to the crime scene people that she hadn't been dead long when we found her.

I thought about my mother's comment. What were the chances of a stranger breaking into the school and killing Georgia over a potential housing development? Slim to none. But what about a stranger breaking in period? Although I hated to think about it, crimes in schools were on the rise.

I went to page two. *Section II. Questions/Observations: 1. Was Georgia murdered? 2. If so, how? Was it the bassoon? 3. How did the murderer get out of the room? Through the door in the storage room?* I needed to get a look at that.

I flipped over five pages to leave room for more questions and wrote, *Section III. Suspects:* Who had been there at the time? *Marvin Slade. Carla Bickford. Connie Gilbert.*

Who else?

*Coach Kent Smith. Football players. Other teachers? Students?* I could rule out Tommy, but what about his classmates? Would any of them have a reason to kill Georgia?

Perhaps it had been someone who didn't work at the school or attend but had known her. *One of Georgia's acquaintances. Who?* Then I wrote, *A complete stranger.*

I jotted notes about where I thought people had been. Had Connie still been at the school when I found Georgia's body or had she left after I had spoken with her?

I was going to have to do some snooping around the school. That would be difficult because I had no good reason to be there except for play committee meetings. I wondered if Carla would cancel our next meeting due to Georgia's murder. I doubted it. Her credo was probably "The show must go on."

I flipped back to Section II and added a couple more things. *Carla and Georgia were supposed to go out to dinner. Were they friends?*

My stomach growled. The milk shake hadn't lasted long. I laid the pen on the notebook and noticed for the first time since I'd arrived how lifeless the house felt. Sammie and Charlie were still at my folks' house. Tommy and Karen were both working.

I should do something productive like finish sewing the curtains for the baby's room. In a frenzy of homemaking insanity, I'd decided to make everything myself. Thus, patterns and fabric littered a corner of the family room where I kept my sewing machine. I needed to get everything done, but. . .better yet, I could put it off and go see Abbie.

I dialed her number. The phone rang six times; then her machine picked up.

I jiggled my foot in frustration. As soon as the message ended, I began yammering. "Abbie, where are you? I need you. I want to talk. Please call—"

I heard a click. "Trish?" Abbie breathed into the receiver. "Sorry."

"Are you monitoring your calls?"

"Sort of. I heard about Georgia. I was going to call you shortly. Are you okay?"

"I'm okay, but I need company," I said. "I'm alone."

"Where is everyone?" Abbie didn't really understand how I felt about an empty house. I'm social to the extreme. She loves her solitary life, writing her suspense novels in her store-top apartment.

"My oldest are out doing their normal activities. The youngest ones are at my folks' house. And Max is working late. Again."

"I'm sorry," she repeated. "You know what? I could really use a break. How about I come over and help you work on the nursery?"

"I don't feel like sewing," I said. "I was at the Dairy Delite today and remembered how we used to cruise. It made me miss you and want to go out."

"Oh wow." She laughed. "To be that young again. . .or maybe not. Anyway, that sounds perfect. I'm starving. Yes. Why don't we go to that little Mexican place over in Plummerville? I'll pick you up in, say, thirty minutes?"

By the time Abbie pulled in my driveway, I'd changed into maternity jeans and an orange stretchy shirt—a normal one. I looked like a basketball tummy. I didn't care. I was tired of wearing baggy shirts that pretended to cover everything but only made me look like a cloth-draped pear with legs. The pants felt snug, but they'd just come out of the dryer. Besides, my stomach was getting huge.

At the last minute, I snatched my steno clue notebook from the table and stuffed it into my purse.

Abbie pecked my cheek with a light kiss after I'd crawled into her red Mustang. I loved her car. A convertible. Sometimes in the summer, we'd put the top down and go out cruising like we had when we were teenagers. Only back then, we used an old pickup truck.

"So talk to me."

She always says that. And I always oblige. I proceeded to whine about Max working late when I'd planned a romantic dinner. I was in the middle of telling her about the black dress I'd bought to entice him when she interrupted me.

"Did you tell him ahead of time about your plans?"

I stuck my chin in the air. "Well, no, Miss I'm-on-Max's-Side. I wanted to surprise him."

She smiled. "How could you expect him to know what you were thinking?"

She sounded so reasonable and logical. I didn't want to be reasonable or logical, so I just crossed my arms and frowned at her. "He should come home at night."

She laughed softly. "You know he adores you. Maybe he's just got a lot going on right now."

"You're my best friend," I said. "You're supposed to be on my side. You've always been on my side."

"Okay, okay." She turned a corner, moving the car smoothly from gear to gear. "He's a beast. He treats you horribly, and you're absolutely miserable."

I slapped her arm. "Use sarcasm on me. You're right, of course."

When we reached the restaurant, we got a corner booth. Colorful piñatas hung from the ceiling. Brightly painted panoramas embellished tan plaster walls. Recorded mariachi music blasted from the speakers. We ordered then settled back with chips and salsa. I finally noticed that Abbie didn't look so good. Sort of tense, with lines on her forehead and around her eyes, like she had a headache.

"You okay?" I asked.

"Mostly." She took a sip of iced tea and didn't look at me.

"Are you sure?"

She put down her glass. "Why don't we talk about you? That's why we're here."

She wasn't acting right at all, but Abbie was a private person even with me, and we'd known each other since kindergarten. Sometimes I had to work to get her to open up. In that regard, she was a bit like her grandmother, the woman who had raised her. Although Abbie wasn't the repressive, overly religious person her grandmother had been, she had some of the same personality traits. I'd wait a few minutes and try again.

"So," Abbie met my gaze, "you want to tell me about Georgia?"

I took a deep breath. "Not gory details, really, because it's kind of icky. Especially when we're about to eat."

"We can talk about something else if you want to."

"No. It's fine. I need to talk about it." I took a deep breath and explained how I'd arrived at the band room and when Tommy showed up.

Abbie was shaking her head.

"What?" I asked.

"I know it's horrible, but still. . .bashed in the head in the band room. Only you could find someone in a situation like that. Are you going to play sleuth?"

I must have blushed, because Abbie smiled. "You can't help it, can you? You're terribly curious."

"Well, there is that, but I'm also a little bit worried. I'm pretty sure she was murdered."

"Was there any doubt?" Abbie asked.

I shrugged. "You know how noncommittal the cops are. I guess it could have been an accident. She could have fallen and hit her head, but some things in the room were wrecked. Like there'd been a struggle."

"Sounds like a fight to me," Abbie said. "Why are you worried?"

"Tommy was questioned."

She raised her eyebrows. "Really?"

"Yes, but I can't imagine why except that he was there with me. What possible motive could he have?" I went on to tell her all the other people I considered possible suspects.

Abbie nodded. "You know that Georgia moved in with her granny Nettie two years ago? Nettie isn't doing well."

"Really?" I fumbled in my purse for my notebook. "Nettie Winters? How do you know that?"

"Nettie was quite a gardener. Remember? That's where I used to get my cut flowers and herbs."

"Yes, now that you mention it. What's wrong with her?"

"Not sure, but her health is failing." Abbie frowned. "So you *are* going to play sleuth?"

I shrugged. "Maybe. Maybe not. But Mr. Bossy Police Person Detective Eric Scott told me to mind my own business. I hate it when he does that."

Abbie picked up a chip and jabbed it in the salsa.

"He was in a horrible mood. He practically yelled at Carla; not that she didn't deserve it, but usually he's cooler than that." I took a swig of water. "You know what was really weird? Corporal Fletcher implied something odd was going on."

Abbie chewed her chip hard.

"You know Detective Scott's daughter is living with him now. I met her today. She's not a happy camper. I wonder why he never got married again." I stuffed a salsa-laden chip into my mouth then attempted to speak through it. "It's really no wonder. He's personality challenged."

Our server arrived with our food. Abbie and I asked the Lord to bless the food; then I dug into my taco salad with gusto, in spite of knowing that even if it was blessed, I'd pay later with acid reflux. We ate in silence for a few minutes; then I noticed Abbie was just pushing her tacos around her plate.

"Are you okay, Abs?" I asked. "You're not sick, are you? You don't look so hot. The way you're acting, you'd think that you had a run-in with Detective Scott, too."

Abbie's fork hit the plate.

That got my attention. "Did you? Did he give you a ticket or something?"

"I wish it was that." Her lips were pursed.

I put my fork down. "Stop doing that with your mouth. You look like your grandmother, and that gives me the creeps."

She tried to relax her lips but didn't succeed.

"Abs, he didn't arrest you for something, did he? You go to all lengths to research your books, but you didn't do anything wrong, did you? Just for your books? I mean, that would be kind of funny if you didn't get a record because of it."

She coughed and shook her head.

"Well then, what?"

She took a deep breath but avoided my eyes. "He asked me out."

5

I felt stupid. Why hadn't I seen this coming? During the investigation into Jim Bob's murder, I'd noticed Detective Scott watching Abbie with appreciation. Of course, with her long red hair and legs that go on forever, most guys watched her that way. I'd be jealous if I didn't love her. Still, if I hadn't been intuitive enough to see this, how in the world did I think I could solve a crime?

I reached across the table and touched her hand. "Are you going?"

She finally met my eyes. "No."

I pushed my plate away. "I think it's time you talk to me."

"I don't want to talk about it."

"I'm not going to let this slide, so you might as well give it up."

She glared at me. "Fine. Then you might as well know."

I leaned back and waited while she picked at the food on her plate.

"You know somebody at the sheriff's office fobbed me off on Eric a year and a half ago, right?"

"You mean to ask writing questions? Like a consultant? That wasn't your idea?"

She shook her head. "No, it wasn't. My old consultant retired. I have no idea why I ended up with Eric, but I did. My old consultant just kept telling me to go with the flow. Eric had the experience I needed for my books. Things have been okay. I only talk to him when it's necessary." She looked away from me. "This time, I was sitting in his office with a list of questions, but he wasn't really paying much attention, which frustrated me. Finally, I asked him if I should come back at a better time. He bounced his pen a few times and then asked me out."

I knew Detective Scott's pen bouncing routine. It meant he was either thinking or disturbed. "So you turned him down?"

"I was so shocked I lost my voice for a second." She bounced her index finger on the table in what seemed like a subconscious imitation of Detective Scott. "I didn't know how to respond, so I just stood up and said, 'I'm sorry. I can't.' Then I walked out of his office." She blinked back the tears in her eyes. "He can shut down the whole sheriff's office to me. Then where would I get my questions answered?"

I suspected that wasn't her real reason for being near tears. Detective Scott had always brought strong emotions out of her, I just didn't know why. "Did he say he wouldn't answer any more of your questions?"

"No," she said. "But I didn't give him a chance to say anything."

"I know he's persistent and obnoxiously pushy, but he doesn't strike me as vengeful." I reached across the table and patted her hand. "Why did you turn him down, anyway? You're both single."

She stared at me with her eyebrows raised. "You just said he's stubborn, pushy, and obnoxious. Why would I date him?"

"Because," I said.

"Because?"

"Well, why not?" I asked.

She gave me the smarty-pants smile that used to drive me nuts when we were in school. "Because. That's all I'm going to say."

Our server came and asked us if we were done. Abbie said yes. I said no. I wanted dessert. He took my order for biscochitos and carried our plates away.

"You're eating more than usual tonight," Abbie said.

"You can share the cookies with me."

"I hate them. Anise with cinnamon just doesn't do it for me."

I waved my hand in the air. "Don't try to change the subject. Why won't you go out with him? Do you dislike him that much?"

Her nostrils flared. "And you say *he's* pushy?" She took a deep breath. "Don't you remember why my ex-husband left me? He said I was too intense. Too absorbed in my work."

When she'd been married, Abbie worked as a journalist. Her husband was a cop. "You were both so young," I said. "You were both busy."

"I've only gotten more intense," she said, as though I hadn't spoken. "I don't want to. . ." She let her words fade as she picked up her napkin and shredded it into pieces.

I knew what she meant. Her husband had gotten sympathy from a couple of other women. She still blamed herself and was terribly afraid of another relationship.

"Abbie, you're older now. You really have changed."

The mustached server delivered my cookies and refilled my water and Abbie's tea.

"Yes. I'm worse." She shook her head. "I've been alone too long. I like my space and my apartment. I don't want to share. I don't have the time or nature to be a wife. And now his daughter is living with him? I could never be a stepmother."

"Well, I won't argue with you about that right now, even though I disagree, but for Pete's sake. Detective Scott just asked you out. He didn't ask you to marry him."

She had taken a big swallow of tea, started laughing, and gurgled instead. A few drops of liquid dripped down her chin. I picked up a napkin, reached across the table, and wiped her mouth. "That's better. You need to laugh." I paused. "So, are you going to go out with him?"

187

"No," she said. "No, I'm not. Can we drop it now?"

"There's more to this story, isn't there?"

"Trish. . ."

Her tight lips told me what I needed to know. She wasn't telling me everything, but I also recognized that she wasn't going to say another word tonight. That was fine. I'd find out one way or another.

—

Max wasn't home yet when Abbie dropped me at my house at eight. My mother delivered Charlie and Sammie at eight thirty. I felt out of sorts as I put the little kids to bed, wishing my husband were home.

"Granddad has a new calf," Charlie said as I tucked him in.

"I love calves." I sat on the edge of his bed and wished I could run my fingers through his spiky red hair, but he wasn't keen about that kind of attention from me anymore. "They're so wobbly at first, then they start running around and jumping, acting like little kids on the playground."

Charlie rubbed his eyes. "I want cows when I grow up. I can work with Granddad. I'll be a farmer, too."

I smiled. "That would be great, honey." Even as I said the words, I thought about the hard life my father had lived. Only lately had he been able to relax because my mother was making good money at her doughnut shop. I also knew what Max's wealthy parents would think if any of their grandchildren went into farming. When I was dating Max, I overheard my mother-in-law say to him, "Farmers are fine, dear. We need them, but we don't need to date them." I was naive enough to think that as my relationship with Max grew, she would see that I made him happy and change her opinion. Boy, had I been naive.

But I never let her influence me, and I did my best to see that she didn't influence the children. As long as what they chose to do was honest and moral and made them happy, I would never dissuade them from their dreams, no matter what paths they chose.

A few minutes later, I finished praying with Sammie and was about to turn off her light and shut her door when she sat straight up in bed. Her blond hair fell over her face. "Mommy?"

"Yes?"

"Grandmom says she never sees you anymore."

There we have it. My mother's contribution to survival of the fittest. Evolution mother style. Traits handed from one generation to another. In this case, the fine art of manipulation.

"She says that all the time, sweetie. I'll call her tomorrow." I turned out the light.

"You prob'ly should." Sammie snuggled back under her covers. "She almost cried when she said it."

"Good night." I shut the door.

Back in the kitchen, I heard a car door slam, and a moment later, Karen, my stepdaughter, shot through the back door with her purse and a white bag in her hand.

She smiled at me and tossed the bag on the table. "Wow, Mom. I heard you and Tommy found Ms. Winters. You gonna solve the mystery?"

"I don't think your father would be thrilled about that." I already felt a little guilty about starting a clue notebook.

"You've gotta convince Dad to let you do it. You have to. At least we can trust you." Her expression turned grim.

"What do you mean by that?"

She put her purse on a chair and faced me. "Well, most of the kids don't think the cops are looking out for us. I mean, they searched Tommy's locker." She crossed her arms. "Oh please! Tommy?"

"The police aren't against you." I felt a bit hypocritical saying that given my own attitude toward a certain detective.

"They also suspect Mr. Slade. I mean, really. Mr. Slade? All you have to do is look at him to know he couldn't kill anybody. He's my favorite teacher."

While I was sympathetic because Marvin Slade had the kind of looks that made a woman want to take him home and feed him, I knew that had little to do with murderous intentions. "Some of the most innocent-looking people commit murder," I said.

"I know he didn't do it, but it looks bad for him."

"Why?"

"He and Ms. Winters haven't been getting along." Karen stared at me. "Please, Mom."

"But that's good motivation for murder."

"Maybe, but I don't believe it," Karen said. "You have to do this."

Why did I feel this pressing need to investigate? Was it just Karen's request? Or was it because I had an insatiable curiosity and had been involved in a previous murder investigation? Or maybe I had some sort of crusader inside me that had to help the cops fight evil?

I sighed. I did have a sense of wanting to see justice done. That made my decision inevitable and meant that I was going to have to be honest with Max and tell him what I was going to do.

Karen could tell I was weakening. "I can let you know if I hear anything at school."

My stomach twisted. "No, Karen. Please. If this was murder, and it looks like it was, I don't want you involved."

She snorted. "The person who did it can't be anybody I know. Really." She caught my glance. "Oh, okay. As long as you promise to investigate."

"I promise, *if* Dad's okay with it," I said. "Now, how was work at the pretzel stand?"

"Cool. Brought you leftovers. I know how you like them." She pointed at the bag on the table.

"Thanks, honey."

"Well, I gotta finish my homework." She trotted from the room.

I slipped a cinnamon sugar pretzel from the bag, took a big bite, and chewed while I pondered Georgia's death from all angles. Then I caught myself reaching into the bag for a second pretzel and stopped. Overeating was developing into a bad habit. If I wasn't careful, I'd be the size of Texas by the time I had the baby. That wasn't normally a problem for me. When I wasn't pregnant, I had trouble remembering to eat. But when I was expecting, I could happily consume copious amounts of food all day. Eat and sleep. In fact, right now, the tiredness I'd fought all day was seeping into my bones, making me feel like jelly. I needed to get to bed even if Max wasn't home. And I'd take my Bible study with me. I'd get some work done before I fell asleep.

Awhile later, I woke to Max's beautiful face hovering over mine.

"Hi." He brushed the hair from my eyes and kissed me. Then he picked up my Bible and the study book from where they'd fallen on the bed beside me and placed them on the nightstand. "Guess you fell asleep doing this?"

"I fell asleep before I read the first word." I tried to extricate my arms from the covers to pull him into a hug, but he stood up before I could.

"How are you?" he asked.

"Put out." My whine can rival Sammie's. "I had a special dinner planned for you tonight. I had steaks ready and arranged for the kids to be away."

He frowned and swiped his hand through his hair. "I'm sorry, but you should have told me earlier. I could have rearranged my meetings."

"I wanted to surprise you," I said.

He leaned over and kissed me again. For a minute, I thought he was going to be romantic, but he straightened and stepped back. "How are you feeling now? Are you okay about Georgia?"

"Abbie and I went out to dinner, so I talked with her about it. Right now I'm just achy and tired."

"Oh." He walked over to his dresser and pulled off his tie. "Well, I'm glad you're okay. I'm just sorry you had to be the one to find her."

"Well, it's not like it hasn't happened before."

"Don't remind me." He dropped the tie on the dresser.

I watched him with one eye because I was having trouble keeping both open. "What's the big deal with all the meetings?"

He met my gaze briefly in the dresser mirror then turned and began to unbutton his shirt.

"Dad and I have several projects going on."

"More self-storage centers?"

"We're looking into that," he said.

Max and his father were building a self-storage empire that had started with our facility in Four Oaks.

"I'll be back in a minute," Max said. "Then we can finish talking."

Through almost closed eyelids, I watched him walk to the bathroom to take his shower. To say that Max is good-looking would be an understatement. Dark hair, green eyes, and chiseled cheeks and chin—he could be the cover model for a romance novel. And he looked good coming and going.

I heard the water in the shower start and decided I would try to resurrect my romantic evening. I wanted to cuddle with my husband. I settled back under the covers. My eyelids drifted shut. The next thing I felt was Max leaning over me to turn off the light. I tried to force my eyes open.

"Good night," he whispered and rolled over with his back to me.

He obviously wasn't in the mood for cuddling, but I did need to tell him about my clue notebook. "Max?"

"Mmm?" He settled deeper under the blankets.

"You're not worried that I found Georgia Winters?"

He inhaled. I'd caught him off guard. He rolled over to face me. "Is there a reason I should be?"

"I'm collecting clues in a notebook." I held my breath.

He flopped onto his back. "I can't say I'm surprised."

"Detective Scott threatened me. He said he would tell you."

"If he thinks threats will work, he doesn't know you as well as I do." Max sounded resigned.

"Well, he was in a horrible mood. Did you know that he asked Abbie out?"

Max sighed. "What does him asking Abbie out have to do with you collecting clues?"

"Well, she turned him down."

"Okay. . .and?"

Max wasn't putting it all together. "Because of that, he was in a really bad mood."

Max grunted.

"And tonight Karen told me that Marvin Slade is a suspect. She asked me to solve the mystery."

"The band teacher?"

"Yes, but how could he do it? As murderers go, he doesn't fit. He's just a skinny musician. Well, skinny or not, I guess he could have murdered someone, but if I had to pick someone right now, I'd be more inclined to think it was Carla. I'm sure she could take a grown man if she wanted to. Connie is more iffy, but a possibility." I paused and remembered something I'd need to add to my notebook. "You know what? Carla said that Connie and Georgia were fighting. And the football coach was around. He could have done it easily, but why would he kill her? Maybe he and Georgia were dating." I bit my lip and thought.

"There's a good chance it was a random crime, too," Max said. "Maybe drug related."

"Drugs?" The thought horrified me.

I heard the smile in his voice. "Honey, Four Oaks isn't Utopia. There's always a good possibility that someone was looking for something."

I chewed on the inside of my cheek. I wasn't having any trouble keeping my eyes open now. "My mother said it was a mob hit because a new housing development will eventually bring in gambling and all manner of crime. She actually used the word *avarice*."

Max coughed then laughed. "Only your mother could come up with something like that."

"Yeah, I suppose."

We lay silently for a minute; then Max yawned and apologized. "Just promise me that you won't put yourself in danger. Last time was plenty for me."

"I never do that on purpose." I felt put out that he would think I was that stupid. "And I didn't find Georgia on purpose, either. I was just there for a play committee meeting. It's not like I go out looking for trouble."

He laughed. "You don't need to. It always finds you."

"Well, this time I don't think I have anything to worry about. I'm not a suspect. I hardly knew Georgia." I briefly thought about Tommy. "It's not like she was *my* teacher or anything."

"I'm not sure I like the idea of you collecting clues, but I'm not going to try to stop you. I don't think I could." He leaned over to kiss me again then rolled over on his side.

I was almost disappointed that he'd given in so quickly. I didn't want him to rampage like he had during the other murder investigation, but I wished he had tried a little harder to talk me out of it. I could have had fun with that. However, when he began snoring less than two minutes later, I realized he was exhausted.

So was I, but, perversely, now I was having trouble quieting my mind, which wandered from Georgia to Detective Scott and Abbie and finally to the housing development. My last thought was how so many times we think we know someone, or we understand a situation and have everything figured out, but we really don't. And that was exactly why it was going to be hard to figure out who murdered Georgia. No one is ever totally what he or she appears to be on the outside.

6

On Tuesday morning, Max got the little kids ready for school, and I fed them. While I ate breakfast, I pulled out my clue notebook and added, *Carla said Connie and Georgia were fighting. Were the coach and Georgia dating? Was it a random crime? Something to do with drugs?*

I half listened to the television, waiting for the local news, hoping to hear more about Georgia's death. A cheerful morning show host was running down national news, although what was considered important amazed me. She rambled on about the latest cell phone issues, including batteries that blow up. Then she mentioned the newest diet rage and a drug that helped erase bad memories and made coping with pressure easier, often used by musicians to enhance their concert performances.

"Now to the local news," she said. "The body of Four Oaks English teacher Georgia Winters was discovered yesterday in the band room of Four Oaks High School. Local law enforcement will only say that the death is being treated as suspicious."

The picture on the screen cut to Carla in front of the school. She looked surprisingly good on television, but she said nothing I didn't already know, just that she and the authorities were doing everything in their power to keep the children safe.

I was relieved no one mentioned that I had found the body. I didn't want that kind of attention. If Carla's unwillingness to share had a positive side, it was that she wouldn't share the limelight with me.

I turned off the television. On Tuesday mornings, Max carpooled the little kids to school. I kissed everyone as he herded them out to his car. After they left, I went through five changes of clothes before I decided I didn't look good in anything. I gave up trying, yanked on a boring, tight pair of maternity jeans and an equally boring sweater, tucked my steno pad and some play advertising forms into my purse, and drove to Four Oaks Self-Storage. I was happy to run the accounting end of the business from my office at the Four Oaks facility, although I planned to take a leave of absence when I had the baby.

When I walked into the front office, Shirl, the office manager, was talking on the phone. She waved at me to wait until she was done. I plunked my purse on the counter.

After she'd slapped the receiver down, she turned to face me. "I heard about that Winters woman."

I was sure everyone within a hundred-mile radius had heard about the Winters woman.

"So, are you going to solve this mystery?" Shirl asked.

"I'm not sure," I said, even as I removed the notebook from my bag.

She opened a drawer in her desk, pulled out a tube of Avon extra-moisturizing hand lotion, and squirted some into her palm.

"Do you know anything?" I lifted a pen from the desktop and held it poised over the pad.

She shrugged, rubbing her hands together. "Well, Sue, my neighbor's daughter's sister-in-law, works at the school." Shirl's eyes glittered, and I could tell she was just winding up.

"Well, I'll tell you what." Shirl put the lotion away, pulled an emery board from the pencil holder, and began sawing at her nails. "No one is surprised someone bopped that woman. She's got mean as a snake lately. I figure it's probably early menopause. She should have gotten some help. Got some herbs. You know, like black cobash?"

"I think that's black cohash."

Shirl waved a dismissive hand. "Whatever. You do realize that if more people used herbs, the drug companies would have to start charging less for their pills."

"Uh-huh." I wondered what she'd been reading.

"It's true," Shirl said. "That new pharmacist in town sells all sorts of natural stuff. You'd think he'd be afraid of losing money, but he's always giving out advice. And that Georgia needed some kind of help. You do know she threatened to fail Jason."

I shook my head. "I didn't—"

"Jason is the star quarterback on the Four Oaks High School football team. He fails? He's off the team. He goes? The season goes. That happens? Coach Smith probably loses his position."

I snorted. "Well, how stupid is that? Firing a coach because a kid fails. After all, it's just a game—"

*Oops.* Shirl tapped the nail file against her palm and stared at me as if I'd just uttered blasphemy. "Our team hasn't had a losing season in five years," she said icily.

Our team. Like high school football was the be-all and end-all of life. I hadn't understood that level of enthusiasm when I was in high school. Now that I'm an adult, I understand it even less. But this did give the coach a good reason to be a suspect.

A car pulled up in the parking lot. Shirl stared over the counter and through the window. My gaze followed hers.

"That's Connie, the costume lady," Shirl told me.

I didn't bother to remind her that I knew Connie, too, and could easily recognize her from fifteen feet away.

Shirl plunked the nail file back into the pencil holder and thumbed through some paperwork on her desk. "She called me yesterday and said you said I should hold a unit for her. She just bought a whole slew of new costumes." Shirl picked up the lease she'd already printed out and put it and a pen on the counter. "You know she's related to Georgia, don't you? Cousin. She left town right after high school. I don't know what happened, but she moved back here not so long ago."

Somewhere in the recesses of my memory, I realized I did know that. That made me even more curious to know why she and Georgia had been fighting.

The bell over the door rang when Connie walked in. Her eyes were red-rimmed.

"I was surprised you came out today," Shirl said. "I wouldn't be able to function if one of my relatives was murdered."

Connie's face blanched.

"I'm so sorry," I said with double meaning. Even though Connie's name was on my suspect list, I was sorry for her loss. And for Shirl's lack of tact.

"Thank you." Connie sniffled. "I'm sure it was difficult for you. . .finding her."

"Yes, very." I drew in a breath, trying not to remember Georgia on the floor. "Were you at the school when the police arrived?"

"No." Her eyes filled with tears. "I left right after I talked with you."

"Well, it's a good thing you didn't walk down to the band room with Trish," Shirl said. "I can't imagine how horrible it would be to find a relative bludgeoned to death."

If it were possible, Connie's face became whiter.

"Did the police bang on your door and tell you she died?" As usual, Shirl was a bull in a china shop.

Connie sniffled again. "Yes. They went out to the farm. It was horrible. Granny Nettie was there. It was the worst way she could have heard about it, although I'm not sure how much she really understood."

"I'm sorry," I said again.

"Thank you." She pulled her checkbook from her purse. "Well, work helps me cope. Besides, I have to get all this stuff into storage. I'm going to be really busy now."

"Oh?" Shirl shoved the lease toward Connie.

"Someone has to care for Granny Nettie." She swiped a tear from her cheek with the back of her hand. "You know she hasn't been doing so well in the last year. Georgia was caring for her. I helped during the day while Georgia was at work."

"I heard Nettie wasn't well," Shirl said. "What's wrong with her?"

"Mostly old age." Connie signed the lease, wrote a check, and handed both to Shirl. "Georgia was cracking under the pressure, but now she. . ." More tears. "She was having a rough time of it all."

"I can understand," I said.

"That's probably why she was acting the way she was," Shirl said. "A shrew."

"Shirl!" Sometimes I wanted to stuff a sock in her mouth.

She waved a pen in the air. "Well, people talk." She looked at Connie. "I know you heard what they were saying."

She nodded. "Yes. Georgia was ornery lately. It was because of all the pressure." She stopped suddenly and took a deep breath. "I haven't been feeling that well. My heart keeps pounding. I think it's stress."

I felt guilty for having Connie on my list of suspects. She was obviously miserable. Still, that meant nothing. I was pretty sure that some murderers felt remorse.

"You know, there's things to help that," Shirl said authoritatively. "Herbal remedies. I can get you some." She eyed Connie. "But Nettie used to make all that sort of stuff. She'd know what to do. She used to grow her own herbs."

Connie picked up her purse. "We all drink her herbal tea. It's got ginseng in it."

"Gotta be careful with herbs, though," Shirl said. "Pick the wrong ones and. . ." She ran her finger across her neck.

Once again, I wondered what Shirl had been reading—or drinking. This herbal thing was a brand-new topic for her, and I had a feeling I'd be hearing more about it before she got it out of her system.

Connie backed toward the door. "Well, I should get this stuff unloaded. I've got so much to do."

Shirl clucked sympathetically as Connie left the office. We watched her car drive up the parking lot to her new unit.

"Lover's quarrel," Shirl said.

"What?" Sometimes talking to Shirl made my brain feel like it was in a wringer washer.

"A crime of passion. Maybe Marvin or Coach Smith was dating Georgia. And then she broke up with him."

"Seems sort of obvious," I said.

"Isn't it always when it involves love gone bad? People just lose control. Then they murder in cold blood."

I shrugged. "Maybe." Another customer came in, so I went to my office. There, I pulled out my steno pad to make notes.

*Were Georgia and the coach dating? Did he clobber her?*

I chewed my pen. Another important part of solving a crime is looking into the victim's past. Connie had said some interesting things about Georgia.

*Georgia lived with Nettie. Was she overwhelmed taking care of her?*

196

At the familiar sound of a purring engine, I looked out the window. Max pulled into the parking lot. I was surprised to see him. He hadn't said anything about coming into the office today. The bell over the door rang as he came inside.

"Hi, Mr. C.," Shirl said. "I didn't expect you today."

"Good morning. Just need to pick up something I forgot. Any messages?"

"Yes. Your *mother* called. Then your father called. Then your *mother* called again." Shirl felt the same as I did about Max's mother, and that was obvious by her slightly sarcastic emphasis on *mother*.

"Okay. I'll call her in a minute."

He entered my office smiling and kissed me. "You okay?"

"Yeah, especially now," I said. "This is a nice surprise."

He grinned, but it faded when he noticed my notebook. "Clues?"

"Mmm-hmm."

"You're incorrigible."

"Probably."

"That's why I love you, though." His grin returned.

"Because I'm incorrigible?"

"Because being married to you keeps life from becoming boring." He kissed me again, this time longer, and I felt it all the way to my toes.

When he was done, I couldn't speak.

He stepped back and winked at me. He knows exactly how he affects me. "Anyway, I have a couple of things to do. Is that Connie Gilbert I see unloading things?"

I nodded. "Did you know she's related to Georgia?"

Max nodded. I shouldn't have been surprised. He seems to know everybody and everything.

"I was a little shocked that she was out so soon after Georgia's death," I said, "but she's got a bunch of costumes to store. She says she has to take care of Nettie now. Connie doesn't seem to be doing very well."

"I can understand," he said. "Does she have help unloading?"

"Not right now."

"*Hmm.* It looked like she has some heavier boxes. I'll go give her a hand for a couple of minutes."

"That's sweet of you. You want me to come?"

He shook his head. "I don't want you lifting anything."

I settled down to work. Max returned twenty minutes later and disappeared into his office. I needed to get busy getting advertising commitments for the play program. I'd have Max fill out a form for Cunningham & Son. I'd fill out one for Four Oaks Self-Storage.

I took one of the forms and went to Max's office. His door was open a crack, so I pushed it and walked in. He was on the phone and looked up with a frown, holding up a finger to tell me to wait.

He shoved some papers around on his desk. I narrowed my eyes in suspicion.

Because of who I am, how I am, and how I've always been, I recognize a cover-up when I see it. That's because I have the regrettable ability to cover up with the best of them. Something I'm working hard to change.

He mumbled a few uh-huhs then said good-bye and hung up. "I'm sorry, baby. I'm in a hurry to finish something here." As he spoke, he placed a leather portfolio on the desk in front of him over the papers. "I've got a lot to do, and I hadn't planned to come to the office today. I have one more phone call to make. Can you give me just a couple minutes?"

That meant he wanted me to leave. I sighed my objection, but he ignored it and just stared at me.

"Okay. Well, I'll be in my office." I didn't move.

"Great. I'll be there in a minute. And would you please shut the door on your way out?" He picked up the phone again.

I knew when I was defeated. I turned and shut his office door. What was he hiding from me?

At my desk, I watched the lights on the phones. Not too long after Max's turned dark, I heard him leave his office and shut the door.

He appeared in my office. "I have to get going."

"I need you to fill out this form for advertising for Cunningham & Son." I held it out to him.

He put down his briefcase, crossed the room, and took the form and flipped through the pages. "All this for advertising in a school play program?"

"Yep," I said. "That's Carla. Obsessive."

"I'll say." He stuck the form in his briefcase.

"Max, is everything okay?"

He pecked me on the cheek. So different from the passionate kiss of a few minutes before.

"Yes. I'll be home tonight, hopefully at the normal time. I told Tommy that Sherry could come over to dinner tonight. They want to practice for the play."

I wanted to say, "Thanks for asking me first," but I didn't. I just nodded. He turned and left. I didn't understand. One minute he was kissing me with feeling; the next he was like a cold fish. What was going on? I buried my nose in work, trying to ignore my swirling thoughts. Then Shirl hollered from the outer office that she was going out to lunch, emphasizing she had an important appointment.

Normally I would have been curious, because Shirl never goes out to lunch. Instead, she frugally packs a sandwich, which she eats in the conference room in front of a tiny television we had installed for her. There she reads a romance book while she watches her favorite soap opera.

Today, however, I was too busy wondering what Max was hiding to think about Shirl. When her car pulled from the lot, the war began. Bad Trish began to argue with Good Trish.

I wanted to search Max's desk to see if he had left anything behind that would give me a hint about what he was hiding. I could temporarily turn off the security cameras and lock the front door so I wouldn't be caught.

I took a step toward the front door then stopped.

My mother raised me on clichés. They still live in my brain and come back to me in her voice at the appropriate moments. Like when you hear an annoying song on the radio, and the dumbest line in the whole thing repeats itself over and over again in your mind until you think you'll go crazy.

I could hear my mother speaking right now. *"Trish, one day your curiosity is going to get the best of you. You know what they say, don't you? Curiosity killed the cat."* When she told me things like that, she added object lessons when she could, like smashed cats in the road. *"See?"* She'd point with great enthusiasm. *"That cat just had to cross the road. Too busy being curious to watch for cars."*

*Yes, but this is my husband.* I argued pointlessly with her in my head. *He shouldn't keep secrets from me. I'm not a cat, and I'm not crossing the road.*

I looked around the empty office. I didn't have to worry about being smashed by a car unless someone accidentally came barreling through the front window.

No one would ever know. Except me and God.

ood Trish triumphed over Bad Trish. I didn't search Max's office. To reward myself, I got three different flavors of ice cream when I stopped by the Shopper's Super Saver after work to pick up things for dinner.

At the checkout, a young man with more piercings and tattoos than I cared to look at was shoving my purchases into plastic bags with abandon.

"Um, those are eggs there," I said.

"Sure are." He crammed more items into the bag.

I was too tired to argue. Besides, trying to write my check and simultaneously recall whether I had hot fudge at home for the ice cream was daunting enough. That's when I heard Georgia's murder being discussed with great relish at the checkout behind me.

". . . We've never had a tragedy like this at my school before, and I don't intend for it to ever happen again."

I recognized Carla Bickford's voice and turned around to look at her. She was holding court two checkouts down from me like the queen of England, with a sensible purse that coordinated with her proper suit. The whole outfit was an echo of what she'd been wearing the day before.

She met my gaze, and her eyes widened. "Why, Trish. I didn't recognize you from behind."

What did that mean? Was my behind different than it used to be? Had I gained so much pregnancy weight that I'd become unrecognizable? Or did it mean she just never really saw me from this angle before?

With a small wave of her hand, Carla motioned toward me then gazed slowly from person to person, acknowledging her subjects. "Trish is the one who found Georgia."

Everyone's eyes fell on me. The low, confiding pitch of Carla's voice had given her words just enough drama that I wouldn't have been surprised to hear everyone ooh and aah.

I recognized one of my mother's friends in line, and she nodded and smiled at me, as though I had done something terribly special by finding a dead woman.

"Oh wow," my cashier said.

"Dude," the bagger said, looking at me with a sudden new respect in his eyes.

I felt like saying, "Aw, shucks, 'tweren't nothin'."

"Did you throw up?" my cashier asked me breathlessly.

"No." I hated this kind of attention, particularly since it was at Georgia's expense.

My mother's friend had to add her two cents. "Well, everyone should remember that Trish is the one who found Jim Bob in the milk case last spring. She's used to this by now."

"Dude!" The bagger eyed me with awe and carefully bagged the rest of my groceries.

What a thing to be known for. Finding dead people.

My mother's friend wasn't done. "Not only that, but she solves crimes."

"Well, not exactly," I said.

"That's not what your mother says."

The air stilled, as if all the people around me were holding their breath. All eyes were on me. I wanted to disappear. Solving crimes was one thing, but to have the fact advertised all over the county could be dangerous.

"So will you cancel the play?" a woman in line behind Carla asked her.

That got everyone's focus off of me.

"Absolutely not," Carla said. "The show must go on. We can't let anything take us from our duties."

I waited for applause, but it wasn't forthcoming.

Carla sniffed, put her purse strap over her shoulder, and picked up her grocery bag. "We need to get to the bottom of this crime. I'm upping the security in the school. I told the school board at the beginning of the year that we were at risk and needed a school resource officer. We also need cameras in the halls. You never know when a crazy person is going to break in and hold the children hostage. Now I have proof that we are susceptible to attack from the outside."

That was the third time I'd heard someone say a stranger had broken into the school. Was I the only one who didn't believe that?

The bagger dude offered to push my groceries outside to my car. I agreed and ended up walking next to Carla. "So you think a stranger broke into the school?"

"Certainly. You don't think anybody we know could be guilty of this, do you?" Her gaze was challenging.

I shrugged and decided not to give her my opinion at the moment. "Did you know Georgia well? I didn't, although she did grow up around here."

"Well, I knew her better than the other teachers on staff. We ate dinner together on occasion. She was dedicated. Determined that the children should be well educated." Carla's purse slipped off her shoulder, and she shoved it back. "She was under a great deal of pressure to take care of her grandmother, though. I wondered if she should take a leave of absence."

"Did you know that she and Connie were cousins?" I asked.

Carla blinked. "Well, of course I knew that." She stopped in front of a gray Volvo and opened the front door, leaning over and placing her bag on the passenger seat.

Bagger Dude hovered behind me, listening.

"Aren't you worried about the football team?" I asked.

"The football team?" Carla stood up, gripping her purse with both hands, and stared down at me. "Why? Just like our band, our football team is one of the best in the tri-county area. As a result, we get attention from some of the best colleges in the area."

*Rah, rah, rah. Sis boom bah.* I was getting the party line and decided to grab the bull by the horns, to quote another one of my mother's oft-used clichés. "Well, I heard that Georgia was threatening to fail Jason, who is the star quarterback. Wouldn't it be possible that he or Coach Smith had something to do with the attack on Georgia?"

"What?" Carla blinked like a toad in a hailstorm.

I'd plainly caught her off guard, so I pressed my advantage. "I heard that Jason was going to be removed from the team."

She took two steps backward. "It's absolutely ridiculous to think our football team is good only because of one player. Besides, if Jason could be guilty, then any number of our other young people could be guilty." She took several deep breaths. "That would mean her death was some kind of personal vendetta. . . . No, I'm sure this was a stranger."

I thought she was protesting too much. "Well, you never really know what people are going to do. There are rumors—"

"Hearsay," Carla snapped. "You shouldn't be listening to it." A red flush worked up her cheeks. "I don't care if you *do* solve mysteries."

Her hostility seemed a bit over the top to me. Still, I didn't want to stress her out any more than I already had. I forced myself to laugh. "Yep, gossip can be a killer, all right. Especially in a small town."

She visibly relaxed. "Remember our rescheduled meeting tomorrow afternoon. I don't want anything to distract us from our goals. I want to discuss the advertising for the school play. I'd like to see the paid ads throughout the program. And I want the whole thing professionally printed on heavy, good quality paper."

I nodded even though I thought the idea was ridiculous. This was a school play in a public school, for Pete's sake. But what did I know?

"This will raise money for the drama club as well as present our high school in a good light." Carla slipped into the driver's seat. "I'll see you tomorrow afternoon at the meeting."

I turned away and wondered what was wrong with our high school that it had to be presented in such a good light. Well, other than the fact that it had been the scene of a murder.

My spiky-haired bagger followed me to my car with my basket. "Dude, that woman is a freak."

"What?"

He motioned with his head at the back end of Carla's car as she pulled out of the parking lot. "Her. She's a freak."

"How come?" We halted at the back of my SUV, and I popped the back door open.

"Too good for everyone. You know? Like those old bags on the BBC." He started loading my groceries. "She acts like she's on drugs, man."

I had a feeling he would know.

"You know what they say about the coach, don't you?" He turned to stare at me.

"No."

"Steroids."

I stared at him in disbelief. "Steroids? You can't be serious."

"Serious as a heart attack." He shrugged. "Took 'em a long time. Affected his head." He tapped his temple then slammed the car door shut. "Now he makes sure his players do well on tests, if you get my drift."

"Steroids?" I asked. "Do they help on tests?"

He laughed and stared at me. I felt uncomfortable under his scrutiny. "He has other ways."

"How do you know this?" I asked.

His eyes narrowed. "I hear things. Listen, I gotta get back to work."

"Okay." I turned to my SUV and used the remote to open the locks.

"Hey, lady."

I turned.

Bagger Dude scratched his arm. "Be careful about askin' questions." He swiveled on his sneakered foot and headed back to the store.

That sounded like a threat. I shivered, got into the car, and locked my doors. I needed to write down what I'd just heard. I pulled a pen and my steno pad from my purse.

*Bagger Dude says Coach used steroids and they messed up his head. He arranges for players to pass tests in order to stay on the team. How?*

*Carla is defensive. Team isn't dependent on just one player.* I stopped and thought carefully about her words. *Carla never denied that Jason or the coach had done anything wrong. But she insists that it was a stranger who killed Georgia.*

After staring at the words, I shut the steno pad and tucked it in my purse, along with the pen. As I started my SUV, I noticed my wedding rings needed to be cleaned. That's when it dawned on me that Carla hadn't been wearing any rings. Not even an engagement ring. Strange. I thought she had a fiancé.

I drove home, mentally reviewing all of my clues. Murder investigations have a way of peeling away people's veneer of civility. Before I was done, I was going to know some people in my town a lot better than they wanted to be known.

—

Water flew from my salad spinner as I twirled it in the kitchen sink. I had my Bible study open on the counter, trying to meditate on the Scripture. *Be on your guard; stand firm in the faith; be men of courage, be strong. Do everything in love.* As I thought about that, the back door opened. I turned. Tommy and Sherry walked into the room frowning, bringing with them a dark atmosphere of despair.

Sherry met my eyes. "Hello, Mrs. Cunningham."

"Hey, Mom," Tommy said.

Neither smiled.

"I hope you like steak, Sherry." I needed to use the steaks I'd thawed the night before, so I had bought a couple more for dinner tonight. They were cooking on the gas grill out on the patio, manned by Max, who was in slightly better spirits. At least he'd seemed that way when he pulled me into an enthusiastic kiss a few minutes ago that ended only when Sammie interrupted us.

Sherry offered to help me, and Tommy left to take his books to his room. Karen came traipsing in and gave Sherry and me a hand carrying things to the table.

In a couple of minutes, we were all seated at the dining room table except Charlie. He came straggling in, a sour expression on his face.

"You okay?" I asked as he sat down.

"Yeah," he mumbled.

Max asked the blessing. For a few minutes, no one said a word. Tommy and Sherry kept exchanging glances; then Sherry dropped her fork on her plate with a clatter.

"I'm going to ask her, Tommy."

His knuckles turned white on his water glass. "Sherry, remember?"

"I know I promised, but she can help us. You're the one who told me she's great at solving mysteries."

Max stopped chewing.

"I already asked her to do it last night," Karen said.

Charlie looked up, and for the first time since he entered the room, his eyes lit up. "You gonna ask Mom to help you solve a mystery? She can do it, you know, no matter what anybody says."

Sammie grinned. "Yeah, Mommy can help."

I couldn't resist. "What do you guys need help with?"

Tommy was frowning at Sherry in exactly the same way Max was at me, glittery green eyes with creases between the brows.

"I've got to do it. I'm sorry." Sherry turned teary eyes to me. "Tommy is a suspect in the attack on Ms. Winters."

"What?" Max's gaze fell on me and then slid to his eldest son. "Tommy?"

Tommy glared at Sherry. "I told you to wait until I talked to Dad."

She waved a hand in the air. "I overheard Corporal Fletcher. And my dad is coming to get me after dinner because my car's in the shop. He doesn't. . .want Tommy to drive me home. I think it's because he wonders if Tommy did it."

"Is this true?" Max asked softly, glancing at me. I knew what he was thinking. He wondered if I knew and hadn't told him. I wasn't fooled by the tone of his voice. He speaks very softly when he's really upset.

"You can't really be a suspect. You just happened to be there, right?" I looked at our eldest. He wouldn't meet my gaze.

Charlie bounced in his chair. "Well, Deep Freeze Winters didn't like you much, did she?"

I turned to him. "You called her Deep Freeze?"

"That's what Tommy and everyone called her. Because of her last name. Winters." Charlie sounded as though that was the coolest thing in the world, no pun intended.

I didn't have time to consider that, because Sherry was very near hyperventilation as she reached across the table to grab at my hand. "Please, Mrs. Cunningham."

I squeezed her hand while I tried to untangle my thoughts. *Tommy had absolutely no motivation in the world to kill Georgia. . .right?*

Max cleared his throat. "Why would Eric, uh, Detective Scott, be looking at Tommy as a suspect? Why didn't someone tell me about this?" He favored me with a quick, narrow-eyed stare that made me feel defensive.

"Last night on the phone, I told you they had interviewed Tommy. You said it didn't matter. They were doing that to everyone. I mean, how could Tommy be a real suspect?" My voice got louder. "If I haven't learned anything else, I've learned that a good suspect has to have a good motive. That's the key factor in solving crimes, you know. Motivation. Well, motivation and. . .accessibility."

Tommy, Sherry, and Karen stared at me. I could have sworn they weren't breathing. Then a chill made the hair on my arms stand up, because I realized they knew something I didn't.

Max leaned forward. "Son?"

Sherry and Tommy exchanged glances. "Tell them, Tommy. If you don't, I will."

Tommy's shoulders sagged. "Well, Ms. Winters said I helped Jason cheat on an English exam. That's why I was looking for her the day she was killed. I wanted to tell her I didn't do it."

"What?" Max and I both said.

Sherry slapped her hand on the table. "He didn't cheat. Neither did Jason.

The problem was we studied together, so our answers were similar. She said she wasn't going to let Tommy be in the play. Maybe get him expelled. And she was going to get Jason kicked off the football team."

Max was breathing harder across the table.

"What's 'expelled,' Mommy?" Sammie asked.

"Kicked out of school," I said absentmindedly. Even though I was on the verge of panic, the accusation made no sense to me. Why would Georgia think Tommy was guilty and not Sherry—not that I wanted Sherry expelled either, for several reasons. One, I liked her. Two, she wasn't guilty. Three, her father would blame Tommy, and vicariously, I would be to blame, too.

I turned to the teenagers. "Is this because of Coach Smith?"

The teenagers looked at each other.

"What are you talking about?" Max asked me.

"I heard he arranges for his players to get good grades." All three teenagers were staring at the table. I wanted to say something about the drugs, but I'd wait until I talked to Max. "Why was Georgia Winters fixated on Tommy?"

Max glanced at me then turned back to the kids.

Tommy finally looked up. "I don't know. She used to like me."

Sherry met my gaze, and I read a silent plea.

"This could really mess up my college plans," Tommy said.

I felt as close to hyperventilation as Sherry was acting. Yes, cheating would certainly mess up Tommy's college plans. So would being accused of Georgia's murder.

Max stood and told Tommy to meet him in his office. Charlie scampered upstairs to his room. Sammie followed him with a purposeful look on her face. I had a feeling she wanted him to explain to her more about what was going on. She figured Charlie would know because he loved crime and detective shows. Karen and Sherry carried leftovers into the kitchen.

I stacked dirty dinner plates at the dining room table, ignoring my husband, who was standing next to his chair. I didn't like his body language, which was all stiff like a mad dog. "Trish—"

"Max, don't say a word. I'm just keeping clues in a notebook." I began to gather up silverware. "I didn't know any of this. But I heard something today about drug use, too. That Coach Smith used drugs to help his players."

Max was breathing hard again. "Was that from a reliable source?"

I thought about Bagger Dude. "No, probably not."

"Sherry shouldn't have asked you to investigate. Her father is the detective." Max shook his head. "I thought Tommy was with you when you discovered Georgia."

I looked up at him. "Well, he was. Sort of. I mean, he got there after I got there. I don't know where he'd been. I really didn't think it was that big a deal."

I gulped. "This looks bad, Max. I can't honestly say that Tommy didn't do it, although I *know* he didn't."

Max had a hard, cold look in his eyes that I rarely saw. "I need to go talk to Tommy. We'll be in my office." He whirled on his heel and strode down the hall.

The older girls helped me clean the kitchen. None of us spoke. I was surprised that Sherry stayed, since it appeared Tommy would be busy the rest of the evening, but she lingered even after the dishes were done and Karen had left the room.

"I thought your dad was coming to get you," I said.

"He is, shortly." She crossed her arms. "I wanted to talk to you alone, though."

"Okay." I motioned to the kitchen table. I hoped this wasn't going to be something like a confession of true love for my son. I wasn't ready for anything like that. But my worry was squelched when I saw a steely flash in her eyes. The look wasn't that of a young lady about to announce her true love.

As we sat down, I studied her face. She had the angular look of Detective Scott, but her bones were finer. She still hadn't grown into her features, and she would never be a classic beauty, but I could tell that when she hit her midtwenties, men would be falling all over her.

She placed her elbows on the table and clasped her hands together as if in supplication. "Mrs. Cunningham, please solve this mystery."

"Call me Mrs. C.," I said to distract her, because I didn't know how to reply.

She nodded. "Okay, but please? Solve the mystery."

"Sherry, you know your dad doesn't want me involved." I wasn't about to tell her I was already keeping notes. Her intense gaze made me uneasy. My fingers danced a rhythm on the table while I tried to figure a way out of this conversation.

"My dad can be pretty pushy," she admitted.

"That's putting it mildly," I murmured, hoping I would never again have another interview session with him.

"Yeah, and he really likes to get confessions out of people. He took classes to learn how to do that." She sighed. "I've never been able to keep the truth from him—at least in the long run. Sometimes being a cop's kid is really, really hard. I mean, I have to live up to all these *standards*. Even when I wasn't living with him. Now it's worse."

I could only imagine. And to make things harder, her mom wasn't around to balance things out. "I understand he's tough. We've had, uh, discussions in the past."

She returned my smile. "Well, he has made a couple comments about the Cunningham stubbornness."

I felt a brief sense of accomplishment that the bullheaded detective thought I was worthy of comment.

"My dad is a really good cop," she said. "I can admit that, even if I don't want to live with him. But see, he can't find out things like you can. People treat cops differently than they would regular folks. Honestly, cops act different, too." She paused and eyed me. "And I'm in an even better place to find out things. We could work together. You and me."

I stared at her in disbelief. "No way. Not only is that unsafe, but your father would find a reason to lock me up and throw away the key." I stood, placed my hands flat on the table, and stared down at her. "At the very least, he'd accuse me of contributing to your delinquency."

"Well, then, let's hope he doesn't find out." She stood, too, and faced me across the table. "I've thought a lot about this. My aunt is at our house, and that's distracting my dad. She could be a problem, but I can work around her. I have to go to school anyway. That's where I'm going to look for things."

"I don't—"

"How can it be dangerous?" she continued. "I'll just be listening. Most adults don't pay attention to kids, and they say a lot of things when they think we're not listening. I could start writing things down like Tommy says you do, and we could compare notes."

So much for not telling her about my notebook. I wanted to shake her. Was this how frustrated Max felt with me sometimes? Tiredness hit me. I needed to sleep. I'd be able to think better tomorrow morning.

I met her gaze. "No, I can't let you do it. It's bad enough for adults."

Sherry lifted her chin. "Actually, I'm eighteen. I *am* an adult."

At my frown, she nodded. "It's true. Because of the divorce and all, I repeated first grade."

"That doesn't mean your father won't be mad when he finds out. And, believe me, somehow he'll find out. It also doesn't mean that you'll be safe. I'll feel responsible."

She leaned across the table, facing me nose to nose. "Mrs. C., if you won't let me help you, I'm doing it myself. No one is going to stop me."

In the end, what could I say?

8

So Cunningham & Son will buy an ad for the program, right?" I asked Max as he passed through the kitchen behind me.

He grunted in the affirmative.

"Are you still mad at me?" I shoved the last of the dirty cereal bowls into the dishwasher.

"I was never mad at you."

"Well, irritated, then?" I turned to face him.

He was standing by the door to the garage dressed in his usual Wednesday navy pinstripe power suit. Normally it made me want to loosen his red tie and smother him with kisses, but today he looked icy and formidable. "I just wish someone had told me that the police suspected Tommy."

I opened my mouth to protest, and he raised his hands in a gesture of surrender.

"I understand what you said. I guess there's no way you could have known that Tommy was a serious suspect. I'm not blaming you."

"But you're irritated with me."

He frowned. "Why would you say that?"

I crossed my arms. "You hardly talked to me last night. You didn't even kiss me good night."

That's when he finally smiled. "Honey, you went to bed early while I was still talking to Tommy. You were sound asleep when I came upstairs. I did kiss you; you just didn't wake up."

That was no excuse, as far as I was concerned. "So you're going to talk to Carla today about Tommy cheating?" I turned and shut the dishwasher door harder than I intended. "I can do it, you know. Besides, I'm mad at her because she didn't say anything to me about all this yesterday at the store."

"I'm sure you could talk to her just fine, but I'll take care of it." I glanced at him over my shoulder, and he raised an eyebrow. I knew he was thinking he didn't want to set me loose on Carla. That was wise. "I don't need any help, okay? And I don't think you should be involved anymore. Knowing that Eric is seriously looking at Tommy and some of the other people at the school as suspects scares me. It's probable the murderer isn't just some stranger who happened to be passing by."

At last. Someone saw the crime the way I did. I pulled the kids' lunches from the refrigerator. "Do you remember when I was investigating Jim Bob's murder?"

"That would be hard to forget," he murmured in a facetious tone I couldn't miss.

I ignored that and pressed my point while I slipped cookies into each lunch container. "Well, after you got all obsessive about me doing that, and we had a huge fight, you said you were going to stop being so bossy and overbearing."

"Yes, I know, but that was before. . ." His voice drifted off.

I dropped the last package of cookies into the lunches and turned to face him. "Before what?"

He inhaled and averted his gaze. "Before Tommy was involved."

"And you don't think that's a good reason for me to help?" I planted my hands on my hips. "Lots of people think I have a talent for being a sleuth. My mother, for one."

Max closed his eyes for a moment and took a deep breath. He opened them again. "Trish, I'm positive that you're a good sleuth. You have that sort of mind. But right now, you're pregnant."

"Max, we agreed the night before last. I've already started my clue notebook. I can sleuth and not be in danger."

A grim smile flashed across his lips. "And pigs fly."

Hearing a cliché of my mother's coming from the mouth of my sophisticated husband made me laugh. "You don't need to worry. I have plans."

His nostrils flared. "Plans? Like what kind of plans?"

"I'm getting off work early today for a play committee meeting. But before I go to the school, I'm going to Ma's shop to ask her to buy a full-page ad in the school play program. I also want to see if she's heard anything that would be useful. Then I'm going to buy doughnuts to take to the meeting. You know the effect my mother's doughnuts have on people. Makes them giddy. Maybe someone will talk." I met his gaze. "That should be harmless enough."

"Right." He eyed me. "Will all the main suspects be there?"

"Well, the football team and the football coach won't be there." I stared at him. "But lots of other people will be there."

"You mean lots of other *suspects* will be there." He sighed. "Oh, all right. I'm not going to be able to stop you, anyway." The wrinkles on his forehead deepened.

"Is anything else wrong?" I asked.

He picked up his briefcase. "Isn't the problem with Tommy enough?"

I relented, walked over, and kissed him. "Don't worry, Max. Everything will be fine."

"I wish I could believe that," he said.

❦

Doris's Doughnuts are a favorite with everyone, from construction workers to cops. My mother started the business years ago in a little strip mall, selling coffee and doughnuts made from recipes perfected when I was just a tot. Now she has added other pastries, along with breakfast and lunch sandwiches.

When I pulled up, I could see that she had plenty of customers, even though it was after lunch. I grabbed my purse, crawled from my SUV, and took a deep breath to prepare myself to enter the fray.

Over half the tables in the dining area were filled, and heads turned when I walked through the door. A few people waved. Gail, my mother's best friend and right-hand gal, was stacking blue coffee mugs behind the counter.

She looked up and stared at me. "Doris," she yelled. "You'd never believe who just walked in." Her voice was loud enough for people out in the parking lot to hear her.

"Who?" My mother's equally loud voice roared from the back room.

I braced myself for what was coming.

Gail cocked an ample hip against the counter. "I'm not sure I remember her name. It's been so long."

"Oh, come on." April May Winters, my mother's left-hand gal, paused in the midst of making an espresso. "Don't give her a hard time." She smiled at me, her bright hazel eyes sparkling.

Something niggled at my brain about April—something my mother had said—but I didn't have a chance to explore my thoughts, because my mother walked out of the back room, mouth first, wiping her hands on a towel.

". . .must mean my daughter. Although I don't know if I would even recognize her. I haven't seen her in so long. I talk to her friend Abbie more than I talk to her. *She's* coming to dinner on Friday."

I took a deep breath. "Hi, Ma. You know we'll be at your house on Friday, too."

She slapped the towel down on the counter, crossed her arms, and glared at me. I'd seen her just the previous weekend, but she conveniently didn't mention that. For a short time after Jim Bob's murder was solved, I'd been in her good graces. She was proud that I had, as she put it, single-handedly solved the murder for the police. I hadn't, of course, but no one can convince my mother of anything she doesn't want to believe. My notoriety wore off after a couple of weeks, and things returned to normal, which meant she was back to manipulation and minor insults. But her present glare was not normal.

I leaned my elbows on the counter and stared down through the glass at the fatty circles. "I need two dozen doughnuts. Your choice." I eyed my mother and lowered my voice. "What's wrong, Ma?"

Gail harrumphed, grabbed a box, and snatched up doughnuts like she was picking Japanese beetles from a prize rosebush.

"I heard Tommy is a suspect in the attack on Georgia Winters," Ma said in a loud voice. "The police questioned him. And you didn't even call me."

The murmurs from the room behind me stopped. If the whole world hadn't known about Tommy before, it did now.

"He wasn't accused of a crime, Ma. Don't you think I have enough on my mind right now without worrying about who knows what?"

"And even worse than anything," she continued as though I hadn't said a word, "you were once again involved in a criminal investigation and didn't call me. I had to call you, remember? I mean, really. You find that Winters woman sprawled all over the band room, drenched in her own blood, and you didn't even see fit to let your own mother know. Why, I attended the garden club every month for years with Georgia's grandmother, not that you would recall. I've known her since before you were born. You know, one day I'll be dead and buried next to your father, and. . ."

She ranted on, but I wasn't listening. I had just remembered that my mother told me Georgia was thinking of selling the farm and April's last name was Winters. Was she a relation?

"Trish, are you listening to me?"

I looked up at my mother. She was standing directly in front of me. I hadn't even seen her move.

"Sorry, Ma." I needed to distract her. I leaned harder against the counter. "Being pregnant and all. . .I can't quite. . .well, I'm just so tired. . . ." I ended on a sigh, letting my words fade into the air. Inwardly, I smiled at my acting job. It's only fair that once in a while I turn the tables on the master manipulator, especially when it's to my benefit.

Her expression immediately changed to one of concern. "For heaven's sake! Why are you standing there? Go sit down. Are you trying to kill my newest grandchild before it's born?" She turned to April. "Make her a decaf latte with whole milk right now. I'll make a turkey club."

"But, Ma, I'm not hungry. I'm—"

"Don't argue with me, young lady." She pointed toward an empty table. "You're going to eat. Go sit down."

I ignored the surreptitious stares from everyone seated in the dining area and glanced at my watch as I obeyed my mother's orders. Fortunately, I had plenty of time to snack and still arrive at the high school early. I wanted to check out the band room.

Less than five minutes later, April delivered my sandwich and drink.

I waved at a chair. "Can you take a break for a couple of minutes?"

She glanced over at my mother, who was making an espresso for a local dentist. "Doris? You mind if I sit down with Trish?"

"I'd like the company," I whined for my mother's benefit as I tried to look drawn and weak. "It'll help me eat."

"Sure. Go on," Ma said. "It's time for your break, anyway. Besides, it'll do Trish good."

I took a bite of my sandwich while April grabbed a cup of coffee and a chocolate biscotti. By the time she joined me, I had made a big dent in my sandwich.

She dropped into a chair across from me and smiled, then took a sip of coffee.

I wiped my mouth. "You wouldn't happen to be related to Georgia Winters, would you?"

April's smile died as if I'd slapped her. "Yes, I am. On my dad's side. The whole thing isn't a great topic with my family, and it's even worse right now."

I took a deep breath. "I don't want to be insensitive, but why?"

April rubbed her fingers on the coffee mug. "I'm really not sure. We think Granny Nettie is going senile. Georgia was taking care of her, but Granny was starting to need more care, like a home, so when Connie moved back, she started pitching in during the day while Georgia was at work. But then she started fighting with Georgia."

"Why?"

"Well, Georgia was getting tired. The farm was too much to take care of on top of everything else. She wanted to sell everything. But here's the rub. She wanted to put Granny Nettie in a home. Connie didn't. She thought things should continue the way they were."

"So what's the relationship between Georgia, Connie, and Nettie? Why were they caring for her?"

"She's their aunt. Her husband died really young in some farming accident. They didn't have kids, so when Georgia and Connie were young, they spent every summer with her on the farm, and she just started treating them like her kids." April clicked her fingernail on the side of her coffee mug. "Things aren't good right now. And without Georgia, we're all sure Granny Nettie will have to go to a home. But Connie is insisting no. The bad thing is that Granny is losing things."

"Losing things? Like misplacing them?"

"That's what they say. It's that senile thing. She puts things places to keep them safe. Like, once she put her purse behind the ironing board in the laundry room. No one found it for days. But the really bad thing is that she's misplaced some valuable jewelry and knickknacks. Family heirlooms, I hear. The girls looked high and low for everything but found nothing."

"I'm sorry. That's horrible."

"Yeah. That's why Georgia wanted to put Granny Nettie in a home and sell everything. Besides, she didn't want the responsibility anymore. And she wanted Connie to go back where she came from."

"Where was that?" I asked.

"Some town in Virginia. Charlotte something or other."

"So did Connie move here to help with Nettie?"

April shook her head. "Sort of. But she was also friends with that principal. You know? At the high school? I think she lived in that Charlotte place for a while, too."

A group of six construction workers walked through the front door.

"April!" Gail hollered. "We need you."

"Be there in a sec." April took a last sip of coffee and shoved the rest of the biscotti in her mouth.

"Thanks," I said.

"Your mom said you're going to solve this mystery." April stood and picked up her coffee cup. "I think you should. Even if it makes my family look bad. I feel really bad for Granny Nettie. I don't know what's going to happen to her now, but I'm glad I don't have to take care of her."

As she walked back behind the counter, I pulled my clue notebook from my purse. As I finished my sandwich, I studied the clues I'd already written. Then I jotted down what April had told me.

*Nettie treated Connie and Georgia like her own kids. Connie and Georgia fought about selling the farm and putting Nettie in a home. Georgia wanted to sell. Connie didn't. Nettie is losing her memory and losing things. (Is that important?)*

I chewed the end of my pen. Money was a great motivation for murder. Had Connie killed her cousin? When she came to the self-storage facility the day before, she acted upset about Georgia's murder, but maybe that's all it was—an act. And Connie and Carla knew each other from. . .where was it? Was it Charlottesville? I made another note in my notebook.

A glance at my watch told me I'd better move on. I had a meeting to attend and more investigating to do.

Before I left, I convinced my mother to run a full-page ad in the play program. Really, all I had to do was tell her that the Cunninghams were doing the same. That's one area where my mother and I are in perfect agreement. The way we feel about Max's family.

———

I arrived a bit early for the play committee meeting, pausing for a deep breath at the band room door. My gaze slid around the room. To my relief, everything was in order.

"Marvin?" The baby was kicking my ribs and making it hard for me to breathe.

He didn't answer. The room was empty. I laid the boxes of doughnuts on a table and decided to take a quick look around before anyone arrived. I needed to see how the lock worked on the door in the instrument storage room that led out to the main hallway.

The storage room hadn't changed since I had been in the band. The various-sized wooden slots held instrument cases. There were only two high windows in the room. No way to escape through them. I walked over to the door that led from the room to the hall. When I had attended school here, the door was left open, and we could come and go as we pleased. Now a lock had been installed—a dead bolt that had to be unlocked with a key.

How did someone kill Georgia and escape from the room, leaving the only entrance to the band room blocked by a chair?

A sound behind me made me jump. I spun around, and Marvin was standing in the doorway to the storage room.

He took a step into the small room. "Mrs. Cunningham, what are you doing here?"

"Call me Trish, please," I said quickly.

I'd done just what I promised Max I wouldn't do. Put myself in a dangerous situation. How easy it would be for Marvin to bash me over the head with an instrument right now and leave me here, then claim he'd been somewhere else. Everyone would think we had a serial instrument basher at the school.

"Uh. . .I used to play the clarinet in marching band. I wondered if things had changed since then. They haven't." I pointed in the general direction of where I'd stored my instrument. "That's where my slot was."

He nodded. "Not a lot has changed around here at least in terms of the physical building. Lots of other things have changed, though."

His body language wasn't that of someone ready to attack me, so I relaxed a bit and motioned toward the door to the hall. "I guess that's one of the changes. We used to be able to come in and out of that door."

"That was done before I came. I keep it locked so that kids can't use the room to make out or steal instruments and pawn them."

"Pawn them?"

"Oh yeah," he said. "They use the money to buy drugs."

My little ideal world just kept crashing in around me. Was I so naive?

He looked over his shoulder. "Say, did you bring the doughnuts?"

"Yes," I said. "Help yourself."

"I'm really hungry." He turned and walked back into the band room.

I took a deep breath of relief, but I could see that keeping my promise to Max to stay out of danger while I gathered clues was going to be harder than I thought.

By the time I walked out of the storage room, Marvin was stuffing his face with a doughnut as if he hadn't eaten in a week. With powdered sugar on his lips, his dress shirt hanging limply on broad, bony shoulders, and pants resting low on his narrow hips, he looked a bit like a scarecrow.

Carla strode into the room and greeted me with a nod and Marvin with a cool glance. She had a clipboard in her hands with papers half an inch thick piled on it. I guessed Max had already talked with her, but she gave me no indication either way, just acknowledged me with that slight nod. I had a feeling she had difficulty focusing on more than one thing at a time. What I didn't understand was why the principal of the school was so involved in the play. Didn't she have office things to do?

When she noticed the boxes I'd brought, she put the clipboard down and chose a cake doughnut, which she delicately nibbled, dabbing her lips with her napkin after each bite.

Other people arrived, including a woman who looked so much like Detective Scott, I knew she had to be his sister. She headed straight for me. That's when I noticed she walked with a cane and a decided limp.

"You've got to be Trish Cunningham," she said when she reached me. "I'm Elissa Scott."

She held out her hand, which I automatically clasped. Her grip was firm and strong. She was tall, with gray eyes and an assessing gaze. I wondered why she was here.

"I'm glad to meet you. I heard you were living with Detective Scott."

"Ah yes." She glanced around at the people gathering in the room then back at me. "News does fly around here."

"Yep." I grinned. "But I also know your niece."

She smiled. "She speaks highly of you and your family."

"She might like me, but I'm not sure your brother does."

Elissa laughed. "Don't worry about him. If he didn't like you, you'd know for sure." Her gaze swept over me. "So, when is your baby due?"

"Less than a month."

"All right, ladies and gentlemen, we need to start this meeting." Carla slapped her clipboard down on Marvin's music stand, interrupting my conversation with Elissa. Marvin's baton fell to the floor, and anger flashed in his eyes as he bent over to pick it up. I was trying to figure out the dynamics between him and Carla when, from the side of my eye, I saw motion at the band room door and turned to see Sherry waving wildly through the window.

I nudged Elissa with my arm. "Does Sherry want me or you?"

Elissa looked over at her niece, who was now pointing with thrusts of her index finger in our direction. "You, I think."

"Excuse me," I murmured. I crossed the room and opened the door. "What's up?"

"Mrs. C., I have to talk to you." The tone of her voice was low and urgent.

"Trish?" Carla said behind me. "We must start this meeting now."

I glanced around and realized that everyone was seated and staring at me. I turned back to Sherry. "All right, why don't you call my cell phone in about an hour?"

"You don't understand," she said. "My dad is on a rampage."

Her anxiety was catching, and my stomach clenched, but I needed to be cool. "I'm not surprised. He's rampaged before."

"No." The poor child was wringing her hands. "Not like this."

"Trish?" Carla repeated in her bossy tone.

"I have to get back to the meeting. I'll call you when I'm done." I patted Sherry's arm. "Don't worry. Things will be fine." I was trying to assure her even though I didn't believe it myself.

Her shoulders slumped. "Just be prepared, okay?" She turned and walked slowly down the hall, leaving me feeling anxious.

I tried to ignore the dread that settled in my stomach as I shut the door. Elissa saved me a seat next to her and patted it. She'd hung her cane on the back of her chair.

"What's up?" she whispered.

"She says her dad is on a rampage."

Elissa snorted, which relieved some of my tension. I had a feeling I was going to like her, but she didn't have a chance to say anything, because Carla glanced at us and pointedly cleared her throat.

"I have drawn up a tentative schedule of when everyone's tasks should be completed." She motioned imperiously at Marvin. "Please hand this out." Then she frowned and looked around the room. "Where is Connie? Marvin, do you know?"

"No, I don't," he said in a flat tone without looking at her. He continued passing out papers as Carla had ordered.

"Well, that's. . ." Carla took a breath. "Well, we'll just work around her, then. You." She pointed at Elissa. "You said you wanted to help somehow. You can help Connie with costumes. You'll need to get in touch with her."

She turned to me. "Now, Trish, please tell us whom you have approached for advertising."

I pulled a folded piece of paper from my purse. It wasn't really a list—I was just pretending—but I didn't need a reminder of the two whole people I'd already talked to. I would just do some quick faking for the rest.

I had opened my mouth to begin my recitation when the door flew open and Detective Eric Scott strode into the room.

Everyone stared at him. I thought Carla was going to have a stroke.

"We're having a meeting here," she said.

"Excuse me. Sheriff's office business." He scanned the room, his gaze skimming over his sister, then locking with mine.

"Trish," he said. "I'd like a word with you. Will you please come with me?"

9

Detective Scott motioned for me to go ahead of him and pulled the band room door shut.

"Why do you do things like this?" I demanded. "Everyone's going to think I killed Georgia or something."

He pointed up the hall as if I hadn't spoken, which didn't surprise me. "Let's go outside to my car."

I stopped midstep. "Can't we talk here? I don't feel like going outside. I need to be in that meeting." The truth was I couldn't have cared less about the meeting, but I was in no mood to talk to him. Sherry had correctly called it. Her father was on a rampage, although it wouldn't be apparent to the casual observer. Self-controlled types like Detective Scott and Max, and even my father, show their emotions in subtle ways, like clenched jaws, stiff bodies, and deceptively low-pitched voices. Not in loud outbursts like my mother. Subtlety was much more intimidating to me.

"We're going outside," he said in a flat tone.

I met his intimidating gaze and shrugged. I would go with him because he was an officer of the law. He had the badge and the gun. However, I would not let myself be browbeaten.

"I've been thinking about all of this," I said breathlessly as I tried to keep pace with him. "Because of that chair behind the door to the band room, there's no way anyone could have left after they bashed in Georgia's head. . .unless they went through the door in the instrument storage room. The door to the instrument room is locked with a dead bolt that you need a key to unlock. Who all has keys? I imagine Marvin does. So would Carla. Actually, so would anybody who had school access. Keys can be copied."

He grunted.

"I wish you would slow down," I grumbled. "I can't breathe."

He did, just a smidgeon.

"This way," he said when we reached the front doors.

He held one open for me, and I walked through. My thoughts were gaining momentum. "Really, now that I think about it, I can't be sure Georgia was bashed with the bassoon. I didn't look at it closely, but I should have. It seems to me there should have been more blood all over the place."

He was walking more quickly now, ahead of me. I trailed behind him, down the sidewalk to his car. When he got there, he turned and faced me with crossed arms.

"What?" I was trying to catch my breath. The baby was kicking my ribs and pressing up against my lungs. "So? Was she bashed with the bassoon?"

"You know I can't give you details."

"Well, you should. I'm not my mother. I'm trustworthy. I could help you." The look in his eyes would have frozen most people to death, but not me. I was too keyed up now to be immobilized by the likes of a rampaging detective. "So what do you want, anyway?"

He looked down at me. "You're investigating the attack on Georgia Winters even though I told you not to."

"Max knows. I told him. Besides, I'm just checking up on things and writing down notes." I stretched my back muscles, which felt like massive, twisted rubber bands.

"Like my daughter is checking up on things?" He said the words so softly, I almost missed them.

Suddenly everything was clear. Detective Scott's rampaging. Sherry's fear. She'd been caught, and she was probably in trouble.

Oh, who was I kidding? *I* was in trouble. I wondered how he'd found out she was looking into things. Then I realized that was stupid. He was a master interrogator. He probably tortured her with his tapping pen.

I met his scowl with crossed arms, mirroring his stubborn stance. "Writing down notes won't hurt anybody."

A satisfied gleam filled his eyes. "So you knew what she was doing?"

"I didn't say that." When would I ever learn to keep my mouth shut? "And writing things down isn't dangerous," I reiterated.

"That depends on how the information is obtained. And it sometimes shows a decided lack of good judgment, especially when people are dabbling where they shouldn't."

"So why don't you tell me exactly how you feel?" I snapped. "Like you don't think I have good judgment?"

He took a deep breath. "Listen, my daughter is stubborn—"

My snort of laughter stopped him.

"What do you find so amusing?" he asked. "There is nothing funny at all about this situation."

"Well, yeah, there is. It's *you* saying *Sherry* is stubborn. Did you expect something different? She's *your* daughter. That alone is enough, really, but come on, Detective. She's also a teenager. And teenager is synonymous with stubborn."

"What do you mean she's my. . ." He shook his head and took a deep breath. "Her age has nothing to do with this. Poor judgment is poor judgment." His eyes flashed.

"So both of us have poor judgment?"

"You said it, not me," he growled.

Poor Sherry—having to deal with him on a regular basis. If only Abbie knew how badly they needed a steadying influence.

"I need to ask you about her, Tommy, and this—"

"Her and Tommy?" I narrowed my eyes at him. "Is that why you're so snippy? Because of Tommy and your daughter? And what about Tommy, Detective Scott? Is he a suspect? Because this whole thing is ruining his reputation. Today my mother informed everyone within fifty miles that you'd questioned him. Not that I should be surprised about that. She has a big mouth. But I really need to know. Is Tommy a suspect?"

The emotion in the detective's eyes died, and his expression flattened. "You know I'm not going to discuss that."

Now I was starting to lose my temper, and, unfortunately, I couldn't control myself nearly as well as he could. "Tommy is my son!"

"And he's almost eighteen," Detective Scott said.

We stared at each other, both of us breathing hard.

"Well, your daughter *is* eighteen. She's officially an adult, so she can do what she likes." I dropped my arms and frowned at him. "And Tommy isn't guilty. How could he be? Even your daughter likes him. That has to mean something."

"Sherry is still immature and doesn't have good sense—"

He snapped his jaw shut. He must have seen the look in my eyes.

We glared at each other. A true standoff. He gave in first.

"I'm sorry. This isn't personal. Or it shouldn't be. Tommy hasn't been charged with anything. But I'm not going to discuss that any further with you."

"I consider your attitude very personal." I wanted to stomp on his toes, but that would be considered assaulting a police officer. I backed up a step. "Are we done?"

"No," the detective said. "I want to know who you've been talking to."

I stared up at him. "Besides Abbie, you mean?"

Touché. He stared at me like a dog with a new food dish.

I tried not to smile with satisfaction. "I'm sure that whole experience put you in a bad mood, but just because she's my best friend doesn't mean you have to take it out on me and Tommy. Besides, why should I tell you anything I find out? You won't tell me anything." Even as I said the words, I knew how immature I sounded. Anger had a way of doing that to me.

His fingers twitched, and he inhaled several times. "I can arrest you for obstruction."

"I doubt that," I said. "I watch television. I'm not obstructing anything. You have no proof I even know anything that would help you with the case. In fact, you're obstructing me. You pulled me out of a meeting and—"

I heard footsteps. The detective's gaze flickered over my shoulder.

"Hey there, Mrs. C. You feelin' okay?" Corporal Fletcher's voice boomed at us.

I turned my back to Detective Scott and faced the corporal. "No. I'm *not* okay."

Behind me I heard Detective Scott's ragged sigh. "Great timing, Fletcher."

Corporal Fletcher's round face drooped. "Sorry, Sarge. Did I interrupt?"

"Yes," Detective Scott said.

"No," I said.

Corporal Fletcher's eyes widened, and his bushy brows rose nearly to his hairline.

"I'm not done talking to you," Detective Scott said.

"Well, I'm done talking to you." I was too mad to even pray and ask God to help me get rid of my anger.

"Trish," Detective Scott said. "If you insist on investigating, be careful."

He sounded so worried I wanted to cave in, but I didn't. No way would I share my notes *or* my best friend with someone who thought my son was a criminal and a bad influence.

I was walking past Corporal Fletcher who looked as worried as the detective sounded.

"Mrs. C., we mean it," the corporal said. He glanced over my head at Detective Scott in some sort of unspoken communication. "Maybe you could even avoid, er, socializing at the school for a while."

As I walked away, I wondered what that meant, but I wouldn't lower myself to turn around and ask.

---

On my way home, I talked to Sherry on the phone, and she apologized for her father's actions. She sounded as if she were about to cry, so I didn't tell her how mad I really was—at her and her father. I didn't like being stuck between the two of them. When I tried once more to talk her out of investigating, she just argued with me. Truthfully, I could understand Detective Scott's frustration with her, and I ended the conversation a little abruptly, ignoring her hurt tone.

Max's car was in the driveway when I got home. I was still steaming mad and ready to dump everything on my husband. I wanted him to sic one of his flashy lawyer friends on Detective Sergeant Eric Scott the know-it-all.

I slammed the door between the kitchen and the garage and flung my purse down on the kitchen table. "Max?" I yelled.

No answer. I stalked down the hall to the front of the house where his office was. The door was shut.

"Max?" I grabbed the knob and pushed. *Locked.*

After a stunned moment, I pressed my ear against the door. I heard murmurs from inside. He was on the phone. My temper, which was already in high gear, roared into overdrive. I wanted to pound the door with my fists, but instead, I took a deep breath and waited.

The murmuring stopped, and then I heard the sounds of Max's shoes on the wood floor. The lock clicked, and he opened the door.

"Why did you lock me out?" I demanded.

"Because I didn't want to be interrupted." Max looked even more tired than he had that morning.

"What's wrong? Did the talk go badly with Carla? Is Tommy going to be expelled or something?"

"The cheating isn't going to be a problem. She knows he didn't do that." He put his hands on my shoulders and turned me around. "Let's go to the kitchen. I could use a glass of lemonade before I go back to work."

"But—" I stopped. "You're going back to work? Why?"

"Because I have to." Max gently prodded me down the hall.

"What if I wanted to spend time with you? I hardly ever see you anymore."

"We're both pretty busy," Max said as we walked into the kitchen.

"Well, do you have time to talk right now?"

"A few minutes," he said.

I bit back a sarcastic comment about making an appointment in the future. "Well, you wouldn't believe what happened today."

"What?" Max murmured as he pulled open the refrigerator and pulled out the pitcher of lemonade. "Want some?"

"Yes, please." I crossed my arms. "Sherry is insisting on investigating Georgia's murder. To save Tommy. And now Detective Scott is mad at me."

Max set the pitcher on the counter and turned to face me. "Sherry is investigating? Because of Tommy? You knew this?"

I nodded. "Yes. And what choice did I have? Last night she told me she wanted the two of us to investigate together. I told her no. She argued and said she'd do it without me if I wouldn't agree to work with her."

Max frowned at me as if it were all my fault.

"Stop looking at me like that." I dropped into a chair and waved my hand. "What was I supposed to do? I know she'd do it on her own anyway. She's stubborn."

His green eyes narrowed. "I guess you would know."

"That's not nice."

"Well, maybe you should have told Eric. Wouldn't you have wanted someone to tell us if it were one of our kids?"

Max had a point, and I didn't like it. "I guess I was just burying my head in the sand. But Detective Scott found out today and yelled at me."

"Did you get it straightened out?" Max pulled two glasses from the cupboard.

"Not really," I said. "I, uh, sort of yelled back at him."

Max glanced at me over his shoulder. "You yelled at him? That probably wasn't real sm— Um, productive."

Max had almost said "smart." That hurt me. "Detective Scott deserved it. He insinuated that Tommy was guilty and that he didn't want Sherry involved with him."

Max poured the lemonade and handed me a glass. "Are you sure you didn't misunderstand him?"

"Well, it's possible," I said grudgingly and slouched in the chair and took a sip as I considered how I felt. "It's really possible. I'm afraid, Max, and my fear could be coloring everything. I don't like the way things are going right now. Not with the kids involved."

"Yeah, me, too." He leaned back against the counter.

"Do you think they're safe at school?"

He hesitated before he answered. "I want to think so."

"Did you know that Karen wanted to investigate, too?"

Max put his glass down hard on the counter. "This keeps getting worse. I hope you told her no."

"Of course I did, but I can't stop what they do at school. And Detective Scott keeps questioning me."

Max stared at me. "I don't think Eric seriously believes that Tommy murdered Georgia."

"Well then, why won't he leave us alone?" I asked.

"He's doing his job, that's all. And I suspect he's making sure you tell him everything you saw that's relevant. The faster he gets this crime solved, the faster some things get back to normal."

Max turned around and stared out the window above the sink. Something else was bugging him. Could today's conversation behind a locked door have anything to do with what he had hidden from me on his desk at work? He took a deep breath then picked up the pitcher.

"Max, what's wrong?"

His fingers tightened on the handle of the pitcher as he put it in the refrigerator. "That's a silly question."

"Well, you act like you're keeping secrets from me," I said. "Remember when Jim Bob was murdered? We agreed. No more secrets. I kept my word. I told you when I was keeping notes. Today you had your office door locked. You were also shoving something around on your desk at work yesterday. What was that about?"

Max took a deep breath. Then he turned to face me. "I have a lot of things on my mind right now and—"

The door to the garage flew open and banged against the wall. Karen burst into the kitchen, followed by Sherry.

"Tommy is at the sheriff's office," Karen said.

"What?" Max and I said at the same time.

Sherry started crying. "My dad took Tommy in for questioning. This is all my fault."

# 10

Max knows lawyers with Harvard educations because he went to Harvard, and he takes full advantage of their services when he needs them. I was familiar with the man he hired to represent Tommy. Calvin Schiller had represented me during the investigation into Jim Bob Jenkins's murder months ago.

I hadn't liked Calvin's attitude back then, and it hadn't changed. When we arrived at the sheriff's office, he was waiting for us in the lobby. He glanced at me as if I were a wad of gum stuck on the bottom of his shoe. Then he smiled at Max.

"Everything is fine," he said in his newscaster quality voice. "They can't question him until I get to the interview room. It'll be short and sweet, believe me." I imagined Calvin came across well in court. His gray suit hung on his portly body with the perfection one can buy only from a personal tailor. He looked to be the perfect combination of sophistication and aged wisdom.

"Should we go with you?" I asked. "I'd really like to be there."

Calvin lost his self-possession for a moment and looked horrified. "No," he said quickly. "I'll take care of everything."

I glanced at Max and read his thoughts. I should butt out.

I tamped down my protective nature while the two of them talked in hushed tones. Max had relaxed. I guessed everything would be fine. Calvin might be a snob, but he was a smart snob. If he said things were okay, I believed him. I told Max I'd meet him outside; then I went out to the SUV. I had some thoughts to put in my notebook.

As I walked to the vehicle, I pulled out my phone. Before I could do anything else, I had to console Sherry, who had begged me to call her with any news.

She answered on the first half of the first ring. "Mrs. C., is Tommy okay?"

"The lawyer is here and assures us things are fine." I unlocked the doors to the SUV and plopped into the passenger seat and shut the door.

Her rapid breaths hissed through the speaker. "Well, this is my fault."

I was relieved she thought so. She should leave the investigation in more capable hands. Like mine and her father's.

"So you'll stop sleuthing, right?" I asked. "Stop asking questions?"

"No way," she said.

I was momentarily speechless, which was just as well, because she obviously had more to tell me.

"I have to keep going on this. I'm in a great position to hear things at the school. Like I said, no one pays much attention to me. I can find out stuff even you can't. I've already learned a couple of interesting things."

As much as I wanted to know the interesting things she'd found out, I was more afraid of her father's reaction. "Sherry, you, uh, said Tommy being hauled down here was your fault for investigating. What did you have in your notebook?"

"Not much. Just a few things. But enough that Daddy knew what I was doing."

"But if your investigating got Tommy in trouble, shouldn't you stop before something else happens?"

She laughed—just a little maniacally, I thought. "Oh, I didn't mean it was because I investigated. It was my fault because I was stupid enough to leave my notebook where Daddy could find it."

Her statement was illogically logical. Shades of me. That was scary.

"I don't know about this—"

"Don't worry, Mrs. C. I'll be fine."

"Your father is frantic with worry. I understand how he feels."

I felt anger in her silence.

"Sherry—"

"Does that mean you don't want to hear what I've found out?"

"If I can't talk you out of investigating, will you promise me something?"

"What?" she asked.

"Keep your cell phone with you at all times. Don't put yourself in any dangerous situations. Make sure your dad knows where you are."

"I will. I promise."

She had agreed too quickly, and her promise was about as useless as mine was to Max. Sometimes dangerous situations just happen. I had to think of a way to get her to stop, but in the meantime, I did want to know what she had discovered.

"All right. Tell me what you learned."

"I volunteer in the library sometimes, and the librarians are always gossiping. They think Mr. Slade likes the costume lady."

"Connie Gilbert?"

"Yeah. And Ms. Winters and Ms. Gilbert, the costume lady, had a huge fight the day Ms. Winters was murdered. In the library. Ms. Gilbert was in there using the computer."

"The librarian said something about an argument."

"Well, Ms. Winters made Ms. Gilbert get off the computer and leave the library."

"Do you know why?"

"Nope, but they were both really mad. I wonder if there was some sort of love triangle going on between Ms. Winters, Mr. Slade, and Ms. Gilbert." Sherry's breath came faster. "Maybe Mr. Slade and Ms. Gilbert were. . .you know."

I didn't want Sherry to be thinking about things like. . .you know. Especially since she was interested in my son.

"Maybe that's why Ms. Winters is dead," Sherry said.

Love triangles. That meant potential hostility. Lots of it. "This is really serious. You shouldn't—"

"And Ms. Bickford has a plan," she announced.

"A plan? What kind of a plan?"

"I don't know. I overheard that when I was in the library, too. You should have heard that librarian." Sherry giggled. "She hates cops and was bragging that she was questioned and didn't give in. I don't think she knows who my dad is."

"I can guarantee she doesn't know who your dad is, or you wouldn't be in there helping her." I questioned Sherry for more details about Carla, but she had none.

"There's an emergency closed-door school board meeting tonight," she said. "Oh, and one more thing."

"What's that?"

"This is really strange. My dad told me not to eat or drink anything that anyone gives me. Only what I bring to school myself."

"Why?" I remembered what Corporal Fletcher had said about socializing at the school.

"He wouldn't say, but I already told Tommy."

That changed things. The danger wasn't hypothetical anymore; it was very real.

"Sherry. . ." I wanted to try to stop her from investigating further.

"Don't say it, Mrs. C. You can't talk me out of it. So I'll call you if I find out anything else." Then she hung up.

I pushed the END button on my cell phone. Sherry was right. She *could* find out things that no one else could. However, the more I learned, the more concerned I was.

Max made a good point earlier. I would want to know if one of my kids was behaving like Sherry. As much as I dreaded doing it, I had to let Detective Scott know she was pursuing her investigation.

In the meantime, I needed to add to my notes. I got my clue notebook and awkwardly balanced it on the purse on my knees. I added, *Connie and Georgia had a big fight in the library. Georgia made Connie get off the computer. Possible love triangle between Georgia, Marvin, and Connie. Carla has a plan.*

*Detective Scott told Sherry not to eat or drink at the school.*

I paused to reflect on that point. Did that mean that Georgia hadn't been bashed in the head? Maybe she'd been poisoned? I tapped my pen furiously on the paper, rereading everything I'd written.

I was flipping through my pages when a tap on the window made me jump. I looked up and saw Corporal Fletcher standing there in his uniform.

"Hey," I said, after I rolled down the window.

"Hi, Mrs. C. You okay?"

"Yep."

He looked at the notebook in my hand then back up at me with a sharpened gaze. "Keeping notes?"

I slapped the notebook shut. "Yes. Now perhaps you can tell me why I should avoid socializing at the school."

He cleared his throat and wouldn't meet my eyes. "Just trust me, Mrs. C."

"You mean, like don't ingest anything anyone gives me?"

"Um, yeah."

The way the cops had to pussyfoot around irritated me.

After glancing over the top of my SUV, he rubbed his shoe on the pavement then met my gaze. "Listen, Sarge is a good guy, really."

"Well, you couldn't prove it by me," I said irritably.

"He's worried and under a great deal of pressure to solve this case." Corporal Fletcher sighed. "I shouldn't talk about this, but he, um, really likes your friend."

"Really? Well that's too bad. I wouldn't wish him on anyone."

"Come on, Mrs. C. That's a little harsh."

"Well, he was really rude to me today."

"He's worried about you and about Sherry."

"Then he should say that instead of acting like a jerk."

The corporal shook his head. "You know what our jobs are like. We aren't trained to be sweethearts."

"Maybe not, but I still don't like it."

"Listen, you only see his cop side. Really, he's a great guy." Corporal Fletcher was so earnest.

"Abbie thinks he's going to get even with her for turning him down. Like not helping her research her books anymore."

"That's not like him at all."

"Well, after we had our *discussion* this afternoon, and he found out I knew about Abbie, he immediately went and pulled Tommy in for questioning."

The corporal shook his head. "One had nothing to do with the other." He leaned toward me. "He wouldn't hurt her. He likes her a lot." He eyed me with one slightly raised brow.

I met his gaze, and the truth finally dawned on me. "You want us to play matchmaker, don't you? I can't believe you. No. I don't think so, Corporal Fletcher. You don't know Abbie. She's—"

He put his arms behind his back and stared at me with no expression.

"Oh yeah," I said. "Go hide behind your blank cop look. I'm a mother. I can read minds."

The corner of his mouth twitched. "He makes good money. He owns his own house. He's stable." He winked at me. "He thinks your friend is a knockout."

"He thinks Abbie is. . .well, I have to agree. I'm glad he noticed, because she is. But, really. He has an angry daughter. He's annoyingly persistent. He carries a gun, and he has irregular hours."

"Mmm," was all Corporal Fletcher said.

"Mmm," I imitated him. "I hate it when you guys *mmm*." Then a sudden thought crossed my mind. "Did Detective Scott request to be Abbie's consultant?"

For a moment, I didn't think Corporal Fletcher would answer. Then he nodded.

Perhaps the corporal was right. If Detective Scott wanted to see Abbie that badly, she should at least go out with him. Maybe he would be nicer to me if he was dating her.

"So?" Corporal Fletcher asked.

"Oh, okay. Fine. I'll give it some thought." I eyed him. "So, while you're being so friendly and all, how close are you to solving the murder?"

The amused look in his eyes died. "It's an ongoing investigation."

"I know, but why would someone kill Georgia?"

Corporal Fletcher stood taller and put his hands to his side. "Mrs. C., you know better. I can't talk about that."

"Not even just saying yes or no? Like, if I ask a question, you could just nod or shake your head?"

"Not even," he said.

"Figures," I grumbled. "Well, I'm keeping my ears open, anyway."

He leaned forward and put his hands on the car. "What have you heard?"

"Is that fair?" I said to the corporal. "You won't tell me anything, but you expect me to share?"

"You should tell us anything you know that could be useful," he droned.

I shrugged. "I have very little information, but I plan to talk to some other people." I took a deep breath. "Sherry is still insisting on asking questions, too, even though her father told her not to." I felt like a traitor.

"That young lady has real issues." The corporal leaned against my SUV. "You know I should tell Sarge she's still up to that."

"I agree. Better you tell him than me. You know, Corporal Fletcher, I *am* a mom, and despite how irresponsible Detective Scott thinks I am, I don't want anyone's kid in danger."

"He doesn't think that, and neither do I."

"Earlier today he implied I lacked good judgment."

"He was just frustrated. Really, we just think you're. . ." He stuck his thumb in his belt. "Well, we think you're overzealous."

I had to smile at that. "That's a nice way to say that I'm terribly annoying. All right. I'll let you know if I find out anything important."

The front door of the building opened, and Max and Calvin Schiller strode out onto the sidewalk and headed toward the parking lot.

Corporal Fletcher straightened, a frown etching deep lines in his forehead. "You investigating this is not a good idea, Mrs. C."

"Why not?" I asked.

"I don't have to tell you that. You know exactly what can happen when a murderer gets mad."

11

When I walked into the self-storage office on Thursday morning, Shirl greeted me with a toothpaste commercial smile. Stranger still, I saw books on her desk that weren't her usual bodice-ripping fare. But the oddest thing of all was the lineup of assorted sizes of bottles and plastic bags filled with dried green and brown weedy-looking stuff.

"Hope the cops don't come by. It looks like you're dealing drugs." I grabbed the mail. "I assume these are legal?"

She sniffed and waved her arm over the assembled plastic containers. "These are herbs." She pronounced the *h*. "They're going to keep me from having to ever use pharmaceutical drugs again."

*Pharmaceutical.* That was a big word. I glanced over her collection and wondered if one of them was black *cobash*.

She tapped the stack of books. "I'm studying these now. That's where I've been going at lunch. To classes. My pharmacist teaches them."

"Oh." I thumbed through the envelopes looking for bills to pay.

She narrowed her eyes and stared at me. "You really do look like you could use something. You're pale and puffy, and you look tense. There's herbs for that, too, you know."

"Puffy?" I looked at my fingers. "I'm puffy?"

She looked me up and down. "Your ankles maybe. It could just be all the weight you've gained, but you're probably holding water, too."

"All the weight I've gained? My ankles are puffy?" I knew my pants were tight, but. . .

Shirl stared pointedly at my hips. "Well, it's to be expected. Mr. C. said you're eating like three times as much as normal."

"He said that?"

Before Shirl could answer, she was distracted by someone outside. "Now who is that, I wonder?"

I didn't care. I had my leg extended so I could stare at my ankle. It did look swollen. I had to call Max right away and ask him if he thought I was fat. Was that why he was avoiding me lately?

Shirl squinted. "That guy out there sure looks familiar, but he hasn't been here before, I know that. I know all of our customers by sight and name."

Finally, I turned and peered through the large front window at the man getting out of his car. I would have recognized his lanky frame anywhere.

"It's Marvin Slade," I said to Shirl.

"Marvin Slade?" Shirl stood and leaned over the counter to stare at him as he walked up the sidewalk to the front door. "Name sounds familiar."

"It should. He's the band director at the high school."

Shirl harrumphed. "One of the suspects, you mean."

Marvin met my gaze through the glass as he grabbed the doorknob.

Shirl was breathing hard. "We need to get him out of here as quickly as possible, Mrs. C. We don't need murderers coming. . ."

"Hi, Marvin," I said over her voice. "What can we do for you?"

"I'm just here to check something in Connie's new storage unit. Costume stuff." He pulled a shiny key from his pocket. "I have the key and the code to get through the gate. Is it okay for me to go in there?"

"As long as you have the key and the code, you can go into the unit."

Shirl made noises behind me, opening a file drawer and slamming it, but I ignored her.

"Is Connie okay?" I asked.

He shrugged. "How should I know?"

"Well, that's what I thought," Shirl said.

We both turned toward her.

She waved a contract in my face. "Connie's got Georgia down as her emergency contact, not Marvin."

He swallowed and turned his watery gaze on me.

I felt sorry for him and wanted to agree with what my daughter had said. This man couldn't possibly be a murderer. Still, some of the worst killers in history looked and acted harmless in public.

"What does that mean?" he asked. "I can't go in?"

Shirl sniffed. "Well—"

"It's fine," I said to Shirl. "You know the rules. When someone has the key, they can go in. Besides, I'm part of all this, too, because of the play." I turned to him. "You can go in. You've got my permission."

Marvin's wide, bony shoulders were hunched over as if he were in pain. He looked like a hound dog someone had hit with salt pellets from a shotgun. He smiled weakly at me. "I don't know where her units are."

"I'll show you." I motioned to the door. "I'll walk up there. Once you get through the gate, you can follow me in your car."

As I walked behind him to the front door, I heard Shirl clear her throat.

"Now I know where I saw you," she blurted out. "At the pharmacy. Night before last, around seven."

Marvin turned and eyed her over my shoulder as though she were a stalker. I didn't blame him.

"Shirl has a memory for faces," I explained. "That's why she's so good at her job here." I didn't bother to tell him she could rival my mother for collecting gossip and facts about people.

"Oh." He still looked at her with drawn brows. "Well, I'll be going then." He edged toward the door.

"You be careful," Shirl said. "What with your heart and all, we wouldn't want you to keel over dead in the parking lot."

My mouth dropped open, probably in a good imitation of Marvin's. Whatever herbs Shirl was taking seemed to have short-circuited what little control she normally had on her mouth. I had my back to her, so when Marvin glanced at me with wide eyes, I rolled mine toward the ceiling and mouthed, "I'm sorry."

He dipped his head in acknowledgment, turned, and left without further comment.

"He's a weirdo," Shirl said behind me.

It takes one to know one, as my mother would say.

I faced her. "How do you know he has a heart problem?"

"I heard him talking to my new pharmacist about some kind of heart medicine."

"And you just stood there and listened?"

She shrugged. "Can't help but overhear things, the place is so small."

"Well, why is he a weirdo?"

"He's known as a ladies' man. Now that I've seen him, I'm shocked. Can you believe it, the way he looks with that bald head and elf ears? I heard he's always dating someone." Shirl shook her head. "Makes you wonder what he's got going for himself. Can you imagine?"

No, I couldn't. Nor did I want to.

"I'm going to show him where Connie's unit is." I twisted the knob on the front door.

"If you're not back in five minutes, I'm calling the cops and coming up there with a baseball bat. I keep one in my car, you know." Shirl opened a large tote bag and began stuffing her various bottles and bags into its depths. "You shouldn't be alone with a murderer."

"We don't know he's a murderer."

"And we don't know he isn't. I'll tell you what. There's just something not right about a man like that. Ugly as a catfish but gets women. You mind my words. It's a black widower thing. Some kind of attraction that normal women can't feel, but the victims. . .they're needy."

"Shirl!"

"You know it's true. Now, if he looked like Mr. C., I could understand it. I mean all the women swoon over him. He's as nice as he is good-looking. You should hear what they say when he walks away, especially about his. . ." She glanced quickly at me then away again. "Well, anyway, he just gets better looking as time goes by. I'm surprised you don't have to put a ball and chain on him to keep him from wandering."

Just what I needed to hear when I was already feeling fat and undesirable. Unwelcome feelings of insecurity crammed my mind with pictures of model-like women swarming all over my husband. And me with my tight maternity pants, fat behind, and swollen ankles. Why hadn't I noticed I was gaining that much weight? I had to get away from Shirl because I had a sudden urge to cry.

—

I met Marvin at the entrance to the climate-controlled building and showed him how to use the code. We stepped inside, and I pointed to Connie's units, keeping a good five feet between us. I intended to question him, and if he made a move toward me, I would be able to escape. My first goal was to determine which of the two women he had been interested in.

"I'm really sorry about your loss," I said.

His forehead wrinkled in a frown. "My loss?"

"Um, yeah. Georgia?" I backed up a few steps toward the door, getting ready to run if I had to.

He blinked. "Why would I care about her? All she did was make people's lives miserable. Well, at least Connie's."

He sounded angry. I pressed my body against the door. "Have you seen Connie lately?"

"Yes," he said. "Why do you want to know?"

I shrugged. "Just wondered. So, are you on your break or lunch or something?"

"Break?" he asked.

"Yeah. I'm surprised you aren't at school today."

His eyes flashed with annoyance. "Yeah, a break."

This wasn't going to be productive at all, and he was making me nervous.

Suddenly, his eyes met mine, and his face darkened with anger. "I know what you're doing."

"You do?"

"You're trying to solve this mystery, aren't you? I've heard about you."

I stepped backward toward the door until I felt it against my back.

"I didn't kill her," he said.

I groped behind me for the door handle. "Um, that's great. I'm glad. You could go to jail for that. And be executed. . .and all." Shirl's words about him being a murderer kept ringing in my head. "Do you need anything else?"

He shook his head. "No, nothing. I'm fine. Thank you."

I yanked the door open, rushed down the parking lot, and flung open the door to the office.

Shirl looked up from her computer. "Well? Did he try to kill you?"

"Would I be standing here if he had?" I giggled, but it was from nervousness. "In fact, he assured me he hadn't killed her."

Shirl snorted. "Mark my words. Something's up with him."

I walked back to my office and fired up my computer, trying to quell the shakiness in my knees. After checking through some e-mails and opening the bills, I had calmed down enough to think logically. Maybe I should look over my notes. I needed to start thinking of intelligent questions to find the answers to.

A big one: *Motive. What reason would the suspects who had access to Georgia have to murder her?*

I looked at my suspect list. I had to find out more about everyone. Including Georgia. But I could jot down a few ideas.

*Marvin Slade—pawning instruments? He had a key. He was there.*

*Carla Bickford—has a plan. What plan—is it what she mentioned about upping the school security system?*

*Connie Gilbert—angry with Georgia? Why? Fighting over selling the farm?*

*Coach Kent Smith—giving kids steroids? Didn't want Jason kicked off the team?*

No other suspects made sense.

"That Marvin person is leaving," Shirl yelled from the other office. "Now what do you suppose he was doing? Hiding a murder weapon?"

"I doubt it," I yelled back. I didn't tell her my suspicions.

I jotted down, *How: Was she murdered with the bassoon, or was it poison?*

I needed to find out more about the people involved in this, and I knew one person who had access to information from all over town.

I called Doris's Doughnuts, and my mother answered. She must have seen my name on caller ID. "Trish, I hope this isn't bad news. I've been worried sick about you. Just sick."

I felt guilty for leading her on the day before. "I'm fine, Ma. I just have a question for you."

"Are you sure you're fine? You should go to the doctor."

"I am. Tomorrow. Listen, I need to know everything you know about Georgia, Marvin Slade, Connie Gilbert, Carla Bickford, and Kent Smith."

"Well, hallelujah and pass the offering plate. You *are* solving this mystery." I heard her hand rubbing on the receiver as she covered it. "Girls," she yelled. "You wouldn't believe it, but Trish is going to solve this mystery."

"Ma, please. Don't advertise the fact."

She laughed. "Nobody here is going to tell anyone."

Right. And doughnuts are fat free.

"I'll do some asking around." She sounded excited.

"That would be great. And you're watching Charlie and Sammie tonight so I can go to Bible study, right?"

"Yes," she said.

Maybe this would put me back in her good graces for a while. I hung up and tucked my steno pad back into my purse. I would go even though I hadn't finished studying and just fake my way through the study. That made me feel very guilty.

———

I picked up Charlie and Sammie from the sitter's, and Charlie babbled all the way home about getting a pine snake. He'd wanted a snake for a long time now, but I wasn't ready for a reptile in my house.

When I pulled into the driveway, I was surprised to see Max's car. That reminded me of my conversation with Shirl, which reminded me how good-looking Max was and how we'd had so little time together lately. Like he'd been avoiding me.

Charlie was still blabbering at me when I got out of the vehicle.

"It's just a little pine snake," he said.

"Not right now," I said as I walked inside the house.

"But—"

"No," I said again. "We've talked about this enough, Charlie. I told you, no snake right now."

"Maybe I should just go somewhere like a private school to live. Then I could have a snake. I could have anything I wanted." Charlie stalked past me, through the kitchen, and into the family room.

The phone started ringing before I could follow him and discuss his sour attitude. I didn't need this on top of my raging hormones.

Max walked into the kitchen. I blew him a kiss and yanked the receiver from the wall. "Hello."

"Patricia."

Only one person in the world calls me Patricia. Lady Angelica Louise Carmichael Cunningham, otherwise known as Max's mother. She's not a literal lady. She just plays one in real life. That's not nice to say, of course, but she's not nice. At least not to me. Max was passing behind me with his briefcase.

"Hello, Angelica."

Max put the briefcase on a kitchen chair and held out his hand. "Give me the phone," he mouthed.

"Hang on. Max wants to talk to you." I handed the phone to him.

Without even so much as a smile, he removed it from my hand.

"Mother?" he said into the mouthpiece. "I'm on my way to Dad's office now. . .no." After a pause, he glanced at me. "No."

Max was being more abrupt than usual with his mother. Normally they treated each other with cool dignity and just a touch of affection at special times, like birthdays and Christmas. On occasion he'd get irritated with her and treat her with gentle disdain, much like his father did. The only time I'd ever seen him angry with her beyond reason was when she had insulted me in front of him. She learned quickly. Now she waits until he's not around. She knows I'm not a sissy, and I'm not going to go whining to my husband. I like to settle my own differences.

I busied myself doing nothing at the kitchen sink so I could listen, but Max left the room with the phone. I was tempted to follow him. His odd behavior the last few days in combination with this cryptic phone call was enough to make me start a mystery notebook dedicated just to him.

As I emptied the dishwasher, Karen passed through the kitchen on her way to work. "Hey, Mom, you're still working on the mystery, right?"

"Yes," I said.

"Good, because things are getting really bad at school. Mr. Slade wasn't there today."

"What?" I turned around. "He wasn't there all day?"

"No." She opened the door to the garage. "Oh, I'm going to the football game Saturday night."

"Sure, that's fine."

She left, closing the door gently behind her, and I turned back to the sink. Why had he led me to believe he had been at school today?

Karen's mention of the football game gave me an idea. Maybe I could collect clues there.

When Max returned to the kitchen, I stood in his path. "I'm going to the football game on Saturday. You want to go?"

Max raised one eyebrow. "You don't like football." He knew exactly why I wanted to go to the game.

I stuck my chin in the air. "I think I should support the school right now, given everything that's going on."

"Right," he said. "Yes, I'll go. If for no other reason than to watch out for you."

"That would be great." I paused. "Max, are you still attracted to me?"

He blinked. "Why would you ask me that?"

"Because Shirl said that you said I was eating three times as much as normal."

He laughed. "You are." He slipped his arm around me and pulled me into a hug. I opened my mouth to protest, but he leaned down and cut me off with a kiss. When Max sets out to deflect my attention, he does a great job.

It wasn't until after he'd left to take the kids to my parents' house that I realized he'd also deflected my attention from asking more about his mother's phone call.

———

During Bible study at church, one of the women brought up the scripture from Romans about food and eating, "If your brother is distressed because of what you eat, you are no longer acting in love." The group discussed this at some length, and I tried to fake my way through, but I was distracted by all the other things on my mind and couldn't concentrate. I didn't understand what that had to do with a lesson on the fruit of the Spirit, particularly love. Afterward, as I was leaving, Marion, the leader, called to me. My stomach clenched, thinking she noticed somehow that I hadn't done my work. I hated to disappoint her, she was so nice.

"Trish, I'm glad I caught you."

I smiled.

"I just want you to know how sorry I am that you're involved in such a tragedy. I spoke with Georgia on numerous occasions about the Lord when I went to visit her and Nettie, and I'm confident that no matter how horribly she died, she is now rejoicing in heaven."

My heart felt instantly lighter. I hadn't realized how badly not knowing that had bothered me.

"I'm on the school board, you know." She leaned closer to me. "I'm telling you this just to keep you from worrying about your children. Coach Smith and Marvin Slade have been put on administrative leave."

"Really?"

"Yes." She patted my arm. "Just know that I'm praying for you."

As I left the church, I felt warmed by her compassion, but that was mixed with anger. Why had Marvin led me to believe he was going into Connie's storage unit for school play purposes if he was on administrative leave?

**12**

One of the worst parts of pregnancy are the frequent doctor visits toward the end. Since I was starting my ninth month, I was now going each Friday morning to be poked and prodded in personal places.

The paper gown felt rough on my skin as I pulled myself up on the examining table. I determinedly avoided looking at my ankles. I was glad I couldn't see my rear end.

I wanted to distract myself from my fat flaws by rechecking my steno pad, but it was across the room in my purse, and I didn't feel like clambering off the table to get it.

I heard a knock. "Come in."

Dr. Williams breezed in and smiled at me. Her gray-haired bob was cut just below her ears. "So, Trish, how are you feeling?" She motioned for me to get into position.

"Oh, pretty rotten, really," I said. "I'm exhausted. My ankles look fat. My pants are tight. And I'm really cranky."

"That good, hmm?" When she was done with her exam, she patted my knee and told me to sit up. "Things look great with the baby. Right on target, although you need to remember that you had Sammie a couple of weeks early." She slipped her gloves off and dropped them into the wastebasket. "Everything you've mentioned is perfectly normal for most women. However, you've gained more weight than I would have liked. Especially within the last few weeks. I know you were thin to begin with, but gaining this much weight isn't good."

I wanted to sink through the floor. "Are you saying I'm fat?"

"I want you to stop eating for two now." She made a note on my chart. "Just cut out the sweets. That should do it." She closed my folder. "Do you have any other questions for me?"

"Yes. Would herbal teas help me?"

From Dr. Williams's immediate frown and the way she put her hands on her hips, I might as well have said, "Do you mind if I sniff glue?"

"Do not use anything like that unless you check with me first," she ordered. "Herbs. . .and drugs can be dangerous to babies. In fact, they can be dangerous, period."

———

I was discouraged. Even my doctor thought I was fat. To distract myself, I decided to hit up some places for advertising on my way back to the office. I started at the Shopper's Super Saver. Then I stopped at Bo's Burger Barn, where I bought some onion rings to soothe my emotions. The doctor had said no *sweets*. She hadn't said no onion rings.

I ended my trip at the dry cleaners where I always take Max's suits. The owner's daughter, a cute teenager, was behind the counter and smiled at me as I walked in. "Hey, Mrs. C."

"Hi." I put my purse on the counter and explained why I had come.

"I think Dad's already helping," she said. "We dry-cleaned some of the costumes for the play. Mr. Slade came and picked them up."

"He did? When?"

She bit her lip and thought. "Well, it wasn't yesterday, because I wasn't here. It was probably Wednesday."

The day before he came out to Four Oaks Self-Storage. Was he helping Connie work on costumes even though he was on leave? I shifted my purse strap to my other shoulder.

The owner's daughter put her elbows on the counter. "You know, Mr. Slade acted really weird."

"Like how?"

"Well, I found some papers in the pockets of the clothes and put them aside like I always do. Dad drilled that into me for years and years. When Mr. Slade came, I handed them to him. He got all upset and grabbed them from my hands."

"Really? What were the papers?"

She shrugged. "Dunno. They just looked like receipts to me, and maybe some bills."

"Were all the clothes costumes?"

She frowned at me. "Dunno." Her gaze flickered over my shoulder as a buzzer signaled someone entering the shop. There probably wasn't much more she could tell me, anyway.

"Thank you," I said. "And I'll make sure to mention in the program that your father is helping."

"Thanks." She turned to the new customer.

My cell phone rang as I got into my car.

"Hello."

"Mrs. C.!" Heavy breathing wooshed through the receiver. "You wouldn't believe what just happened!"

"Shirl? Stop yelling. I can't understand you."

"The police were all over the place!"

"What?"

"The place was crawling with cops. Looked like an FOP meeting or something."

"FOP. . .what is. . .never mind. Just tell me what's going on." I turned the key in the ignition, my heart pounding.

"They searched Connie's units. All of them." Shirl was breathing so hard, it sounded like she was standing in a windstorm.

"I'm on my way." I started to put my SUV in reverse.

"Wait!" she said.

"Shirl—"

"Just hang on. You shouldn't drive when you talk on the phone. You know how deadly that can be. It's bad enough people are keeling over at the high school and—"

"I'm about to get irritated with you," I said. "I want to know what's going on *right now*."

"Hang on." She paused.

"Shirl?"

"Just hang on, I said. Mr. C. wants to talk to you."

I wanted to scream into the empty air.

"Trish." His deep voice sounded calm. "Hang on while I go to my office."

If one more person told me to hang on, I was going to hang up. The phone clicked; then he picked up again. "Honey, Shirl's in an uproar, but things are fine." He laughed. "She loves drama."

That was an understatement. My heartbeat slowed. "Why were the cops there?"

"They said it was routine."

"They always say that." My mind went in a million directions. Had Marvin put something in a unit? "So they did search Connie's units like Shirl said?"

"Yes. It's part of the investigation. They had a search warrant."

I tapped my fingers on the steering wheel. "Are they gone now?"

"Yes."

"Was Detective Scott there? Did they take anything away?"

"Yes, he was here. And, yes, I think they took some things away."

Oh, I wished I had been there. "Is Connie a suspect?"

"Honey, I don't know," he said. "What I want to know is what the doctor said today."

"Oh, I'm fine. The baby's fine." I didn't mention how fat I was getting.

"Good. Well, I'm headed out to Baltimore. Shirl is calming down."

"Would you please tell her that I'll be there in about an hour?"

"Sure."

We exchanged telephone smooches, and after we hung up, I pulled my steno pad from my purse and made some notes. After staring at what I'd written for two minutes, I knew exactly what I had to do next.

## 13

That I would willingly appear in Detective Eric Scott's office was a minor miracle. He must have thought so, too, because his face was screwed up in a quizzical frown.

"Have a seat." He pointed to the chair in front of his desk. "You know we were out at Four Oaks Self-Storage this morning, right? We talked to Max."

"Yes, and that's why I'm here."

He took a deep breath. "We had a warrant." Dark, puffy circles under his eyes and the tension lines creasing his forehead made me inclined to feel sorry for him.

"I don't care about that. It's fine. I'm just here to help you."

He winced. "To help me?"

By his tone of voice, I could tell my offer of help wasn't welcome. My sympathy faded, and I bit back an angry retort. "Don't panic. It's just something you should know." I reached into my purse and pulled out my steno pad.

"Is that what I think it is?" he asked.

"My clue notebook." I licked a finger and flipped the pages.

A stream of breath hissed through his lips.

I glanced up at him. "Oh, come on. Stop with all the sighs. Can't you just accept the fact that I collect clues and quit making a big deal out of it?"

He shook his head. "No. You're a civilian. You're not a trained police officer. It isn't safe."

"You sometimes use informants, don't you? Besides, I came here of my own free will, out of the goodness of my heart, to tell you something. The least you could do is be friendly."

He tapped his pen on the desk and stared at me. "Fine. What is it?"

I put my finger on the page. "Connie just got her new unit last Tuesday. The day after the murder."

He pursed his lips. "Okay."

"On Thursday, Marvin came to Self-Storage with a key to look inside one of Connie's units."

"Shirl told us that," Detective Scott said. "And Max assured us that's on this side of legal. If someone has the key and the code."

"Yep. The thing is, he insinuated he was there for school play business." I stared at the detective. "But he was already on administrative leave. He had no business there. If I had known that, I probably wouldn't have allowed him in."

"So?"

"Well, I did wonder if he was planting something or hiding something."

"Mmm." Detective Scott's eyes narrowed. "Anything else?"

I flipped to the page in my notebook that I'd just filled out. "I was at the dry cleaners just a few minutes ago. Connie had a bunch of costumes there to be cleaned. Marvin went to get them on Wednesday. That was the day before he looked in Connie's unit."

The detective stopped moving. "And?"

"The girl who works there said she had pulled some papers out of the pockets of a few of the costumes. She handed them to him. He got upset. Then he took all the costumes and left."

Detective Scott leaned forward. "What kind of papers?"

"She said some bills and some receipts and things like that."

He tapped his pen harder. "Trish, you shouldn't be—"

"I didn't purposely try to dig up this information. I went to the dry cleaners to ask them to advertise in the play program." I flipped through my notes. "Were you aware that people are saying Coach Smith helped football players cheat so they could stay on the team? And there are rumors that he used steroids." I bit my lip for a second. "In fact, some bagger kid at the Shopper's Super Saver insinuated that the coach was giving the players something."

Detective Scott cleared his throat. I met his gaze, but his eyes were shuttered. "What kid told you this?"

I shrugged. "I don't know his name. Spiky hair, piercings, tattoos, smoker, says 'dude' all the time, and looks and acts like he's done his own share of drugs."

"I see."

"That's all." I stuffed my steno pad back in my purse. "I'm trying not to get into trouble."

"Right." His sarcastic tone left little doubt of his opinion on that matter. He got up, walked around his desk, and stood by the door to his office. "Trish, I do appreciate the fact that you came to talk to me. That's good."

"But? I can hear a *but* in there."

He sighed again. "But I'm worried. This isn't a game."

"I'm not playing a game."

"Maybe you don't think you are, just like my daughter doesn't think she is."

I hiked my purse strap higher on my shoulder. "May I give you a piece of advice about your daughter, Detective?"

"Can I stop you?"

I glared at him. "Yes, you can. Just say no."

He closed his eyes and pinched the top of his nose; then he looked at me again. "I'm sorry. That was rude."

"Yes, it was." I debated saying anything at all, since he'd irritated me once again, but then I remembered the bitter tone in Sherry's voice when she talked about her father. "One thing I have experience with is being a parent to a teenager. It's not like sleuthing. It's something I really understand."

"So go ahead." He leaned against the door frame. "I might be able to use some advice."

His admission surprised me, and for the first time since I'd met him, he looked vulnerable. "Sherry is angry right now. What she could use is some unconditional love from you. Do some fun things together, Detective. Spend time with her, but don't spend that time nagging her or lecturing her." I took a deep breath. "Have you ever listened to her laugh? She's got a wonderful laugh."

He swallowed and blinked hard.

I smiled. "In order for a parent to really make an impact, a kid has to know how much they care. Communication with understanding is the key, even when the kid doesn't act like they're listening." I walked out the door; then I stopped and glanced at him over my shoulder. "That goes for adults, too, by the way. You can't expect people to read your mind about all the things you don't say."

—

My mother's farm kitchen smelled of roasting meat, boiling potatoes, and green beans cooked in ham stock, making me feel homey.

"I hope you're feeling better now," my mother said to me as she handed me a baking sheet for rolls. "I found out some things to help you solve this mystery, but I don't want to be blamed for killing my grandchild by putting you into shock."

"If finding Georgia didn't put me into shock, I doubt what you have to say will." I placed refrigerator roll dough that Ma had made earlier on the baking sheet.

"You can never tell," Ma said. "Could be something simple added to everything else, like building blocks. One last block on top of the pile, and the whole thing falls to pieces all over the place."

"Well then, be gentle with your blocks." I rinsed off my hands and put the rolls in the oven.

"Don't be smart with me, missy," she said.

"Sorry. But you can tell me."

Ma put her hands on her hips. "Well, if you pass out, don't blame me."

Sounds of the television came from the family room where the men were assembled. Men didn't work in the kitchen at my mother's house.

Ma put tea bags in a pitcher and poured boiling hot sugar water over them. "Well, Gail was talking to her hairdresser, whose daughter, Twila, is the principal's new secretary at the school."

"Mmm-hmm." She must have been the poor person Carla had called and barked at the day I'd been in her office.

"Well," Ma continued, "seems Twila comes home mad most days. That Bickford woman is impossible to work for."

"I can imagine. She comes across like a dictator."

"Hitler. Everything has to be her way. No one can have any thoughts but her." Ma turned and stared at me. "Thing is, that Carla was all buddy-buddy with Georgia, but not at the end."

"Really?"

"Yep. They had a big fight the day before Georgia up and got herself killed."

"What about?"

Ma shook her head. "Who knows? But Twila says Georgia tore out of Carla's office like she'd stumbled onto a yellow jacket nest."

Right then, Abbie's shadow appeared at the back door. I had a sense of déjà vu. From the time we became friends in kindergarten, Abbie loved coming to my house. She was raised by her grandmother, a very rigid woman who demanded more perfectionism than any kid was capable of. The woman had held grudges like kittens, bringing them out daily for feeding and petting. My mother might have a sharp tongue and be a master of manipulation, but at least I was allowed to be a kid.

"Hi." Abbie stepped into the kitchen, and I gave her a big hug. She smiled, but it didn't reach her eyes.

"Glad you could make it," my mother said to her. "Put your pocketbook down and cut the pork roast, please. You always do it best. The platter is right there."

Abbie obeyed. I checked on the rolls.

"You working on another book?" Ma asked Abbie.

"Yes." She sliced through the meat with a firm hand.

"Some crime thing?"

"Mmm-hmm."

Ma pointed at the beans, and I took the hint, turning off the heat.

"Well, you need to be careful with all that kind of thing," Ma said. "Crime and cops and things."

Abbie glanced over her shoulder. "Why?"

"Well, for one thing, that sheriff person was asking about you."

Abbie's body went stiff. I glanced at my mother.

"Detective Scott?" I asked.

"No, no," Ma said. "Not that one. Shorter, rounder. Looks like Santa Claus."

"That's Corporal Fletcher," I said.

My mother nodded. "That's the one. He's a pervert."

I choked and laughed at the same time, and it turned into a coughing fit. When I finally recovered, I stared at my mother in disbelief. "Corporal Fletcher?

Ma, there's no way. He's a really nice guy. Why would you think that?"

She pursed her lips. "He was asking after Abbie. Did I know her? Was she available?"

"He asked you that?" I couldn't believe he would be so blunt.

My mother snorted. "Well, not in so many words, but I can read between the lines." She clucked her tongue and turned an indignant glance on Abbie. "He's married. Gail said he's got four kids and two grandkids. You, young lady, need to be aware he's got his eye on you. Hard to believe, isn't it? He should be upholding the law, and here he is, an old married man, looking at you with lust in his heart."

I started laughing.

"It isn't funny." Ma's nostrils flared in indignation.

"I think you misunderstood," I said. "He wasn't asking for himself. He was asking for Detective Scott."

Abbie glared at me over her shoulder then turned back to the roast, slapping slices of pork on the platter as if she were swatting flies.

"How do you know that?" my mother demanded.

"Trust me," I said. "I know."

Sammie bounced into the kitchen. "I'm starving. When are we going to eat?"

"Let's talk about this after dinner," I suggested.

Abbie didn't say a word while we carried food to the table and avoided my glances.

After we were all seated and the food had been blessed and passed around, Ma inhaled dramatically.

"I heard someone is coming in with a housing development," she said. "I don't know what things are coming to." She jabbed at a piece of pork roast on her plate.

"Can't say I'm real keen about a change like that, either," Daddy said.

Max glanced at me. "Change is inevitable."

I laughed. "Well, maybe Daddy can sell the farm and make a million."

My mother's head jerked in my direction. "Trish, how could you say that? I can't imagine. . .why—"

"I'm sure Trish was joking." Daddy's narrowed eyes gleamed a warning at me.

"Well, I should hope so." Ma glowered at me. "This farm will be sold over my dead body."

"Come on, Ma. Don't take everything so seriously." I hadn't expected such a strong reaction.

She grabbed the bowl of mashed potatoes and slopped some onto her plate. "Well, it's just that so many people are selling out. What's going to become of us? And what about my grandchildren? What if one of them wants to be a farmer?"

The tone of her voice rose a notch. "What if *all* the farmers sell out?" Her voice broke from emotion.

"No one is going to sell the farm," Daddy said and lifted an eyebrow at me, which meant he wanted me to apologize.

"I'm sorry, Ma," I said obediently.

"Well, I should hope so." She huffed to herself for a few minutes while we all ate in silence. Everyone except Abbie. She was eating very little. Worse than anything else, she wouldn't look at me.

We were almost done eating when Charlie piped up. "Tommy might go to jail. And then I would go to a private boarding school to make sure I don't end up as bad as him."

Where in the world would Charlie get that idea? My mother-in-law?

Karen snorted. "You in private boarding school? They wouldn't take you."

"Tommy has love notes from a girl," Sammie chimed in.

The tips of Tommy's ears turned red. "I have no privacy at all."

Charlie crossed his eyes. "Tommy and Sherry sittin' in a tree, k-i-s—"

"Charlie, stop it." Max's stern, green-eyed gaze was enough to make Charlie back off.

Ma *tsk-tsked*. "I think it's amazing how much influence you have over those children, Trish. Charlie acts just like you did, all rough and ready to fight." Her expression grew speculative. "Tommy, do you have a girlfriend?"

Tommy mumbled something and stuffed a spoonful of mashed potatoes into his mouth. Max tactfully changed the topic, and my mother dropped the topic for the moment, but I knew I'd hear more. After supper she began whipping through the dishes in her usual efficient manner. I cleaned the counters. Abbie was drying pots and still hadn't spoken to me.

"So, is Tommy in love?" Ma asked. "I was a little worried about him. He hasn't had any real interest in girls."

"Ma!"

"Well, it's not normal. Boys his age should be falling in love every week." She grabbed the meat platter and sponged the grease from it. "Well, who is she? Someone I know?"

I sighed. "She's Detective Scott's daughter."

Abbie pursed her lips and rubbed the lid of a pot so hard I thought she would break off the handle.

"Oh my," my mother said. "And Tommy is a murder suspect? That's got to be awkward."

"He's not a murder suspect," I said.

"That remains to be seen. How the family will live down a murder trial is beyond me." Ma waved us toward the kitchen table. "Now you girls sit down and tell me exactly what's going on with all these policemen. What does this Detective

Scott want with Abbie?"

I didn't know how much to say in front of my mother for fear that Abbie's potential love life would be a topic of conversation for the whole world to hear at Doris's Doughnuts. But on the other hand, if I didn't tell my mother something, she would speculate with Gail and April May about it for weeks in public.

Abbie's face looked like she'd been pickled.

"Okay, Ma. You gotta keep this quiet." I might as well ask a cow not to chew its cud.

Ma was indignant. "I don't gossip."

I'm always amazed at how out of touch people are with themselves. But that wasn't important right now. What really bothered me was the glare coming from Abbie's eyes.

"I'm sorry," I whispered to her.

My mother crossed her arms. "Just spit it out."

"Corporal Fletcher is asking about Abbie because Detective Scott is interested in her. He wants me to help get the two of them together."

"This is so humiliating." Abbie put her head in her hands.

My mother frowned. "Now don't you overreact. Nothing good ever comes from that. This Detective Scott, he's the tall one with blond hair, right?"

I nodded.

He's been coming into the store for years," she said. "What is he? Not just a deputy, right?"

"Nope," I said. "He's a sergeant."

"He's not married, is he?" Ma asked.

"No, he's not. He's divorced."

Her breath hissed through her teeth. "How long ago?"

"About twelve years," Abbie said.

"How do you know this?" Ma asked her.

"Because he's been helping me with my books."

"Then why in the world wouldn't—"

"They've known each other a lot longer than that," I said.

Abbie eyed me over her hands, and I knew I was in big trouble.

"I see." My mother watched Abbie with a speculative gaze. "Well, I do know he's a good law enforcement officer. After all, he listened to Trish's advice during that whole Jim Bob Jenkins murder fiasco."

"Ma, he didn't listen—"

She waved her hands in a dismissive motion. "You're too modest, Trish. You solved that murder. And now you're going to solve this one." She leaned toward me. "I heard tell that Connie Gilbert, the principal, the coach, and that band teacher fellow have all been at the sheriff's office."

Before I could say anything, Sammie ran into the kitchen and begged Ma to come play a game with her. My mother's face brightened. She dried her hands and even left a wet pot in the drainer. Then she followed Sammie out of the room.

Abbie put her dish towel down and wouldn't meet my gaze.

"Abs—"

"I have to go. I have a book to write." She snatched up her purse and headed for the back door.

I followed. "I'm sorry."

The door banged shut behind us.

She whirled around to face me, gravel crunching under her shoes. "Did you agree to help fix me up with Eric?"

"I said I'd think about it."

"I can't believe it. You know how I feel."

"You've made it pretty clear."

"Of all people, you should understand." She looked like she might cry.

"I think I might understand better than you think."

"You're not acting like it." Abbie opened her car door.

I took a deep breath. I was about to cross a line, risking my relationship with my best friend. "This is deeper than Detective Scott. Or your emotions."

She tossed her purse onto the passenger seat.

"Don't you see?" I said. "You're becoming your grandmother."

Abbie's body stiffened, and she looked over her shoulder at me. "Did I just hear you right?"

"Yes, you did." My voice grew stronger. "Don't you remember? You said you'd never be like her, yet here you are, living by yourself, withdrawing from people, and walking away from a potential relationship with a guy because you have a grudge."

"I. . .don't. . .have. . .a. . .grudge." She climbed into her car.

"Yes, I think you do. For some reason, you're mad at him over something in the past. Has he apologized to you?"

"I won't talk to him about it," she whispered.

That confirmed my suspicions. "Did he try?"

"Yes."

I dug the toe of my shoe into the gravel. "Abbie, I know you might never speak to me again, but you've got to let it go. At least forgive him. There's a reason that's in the Bible. It's emotionally healthy. If you don't date him because he's not your type, that's one thing. But not because of something in the distant past. Look what grudges did to your grandmother. Remember her funeral? Who was there?"

I waited for Abbie to say something, but she didn't. She just jammed the key into the ignition.

"Call me when you're ready to talk." I turned around and walked slowly to the house, hoping she would call my name, but she didn't. The car door slammed, the engine started, and she sped out of the driveway.

My eyes filled with tears. I might have just lost my best friend.

**14**

Saturday was cleaning day. Everyone pitched in for two hours to get the house in shape. Then Max took the kids out in the afternoon without me—something he started months ago after we realized that Karen was resentful of all the attention he paid to me.

As I swished my mop across the kitchen floor, I thought about my bad parting with Abbie the night before, and I hurt, like a lead-weighted fishhook was hanging from my heart. I kept wondering how I could have said things differently.

I'd tried to call her all morning, but she didn't pick up, and I left five different messages. I was so distressed, I hadn't even bothered to write the information my mother had given me about Georgia's murder in my steno pad.

I was debating about driving to Abbie's apartment and banging down her door when the beep of my cell interrupted my thoughts. I dropped my mop and raced to get it, hoping it was her, but it wasn't. It was Sherry.

My whole body slumped. I had assumed she wasn't investigating anymore, because I hadn't heard from her. So her calling me now either meant bad news—that is, her father was rampaging even after my great advice to him, or she had more new clues. That would mean that sooner or later her father would be rampaging again.

"Hi, Sherry," I said.

"Did you know that Connie Gilbert is a suspect in Ms. Winters's murder?" She wasted no time on nonessentials.

"Yes." I dropped onto a kitchen chair.

"Well, Aunt Elissa is going to handle the costumes for the play. Ms. Bickford asked her to, and we're going to pick up some things from Connie today. Aunt Elissa thought you might like to come."

A distraction. That would be a better alternative than being arrested for bashing in Abbie's front door. Besides, with Elissa along, I wouldn't be responsible for Sherry's being involved in the investigation. That meant I'd be free to gather all the clues I could. Not only that, but I wanted to get to know Elissa a little better.

---

Elissa drove her Mazda as though she were in a car chase on a reality cop show. The daredevil in me appreciated her skill. The mommy in me was scared to death.

Sherry must have sensed my emotions. She leaned forward from the tiny backseat and said, "Don't worry. Aunt Elissa has had training driving cars. She used to be a cop, like Dad."

Elissa was a cop? I glanced over at her.

"It's true," she said.

I didn't have a chance to pursue my questions, like why she walked with a cane, because she roared up Nettie's driveway and skidded to a stop, tires spitting gravel.

Sherry headed for the front door of the house, followed by Elissa. I walked more slowly, looking around. Nettie's farm had changed since I'd been here last. Contrary to what my mother believed, I did remember that she used to attend garden club meetings here. Even at that young age, I'd been impressed by the color-coordinated flower beds that Nettie had created. But now everything had changed. Weeds grew profusely in gardens that had once been tended with great care.

Elissa rang the bell. I joined her and Sherry on the front porch.

When Connie answered, she barely glanced at us. "Come in." She held the door open.

The wide foyer led into a gloomy, wood-floored hallway that was lined with furniture. On the right side, a staircase disappeared into the darkened upstairs. The air was stuffy and smelled of mothballs, toast, and the floral perfume I'd smelled in Georgia's classroom. It must be Connie's scent.

"I'm sorry about your loss," Elissa said to Connie once we were all inside.

Tears welled in her eyes. "It's been horrible. Georgia and I didn't always get along, but she. . ." She took a deep breath. "Well, I know you didn't come to listen to me cry."

"It's okay." Elissa patted her shoulder.

"I'm a suspect, you know." More tears glistened in Connie's eyes. "The police think I killed her."

Connie's tears might have been real, but in the dismal atmosphere of the Victorian farmhouse, I couldn't tell.

She turned to Elissa. "Thank you for doing the costumes. I suppose I could just decide not to provide costumes for the play, but I won't do that to the kids. Trish, I've lost one of the keys to my storage units. I'd really like to keep the one I have left. Would you like me to pay for a new lock?"

"I have a master," I said. "We'll use that."

She turned to Sherry. "Would you please give me a hand getting some boxes from upstairs?"

"Sure." Sherry responded eagerly.

Connie motioned with her hand toward a room to her right. "Why don't you two wait in the parlor while we get the costumes."

I was hesitant to let Sherry go alone with Connie, but Elissa didn't seem worried. While Sherry trailed Connie up the creaking wood staircase, I followed Elissa into the parlor, passing a long, narrow, marble-topped table in the hall, on top of which lay a bag from the drugstore.

Heavy red drapes hung on the tall parlor windows. Dark wood furniture and uncomfortable-looking velvet covered sofas filled the room. In true Victorian fashion, ornate tables were covered with knickknacks.

Elissa turned a sharp eye to me. "I know what she's doing."

"Huh?"

"My niece." Elissa began walking the perimeter of the room, eyeing everything. "She's trying to solve this mystery. She's worried about her boyfriend—your son. Corporal Fletcher told me." Her lips curled into a small smile. "He thought I might handle that piece of information better than her father."

Yea for Corporal Fletcher. I liked him better and better. The heaviness of responsibility for Sherry dropped from my shoulders. "Oh, I'm so glad. So you talked her out of it, right?"

Elissa laughed. "You're joking, of course."

"Well, I was hoping."

"No, I wasn't able to talk her out of it. Sherry comes by her stubbornness honestly. She'd continue even if we told her not to."

"Don't you think her investigating is dangerous?"

A flicker of concern passed over Elissa's face. "Yes, it could be. That's why I'm getting as involved as I can, especially with the play. I have a feeling things are going to get worse before they get better, and this way I can assure her father I'm taking care of her." She glanced around the room then gave me a quick smile. "Now let's get busy. Just don't touch anything."

I glanced at the coffee table and noticed a newspaper from Charlottesville, Virginia. "Look at this."

Elissa joined me.

"This is where Connie used to live," I said.

She stared at the paper. "Obituary section. Interesting."

Most of the deceased were elderly people, but one notice caught my eye. A very nice-looking man, maybe in his thirties. Aaron Bryant.

"Remember that name," Elissa murmured, pointing to the news photo.

Two thick books about antiques were piled on the other end of the table. I walked over to look at them. Peeking out from underneath the pile was a piece of paper on which I spotted a familiar fleur-de-lis.

I pointed at it. "I've seen something like this before."

Elissa joined me. "Oh, I recognize that. It's a receipt from a chain of pawn shops in Baltimore."

"I saw one of these on Marvin's desk at school," I said.

Elissa met my gaze with a frown, but before we could look more carefully at the paper, we heard Sherry's voice, followed by footsteps on the stairs. She and Connie were on their way down. No more time to snoop.

Their hands were full of costumes in plastic cleaner bags.

"I'll start carrying these out to the car," Sherry said.

Elissa nodded at her.

"Some of these costumes will need alterations," Connie said. "When the time comes, I'll need to show you how I do that without ruining the costumes. I have all the kids' sizes on forms that I left on Marvin's desk. I'll get those for you."

"That sounds good," Elissa said. "But are you sure you're up to it?" She nodded at the obituary on the table. "Have you lost more than one relative? That would be very painful."

Connie reached over to pick up the paper, her eyes tearing up again. "Well, in a manner of speaking." She swallowed. "Aaron and I were talking about getting engaged. It was a tragedy. He died the day before Georgia."

An elderly woman walked into the room carrying the plastic shopping bag from the drug store. "Did you bring this?" she asked in my general direction.

"I did, Granny," Connie said.

With gnarled hands, Nettie sifted through the bag. "I need my medicine." She turned to Connie. "Did you bring my medicine?"

"Yes. It's in there."

The older woman began pulling out the contents and strewing them on the couch.

Connie caught Nettie's arm. "Granny, we'll get to all this in a minute. Wait until our company leaves, okay?"

Nettie held up a box. "What's this? A watch? Did you get a new watch?"

"Yes," Connie said.

"Why?" Nettie asked. "You had one. A pretty one."

"Yes, but I broke it." She took the bag from Nettie's hand and replaced the items inside.

"Where is it?" Nettie asked.

"I gave it to Aaron to get it fixed—" Connie's voice broke, and she pressed her fingers against her eyes.

I felt so sorry for her I didn't want to believe she was a murderer. "There are a lot of broken watches going around," I said by way of distraction.

"What?" Connie glanced at me.

"Oh, Carla broke her watch, too. One of the links. A beautiful thing. Gold. Looked expensive."

Nettie clapped her hands. "Carla. That's Georgia's friend. She comes a lot. We always have nice dinners." She paused and looked around the room. "Where is Georgia?"

My heart ached for her.

"Granny, it's time for your lunch." Connie placed the watch back in the shopping bag then turned to us. "I'm sorry. I really can't talk anymore."

"We understand." Elissa's expression matched my feelings—sympathy mixed with suspicion.

Sherry still hadn't come back, so we picked up the rest of the costumes to carry them outside.

Connie walked us to the door and murmured a quick good-bye as we stepped onto the porch. As the front door closed, Sherry walked around the corner of the house. She hurried over to me and took the costumes from my arms.

"Where were you?" Elissa asked.

"Checking out the gardens and stuff. Since Daddy implied poison, I was looking to see if there was anything suspicious. I didn't touch anything, though."

"And?" I asked.

"Well, there's this huge garden shed back there with all sorts of things in it. Squealing hinges. . .I was afraid someone would hear me. The shelves are filled with bags and bottles and stuff. Rat poison, bug poison. You name it, it's there."

We all climbed into the car, and Elissa turned the key, shifted into gear, and careened down the driveway. "There's something with the boyfriend," she said. "According to the article, he died very suddenly. Seems strange that two people in Connie's life died without warning. It would be interesting to find out more about Aaron Bryant."

"And what about the pawn shop?" I explained to Sherry about the receipts. "Marvin said something about pawning school instruments the other day. But that wouldn't bring in a lot of money. Do you think Connie is pawning Nettie's belongings? There are a lot of valuable things in that house. And there were books about antiques on the coffee table."

Sherry had her head between the two front seats. "Maybe that's why Connie killed Georgia. To take the stuff and sell it."

Elissa glanced at her niece. "We don't know that Connie killed Georgia."

I frowned. "Besides, if Connie wanted money, she could have sold the whole farm. Georgia wanted to. Then Connie would have had half of everything. But she didn't want to."

"I'm going to make a few calls on Monday morning," Elissa said. "We're missing something here."

---

The Four Oaks High School marching band was leaving the field after halftime. The show had fallen flat, as if the band members were moving in a fog. The football team was losing. Jason had fumbled several plays. Without Coach Smith and Marvin Slade, the kids weren't holding together well.

I left Max with Charlie and Sammie on the bleachers so I could stretch my stiff body, as well as take a bathroom break—something that was occurring with more frequency. I noticed Detective Scott in attendance. He was in close conversation with a woman whose casual appearance didn't cover the fact that she was a cop. I desperately wished I could be privy to what they were talking about.

I passed Carla Bickford in a huddle with several parents. She was still wearing a suit, although this one was more casual, with pants and a loose jacket. I imagined her closet full of rows of suits, sorted by color.

Ten minutes later, when I was washing my hands in the bathroom, two women I knew by sight, who were also parents of high school students, walked in together. One had red hair that could only come from a bottle. The other was a natural mousy brown. They were so busy talking they didn't even look at me.

"She is just too big for her britches," the redhead said.

"Oh yeah. She thinks she's better than the rest of us, that's for sure. I heard her family in Virginia was dirt poor."

The conversation stopped when they noticed me standing there.

"Trish, how are you?" the one with brown hair said.

I rubbed my stomach. "Besides feeling like I'm going to pop, I'm fine."

She nodded. "How awful about Georgia."

Both women watched me closely, and I recognized the look. They were eager for information and thought I could provide some, but I didn't want to. "Yes, it was awful."

When I said nothing else, the redhead began to speak. "My husband is on the school board, but I'm still thinking of removing our daughter from the school. Even with a police officer here, I just don't feel like it's safe."

The other woman nodded in agreement. "School resource officer, they call her."

I wondered if that was the young woman Detective Scott had been talking to earlier. "So she's assigned to the school now?"

"Just came on," the brown-haired woman said. "Has her own office and everything."

"Of course, Carla is going to do everything in her power to put a positive spin on this," the other one said. "Make it look like it was all her idea, even though it wasn't. It was the school board's."

"She's becoming a dictator."

That wasn't a stretch for Carla.

"Well, you know why, don't you?" the redhead asked.

"Yes. She probably wants to keep moving on. Leave her past behind."

They began joking about what kinds of pasts someone would want to leave behind. I'd learn nothing else here. Besides, I was hungry. I left the bathroom and detoured to the concession stand. There I considered buying a hot dog, which I love to eat with lots of onions and mustard. As I debated whether the momentary pleasure would be worth the price of acid reflux later, I caught a glimpse of Carla Bickford out of the side of my eye. She was stalking Marvin Slade, who was walking with two uniformed band members. I was surprised to see him, since he'd been put on leave. When Carla finally reached him, she tapped his shoulder. He whirled around and frowned at her. I wasn't close enough to hear their words, but I surmised from the way the two band members hurried away that the conversation wasn't pleasant.

Marvin's voice grew loud, and Carla pointed toward the parking lot. When he finally walked away, she patted her hair and headed for the bleachers. My curiosity got the best of me, and I followed Marvin, moving as fast as I could.

"Marvin, wait," I yelled.

His startled gaze met mine, and he hurried toward his car. When he reached it, I thought he might ignore me and take off, but his shoulders slumped, and he leaned hard on the roof of the car.

"Hello, Mrs. Cunningham," he said when I reached him.

"Hi." The baby was kicking my ribs again, and I felt a slight twinge in my abdomen. I wondered if it was a protest at any fast movement on my part. I needed to slow down. I opened my mouth to tell Marvin that I didn't appreciate his deception, but he started talking first.

"I know what you want."

"No, I'm not sure you do," I said. "I'm angry because you lied to me at Four Oaks Self-Storage. You led me to believe you were still teaching."

He smiled sadly. "The second part of that statement is the truth. I did lead you to believe that, but I never came out and said it."

"Sin of omission."

He shrugged. "What can I say?"

"So why were you there?"

He reached for the car door handle. "Let's just say, I'm a fool in love trying to save someone from herself."

"What?"

"In love for the first time in my life."

"Connie?"

He looked over my shoulder, and I saw his eyes flicker. He flung the door open and scrambled inside. "I gotta go."

He turned on the ignition and threw the car into gear. I backed away just in time for him to squeal away.

"If I didn't know better, I'd think he was avoiding me," a voice said over my shoulder.

I turned around. Coach Smith was standing right behind me. Based on the muscles in his shoulders and arms, I had no problem believing he took steroids.

"Did you want to talk to him?" I asked.

"As a matter of fact, I did. He's been snooping around. . ." His voice trailed off, and he looked at me. "But I'll catch him later."

"I thought you were on administrative leave."

The anger that lit his eyes frightened me. "I am. But I came to watch my team play. At least the kids will know I'm here." The big man turned and walked away.

I looked past him and saw Detective Scott, who watched the coach until he disappeared into the crowd. I headed for the concession stand, and the detective jogged over to join me.

I kept walking. "What do you want? Now everyone here will think I'm guilty of something."

"No, they won't." He entered into step with me. "I'm human, too, you know. I do talk to people about things besides police business. I even have friends, although that might be hard for you to believe."

He had a point there. "So you're walking with me just to shoot the breeze?"

"No." He smiled down at me. "I do have a purpose, but people don't have to know that. I want to know what you and Marvin were talking about."

I stopped abruptly and looked up at him. "I told him I didn't appreciate him lying to me. Then he said something very interesting."

"And that was?"

I explained what Marvin had said. "You know, that's really weird. I think he's talking about Connie."

"Mmm." Detective Scott nodded. "Did the coach say anything?"

"He insinuated that Marvin was snooping around."

"I see."

We began walking again. The young woman he'd been talking to earlier motioned for his attention. Before he left, he looked at me. "Trish, be careful."

I met his serious gaze. Then he turned away, and I returned to the concession stand.

"Tell me you're not thinking about a hot dog with onions," a voice said in my ear. "You know you'll suffer all night." Max looked down at me. "How about I buy you a hot dog with just mustard?"

Shortly, Max was carrying drinks for four, along with a bag that contained two funnel cakes. Charlie and Sammie helped me carry five hot dogs. The kids were chattering, but I wasn't paying attention to them. I'd stopped in my tracks, as had everyone else around me.

There, in the shadows next to the bleachers, Detective Scott was kneeling on the ground with his knee in Coach Smith's back, handcuffing him. The young woman the detective had been talking to earlier stood in a typical cop stance, with her gun pointed at the coach's head.

**15**

On Monday morning, I was so glued to the local news for information about Coach Smith that I didn't pay attention to Max until he kissed me good-bye.

I looked him up and down. He was wearing his best charcoal pinstripe suit. "A meeting?"

"The board of directors," he said. "Lunch and a meeting afterward. But first I have to stop at the office in Rockville."

"Okay. That's good to know. This afternoon I have to go by the high school and drop off all the advertisement agreements, so I'll be leaving work a couple hours early."

He nodded as he clipped his cell phone to the holder on his belt.

I turned back to the television in time to see the wholesome, blond newscaster purse his lips in an expression of disgust.

"Coach Kent Smith of the Four Oaks High School was arrested on Saturday night for suspicion of providing drugs to minors," he said. "He's still in jail pending arraignment today."

"I guess they didn't let him out on bail over the weekend," Max said as he opened the garage door. "They'll probably set bail today, and he'll be out."

"They should lock him up and throw away the key," I murmured.

As I drove to work, I thought about Coach Smith. I needed to update my clue list with all the information I'd gathered over the weekend. Townspeople's speculation was rampant, and I'd gotten an earful at church the day before. The coach had murdered Georgia because she found out what he was doing. He was part of a bigger drug ring with ties in Baltimore. And then there was my mother's favorite broken record. He was the head of an international crime ring that had infiltrated our town to bring in gambling casinos.

Based on what I knew, I tended to believe he'd been arrested for providing drugs to some of his players to improve their performance. I remembered the newscast I'd seen about a performance-enhancing drug and wondered if that was the one he'd given them. No matter what, arrest was too good for a man who would do that to teenagers. Whether he murdered Georgia remained to be seen.

When I pulled into the parking lot at Four Oaks Self-Storage, I was so focused on my speculation about Coach Smith, it took a moment to register the fact that a shiny red Mercedes was hogging Max's parking space. I knew who it belonged to, and I wanted to make a fast U-turn. As I opened the front door of the building, I caught a whiff of Chanel. My mother-in-law's favorite scent.

Shirl was standing behind the front desk, hands on her hips and a scowl on her face. She motioned with her head toward the closed door of Max's office. "Her Highness is in there," she whispered.

"What does she want?" I whispered back. "Is she waiting for Max? He's not planning to be here today."

Shirl shook her head. "She was asking when you were going to come into work." Shirl paused and sniffed. "I had some messages for Mr. C., so when I called to give him those, I told him that *she* was making herself at home in his chair."

So Angelica was here to see me. Shirl knew and was trying to protect me. A nervous quiver sped up my back.

From the side of my eye, I saw the office door open, and Angelica's perfectly made-up eyes met mine. "Patricia? Will you please join me for a moment?" Her cool, cultured voice always annoyed me. Possibly because I couldn't achieve the same effect, no matter how hard I tried. She didn't wait for me to answer, just turned on her Gucci heels and disappeared again.

Her tone of voice, combined with the way she presumed to take over Max's office, obliterated my nervousness.

I handed my purse to Shirl, but before I could enter the lion's den, she patted my arm. "Don't you worry none, Mrs. C. You got more class on a bad day than she does on her best."

I didn't agree, but I met her gaze with gratitude, and she smiled. That gave me the extra push I needed. I strode into Max's office, shutting the door behind me. Whatever Angelica had come to tell me, Shirl didn't need to hear.

Angelica was seated behind Max's desk. Without an audience, her smile was gone. In its place was an icy frown. However, if she thought that would scare me, she was mistaken.

She sniffed gently. "I came by to pick up some papers for Max and his father about the new housing development, but I'm glad you're here. I have something I need to discuss with you."

It took every ounce of my fruit of the Spirit self-control not to gasp. "Housing development?"

"The one they have planned for Four Oaks." She raised one delicate eyebrow. "You mean, Max didn't tell you?"

I refused to make it appear as though Max had kept this a secret from me. "Oh yes. That."

"Please sit down." She pointed at a chair in front of Max's desk.

"If you don't mind, I'll stand."

"Do as you like. You usually do. But you might wish to be seated when I tell you this."

The gloves were off, so to speak. I knew for sure this conversation wasn't going to be pleasant.

"Your father-in-law and I want to see that Charles goes to a private boarding school in Bethesda."

"What?" I locked my knees.

"He is, after all, our youngest grandson."

I couldn't catch my breath, like the time I fell off a swing when I was little and had the air knocked out of me. Suddenly everything was clear. Max's hidden papers and behind-closed-doors phone calls. Charlie's attitude and comments.

Angelica's mouth was set in a slight smile. "I felt you should know. Particularly since your actions precipitated our decision. Of course, I warned Max when he married you."

Not only were the gloves off, but she was flexing her claws. "My actions? What do you mean by that?"

She shook her head as though I was an unfortunate, stupid child. "You can't stay out of trouble. You allow the children to run wild. Their futures are at stake. It's too late for Thomas, but it's not for Charles. I talked to Max a few days ago and have started making arrangements at the school."

I remembered my mother's comment that I was influencing the kids and not always positively. That made me feel guilty, but unlike many people, when I feel guilty, I don't crumble. I get mad. The Bible study about the fruit of the Spirit flickered through my mind, but I dismissed its words of wisdom.

"Does Max know you're telling me this?" I could barely see her for the red haze in front of my eyes..

She sighed. "No, he doesn't. Whenever I talk to him about it, he adamantly defends you."

Well, at least he did that.

"But I'm going to insist," she added.

Her tiny smile made me truly regret I couldn't lapse into the Trish of years ago. I allowed myself the luxury of imagining how good it would feel to fling myself across the desk, tackle Angelica, and throw her to the ground. I'd yank her hair, messing up her perfect hairdo, pulling until she screamed. The temptation was so great, I leaned forward, clenching and unclenching my fists.

Fortunately, before I could do anything, the door opened behind me. Angelica's smile died.

I stepped back, away from temptation. "I'm not going to discuss this further with you. Max can tell me the rest."

"The rest of what?"

I turned. Max was frozen in the doorway. When no one spoke, he walked over and stood next to me.

"Trish?" He squeezed my shoulder.

I met his gaze, but I couldn't see for my tears. I couldn't believe he'd betrayed me.

"Ask your mother." I jerked away from him and rushed from the office.

He didn't follow. I heard his voice rumbling and could tell from the tone that he was angry.

So was I. At him and his whole stupid, stuck-up family.

Shirl wasn't even pretending to work. "Mrs. C., is there anything I can do?"

"No, thank you. Just hand me my purse."

She did.

As I opened the front door, I said over my shoulder, "I'll be gone for a while."

I felt sick and vulnerable as I pulled my SUV from the parking lot. Where could I go to hide from everyone? I desperately wanted to go to Abbie's, but she still hadn't returned my calls. I could think of only one other place I would feel safe.

———

When I pulled up to my folks' farm, I thought Daddy wouldn't be there, but I was relieved to see his truck parked near the barn.

After nearly falling out of the SUV, I stumbled over the rough ground and pulled a side barn door open, unable to see clearly through the blur of tears in my eyes. Buddy the border collie greeted me first. My gaze followed the sound of Daddy's distinctive off-key humming to where he was pulling the contents out of some white metal storage cabinets. He'd been using them as long as I could remember, repainting them every five years.

"Daddy?"

He whirled around at the sound of my voice. "Sugar bug, what are you doing here? I thought you'd be at work."

"I was, but—" My lower lip started to tremble.

He wiped his hands on a cloth and crossed the expanse between us with large strides.

I couldn't do anything but stand there and cry.

He put his hands on my shoulders and looked me up and down. "What's wrong, honey?"

I swallowed and sniffled. "I. . .I can't really talk yet."

Worry darkened his eyes. "But the baby's okay? Nothing's happened to anybody?"

I hiccupped. "Everyone is safe." Buddy licked my hand, and I scratched his head.

"Okay." He dropped his arms. "You just take a minute and get yourself together, then tell me what's going on." He waved toward the junk on the floor.

"I could use the break."

I inhaled. "Lady Angelica. . ." I felt a tear on my cheek. "Well, she came by the office and told me she wants to put Charlie in boarding school. Because I'm a bad mother."

Daddy snorted. "Who does she think she is? The queen?"

"Probably," I murmured. "Daddy, I was really tempted to grab her and beat her up. It took everything I had not to do it. Maybe I really am a bad mother. What kind of grown woman thinks things like that? And a Christian woman to boot."

A quick grin passed over his face. "You'd be surprised." Then he frowned. "So, what does Max have to say about all of this?"

Fresh tears burned my eyes. "That's the thing. I'm not sure." I inhaled. "He showed up shortly after she told me, and I left him there. I was just so angry that he hasn't said anything to me about this. Why wouldn't he tell me?"

"That's a good question."

"And that's not all. You know that housing development Mom has been yakking about?"

Daddy nodded.

"Well, Max and his dad are behind that." I rubbed my arms. "Why didn't he tell me about this, either? Why did I have to hear it from Her Royal Highness?"

Daddy shook his head silently.

"And now Tommy is being investigated for murder. And Abbie won't speak to me anymore because I said she was acting like her grandmother." I was close to wailing.

The muscles in Daddy's jaw worked, a sure sign he was holding back what he really wanted to say.

"Is there something wrong with me?" I met his gaze. "Why wouldn't Max trust me?"

Daddy took a deep breath. "I can't say what Max was thinking. Sometimes, though, men are fools."

I couldn't keep my tears under control. "I. . .I need to be alone for a little while. You mind if I sit up in the loft?"

He brushed a piece of hair from my eyes. "You don't even have to ask. You go. And I'll be praying. For all of us." Daddy rarely got mad, but I saw a spark of anger in his eyes. His defending me made me feel good.

"Thank you," I whispered.

"Can you get up there okay?" He looked down at my belly.

"Yeah. I'll go around to the top."

He didn't try to stop me, and he held Buddy so he wouldn't follow me. One thing about my Daddy, he knew me well enough to know what I needed. He'd always been sensitive that way, helping to counteract my mother's sharp tongue.

The loft was warm and smelled of hay and livestock. I realized I should have gotten a drink. My mouth felt sticky. I'd get some water in a little while. For now, I pulled myself up onto a hay bale and leaned against another. I closed my eyes and let the smell of the barn roll over me. Hay, cattle—all of it comforted me. This was where my roots were. I was a farm girl, a redneck. And proud of it. But despite growing up and all the changes God had made in me, I was afraid that underneath it all, I'd always be a girl who was ready to fight at the drop of a hat. I wanted so badly to act kind, to be a godly Proverbs 31 woman. But how could I when I was overwhelmed by my feelings?

Had I made a mistake when I married Max? Was I denying his children their true birthright just by being their mother? Or worse, had he been so desperate for his kids to have a mom that he settled for the first available woman who came along at church? Max and I had some problems in the past, but nothing like this. Our love and passion had been enough to overcome our differences, and I'd assumed we'd always have that. But now I wasn't sure. I wondered if his recent secretiveness, combined with his lack of attention, was an indication that his decision to marry me had been nothing more than rebellion against his upbringing. I'd always had that fear in the back of my head. That he'd get over his initial attraction to me and be sorry we got married. Was that happening now?

Tears spilled down my face, spotting the shirt that stretched over my swollen tummy. I felt another twinge, and the baby kicked. I closed my eyes, praying in desperation.

Several minutes later, when I heard the distinctive purr of Max's car pulling up to the barn, I wasn't surprised. He knew me well enough to eventually figure out where I'd go. I sat up straight and waited.

16

The rumbles of Max's voice and Daddy's angry replies came up through the floorboards of the hayloft. During each lull in their argument, I expected to hear Max's steps on the ladder, but then the two would start all over. Gradually, though, I heard only murmurs.

When Max finally climbed up to the loft and appeared through the square entrance in the floor, I turned my head away from him.

He walked across the wood floorboards and stopped in front of me, looking down. "I'm sorry."

A blanket apology. Was that supposed to make everything okay? I refused to meet his eyes, just stared at his feet, thinking how strange his shiny black shoes looked on the rough, dusty floor. I studied his laces in an effort to distract myself enough to avoid crying or losing my temper. I was in danger of both.

Max shifted from foot to foot, but I didn't invite him to sit down. "Your father reamed me out."

"Yeah, I heard."

I wasn't sure what to say next, and he must not have been either. The silence stretched into several minutes as I pulled pieces of hay from the bale under me, bent them in half, then crushed them and tossed them to the floor.

I couldn't stand the silence any longer. "You should have told me everything. You don't trust me."

"That's not true."

"Then why couldn't you tell me any of this?" I asked through clenched teeth.

Max sat on a bale of hay next to mine, but he didn't touch me. "I didn't tell you about the housing development because we were still trying to figure out if it was feasible."

"And you couldn't talk to me about it?"

"I knew how you'd feel, and. . ." He paused and took a breath.

"And what?" I asked.

"I knew how you'd react." He glanced at me and shrugged. "I didn't want to fight about it until I knew there was a reason to fight. I'm sorry. I just wasn't up to that."

"You didn't want to fight. . . . Am I that hard to get along with?"

"Honestly? Sometimes. Especially lately." He shifted on the bale. "We're both a little touchy right now."

"What about *Charles* and the boarding school? Were you afraid to tell me that, too?"

Max nodded. "As far as I was concerned, that was a nonissue. The idea was Mother's, and there was no way I was ever going to agree to it."

"You should have told me anyway."

He inhaled. "Yes, probably. But. . ."

"But you were worried about my reaction to that, too?"

"In a word, yes."

I could add this to my recent list of failures. Not only was my husband holding back the truth from me because he was afraid I'd overreact, but my best friend wasn't talking to me because I'd hurt her feelings with my big mouth. My mother thought I was a bad influence on the children. My mother-in-law agreed with that, too, which led, of course, to her implication that Tommy was a criminal. Not only that, but I wasn't working on a Bible study I so obviously needed. I felt like the biggest loser in the whole world—and that made me even madder.

"And. . .there's something else," Max said.

I looked up at him, so angry I felt sick. "What else could there possibly be?"

He took a deep breath. "Well, Dad wants to partially retire. He wants to turn more of the business over to me." Max glanced at his watch. "In fact, that's what this board meeting is about. I have to leave pretty soon."

That figured. Even now, in a crisis, business would come first. I knew I was being unfair, but I couldn't help my thoughts, which only served to prove that Max's comment about my irritability was right. "Well, can you spare sixty seconds to tell me why your dad wants to semiretire?"

Max ignored the sarcasm in my tone. "He had a scare not too long ago. He thought he had cancer." Max paused and swallowed. "When the doctors said the tumor was benign, Dad decided it was time to start enjoying life."

"The tumor?" I felt like the bottom of my world had fallen out, but anger surfaced again. "And you couldn't tell me *that*, either? Something that bothered you so badly?"

Max spread his hands. "Dad didn't want me to tell anyone. Not even Mother. She just found out, which is probably why she had that outburst in my office."

For once in my life, as impossible as it seemed, I felt sorry for my mother-in-law. "So that's where you get your secrecy from? Your father? What is this? Some sort of secret, manly Cunningham society, even though we agreed—no more secrets?"

Max blinked, and his eyes glinted bright green. "I don't think it's secrecy. I just don't see the reason to address issues until it's necessary."

"As far as I'm concerned, they become issues as soon as you become aware of them."

"Sorry, I don't agree." His lips snapped shut. He was as angry as I was.

"I'm your wife, Max."

His cell phone rang. He sighed, pulled it from his belt, and looked at the screen. "That's Dad." He gave me a quick glance. "I need to get it."

"You do that." I stood to my feet.

He reached for my hand. "Trish."

I backed away before he could touch me. The phone kept ringing.

He pushed the button. "Hey, Dad. Hang on. . . . No, I'm not on my way yet. . . . Yes, I know I'm supposed to be there shortly." Max put his hand over the mouthpiece.

"You go on and talk," I said.

Max looked like he was deliberating then held the phone to his ear again.

"It's fine, Max." My voice cracked. "I have some things to do at work. Besides, I can't talk about this anymore."

I whirled around and headed for the big open doors at the front of the barn. I heard the thud of Max's heels behind me, along with his voice on the phone. I knew I shouldn't walk away, but I was hurt and—once again—acting out my anger. I needed to get away from him before I said anything I'd regret.

---

"I'll tell you what," Shirl said as I stepped into the office. "You should have been here for that showdown between Mr. C. and Lady Angelica."

"I'm glad I missed it." I pulled some bills from the mail on the counter.

"You've been crying, haven't you?" She looked me up and down. "I'd like to give that woman a piece of my mind, what with you being pregnant and all. What was she thinking? Are you sure you should be here?"

"Yes. I'm better off working, believe me. Besides, after lunch I need to drop some forms off at the school for Carla."

Shirl turned and glared at her computer monitor. "I'm not so sure *I'm* better off being here. I've got one fine kettle of fish to deal with." Her fingers *tap-tap-tapped* on the desk.

I didn't want to know what was wrong. I couldn't care less right now, as upset as I was with Max, but I debated whether I should ask Shirl what she meant. If I did, it could end up in a very long conversation in which I didn't want to be involved. Like about her herb business. Still, if I didn't ask, she'd corner me at some point anyway. Besides, she'd stuck up for me this morning.

"So what's wrong?"

"Connie's check is bouncing all over the place."

Of all the things Shirl might have said, I wasn't expecting that. "I'm surprised."

"Ha. You shouldn't be. It's a habit, I'm afraid." Shirl slapped her palm on the counter and glared up at me over her glasses. "She said it would never happen again, and I believed her. She's been good for a while now."

"You mean she's bounced other checks?"

"Yes. And I'm not going to cut her any slack anymore. From now on, it's all credit card payments or she's out of here. I don't care if she does rent all those units." Shirl's chin trembled with indignation.

Shirl's loyalty to me, Max, and our business was the reason I loved having her work for us. She might be annoying, spinning off in so many directions I could hardly keep track, but she was like a guard dog when it came to our finances. When I took time off after the baby was born, I knew Shirl would run things just fine.

"I know you'll do the right thing." I took some bills from the counter and began to walk to my office when Shirl's voice stopped me.

"And to make things worse, that Coach Kent Smith got out on bail."

My stomach flip-flopped. Did that mean we had a murderer loose in Four Oaks?

---

When I heaved my body through the front door of the high school, I headed directly for the office, carrying my folder of forms.

There I saw Sue, one of the school secretaries, eating a candy bar. I didn't recognize the other secretary.

She looked up at me with a frown. "Yes?"

"I'm here to deliver these to Carla. Can I leave them with you?"

"No, that's not a good idea." Her nameplate said TWILA. Carla's unhappy secretary.

"How come?" I asked.

"It would be better if you delivered them to her in person. If you leave them with me, she's going to be mad because I saw them first. Or something stupid like that."

Things *were* bad. "Okay, where is she then?"

"She's gone to see if rumors are true that Coach Smith was here talking to some kids. She's also chasing down Connie Gilbert, who got here a little while ago, and she also mumbled something about seeing Marvin in the band room. Carla has *nothing* good to say about Connie. They recently had a telephone yelling match. And *Connie* was here to chase down Marvin Slade to get the play's costume list from him." She paused for a deep breath. "He gave his notice today and was cleaning out his desk. Lucky him."

Sue nodded and swallowed a bit of candy bar as she nervously glanced toward the hallway through the glass wall. "She's upset because her fiancé died."

"Connie's fiancé?" I asked.

"No," Sue said. "Carla's."

"What?" Way too many people were dying.

Twila jabbed a pen into the blotter on her desk. "To tell the truth, I was surprised she even had a fiancé. I mean, who would want her?"

"Don't say that." Sue took a nervous gulp from a can of soda.

"Whatever." Twila sniffed. "This school is like some sort of Peyton Place. Georgia admiring the coach's muscles in the gym, dating him a couple of times, then having nothing else to do with him. Marvin sniffing after that costume woman, although that's better than last year when he dated most of the females working here. And Queen Carla mourning over Ronnie. I wonder if he even existed. No one ever met him."

"You better be careful what you say." Sue glanced around as though checking for secret cameras.

Twila exhaled with exasperation. "I don't care anymore. It's always all about her. Her life. Her fiancé. Her, her, her. She's so possessive. I don't even dare touch any of her stuff. My first day on the job, I took her coffee cup from her office and washed it out, and you'd have thought I'd committed the unpardonable. Really, Sue. You and I should just walk out."

"I can't afford to do that," Sue whined. "I got kids and haven't gotten an alimony check in months."

Twila rolled her eyes.

"Well, she *is* going on vacation, remember?" Sue said. "Like tomorrow or the next day. Sort of spur of the moment."

"So, what do you guys think happened to Georgia?"

They turned and looked at me as if they'd forgotten I was there.

Sue's eyes grew round. "I think she was poisoned. By Coach Smith. For dissing him."

Twila shook her head firmly. "I don't think so. This is one thing I agree with Carla about. Georgia's death was an accident. No matter what the cops say. She was always drinking these herbals teas she mixed up at home. A special blend that gave her energy and suppressed her appetite. You gotta be careful with things like that. Too many stimulants can kill you."

"I still think it was Coach Smith." Sue surprised me by defending her opinion. "The guy was freaking out when Georgia refused to date him anymore. Or it was Marvin. He asked me out once." She shivered. "You know, I could be dead right now."

"Well, with the coach, it was just his ego," Twila said. "He had other girls, believe me. A lot of good they'll do him in jail."

As the two debated, I decided to go chase down Carla and get this over with. I left the office just in time. The secretaries' conversation had moved into a discussion about how Coach Smith was probably going to come back, shoot them all dead with a shotgun, spalttering the walls with blood.

My mouth still felt dry, and I needed a drink of water badly. I was about to go in search of a vending machine when I saw Tommy heading my way.

"Hey, Mom." He had half a doughnut in his hand.

"Hi, honey." I stood on my tiptoes and pecked him on the cheek, figuring it was fine since no one else was around. "Where'd you get that, and what are you still doing here?"

"Trying to keep my part in the play." He grinned sheepishly. "We just finished practicing with the new teachers in charge. I'm sucking up to everyone. I brought doughnuts." He took another bite.

"Did you see Marvin Slade?"

Tommy's smile died. "Yeah. Just a couple minutes ago. It's really sad. He was in the band room packing his stuff. I left him some doughnuts, too."

"Where's Sherry?"

He shrugged. "Probably in the auditorium. I left right after practice."

"Well, aren't you two—?"

"Mom, the way things are right now, I can't go there, okay?"

I blinked at the vehemence in his voice. "Has Detective Scott questioned you again?"

"No. And I'm going to do my best to make sure he doesn't have to." Tommy edged away from me. "Listen, I gotta go now. Gotta get to work." He turned and jogged on up the hall, and I resumed my walk toward the band room.

When I passed the doors to the auditorium, I saw teenagers were milling around the room. Sherry was there, too, and she looked up and waved at me. I waved back, even as I picked up my step and hurried on, trying to avoid her, but it did no good. She made a beeline for me, rushing out into the hallway.

"Hi, Mrs. C. I have a message from Aunt Elissa for you."

I slowed down, and she fell into step next to me. "What's that?"

"Well, seems that receipt you guys saw at Connie's was from a pawn shop in Baltimore. They have a number of things there that fit the description of things that are missing from Nettie Winters's house."

I stopped in my tracks. "You're kidding."

She shook her head. "Aunt Elissa thinks either Connie or Georgia was pawning things. I wonder if it wasn't Connie and she murdered Georgia because she found out. And that's not all."

"What else?"

"Well, that boyfriend of Connie's? The fiancé? He died in a suspicious death. It looks like someone broke into his house to rob him and shot him to death."

I began walking again, trying to piece things together in my mind.

"I think Aunt Elissa is helping Dad or something, because before she talked about the whole thing with me, but now she won't. And she's been in to talk to Ms. Bickford. Everyone's a traitor, I guess." She paused. "Mrs. C., have you seen Tommy?"

I glanced at Sherry. "Yes, he's on his way to work."

"He's ignoring me." Her mouth quivered like she was going to cry.

I touched her arm. "You understand why, don't you?"

Her eyes flashed, and her lips firmed. I knew exactly how she was feeling and felt very, very sorry for Detective Scott. He'd better handle the situation differently, or he would drive her away.

"I'm going to clear Tommy's name once and for all." She crossed her arms. "I don't care what anybody says. Then, when we practice our kiss, I won't feel like I'm pressing my lips on a cardboard cutout. When we first started practicing, there was some real feeling."

Oh, great. That's all I needed to hear about. Passionate kisses between my son and a girl. I wanted to clap my hands over my ears and say, "La la la la la la, I can't hear you," but that would have been too obvious. Instead, I glanced up at the ceiling so I could recover my equilibrium.

"Mrs. C.?"

"Mmm?" I twisted my head, trying to decide if the brown water stain right above my head looked more like a dog or a cow.

"Are you mad at me, too?"

The tone of her voice was so forlorn, I felt terrible. I met her gaze again. "No, I'm not." I knew what it was like to be in love with a Cunningham man. Once it happens, you just can't help yourself.

"Where are you going?" Sherry asked.

"I'm looking for Carla—Ms. Bickford. Her secretary said she was meeting Marvin in the band room. She was also looking for Connie."

"I'll come with you."

I began to argue with her but decided I wanted company. With the school practically empty, I didn't want to be alone with my imagination.

"We have a substitute band teacher," Sherry said as we walked toward the band room. "And someone else is taking Ms. Winters's class for the rest of the year."

"Your aunt will still be doing the costumes, right?"

"Yeah. Aunt Elissa wants to talk to you about that. She wants your help."

When I reached the band room door, I had a weird sense of déjà vu. I didn't like the chill that crept over my head, making my hair feel like it was standing on end. Sherry's presence offered small comfort, especially since I was responsible for her safety.

I pushed the door open. The lights were on. So was a DVD, playing the movie *Arsenic and Old Lace*.

"Carla?" I called.

No answer.

"Marvin?"

No answer.

"This is sort of creepy," Sherry said.

"Yeah, tell me about it."

A box of doughnuts lay on Marvin's old desk. Beside that was a packing box partially filled with music books. Then I noticed splotches of liquid dotting the floor next to a shattered ceramic mug and a half-eaten doughnut.

Sherry's breath hissed through her teeth.

From the television, Mortimer Brewster said, "You. . . Get out of here! D'ya wanna be poisoned? D'ya wanna be murdered? D'ya wanna be killed?"

The words were ironic given that Marvin Slade was in a heap on the floor.

17

Slouched on a chair in the hallway of the school with my eyes closed, I felt heavy, like someone had opened the top of my head and poured in concrete. With emergency personnel and cops in and out, I paid no attention to the sounds of the footsteps around me until someone stopped next to me.

I opened my eyes and looked into the eyes of Detective Scott.

"I might have known." His tone was resigned.

I wasn't surprised to see him. Sherry had called him as soon as we discovered Marvin on the floor. I tried to sit up straight, but I didn't have the energy. "He's okay, right? He had a pulse. I watched the paramedics take him away."

"He's alive." Detective Scott's gaze searched my face. "How about you? How are you feeling?"

"Numb."

"You're pale."

"Probably just shock."

His searching gaze made me feel defensive.

"I had a good reason to be here, you know."

"I'm not surprised. You usually do."

The heaviness in my legs increased. "Tommy did, too."

He drew a sharp breath. "Tommy was here?"

Me and my big mouth. Still, Detective Scott would find out sooner or later. "Yes. He was bribing teachers with doughnuts."

I didn't like the look on the detective's face. Corporal Fletcher appeared, and when I tried to smile at him, my mouth wouldn't work. I took a deep breath, and my vision turned to spots. I began to slide out of the chair.

"Oh, hey!" The corporal rushed forward and grabbed me under the arms.

Next thing I knew, I was laid out on the floor, and Detective Scott was kneeling next to me with his finger on my pulse. "Fletcher, get the paramedics."

"Yessir." The corporal walked down the hall, talking into the mike on his shoulder.

My mind felt muddled. "No ambulance," I whispered.

"Yes, an ambulance," Detective Scott said.

"I don't want to go to the emergency room." I spoke louder and tried to clear my vision. "You don't understand, Detective Scott. They know me by name there." I felt the baby kick. I forced myself to relax and take deep breaths.

273

Detective Scott stared at me, eyebrows in a deep V. "Would you please just do something without arguing? Just this once?"

Since I had just slid out of the chair, I decided to agree. "Okay."

"Okay?" His eyes widened. "Just like that? Okay?"

"Yes. Okay." I took another deep breath and felt the fog in my head lifting. Maybe I just needed to remember to breathe. "How is Sherry?"

"Fine." The way he answered told me he was annoyed with her.

I met his gaze straight on, or tried to. "Don't blame her, Detective. Neither of us was investigating. I was here to find Carla to deliver advertising commitments. Sherry was just walking with me. She's a good girl, you know, but she's very vulnerable right now."

He closed his eyes for a moment then opened them again. "I know."

I decided to let the topic drop. There was only so much I could do for either of them, and now wasn't the time for an in-depth conversation. I took more deep breaths and began feeling a bit better.

"I'm going to need to question you, but it can wait until later on," he said.

"It wasn't just an accident then?" I asked. "Was Marvin attacked? Like hit? I didn't see any blood or anything."

Detective Scott stared at me, and I could almost see the cogs in his brain working. "I don't think so."

I felt a brief sense of relief. "I was afraid Coach Smith had come in and bashed Marvin over the head." Then I realized what the detective had said. "What do you mean, 'I don't think so'? Do you think someone did something to Marvin? Like, he ate something funny?" I began to panic, thinking about Tommy and the doughnuts. "He probably had a heart attack. I know that—"

"You need to calm down." Detective Scott patted my arm.

"I hate it when people say that to me." I struggled to sit up.

In a gentle manner that belied his irritated scowl, Detective Scott reached an arm around my shoulders, helped me sit up, then propped me against the wall.

Corporal Fletcher joined us again, and the detective stood.

I looked up at both of them. "Do you think this has anything to do with Georgia?"

"Stop talking," Detective Scott ordered.

"Yes, but what happened to Marvin? If he wasn't bashed in the head, then was he poisoned? Coach was out on bail." I looked up and down the hall, expecting to see Carla marching around giving orders. "Where is Carla?"

"On her way back," he said. "She'd gone home."

"What about Connie? She was here, too, you know."

Detective Scott exchanged glances with Corporal Fletcher, whose forehead was creased with worry. "We're not going to discuss this right now. I'll come by your house later." The detective motioned to another deputy. "Watch her until the paramedics get here." He crooked a finger at the corporal. "Fletcher, come with me. I'm afraid this is my fault, although I told Marvin not to come here."

⸺

Linda Faye King, the emergency room nurse wrapped the blood pressure cuff around my arm. "Well, we haven't seen you in quite some time. I figured you were trying to be careful, given you're pregnant and all, but here you are."

The implication, of course, was that I was still as foolish as ever, even risking my baby's well-being.

"I'm just a little dizzy is all," I said. "I think maybe I hold my breath when I get stressed. And. . .I've had a few tiny pings in my abdomen. Probably Braxton Hicks."

"Lots of people have false labor pains, but we'll see." She pursed her lips and pumped up the cuff. "Dizziness can be a sign of lots of things. Like the placenta could be detaching, and the baby could die."

Fear gripped my stomach. "Well, I'm not—"

"Well, your blood pressure is fine. That's a good sign." She paused. "You know, we had a lady in here last week who lost her baby. Poor thing. Stillbirth. Imagine."

I was going to throw up.

"The lady's mother was already in here with some sort of heart palpitations. Those coincidences happen a lot—like Nettie Winters and her niece a couple weeks ago." Linda Faye efficiently folded up her blood pressure cuff. "I mean, can you believe that? All in one family? On the same day?"

"I'm not sure I follow." And I couldn't imagine she should be telling me all this stuff, but then again, she always did have a big mouth.

"Connie was in here, too—the same day as Nettie. Heart pounding."

I had another wave of dizziness.

"And here we are again," Linda Faye continued. "You and Marvin Slade here at the same time. Then the police were here, too, and—"

The curtain to the room was swept aside by Bill Starling, our general practitioner and regular physician at the hospital. Linda Faye shut up like someone had slapped her. That's what I thought. She shouldn't have been telling me all of this.

"Surprise, surprise." Bill smirked. "Imagine seeing Trish Cunningham in the emergency room. I guess I'd better call your obstetrician."

Max appeared behind Bill. That's when I started to cry.

⸺

Two hours later, I sat on my bed, wearing one of Max's old shirts over black leggings. Whenever I feel insecure, wearing something of his helps me, even now, when we were still at odds. My favorite pink, cross-eyed bunny slippers lay on the floor, and I was wrapped up in my favorite afghan.

The baby was fine. For that I was very grateful. But my doctor said I had to be careful now, especially because I'd been having minor contractions. I was also dehydrated and probably stressed. They'd given me fluids to get my metabolism back in order.

I'd had some problems with dizziness at the beginning of my pregnancy, as well, so my present reaction wasn't totally unexpected.

"Honey? You awake?" Max walked into the bedroom carrying a cup of hot chocolate and my steno pad, my Bible study, and a pen. "I thought you'd like these." He set everything down on the nightstand and stood next to the bed.

"Thank you." I reached for the hot chocolate and took a sip to avoid meeting his eyes.

We hadn't yet spoken about our argument earlier in the day. We were awkward with each other, a little like acquaintances instead of husband and wife. I suspected that his bringing my notebook was a form of apology. Besides which, he probably thought I'd be writing down notes anyway, so he might as well accept it.

"We need to talk, I guess." I put the mug back on the nightstand.

"Yes." He brushed a strand of hair from my face. "But not now. Let's do it later when we won't be interrupted."

"All right." Normally, I like to get things over with, but I was glad for the reprieve. I still felt too raw and hadn't had time to sort things out in my head.

His eyes watered. "Baby, just know that I love you more than anything in the world. If anything happened to you. . . Well, we'll work all this out."

Tears came to my eyes. I leaned against him, and he hugged me.

Karen appeared at the bedroom door. "Mom, are you okay?"

"Yes, honey." I saw the worry in her eyes and felt bad. "Really, I'm just fine."

She smiled. "Good. Grandmom is here. She brought Charlie and Sammie home." After a last glance at me, she turned and left.

"I have to go see to the kids." Max headed for the door talking over his shoulder. "Your mother is making dinner."

"Do the little kids know what happened?"

"I'm not sure if your mother told them or not. If not, I will." Max stopped and turned around. "I want you to know that I'm going to try to stop the housing development project. I don't know if I can, but I'll try."

"Max—"

"I didn't bring it up to discuss it right now. But you're more important to me than any business venture. That's the least I can do."

As I watched him leave, I wasn't sure how I felt about the whole thing anymore. I still felt betrayed by his lack of trust in me, but how much of that was my fault?

A few minutes later, buoyed by the warmth of the hot chocolate and the green and white afghan, I finally relaxed. The baby was pressed up against my ribs, making it hard to breathe, but I didn't care. I was just grateful everything was okay.

I picked up my Bible study book and opened it to the latest lesson. The main scripture was 1 John 3:18: "Dear children, let us not love with words or tongue but with actions and in truth." The words niggled at my brain. I knew there was something the Lord was trying to tell me, but the words grew blurry under my tired gaze. I set the book aside, rolled over on my side, and drifted to sleep, only to be awakened shortly by the sounds of my mother's voice and my youngest children's footsteps on the stairs.

"Land sakes. Your mother is a magnet for crime lately. But then she's always been in trouble. Did I ever tell you kids about the time she was twelve, and she took Abbie for a ride in her granddaddy's truck? Gonna herd cattle, was what she said later. I thought my heart would stop in my chest when I saw the two of them rolling by in the pasture, cattle scattering to the wind and. . ."

I'd heard that story approximately ten thousand times. So had everyone else in the family. While she stood just inside the doorway, droning on and on, Sammie and Charlie burst into the room. Sammie caught herself just before she jumped on the bed. I hugged her and eyed Charlie over her head. His lips were in a thin line, and his body was tense.

"I'm fine," I mouthed at him.

His body relaxed.

When my mother was finally done with her narrative, she put her hands on her hips. "Well, missy, you managed not to kill my latest grandchild."

"Everything is fine." I hoped she wouldn't keep hounding me. I wasn't up to sparring right now.

She stared at me, eyelids blinking. In a flash of perception, I realized she had been worried sick about me and the baby. Because her tongue is so sharp, I tend to forget she's vulnerable.

"I'm sorry to worry you," I said.

She shrugged. "Well, I should be used to it. Now, you're going to rest tonight. I'll take care of everything here. I'll call you when it's ready." She motioned to Charlie and Sammie. "Come on, kids. Let's cook."

"Thank you," I whispered. She didn't hear me, but I wasn't thanking just her. I was also thanking the Lord. I had a lot to be grateful for, and lately I seemed to have forgotten that.

I'd been ordered to be still and rest, but that didn't mean I couldn't think. I grabbed my clue notebook and pen from the nightstand.

I had a lot of clues to write down.

*Carla bullies Twila. Carla was buddy-buddy with Georgia but had a fight with her the day before Georgia was killed. Carla has a fiancé named Ronnie who gave her a watch. My four main suspects have all been at the sheriff's office for questioning. Is Marvin in love with Connie? Coach was arrested for giving drugs to kids. Georgia dated Coach a couple of times then dumped him. Receipt at Connie's was from a pawn shop in Baltimore. Connie had a boyfriend named Aaron Bryant who was killed in Charlottesville the day before Georgia was murdered.*

As I tapped my pen on my bottom lip, my mind went back to Marvin. Maybe he had a heart attack. Shirl said he was talking to the pharmacist about heart medications.

Nothing made sense to me.

While I was staring at what I'd written, I saw motion at my bedroom door and looked up.

Abbie was standing in the doorway.

Abbie didn't move. I remembered when we were little, spending nights huddled together with a flashlight under the covers during weekend sleepovers. Whispering all the secrets that little girls keep. As we got older, giggling about boys and the other girls. In many ways, she knew me better than Max ever would.

"Do you mind if I come in?" she asked.

"You have to ask?" I could hardly breathe.

She approached my bed slowly. "I wasn't so sure you'd want to see me."

"Why would you think that?" I put my notebook on the bed beside me.

"I figured you were mad at me. I haven't returned your calls."

I shook my head. "I was afraid I'd driven you away." I sniffled back tears. "I've got such a big mouth. I'm sorry."

"No," she said. "I'm sorry."

She held out her index finger, and I held out mine. We touched the tips. Our old sign of friendship. When we were little, we'd pricked our fingers, made them bleed, and held them together. Blood sisters.

Abbie is rarely demonstrative, so that meant more than any words she could say. Relief poured over me. I hadn't ruined one of the most important relationships of my life. I pulled her into a hug. "How come you didn't answer the phone?" I mumbled into her shoulder.

"Because I went away. I had to have time to think." She let go of me and straightened up.

I sat back and wiped my nose with my bathrobe sleeve and pointed at the green upholstered chair next to the dresser. "If you can stay, grab that and pull it over here."

She did, shook her shoes off, and propped her legs on the bed.

"Where'd you go?" I leaned back against the headboard.

"To the beach. I sat on the balcony and watched the waves." She sighed. "I concluded that you're right. I'm turning into my grandmother."

I wiped my nose again on my sleeve. "Does that mean you'll date Detective Scott?"

She laughed as she snatched a box of tissues from the bed stand, took one for herself, then handed the rest to me. "I don't know about that, but I am going to deal with some of the issues in my life." She wiped her nose. "Now what's up with you and Max?"

I laughed and blew my nose, then leaned back against the headboard. "How did you know something's up?"

"Because of the way he told me to come up and see you."

I explained our fight to her. When I was done, I took a deep breath. "Am I really that big of a grump?"

She glanced at me then glanced away. "You've always been kind of prickly, but right now you are worse than you've ever been."

I felt so small. "I'm going to have to apologize to him. I hope he'll be able to forgive me."

"Well, you can't take all the blame. He does have that arrogance thing going on, and he should have told you these things despite your grumpiness." She smiled. "But he adores you. You guys will get it straightened out."

"I hope so."

"Trust me."

I rearranged the pillow behind my back. "Now will you tell me why you won't date Detective Scott?"

Abbie's lips narrowed, and I raised my eyebrows at her.

"All right, all right. I'll tell you. Then I want to let it go for a while, okay?"

"Fine."

"It's not that I don't like him. Not at all. In fact, the opposite is true."

"Well then—"

"Eric was the one who told me that my husband was cheating on me. They worked together, you know."

I nodded.

"My husband cheated one too many times. I couldn't take it anymore, but Eric tried to talk me into staying with the marriage. When I walked out, Eric was mad. It was like a good ol' boys' club." She paused. "I thought he was my friend. I thought he'd support me."

"So you felt like he was judging you?"

"Yes. And then he ended up going through a divorce himself."

"Did he apologize?"

"Yes, he did." She swallowed. "I refused to forgive him. . . . At least I refused then."

"And now?"

She took a deep breath and met my gaze with a quick smile. "Now I'm ready to do the right thing. Whatever it is that God wants me to do. Walking in God's love instead of selfishness sometimes means doing the very thing we don't want to do. In my case, that's leaving the past behind."

Abbie's words struck me like a physical blow.

"Did I say something wrong?" she asked. "Your face is all screwed up."

I shook my head. "No. You said exactly the right thing. That's what the Lord has been trying to get through to me." I snatched my Bible off the bed stand and opened it to 1 John 3:18. "Listen to this, Abs. 'Dear children, let us not love with words or tongue but with actions and in truth.' "

She smiled. "That's it, exactly."

She put the Bible back on the nightstand and picked up the notebook "Now I want to hear about your mystery. Maybe I can help."

I laughed. Abbie had helped me solve Jim Bob Jenkins's murder by providing me with an essential piece of information she had gained from researching her crime novels.

She flipped my notebook open. Her eyes widened, and she glanced up at me. "Wow. I'm impressed. This is much more detailed than your last list."

I felt absurdly pleased by her remark. "That means a lot coming from Ms. I-Outline-My-Books-in-Gory-Detail."

She grinned. "Does Max know you're investigating?"

"Yes. He said he can't stop me."

"I believe that." She leaned back and studied my notebook. Then she handed me the notebook and steepled her fingers. "To sum it up, Marvin might have just had a heart attack and it wasn't a murder attempt at all. He's possibly involved in a drug scheme. He's also in love with Connie. Connie stands to inherit Nettie's farm now that Georgia is dead. Oh, and her boyfriend is dead, too, so maybe she murdered two people. Either Georgia or Connie was pawning Nettie's belongings, and Marvin might have been in on it. Maybe he and Connie murdered Georgia with poison.

"Then there's Coach Smith. Besides giving kids drugs, he was dating Georgia, and she dumped him. Carla is a selfish control freak who wants to be better than she is." Abbie flicked the pages with her fingernail. "I wonder how many of them knew about the drug and/or cheating scheme?"

"That's a good question." I sighed.

"Love and greed are powerful motives," Abbie said.

An hour later, we were seated at my dining room table finishing up a meal of fried chicken, mashed potatoes, gravy, and corn pudding. That wasn't going to help my waistline, but I enjoyed it. Since I came downstairs, Sammie had been glued to my side and insisted on sitting next to me at dinner. Charlie had been eyeing me while he continued his usual chattering. Tommy and Karen were at work.

Ma was beginning to clear the table with Abbie's help when someone knocked at the front door. Charlie scampered to get it.

I heard a familiar man's voice and Charlie's higher pitched one jabbering excitedly.

"Hey, look. It's that policeman," he announced as they walked into the dining room.

At that moment, Abbie entered the room through the kitchen door holding an apple pie. Her eyes connected with Detective Scott's. I was afraid she would drop the plate.

He broke eye contact first, shifting his gaze to Max and then to me. "I'm sorry to interrupt. I'd like to talk to you, but I can wait outside until you're done eating."

I had visions of him huddled in a dark, cold car while we sat inside eating apple pie and drinking coffee.

"I'm done." I stood slowly to my feet. "Let's talk now. How about we go into the living room?"

Ma burst out of the kitchen with coffee mugs, which prompted Abbie to plunk the pie on the table. She whirled around and went back into the kitchen.

"What is he doing here?" Ma asked nobody in particular. "Trish has to rest. No more cops and robbers for her today."

Detective Scott smiled. "I won't keep her long."

Ma's fisted hands rested on her hips. "Well, I should hope not. I'm sure she's already helped you plenty. You need to solve the crime so she can have some peace before this baby comes."

I looked over at Max whose expression was resigned; then I looked at the detective. "Let's go get this over with."

Max accompanied us with his hand on the small of my back.

When we got to the family room, Detective Scott eyed me with drawn cheeks and a wrinkled forehead. "Are you okay to do this?"

"Yes. I'm feeling great now. Have a seat." I pointed to one of the overstuffed chairs.

"Thank you." He settled into the chair's depth, reached into his shirt pocket, and pulled out his small notebook and a pen.

I sat on the sofa, and Max sat next to me.

"I was very concerned about you earlier today," Detective Scott said. "I'm glad you're okay."

"Me, too," Max breathed.

I put my hand on his leg, and he put his arm on the sofa behind me.

Detective Scott shifted in the chair. "I want to know what happened from the time you walked into the school."

I told him. Then I mentioned running into Tommy in the hallway.

As I spoke, Max's body stiffened. He looked down at me. "Tommy was there?"

"Don't worry," Detective Scott said quickly. "Tommy is no longer a person of interest. Neither are any of the other students. In fact, after the first day or two, they weren't suspects. We just needed information from them." He paused and eyed me. "That's between you and me."

The detective was finally trusting me with something. I also felt like a load of bricks was lifted off me. Max did, too—I could feel his body relax.

Max removed his arm from around me. "In that case, perhaps I should go get the kids ready for bed. Will you be okay, Trish?"

I nodded.

When he was gone, I focused on the detective. He was studying his notes; then he looked up. "Did you speak with anyone else?"

*Sherry.* I felt panicked, wondering how he was going to react when he found out that his daughter was still trying to solve the mystery. My foot starting wiggling in response to my nerves.

"What is it?" he asked.

"Well, Sherry and I talked."

We were interrupted by Abbie who walked into the room carrying a tray on which were two mugs and two plates holding thick wedges of pie.

"We thought you guys might need something." She set the tray on the coffee table then straightened and met his gaze. "You look tired."

"I am."

"I know this has got to be difficult." She took a deep breath. "When you get done with this case, why don't you give me a call?" She quickly leaned down and kissed my cheek. "I'm going home now. I'm glad you're okay."

As she walked from the room, Detective Scott followed her with his eyes. They shone with a mixture of hope and anxiousness like a teenage boy's. However, once she was out of sight, the expression disappeared, and he turned to face me.

"So, what about Sherry?"

"She was looking for Tommy. He's avoiding her because of you. It upsets her."

The detective's jaw tightened. "What did she say?"

I told him, leaving out the part about Sherry wanting to kiss Tommy. That fell under the topic of *too much information* and meant nothing to the investigation. He didn't seem surprised by what Sherry told me, which made me wonder if she was correct. Elissa was helping her brother.

He tapped his pen on his leg. "I'm going to walk through the whole thing with you again. From the time you pulled into the parking lot."

I nodded and felt a sudden admiration for him. His personal feelings and obvious weariness weren't deterring him from his job. I could learn a lot from his self-discipline. I took a deep breath and answered his questions as he prompted me. He was particularly interested in the conversations I'd had.

When I was done, a tiny grin played on his lips. "Now, is there anything in that notebook of yours that you'd like to share with me?"

I couldn't believe he wanted to know what I thought. I retrieved it from my bedroom. He flipped through the pages and even jotted something down. I tried not to let my sense of satisfaction show, but when he smiled at me, I think he knew how I felt.

A few minutes later, after he left, I went in search of Max. He was talking to Tommy, who had just returned home, so I went upstairs and got ready for bed. After I got under the covers, Max walked into the bedroom. "After my shower, we need to have that talk."

# 19

I leaned back against the headboard, picking my nails and listening to the water run in the bathroom. I knew what I had to do. Apologize. But first, I needed to get one other thing cleared up. By the time Max walked back into the room, I had worked myself into a minor dither.

He sat on the bed and grabbed my hands. "Stop picking. You'll make yourself bleed."

I sat up straight. "Max, I'll never live up to your family. I'm a redneck through and through. I'm afraid you're going to wake up one day and wish you hadn't married me. Your mother always insinuated I forced you into it. Did I? I didn't do anything but fall in love with you. In fact, I tried *not* to fall in love with you. But if I hadn't done that, then I wouldn't have Sammie. Or Karen, Tommy, and Charlie. And this one." I rubbed my big tummy and felt my lower lip tremble. "That would be awful."

"Where is all this coming from?" Max let go of my hands and put his fingers under my chin, forcing me to look at him. "I've never regretted being married to you. You're my balance. You keep me from becoming what my family is." He paused. "Well, at least my mother."

"Don't you think I'm a bad influence on the kids?"

He smiled. "You're the best mother our kids could have."

I blinked back tears. "Really?"

He laughed. "Yes. Your spontaneity and daring is what I love the most about you. You've helped them not be afraid of things. Especially Tommy. Remember how he was when I first married you? The nights you insisted on sitting up with him?"

I thought about the skinny little boy Tommy had been then, tormented by nightmares. "Yes. I love him," I said softly. "I love all our kids."

"I know that." Max stroked my hair. "I didn't even consider my mother's suggestion to put Charlie in a private boarding school. The idea was absurd. The kids need you—they need us as a family. That's why I didn't say anything to you. Besides, you didn't need another reason to dislike my mother."

"But Charlie knew, didn't he? He threatened once that maybe he should go to private school."

Max grimaced. "Unfortunately, my mother said something to him. But I straightened it out. He doesn't really want to go."

He kissed me, walked to his side of the bed, and got under the covers.

I rested my head on his shoulder.

We lay in silence for a few minutes. I inhaled the scent of soap on his skin and felt the slow thump of his heart.

"I'm sorry I've been acting like I have been. So grumpy you couldn't even tell me about the housing development. I've been very selfish."

He sighed. "Well, you were right about that. I should have told you." He stroked my hair. "I'm sorry."

"Have you talked to the board about stopping the project?"

"Not yet. I haven't had time." He shifted. "You know, come to think of it, I think that housing development is one of the reasons that Georgia had it in for Tommy."

"What?" I lifted my head and looked at him. "What do you mean?"

"She wanted to sell the property badly. Nettie was in no condition to make decisions. Dad and I heard about it and approached her. She must have gotten her hopes up. When we determined that the property didn't meet our criteria, she was furious." He sighed. "Connie didn't want to sell. That's why I talked to her that day at Self-Storage. To make sure she understood we weren't going to buy it. She was happy."

"Maybe that's because she was pawning stuff. Someone in the house was." I put my head back on his shoulder. "But if it was her, then why?"

"That's a good question."

Lying with Max in the dark, hearing his soft breathing and feeling his protective embrace, reminded me again how much I loved him.

I took a deep breath and steeled myself. "Max, don't stop the housing project. I know you were doing that just for me. You don't have to. I'm fine."

He inhaled sharply.

"I mean it. Like you said, it's going to happen. It might as well be you and your dad first."

He turned onto his side. "Are you sure?"

"Yes."

"Thank you." He kissed me and pulled me tight. "I've missed spending time with you like this. Time alone."

"What?" I struggled to a sitting position. "You haven't tried to spend any time alone with me lately. Cuddling used to be such a big part of our lives. Now you barely look at me."

He frowned.

"I know it's because I'm fat," I moaned. "And my ankles are fat, too. My pants are tight. I just can't help it. And I eat like a horse. I—"

"Baby. . ."

"Well, I do. And I feel so ugly and—"

He grabbed my hand. "Trish, hush."

"It's true," I whispered.

He pulled me close again. "I'm so sorry. I wasn't reading your signals right."

"What do you mean?" I tried to pry myself loose, but I couldn't.

"Well, you kept telling me how badly your body hurt and how tired you were. I just assumed you didn't want anything to do with me—that you just wanted to be left alone."

"But you were acting like you were avoiding me."

"No." He groaned. "Not at all. I didn't want to bother you. You have no idea how hard the last month has been."

"Really?"

"Really."

I finally untangled myself from his arms. "So you don't think I'm the fattest, ugliest thing you've ever seen in your whole life?"

He laughed. "No. Not at all. I'm nuts about you. I always have been. And I think you're beautiful."

---

I didn't go into work on Tuesday or Wednesday in an effort to rest as ordered. That meant no excuses for not completing sewing for the baby's room. But, by midday Wednesday, I thought I would go insane. The only thing saving me was knowing I was going to help Elissa and Sherry begin to sort through play costumes that afternoon.

Yellow fabric slid under the needle of my whirring sewing machine as I finished a seam on the last set of curtains. My mind was whirring as fast as the machine. I'd tried to call Marvin at the hospital, but he didn't answer his phone. I couldn't find out from anybody what had really happened to him. I kept running all my clues over and over in my head.

I was done with the curtains and had started the ruffle for the bottom of the crib when my home phone rang. I grabbed the portable off the wall in the kitchen.

"Well, I'm glad you're home and not risking my grandchild's life by going to work today."

"Hi, Ma. I can be taught."

She snorted. "I have my doubts about that. What are you doing?"

"Sewing. Then I have to help Sherry and Elissa Scott with costumes for the play."

"You're going to drive?" she demanded. "You know we're having high winds. Where are you going?"

"To the high school. It's not a long drive. It can't possibly hurt anything."

"That place is a bastion of murder and mayhem," she said. "You should pull the kids out."

"Everything is locked down now. During the day only the front door is open, and the resource officer sits there at a desk. After school you can't get in unless you have an appointment. It's safe."

"Well, locks don't stop bad people. In fact, seems to me it would just encourage them to break in. And what if the bad guys are in the school already? We're surrounded by all sorts of criminals, you know." Ma paused. "That's why April is on leave for a few days."

"We're surrounded by criminals, so April's on leave?"

"Yes."

"So, what's the crime?" I asked.

"Just like I said. Gambling. See? People should listen to me."

As usual, my mother's conversational technique made me feel as if I had brain whiplash. "April is gambling?"

"Oh, for heaven's sake. Not April. You should know I'd have better sense than to hire someone who gambled."

I bit my tongue so I wouldn't ask the obvious question: How can you tell when people are gambling—do they have it written on their heads? "Well, who then?"

"It's Connie. *She's* been gambling. Online.

"Connie's gambling online. . . . What does that have to do with April being on leave?"

"She's got to take care of Nettie, of course."

"Where is Connie? And why can't she still watch Nettie?"

"Connie's been stealing stuff from Nettie to pay off her gambling debts." Ma huffed indignantly. "Can you imagine? The family had her arrested last night. Today they're having a big family meeting to figure things out."

Pieces of the mystery puzzle began falling together in my head, but I wasn't sure they were making a complete whole. This did possibly explain April's comment that Nettie was misplacing things. Perhaps it hadn't been Nettie at all. Instead, Connie was taking things to pawn. And was Connie gambling online in the school library? If Georgia had discovered what Connie was doing, that would explain Georgia's anger and their fight in the library. Was Connie the murderer? And that brought up Marvin. He had a copy of a pawn shop receipt on his desk. Was he in on this with her?

"Have you heard anything about Marvin Slade?" I asked.

Ma snorted. "Oh, that one. Yes. This morning Gail's cousin's wife came by. Her husband is on the school board. She told Gail that Marvin was out of the hospital today, but they think maybe he was involved in the drug scheme. You know what they're saying, don't you?"

"No. That's why I asked." I tapped my fingers impatiently on the kitchen table.

"Don't get smart or I won't tell you," she said.

I doubted that. She could never stand not sharing a juicy tidbit of gossip, but I apologized anyway.

She sniffed. "The drugs Coach Smith used were for performance all right, but not just sports. They were supposed to help the kids take tests better. Something called Inderal. People take it for their hearts. Can you imagine? What will they think of next? Coach Smith claims Marvin knew all about it and was helping kids pass tests by cheating."

Now I was really confused. Cheating. Gambling. And a drug called Inderal.

"That principal woman was here this morning to get coffee. Oops. I have to go. We have customers." Ma hung up before I could even say good-bye.

I needed more information. I picked up the phone and called my doctor's office.

A half hour later, my cell phone rang. Sherry's name popped up on the screen, and I hit the TALK button.

"Hey, Sherry."

"Mrs. C., are you still coming to help with costumes this afternoon? Ms. Bickford told me this morning before she left for vacation that she didn't think you'd be coming because you'd been in the hospital."

"I'm still coming. Is your dad okay with you doing that at the high school?"

"Yeah," she said. "Aunt Elissa will be there, and that seems to make him feel better."

That made me feel better, too. Then a thought occurred to me. "I hope we don't have to work in the band room."

"Oh, no," Sherry said. "That would be awful. We'll be in the auditorium behind the stage. And I'll meet you at the side door nearest the auditorium to let you in. Umm, but I have a favor to ask you."

"What's that?"

"Can you go by Ms. Gilbert's house and pick up a few more costumes? We're missing a couple of things. Somebody named April said she found what she thinks we need. Aunt Elissa is at some sort of meeting and will be coming straight here, and my car still isn't working right."

I agreed. I'd be perfectly safe going to Nettie's house, since Connie wasn't there. I promised to be at the school in an hour and a half.

At Nettie's a flustered but smiling April opened the door before I could even knock. That was good. The wind was blowing something fierce, sweeping leaves across the overgrown lawn and whipping my already frizzy hair into a mop.

April grabbed my arm and pulled me inside. "Trish. I'm glad to see you. Just so I can talk to someone who makes sense. Can you stay and have coffee?"

I shook my head. "I'm sorry. I have to get these things over to the high school."

Her smile died. "This place is just creepy. I hate it here." She glanced around. "I get out as much as possible. I left Granny Nettie here for a little while this morning to go pick up a costume from Connie's storage unit. Granny can stay by herself for an hour or so."

"I want a tuna sandwich," a voice called from the parlor.

A flicker of irritation flashed over April's face. "Granny, it's too early to eat."

April looked at me. "She eats all the time. No wonder Connie gambled and Georgia acted like she did. And this house—I've never been anywhere in my life that's so gloomy. There are so many weird noises."

"Old houses are like that." I took a deep breath and wondered why I could still smell Connie's perfume.

"Well, it's weird. Like that—"

I heard one of the noises she was talking about—a distant, metallic-sounding noise. "I know what that is. Sherry was looking around last time she was here and said the hinges on the garden shed squeal. I'll bet the door is blowing in the wind."

Nettie shuffled out of the parlor. "I'm hungry." She noticed me standing there. "Is that Trish?"

April turned to her. "Yes. Trish Cunningham."

Nettie peered at me. "You were here before. Connie isn't here. She was packing to go, and they came and got her. But sometimes I still hear her."

April rolled her eyes. "I'll go get the costumes for you. I've got them folded in a bag."

She walked down the hall and disappeared into the back of the house. Nettie watched her for a minute then turned back to me. "People shouldn't yell. I taught the girls better than that. I'm glad you're not yelling."

"Who's been yelling at you?" I couldn't imagine April raising her voice.

Nettie shook her head. "Connie and that other woman. Georgia's friend. Did you know Connie was packing to leave?"

April returned with a bag. "I'll carry this to the car for you." She turned to Nettie. "You stay here. I'll be right back."

"What is Nettie talking about. . .people yelling?" I asked while I held open the passenger side door of my SUV.

April dropped the bag on the seat and shut the door. "I have no idea. I don't know half of what she's talking about. I guess Connie was arguing with someone." She sighed. "I miss working. Being here is driving me up the wall. Connie got out of jail this morning, but she won't be coming back here right now. I don't know what the family is going to do."

"How come she's out of jail if she stole Nettie's things?"

"The family isn't going to press charges. And most of the stuff has been recovered. They just want her to get some help with her gambling addiction."

"So they don't think she killed Georgia?"

April shrugged. "She says she didn't, but you'd better believe I'm not eating or drinking anything that I didn't bring here myself." She met my gaze. "I'm worried about being poisoned."

That reminded me of my earlier conversation with the nurse at my doctor's office. "Does Nettie take any medications for her heart?"

April nodded. "A beta-blocker."

"Is it called Inderal?"

"I can go inside and look," she said.

"Can you? And call me on my cell phone, okay? I need to get going or I'll be late."

———

When I arrived at the school, I parked in a side lot. As I got out of my car, Carla drove past me in her Volvo. That was odd. I thought that Sue, the school secretary, had said that Carla was leaving for vacation. And Sherry had just mentioned that Carla left this morning. I must have misunderstood.

Sherry was waiting by the side door to let me in. "Hey, Mrs. C. I'm glad you're here. Aunt Elissa just got here. Mr. Slade showed up at the door awhile ago, but I couldn't let him in. I'm under orders from Dad not to let anyone in except for you." She glanced at me with a happy grin. "Tommy talked to me for a little while before he went to work."

We passed through the double doors of the auditorium and walked down the red-carpeted aisle, then up the wooden stairs to the stage. Sherry held the red velvet side curtain back for me, and I walked past her into a wide space where Elissa sat in a molded plastic chair holding a clipboard, her cane hanging on the chair back. The two boxes of costumes we'd gotten from Connie the previous weekend were at her feet.

"Hi, Trish," she said.

We exchanged smiles, and I put my purse and bag on a table.

"We've been sorting through the costumes, checking them against the list Aunt Elissa got from Ms. Bickford." Sherry hung a suit on a hanger and slipped it onto one of two racks.

"Oh," I said. "I wonder how she got that. I thought Connie was supposed to get it from Marvin the day we found him in the band room. . .but, I guess she didn't."

Sherry picked up a man's dress jacket. "This is one of the things that Tommy is going to wear. Isn't it cool?"

I nodded, noting the proprietary way Sherry held the garment and spoke about my son.

Elissa smiled and shifted in her chair. Her cane clattered to the floor.

I picked it up and handed it to her. "Do you mind if I ask what happened?"

She shook her head. "Stupidity. I was running after a kid who had stolen a car. I blew out my knee."

"Is it going to get better?"

She shrugged. "I hope so, but it's a long process."

We were interrupted by ringing from my cell phone. It was April.

"Trish? Sorry. Everything's going crazy. Connie is missing."

"What?"

"Yeah. Anyway, that medicine? You were right about it. It's called Inderal."

"Thanks," I said. "Be careful."

"I will. I gotta go take care of the garden shed. That noise is driving me crazy."

I folded my phone shut and shoved it back into my purse, then glanced up at Sherry and Elissa. "Did you guys know Connie was in jail, but she was let out this morning, and now no one can find her?"

"Yeah," Sherry said. "Aunt Elissa told me a little while ago."

"That means all the suspects from my list are on the loose. I guess for once the high school is the safest place to be. Even Carla is gone. I saw her leaving the parking lot when I arrived. I guess she's leaving for her vacation." I frowned. "You know what? Something just occurred to me. Why is Carla allowed to go on vacation? Isn't she a suspect?"

Elissa nodded. "You're right. She shouldn't be allowed to go."

"I thought she was already gone," Sherry said as she reverently hung up Tommy's jacket. "She took off at lunch today from what I heard."

Elissa glanced at her watch then handed her niece a black jacket. Sherry slipped her arms into the sleeves and twirled around. "This is the one that I'm going to wear in the scenes where I'm dressed to go on my honeymoon with Mortimer Brewster. Isn't it great? You know, we get to kiss at the end, when he carries me off the stage."

I ignored that and began to pull things out of the bag I'd gotten from April. Then Elissa's phone rang, and she yanked it from her pocket.

"Yes?" She listened for a moment then said yes again and hung up. "Listen, ladies. I've got to go do something for a few minutes. I'll be back." She turned to Sherry. "You have your cell phone?"

She patted her pocket. "Was that Dad?"

Elissa nodded. "I'll be calling you to make sure you're all right."

She turned and disappeared through the curtain as Sherry hung the black suit up on the rack. "I know she's helping Dad. Maybe they've found Connie." She turned and faced me. "Did you know that Dad was going to meet that book author today for coffee?"

I looked up at her. "Abbie? Really?"

"Yeah. He likes her, I think. I like that she writes books." Sherry was very still, watching my face.

"I think she likes him, too."

"Do you know her well?"

I smiled. "Yep. She's my best friend."

Sherry relaxed. "Well, in that case, she must be all right."

My smile widened. "That's a nice thing to say." I turned and pulled a garment from the bag I'd gotten from April and held it out. It was a familiar-looking blue linen jacket. "This doesn't look like a costume."

Sherry reached out and touched it. "Smells like perfume."

She was right. It smelled like Connie's distinctive scent. "I don't think this should be here."

Sherry grabbed the bottom of the jacket and held it out to look at it. Something rattled in the pocket. She reached inside and pulled out a folded piece of paper.

My mind snapped back to the day Georgia was murdered. Connie had been wearing this jacket and slipped a folded piece of paper into her pocket. She'd also looked scared. "What does that say?" I asked.

Sherry glanced through it. "It's an e-mail from that guy who died. You know the one in the article you and Aunt Elissa found? He says his family is coming around to the idea that he wants to marry Connie. He wants her to move back to Charlottesville to live."

I heard footsteps on the stairs to the stage. Elissa was back.

"Oh wow." Sherry gazed at me with wide eyes. "Then he says that Carla had been to see him and accused him of giving Connie a family heirloom watch that should have been hers."

The puzzle pieces fell together. I knew who the murderer was. I just didn't know why.

"What's his name?" I asked

The curtain moved and swung aside. I looked up, expecting to see Elissa. Instead, Carla Bickford stood there.

"His name was Aaron Bryant," she said. "Ronnie."

## 21

Sherry and I were frozen in place.

"Well, I'm glad I came back to check on things," Carla said. "I couldn't find you at home, Trish."

"You were looking for me?"

She just smiled and held out her hand. "I'll take that paper, please."

Sherry glanced at me with raised brows, and I nodded. Carla snatched the letter from Sherry's outstretched hand, balled it up, and stuck it in her pocket, then stared at her. "I knew you were snooping around the school." I watched in horrified disbelief as she took a gun from her pocket and pointed it in our direction.

"I don't understand," Sherry said. "Are you the one who killed Georgia?"

"Not on purpose, but it's just as well. She had turned against me. The day before she died, she actually had the nerve to tell me that I was crazy."

She waved the gun at us, and I thought Georgia's words weren't too far from the mark.

Sherry's phone rang. Carla jumped. "Don't even think about getting that," she said.

"Sherry is a cop's daughter," I said. "You kill her, and he'll be after you the rest of your life."

She shrugged. "They won't know it's me. They all think I'm on vacation."

"No, they don't," Sherry said. "Aunt Elissa knows that Trish saw you in the parking lot."

Carla narrowed her eyes. "Then I guess Trish will be mistaken, won't she?" She glanced at me. "And your mother knows I was leaving. I stopped to get coffee."

"I don't think they'll believe you," I said.

"Sure they will. You'll be dead, so no one can argue with me. You are going to leave a note saying the two of you have gone out to Connie's house to return this jacket and pick up something. There, Connie is going to kill you two and kill herself. I intended to kill her to begin with, anyway."

"You wanted Connie to die?" I asked.

"Of course. She took what was mine—Ronnie."

Sherry watched us with huge eyes. "How did Georgia die?"

"I bought coffee for the three of us and doctored Connie's with Inderal." Carla smiled as though she were proud of herself. "Both of them always drank those herbal concoctions with lots of ginseng, which was giving Connie heart palpitations. She also had low blood pressure. I figured the Inderal would finish her off. I wanted Kent Smith to be blamed. Unfortunately for Georgia, she drank Connie's coffee, as well as her own."

"Why blame Coach Smith?" Sherry breathed.

"Because he was threatening me. We were supposed to be working together. Now, that's enough!" Carla waved the gun at us. "One of you get a piece of paper."

Sherry turned and pulled a spiral notebook from her backpack. My mind was whirling.

"Write the note," Carla ordered Sherry.

"So this is all because of Aaron?" I asked.

Carla smiled bitterly. "He was mine. She took him. I thought when she moved here she'd lose interest. Then he'd take me back."

Sherry finished writing the note.

"Let me see." Carla held the gun on me while she read the note. "Okay. Put it on the table."

Sherry obeyed; then Carla held the curtain back so we could walk through.

"Where is Connie now?" I asked, trying to figure out how to get away.

"Right where I left her."

I felt a sharp twinge in my abdomen. A contraction. I doubled over to give myself more time to think.

"Get up," Carla ordered.

"Can't. Starting labor."

She swore. "I'll just have to shoot both of you here then plant the gun on Connie, which I was going to do, anyway. Then she'll be guilty of four murders."

My ploy wasn't working. Maybe I could talk us out of this. Appeal to Carla's mercy for the life of my baby and for Sherry. I slowly stood and glanced at Sherry, whose face was ashen. Then I realized what Carla had said.

"Four murders?"

Carla smiled. "My dearest Ronnie. He was shot with this gun."

My heart thumped. If she could kill someone she loved, there would be no appealing to her mercy.

"My aunt will be back any minute," Sherry said.

"No, she won't." Carla smiled.

"What did you do to her?" I asked, thinking the worst.

"I watched her drive out of the parking lot. I called in an anonymous emergency call. I told them Connie is threatening Marvin—at his house across town. I knew she was helping the cops."

Prickles of anger began to replace my fear. No way was I going to let some monster truck principal kill us.

I met Sherry's gaze and narrowed my eyes at her. She did the same. That's when I knew we would figure out something.

Carla held the curtain aside, keeping her gun trained on us. "Let's go. Close together, please."

The phone in my purse began to ring. Carla jumped, but it didn't distract her. Then Sherry's phone began to ring in her pocket. Perfect. In the cacophony of noise, Carla's gaze and aim wavered just long enough for me to slam her gun arm. Then Sherry slugged Carla in the stomach with a strength that surprised me. The gun clattered to the floor.

Carla lost her balance and fell. But she recovered quickly and scrabbled on the floor for the gun. I kicked it to the back of the stage. Sherry tackled Carla and knocked her to her back.

Carla screamed like a banshee and tried to get up. Sherry boxed her ear then pulled her hair, making her scream louder.

I couldn't believe my eyes. My son had picked the perfect girl.

Suddenly, the doors to the auditorium flew open and cops overran the place. Detective Scott sprinted down the aisle, followed by Corporal Fletcher, who surprised me by how fast he could move. Another deputy leaped up on the stage and handcuffed Carla. Elissa followed behind them, limping on her cane.

"Are you both okay?" Detective Scott yelled as he ran up the stage stairs. "We called Sherry twice. Then Trish. I was frantic when neither of you answered your phones."

"We're fine, Daddy," Sherry said.

"Fletcher, take care of Trish," the detective said as he snatched Sherry into his arms.

The stage was swarming with cops.

Another pain seized my abdomen. I grabbed at the plastic chair and sat down hard.

Corporal Fletcher rushed to my side. "Mrs. C., you don't look so good. Did she hurt you?"

"No." I grimaced in pain. "But I am going to have a baby."

## 22

I love you." Max leaned over my hospital bed and kissed my cheek.

I brushed my fingers over his lips. "Ditto."

He glanced at the bassinet next to my bed. "Rest, now. I'm sure Chris will wake up hungry soon."

After one last kiss, he left the room. I watched him, remembering what Shirl had said—how women liked to watch his. . . Well, she was right. He looked *good*. And I vowed to get back into good shape now that the pregnancy was over.

For once, I was grateful to be in the hospital. I stared at my new son. Despite his early arrival, he was healthy. Delivery had been easy compared to the pregnancy.

From the corner of my eye, I saw a shadow at the door and looked up. Connie and Marvin were standing there. She was holding a present.

I was surprised to see them. "Come in."

"I. . .we. . .came by to thank you," Connie said as they walked softly across the room. She handed me the present and peered into the bassinet. "He's beautiful."

"Thank you." I laid the box on the bed next to me. I wasn't sure what to say after that. "Um, Marvin, what happened to you in the band room? It was a heart attack, right?"

"Yes. All the stress. It wasn't a murder attempt."

"So you're going to stop eating doughnuts?"

He grinned. "Yes."

We were all silent for a few moments.

Connie shifted. "I guess you're wondering why we're here."

"Yes. I am."

She and Marvin glanced at each other.

"We wanted to thank you," Connie repeated. "You saved my life. You told April about the shed door hinges squealing, and the detective said you helped him with some of your observations."

That was news to me. He'd been by to visit and so had Corporal Fletcher, but I guessed neither had said anything because I hadn't been in shape for a discussion at the time.

"I don't know the whole story about the shed."

"Carla had me tied up in there but didn't fasten the door tight. In all that wind, it blew open. When April came out to shut it, she found me. I told the cops on the phone that Carla had gone to your house to get you. She thought you'd be home resting, not helping Elissa and Sherry."

I glanced at Chris and shivered to think how close we'd come to being killed. "Connie, did you know it was Carla?"

"I wasn't sure. I couldn't figure out why she would have killed Georgia. But remember when you told me about the watch?"

I nodded.

"That's when I wondered if Carla had stolen it from Aaron after I gave it to him to have it fixed. But I couldn't go to the police because I was afraid they would blame me for Aaron's murder or something." She paused. "You know what the really horrible thing is?"

I shook my head.

"Georgia and I were together in the band room before she died. We had the coffee that Carla brought us. I couldn't drink mine because I was having heart palpitations, so Georgia drank both cups. We were fighting. She'd found out I was gambling, and she saw what I was doing in the library the day before. She said she'd told Marvin, but he didn't believe her."

Marvin put his arm around her.

"I was so angry with her I stormed out." She swallowed and began to cry. "If I had stayed, I might have been able to call the paramedics in time to save her."

"I'm pretty sure by the time she was having convulsions, it would have been too late," Marvin said.

I looked at him. "Why did Georgia tell you about Connie gambling?"

"She was angry and wanted someone to stop Connie. She thought I could."

This must have been the argument that Karen talked about when she wanted me to solve the murder.

Connie sighed. "Most everything I stole has been recovered." She glanced shyly at Marvin. "He went and got them back. The family is willing to let me take care of Granny Nettie again if I attend classes for my addiction."

I turned to Marvin. "Why aren't you in jail? I thought you were part of the drug and cheating scheme."

He shook his head. "No. Unfortunately, though, I'm the one who gave the idea to Coach Smith. At least about the Inderal." He reddened. "I used to take it to help me perform in concerts. One day I was joking with him that we ought to use it to try to improve the kids' concentration during tests. He took me seriously. And he got Carla involved. She was always out to prove herself. She wanted to move on to a more prestigious school."

"So why were you afraid that day at the football game?"

"Because I was working with the cops to set up Coach Smith, and I was afraid if I talked to him for long, he'd know something was up."

"Oh." My eyelids felt heavy.

"We should let you sleep," Connie said.

I forced my eyes to focus. "Wait a minute. I have two more questions. Marvin, why were you at Self-Storage that day? And why did you get mad at the dry cleaners?"

He laughed. "You are thorough, aren't you?" He glanced at Connie. "When I picked up the dry cleaning as a favor to Connie—trying to get her to notice me—the girl there gave me some papers she'd found in the pockets of a jacket. One of them was a pawn shop receipt. Then I knew that what Georgia had said about Connie was true." His cheeks reddened. "I managed to steal a self-storage key from Connie's house to see if I could find any evidence in her unit of her stealing stuff from Nettie. I did."

"So the cops knew?" I asked.

Connie nodded. "Yes. That's how the family found out."

My eyelids were drooping again. "I'm sorry. I have to nap."

"We understand," Connie said.

I heard their footsteps as they left the room, and I smiled. I love a happy ending.

—————

Two days later, I was sitting in the living room with Chris in my arms. Max was fixing dinner with Karen's help. Tommy, along with Sherry, was helping Sammie with a school project. I was actually enjoying doing nothing, even though I was still sore and tired from the baby's birth. But my brain was doing fine. I had my clue notebook next to me, and I was going over my questions and observations. I needed one more answer before I would be satisfied.

When the doorbell rang, Charlie, as usual, raced to get it.

"Mom!" he yelled. "It's that policeman guy again. And Abbie."

This was a pleasant surprise.

Detective Scott and Abbie walked into the living room, and she made a beeline for Chris.

"He's so adorable," she murmured.

Detective Scott smiled at me. "Congratulations, again."

"Thank you. What are you guys up to? You know Sherry's here, right?" I was worried that he would still object to Sherry and Tommy being together.

"Yes," he said. "It's fine."

"We were out shopping," Abbie said. "We've been invited for dinner. Max wanted to surprise you."

"It *is* a surprise. Especially since you're together."

Detective Scott glanced at her then back at me. "Yes. I guess I have you and Fletcher to thank for that."

I narrowed my eyes. "You need to remember something, Detective. Abbie is one of the most important people in my life. I used to beat kids up in school to protect her."

He grinned at my mock threat. "I don't think you'll have to worry."

"I guess this means you're one of the family now."

"In that case, how about you call me Eric?"

I wasn't sure I could get used to that.

He noticed my notebook. "Still thinking?"

"Yes." I picked it up. "I have one unanswered question."

"Let me see if I can take care of that." He dropped into a chair opposite me and stretched out his legs. He was the most relaxed I'd ever seen him. Abbie sat in the other chair.

"Just like that? I don't have to beg or coerce you?"

"No," he said. "Ask away. I owe you. It was two of your clues that helped me nail Carla."

"Which ones?"

"The one about Carla's fiancé and the one about the watch. The cops in Charlottesville were able to pin Aaron Bryant's murder on her, as well."

"Wow." I felt like I'd been given a gold medal.

Abbie winked at me.

I settled back on the couch. "So you asked Marvin to set the coach up to be caught?"

"Yes, we did. That was the only way we could get to him. Have him think Marvin finally agreed to help. One of the kids told Marvin what was going on. When Marvin confronted Coach Smith, he threatened he'd tell law enforcement that the drugs were Marvin's idea. And Carla would back Coach Smith up, so Marvin came to us first."

I glanced down at my notebook. "I think that's about it. I understand everything else."

"Okay." Eric smiled at me then turned to Abbie. "Why don't I leave the two of you here to talk? I've got a little gift for my daughter." He smiled broadly as he walked away.

"She's in the family room," I said. When he was gone, I turned to Abbie. "What is it?"

"A charm bracelet. He's going to document their life together with charms."

"That is the sweetest thing in the whole world," I said. "He's much more sentimental and sensitive than I thought."

"No." She laughed. "He's not."

I grinned. "Ah. It was your idea."

"Yes, but he thinks it was his, so let's leave it that way."

Abbie was learning fast.

Max walked into the room. "Time to eat."

Abbie stood. "Why don't you let me carry my godson to the dinner table?" She took Chris from my arms and walked from the room.

Max held out his hand, took one of mine, and helped me to my feet. "Have I told you how much I love you?"

"A couple hundred times, I think."

He kissed my forehead. "I have the last few months to make up for."

"You're not the only one," I murmured. I was determined to practice the lesson the Lord had taught me—walking in love.

I picked up my notebook as we left the room. I would retire it with the empty ones in the kitchen drawer.

Max grabbed my hand. "You're not sad it's over, are you?"

"Are you kidding?" I glanced up at him. "I've got enough to do now that Chris has been born. I might just give up my sleuthing hobby."

Max met my gaze with a tiny grin. "Right. And pigs fly."

# KITTY LITTER
# KILLER

1

I've often thought it interesting how an emotion like love—or the perception of love—can make a person act irrationally and do things totally out of character.

Take this morning, for instance. I was sitting in my SUV, Monday mid-morning, in the throes of lethargic indecision, parked in front of Adler's Pet Emporium. Chris, my thirteen-month-old son, was throwing a tantrum in his car seat. I dug my nails into my palms to keep myself from banging my head on the steering wheel with the rhythm of his pounding heels. Not because I was frustrated with him. Temper tantrums were his regular mode of communication lately, so I just tried to ignore them.

No, I had to make a decision. Did I want to be selfish, break my daughter Sammie's heart, and tell her she couldn't have the pedigreed Siamese kitten my mother-in-law had purchased for her? Or would I put up with a house cat because I loved my daughter enough to sacrifice for her? Not to mention adoring my husband, Max, enough to allow his mother to do something like this to me without first asking my permission.

Head banging would momentarily distract me from my dilemma, but despite feeling lethargic, I could no longer avoid making the decision. As my mother would say, "Never put off until tomorrow what you can do today."

I bit a nail and considered the possibilities. The kitten was still at the breeder's. That meant I had time for a desperate act—like coming down with a sudden, raging cat allergy that would kill me if I inhaled enough cat dander. Of course, that would be a lie. And true love doesn't lie.

I turned to look at Chris, whose face was tomato red. "Just hang on, grumpy."

I buttoned my coat against the brisk November cold, got out of the car, and opened the door to the backseat. Chris immediately stopped crying, reached out his arms, and beamed at me. Let anyone tell me that babies aren't born manipulators! I kissed both his cheeks. Then I snugged a hat over his head, zippered his little blue coat, and hefted him from the car.

The pet store occupied one end of a small strip mall in Four Oaks. My mother's doughnut shop occupied the other end. In between were little stores that changed owners on a regular basis because our rural location can't sustain the business. Especially with the advent of megastores that offer impossibly low prices on everything.

I sneezed when I entered Adler's Pet Emporium, an ambitious name for the family-owned business that consisted of only two stores. Maybe I really was allergic.

"Trish Cunningham. What a nice surprise on a Monday morning. You just bring that baby right over here to me. Your mother talks about him all the time." Jaylene Adler reached out for my son from behind the counter. Her big black beehive hair didn't move. She'd had the same hairstyle for as long as I could remember.

I gladly obeyed. She took Chris from my arms, and he smiled broadly, the little charmer. He happily let her remove his hat and coat.

"I do so wish I had more grandbabies. My oldest is almost nine. Peggy's daughter? She's coming into town to visit me for a week while her mama goes on a business trip with her husband."

I remembered Peggy. During high school, she'd attended a private boarding school in Michigan. That's where she lived with her husband. I hadn't seen them in a long time. "How is she doing?"

"Great. Really great. Her husband is really moving up in the world." She tickled Chris's tummy, and he giggled. "So what are you here for?" she asked between coochie-coos.

"Stuff for a new cat. My mother-in-law thought Sammie needed a pet now that she has a new little brother. We're picking up the cat in the next couple of weeks. Siamese."

"You getting it from that breeder out there near Brownsville?" Jaylene asked.

"Yes. Some friend of my mother-in-law's. Hayley, I think her name is?"

"I order all her supplies," Jaylene said. "Now. . .you'll need the works." She nodded toward the back of the store. "Row four, back right corner. You go on while I hold little Chris here, and I'll get my lazy bum of a husband to help you." She turned around. "Hen-*ry*? Little Trish Cunningham is here and needs help."

I found it amusing that I was still Little Trish Cunningham to her. She and Henry had been friends of my family for as long as I could remember.

I wandered to the back of the store, past the dog aisle, and sighed as I glimpsed a sturdy leather collar and leash. A dog would be so much better than a cat. Maybe a border collie like my father's dog, Buddy. Dogs were just so much less elusive and sneaky than cats.

In the back of the store, I picked up a small bag of cat litter, felt something hit my feet, and looked down to see a tiny stream of litter flowing from a hole in the bag.

Henry appeared as I tried in vain to stop the litter dribbling onto my feet and into my shoes.

"Trish, good to see you. I'm lookin' forward to seein' your daddy soon to do a little huntin'."

"He's looking forward to it, too. Keeps us all stocked up in venison." I pointed to the floor. "Um, there's a bit of a mess here. This has a hole in it." His gaze fell on the bag then on the trail of kitty litter that had fallen to the floor. He mumbled something that sounded suspiciously like a swear word as he reached out with meaty hands and took the leaking bag from my arms.

"Jaylene!" he yelled. "We got a mess back here."

I heard her footsteps as she strode to the back of the store, still holding Chris.

"What's wrong that you can't handle?" she asked.

He pointed at the floor. "A hole in the kitty litter."

"Well then, clean it up," she snapped and whirled away. "The dustpan's in the back. I can't help it. It's 'cause of that new WWPS delivery guy. He punched holes in two other bags, too." She marched past a fish tank display. "I'll call the WWPS place and complain."

"Thanks for nothing," he grumbled as he glared at her back.

"And while you're at it," she said from two aisles over, "you need to pack those boxes that have to go out before he gets here."

Jaylene and Henry were getting along as usual, which meant they weren't. Sometimes I find comfort in knowing that some things never change; however, marital discord isn't on my favorites list.

Henry's paunch jiggled as he put the leaky bag aside and picked up a larger one for me. "You'll need more than that."

"Why? It's only a small kitten," I said.

"You'll want to scoop the litter twice a day. Keep the kids from playing in it."

That was a thought that hadn't occurred to me, and I didn't like the picture I got in my head. Maybe a cat wasn't such a good idea after all. But I wouldn't change my mind now.

"I also need a crate," I said.

"Well, you're in luck. We have those in stock here. Won't have to get it from the other store."

I made my choices, and Henry followed me, carrying the heavier items to the counter for me, where Chris burbled happily in Jaylene's arms.

"I'll get that crate," Henry said as he went into the back room.

"While he gets that, you need to pick out a kitty collar." Jaylene pointed to a rack of custom-made collars next to the counter. "This is my specialty, you know. I make these and sell them over the Internet. I also carry a line of pet toys and clothes."

"I know," I said. "I saw your display at the festival last Saturday." Everyone with any kind of business had a booth at the Four Oaks Fall Festival each year.

I stared at the collars, thinking how much the kitten was going to hate wearing one, but to save my time and energy, I didn't argue. I snatched a blue one from the rack.

"So I hear from your mother that Abbie Grenville is getting married," Jaylene said. "To that police detective."

I nodded. My best friend's wedding was in two weeks and six days.

Jaylene handed Chris back to me as she began to ring up my purchases. "What's the detective's name? Scotch?"

"Scott," I said. "Eric Scott."

"Not a local boy, is he?"

"No," I said.

"Well, not like her first husband, which is a good thing. You know that Philip's mama still lives near here." She took a breath. "That Scott fellow. . .he was the one you helped solve that teacher's killing over there at the high school last year, right?"

Obviously Jaylene had been talking to my mother, who is convinced that the cops can't figure out a murder without me. "*He* solved that murder. Not me."

"Well, that's not how your mama tells it," Jaylene said.

"It's not true." I spend way too much time denying the rumors my mother spreads about me—good and bad.

"Anyway," Jaylene continued, "being married to a cop will certainly be handy for Abbie's books. All that scary stuff she writes. I bought a copy of her latest book when she did that book signing thing at the festival, but I'm not going to read it."

I didn't think the books Abbie wrote were *that* scary, just typical suspense.

Jaylene glanced over her shoulder then leaned toward me. "Besides, it might give me ideas." She said the words in a stage whisper.

I winced. "Ideas?"

"You know what her book is about. Killing *somebody* off." She nodded at the door where Henry had disappeared. "Sometimes husbands just get on your nerves."

Abbie would be troubled to know that her book might inspire someone to kill. If only Jaylene would say something nice to Henry and ease the tension in the room.

He wandered out of the back room and came up behind Jaylene. I balanced Chris on my hip.

Jaylene frowned at Henry when he started to paw through papers and receipts in a drawer under the cash register. Several fell to the floor as his search grew more intense. "You seen that receipt for my new rifle?" he asked. "I gotta go back to the gun shop and get somethin' fixed. Goin' huntin' this weekend."

"You got that gun?" Jaylene turned on him as though she were going to hit him.

Henry glanced at me then back at her. "We'll discuss it later."

"You better believe we will. And the stuff in this drawer is just pet store stuff. Why would it be here?"

" 'Cause I put it here." He kept digging.

Jaylene's breath hissed through her teeth, and she turned her back on him. I could see her trying to pull herself together. "Your mama said she's doing the catering for the reception even though she's been out of the catering business for a while."

My mother's shop, Doris's Doughnuts, is gossip central. I was sure everyone knew everything about the wedding since it was one of my mother's favorite latest topics.

"Yep." I glanced at my watch. "In fact, I've got to get going. I promised her I'd stop by so she could see Chris."

Jaylene glanced at Henry. "Take this stuff to Trish's car."

Since Henry was already piling my purchases in his arms, I thought maybe her orders were unnecessary. "Gimme your keys," he growled at me.

I did, and he walked away mumbling. I set Chris on the counter for a moment while I fumbled my wallet out of my purse and started counting out money.

"Weird, Abbie gettin' married, and her ex-husband shows up all the way from New York City," Jaylene murmured as she watched me.

"What?" I glanced up, dropping a five-dollar bill on the floor. Then Chris shoved my purse. It fell over, and though the contents spilled all over the counter and onto the floor at Jaylene's feet, I was too startled by her words to pay much attention. "Philip is in town?"

"Yes." The word sounded harsh as she bent to pick up my belongings.

"Have you seen him?" I asked as I began to stuff things back into my bag.

Jaylene stood up and handed me my cell phone, some tissues, and a small pile of receipts. "Henry saw him. Haven't seen him myself. He's a pitiful excuse for a man."

In a way, that was a true statement. Philip had never been faithful to Abbie, which is why their marriage ended. I wondered if Abbie knew he was in town.

From the corner of my eye, I saw Henry loading my stuff in my SUV. Chris was bouncing on my hip and kicking my thigh.

Jaylene followed my gaze and then rolled her eyes. "He says I'm a tyrant, but if I don't ride him, he'd get nothin' done all day." She took my cash from my hand, and I leaned over to pick up the five-dollar bill. I still had kitty litter on my shoes. I stood up again, and Jaylene slapped my change on the counter. Then she stretched over and rubbed Chris's head. "Bring him back in to see me again."

"Will do," I said. I tucked Chris into his coat, then I slung my purse over one shoulder and my son over the other. Henry handed me my keys on my way out the door.

"You take care now," he said.

"You, too," I murmured.

I could barely think. I was stunned that Philip was back in town. I needed to find out more, and I knew just the place to start. I left my SUV parked where it was and ambled down the sidewalk to Doris's Doughnuts. I was under strict orders to bring Chris by to visit my mother whenever I was running errands. I dared not disobey her. She always seemed to know when I was out and about. A stranger might think she had some sort of supernatural GPS system to keep track of me, but I knew better. She had informants. Besides, today my vehicle was parked within her sight. I had no choice.

As I walked, I speculated about how small my world had become since the birth of my fifth child. Well, technically my second, but I viewed my stepchildren as my very own.

I used to work part-time for our family self-storage business, one of Max's family's ventures. But I'd taken time off after Chris was born, and now the biggest event of my day was buying supplies for a new cat and visiting my mother's shop.

Unlike many women who adore being home all the time, I missed working.

I opened the glass front door of Doris's Doughnuts, and a bell announced my entrance. A blast of cold air blew past me, tangling my already messy hair and riffling the papers hanging on a bulletin board on the wall.

The cheery red and white dining area was almost half full, even at midmorning. Ma's shop was *the* place in town to get a good cup of coffee. It rivaled that of any specialty coffee chain. She'd started out in the catering business, and then she'd opened the shop. Once it began to take off, she stopped catering on a regular basis. And a few years ago, she'd expanded the shop hours, adding lunch sandwiches and other baked goods.

Chris was wiggling in my arms as I walked toward the glass-enclosed counter.

"Well, look who the wind blew in," Gail, my mother's right-hand gal, said. "Doris didn't say she was expecting you. Then again, she doesn't tell me much these days."

"You know everything you need to know," Ma growled at Gail while she snatched Chris from me. "You come right here to your granny."

I let him go and looked at the two women in surprise. They rarely fought. When they did, it was the proverbial battle of the titans and rarely lasted more than a few hours, which was a good thing. The force of their joint anger had the potential to destroy half the town.

"I'm glad your mommy finally decided to come by and visit Grandma," Ma said to Chris, who grinned at her. "Your auntie Abbie has been here for two days straight."

I blew out an exasperated breath. "Of course she's been here, Ma. You're catering her reception. She needs to talk to you about it. Besides, I was here two days ago."

I don't know why I bothered defending myself. It was a lost cause. I dismissed her manipulation and perused the menu.

"We're selling Abbie's latest book." Ma pointed at the counter near the cash register. "She came by with some copies. April May set up a display this morning."

I'd missed it due to my son's squirming, but I looked now, and I was impressed. April had done a good job. The black book cover with the profiles of a man and a woman, with the graphic of a sparkling gray bullet superimposed between them, was simple but attention-grabbing. This book was Abbie's best suspense yet and her first to win real accolades. It read like a true story about a man who plans his ex-wife's murder and almost gets away with it.

"She's going to be a celebrity bride," Ma said. "We might have to keep the paparazzi away from the church during her wedding."

"I doubt that." I grinned at her flair for the dramatic.

"Your mother just wants the publicity so she can expand and leave her friends behind," Gail snarled as she sideswiped my mother on her way to make a shot of espresso for a customer.

Ma glared after her then turned back to me, jiggling Chris on her hip. "Are you and Max still thinking about buying a new house?"

"Maybe—why?" I couldn't decide what to eat.

"Linda Faye King has her real estate license now. And she's working for me part-time in the mornings."

Gail snorted and slammed a ceramic mug on the counter. I blinked, surprised it didn't crack.

Ma rolled her eyes.

"So Linda's not working in the hospital emergency room anymore?" I asked.

"No."

"She says she quit, but. . ." Gail's words trailed off, leaving no doubt that she was suspicious of Linda's exit from her job.

"Linda just got tired of the hospital," Ma snapped. "I told her you and Max need to move, so she's looking for houses for you."

"I didn't say it was a for-sure thing." Had my confidence level so diminished since I'd stopped working that I was letting everyone boss me around?

"You know what they say," Ma intoned. "The early bird gets the worm. You can never be too prepared." My mother has an encyclopedia of platitudes embedded in her brain.

Gail snorted louder and stomped to the back room. I wondered what was up with the two of them. I also realized I wasn't going to be able to stop my mother from doing what she wanted to do once she set her mind to it—like finding me a new house. My best course of action was to just nod and agree. Or change the subject.

"Have you heard anything about Philip Grenville being in town?"

Lips pursed, she nodded. "He came by for a cup of coffee this morning. Linda Faye served him, and we were all polite, but I didn't want to be. I haven't seen him in years. He's really aged. Looks older than he should, and no wonder. Pervert."

"Did you tell Abbie?" How would she feel being so close to her wedding and having her ex-husband show up?

"No. I haven't seen her since he came. Really, why would it be important? That man broke her heart." Ma drew herself up in indignant anger, and Chris laughed in her arms. At least he couldn't understand her words. "Her book should have been about a woman killing her ex-husband instead of a man killing his ex-wife."

"Ma!" I glanced around the shop, hoping the lull in conversations was coincidence and not customers trying to eavesdrop.

"Well, nobody could have blamed Abbie if she'd shot Philip dead. He deserved it years ago. Now she's finally got a chance at happiness with Eric. He's such a nice man. A good man. A successful man."

She sounded a little bit like the Jewish matchmaker in *Fiddler on the Roof*.

Ma kissed the tip of Chris's nose. "I wouldn't have been surprised to hear that some relative of some woman Philip slept with shot him in the head."

I wasn't comfortable with the direction this conversation was going. I lowered my voice, hoping she'd take a hint. "So why is Philip in town? Do you know?"

"Like I told you," Ma said. "To ruin Abbie's wedding."

Someone walked up to the cash register, so Ma handed Chris back to me. He bleated in disappointment, and I stuck a pacifier in his mouth.

As Ma rang up the ticket, she looked over her shoulder at me. "He'd better not bother Abbie. That's all I have to say. Or you and I will pay him a visit, and I'll shoot him myself." Her voice was just as loud as it had been before.

"Well, let's hope he doesn't get killed." I forced a laugh. "You'd be a prime suspect now. You really should be careful about what you say."

Ma waved at the customer as he left. "I'm *always* careful about what I say." She trounced over to the coffee machines.

Ah, the beauty of self-deception. I didn't bother to argue. It's my policy not to argue with someone who is always right.

April May Winters walked up to the register. "You have to admit it's weird timing, given Abbie's new book and her wedding. Maybe Philip thinks he can somehow get a cut of the money she's making."

I shook my head. "Unless an author is a big name, they don't make a lot."

April looked skeptical, but I knew for a fact that Abbie was barely making enough money to live.

"You want something to eat?" April May asked.

"Yeah, I do. A turkey club. And a Mountain Dew. And would you please hand me a sugar cookie for Chris?"

"Mountain Dew?" April asked with raised brows. "Not your regular coffee?"

I shook my head. "No. I've developed a new bad habit. Caffeine in the form of green sugary fizz."

A minute later, as she handed me a paper-wrapped cookie and the drink, face squished into a frown, she glanced over her shoulder at Ma. "If this keeps up with Gail and Doris, I'm going to look for another job."

I frowned. Gail had worked for Ma since she'd started her business. And April had been working here for several years. "You mean this isn't like one of their normal fights?"

She shook her head a smidgen and leaned toward me. "No. I'll tell you about it when I bring you your food."

I got a table and put Chris, whose mouth was still plugged with the pacifier, in a high chair and then dropped into my own chair. Although the dining room was full and people were back to talking again, the place seemed strange without the background of Ma and Gail tossing comments back and forth. I never thought I'd say it, but I missed them ganging up to snipe at me.

April was on her way to my table with my order when a big blue WWPS truck pulled up outside in the parking lot. When the blue-uniformed man leaped from the driver's side and strolled toward the shop door carrying a box, April stopped midstep to stare at him. As far as I could see, every other woman in the place turned to look, too. Even my mother.

"April!" I stage-whispered.

"Huh?" She ripped her gaze from him as he walked through the door.

"You're gaping."

"Oh. . .oh." She almost tripped hurrying with her tray to my table. After she set it down, she slipped into a chair, positioned so she could still see him. "Wow."

I had to admit, the man was fine. I should know. I'm married to a man who has the same kind of effect on women. Still, this guy. . .

"He's new," April said. "His name is Clark."

"As in Clark Kent? Like Superman?"

"Mmm." April smiled. "But his last name is Matthews."

I checked him out. He did have a certain resemblance to the man of steel. I wondered if this was the same guy who had broken open the bags of kitty litter at Adler's Pet Emporium. He and my mother were in conversation at the counter. He told her how good her coffee was and that he could never get enough. Her angry persona melted. Then I heard her giggle. My mother never giggles.

While I wanted to stare at my mother's unusual behavior with the same freakish fascination with which a person rubbernecks at the aftermath of a car wreck, I had to find out from April what was going on with Ma and Gail, so I tore my attention from the front of the shop and put it on April. Chris slapped his chair with open palms and rocked back and forth.

"What's with Gail and Ma?"

"What?" She turned dreamy, unseeing eyes toward me.

I snapped my fingers in front of her face. "Come on, April. Snap out of it." She blinked. "Oh. Sorry."

I leaned toward her. "If you like him so much, why don't you go say hello?"

"Oh, I couldn't do that. He's just too. . .well. . .*no way*."

This did not sound like the April I knew, but whatever. "All right. Then tell me what's going on with Gail and Ma."

April tensed and finally met my eyes directly. "They're fighting. Over Linda."

"Linda?"

"Yeah. Linda Faye King. Your mom hired her part-time to help early in the mornings because Gail has to temporarily come in two hours late. Linda is also helping to cater Abbie's wedding reception. Gail is really mad."

"Why?"

April shrugged. "I don't know. Gail won't say. Linda always seemed nice to me, although sometimes she seems to be living in another dimension."

"How did Ma end up hiring her?" I asked.

"She was here at the right time when your mother was superbusy. Gail hadn't come in yet. She has to take her granddaughter to school right now. Well, Linda's gotten into real estate and comes in here every morning to get coffee. She overheard your mom talking about needing some temporary help in the morning. She needs some extra cash."

Chris spit out his pacifier and began to cry. I gave him the sugar cookie. I'm not above bribing my kids with sweets to get them to cooperate.

April glanced over my shoulder, and her eyes widened.

I turned around to see what she was looking at, and lo and behold, Clark was approaching our table.

"Hey, April."

She gaped up at him with an open mouth and said nothing, so I kicked her under the table.

"Uh. . ." She inhaled. "Hi."

He smiled. The man had it. Whatever "it" was. Like Max. But unlike Max, Clark seemed to know the effect he had on women and used it.

"You doin' okay, April?" Clark stretched, showing off his biceps.

"Uh-huh," she grunted.

"Well, good." His gaze lingered on her, and he rolled back and forth on his black walking shoes.

He had a copy of Abbie's book in his hand. Since April was stunned into silence, I thought I'd fill the gap to give her time to recover.

"Are you going to read that?" I asked.

His gaze slid to me, as if seeing me for the first time, and the fingers of his empty hand drummed a spastic rhythm on his thigh. He glanced down at the book and shook his head. "No. It's for my mom. She's a big mystery reader, and she's been waiting for this one."

"Does she live around here?" I asked.

"Yep. I just moved her into a house outside of town. She hasn't been well, and I'm taking care of her."

"Wow." April drew out the word, making it sound as though Clark had done something supermanly heroic. "That's so nice of you."

I bit my lip to keep from laughing. The man was only doing what most people normally do.

He preened a little bit and shrugged. "Gotta watch out for family, you know."

"Wow," April repeated.

I had a sudden thought that might help April out. "You know what? Abbie Grenville, the author of that book, is my best friend. I could get a bookplate for that book personally autographed for your mother. Then I could deliver it to your house." *With April in tow.*

"Now that would be really nice," he said. "My mother's name is Eunice Matthews."

April stared at him with rapt attention. I was tempted to look more closely to see if she was drooling.

"Well, I guess I'll see you later." He winked at April, waved, turned on his heel, and strolled out of the shop.

I thought April had stopped breathing again. I patted her arm. "It's okay. He only said hello. He didn't declare his undying love or anything." I paused. "Okay, well, he didn't really say hello; he said, 'Hey, April.' "

"I know." She took a deep breath, which relieved me. I had been afraid she was going to faint. "Wow." She turned glazed eyes toward me. "He knows my name."

"April!" Gail hollered. "We need you over here."

"Gail knows your name, too," I murmured.

April stood up, mumbled good-bye to me, and floated back to work. At least she'd been distracted from looking for another job.

As I ate my sandwich, I watched my mother and Gail. They were making wide swaths around each other to avoid accidentally touching, and there was no eye contact between them at all. When they did speak, their words were clipped and harsh. I found myself wishing one of them would just turn to the other and say something nice. Like I'd felt when I observed Jaylene and Henry.

A simple effort on the part of just one of them could end the ongoing hostility.

## 2

As I turned the key in the SUV, my cell phone rang from the depths of my purse. I flung pens, receipts, and other things aside as I dug for it. As was my habit, I didn't bother to look at the screen to check the caller ID.

I jammed the phone against my ear. "Hello?"

"Patricia?"

Only one person in the world calls me by my given name. Lady Angelica Louise Carmichael Cunningham, otherwise known as my mother-in-law.

"Hello, Angelica." Despite my best efforts not to be intimidated, I always find myself speaking more properly with her.

"How are you, dear?"

"I'm fine. How are you?" Angelica never calls me without a reason, so I stiffened in preparation for whatever she was going to say.

"I'm well. How are the children?"

"Everyone is good." I opened the center console in the SUV and pawed through the contents, looking for a headset. I found cleansing wipes, a bottle of germ killer, pens, fast-food napkins, and a slightly used mint. Where was my headset? "The kids are fine. So is Max."

I heard her brief intake of breath and braced myself for what she would say next. "Has Sammie stopped indulging in her unfortunate. . .habit?"

I dropped the lid on the console. It bounced once then shut.

"Mamamamamamamama," Chris chanted from his car seat.

"What's that noise?" Angelica asked. "Are you still there?"

"It's Chris. I'm here." Talking with gritted teeth and stiff lips is nearly impossible.

"Did you hear my question? Has Sammie—"

"Sammie is fine," I said, trying to force my jaw muscles to relax.

"I've spoken to some of my friends and found the name of a child psychiatrist."

*This is a test,* I told myself. *Only a test.* Chris was smacking his hands on his car seat in rhythm with his repetitive monosyllable. Perhaps he was destined to be a drummer.

"Patricia?"

I took a deep breath. "Sammie is going to be fine. She's just developed a habit of picking things up off the floor and putting them in her pockets. It's not a big deal. She's—"

"Kleptomania is a serious mental disorder, dear."

"Klepto. . .what are you saying? What exactly did Max tell you she's doing?"

"Stealing," Angelica said.

I knew my husband would never say such a thing. He had agreed with me that it was probably just a phase. At least that's what he told me.

"She's *not* stealing," I said. "She's a neatnik. She just picks things up off the ground and the floor."

"And puts them in her pockets!" Angelica sighed long and hard. "Sometimes it takes longer for mothers to see the truth about their children."

Well, that might be an accurate statement, but I happen to know that a person's version of the truth can be subjective, based on their perception of reality. And that was the big problem here. Angelica and I rarely perceived reality the same way.

"Sammie says she's worried about Chris," I said. "This didn't start until he began trying to crawl. Unfortunately, Sammie watched a show where a toddler choked to death on something he got off the floor."

"Whatever you believe, dear, but this is why she needs a distraction. Have you made a decision?"

She was referring to the kitten, and I wouldn't let myself be fooled by her use of the endearment. She used words like weapons, wielding them like friendly fire that kills just as dead as enemy fire. I decided to play with her head.

"A decision? Um, about what?"

I heard her delicate sigh. "About the cat, dear. Maxwell said he's leaving it all up to you. . ." Her voice trailed off.

*Which I don't understand at all. . .* I completed her sentence in my head. "Oh yes. The cat." I paused just long enough to irritate her. "Yes, I've made a decision."

"And?" Her tone of voice changed. "This. . .is important. Not just for Sammie."

That was an odd statement for her to make. Was that vulnerability I heard in her voice? I felt a niggle of guilt. Playing with her head—anybody's head—wasn't nice. And the Lord had been trying to teach me to be nice for a long time now. I had only to look at the Adlers to see the end result of not being kind to someone.

"I've decided that Sammie can have the cat."

"Good." Relief laced the satisfaction in her voice. "She needs to pick which kitten she wants from the litter. She gets first choice."

"Why now?" I asked. "They aren't ready to leave their mother yet."

"That's the way it's done, dear," Angelica said. "What time this afternoon after she gets home from school is good? Hayley will be home after we play tennis."

Give someone an inch, and they'll take a mile, as my mother would say. I'd given my mother-in-law just the tiniest bit of leverage by agreeing to the kitten, and now she was taking over, which she'd do in every area of my life if I let her. Just like my mother. But unlike my mother, Angelica doesn't believe I'm good enough to be a Cunningham, along with my many other failures of character. Unfortunately, I resent that.

"Patricia?"

"Tell Hayley around four."

Angelica said good-bye and I hung up, wondering how I got into these things. My life was being controlled by two domineering women, not to mention all the demands from my family. I felt like I was losing myself.

I needed to go back to work. That's all there was to it. Not to the self-storage business. When I left there, we turned the running of daily operations over to our office manager, Shirl. She was doing a great job. We'd even hired help for her.

But maybe I could get a job in another part of the Cunningham family business. Max and his father had recently begun work on a housing development. Perhaps I could help with that. For the first time since I'd gotten up that morning, I felt a twinge of excitement.

⟞⟝

The trees had shed most of their leaves, helped by the strong wind I felt pushing at my SUV as I drove to the cat breeder's place.

I'd texted Max on my cell phone and told him what was going on. Lately we'd developed the habit of text messaging on our phones rather than calling. I enjoyed the new technology. Plus, if he was in a meeting, he could still subtly check his message and even answer me—unlike answering a ringing phone.

Sammie and I stopped briefly at the local Gas 'n' Go to get some juice for her and to satisfy my latest addiction, an ice-cold, bubbly Mountain Dew from the fountain. After that, I continued on to Hayley Whitmore's house. In the backseat, Sammie babbled about cats and school. Fortunately, her presence kept Chris entertained.

"Mommy, look!" Sammie bounced and pointed at a farm we were passing.

A big sign loomed in the field, advertising a cornfield maze. We'd done the maze the last couple of years and enjoyed it.

"Can we go?" she asked.

"We'll talk to Daddy tonight," I said. "I'm sure we can."

Hayley's house was near the Cunningham estate. The Cunninghams had moved to this neighborhood when Max was a teenager. . . . Well, this wasn't a neighborhood like the typical suburban sprawl. Instead, large houses were planted tastefully on acres of carefully manicured land. It was beautiful.

Despite my irritation with Ma for going behind my back to set up house-hunting help, it *was* true that we were considering a new home. Our present home still seemed crowded with the addition of a very active baby, even though my oldest stepson, Tommy, was away at college. My in-laws wanted me and Max to buy property out here, build a home, and be near them. I figured it wasn't because my mother-in-law particularly wanted me nearer to her, but it was more likely that she wanted to make sure the children were raised correctly. More of her influence and less of mine.

I knew Max would like being nearer to his father. He sounded a little nostalgic when he mentioned houses and land for sale in this neighborhood. I tried to act interested, but I couldn't imagine living here. In addition to being closer to my in-laws, living here would mean being farther from my parents and everything I'd known my whole life. Besides, I wouldn't fit in. I was a farm girl. A redneck through and through. Despite the fact that I married a man with money, my clothes still usually came from the racks in Wal-Mart. There was no way I would join the country club and meet the girls twice a week. I hated tennis and golf.

Still. . .was I being selfish?

I found Hayley's place easily because the shiny brass street numbers glowed on an ornate black mailbox. Following the curved, tree-lined driveway, I calculated in my head how much the asphalt had cost. After I rounded a final bend, I saw the house, and my breath caught in my throat. Built in the style of a southern mansion with tall white pillars gracing the front, the building glowed in the setting sun. I felt like donning a Civil War–style gown and saying, *Tara! Home. I'll go home.* Just call me Scarlett.

I parked in the circular driveway, half expecting servants to run from the house to help us from the SUV. Then I turned to Sammie, who was eagerly undoing her seat belt. "Honey, don't pick up anything in the house and put it in your pocket, okay?"

"I know, Mommy." I could hear the sigh in her answer.

She jumped from the car, coat flapping around her legs, more excited than I'd seen her in a long time. As much as I hated to think it, perhaps Angelica had been partially right. Sammie needed a distraction. A new addition to a family, especially one as demanding as Chris, was hard on everyone. And sometimes the kids who are the quietest get lost in the process.

While she ran over to the flower bed full of lovely mums and other fall plantings, I took Chris from his car seat and balanced him on my hip. He started yanking on my hair, messing up the already frizzy blond curls.

When our motley crew was assembled on the massive veranda, I rang the bell and didn't have to wait long. A petite girl, about my height, answered. For a moment, I thought she was a teenager; then I realized this was Hayley. I was surprised by her youth. I had expected she would be older since she was friends with my mother-in-law. Hayley wore a pair of jeans and a black sweater set with pretty gold buttons. I'm small, but I'd gained way too much weight when I was pregnant with Chris—and I still hadn't lost it all. She made me feel frowsy.

"Hayley?" I asked.

"You must be Trish." She looked me up and down and then smiled. The smile was genuine and reached her eyes with warmth that surprised me. "It's nice to meet someone as short as I am. Come on in."

We stepped into the marble-floored foyer. She took our coats and draped them on an antique umbrella stand, and we followed her into a central main hallway. The mellow oak floors looked like refurbished antique wood. Two rooms extended from the hall; one looked like a music room complete with a grand piano. The other was a living room.

Chris babbled, motioning with his arms that he wanted to get down. I jiggled him up and down.

"This is Chris, and this is Sammie." I pressed my free hand on Sammie's head, trying to send a mental message to behave and be good. I needn't have worried. Sammie beamed up at Hayley.

"Thank you for the kitty," she said.

I couldn't have scripted it better myself.

"Oh, aren't you just the sweetie. Your grandmother has already told me all about you. She just loves her grandchildren so much." Hayley glanced at me. "Your in-laws have been over here to dinner recently. We've really hit it off."

I felt a twinge of guilt. Angelica wanted to see the kids more often. I just couldn't stand her attitude toward me. But was I depriving my kids of something they really should have just because I didn't want to deal with her? My mother was just as judgmental of me in her own way, yet our family spent a lot of time at her house.

Hayley took Sammie's hand. "Let's go to the back where you can play with the kittens and decide which one you want."

She motioned for me to follow her.

Two whitish-gray cats with dark-tipped ears, feet, and tails slipped from the living room and dashed in front of me. I noticed a third sitting on top of a bookshelf in the hallway, tail twitching as it watched me walk past. I began to feel like eyes were staring at me from the walls. All my good feelings about doing this for Sammie slipped away, and I wondered if I should have said no. Cats were sneaky. Cats were sly. Cats were. . .

A horrid wail came from somewhere in the house. I skidded to a stop. It sounded like a baby with hormone issues.

"What is that?" I asked.

Hayley looked around at me, then up and down the hall. "I think that was Mr. Chang Lee."

"Mr. Chang Lee?" I pictured a Chinese cook suffering an acute case of appendicitis.

"Yes. My retired champion Siamese. He's the first cat I ever bought. I guess he got out of his room. He's an escape artist."

"Is he sick?"

She stared at me with raised brows. "Sick?"

"He sounds like he's dying."

She laughed. "Heavens, no. That's just the way Siamese cats talk."

My stomach clenched. "Do they all sound like that?"

"To one degree or another. Some are more vocal than others." She laughed again. "Listen, watch yourself. Mr. Lee doesn't like most people except me."

Nervous, I glanced around. "What will he do?"

"Sometimes he attacks people's legs. He's gotten my husband, Leighton, several times, but they've learned to avoid each other. I try to keep Mr. Lee locked up when strangers are here."

Sammie giggled. I wasn't amused. While she chatted with Hayley, I was on the lookout for an attack cat. Then I glanced up at the cat on the bookshelf. Would it leap down on my head as I walked by? It opened its mouth and yowled.

The noises of the cats rattled my brain. Strange for someone who easily tuned out the complaining of an almost-toddler. What if the kitten Sammie picked out was the most vocal of the litter?

I felt something bump up against my leg. I jumped back and looked down into the bluest cat eyes I'd ever seen. The animal had materialized out of nowhere. It looked up at me, opened its mouth, and wailed.

Hayley turned. "Ah, there he is. Mr. Lee." She paused and stared speculatively at me. "Wow, Trish. You're special. He likes you. I've never known that to happen before." She leaned down and scratched his head. "Oh, my whittle kitty," she murmured. "You mama's baby boy, honey bunny?"

I thought I might be sick. Mr. Lee purred.

"Kitty's messy wessy," Hayley said and then straightened and looked at me. "Mr. Lee tends to spread cat litter all over. I'm not sure why. It annoys my husband."

It would annoy me, too. Mr. Lee began rubbing his face on my ankles. There was indeed cat litter on the floor. Great. I hoped our new cat didn't have the same habit. I gently tried to shove him away with my foot, but he stuck like glue, and I was afraid to push the issue, given what Hayley said about his attack tendencies. "Being liked isn't all it's cracked up to be," I mumbled at her.

Hayley laughed. "Oh, wow. You really are funny. Angelica tells me that all the time. Now I understand what she means." She looked down at Sammie. "Okay, now let's go pick out your kitten."

I didn't think Hayley had the right idea about what my mother-in-law meant when she said I was funny, but I wasn't going to explain.

"Angelica is one of the nicest people I know," Hayley said over her shoulder. "She's been good to me. We play tennis regularly. It's just like her to do something sweet like buy a kitten for Sammie."

I wanted to ask her if she had the right Angelica. But she did, of course. Hayley was the kind of woman my mother-in-law had wanted Max to marry. The kind of woman he was married to the first time around. When he married me, Angelica wasn't happy and had always let me know I wasn't quite good enough, thus leading to our present impasse.

On my truly honest days, I admitted to myself that though Angelica's attitude bothered me, I did crave a better relationship with her, but I was clueless as to how to go about getting it.

The cat kept wrapping himself between my feet, and I was having trouble walking.

"Cacacacaca," Chris said, staring at the cat and beating in rhythm with his heel on my leg.

"He's adorable," Hayley said. "I really want children. . .but. . .anyway, maybe someday."

She sounded so wistful that I couldn't help but wonder why they hadn't had any.

We finally reached the back of the house and entered what might have been a family room or a great room—emphasis on "great." Mr. Lee was still pasted to my ankles, but I was momentarily distracted from his attentions by the floor-to-ceiling windows and french doors that covered the wall in front of me. Doors framed by long, striped, sateen curtains led outside to a pool. Well, *pool* is too mundane a word to describe what I saw. This was an artistic creation. Abstract shape, rocks, a waterfall, and a Jacuzzi. I was wowed.

"Mommy, look!" Sammie squealed. "What a pretty pond."

"Swimming pool," I murmured.

Chris squirmed in my arms. "Down," he said firmly, using one of five words he said very clearly.

"No," I told him with an equally firm tone. That was one of his other words, and he learned it from me.

"But it's got rocks," Sammie said. "How can it be a pool?"

"That's part of the decorating." Hayley was staring out the windows. "We just had that put in."

"It's beautiful." As Chris squirmed in my arms, I thought how nice it would be to have a Jacuzzi to relax in and a pool for the kids.

"I've always wanted one," Hayley said. She pointed to a stack of shiny house-decorating magazines and books sitting next to a leaded-glass vase filled with red roses on a glass and iron coffee table. "Leighton did it for me. I wanted to landscape around the pool. See?" She picked up a heavy book, the front of which was illustrated with a pool very similar to hers, surrounded by a garden that would take at least part-time help to maintain. "Isn't it great? I bought this book last weekend to show Leighton what I want to do with the landscaping." Her eyes moved from the pool back to me. "I hope we don't have to move. Anyway, the kittens are in the laundry room. You want to come with me?"

Chris whimpered in frustration, and I jiggled him up and down on my hip as I followed her. Then I noticed the spectacular fireplace, lined with bookcases on both sides, filled mostly with the latest fiction.

A single picture graced the mantel. I went over to look more closely, trying not to step on Mr. Lee, who was no longer wrapped around my ankles but still hanging close by.

"Your wedding?" I pointed at a picture of Hayley in a gown next to a man who looked to be thirty years her senior.

"Yes. That's Leighton." She picked up the picture. "That's from our wedding."

"Did you get married outside?"

"Yes." She set down the photo. "At a botanical garden. We haven't been married long."

"Where are you from?" I asked.

"New York City."

In the picture, Hayley was smiling and holding on to Leighton's hand.

"Your wedding gown was amazing," I said. "My best friend is getting married in a little more than two weeks."

"Really? How exciting. To be in love and have the whole world in front of you." Hayley's eyes sparkled for a moment. Then her gaze became unfocused, and she chewed her bottom lip. Finally, she blinked and stared clearly at me. "Does she live around here?"

I nodded. "Yes. Her name is Abbie Grenville."

"Do you mean that author person?"

"That's the one."

"Mommy, can we see the kittens now, please?" Sammie whispered.

Poor thing. She was trying so hard to behave even though she was nearly vibrating in her excitement.

"Oh sure, honey," Hayley said, taking her hand again. "We'll look at them right now." She glanced at me over her shoulder. "I think I saw your friend this weekend at the fall festival."

"Yes, she had a book signing there. I was there early, helping her set up."

"We were there right around lunch. I was going to look at her book, but Leighton was impatient to leave. He has to eat at regular times. And he only eats certain things."

I followed Hayley through a large gourmet kitchen complete with black granite countertops and cherry cabinets. She opened another door at the far end, revealing a long hallway. I happened to look down at the floor and noticed that Mr. Lee had disappeared.

"I'm getting lost," Sammie mumbled.

Hayley laughed. I understood. This was a lot of house.

Walking down the hall, we passed a room on the left that looked to be a man's study, traditionally decorated in hunter green. Sunlight streamed in through large leaded windows. Two walls were lined with floor-to-ceiling bookshelves. Several display cabinets filled with guns lined a third wall.

"Your husband's office?"

"Yes," Hayley said.

"Does your husband hunt?" I asked.

"Yes. He's even been on safaris." Hayley gave an exaggerated shiver.

I wasn't paying much attention to her. All I could think about was how Max would love a study like this.

"Ggggg." Chris bobbed up and down in my arms, pointing with his chubby finger. I realized he was telling me that Hayley and Sammie were walking away. I hurried after them as they turned into a room on the right, a large laundry room.

The room was amazing. A woman's dream. Wallpaper with climbing vines decorated the walls. A top-of-the-line washer and dryer were surrounded by built-in shelves and cupboards. There was even a phone/intercom system on the wall. A silky-looking Siamese cat perched on the edge of the dryer next to an open box containing several of Jaylene's Kitty Kollers. The cardboard looked like it had been caught in a tape explosion. Jaylene must have been in a frenzy the day she mailed that one out.

Sammie was squatting on the floor next to a terry-lined basket that held five kittens. "Mommy, look," she said.

I had to admit the almost-all-white kittens were adorable.

"Cacacacaca," Chris yelled in my ear as he tried to throw himself from my arms onto the floor. No doubt I would be diagnosed with child-induced hearing loss later in life.

"Will the kittens stay white?" I gasped as I tried to hang on to my hefty son.

"No. They'll start developing gray points soon." Hayley knelt next to Sammie, gently explaining things to her.

I glanced at the rapt expression on my daughter's face and knew absolutely that I'd made the right decision despite my own doubts.

Hayley stood to let Sammie decide which kitten she wanted.

"Does your husband help you with the cats?" I asked Hayley, speaking loudly over Chris's protests.

"Yes. . . ." She frowned. "Well, he did. Right now he's awfully busy. He's thinking about a couple of job offers. But he's promised he'll help me again."

I thought Hayley seemed a little defensive in telling me so much, and I wondered if things were as good as she claimed.

"Caaaa," Chris wailed, pointing at the kittens with his fist.

I jiggled him harder, and as his cries wavered back and forth from loud to louder, I encouraged Sammie to hurry. She finally decided. How, I'll never know, because they all looked alike to me.

Hayley complimented Sammie on her choice and put a tiny blue ribbon on the kitten's neck. Then we followed her back through the house, twisting and turning our way to the front door.

There Mr. Lee materialized as if by magic and was once again glued to my foot. Hayley noticed and smiled.

"You should feel privileged, Trish. I've never known him to do that with a stranger."

I stared down at the cat, trying to communicate my desire for him to leave me alone. *My mother taught me that getting up close and personal with someone I don't know without an invitation is bad manners.*

I was shocked when the cat met my gaze, yowled, twined around my ankles a few times, then strolled to Hayley and sat on his haunches next to her, staring at me. Was he mocking me?

Hayley handed us our coats.

As I bundled up Chris, Hayley looked down at Sammie then back at me.

"You can bring her back to visit the kitten." Her face grew wistful. "You can come often."

That's when I realized Hayley was lonely. I felt bad for her. Although I do believe money can make life easier, it can't take the place of people.

As I put the children in the car, a black BMW streaked up the driveway, pulling around the side of the house. I assumed that was Leighton, and my hunch was confirmed when the man I recognized from the picture on Hayley's mantel walked back around the house.

I waved, and he approached me.

"Hello," he said. "I assume you're Trish Cunningham. Hayley said you were coming this afternoon."

"Yes." I offered him my hand, and he shook it.

Leighton Whitmore's photo hadn't done him justice. He was as tall as Max and good-looking in a way that age doesn't impact. A mere photograph could never reveal the full extent of his charisma. Especially when he smiled like he was doing now.

"Angelica and Andrew have told us all about you, and your husband speaks highly of you."

I smiled even as I wondered when Leighton had met Max. "It's nice to meet you."

"And you, as well," he said. He bent down and spoke to the children. We exchanged a few more pleasantries, then he disappeared inside.

# MAYHEM IN MARYLAND

As I pulled down the driveway, I wondered if they were truly happy. Hayley didn't seem to be. I had a fleeting thought that perhaps Angelica recognized Hayley's loneliness, and that was the reason she invited Hayley to do things. Then I dismissed it. Angelica would never be that sensitive.

---

I called Abbie as soon as I got home, but she couldn't talk. She was on the phone with Eric, who was out of town. I didn't want to interrupt them. Philip's presence in town could wait.

I answered some e-mails, including one from my oldest stepson, Tommy, and another from Eric's daughter, Sherry, who was Tommy's girlfriend—a relationship that had continued after both of them graduated from high school.

Tommy was away at college. He'd had a last-minute change of majors and was studying criminal justice, much to Max's parents' dismay. They wanted him to be a lawyer.

That reminded me of Angelica's opinion about Sammie. I needed Max to assure me that he didn't really think Sammie had a dark future as a kleptocriminal in some prison cell, but he was ensconced in his study.

I glanced at my watch. It was late, and I didn't have time to make dinner. I ordered pizza instead, ignoring the tug of guilt I felt for not planning ahead. While I waited for it to be delivered, I paced the house feeling vaguely restless. Not that I didn't have a lot to do. I had bookkeeping to do for Max. A house to keep. I also had the never-ending piles of laundry. I even had a stack of books from the library, but I wasn't interested in any of them. Frankly, I was just bored.

Most of the women I knew at church were content to be at home or at least wished they could be home. Knowing that piled more guilt on my head because I wasn't content. That made me a failure in my eyes. Aren't all women supposed to adore taking care of their families full-time?

I wandered back into the kitchen. Sammie had tossed her coat on the back of a chair. I picked it up, ready to hang it on a peg next to the back door, but I felt something hard in the pocket. I reached inside and pulled out a squashed, unopened pack of gum and a rock that looked very similar to the rocks in Hayley's flower beds. The package of gum looked like it had been run over by a truck and probably came from the parking lot at the Gas 'n' Go. At least it wasn't used, but it still grossed me out, and I tossed it in the trash. Then I balanced the rock in my palm.

A rock is no big deal, I told myself. Kids always pick up stuff like rocks. But a little voice in the back of my head asked me if maybe Angelica was right. And worse, it told me if I were a better mother and more content maybe Sammie wouldn't have kleptomaniacal tendencies.

"Mom!" Charlie yelled from the family room. "I can't hear Mike over Chris." My middle son spent hours each day on his cell phone with his best friend, Mike. Anyone who says males don't talk as much as females is seriously unobservant. It's just the topics that differ.

I realized my youngest son had been noisy for a while. I'd tuned him out because the sounds were the whiny kind of talking he did for self-entertainment and not because he was in need or wanted attention. I could tell the difference, so I had learned to ignore the noise. Not everyone in the family had the same ability.

I went into the family room, scooped Chris out of his activity center, and carried him with me to the kitchen, where I stuck him in a high chair and covered his round cheeks with kisses. He beamed at me. Something crunched under my feet as I walked to the counter, but I ignored it, not wanting to be reminded of my housekeeping failures. As I cut up a banana for him, I heard the soft padding of bare feet behind me. I turned and saw Max.

"Hey, I really need to talk to you," I said.

"Dadadadadadadada," Chris said, holding out his arms.

Max took Chris's hands in his and blew on them, making whooshing sounds. Chris chortled. Then Max looked at me. "I heard the little guy yakking. I have a feeling he's always going to be vocal."

I smiled. "Probably."

Max came over and snaked his arms around my waist, and I leaned back against him.

Then I felt him shift back and forth. "What's on the floor?"

We both looked down. Me with dread, thinking it had to be Cheerios or something the kids had dropped.

"Is that. . .gravel?" he asked, wiggling his toes.

"No-o-o." I reached down and scooped up a familiar substance. "It's kitty litter. Must have been stuck in my shoes. I have new trainers, and they have deep treads."

While I swept up the pieces of litter, I told him about buying supplies from Adler's Pet Emporium and the hole in the litter bag. Then about our visit to Hayley's house.

"Mother told me you decided Sammie could have the cat." He kissed the top of my head. "Thank you."

I pulled myself from his grasp and turned around. "Do you mean you were worried I would say no?"

"Not worried," he said. "Just hoping you would do it for. . .well, for my mother. . .and Sammie."

"To avoid conflict and hard feelings, you mean?"

"Something like that." He pushed a piece of hair away from my face.

"Well, I'm struggling with hard feelings today." I crossed my arms. "Did you tell your mother that Sammie was stealing?"

The drop of his jaw told me all I needed to know.

"That's what I thought," I said. "I just needed to know for sure."

"I can't remember exactly what I did say, but whatever it was, that wasn't anywhere near the word I used. I can't imagine where she got the idea."

"She called it kleptomania and said she's found a really good psychiatrist for Sammie."

Max shook his head. "I'll talk to her."

"And your mother isn't the only one who's taking over. My mother talked to a real estate agent for us. Linda Faye King. Remember the emergency room nurse? She's into real estate now."

"What?" He raised his eyebrows. "Have we decided to move?"

I shrugged. "Not that I know of, but everybody is making decisions for me. My mother. Your mother. As usual. So I just go along with it all."

He smiled. "You *pretend* to go along with it and then just quietly do what you want to do."

I considered that and frowned. "That's a bit passive-aggressive, isn't it?"

He laughed. "No. Not in you. You just avoid making scenes, which is a good thing, as far as I'm concerned."

"Oh. Okay." I stared up into his green eyes. "I had a fleeting thought today about living out near your parents."

Surprise lit his face, making his eyes greener. "Really?"

"The cat breeder lives out there. Hayley Whitmore. Her house is too huge for my taste, but I liked the deck and the pool."

"Whitmore? Leighton and Hayley?"

"Yep," I said. "And Leighton said you know him."

"I've met him through my father." A quick frown wrinkled Max's forehead, and then it slipped away. "Anyway, you liked their house?"

"Not *their* house. It was way too pretentious. Like Tara from *Gone with the Wind*. But I just thought about you and how happy you'd be out there and. . ."

He kissed me soundly on the lips, and I felt it down to my toes. When he was done, he stepped back and smiled while I pulled myself together. He knows what he does to me.

"So we can, um, talk about it," I finally said when my heart slowed.

"We don't have to decide right now," he said.

I heard the back door open, and Karen, my stepdaughter, rushed into the kitchen from work, her long hair swinging in her face.

"Caaaaaaaa," Chris squealed.

Karen dropped a kiss on his head and then looked at us. "Dad. Mom." She dropped a bag of pretzels on the table and reached for the refrigerator door. After a quick look inside the fridge, she slammed the door. "What's for dinner?"

"Pizza," I said.

"Pizza again?" She screwed her pretty face into a frown.

Even my kids were heaping burning coals of guilt on my head.

"Yes, *again*." I tried not to snarl, and I also avoided Max's eyes in case he felt the same way Karen did.

Charlie exploded into the kitchen from the other direction, clinging to his cell phone and just missing ramming into Karen.

"Watch it, moron," she said.

Charlie stuck his tongue out at her.

"Stop now, you two, before you get started," Max warned.

She rolled her eyes. Charlie grinned and turned to me and Max, waving his phone in our faces.

"Mike's brother got caught today with drugs. He's in big trouble. It's called estisee."

"Ecstasy," Karen said. "And he's a moron, too. I see him at the mall all the time."

"Karen. . ." Max met her gaze, and she tightened her lips into a thin line.

"He's in such big trouble," Charlie said. "Grounded for life." He bounced out of the kitchen.

I was glad that Mike's parents were taking a hard stand.

"Dadadadada," Chris intoned from his high chair.

"I see him at the mall with a group of kids he goes to junior college with. At least there will be one less idiot loose in the mall." Karen sniffed. Max cleared his throat, and she tossed her hair. "You gotta admit it's stupid."

Well, we couldn't really argue with her point. And with that proclamation, she asked me to call her when the pizza arrived, mumbled about tons of homework, and disappeared down the hall.

I had to admit I was jealous. Karen had a life. She got out of the house.

I wrapped my arms around Max. "Honey, I think I want to go back to work part-time. Outside the home."

He blinked in surprise. "Where? Back at Self-Storage?"

"No." I looked up at him. "Shirl's doing fine managing everything. I need something else."

His expression was wistful. "I kind of thought you were happy at home."

Sometimes men are clueless. They see only what they want to see. Max liked me being home. He's old-fashioned that way. His mother was always home when he was young. Not that she was the typical suburban housewife type—well, she was typical for her social class. That meant lunch at the club after a nice game of tennis. She had no money worries, so she could do that. But she was "home."

I had no money worries, either. If I wanted to, I could go enjoy a nice game of tennis with my mother-in-law, but I don't like tennis.

"I'm happy enough, but I miss the social interaction. I miss the regimentation. I miss having a purpose."

"Taking care of our home and kids isn't purpose enough?" he asked.

"Would it be for you?" I thought I had him there.

"Chris is getting on your nerves, isn't he? It's the teething thing."

Max wasn't getting it. Or he didn't want to. "No. I just ignore Chris's grumpiness. That's not it. I just want to get out." I took a deep breath. "I had a really good thought. How about I work for your company?"

He stepped back, surprise lighting his eyes again. "You mean, work for Cunningham and Son?"

"Well, your dad is semiretired. Seems to me you could use a partner."

Max blinked like a toad in a hailstorm.

"What's wrong?" I frowned at him. "You wouldn't want to work with me? You worked with me at Storage part-time. I do bookkeeping work for you here at home. You don't think I could do it?"

"Well, it's not that, exactly. . . ." He started to back away from me.

"You're afraid of what your parents will think?"

"No. . . ."

I planted my fists on my hips. "Is it because I didn't go to Harvard?"

"Um, no. . . ."

"Well, what is it, then?"

"I'm not sure—"

The doorbell rang. The pizza had arrived.

"I'll go get that," Max said and quickly left the room.

"Fine," I grumbled, my feelings hurt. I thought maybe he'd go with my idea. Especially after I held out the olive branch of living near his parents.

O n Tuesday afternoon, I prepared to meet Abbie and my mother at the church hall. Abbie was supposed to get there earlier than us to fiddle with the decorations she was going to use. As I passed through my kitchen on the way to the garage, the yellow walls glowed, and I felt just as radiant. Max had come home early so he could watch the little kids for me while I was gone. But he'd come home before the time we'd discussed and managed to sidetrack me. Not that he has to work hard to sidetrack me. But as a result, I had totally forgiven him of his insensitivity the night before and even felt hopeful. I figured I'd attack Max's doubts about me working at Cunningham and Son like water wearing away a rock. Slowly and over a period of time.

I was leaving a bit early in hopes of getting a chance to talk to Abbie at the fellowship hall before my mother got there. I tried to reach her by phone to tell her, but when I got her voice mail, I left a message confirming that Ma and I would see her shortly. I wanted to tell her about Philip.

I saw a sign for the Gas 'n' Go, which happens to be near the church hall. My mouth watered. Funny how addiction affects the body. I pulled into the parking lot and the debate began. *Must have Mountain Dew,* one voice in my head whispered. *Just say no,* another retorted. I sighed.

Then in my rearview mirror, I saw a WWPS truck whiz by on the road. That reminded me of Doris's Doughnuts and my mother. . .her constant nagging and how tired I got of people telling me what to do.

I ordered the voices in my head to be quiet, grabbed my official I Get My Get-Up-'n'-Go from Gas 'n' Go plastic refillable cup, and climbed from my SUV. Inside, I nodded at Pat, the clerk, and headed straight for the soda machine, half expecting to see a little good imp and a little bad imp sitting on the counter ready to continue the argument.

As the fizzy liquid flowed over chipped ice in my cup, I told myself I needed to break the habit.

Back outside, I was climbing into my SUV when I heard the sound of a car window sliding down. Then someone called my name.

I turned and saw Linda Faye King in a tiny hybrid car parked right next to me. She looked totally put together in nicely cut brown slacks and a silky gold sweater. She tossed a leather briefcase on top of a jacket on the passenger seat.

"Hey," I said.

"I'm glad I caught you." She sounded a bit breathless. "I'm supposed to meet your mother at the reception hall, but I just got a call. I have to meet a real estate client. I drove by the church, but your mother wasn't there. She's not answering her cell phone, either. Can you tell her for me?"

"Yep. No problem." I took a sip of my drink. So good. Unfortunately, the word that came to mind was *ecstasy*.

"Oh." Linda reached into her purse and pulled out a gold business card holder with her red-tipped fingers. "You and I need to get together and discuss what you're looking for in a house. I have several listings now that might suit you." She handed me the card. "You can reach me at these numbers." A diamond tennis bracelet dangled from her wrist.

I wondered if the bracelet was a gift. It didn't look like the purchase of a newly minted real estate agent who needed a part-time job. "Okay," I said, even though I had no intention of following through. At least not right now.

We said our good-byes. Linda headed off in one direction, and I headed in the other toward the church hall. This wooded countryside wasn't developed. I saw FOR SALE signs along the road that I hadn't paid attention to before. Linda's name was on the bottom of each of them.

I pulled into the parking lot in front of the church fellowship hall. Ma and Abbie both attended this church. The congregation had recently bought this property and put up the building. Plans were in the works for a sanctuary to follow in the spring. But for now, the members used the multipurpose building for their worship services as well as social events, prayer meetings, and other group activities.

Backed up against the woods, the soft peach brick of the building glowed in the afternoon sun. Abbie wasn't here. I glanced at my watch and wondered where she was.

I rubbed my arms, feeling a tingle of excitement. My best friend since I was little was getting married. My matron of honor dress hung in my closet, and I couldn't wait to wear it. I'd been Abbie's maid of honor when she married Philip, but this time was different. This time I liked her husband-to-be, Eric Scott. I'd met him right after I found the body of Jim Bob Jenkins in the milk case of our local grocery store. Eric had been the lead detective in the murder investigation.

He'd pursued Abbie long and hard and finally convinced her to try again with him. A new chance for love.

Just as I stepped from my SUV and shut the door, my mother roared up in her catering van. I waited for her.

When she jerked her body from the vehicle, I knew something was wrong. "Hey, Ma. You—"

"I am just so mad I could spit nails." She slammed the door shut.

"I'm sorry. What's—"

"After all, it is *my* business, you know." She strode toward the building.

I followed in the wake of her hostility. "Yes, I—"

"And my name is on that sign. Big as day, it says 'Doris's Doughnuts.' " She stomped up the step to the cement walkway.

Breathlessly I joined her. "Yes, it—"

"That means *I'm the boss.*" She glared at me, stuck the key in the lock, turned it, and flung open the door to the church hall, banging it on the side of the building. Then she stalked through the opening with me trailing behind her. "Where is Linda?"

"She can't make it," I gasped.

Ma paused. "What?"

"I saw her at the Gas 'n' Go. She asked me to tell you she had an emergency and can't make it. Something to do with a client."

"Well, that just makes my day complete." Ma strode to the kitchen area and began flinging open cupboards. "I hope the women in charge of the morning Bible study put everything back the way it's all supposed to be. They usually don't, you know. And they just had a luncheon." She sniffed the air. "What is that smell?"

I shrugged and grunted. Saying anything was taking the risk of having my head bitten off. As Ma scurried around trying to find the source of the odor, I examined the kitchen. It was a cook's dream and a good indication of how important socializing was to the church members. There was plenty of counter space and cupboards. A large center island held an additional sink, which I couldn't fully see at the moment because of the bags that covered the surface.

On the edge of the island lay a copy of Abbie's new book. She had said she would be here earlier in the day to drop some things off and look at the supplies in the kitchen cupboards to make sure she didn't need to buy anything else.

I sneaked a look inside the bags and found packages of plain blue napkins, matching paper plates, and plastic cups, along with plastic flatware.

"It's the trash," Ma said.

I glanced up at her. "What?"

"The smell is coming from the trash." She snatched the plastic bag from the metal can, grumbling under her breath that she couldn't depend on anybody to help her.

"Do you want me to take that out?" I dropped the napkins back into the bag.

"No." Ma stomped across the tiled floor to the back door. "You try to find the punch bowl. Who knows where that is."

I heard the squeaky front door swing open. Both of us turned, and Abbie walked in carrying a drink from McDonald's.

"Well, at least the bride-to-be is faithful," Ma grumbled.

Abbie met my gaze with raised brows. Ma disappeared outside, and I heard her footsteps clomping down the stairs that led to the parking lot and yard behind the church.

"Hey," I said.

"Hi." Abbie crossed the room and kissed my cheek.

"Where were you? I thought you'd be here before me."

"I was." She dropped her coat on the counter, followed by a wool blazer with dull brass buttons.

I looked more closely at her. "Are you okay?"

"I'm fine." She brought the straw in her drink to her mouth and didn't meet my eyes. I didn't believe her reply. Her eyelids were red rimmed.

"Abbie, have you been crying?" An awful thought occurred to me. "Have you and Eric been fighting?"

She shook her head. "No. He's out of town, remember? At that training school." She took a deep breath and seemed to pull herself together. "Did you see the napkins?"

"Yep. Sort of. . .plain, aren't they?"

She half smiled. "Nothing formal. This wedding is going to be different from my first. I don't want to take any chance of. . .flashbacks."

I looked up at Abbie in time to see a quick frown crease her forehead, then it was gone. If I hadn't known her so well, I wouldn't have noticed it.

"That's probably a good idea. When you married Philip, it was a formal affair, all gold and white and perfect, and look how that turned out. But this is the real thing."

She thunked her half-finished drink on the counter and rubbed the middle of her forehead with her index finger.

"Are you okay, Abs? Do you have a headache?"

"No, not a headache." She met my gaze with a shaky smile. "Everything is just fine."

Her attention fell to the book on the counter. "Is this yours?"

I shook my head. "No. I thought it was yours."

The back door swung open, clattered against the wall, and Ma stumbled in, coughing, her hand over her mouth.

I dropped the napkins on the counter and rushed to her side. "Ma? Are you okay?"

She shook her head and dropped her hand to point toward the back door. Her face was as white as the boxes she packed doughnuts in.

"Ma? Are you sick?"

She swallowed hard as she shook her head again. "No. Yes. Not yet." She took a deep, trembly breath. "Don't go out there!"

I couldn't imagine what was so bad in the trash outside that she'd had this reaction.

She shocked both of us by grasping Abbie's arm then dragging her across the room to the counter where Ma had set her purse. "It's Philip. He's outside on the ground."

She yanked her cell phone from her handbag. The color returned to her face in two tiny red patches on her cheeks. Somehow that was worse than her dead white face. She punched in some numbers.

"Philip? As in Philip Grenville?" A tremor of apprehension wormed up my back.

Ma nodded. "Don't go out there."

Abbie wasn't moving, and Ma released her arm and took a deep breath. "Hello? 911? I need to report a shooting."

Mute and motionless, I listened to Ma bark orders at the dispatcher.

"Yes, he's dead," Ma said into the phone. "Yes, I know who it is." She reached over and clasped Abbie's arm again. "His name is Philip Grenville."

I had the proverbial breath-caught-in-my-throat reaction to that. Abbie's face blanched so white she could have played the part of a vampire in an old horror flick.

I didn't hear the rest of what my mother said because Abbie burst into motion, escaping Ma's grip—not a small feat—and heading for the back door.

"Trish." Ma frantically caught my eye and put her hand over the receiver. "Don't let her see him. I. . .think a hunter shot him. It's. . .bad."

She didn't have to say more. I was already running after Abbie. As she snatched the door open, I grabbed at her arm, but she jerked away from me, almost stumbling down the wooden stairs.

"Abbie. Stop!"

She didn't listen. By the time I caught up with her, she was kneeling in the sparse grass beside Philip's body.

I'd seen dead bodies before. Two to be exact. The first was Jim Bob Jenkins. The second was Georgia Winters, a teacher at the high school. But this was different. Philip was someone I had known well at one time.

Abbie was murmuring Philip's name, pushing at his body. I guess shock shielded her from seeing harsh reality.

I glanced at him. What looked like bruises marred one side of his face. I averted my gaze so I wouldn't see the rest. "Abbie, you shouldn't—"

"Shut up," she snapped. She finally tugged one of his hands from under his body and put her finger on his wrist.

I couldn't stop her, but I knew checking for vital signs was a waste of time. He was dead.

My stomach roiled, and I was trying desperately to keep my gaze off his inert form. I swallowed hard. I put my hand on Abbie's shoulder. "Come on. You can't do anything for him. We need to wait for help to arrive." And I had to get back inside before I lost control of my stomach.

This time she listened to me. She stood and swayed. I gripped her arm to steady her.

"I just talked to him," she said softly. "Just this afternoon."

My heart skipped. I stared up into her tear-filled eyes. "What?"

She wiped tears from her cheeks and left a streak of Philip's blood on her parchment-white skin. My stomach turned.

"And he came to my book signing at the festival."

"I didn't see him there," I said.

"He came after you left. I wouldn't talk to him." Her voice was getting higher. "He called me this morning. Then he showed up here."

"You never said anything about it. You didn't tell me he was in town."

"I—I told him to get lost." Her nose was running, and I searched my pockets for a tissue but came up empty-handed.

"It was like he was stalking me," she said. "I didn't tell anybody. Not even Eric. I just couldn't tell him. Not yet."

"Oh, Abs. . ." My voice trailed off. She was wrong if she thought nobody knew. Someone always knows. Especially in this town. Unfortunately, the ones who *didn't* know were the people she should have told to begin with.

"What am I going to do?" She hiccuped.

"I don't know." I wouldn't say what I was really thinking—like this wasn't a good way for the detective to find out his fiancée had been in touch with her estranged ex-husband and kept it a secret. Especially so close to their wedding day.

I tugged at Abbie's arm. "Come on. We need to go inside. We've already messed up the crime scene."

"Crime scene?" Her eyes grew wide. "You don't think this was a hunting accident?"

I glanced around. The church was in an isolated location, a no-hunting zone, next to the woods. It *was* hunting season. "Maybe. I guess it could have been." But even as I said the words, I didn't believe them. Something inside me was tingling. I wasn't sure why, but my gut told me this wasn't an accident.

4

Forty minutes later, the building was crawling with deputies, emergency workers, and then the medical examiner guy. I knew the drill. We had all been separated and given an initial interview. I sat in a front room of the church hall with a bored deputy watching over me.

I kept glancing out the window. Unfortunately, the view was of the front parking lot, not the back. I watched vehicles arriving, including several state police cars. I wondered why they were here.

My thoughts were muddled. Questions tumbled one over the other in my head. Like how did Philip get here? There hadn't been any cars in the parking lot when I came.

From the corner of my eye, I saw another sheriff's office car pull up. A familiar Santa Claus–like figure got out. Corporal Nick Fletcher. I had been wishing Eric was here, but the corporal was just as good. He was one of Eric's best friends, as well as a close working companion.

He entered the building, and I hoped he'd come find me. I wasn't disappointed. I heard footsteps outside the room, then the door swung open. He walked in, and I shot to my feet.

He nodded at the deputy, eyes dark under drawn brows and deep furrows in his forehead. "Hey, Mrs. C."

"Corporal Fletcher. I'm so glad you're here."

A brief, warm smile passed over his lips. "Always good to see you, but I have to say, I don't like the circumstances. Better if it was social. Like Abbie and Eric's wedding."

"Isn't that the truth," I said.

He shook his head. "This is bad."

His tight inflection said it all. Anxiety clawed at my brain. "Was Philip shot by accident?"

He and the younger deputy exchanged brief glances before Fletcher answered me. "Any kind of death like this is treated as suspicious until proven otherwise."

"Are you helping with the investigation, then?"

He shook his head. "I'm not here officially. Eric called and asked me to stop by to make sure Abbie was okay."

"I don't understand," I said. "Why aren't you official?"

The deputy behind me stared at the wall.

"You gotta understand, Mrs. C. It's a conflict of interest. The victim is the ex-husband of my superior officer's fiancée. I can't be involved."

"Does that mean Eric can't be involved in the investigation, either?"

"Absolutely not. In fact, they've already brought in the state police."

"The state police? That's why they're here?"

He nodded. "That way, our agency can't be accused of conflict of interest."

"Well, at least Abbie couldn't have done it." I took a deep breath. "Neither could I. We weren't anywhere near here."

I thought he'd look relieved, but he didn't.

"What's wrong?" I asked.

He shifted on his feet, and his belt creaked. "Things aren't always that easily dismissed. They're going to be extra careful not to show favoritism since Abbie is involved and she's Eric's fiancée."

"What does that mean?" I asked.

"She'll be treated fine if things are as they seem, but they can't afford to lose a case due to poor investigation. And the investigation will include looking into the lives of everyone involved. Now I'd better go see what's going on." His lips were set in a grim line. "You gotta stay out of this, Mrs. C. I've had about enough of rescuing you from the hands of murderers."

The deputy opened the door for Corporal Fletcher, who disappeared.

"Do you know how long I'm going to be here?" I asked the deputy.

"No, ma'am," he said.

"I need to make a phone call."

He inhaled and frowned.

The tense atmosphere made me cranky. "I just need to tell my husband where I am so he doesn't worry. Is that okay?"

He sighed. "Yes, ma'am. I need to listen, though."

"That's fine. I don't care who hears." He'd be bored to tears by my conversation, I was sure.

When Max picked up the phone, I heard Chris crying in the background.

"Hi, honey," I said. "Things okay there?" I wasn't sure how to tell him I was once again involved in a crime.

"Yes." He sighed. "I'll be glad when teething is over. Chris is so much louder than Sammie ever was. Although I'm beginning to wonder if this is just his personality. And Charlie's snake escaped. We're still looking for it."

Neither fact surprised me. "I'm sorry, honey. Chris isn't an easy baby. And Charlie is so excited about his new snake, he walks around with it all the time. But then sometimes he puts it down to do something and forgets."

I felt the deputy's gaze on me.

"Hang on, Trish," Max said. I heard the muffled voices of my kids through the receiver. "Honey, I have to go. Will you be home soon?"

"I'm not sure. I have something to tell you." I took a deep breath, worried about Max's reaction to Philip's murder.

"Hang on again," he said. I heard his hand cover the receiver and then his muffled voice. "Charlie! Tell me you did not put your snake in Karen's room." He paused. "Go get it *now*." His hand rustled on the receiver. "Okay, I'm back. Now, what?"

"Um, Max, something bad has happened."

There was a slight pause on his end. "Worse than a missing snake, a teething baby, and an angry teenager?"

"Yes. Much worse."

He inhaled. "What?"

"Philip is dead."

Max didn't say anything for a second. I could almost hear his brain clicking. "That's Abbie's ex-husband," I said.

"Oh, wow." Max paused. "That's too bad. Was he in an accident?"

"No." I glanced up at the deputy and decided not to say anything more about Abbie.

"What happened?"

I swallowed. "He was, ah, shot. Killed."

"You mean, on the job? He was still a police officer, right?"

"I think he was, but no, it wasn't job related—that I know of."

Max's breath hissed in the receiver. "He was murdered?"

"I don't know."

"You mean, he was in town?" Max asked. "Here?"

The deputy cleared his throat.

"Max, I have to go."

"Wait. Tell me you didn't find the body. Please?"

I picked my nails. "Well, not exactly."

"Not exactly?"

"No." Movement in the parking lot caught my attention. Another police car had arrived. This one unmarked. A woman built like a bulldog stepped from the vehicle. I watched her stride toward the building.

"Where are you?" Max's tone was a mixture of concern and irritation.

"I'm at Ma's church fellowship hall. And no, I didn't find Philip. My mother found him."

"Your mother. . .what? She found him at church?" Chris's wails in the background grew louder.

"Yeah. He was in the back on the pavement behind the church hall."

"Shot?" I heard Charlie's voice in the background and Karen yelling at him. "There's no way you could have been involved, right?" Max asked breathlessly.

My poor husband. He's always having to pick up the pieces when I do something outrageous.

Somebody walked into the room behind me, but I didn't pay attention. "No. No way."

"Good," Max said.

"Mrs. Cunningham, you need to get off the phone," the deputy said. "We need to take you to the sheriff's office for questioning."

My stomach clenched, and I nodded. "Max, I've got to go. They want to question me at the sheriff's office."

"Do you want me to come down there and meet you?"

"No. I'm fine." I stood to follow the deputy. I could just imagine Max in the foyer of the sheriff's office with a screaming baby, Sammie, Charlie, and a snake.

"All right, baby. Call me as soon as you can. I love you."

"Okay, and I love you, too." I hung up and stuck the phone in my pocket.

Quite awhile later, at the sheriff's office, a deputy walked me to an interview room. Having been involved with two other murder investigations, I knew the drill. But the bad thing was, I'd finally gotten used to Detective Eric Scott, and he wasn't here. I was going to have to deal with someone new.

I waited for a few minutes, biting my nails, wondering where Abbie was. Then the woman I'd seen exiting her car at the church hall rolled into the room like a Mack truck, shutting the door behind her. She carried Abbie's book in a plastic bag.

The skin on her face had seen more sun than moisturizer or makeup. I imagined she intimidated most people with her size and her attitude. When I meet someone with a chip on their shoulder, I always want to knock it off, and hers was so large, it would be a fun challenge.

I had a sudden, vivid memory from high school, when I rumbled with a girl who reminded me of this woman. She had insulted Abbie, who was shy and wouldn't stand up for herself. Although bruised and a little bloody, I'd prevailed in the fight, despite our differences in size, much to my delight and my parents' chagrin.

Given that I felt the same way about the woman standing in front of me right now, I could tell the Lord still had a lot of stuff to work out of me.

"Mrs. Cunningham?"

I stared up at her. "Yes?"

"Thank you for waiting for me. I'm Detective Reid with the state police. We're temporarily using the sheriff's office for interviews."

"You're welcome." *Like I had a choice?* My antenna was up. Her eyes were flat and unemotional, and she eyed me like a praying mantis would size up its prey. She was a force to be reckoned with.

She yanked out a chair and sat down. Then she pulled out a notebook and pen from her pocket. She ran the tip of the pen slowly down several pages, as though reading her notes. I knew she was faking.

"So, Mrs. Cunningham." She glanced up quickly. "Did you know the deceased?"

"Yes, I did."

She stared at me. "How did you know him?"

"He is. . .was. . .the ex-husband of my best friend, Abbie Grenville."

"Uh-huh." She ran her pen down the list again. Then stared at me from eyes untouched by makeup. "How well did you know him?"

I shrugged. "I hadn't seen him in years. So—not well anymore, I guess."

"Years," she repeated. "So that means you haven't seen him lately?"

"Yes. That's what that means." I wished with all my heart that Eric would walk into the room and take over the questioning.

"Were you aware of his recent whereabouts?"

"If by that you mean, was I aware that he was in town? Yes. But I hadn't seen him."

She continued her interrogation, asking me detailed questions about my steps from the time I arrived at the church to the time the first deputy came on the scene. I had to describe Philip's body and what Abbie had done when we were outside.

When I was done with my recitation, she inhaled and exhaled slowly and then dangled Abbie's novel in the plastic bag in front of my eyes. "Is this yours?"

"No," I said. "It isn't."

It wasn't Abbie's. It wasn't mine. It wasn't my mother's. Whose was it? I wondered if the detective was going to read it. If so, it wasn't going to look good for Abbie. An ex-spouse shooting an ex-spouse?

"What time did you arrive at the church hall?" she snapped.

"Around four," I said.

"When you arrived, was Abbie Grenville there?"

"No," I said.

"When did she arrive?"

"About fifteen minutes after my mom and I got there."

I met Detective Reid's cold, watchful gaze. "And had she been there earlier?"

"Yes," I said. My thoughts dropped in line like playing cards in a game of solitaire. Of course Abbie had been there earlier. That meant she theoretically could have killed Philip.

The detective stood. "Thank you. That will be all."

5

When I was finally driven back to my car in the church fellowship hall parking lot, it was dark. I was shaking. I'd been interviewed before—after both murder investigations I was involved in—but Eric was a whole different kind of person than Detective Reid. He at least had an innate kindness. She seemed to have no soul.

My mother had called my cell and left me a message that she was headed home after her interview at the sheriff's office to make dinner and that she'd called Max and invited him. He'd accepted, to my relief. I needed to be around my family. All of them.

Abbie's car was still in the parking lot. That wasn't good news. Inside my SUV, I called Eric's cell phone and left a message for him. Then I tried to reach Abbie, but she didn't answer.

As I drove to my folks' house, my mind continued to turn questions over again and again so rapidly, I felt nauseated. What had Philip been doing back in town? And why had he been trying to talk to Abbie? Why was he at the church? What time had he been shot? Was it murder or an accident? And, the very worst thought, was Abbie a suspect?

When I pulled up to the farm, Max wasn't there yet. Daddy was walking from the barn to the house illuminated by the lights he'd installed on the outbuildings. He met me and pulled me into a bear hug as soon as I got out of my vehicle. My purse banged against our legs. "Sugar bug, you managed to get involved in trouble again."

I snuggled against him, feeling his warmth against the cold fall air. "Not me this time, Daddy," I said into his shoulder. "Ma found Philip. And it's Abbie I'm worried about."

He sighed. The scent of the outside lingered in his heavy coat, reminding me of childhood and safety and good things. How I wished right now that Abbie and I were still kids and she was visiting me. We'd go running up to my bedroom to share secrets. And we'd be ignorant of what it was like to be adults.

"I'm praying for her," Daddy said. "Your mother was pretty upset—and not just about finding Philip. She overheard someone say something about evidence pointing at Abbie." He backed up and took my chin in his hand. "Sugar bug, we've all got good reason to be upset. There's something you should know."

I frowned up at him.

"And if the police ask me, I'll have to tell the truth."

I felt my breath come faster. "What is it?"

He took a deep breath. "When Abbie was writing her book, she asked me to help her learn about guns. Remember?"

I nodded.

"Well, I helped her learn to shoot a 30-06."

I thought about Daddy's rifles, which he kept in a cabinet in the barn. "That's your favorite hunting rifle, and. . ." I realized where he was going. "That's the kind of gun she used in her book." I felt my voice growing shrill. "I don't know what Philip was shot with."

Daddy rubbed my arms. "Hopefully it wasn't a rifle like that. And maybe no one will ask me about it. But I think I'm in the acknowledgments of her book."

My earlier anxiety gripped me like a vise. "I have to try to reach Eric again." I pulled away from Daddy and reached into my purse.

Daddy patted my arm. "Trish, you've got to remember that God is in control."

"Right."

I wondered if he heard the sarcasm in my voice. Daddy said nothing, just patted me one more time then headed for the house, which was good, because I didn't want him to know my momentary angry thoughts. Like why had God allowed this to happen? Abbie finally had a chance to be happy with a new man, and along comes her ex-husband to ruin her life again by getting killed. Not that he'd done it on purpose.

I forced myself to breathe deeply while I punched in Eric's number. This time he answered.

"Trish? Is Abbie okay? I haven't been able to reach her. Tell me what's happened."

"Didn't Corporal Fletcher tell you?" I asked.

"Yes, but I want to hear it from you."

His voice had a desperate edge that made me shiver in the cold air. I forced my voice to remain calm. "Ma found Philip dead behind the church hall. Abbie and I were there. We were all taken to the sheriff's office for questioning by a bulldog state police detective."

"Reid," he said.

"Yep. You know her?"

"*Of* her," he said. "So what happened exactly?"

I explained everything. "And I'm really worried about Abbie. . . ."

"Why, exactly?" he asked.

"Because she moved the body to check his pulse. And because of the book on the counter that didn't belong to her or me or Ma—"

"Whose book was it? Do you know?"

"I have no idea, but, Eric. . .she could have done it. She was there alone before Ma and I got there. And you know what her latest book is about, don't you?"

I heard him groan.

"Eric, Abbie told me that—"

"Stop," he snapped. "Don't tell me anything she said to you. If I know and it's something they haven't discovered yet, I'll have to tell them. And I can't deal with all of this from out here. I'll be home tomorrow. I'll see her then."

"Yes. Okay." The awkward position Eric was in finally hit me. Torn between two worlds. His occupation and his fiancée. His job was to support the men and women investigating this case, even at the expense of people's comfort. But he wanted more than anything to protect Abbie. How could he do both?

He made me promise to get in touch with him if anything else happened. He also requested that I watch over Abbie—something both of us knew he didn't have to ask.

As I put my phone in my pocket, I realized I hadn't seen Buddy, my father's dog. Usually he'd have greeted me with enthusiasm. I wondered where he was. I shivered again, but before I could head for the house and warmth, Max and the kids arrived.

I waited. Charlie and Sammie scrambled from the car, and Karen took Chris from his car seat and followed more slowly. They all greeted me with a chorus of "Hi, Mom" and went inside.

When Max got out, I threw myself into his arms like Sammie does. The problem is, I'm not as small as our daughter, so Max fell back against the car.

"Hey, hey," he said when he'd regained his balance. He wrapped his arms around me and kissed the top of my head. Then he lifted my chin and made me meet his gaze.

"So how are you? Okay? You survived questioning?"

"Yes. They had to turn everything over to the state police since Abbie is engaged to Eric."

"That doesn't surprise me," he said. "How is she?"

"I haven't talked to her since they separated us at the fellowship hall." I took his arm, and we walked toward the house.

"Did you tell the kids?" I asked.

"I said something to Karen but not to the little kids." He shook his head. "I wanted to wait until we knew more details. I'm not sure how much they really need to know."

"Good," I said. "I'm really worried about Abbie."

He glanced down at me. "Why?"

"They were questioning her at the sheriff's office, and that detective woman is awful." I gave him the abbreviated version as we stepped through the back door and into the mudroom. There we shucked off our coats and headed into the kitchen, where my mother was working.

The steamy, warm, delicious-smelling air seemed completely at odds with the icy worry that had wrapped itself around my heart.

"This sounds pretty serious for Abbie," Max said when I was finished.

"Oh, it's serious," my mother piped up. She was cooking a spread worthy of Thanksgiving and Christmas combined. Her solution for any kind of calamity is food and lots of it.

Max glanced from her to me. "I can get Abbie a lawyer if she needs one." He knows lots of great lawyers. Tough, Harvard-educated lawyers.

I felt a sense of relief. "Thank you, honey."

He kissed me again and then greeted Ma with a kiss on her cheek.

Daddy walked into the kitchen, followed by Charlie and Sammie. "Hello, Max."

"Simon," Max said and gripped Daddy in a quick guy hug.

Sammie rushed Max and grabbed him around the hips. "We're going out to look at some new calves. Wanna come?"

"You bet," Max said. Then he turned to me. "You gonna be okay, baby?"

I waved him on. "Yep. You go. I need to help Ma here."

Charlie chased Sammie out to the mudroom where they pulled on their coats. I heard Chris in the other room where Karen was watching television. Daddy and Max followed more slowly, putting on their outer garments.

"Have you talked to Abbie?" Ma asked as soon as the back door was shut.

"No. I can't reach her. I'm really worried. Especially since I talked to Eric and Corporal Fletcher. Both of them sound worried." I explained to her what they had said to me.

Ma sighed.

"So you're sure he was murdered, and you think they suspect her?" I asked.

"Yes. Especially the way they took her out of there. And then you know they found Philip's car just up the road."

"They did? Why didn't we see it?"

"The other direction. None of us passed it on the way to the hall."

"How do you know this?" I asked.

"I overheard them talking in another room." Ma smiled for the first time since I'd arrived. "People assume since I have gray hair I can't hear."

Assuming anything about my mother is a mistake. And it was my opinion that her hearing was finely tuned by daily practice at the shop. How else would she be able to pick up the choice bits of gossip she did, if she didn't have the hearing of a bat?

She pointed at the refrigerator. "Slice the ham that's in there." She worked at the counter with hard motions, but she glanced at me from the corner of her eye.

"You need to solve this mystery. You have to help Abbie."

"I gave up solving mysteries, Ma. You know that. Last time was too much. I almost got killed, and Chris would have been killed with me. It's not worth it."

"You can do it and be safe. God will protect you. Don't you care about your best friend?"

I thought it was a little presumptuous to assume God would automatically protect me, especially when I hadn't even prayed about it yet.

Ma was making chicken. In addition to the ham.

"Fried chicken *and* ham?" I asked. "It's like a holiday or something."

Ma's hand hit the counter with a thud, and she stood still, looking out the kitchen window where Daddy, Max, Sammie, and Charlie stood at the fence watching the new calves in the field. "Sometimes it's good to just celebrate being alive."

I'm so used to fending off my mother's sarcastic comments and odd ideas that when she says something profound, I'm speechless. I walked over and hugged her shoulders.

She patted my hands. "You've got to help Abbie." Her tone was unusually soft. "I don't want to see her wedding postponed. I have a feeling about this, and it's not good."

Ma's insistence tore at my resolve. "I promise I'll think about it." I went back to slicing ham.

"I'll help," Ma said. "I can collect information, too."

I glanced at her with horror. "Ma, no—"

"Don't argue with me." She faced me with blazing eyes. "Abbie is like a daughter to us. And she's like a sister to you. Family. Maybe not by blood, but in our hearts."

I put my hands up in surrender. "You're right, Ma. She *is* family. I just don't want anyone to be hurt. . .any more than they have been already."

Her body deflated. "Don't think I'm insensitive to how you feel."

I wasn't sure what she meant. Besides, sensitivity wasn't one of my mother's strong points, so I had my doubts. But she was in an unusual mood tonight, and I was seeing a side of her I rarely glimpsed.

Her shoulders drooped. "I never thought before how it felt to find a dead person," she said. "Now I know."

I swallowed. "It is awful. It's the shock of seeing the shell of a person. Knowing they were there but are now gone."

"Exactly." She sniffed and straightened.

I knew that in a weird way, she was apologizing to me for not understanding the other times I'd been involved in murder. I was grateful.

"Well, gracious." Ma rinsed off her hands and went back to work on the chicken. "This dinner isn't going to put itself on the table. Let's get to work."

Later, when we were all seated at the dining room table, the blessing said and the food passed, Ma glanced at me. "In all the. . .confusion today, I forgot. Jaylene came by the shop and told me you bought some things for a cat?"

Sammie bounced in her chair. "I'm getting a kitten. Grandmother Cunningham is buying it for me."

"What?" My mother stared at me. "I didn't know about this. Trish? You aren't that fond of cats—especially inside."

"I know, but. . ."

"You let that woman—"

"I think it's wonderful that Trish is doing this for Sammie," Daddy said before Ma could finish her thought.

I met Max's glance, and he winked at me. He knows how my mother feels about his mother, but she usually wasn't so vocal in front of the children.

Ma realized what she'd almost done and had the grace to blush. "Well now, I suppose that's a good thing. After all, Charlie's got his snake."

"After months of nagging," I said.

Karen glared at her little brother. "He purposefully put the snake in my bed today."

"I can't help it that he fell off my shoulder," Charlie said.

Karen glared at him. "Well, I hope Sammie's cat eats your snake."

Sammie's eyes grew huge. "No! That's not nice at all."

"Karen," Max said. "Don't start, please."

Karen and Charlie were always like water and oil. He knew just how to push her buttons to get her to react.

The normalcy of their bantering helped me to relax, although I was forcing myself to eat because I knew I needed to, despite my stomach's protests. I felt Max's gaze and looked up at him.

*I love you,* he mouthed.

We all ate in silence for a while, and then Ma put her fork down. "Well, did your daddy tell you that Buddy took sick last week? Vet says he's not doing well. He mostly stays in the barn now. And we let him sleep in the house at night."

That explained why Buddy hadn't greeted me when I arrived.

"Gotta get another dog, I guess," Daddy said. "I should do it before Buddy. . ." His voice trailed off.

"Does that mean he's going to die?" Charlie never missed a thing.

"Yes," Ma said. "And he'll go to doggy heaven. Now would anyone like more mashed potatoes?"

I met Daddy's gaze. He smiled at me, but his eyes were watering. He and

Buddy were inseparable. I felt tears well up in my own eyes.

He saw them and reached across the table and patted my hand. "Buddy lived a good long life. It's the cycle of things, sugar bug. You know that. For everything there is a season. A time to be born and a time to die."

"I know." I swallowed and thought about that. Buddy was old for a dog. And though it was sad, he'd lived out his full years. But what about Philip? His life had been cut short. Even though I hadn't liked him for what he did to Abbie, I never would have wished him dead in a pool of blood on the ground.

After the kids left the table, the four adults sat and drank decaf coffee, pretending everything was normal. Max talked about Tommy at college. But my mind wasn't in what anyone was saying. I kept thinking about Abbie.

"You know what's weird?" I said during a lull in the conversation. "Jaylene said Henry knew that Philip was back in town. She was pretty nasty about Philip."

"Doesn't surprise me none," Ma said. "The Adlers hated him."

I glanced at her, surprised. "Why?"

Ma shrugged. "Not really sure, but you can start your investigation by talking to Jaylene."

From the corner of my eye, I saw Max's head swivel toward me. I didn't look at him, but I knew I'd hear about this later. Max didn't want me to investigate any more than I wanted to.

"We can get this done fast," Ma said. "That detective isn't nearly as smart as she'd like to think. You wouldn't believe the questions she asked me."

Unfortunately, I thought the bulldog was a lot smarter than Ma gave her credit for. I just hoped she was smart enough to see that Abbie wasn't guilty of murder.

Had I decided to do it? I didn't want to do it. I wanted to pretend everything was okay and just let the police handle it. I thought about everything Ma had said. Abbie was my best friend. Closer than a sister. Did I have a choice?

6

After a terse "We have to talk," Max took the kids home so I could stop by Abbie's apartment in town. She still wasn't answering her phone. Ma sent several plates of food along with me, despite my arguments that Abbie wouldn't be eating. When I pulled up, her car was there, parked along the street. She lived above a shop in downtown Four Oaks.

I sat in my SUV for a moment, gathering my emotions. Abbie and I were opposites. I was a fiery volcano. She was an icy mountain spring. She always held her counsel, maintaining rigid control of herself and everything in her life, even when she was falling apart inside. I tended to fly off all over the place. To act and speak before I thought.

But now I needed to temper myself. Be confident and strong for her and watch my tongue, even though I felt like coming apart.

Balancing my load of food, I walked up the stairs to her apartment and banged on her door.

"Abbie, I know you're in there. I'll use my key if you don't answer."

I heard her steps coming to the door, then the lock turning.

I expected her to look bad, but I tried not to gasp at her appearance. Abbie rarely let herself be seen without being perfectly made up. Mascara ran in dark trails from her bloodshot eyes down her white cheeks. The only other color on her face was her red nose and eyes. She motioned me in, turned, and walked to the couch, where she dropped into a corner and pulled a blanket around her shoulders. Only one lamp was on in the room. A small, decorative brass thing that only served to prove how dark the rest of the apartment was.

I held up the plates that my mother had sent. "Ma sent food. Do you want something?"

"I would throw up," she said.

"That's what I told Ma." I turned on another light so I wouldn't fall over anything. Abbie blinked but didn't complain. She had a half-empty box of tissues next to her. The coffee table was littered with wadded, used tissues, but there was no sign of any kind of nourishment.

"I'll put this away. And I'm making you some tea. Don't argue." I took the food to the kitchen and put it in the refrigerator. Then I put water in the teakettle and set it on the range.

While I waited, I straightened things up. The kitchen was as big a mess as

Abbie. Another indication she was falling apart.

After the tea was made, I carried two cups to the living room, along with a trash bag. After putting the cups on the coffee table, I turned on another light. Then I gathered up all the used tissues. "This won't do, you know," I said. "You can't sit here in the dark. You can't let them get to you."

I heard sniffling and turned to look at her. She was crying. "I—I just talked to June. Philip's mother."

"Oh, Abs. . ." I sat next to her and hugged her. "That's brave of you."

I felt her tears wet on my cheek and her body shaking. My tall, cool friend was trembling.

"They think I did it," she said. "That detective was so hostile. She questioned me for hours. So invasive. I feel violated. And I just wanted to tell June that I didn't kill him."

"Did she believe you?" I asked. I knew the two women had been in contact over the years.

"Yes." Abbie sniffed. "I think so."

"Good." I held her more tightly, and for once, she let me. "I can't even imagine how you feel. I'm so sorry. Have you talked to Eric?"

She hiccuped. "Yes, just for a minute. I told him I didn't want to discuss things until he returns. This is a nightmare."

I agreed, but I didn't say that. I finally let her go and handed her a cup of tea. "Drink this."

She wanted to refuse, but I just glared at her. After a brief battle of wills, she took the cup.

"Max can find you a good lawyer," I said.

Abbie's lips trembled. "I don't want to have to have a lawyer. When a suspect *lawyers up*, the cops see it as suspicious behavior."

I shook my head. "They're already looking at you with suspicion, remember?"

She swallowed. "It's worse than you think," she whispered. Tears filled her eyes again, and her nose started running.

"Blow your nose and then tell me why."

She obeyed and then took several deep, halting breaths. "I don't know if I can."

"Spit it out," I said.

"Philip was there with me at the church. Maybe even right before he was killed."

My vision seemed to go black, and I could only see Abbie through a tiny pinpoint. "With you?"

She nodded and started crying again. "That was the third time I'd seen him." My chest constricted.

"The first time was at my book signing at the festival. I was so mad that he was there. I wouldn't talk to him, and he finally left. In a big hurry. Today he ran into me at the Gas 'n' Go. We argued. I—I was very angry. I left him there. After I arrived at the church, he showed up. That's why I left and went to McDonald's."

"How did he know you were at the church? Did you tell him you were going there?"

She shook her head. "But the police know we were at the store together. They found a receipt in his pocket from the Gas 'n' Go, so they went out there and looked at the security tapes. Our argument is there to see." Her mouth twisted. "The thing is, I never saw him buy anything. But maybe he did after I left."

I was having trouble breathing. She picked up her tea but was trembling too hard to drink any, so she put the cup back down.

"Remember how manipulative he used to be?" she asked. "How he always made me feel like he was right and I was wrong?"

"Yes. That used to make me feel so horrible for you." I closed my eyes then opened them again. "There's no way they can say you did it, right? His shooting wasn't close and personal."

She clasped her hands so tightly, her knuckles were white. "Yes, they could say I did it. I was angry. I locked the door and left him standing in the front parking lot. He could have walked around back. There's a road that skims around the church property. They could say I might have driven up there, stopped the car, and shot him."

"With what?"

"My hunting rifle."

I know my mouth fell open. "You have a hunting rifle?"

"Had," she said. "I had one."

"When?"

"When my grandmother died and left me everything, there were some guns in her stuff that had belonged to some of the men in her family."

"Do you have them now?"

"No. I gave them to Philip when we were married. But they were listed in her will, and I was the sole beneficiary. And now he's dead. With a shot from a rifle. What if it's like one that I had?"

"How would the cops know that? Tell me you didn't tell them?"

She closed her eyes and then opened them again. "Do you have any idea what that kind of interrogation is like? I didn't. Even though I know cops. I've never been on that side of the table. By the time she was done with me, I was ready to admit anything just to be able to leave." Fresh tears dripped down her face. "I'm so stupid."

"I think you mean naive." I leaned over and hugged her again then sat back. "So did Philip have his car with him?"

"Yeah," she said. "A blue Honda."

"Remember, there was no Honda in the parking lot when we were in the hall right before Ma found him."

Her eyes grew wide. "I didn't even think about that. Where was his car?"

"Down the road. Ma overheard the deputies talking about it."

"That's weird," Abbie said.

I nodded. "Yes, it is. And did he have a copy of your book with him when you saw him?"

She shook her head. "No. That's weird, too. I don't know where that book came from."

I thought it was strange, too. "Hey, I talked to Eric tonight. He said he's coming home tomorrow."

"Yeah." She stared at me with glazed eyes. "I think we need to postpone the wedding. He disagrees."

"I do, too," I said. "We all finally convinced you to get married, and now you're talking about postponing it?"

A tremulous grin crossed her lips; then it died, and she started crying again. "Trish, I can't get married in a jail cell."

"You aren't going to jail." I sat up straight. I knew without a doubt what I had to do. "I'm going to solve this mystery. I refuse to let them take you down."

For a moment, I saw a glint of hope in her eyes. Then she blinked and shook her head violently. "No. I can't let you. It's too dangerous."

"You can't stop me." I stood and went over to her desk and started rummaging for some paper and a pencil.

"What are you doing?" she asked.

"I'm going to take notes. And when I get home, I'm going to transfer them to a steno pad." I whirled around to face her and waved the pen at her like a baton. "Start talking, Abbie. I want to know everything you can possibly remember."

When I got home, Max met me in the kitchen.

I dropped my purse on the table, feeling like I was a hundred years old. His expression was a mixture of concern and determination.

I wanted to avoid the discussion I knew we were going to have. "How are the kids?"

"Karen is giving Chris a bath. Charlie is doing some homework. And Sammie is doing some kind of project in her room."

"Good."

"How is Abbie?" He began rubbing my shoulders. His way of softening me up before telling me he didn't want me to investigate.

But his tender touch got to me, and the tough shell I'd portrayed to Abbie began to crack under his attention. I bit my lip trying to keep myself from blubbering.

"Honey?" He turned me around and stared into my eyes.

"Abbie's not good. Not at all." I disengaged myself from his grasp and went to the sink for a glass of water, just to have something to do so I wouldn't fall apart. "I'm sorry you had to deal with the kids all evening. I know you have a lot going on. I'm just. . ."

"It's fine. Really. I'm so sorry about Abbie. The timing is terrible."

"Yes, it is." I filled a glass, took a sip, and stared at the dark night through the window. "She's talking about calling off the wedding." Tears filled my eyes, and I couldn't see. "The bad thing is, she might have to."

"I can see why she'd say that," he said. "The investigation might go on for a while."

I whirled around. "Yes. I know that. But it's worse than just that. Things don't look good for her because she could have shot Philip." The pitch of my voice kept rising. "He was there with her at the church. Alone."

Shock rippled across his face. "Whew."

"Yeah, whew," I said.

"I'm serious about helping her find a good lawyer." He leaned his hip against the counter. "I'm sorry to say this, but she might need one, given that fact. I'm sorry, baby." He paused and studied me. "You're not going to get involved. Right?"

I took a deep breath, stepped toward him, and met his gaze with my chin in the air. "Yes, I am. I'm going to at least try to solve this mystery."

His nostrils flared. "I was hoping I'd misunderstood things at your mother's. I thought you'd had it with solving mysteries."

"I have—last time scared me so bad. But this is Abbie we're talking about."

He crossed his arms. "I don't like it. Let the police do their job."

"You're the one who just said it sounded like she might actually need that lawyer. I've got to find out what happened. That detective is. . .well, awful."

He ran his fingers through his hair. "It terrifies me." After he took a couple of deep breaths, he shook his head. "No. I can't agree to it. I just have a feeling about this."

I did, too, and it scared me. I blinked back tears, turned away from him, and leaned my forehead against the cool metal of the refrigerator. "You didn't see her, Max. You know how Abbie is. Tall. Cool. Always perfect. She was crumpled up in a ball in the corner of her couch." I started to cry. "That detective ripped her to shreds."

I heard his steps cross the kitchen floor, and he wrapped his arms around me. I leaned back against his chest.

"What if his murder had nothing to do with anyone around here?" Max asked. "What if it had to do with his job? Some kind of drug dealer or something. What then?"

"Then it will be obvious real soon, won't it?" I pulled away from his grasp and turned around. "The killer would have to be a stranger. How many strangers come into town unnoticed? I could find that out easily enough."

"That wasn't my point, and you know it," he said.

"I know what your point was. It could be dangerous. But. . .Abbie." I leaned hard into his chest, smashing my nose flat. "I can't let it go. Please, Max, you have to understand." My voice was muffled.

"So you're just going to collect clues?" he asked softly. "In a notebook."

"Yes." I pulled away from him and looked up into his face. "Wouldn't you do whatever you could to help someone you loved?"

"Yes, but I would also do anything I could to *protect* someone I love."

I knew he was referring to me, but I also knew I'd won my point.

We stood in silence for several moments. The tick-tocks of the grandfather clock in the living room echoed down the hall, reminding me of the passing of time. The short amount of time before Abbie's wedding.

"I can't stop you," Max said finally. "I'm not going to try, because it'll be pointless. Because we'll fight, you'll feel guilty, and I'll feel mean. Just please be careful. And. . .I know you will. . .but please keep the kids out of it."

"Yes. Yes, I will." I totally understood his concern, and for once, I wasn't even offended that he would make a comment like that or imply that I was stupid. "I'll hire a babysitter for Chris and work only when the kids are in school."

Our eyes met, and he gave me a slight grin. "You're incorrigible."

I rubbed my hands up and down his arms. "I'm trying to grow up. Trying to be more careful."

"I know," he said.

"I don't want to talk anymore about this tonight." I heard my youngest begin to cry upstairs, followed by Karen's voice and Charlie's yell to cut out the noise. "I'll go take care of him. See the kids to bed. Take a long, hot bath." I twined my arms around Max's neck and hugged him hard. "Then I want to lie in bed next to you. I want you to hold me tight, and I want to forget about everything."

7

On Wednesday morning, after I saw the kids off to school and got Chris settled in his playpen, I called Abbie to make sure she was okay. She assured me she was fine, but I knew she was lying. That just gave me more incentive to get to work.

I hadn't slept well, so I made an extrastrong pot of coffee. Then, I took one of my new steno pads from the kitchen drawer and reached in my purse for the notes I'd taken at Abbie's the night before. I stared at my scrawls and felt overwhelmed. I had no clear suspects. No idea where to start. Well, truth be told, there *was* one clear suspect. Abbie. And if I were really honest with myself, in Detective Reid's place, I would be looking hard at her, too. But unlike the detective, I had the advantage of knowing Abbie. And I knew for certain that she hadn't killed Philip.

I tapped my pen on the table and considered my tendency to jump into things without thinking about the consequences. I'd paid dearly for that impulsiveness repeatedly throughout my life. Until this year, the staff at the emergency room knew me by name because of all the times I had thoughtlessly participated in activities that led to some mishap. Like skateboarding with Tommy and his friends at the park, even though I hadn't skateboarded since I was a kid.

But this past year, since my last pregnancy, a sense of my own mortality had finally penetrated my dense brain. And even more important than that was the realization that I wasn't an island. I needed to consider the consequences of my own actions in the lives of others, particularly those I loved most and who depended on me.

Looking back at the last two mysteries I'd been involved in, I knew I had been impulsive. And I wondered if I'd really given my investigations to the Lord.

However, that wasn't relevant. What mattered was here and now. This time I would. I had to. I couldn't do this on my own. And this time, the circumstances were even more pressing. At best, Abbie might have to postpone her wedding. At worst, she could be thrown in jail.

I bowed my head and asked for guidance. Then I asked God to have mercy on my best friend.

When I was done, I flipped open the steno pad. One key to finding a murderer is knowing the steps that the victim took minutes, hours, and weeks before his or her death. Philip was pretty much an unknown to me. I hadn't seen him in years.

And I'd had no idea he was back in town until Jaylene had mentioned him.

I'd have to begin with what Abbie told me and build on that.

I titled the entry "Philip's Actions." Then I wrote what I knew about Philip.

> *Philip showed up at Abbie's book signing at the fall festival the weekend before. She refused to talk to him, and he left abruptly. Why?*
>
> *He caught up with her again at the Gas 'n' Go on the day he was murdered. How did he know she was there? Was he following her? Or was it a coincidence?*
>
> *She refused to talk to him. They fought. He left. Then he went to the church. How did he know she was at the church?*
>
> *She didn't want to talk to him, so she left and went to McDonald's.*

I needed to begin a list of questions I had to answer, so I wrote:

> *Why was Philip's car parked down the road?*
> *What did Philip want to talk to Abbie about?*
> *Where did Abbie's novel come from, and why was it at the church?*
> *Why did he leave the fall festival so quickly? Because he was mad like he used to get at her?*
> *How did he know she was at the Gas 'n' Go and the church the day he was killed? Was he following Abbie? Or coincidence?*
> *Why was he back in town?*

When I'd investigated the two other murders, the suspects had all been present and accounted for at the time. This time, I had no clear suspects. And no obvious reasons that I knew of why someone would kill a man who hadn't been in town in years.

The only people on the scene had been me, Ma, and Abbie. And none of us had done it. I tapped the pen on my chin. Linda had been out there, but did she even know Philip?

To Detective Reid, it might appear that Abbie had good motivation. Philip suddenly returned after years, right before her marriage to Eric, who was an old friend and work buddy of Philip's. But aside from his presence disrupting her life, what good reason would she have to shoot him now?

Then there was Abbie herself. She sometimes holds bits of information back. And I often didn't know what she was really thinking about a certain situation, incident, or person until long after the fact. She was trying to change, but a situation like this might make her retreat again. I couldn't depend on the fact that she was telling me everything. I would have to question her again.

The thing that scared me to death was that she had been in the right place at the right time to kill Philip. She had owned a rifle and was an experienced shot, thanks to my father. And then there was her recently published book. The one about a man who shoots his ex-wife and almost gets away with it.

I tapped my pen against my teeth. How could I approach this?

Trying to approach the mystery by looking for rifle owners wouldn't get me anywhere. We lived in a rural area where most households had rifles because so many people hunted.

I wondered about Max's statement that maybe the murderer was someone Philip had dealt with as a cop. Someone who had followed him here from New York. That was a possibility.

And what about Philip's behavior? That was the most puzzling thing of all. He seemed to have been almost stalking Abbie. Why now? After all these years?

I knew of only two people besides Abbie who were angry with Philip. The Adlers. I'd start at the Pet Emporium. I'd buy another Kitty Koller. Then I'd stop by Ma's shop. I never knew what kinds of clues I'd pick up there.

I also wanted to talk to Eric. In person, preferably. I glanced at my watch. He would be at work now. I grabbed my cell and dialed, thinking of all my arguments to get him to agree to see me. Eric answered on the second ring.

"Trish, I was going to call you. Can you come to my office? I want to talk."

Well, that was easy. "I was just going to ask you if I could do that."

"Good," he said.

We agreed on a time and hung up. I took a deep breath. There was one other thing I had to do even though it made me feel sick. I needed to go back to the murder scene. I probably wouldn't find anything, but it might help jog something in my head. That meant I had to get a key to the church hall from my mother. And I had to find out when the police would be finished with the scene. Maybe Eric would be able to tell me.

I put the pen down, slapped my notebook shut, tucked it into my purse, and stood. The first thing was to find a babysitter for Chris.

I was counting down to Abbie's wedding. I intended to see that everything went as planned.

～～～

After a quick call to Ma for babysitter advice, which she gave me only if I promised to stop by the shop, I decided on Gladys, who went to church with my mother and had lived in a house across the street from my folks' farm since I was a kid. She watched her great-grandchildren on a regular basis, so I wasn't putting her out. She was perfect.

Gladys's house smelled like laundry detergent and cinnamon. A strange but very appealing combination. She had a round face that matched her round waist. When I was little, I visited her often, and she'd ply me with chocolate chip cookies by the dozen and homemade root beer by the gallon.

"Well now, Trish, you just come right on in here. And here's that adorable little boy your mama's brought by." She reached out and took Chris right from my arms. He beamed at her.

"Can I get you somethin' to drink?"

"No, thank you." I was eager to begin my clue collecting.

"Your mama told me you're going to solve this dreadful crime. Someone like Philip Grenville wasn't the kind of person you'd want your daughter to marry, but nobody deserves to die that young and in such a tragic way."

I agreed wholeheartedly. "I don't know where to start."

"Well, your mama says you're the best sleuth around, so I'm sure you can do it."

"I'm not sure I agree with that." I wished my mother would keep her mouth shut about my investigating. "I don't even know how to start this time."

"Well, you just need to clear your head." I followed her into the family room, where she put Chris on the carpeted floor next to a baby very near his age. Then she turned to me. "You know what I think?"

I shook my head, knowing she was about to tell me.

"You need to look at people without moral values. Or people who are strangers in town."

I wanted to ask her how I could determine whether people had moral values, given that some of the worst killers in history seemed like the salt of the earth. However, her idea about strangers in town was one that I needed to examine. "Do you have any suggestions? Do you know of anyone who has been in town recently who doesn't live here?"

Gladys pursed her lips and *tsk*ed. Then she planted herself on a brown, suedelike sofa. "Why, yes, I do. The good-looking boy. The one everyone fawns over, including two of my granddaughters." Gladys *tsk-tsk*ed again. "Why, even your mother goes googly-eyed. I've never seen Doris have no sense like that before."

There was only one man who fit that bill. "Do you mean Clark? The WWPS delivery guy?"

"That's the one."

"Well, why? He's just a delivery guy. What in the world would he have in common with Philip?"

She snorted. "He's just too good-looking for his own good. He was a model, you know. In New York. Still goes up there a couple times a month."

That explained the fact that he knew he looked good. "I've never seen his picture anywhere," I said.

"Well, of course you haven't. My lands, Trish. You wouldn't read those kinds of magazines."

"What. . ."

Gladys raised an eyebrow.

"Oh," I said. I didn't bother to ask how *she* knew. "Does my mother know?"

Gladys shrugged. "Your mother is too smitten by him. She refuses to believe it."

That was odd, but then, Ma was unpredictable. This was an interesting fact. Philip was from New York. Clark was from New York. "Why is he here? Do you know?"

She shook her head. "Something about his mama, I think. Philip moved her to a nice trailer on the other side of Brownsville. You know. . .in the next county."

I remembered Clark had said something about his mother being sick. This was more and more interesting. I needed to get that autographed bookplate for her and deliver it personally.

"Models do drugs and. . .do other things for money," Gladys said. "I see it enough on the news. Like all those actors and actresses."

I nodded as if in agreement, but I didn't like to make blanket assumptions like that.

"Mark it down," she said. "There's something funny with him. It's not right for a man to do *that* kind of thing. Modeling, indeed."

I left "do *that* kind of thing" alone and said my good-byes. Chris didn't even look up when I walked out the door. I may have found the person I could leave Chris with when I started working with Max. And I'd made up my mind about that. Once I solved this mystery and got Abbie married off, I was determined to work at Cunningham and Son.

———

I walked into Adler's Pet Emporium. No one was behind the counter, and I yelled hello while I picked out another Kitty Koller.

Jaylene walked out of the back room and frowned at me. "Did you forget something last time you were here?"

She might as well have tossed a bucket of ice water over me. That was the effect of her cold voice and attitude.

I pointed to the Kitty Koller rack. "No, I just wanted another one of these."

Her attitude didn't change. "That's not the only reason you're here, is it?"

I shrugged. "Well, I did want to ask you some questions."

"I knew it. I knew that's what you were doing. Your mother says you're trying to solve Philip Grenville's murder. To save Abbie from going to jail." She glared at me. "Well, you won't find any suspects here. I told your mother that this morning when she walked in here and started demanding answers to her questions. I've never been so offended in my life."

I wondered what my mother had asked Jaylene. I'd never known her to act so hostile, especially to an old family friend.

"Well, honestly," I said, "I *don't* want my friend to go to jail. So I'm asking questions of everyone I know. I'm not accusing anyone of anything."

Jaylene crossed her arms and stared hard at me. "Well, you'd better not. That's all I have to say."

After my little chat with Gladys, maybe I'd do well to begin with questions about Clark. Not that I could imagine how he would fit into Philip's murder. Still, it would serve to distract Jaylene. "Do you remember those holes in the cat litter bags?"

Her eyes widened. I'd surprised her. "Yes. What about it?"

"Well, I wondered if you knew anything about that delivery guy. Clark? One of my, um, friends is interested in him. But if he's irresponsible, I want to discourage her." April May *was* a friend. And she *was* interested.

Jaylene relaxed a fraction. "I don't know anything about him except that he's too cocky for someone who works at WWPS. I called them and complained."

"How long has he been coming in here?"

"Only a few weeks. The WWPS company said he was new. Sloppy is what I said."

I pulled some cash from my wallet to pay for the Kitty Koller. "Well, maybe he's not the kind of person she needs to hang out with if you think he hasn't got good character."

She snatched the money from my hand. "Good character is in short supply around here."

I wasn't sure what she meant, but it did remind me of Philip. "Listen, that reminds me that you said Henry had seen Philip in town. I wondered if you knew why he was here."

"Well, why would we know that?" She eyed me with a narrowed glance then slapped some change into my hand. "I'm sure *I* don't know, and Henry wouldn't know, would he? It's not like Philip's a relative of mine or Henry's, is it?"

"Why do you say that?" I asked as I put the money back into my wallet.

She huffed. "He was scum. Just plain scum. But you would know that, wouldn't you? Because of Abbie?"

I couldn't help the look of surprise that I know crossed my face. "Scum?"

She put her hands on her hips. "If I don't hear Philip Grenville's name ever again, I'll be happy. And don't think you can pin this on Henry."

Her vehemence was like a physical blow. "What?"

"Philip's murder. You can't pin that on Henry."

"Why would I pin it on Henry? What does Henry have to do with Philip?"

She glared at me. "Nothing. Absolutely nothing. Isn't that what I said? Now I have things to do, unless you need to buy something else."

My lie-meter alarm, honed from being the mother of five, was clanging like

Ma's old dinner bell. Jaylene was covering up something that had to do with Henry and Philip.

I heard some rustling in the back room, then Henry came charging into the store. "Jaylene, I—"

"Trish is just leaving," she said.

Henry finally noticed me. "Trish."

"Henry," I said.

"She's trying to prove that we murdered Philip."

"That's not what I said at all." I couldn't believe how people jumped to conclusions.

Henry's lip curled. "Well, I wouldn't be so ready to defend Abbie. You know she can handle a rifle as easy as a guy can."

"What—"

The door to the shop opened, and Jaylene glanced over my shoulder. Her eyes narrowed.

I turned and saw Clark walking determinedly down the aisle.

"Abbie coulda done it," Henry said, undeterred by the intrusion. "Your daddy taught her, you know."

Clark reached the counter, and Jaylene stood there with her arms crossed, glaring at him.

"I ain't takin' it back. I called your company and complained. Because you busted open those bags of cat litter."

Clark smiled at her. White teeth. Full wattage. Lit up the room. The guy was good-looking, no doubt about it. "I just came by to apologize," he said. "I'll pay for them."

I watched Jaylene's frown diminish. He was a charmer, all right, if he could accomplish that with her.

"I'll try not to let it happen again." He looked at Henry. "Sir. . ."

Henry nodded.

Then Clark turned to me. His fingertips danced a rhythm against his thighs. His smile faded, and a tiny frown creased the skin between his brows.

"I met you. . . ."

I didn't like the fact that I wasn't memorable. If I were tall and striking like Abbie, he wouldn't have forgotten. "I'm Doris's daughter. Doris's Doughnuts? I met you the other day."

"That's right." He grinned. "I'm headed down there in a minute. Say, you're the one who's gonna take the bookplate to my mother."

I'd be doing that as soon as possible. I wanted to know more about the handsome Clark Matthews. "Yes. I'll do that soon."

"Good. She's excited about it." He looked me up and down. Then he frowned again. "Abbie. Isn't she the one whose husband just—"

"Ex-husband," I snapped. "Yes. He was killed."

"Ah. I'm sorry. Bad thing. You wouldn't think it would happen around here in Four Oaks." He turned back to Jaylene. "I promise I'll do better in the future. I can't afford to lose my job."

He continued to talk. I edged toward the door. I had a few other things to find out, but I knew one thing for sure. I wasn't going to get any more answers from Jaylene. At least not today.

———

At Doris's Doughnuts, things were hectic. Linda was cleaning a table and chatting with some customers. April May was making sandwiches, and Ma was stomping around the coffee machines, wiping them down hard with a white rag. The scowl on her face was an indication she was in a bad mood. I hoped it wasn't something I'd done.

"Hi, Ma."

She glanced at me. "Well, you came. At least some people do what they say." She slapped the rag on the counter.

I breathed a sigh of relief. That sounded promising. Someone else was the object of her wrath, not me.

"So what's wrong?" I asked. "Oh, and can I have a Mountain Dew, please?"

"What's wrong?" She jammed her fists into her hips. "You ask me what's wrong?"

"Yes," I said. "That's what I asked."

"Well, I'll tell you what. You think people are friends. And then this." She yanked a glass from the stack on the counter and filled it with ice and soda for me.

"Uh-huh." I waited.

When she was done, she slid the glass toward me. "I don't know why I bother."

"Me, either," I murmured to pacify her.

"That's what I get for having friends."

"What happened?" I drew in a mouthful of drink through my straw.

"It's Gail. She called and said she wasn't coming in. Then she said she was taking the rest of the week off."

I almost dropped my glass. "What? She never takes time off except to go to North Carolina once a year."

"Well, people change, now, don't they?" Ma rubbed hard on the counter.

Gail was a legendary stick-in-the-mud. Never altering her routine. That she would suddenly do this meant that things between them were more seriously wrong than I had thought.

"Don't you think you should talk to her?" I asked. "You guys have been friends for years."

"Isn't that what I just said? She shouldn't do this." Ma shook her head. "No. I'm not the one who walked out of here."

While my mother was in this state, I wouldn't be able to convince her to do anything, so maybe a change of topic was in order.

I leaned closer to her so she wouldn't have to talk loudly, although I knew it was a lost cause. "What did you ask Jaylene this morning? She was really upset when I went over there."

"I asked her if she or Henry killed Philip Grenville," Ma said, as loud as ever. "The Adlers have hated Philip forever. I don't know why."

I drew in a deep breath. That was a new low on Ma's lack of subtlety list. And it explained why Jaylene was so hostile. "So if she or Henry had committed murder, you expected her to answer that question honestly?"

Ma blinked. "Well, of course I would. I've known her for years. She goes to church twice a week, and Henry hunts with your father."

I couldn't even think of a reply to that skewed logic, and that was fine because when Ma glanced up over my head, all the tension etching her face melted. She suddenly looked ten years younger. I turned around to see what caused the miracle. I should have guessed. Clark, the studly WWPS man, was walking into the shop.

Seeing him reminded me of Gladys's comments. I could picture Clark as a model, but I didn't want to pursue that further in my head because the pictures weren't edifying. Still, he was from New York. Relatively new in town.

He stopped midway to the counter, and his gaze cut across the room. I followed it. He and Linda were making serious eye contact. She smiled and waved at him. He smiled back then proceeded to the counter and handed some boxes to Ma.

I glanced at April May, who was making a breakfast sandwich behind the counter. I hoped she hadn't noticed the little interchange, but she had. Her arms were frozen. With a roll in one hand and a piece of bacon in the other, she gazed from him to Linda with wide eyes. Then her eyelids dropped. She pursed her lips and set about making the sandwich with deliberate, hard motions. She'd seen exactly what I had seen. Something was going on between Clark and Linda.

I leaned against the counter to watch the soap opera.

Ma, oblivious to everything, just kept chatting with Clark. I heard him compliment her coffee. Linda went back to cleaning tables. April finished the sandwich and, with a stiff back, delivered it to a customer. I felt sorry for her. Clark finished his business, then he smiled at April as she returned to the counter. She just nodded at him and brushed past him and back behind the counter. He frowned. I found myself inwardly cheering for April May.

As he swaggered toward the door to leave, he waved at Linda again, and she held up six fingers. I assumed they were meeting later on.

I watched him leave. Two kids pulled up in front of the shop. He exchanged high fives with them. I turned back to the counter, thinking that outside would be a friendlier place than inside the shop right now.

Ma was swiping her rag across the countertop again.

"You eating?" she asked, back to her grumpy self.

"No," I murmured. "I need to borrow your key to the church."

She glanced sharply at me. "You are going to solve this mystery, aren't you? That's good. It means I don't have to do it myself."

"Yes. I'm looking into it." I wanted to say that I was going to try to solve it if for no other reason than to protect Ma from her own mouth.

"I talked to Abbie, and she told me to put off reception plans, but I'm not going to. I told her that. I told her you'd solve this mystery."

"I'm hoping the police are done at the fellowship hall."

"I'm sure they will be. They assured the pastor they'd be done as soon as possible. He wants to hold a prayer meeting there this afternoon so people don't feel so strange about being there." She frowned. "They need to do something. The ladies are having a holiday tea on Friday, and a few of the women are going to do some prep work tonight."

I felt sorry for the church members. Their new building was stained, at least figuratively, by a shooting.

"I won't be going," Ma said through narrowed lips.

"Why not?" She'd never missed the tea before.

"Because Gail is in charge."

"Ma, that's child—"

"Wait here," Ma said, cutting me off. "I need to use the bathroom, and then I'll give you my extra fellowship hall key. I can get my other one back from Linda." She strode to the back room.

She knew what I was going to say and didn't want to hear it. Even though it wasn't my fault, I felt bad about the issues between the two women.

Linda had finished talking and wiping tables and was back behind the counter, where she put her rag on the edge of the sink. Then she joined April May, whose mouth was clamped tightly shut. The atmosphere in Doris's Doughnuts was tense today. The only one who didn't seem to notice was Linda.

"You need any help?" Linda asked April with a bright smile on her face—the same one she always used in the hospital emergency room. Was she even aware of how April felt? I remembered what April had said about Linda living in a different dimension.

April gave Linda a sidelong glance then handed her an order form. "Finish this. It's for table three." Then she laid down her knife, wiped her hands, snatched the rag from the sink, and went to bus tables.

Linda stared wide-eyed at April's back, then she began to make the sandwiches.

She must have felt my eyes on her because she looked up. "Doris says your friend is a suspect."

"'Person of interest' would be a better term. But then, so am I, and so is my mother. And probably any number of other people."

"I watch those shows on television, and you know what they say. Usually the spouse is the one who's guilty."

April May glanced at me from a table she was cleaning and rolled her eyes. I could pretty safely say she'd joined Gail's "I Don't Like Linda" club.

"Abbie and Philip were divorced a long time ago," I said. "She wasn't his spouse."

Linda leaned toward me. "I saw her signing books at the fall festival. I bought one from her. I've heard some things. I was talking to your mother about it this morning."

"Like what?" I asked.

Her gaze shifted. "I don't want to spread gossip."

Like I believed that. I remembered her big mouth when she worked at the hospital. I'd let her play hard to get. I knew from experience that the best way to get someone to give up a piece of information is to feign disinterest.

"I understand how you feel," I said. "I don't blame you at all for not talking about it." I turned my attention to the bulletin board, where I saw a business card advertising Hayley's purebred Siamese cats.

"People say that Philip was holding something over Abbie," Linda said.

My ruse worked. I barely avoided smiling when I turned back to her. "Like what?"

"I saw them at the festival. They argued. I think he knew some secret about her or something. And because she was making it big with her latest book, he came back to bribe her with something that would ruin her career. Or maybe destroy her new relationship with that detective."

"Like what kind of secret?"

"I'm not sure. Maybe something about why they broke up."

"Oh."

She nodded sagely as though she knew all, then she went back to making sandwiches.

"Does Hayley Whitmore come in here for coffee?" I asked whoever was listening. For some reason, thoughts of her haunted me. I suspected, but didn't want to admit to myself, that my curiosity stemmed from the fact that Hayley was near my age and very close to my mother-in-law.

"Yeah," April said. "Like twice a week. She says we make her laugh."

Along with me, my mother and her cohorts were amusing to Hayley. I wondered if she and Angelica made fun of all of us while they sipped iced tea at the country club.

Ma returned with a key dangling between her fingers. "Here you go. The key to the church hall. I'll need it back, but I'm glad you're doing this. Visiting the murder scene. What are you looking for?"

"I don't know." I glanced around the full shop. Coming here had been stupid. At this point, anyone could have murdered Philip. I didn't need my plans advertised. Of course, Ma would advertise them anyway. I needed to be careful what I told her.

"Well now, that's not smart. You need a plan." Ma frowned. "You need to look for evidence. Like in the corners of things. Somebody was out there before we got there. Somebody killed Philip, and it wasn't Abbie, even though, heaven knows, she had every reason to. Especially if he was threatening her."

"Ma, you don't know that. And I'm sure the police have gathered all the evidence there is to gather."

"Police." She made a rude sound. "Well, why else was Philip there if he wasn't threatening her? What in the world was he doing back in Four Oaks?"

That was the question I intended to answer. And I hoped I could do it before my mother inadvertently convinced the whole town that Abbie had offed Philip.

8

My next stop was to see Eric. When I walked through the doors at the sheriff's office, I felt a tremor of apprehension as I recalled my interview the night before with Detective Reid. The fact that I was here again on my own accord was a testimony to my love for my best friend.

The girl behind a wall of bulletproof glass at the front desk called Eric and then told me to have a seat. Shortly after that, a deputy came to escort me and buzzed me through a locked door. When we reached Eric's office, he was sitting at his desk. Pain so twisted his face, I felt like a voyeur looking at him.

"Sir?" the deputy said.

Eric glanced up and grimaced with what was probably supposed to be a smile. "Trish. Please come in."

"Hey," I said as I dropped into a chair in front of his desk. The deputy shut the door.

I noticed some new pictures displayed on his credenza. His and Abbie's engagement pictures. He, Abbie, and his daughter, Sherry, were all grinning broadly. My heart ached.

"Have you talked to Sherry?" I asked.

He drew a deep breath. "I'd planned to call her as soon as I talked to you. I don't want her to hear about this before I tell her. This is the end of her first college term. I hate that it might affect her exams."

"It's going to be hard on her," I said. "She'll be frantic with worry."

"I know," he said softly. "She's so excited I'm marrying Abbie."

I leaned forward and put my elbows on his desk. "You wanted to talk to me?"

He sighed. "Yes."

"Before we start, can you tell me if Philip's death is a murder?" I asked.

"Suspicious," he said.

"But that's always the way it is, right?" I asked. "With an unexpected violent death like this?"

"Yes." He brushed his fingers through his hair.

"Detective Reid is not on my top-ten list of people to invite to Christmas dinner."

One side of his mouth quirked. "A number of people feel that way."

"So Corporal Fletcher said the state police are involved to avoid conflict of interest. I'm not sure that makes sense to me, but I understand what it means."

He sighed. "It's just to keep things from being muddled. If we investigate, Abbie might be given some sort of preferential treatment, and important evidence could be overlooked."

"Why is preferential treatment a big deal? Especially when we both know she didn't do it?"

"A suspect could get off in court if a lawyer can prove we didn't handle an investigation correctly."

"Are all the state police people as friendly as Detective Reid? Do you know any of them?"

"I know some of them," he said. "And friendly? Define friendly."

"That's a good point," I said. "They are, after all, cops."

He narrowed his eyes. "What does that mean?"

"Surface friendly, but underneath you're suspicious of everyone. Always looking for bad guys. You're out to nail our hides to the wall."

That made him smile. "Yes and no. We're trained to observe. We can't afford blanket trust in people. And in suspicious circumstances, we have to look at everyone involved as a person of interest. Our jobs make us that way. If you were lied to as much as we are, you'd be the same." He paused. "Besides, we're not all just surface friendly. Look at me. Look at Fletcher."

I rolled my eyes. "Please, Eric. I remember when I first met you."

"Well, at first, you were a person of interest in a murder case. You wouldn't expect me to be friendly." He eyed me with a slight smile. "And you—"

"Didn't tell you the whole truth. I know." My face grew warm. "But I didn't lie, either. I just avoided the truth."

"See?"

"Yeah, well, whatever." I didn't like to remember that I had tried to deceive Eric during Jim Bob's murder investigation. "Anyway, I don't like the way this is going at all." I tap-danced my fingers on the chair arms. "The state police people aren't going to care about Abbie."

He smiled grimly. "That's the whole point of having them investigate."

"Will they question all of us again?"

"No doubt," he said.

"So what's the procedure for something like this?" I asked. "How long do they investigate at the scene?"

He eyed me. "In this case, I assume they were back there first thing this morning, but I. . . They aren't talking to me about it. It's a tough scene, though. The shooter was way off in the woods. They had to comb the whole area."

"Do you think they're done now?"

He glanced at his watch. "I imagine. They were getting a lot of pressure from the church people because there's some big event coming up, and they need the building."

"Yeah. It's a ladies' holiday tea."

He nodded. "That's right." Then he suddenly squinted at me. "Why do you want to know?"

I shrugged. "Just curious. So what did you want to talk about?"

"Abbie," he said.

"I sort of figured." I settled back in the chair and crossed my legs. "What do you want to discuss about her?"

He met my gaze with tired eyes. "She's withdrawn. She's talking about canceling the wedding. I don't know what to do because she won't talk to me. Is she talking to you?"

"In dibs and dabs, but probably a little more than she's talking to you."

"That wouldn't be hard," he said dryly.

"Her reaction doesn't surprise me," I said. "She's always been that way. When she's in pain, she withdraws."

"It's killing me. I need her to talk to me." I saw a flash of anger in his eyes. "Does she think she's the only one this is impacting?"

I shook my head. "No. Not at all. And that's why she's withdrawn. She's worried she's going to affect your career. And I think underneath, she's worried that you're mad."

"Well, truthfully, I am." He stood and paced the length of his desk. "Why couldn't she have told me that Philip had contacted her? I look like an idiot." He stopped and inhaled, then met my gaze. "I'm not allowed to have any part in this investigation. I don't know much of what's going on, and she won't even confide in me. Do you know how frustrating that is?"

"Yes, I can imagine." I thought of all the times he hadn't answered my questions. I could be childish and point that out, but instead, I felt compassion for him.

Eric dropped into his chair, grabbed a pen, and started tapping it on the desktop. A vein in his temple pulsed. He was much more worried than he was letting on.

"So you don't know why Philip was in town, then?" I asked.

His gaze slid over me, then to his desk, then back to me. "I don't know why he was in town, but. . .I did know he was here."

I grasped the arms of my chair. "You did? And you didn't tell Abbie? Eric, what's the difference between you not telling her and her not telling you?"

"Plenty," he said. "For one thing, he wasn't hounding me."

I had to give him that. "Do you know what he was doing?"

"Well, I knew he had been visiting his mother. He did that periodically. And I always kept track of him because I *didn't* want him bugging Abbie. We usually talked about our investigations. Like I told him I'd recently been assigned to work with Narcotics on a special case." Eric stopped and drew in a deep breath. "Trish, you have to understand that I was concerned about him. I wanted to protect Abbie, but I was still concerned about Philip. That's why I kept in contact with him. I wanted more than anything for him to get his life straightened out."

"I understand," I said softly.

"The strange thing is, he called me and left a message the day he was shot. Just said he wanted to talk to me—had something to tell me." Eric tapped his pen harder. "I was in a class, but I wish I'd answered. Maybe he wouldn't have died."

"When did he call you?" I asked.

"Based on everything I know now, about an hour before he was shot."

I made a mental note about that because the timing was curious. "I know he moved to New York City. Has he been there all this time?"

Eric nodded. "Yes. He was working for the NYPD. He did pretty well. Moved up the ladder. Worked as a detective and in Narcotics. Made lieutenant. Never married again, just had a string of girlfriends."

Eric sighed. "You know he was a good friend when we were in the academy together, right?"

I nodded.

"Then he was a fellow officer. There's something about that. A camaraderie that I can't explain." Eric's eyes boring into mine seemed to beg me to understand, then he looked away. "When he was first married to Abbie, things were fine. But after a while, I began to realize things weren't right. Eventually I saw what he was doing with other women." He rubbed the skin between his eyebrows. "She came to me and tried to talk to me about some things. I blew her off. He was my friend. A fellow cop. A brother of sorts. That hurt her bad."

"I know," I said. "I'm just glad she got over it and is giving you a chance now. Neither one of you is the same person you were back then."

"Yes." For a moment, his face brightened, and then the light died.

I decided a change of subject would be good. "Philip's timing in being here is interesting, don't you think?"

Eric's eyes focused on me again. "Well, I wouldn't say 'interesting' is the best choice of words, given how things have turned out. More like disturbing."

"There has to be a reason he was here," I said. "I just wish Abbie had me or Daddy with her when Philip first approached her. We could have helped."

"I wish she had, too. Things might have been different." He glanced at the desk then up at me. "Do you know something I don't know about Abbie? A secret reason she could have had to murder Philip? Or have him murdered?"

"What?" I shot forward in my chair. "Do you mean you think she did it? I can't believe it. What are you—"

"No!" He stretched out his right hand as if he were directing traffic and telling me to stop. "Please, Trish. I know her better than that. But she is very deep. I know there are layers in her that I haven't begun to see. I just don't want something coming to light that will hurt her." He rubbed his eyes. "I don't want someone else discovering something."

"Like the bulldog, you mean?" I took a deep breath. "You want me to look into things?"

He met my gaze with wide eyes. "You're kidding, right?"

A brief surge of irritation washed over me. "Do I look like I'm kidding? This is a serious conversation, is it not?"

"Yes, it is a serious conversation, and no, you don't look like you're kidding. I was being facetious. I know perfectly well how you are. In fact, you're probably already looking into things. That's why you wanted to know about the crime scene."

I felt warmth on my cheeks.

"I'm right, aren't I?" he asked. "And you have one of those notebooks in your purse, don't you?"

Body language plays a big part in police interrogation and interviewing. Mine gave me up.

"You do," he said. "Admit it."

"Yes, I do."

"Trish, you need to stay out of this." He shifted in his chair and it creaked. "For a number of reasons."

I shook my head. "My best friend is a suspect. I can't let this go."

"I'm asking you to. She'll be fine." Even as he said it, I could tell he wasn't sure he believed it himself.

I felt angry all over again when I thought of Abbie huddled on her couch, crying. "You weren't there after she was interviewed. You didn't see the shape she was in." I described how I found her the night before.

Eric blinked. "She never told me that."

"Well, of course she didn't. She doesn't want to compromise you." I placed my hands on his desk. "I know I can do this."

He leaned back in his chair. "I know you can, too, but there's so much at stake. Your getting involved could make a messy situation messier—not to mention being dangerous for you."

I wasn't going to press the point. I already knew what I was going to do. And I wondered before all this ended if Eric might welcome my help.

His phone rang.

"Excuse me," he said. After a few uh-huhs and glances at me, he put the phone down. "Detective Reid would like to see you. She's here in the building, and she's sending someone to get you."

"How did she know I was here?"

"The walls have eyes." A grim smile passed over his face. "I think I'm going to need to watch my step."

As I waited for Detective Reid in the bland interview room, I remembered the first time I had been here, interviewed by Eric. At the time, I'd thought that was a bad situation. Things had certainly gone from bad to worse. After being kept waiting what I presumed was a suitable amount of time to keep me off balance, Detective Reid walked in.

"Good morning, Mrs. Cunningham."

"Hello." I put my elbows on the table and stared at her.

She dropped onto a chair across from me. "I'd just like to go over your statement again."

I nodded.

She pulled out a piece of paper and read each answer I'd given her. Each time she looked up at me, I nodded.

"Well, that's about it," she said as she stood.

I waited. I had a feeling I was about to find out her real purpose for asking me here.

As she gathered her papers in her arms, she glanced at her telephone then back at me. "Why were you here today?"

I had to tread carefully, and I wasn't sure what to say. I didn't want to put Eric on the spot, although I had a feeling he already was.

"I came to see Eric Scott."

"About?"

"He's about to marry my best friend. He was concerned about her well-being because he hasn't seen her since Philip died."

"He hasn't seen her?" The surprise was evident on Detective Reid's face, but she got control of herself quickly.

"No."

"Mmm." She headed toward the door.

I braced myself, thinking about Lieutenant Columbo on television. He used to do the same thing. Make the suspect feel like they were home free, then turn around and fire questions. I wasn't disappointed. She whirled around to face me again.

"Were you aware that Abbie Grenville met Philip Grenville at the Gas 'n' Go the day he was murdered?"

"Yes," I said.

"You didn't tell me this yesterday," she said, her flat, cold eyes nailing me to the chair.

"I didn't know yesterday," I said.

She nodded very slowly. "I see. And where did you find this out?"

"From Abbie," I said.

"And when did you speak to her?"

"Last night," I said.

"I see." Detective Reid put her hand on the doorknob. "Is there anything else you know that you believe would be pertinent to the case?"

I shrugged. "I have no idea what I know that you think might be pertinent."

The detective smiled grimly. "You have quite the reputation."

I stood, picked up my purse, and slung it over my shoulder. "I've lived in Four Oaks all my life. I'm sure you're going to hear all sorts of things about me."

She stared down at me. "Don't get in my way, Mrs. Cunningham. This is not a game of Sherlock Holmes. *I* don't appreciate civilians getting involved in my investigations."

"Frankly, Detective Reid, I don't know any law enforcement officer who does like civilians involved in their investigations."

She stared at me with narrowed eyes.

Detective Reid was a formidable foe. She smiled slowly, looking like a shark, then motioned for me to go ahead of her so she could escort me from the building.

I returned her smile as I passed her and saw a flicker in her eye. I had a feeling this wasn't the last of my little chats with the detective.

## 9

I stopped to eat lunch at Bo's Burger Barn, but I didn't have much of an appetite. When I ended up pushing my onion rings around the half-eaten cheeseburger on my plate, I realized it was pointless. I wasn't going to finish. I shoved the whole thing aside and pulled the steno pad out of my purse. I needed to write notes about what I had learned that morning.

I looked at what I'd already written about Philip. To that, I added:

*Philip called Eric an hour before he was shot.*

Then I flipped a few pages ahead, titled the page "Suspects," and began to write.

*Jaylene and Henry Adler. They hated Philip. Why? And why is Jaylene so defensive that Henry had nothing to do with Philip's murder?*
*Clark Matthews? New in town. Worked in New York City as a "model." Could have had a run-in with Philip there.*

He just didn't seem like a viable suspect to me, but I had so little to go on, I needed to follow every lead I had.

I tried to take a sip of my Mountain Dew and sucked up nothing through the straw but water from the melted ice. I'd been here a long time. I was avoiding my next stop. It was the one I was dreading. Back to the murder scene.

My cell phone rang as I finished paying for my lunch. I looked at the screen. It was Eric's daughter, Sherry.

"Hi, hon," I said as I walked out into the cold air. I tugged my coat tight around me.

"Mrs. C.!" She was yelling so loud, I had to pull the phone away from my ear. "You'vegottosolvethismysterysoDadcanmarryAbbie!"

Sherry was frantic. I understood. That was how I felt on the inside. "I guess you talked to your father?"

"Yes! And I need to come home, but he won't let me."

I jammed the phone between my head and my shoulder and dug through the mess in my purse for my keys. I needed to clean it out. "There's not much you could do here," I said. "It doesn't make sense for you to miss school. And you need to calm down. Getting hysterical isn't going to help."

I heard her take a deep breath. "I'm sorry."

"It's fine. I understand totally. This has been a nightmare."

"So are you going to solve this?"

"I'm going to try." I unlocked my SUV and climbed in. The sun had been shining through the windows, and I was grateful for the relative warmth of the interior.

"I'm going to call you when I can," she said. "And Tommy might have some ideas, too. I talked to him."

"That's fine. I can use all the input I can get."

Unlike Detective Reid, I welcomed help from any source. And a college student at a distance might have a different perspective.

Sherry interrogated me for the next twenty minutes while I drove to the fellowship hall. I told her everything I knew. Then we said our good-byes.

Before I reached the fellowship hall, I turned onto the road Abbie had told me about. The one that passed around the church property and would have allowed someone access through the woods to the back of the property where Philip had been shot. I drove slowly and noticed a dirt road leading back into the trees. If I had my bearings right, this headed toward the hall.

I pulled my SUV into the entrance, trying to avoid tree limbs that threatened to scrape the paint off the side of my vehicle. The road narrowed, and the woods closed in around me. I stopped. Perhaps this was only a parking place for hunters or kids.

If nothing else, this isolated spot would have made a great hiding place for a vehicle while the murderer shot Philip. I wished I could investigate more, but I felt uneasy. I backed up, pulled onto the road, and headed for the fellowship hall.

The yellow police tape had been removed from the church property. Things looked normal. I let myself into the building. I wasn't really expecting to find anything. I was sure the police had been thorough. I just wanted to get a sense of things. Maybe some flash of insight.

I looked all over the kitchen. In corners and cupboards. But I found nothing. Then I leaned against the kitchen island and tried to imagine what had happened. What had Philip done after Abbie left for McDonald's? Why had he gone to the backyard of the church?

I mentally shook myself. I was only postponing the inevitable. Going outside. Where a single shot from a rifle had ended Philip's life.

As I walked down the steps, I averted my gaze from where Philip had bled to death. Instead, I glanced up into the woods. Who had been up there? I could almost imagine eyes gazing at me.

I heard the distant sound of a car engine, and it brought me back to reality.

After a stabilizing breath, I approached the spot where Philip's body had been. I hated the thought that he had died so unexpectedly. As he died, had he known it was the end? Had he known the Lord?

I glanced up at the woods. A breeze whispered through the bare trees, and I shivered in my coat. This spot was so isolated. A great place to commit a murder. I wondered what the police looked at. There was something called a line of sight, I thought, but I knew very little about crime scene investigation.

The sound of the car engine came closer; then I heard a vehicle pull in front of the building. The engine stopped. Then a car door opened and slammed shut.

I felt a brief surge of panic, thinking maybe I should hide. But that was silly. My SUV was parked right out front. Besides, the scene had been cleared. I could conceivably be here for church business.

Squaring my shoulders, I jogged up the back stairs, mentally fortifying my excuses for being here. I yanked the door open and came face-to-face with Corporal Fletcher.

"Mrs. C.," he said as he moved aside and made a motion for me to enter the room.

I'd never seen him angry, but there was no doubt that at this moment, he was furious. At me. Under his bushy brows, his eyes were emitting sparks. All the reasons for my presence here fled my brain.

He shut the back door with more force than necessary then settled his full gaze on me. "Didn't I tell you to stay away from all of this?"

I felt as if the fire from his eyes was burning my retinas as we stared at each other. "Yes, you did, but I needed to, um, do something for, uh, my mother. . . ." My voice trailed away.

The slight shaking of his head told me he saw right through my half-truth. "I was not joking when I told you to stay away."

I have the unfortunate inability to stay intimidated for long, and the corporal's anger triggered my self-defense mechanism. "I'm not a child, Corporal Fletcher. And I'm not here just playing around."

He took a deep breath. "I know why you're here. Eric told me you'd been to his office. And you offered to investigate."

"He told you that?"

"Yes. And he also told me that he tried to dissuade you. And yet here you are."

"How did you know I was coming *here*?"

"Because you asked him if the state police were through with the scene. And I also happened to see you from the woods."

"You mean. . ."

"Yeah. I was up in the woods looking things over." The sparks in his eyes had turned to flaming embers. "You got any idea how easy it would have been to pick you off? If I had been someone with, let's say, bad intentions? Like maybe the same person who shot a hole in Philip Grenville?" His voice had risen to a loud growl.

I swallowed then felt unexpected tears prickle my eyelids, so I looked down at my feet. To have kindhearted Corporal Fletcher so angry with me hurt.

"Mrs. C., can't you understand what I'm saying? I got too much to worry about right now without you in the mix. I don't have time for this." He turned away from me and began pacing.

I let him pace for a minute or so, hoping it would calm him down. Then I glanced up at him. He stopped walking and met my gaze. I felt a tear run down my cheek.

"Aw, man." His bunched facial muscles relaxed, and the flame in his eyes died. "I made you cry." He swore under his breath. "I'm sorry."

I shook my head and sniffled. "It isn't just you. I'm so worried. Abbie is my closest friend. In some ways, she's closer to me than Max. She finally has a chance to be happy. . . ." I gripped the kitchen island tightly with my hands. "That wedding has got to happen."

"That's the way I feel about Eric." Corporal Fletcher eyed me for a long time, and I could tell he was deciding whether he wanted to say anything else to me.

I waited.

"I'm here doing what you're doing," he said finally. "I'm here on my own time, and I'm telling you 'cause I don't want Eric to know. I don't want *anyone* to know, including Abbie. I could get in trouble. You gotta promise me, Mrs. C."

"You're not going to tell Eric?"

The corporal shook his head. "No way. He's my commanding officer. He can't know. He'd have to order me to stop. I wouldn't want to break my word to him. And I wouldn't want him to get in trouble for what I'm doing."

"Okay. You've got my word." The corporal's confession surprised me, yet at the same time it didn't. "So you're really doing the same thing I am? Trying to help Abbie and Eric?"

"Yes. At the risk of being charged with misconduct and insubordination if someone finds out."

"But you were here the night they were collecting evidence. Why did you come back today? What more could you find out? Do you think they did a sloppy job investigating?"

He shook his head. "I don't think they missed anything, but I wanted to revisit the scene. Just to think about what happened." He motioned toward the back door. "I'm going to look out there."

"You mind if I come?"

"Nope. Glad for the company."

I felt much safer with the corporal along. I stayed quiet so as not to disturb him. He stood looking up into the woods.

"Great place for a shooting," he finally said. "Easy access. Easy escape."

"But why was Philip out here?" I asked. "Why was his car parked down the road? Abbie said when she left that he was out front."

He glanced at me. "That's one of my questions. Doesn't make much sense, does it? Unless someone made him come out here. Or walked out here with him." Corporal Fletcher took a deep breath. "That's the thing. Who knew he was here? This was at least slightly premeditated. Even if someone by chance had a gun in the trunk of their car, they still had to know Philip was out here alone and then hide their car and shoot him. You see why it looks bad for Abbie? And why Eric is concerned even though he won't admit it?"

My stomach rolled into a knot. "Yep, I see. And I don't even know who the suspects are. The other times I've been involved with a murder, they were obvious. This time the only obvious suspect is Abbie, and I know she's not guilty."

"You know that. I know that. Eric knows that, but she's lookin' real good as a suspect, Mrs. C. If I was the lead on this case, I'd be lookin' pretty close at her. There's stuff that points at her, and—"

My mouth went dry. "Like what?"

He shifted from one foot to the other. "Not sure I can tell you that. Don't want to be accused of compromising the investigation."

I wanted to stomp my feet and scream that the investigation was already compromised if they were looking at Abbie.

Corporal Fletcher's attention had left me, and he was looking at the ground where Philip's body had been. I refused to look down.

"Mm-hmm," he said. Then he knelt.

The thought of kneeling anywhere near where the blood had been made me feel like the onion rings, cheeseburger, and Mountain Dew were congealing in my stomach. I turned my face toward the woods and tried to clear my mind.

"This is interesting," Corporal Fletcher said. I glanced at his head out of the corner of my eye. He stood and wiped his knees with one hand and held out something for me to see with the other. "They found some of this the other night. I wanna know what you think."

That got my attention. "That looks like a tiny piece of. . .gravel. . .wait." I bent over his hand. "That's cat litter. I know because I just bought some for Sammie's new kitten."

He grinned. "A clue for you, Mrs. C."

"Cat litter." I thought about the Adlers.

The corporal's eyes narrowed. "You got a thought about this, don't you?" He dropped the piece of litter and stared at me.

I shrugged. "I'm not sure."

"Okay, we'll come back to that in a minute. Right now I want you to think back about the body."

My stomach lurched. "I don't want to. I feel like throwing up."

Corporal Fletcher nodded. "I understand. Just try to think of it as a body, not a person."

My mind didn't seem to want to make that differentiation, but I took a deep breath and ordered my stomach to behave. "Okay."

"Did you see his face?"

"How am I supposed to think of it as just a body when you want me to think about his face?" I snapped.

Corporal Fletcher patted my arm again. "I'm sorry. I wouldn't ask if it wasn't important. So did you see his face?"

I swallowed hard. "Yes. For a few seconds."

"Anything you noticed? Different from a normal face?"

I thought about it. Philip's eyes had been closed. And there had been some discoloration around his eye. I looked up at Corporal Fletcher. "Like. . .bruises? Maybe a black eye?"

He nodded. "Good so far."

"Oh, I see. This is a guessing game. It's a clue. Evidence. But you're not going to tell me. So you can't be accused of compromising anything."

"You got it."

I bit my lip and thought about it. Then I realized what he was getting at. "Someone hit Philip. And it wasn't at the time of his murder. It was before."

Corporal Fletcher smiled. "Smart cookie."

I felt proud, like I'd passed a test. "So someone was possibly angry enough at him to hit him. And that same person could have been angry enough to kill him."

"Bingo. And you figured it out yourself. I didn't tell you."

Black eye. Fight. Anger. Once again, I thought of the Adlers.

As if he could read my face and knew I had some suspicions, Corporal Fletcher motioned to the stairs. "Let's go inside and talk."

I glanced around, suddenly feeling uncomfortable. "You know, it would be just as easy for someone to shoot both of us out here."

He smiled. "I've been listening for cars. Haven't heard a thing."

Back inside the church hall, we stood in the kitchen. I was on one side of the island, and he was on the other.

"You're not going to stop looking into this, are you?" he asked.

Feeling a little bit like Charlie when he was rebelling, I crossed my arms. "No, I'm not going to stop looking into this."

"You got one of those notebooks in your purse, don't you?"

"Yes." I glared at him. "Yes, I do." It was annoying that he and Eric knew me so well.

He held up his hand, placating me. "It's okay." His gaze was searching. "I trust you, Mrs. C. You're good people. And you got good instincts, too. Seeing as how I can't stop you from doing this, how about a partnership?"

"Partnership? Just a few minutes ago you were lecturing me about being involved. Now you want to partner with me?"

"Well, I can change my mind." He paced the kitchen again. "I got my reasons. Among them, it'll be easier to keep tabs on you. Plus, you can find out things that I can't." He stopped pacing and stared at me. "And that way, you have to tell me what *you* know."

"And in turn, that means you'll have to tell me what you know?"

At his pause, I knew this wasn't going to be an equal deal. That figured. "Why should I partner with you when you aren't going to share with me?"

"I'll be straight with you, Mrs. C. It's bad enough I'm doing this on my own time. But I got certain rules I won't cross. One of them is sharing official evidence in an investigation. Not that I'm going to know all the evidence. But still, even if I told you what I know, that could jeopardize the case."

"Well, I won't—"

"Okay, I'll put it this way. If it ever came out that I was telling you things only the cops know, a murderer could go free, and I could lose my job and my pension. But if it's something you could easily know, I'll tell you. Or we'll play another guessing game."

I had to understand that. "Can I at least tell Max?"

Corporal Fletcher blinked.

"He's worried sick about my doing this. It would relieve his mind, and he won't tell a soul."

Corporal Fletcher studied me then finally nodded. "I'll trust you two. Just remember. This could really hurt my career."

That's when I realized how much Eric meant to Corporal Fletcher. That he would go to this length to help him said a lot about their friendship. I could relate to that kind of loyalty. Abbie and Eric had to succeed with two good friends who would risk everything for them.

"All right. I agree. We'll work together." I suddenly felt like Watson to his Sherlock Holmes.

"Okay, so spill. What's in that notebook of yours?"

I pulled out my notebook and read my few clues to him. Then I told him about the Adlers and the kitty litter.

"I can look into that," he said. "See if there's something someone knows. Be careful, Mrs. C. Sounds like they're angry."

"They're definitely that," I said. "And I'm sorry. I don't know a lot yet."

"But it's a beginning."

"So I guess I'll call you when I learn anything," I said.

"Yes. I'll give you my cell phone number." He pulled out a business card and a pen and jotted his number on the back. Then he handed it to me.

He grinned at me. "This is very unusual for me. To ask for help from someone like you."

"Someone like me?"

"A civilian who isn't an informant. It's against all proper procedure."

I smiled back. "Well, you'll find me to be a good partner." I paused. "Can you tell me if Abbie is the only person of interest?"

He shrugged. "She's looking the best. There might be others, but I don't know for sure. Since this went to the state, I'm not privy to much."

A few minutes later, I watched him climb into his car. As I opened the door to my SUV, I looked down at the gravel. A gold-colored button lay flattened on the ground. I wondered if it was Abbie's. I picked it up. Too bad. But a flattened button was the least of her worries.

10

Before I pulled out of the parking lot, I glanced at my watch. I had a little more time before I had to pick up Chris. I wanted to find out how Abbie was doing. I called her and she picked up right away, which surprised me.

"Hi," I said. "Are you okay?"

"Better than last night in some ways, but I need to talk to you."

"I'm on my way to your house right now."

Twenty minutes later, I was in her living room. She had applied makeup and was dressed in a nice pair of jeans and a tailored shirt, all of which was a good sign because it meant she was trying to regain some control of her life. However, the circles under her bloodshot eyes and the drawn expression on her face told the real story.

After I hugged her, I looked around. She had made an effort to straighten up. I was glad for that because it meant she had some fight in her.

"Have you eaten anything?" I asked.

"I forced myself to eat lunch—some of what your mother sent over," she said.

"Good," I said. "You want me to make some coffee or tea?"

She shook her head.

"Okay." I dropped into a chair and put my purse at my feet. "I've been to see Eric."

"I know. He called and told me." She swallowed and blinked. "He doesn't say so, but I can hear in his voice that he's angry with me for not telling him about Philip."

"Do you blame him? I was a little irritated myself. You do have a habit of keeping things to yourself."

"You're right." She took a deep breath. "And I'm trying. That's why I asked you to come. Because I need to come clean and tell you everything."

My heart plummeted. "What do you mean, *everything*? Abbie, what else could there be?" I realized immediately how harsh I'd sounded. "I'm sorry. I didn't mean that."

"Yes, you did." She stuck her chin in the air. "And I suppose you've told me every little detail about your life? There's *nothing* I don't know?"

Some color had returned to her face. Perhaps the two of us semiquarreling wasn't a bad thing.

"Okay," I said. "You have a point. Except that I'm not a suspect in a murder."

"And that's why I'm telling you this. Because I am—now. I wasn't before."

That made sense in an odd way. "Have you told Eric what you're about to tell me?"

"I sent him an e-mail. I haven't heard back." She was pumping her leg up and down, a nervous habit she'd had since she was a kid. She had tried to conquer it as an adult, but the bouncing returned when she was stressed out.

"Philip wrote me a letter two weeks ago. I returned it to him unopened. With a letter of my own telling him to leave me alone. I know it sounded. . .almost threatening."

"And the police found it?"

"Yes. He had it with him at his mother's house."

"So you didn't look at his letter at all?"

"No. I just didn't want to be reminded of the past." She picked up a pillow and put it in her lap. "You remember back then, right?"

"Yeah, I do," I said.

"I thought we'd be happy forever," Abbie murmured. "I thought he loved me. But then I started hearing all the rumors of other women."

I nodded but didn't speak. I couldn't because I still carried some anger in my heart against the man—now dead—who had devastated my best friend.

"Um, the last couple of times I confronted him, he hit me." She wouldn't meet my gaze.

"Hit you?" I felt like *I'd* been punched. "He hit you? And you never told me?"

She blushed but looked defensive, too. "I was so humiliated at the time, dealing with his infidelities. Like everyone was staring at me. And it only happened a couple of times."

"But I'm your best friend. Why couldn't you tell me? Eric asked me today if there were things in your past that you were keeping secret. I assured him there weren't, but you're like a book of secrets."

"I was so young at the time. He was a cop. He wore a badge and carried a gun. When he spoke, people listened. He held that over my head. You know. . .while we were married, he used to tell me that he could. . .make me disappear? I was terrified."

I was gritting my teeth and trying not to hate a dead man. "So what happened? I know he supposedly just walked out of your life. Is that really how it went?"

"Yes, pretty much. Well, I took pictures of the last batch of bruises he left on me. I made copies and put them in a safe-deposit box, but I didn't need them." She frowned. "Something else happened. I'm not sure what, but he came home in an unusual mood one night. Unfocused. Maybe a little scared. He methodically started packing a suitcase. Said he was leaving me and leaving town."

"That was good, right?"

"Well, yes, but weird, too. I didn't understand. But that's when I did the first thing I can say makes me proud. I went immediately to a lawyer and filed for divorce. He assured me that with the proof I had, I was fine. Then I went home, packed up the rest of Philip's things, put them in the garage, and changed the locks on the house. I had him served with the papers. I also sent him a letter."

"A letter?"

"Yes. Unfortunately, that letter was even more hostile than the one I just sent him two weeks ago. I basically threatened him with retaliation if he tried to talk to me again."

"Violence?"

"No." She inhaled. "But I didn't say exactly what. I don't remember what I said, but it was something along the lines of 'If you bother me again, I will make sure it's the last time.' I meant, of course, that I would drag him into court.

"But, Trish, he kept the letter, along with the divorce papers. The investigators found it, too, along with the one I sent him two weeks ago. Between the two of those letters, I pretty much spelled out exactly what he had done to me back then. So the police know everything."

"Oh boy." I didn't know what else to say, but I understood why Detective Reid was looking so closely at Abbie. Suspicion of revenge.

"Maybe you don't understand," Abbie said softly. "It's been nine years. When I suddenly got a letter out of the blue and then Philip showed up and started following me, I panicked. I realized I was still afraid of him."

"I can understand that," I said.

"You know what's really bad?" Abbie bit down on her lower lip.

"Um, everything?"

That earned me an eye roll from her, despite the seriousness of the topic. "My emotions. They're so mixed. That's making the interviews and everything harder, because I walk in there feeling bad and walk out even worse off."

"The system is designed to break you down," I said.

"Yes, I know that, but this is much deeper." Her fingers spasmodically clutched at the pillow in her lap. "I feel like such a bad person to even say this, but there was a part of me that was relieved Philip was dead. That meant there was no potential for him to contact me again. I could finally really and truly move on." She glanced at me. "That's horrible, isn't it?"

"No," I said. "Normal, I think. Remember how I felt a bit of relief when Jim Bob died?"

Some of the tension on her face left. "I'd forgotten that. But. . .here's where it gets all mixed up." She pulled the pillow to her chest as if to protect herself. "After that initial feeling of relief, I was hit with horrible sorrow. Like I'd lost the marriage all over again. And then I wondered if there was more I could have done to make it work. Was it my fault? And was I responsible for his not following the

Lord?" She hiccuped and swallowed. "The guilt has been unbelievable. And it's made me wonder if everything that's happening now is some kind of judgment from God. That I don't deserve. . .Eric. . .or happiness. . ." She dropped her head into the pillow and cried silently, shoulders shaking.

That I couldn't hear her cries made them all the worse. I began to cry, too, and scooted over to the sofa to hold her.

"I'm sorry," I murmured as I rubbed her back. "I'm so, so sorry."

After several minutes, I felt her sobs die. She inhaled, and I knew she was done.

I sat back and handed her another tissue. "You're probably going to have to wash that pillow."

She smiled weakly. "It is a mess, isn't it?" She laid it back on her lap. "I'm sorry for being such a wreck."

"Don't you ever apologize to me for anything like that." I clenched my fists, wanting to pound on something. "Abbie, this is *not* God's judgment. You don't *really* believe that, do you?"

"In the darkest night, I do." She paused and frowned. "In the light of day? Maybe I don't then. I'm just so tired and worn out from all the questions. I feel like I've been. . .battered."

Enough was enough. I grabbed my purse, yanked my notebook and pen from its depths, and settled back on the couch.

Abbie's face brightened. "You really are going to try to solve this? Eric said you might. And he also said he told you not to."

"Has that ever stopped me before?" I asked.

"No. And I have to say at this point, I'm relieved."

I wished I could tell her that Corporal Fletcher was working with me, because that would double her sense of security, but I couldn't.

"Do you think I would let you do this alone?" I held the pen over the steno pad. "I can't be there in the interview room with you to protect you from the bulldog, but I can try to solve this mystery so she'll leave you alone." I grinned. "I could take her, you know."

Abbie did break a smile for that. "Oh, I'm sure you could."

The atmosphere momentarily lightened. I sat back. "Let's get busy. Is there anything else you think would help me?"

"I've been thinking a lot about the fall festival, where I first saw Philip," Abbie said. "He was acting odd there. I didn't realize it at the time because I was so traumatized to see him and distracted with signing my books. But I realized he left very abruptly after he mumbled something about getting back to me."

I tapped my pen on my notebook. "This could have something to do with the past." I told Abbie about the Adlers.

She nodded. "They did hate him. I was never sure why."

I had a sudden, brilliant idea. "Do you think his mother would talk to me? June?"

Abbie's face lit up. "Yes, I think she would."

"Will you call her and ask her and then let me know? Would you feel awkward doing that?"

"No. We do talk now and then."

"Do you want to go with me to see her?"

Abbie shook her head violently. "No. She and I have already agreed that to see each other right now would be too emotional."

I glanced at my watch. "I need to get Charlie at the YMCA. He's there with Mike. I also need to pick up Chris from the sitter. And Sammie will be home shortly. Oh." I reached into my purse, pulled out the button, and held it out to her. "I found one of your buttons in the parking lot of the church hall. It must have fallen off the other night. It's flattened. I don't think you can do much with it."

"Thanks," she said as she took it from my hand. Her cell phone rang. When she answered, she paled, said, "Yes. . .yes," then hung up.

"That was the state police. They're coming to get me to take me down for more questioning." She took a shuddering breath. "I don't know if I'm going to survive this."

I wanted to take Abbie's place and face down Detective Reid, but I knew I couldn't.

"This makes me all the more determined to find out who killed Philip," I said. "I've waited a long time for you to be happy. You *are* going to get married in a little over two weeks."

⸺

When I picked up Chris from the sitter, he didn't want to leave. I had mixed emotions about that, which, given my desire to go back to work, was amusing. The mother ego part of me wanted him to be clingy. The other part of me was relieved that he was happy with Gladys. That meant I was free to pursue a new job after I solved Philip's murder.

Gladys laughed as she handed my grumpy son to me, wrapped up in his coat. "He's a cute one. And such a good boy."

*For everyone but his family, it seems,* I thought as he drilled his heels into my sides and complained in my ear.

Her smile suddenly died. "Trish, you've got to do something about your mother and Gail. This disagreement of theirs has gone on long enough. It's starting to impact everything, including the church. The phone lines are burning up."

I was surprised by her vehemence. "What can *I* do?"

"Really, it's your responsibility as your mother's daughter to help her. You can start by trying to talk some sense into both of them. This is just not a healthy situation. Not in any way, shape, or form."

I fought resentment a few minutes later as I tucked Chris into his car seat. Gladys's words settled around me like a noose. How was resolving my mother's fight with Gail *my* responsibility? They were both adults. And I doubted I would be able to talk sense into either woman as stubborn as they were.

I picked up Charlie and made it home just in time for Sammie to arrive. I fed everyone snacks and put an exhausted Chris down for a nap. Then I began to prepare dinner. Not exactly from scratch, since I was making spaghetti with bottled sauce and frozen meatballs, but at least I was cooking instead of ordering pizza.

While the sauce simmered, I put water on to boil for the noodles. Then I sat at the table with my notebook.

After reading through what I'd already written, I jotted down "kitty litter" and thought about that. Weird that it would be next to Philip's body. Especially since he was shot from the woods. Where had the litter come from? Had it been on someone's shoes? Philip's? Or someone else's?

I tapped the pen on the paper. The kitty litter was definitely a clue. How, I wasn't sure. But I needed suspects. The one thing Gladys had said that really made sense to me was to look for people who were strangers in town. Clark was one, and he'd definitely been exposed to kitty litter because of the busted bags he'd delivered to the Adlers' store.

Then there were the Adlers, who had hated Philip for years.

*Kitty litter.* I frowned. The water for my spaghetti began to boil. I jumped up from the table and put noodles in the pot. As I stirred the sauce, I watched the pasta turning over and over in the water. That's how my brain felt. Like my thoughts were tangled, churning spaghetti noodles. I hoped I could think straight quickly enough to solve this mystery before my best friend's wedding date.

———

Chris had more sauce from his chopped-up spaghetti on his mouth than in it. Max smiled at him, and he grinned back. "Dadadadadada."

"He's happy tonight," Max said as if that had never occurred before.

"I think he likes the babysitter," I said. "He didn't want to leave."

Charlie was pushing his spaghetti around on his plate, for once not stuffing his face so fast that remnants landed on his chin.

"Are you feeling okay, honey?" I asked. I was trying to be as normal as possible for my family.

His face squished into a terrible frown. "When is Aunt Abbie going to jail?"

Sammie's mouth dropped open, and she turned to Charlie, big blue eyes filling with tears. "Aunt Abbie is going to jail?"

Charlie nodded solemnly. "I heard in school she killed her husband."

"But Aunt Abbie doesn't have a husband yet," Sammie said. "Did she kill Uncle Eric?"

I glanced desperately at Max. We'd foolishly put off telling the little kids about Abbie, thinking the news wouldn't spread that fast. I didn't know how to tell them. I was afraid I'd cry, and I didn't want them to know how upset I was.

"Aunt Abbie didn't kill anyone," Max said. "Yesterday, Aunt Abbie's ex-husband, Philip, was killed. That's all."

"Yeah, but I heard that she shot him—"

"She didn't," Max told Charlie firmly. "You know your aunt Abbie wouldn't do anything like that."

Sammie looked at me for confirmation. "It's true." I forced myself to smile. "Aunt Abbie didn't shoot anyone. Now I have a great idea. Do you guys remember that cornfield maze we went to last year?"

The kids' expressions immediately brightened.

"I thought maybe we could go this weekend." I glanced at Max. "Friday night?"

He nodded. "Excellent idea. We'll do the maze, take a hayride, eat s'mores, and drink hot chocolate."

Maybe by then, Philip's murder would be solved. I could only hope.

After dinner, I gave Abbie a quick call to make sure she had survived her time at the state police barracks. She was as good as could be expected. She said that Eric was on his way to her house. He'd read her e-mail, and everything was okay; I knew she'd be in good hands. She also told me that she had spoken with June, who said she'd be delighted to meet with me. After Abbie gave me June's phone number, we exchanged "I love you's" and hung up.

Max and I went to the living room while Sammie and Charlie cleared the table and cleaned the kitchen. Chris was in his high chair in the kitchen with the kids, so Max and I could have a few moments of alone time.

"That was a good meal." He sat on the sofa, and I dropped down next to him. "And a good idea about the cornfield maze. The kids will love it."

"I think we all will."

"How is Abbie?" he asked. "Does she need a lawyer?"

"I'm afraid she's going to." I told him about my visit and how she'd been called to the state police barracks.

"It's not unusual in a case like this that she would be questioned over and over again, especially given what you've told me." He took my hand. "You're still investigating this?"

"Yes, I am. But I do have some news that might make you feel better about it.

Corporal Fletcher is working with me to find out more about Philip's murder."

"Oh?" Max's surprise was evident by his raised brows. "That's a little. . .irregular, isn't it? Like, against the rules?"

I smiled at his choice of words. "Yes, it is irregular. He could get in trouble if someone knew. I'm the only one who knows. And now you know, but he made me promise we wouldn't say a word."

"I certainly won't," Max said. "This means you're just collecting clues, right? He'll handle the tough stuff?"

"Yes." I wasn't sure what Max meant by "the tough stuff," but agreeing with his summation was the easiest thing to do.

He bent down to kiss me, which is normally one of my very favorite activities, but because I was too distracted to indulge tonight, I didn't encourage him.

He lifted his head. "I guess that means you're not done talking?"

"No," I said.

He sighed. "Okay."

"Do you remember Ma's neighbor Gladys?"

"You mean the one whose shed you almost burned down when you were eight and decided you needed to learn how to smoke?"

I slapped his arm. "Don't remind me of my past. I wasn't always a good kid."

"Wasn't *always* a good kid?" he asked. "How about *hardly ever*? Your middle name was Trouble."

At my frown, he laughed. "It's true. And you can't say you're not glad our kids aren't like you."

"Well, that's true. I am glad." I couldn't imagine being mother to a child like I had been. But then, my parents were a little odd. Ma always sniped at me, and my daddy spoiled me rotten. I was blessed to have grown up semi-normal, although I was still prone to personality issues that I was trying to work on with God's help. Like selfishness.

"So what about Gladys?" Max asked.

"I think I'm going to leave Chris there when I go back to work part-time."

Max's smile died. "I didn't know your working was a done deal. We haven't really discussed it."

"Yes, we have." I leaned against his shoulder. "Remember? I told you I want to work at Cunningham and Son."

He shook his head. "I was hoping you wouldn't mention that again. I just don't think it's a good idea."

"Well, we worked together at Self-Storage."

He sighed. "Yes, but I was only there sometimes while we were building the other facilities." He paused and squeezed my hand. "I'm worried about it affecting our relationship."

I sat up straight. "But we get along well. . .okay, most of the time."

He stared at me. "I'm just not sure we'd get along working together and living together."

"Does that mean I'm quarrelsome?"

He sighed. "I'm not sure I can explain it right now. Besides, my father wants me to consider a new partner."

"I wanted to be your new partner," I said.

Max avoided my eyes. "Dad has several people in mind. My mother is pushing one in particular, and he doesn't want to battle her."

"Your dad is basically retired, isn't he? How can he make suggestions like that?"

"He's still on the board of directors. And he's still my adviser."

I pulled my hand from his. "So a new partner would be someone who isn't family?"

"Yes. You know who he is. Leighton Whitmore."

"Leighton Whitmore?"

"Yes. I'm not sure about him. I'm still looking into his background and experience." He stared at the wall over my head for a moment, then looked back at me. "I'm sorry."

Irritation slapped at me like an ocean wave. "You know I'm good at what I do, Max. Accounting. Running an office. And I was great with the customers at Four Oaks Self-Storage. It's not like I'm a loose cannon or something. And I care for the company. A stranger would never care like I do."

Max stroked a piece of hair out of my face. "Honey, think about your talents. You have all sorts of options."

He was using his soothing voice. The one he used with the children when they were unreasonable.

I scooted away from him. "And what would those talents be? Why don't you tell me since you're such a know-it-all? Do you mean doing laundry, cooking dinner, and taking care of the children?"

"You know I don't mean that," he said. "Although all of those are commendable qualities and nothing to be ashamed of."

I took a deep breath and tried to regain my composure, but I couldn't. Too many emotions and conflicts warred in me, and worry about Abbie was top on the list.

I jumped to my feet. "I need to go take a bath now."

"Trish. . ." Max reached out a placating hand.

"It's fine. We can talk later. Seriously. I don't want to quarrel."

To his credit, he just let me go. I knew I was being unfair by walking out, but I didn't want to chance a fight. I felt ready to snap.

As I stepped into the tub, Gladys's last words about my mother crept back into my mind, and once again, I felt the responsibility hanging on me. That made me angry. Why was it my responsibility to fix the problem between Ma and Gail? What could I do, really?

And then there was my mother-in-law, Angelica. Our relationship had been strained since the day I met her. Her digs at me hurt. She'd made it very clear I wasn't the ideal daughter-in-law. I had responded by shutting her out of my life and, to a degree, out of the kids' lives. I had a feeling that God was dealing with me about my relationship with Angelica. The problem was, I didn't want to listen.

I deliberately turned my mind to other things, and in just a few minutes, the heat of the bathwater began to loosen the tension in my muscles. I let my brain run on autopilot. I thought about Abbie, Philip, the Adlers, Clark, kitty litter, and Cunningham and Son. How could Max be thinking about hiring someone like Leighton? He wasn't family. He wasn't even from around here. They'd just moved here from. . . I sat up abruptly, splashing the floor with water. Leighton and Hayley had lived in New York City. They were new in town. He was a hunter and owned rifles. And they had kitty litter.

What connection would they have with Philip? Or did I just want them to be guilty of something because the Cunninghams thought they were so perfect?

# 11

It was Thursday morning—two weeks and two days before Abbie's wedding. Once again, I'd slept fitfully. While the kids got ready for school, I sat at the table in the kitchen and perused my clue notebook.

Under "Suspects," I quickly jotted down "Hayley and Leighton Whitmore" before I could lecture myself about being biased. Instead, I told myself that a good sleuth follows up all possible leads, no matter what.

When Max walked into the kitchen in a classic gray suit, I murmured hello but kept my eyes on my words. I was still slightly irritated with him.

He bent over to kiss my temple. "I'm sorry about last night. I've given it a lot of thought, and I might have a job idea for you. Just let me think a little bit more, okay?"

I glanced up at him in surprise. "Really? At Cunningham and Son?"

"Yes and no." He grinned. "I'm not going to say anything else right now, so don't ask."

He disappeared through the door to the garage. I felt humbled. Even though Max wanted me home full-time, he loved me enough to want me to be happy. Self-reproach knocked aside my self-righteous crankiness. Max loved me. Enough to allow me to be happy, despite what he wanted. Love sometimes means making choices we don't want to make for the sake of someone else. Doing things we don't want to do. I had a feeling this was a lesson the Lord was trying to teach me. And class wasn't over yet.

Maybe I could hurry my lesson along by trying to help my mother. My first stop after dropping off Chris at the sitter's would be to visit Gail. Maybe I *could* make a difference.

---

Gail's house had once stood alone in the middle of ten acres, but as her family grew, she and her husband had subdivided the property, giving each child an acre on which to build a home. That said something about her that went beyond her weirdness and sniping at me. She was loyal to the people she loved, and they returned that loyalty. That was another reason I was surprised by the intensity of the bitterness between her and Ma.

I pulled into the driveway and saw a curtain twitch on one of the front windows. When I got to the door, I rang the bell and waited. Finally, Gail opened the door just enough for me to see her.

"What do you want? If your mother sent you, you can tell her to be happy with Linda."

"She didn't send me," I said. "I came on my own."

Gail didn't move; she just stood like a sentry at the door.

"Can I please come in and talk?" I asked.

Her eyes narrowed. "You're sure you're not here because your mother sent you?"

"Yes, I'm sure." I was trying to think of something that would make her open the door to me. And something that would start the conversation without talking directly about her and Ma. "I—I want to talk to you about Linda."

The mention of Linda's name lit a fire in Gail's eyes. I'd said the right thing. She flung the door open and motioned for me to come in.

"Just go to the living room." She nodded to a room to our left where a soap opera played on the television. "You want anything to drink?"

I shook my head. "No, thank you. I won't be long."

I sat on a beige and blue plaid couch. She dropped heavily into a beige recliner. I looked at her more closely, concerned by the lines in her face. Despite her propensity for joining my mother in marathon Trish-sniping sessions, I liked her. Probably because she'd been my mother's faithful friend for longer than I could remember. Loyalty is something I prize.

"Now," she said, "what do you want to know about that tramp?"

"Linda?"

"Certainly. There aren't any other tramps we were talking about, are there?"

"Well, if—"

"Linda's takin' your ma for a ride. I tried to warn her, but she won't listen to me. I don't have the energy to deal with it right now, but I'll tell you what. She said she needs extra money, but I'm not sure. I think the girl wants something."

"Why do you say that?" I asked. "I thought she was pretty nice. A little dense, maybe."

"Well, that shows you what you know," Gail said.

I found comfort in her familiar dig at me.

"Don't let her fool you. Linda Faye went to school with my daughter. I know what she used to do. She acts ignorant and then stabs you in the back."

"I guess I don't know her that well. But people can change."

Gail snorted. "Change? I doubt that. If you dye a zebra, you still have a zebra."

"Yes, I guess that's true. Only God can change a person's heart."

"And He's got His work cut out for Him with people like Linda." Gail's eyes narrowed, and she leaned forward. "I wouldn't be surprised if she killed Philip Grenville. You do know that she slept with him, too, don't you? She hated him."

Surprise rocked my mind. "I had no idea." Philip's transgressions had cut a wider swath through Four Oaks than I had imagined.

"Oh yes. Back when she lived out with her mama."

"Did she tell you that?"

"No. Philip tried to keep it hush-hush, and so did the women he was involved with. And he made the rounds, believe you me. Seducing them with his uniform and badge. Poor Abbie didn't know the half of it."

"Maybe she did," I murmured. "Do you know who any of the other women were besides Linda?"

Gail's face was twisted in anger. "He made passes at my daughter, Terry, too, but he didn't make any headway. I can't remember who else there was."

"So had he been in touch with Linda?"

"Yes. I overheard her tell one of her friends about it. First time at the fall festival. He wanted to meet with her, and that made her mad."

I had already thought it odd that Philip had contacted Abbie. Now he had made contact with Linda.

"But she's slick." Gail's eyes narrowed again. "Philip came into the shop for coffee, and Linda was as nice as pie to him."

"Maybe that's because she was at work. Or she thought that if she was nice to him, he'd leave her alone?"

Gail snorted. "No. Something's up." She breathed deeply, and her eyes drifted shut.

"Are you okay?" I asked.

Her lids snapped open. "I'm fine. Just tired. It's my daughter. She's having a hard time. Single mom, you know. She lost her job then got another one. She works with kids at the YMCA, but the hours are terrible. I have to drive my grandbaby to school for a while."

A smile flickered briefly over Gail's lips. "She's in the fourth grade, you know, in a private school. No buses. We pay for it."

I nodded. "It's wonderful that you do that."

Gail's face hardened again. "Terry had just started dating someone, and it looked good for her. Met him through the kids she works with. Then Linda came along and stole him."

*Ah.* Now the truth came out. Gail's real reason for disliking Linda. "So she took your daughter's boyfriend? Who was it?"

Gail huffed. "Clark Matthews. And then your ma has the nerve to hire Linda after she did that. I can't believe it."

Clark's name kept popping up. And he was beginning to sound like the proverbial Lothario. This also began to explain the rift between Ma and Gail. "Well, why *did* Ma hire Linda? Did she know about all that?"

"No, but she should have had more sense." Gail huffed. "I told her after she hired her, but she said she needed the help 'cause I wasn't there." She took a deep breath. "Now why didn't she just fire Linda?"

I understood how Gail felt. But I knew that my mother couldn't just fire someone based on Gail's grudge. Was it possible this situation might not have a good ending?

"You two have been friends for so long," I said.

"That's my point," she said. "I'm her friend. And she chose someone else." She blinked rapidly, and for just a minute, I saw the real emotion behind the anger. Hurt. And I thought she might cry.

"I'm sorry it's turned out this way," I said. "I know Ma misses you."

Gail recovered and snorted again. "If she missed me, she would get rid of that hussy."

—

Although I'd failed in my mission to mend the rift between Gail and my mother, I had tried. I'd learned a few more interesting facts for my clue notebook. And I hoped my talk with Philip's mother, June, would be as enlightening.

On my way to her house, I called Sherry to update her like I'd promised. She didn't answer, so I left her a message telling her what I could and explaining I'd be busy most of the day. I wasn't keen about talking to her, so I hoped she wouldn't call back. I was walking a fine line trying to keep the things secret that needed to be kept secret.

June Grenville lived alone in a neat, long ranch home in a tiny town about twenty miles from me. She'd lived there for years. Nothing had changed since I'd last been here. That was when Abbie and Philip were married.

I took a deep breath and walked to the front porch, which was surrounded by tidy square flower beds and neatly trimmed evergreen shrubs.

The door opened shortly after I knocked. I was surprised. June didn't look a day older than the last time I'd seen her, despite the grief etched on her face. Her hair was a little bit different. Not as long. Now it hung in a pale blond pageboy.

"Trish, how nice to see you. Please come in." She opened the door wide.

I walked past her into a tiled foyer, then I turned to face her. "Thank you for seeing me. I know this is a bad time."

"Bad time. Yes. . .and no."

That was a strange statement. I must have frowned.

"I'll explain in a few minutes," she said with a tiny smile that revealed laugh lines around her eyes. "Please come and sit down. Can I get you anything?"

"No, thank you," I said.

She took me to her living room in the front of the house where modern furniture and glass-topped tables adorned a celery-colored carpet.

I sat on the couch, and she sat across from me in a chair.

"So what can I do for you?" she asked. "Abbie indicated that you wanted to talk to me, but she didn't say why, except that it had to do with Philip."

"Abbie didn't tell you anything?" I asked.

"Just that the police questioned her regarding Philip's death."

"She didn't do it," I blurted out defensively.

June held up a hand. "I don't believe for a minute that Abbie did it." She rubbed her temple. "The police have been here talking to me. I know Abbie understated the issue to me. They kept asking me about her relationship with Philip. Past and present. Like they think she might have done it."

"She's probably considered a suspect." I knew that was as close as I could come to telling her the truth without compromising my promise to Corporal Fletcher.

June leaned forward with an intense gaze. "So why are you here?"

Trying to explain my penchant for sleuthing was hard enough with my family. Explaining it to a relative stranger made me feel weird and maybe a bit presumptuous. "Well, I'm afraid she's going to be arrested, so I'm. . .well, I guess I'm investigating."

June's eyes widened. "Really? Trying to solve my son's. . .murder?"

"Um. . .yes," I said.

"Well now, that's fascinating. Why would you do that? Don't you think the police can handle the investigation?"

I shrugged. "If it was Eric leading the investigation, yes. But this detective seems to have it in for Abbie." I paused and considered my next words. "I could be wrong about it. Maybe it's just the detective's personality, but I want to look into it myself. I can find out things I know the cops can't. And I have a way to get what I discover back to the police."

"Good," she said. "I must admit that Detective Reid's visits here haven't been the best experience for me, and I'm Philip's mother. She's not a nice person. The worst thing is, I expect she'll be back." June gazed at me with eyes that burned with emotion. I could tell she was trying to figure out what made me tick. "So what makes you think you can solve this? You don't have any police background, do you?"

"If you count being involved in two other murder investigations, then yes." I told her about Jim Bob and Georgia Winters. I also explained that Max wasn't thrilled with what I was doing.

"I should think not," June said. "But I can see you're determined. And I want to see Abbie cleared as much as you do." I squirmed under June's steady, assessing gaze. Then I saw the change in her eyes when she made up her mind. "I believe you might be able to do this."

Her expression of confidence made me feel better, but I was still confused by her emotional state. She wasn't behaving at all like I would expect a grieving mother to act. "So you do believe Philip was murdered—that it wasn't just an unfortunate accident?"

"Don't you?" she asked. "What is the likelihood that he was shot with a stray bullet from a hunter's rifle? In an area posted No Hunting? In that location near the church?"

I nodded. "I feel exactly like you do, which is why I'm here. The police don't appreciate my help, by the way."

"I don't imagine they do." She stood and walked to a side table that was covered with framed pictures. She picked up two and held them out to me. I took the first from her hand. It was Abbie and Philip at their wedding. I had a similar picture in an album at home.

I glanced up at June to ask why she'd shown me the photo, but the two tiny trickles of tears running down her cheeks stopped me. At last. Signs of mourning.

"I'm sorry," I said. "I feel insensitive."

She sniffed. "It's fine, Trish, really. Please ignore my tears. I just want you to know that the day Abbie married Philip, she became like another daughter to me. That hasn't changed." She handed the next picture to me. This one was a family shot of her, Philip, and a younger woman.

"Is that your daughter?"

June nodded. "Mary. This was taken a few years ago during one of his brief visits here."

If body language in the picture was any indication of relationships, Mary and Philip didn't get along well. He had his arm around her shoulders, but they were stiff. I could have put a fist between their bodies. "How often did Philip visit?"

"Regularly and on holidays."

That meant Philip was in town many times without contacting Abbie.

"Mary will be here tomorrow. We're going to bury Philip Sunday afternoon in a private service. Then she's going to stay with me for a while." She took the pictures from me. Tears still flowed down her cheeks. Ignoring her obvious pain was difficult. While her initial lack of expression had been puzzling, this was much worse. I wanted to either hold her in my arms or leave so she could be alone. I could only imagine the grief of losing a child. I took a deep breath and steeled myself for the questions I had to ask.

"I guess I was always a little surprised that you weren't angry at Abbie for the end of the marriage."

"How could I be? We all knew how Philip was changing for the worse." She placed the picture back on the table and stroked the glass. "He wasn't always like that, you know. Something changed. It might have been his work—I don't know. Or his father's death. But Philip got worse after he married Abbie. It was like the responsibility of marriage brought out the worst in him." She turned around and gazed at me. "I always suspected that he hurt her."

I said nothing. I didn't know if Abbie wanted anyone to know.

June's glance was sharp. "You don't have to say anything. I know. I just wish I'd had the courage back then to step in. Maybe things would have been different—"

"I think we all have regrets," I said.

She dropped back into her chair and visibly drew herself back together. "How will you proceed?"

"First, I want to figure out why Philip came back after all this time. Why he wanted to talk to Abbie so badly."

"Oh, I can tell you that."

I almost fell out of my chair. I was finally going to get an answer to my question, and so easily.

June fingered the edge of her shirt. "Most people didn't know that he came back on a regular basis to visit since he made sure no one knew he was here. He was never successful in his relationships, but he did take care of me. Too many people around here didn't like him. But this time was different. He. . ."

I waited for her to finish. Her mouth worked; it was obvious that what she had to say was painful. Then she met my gaze with her tear-filled eyes. "He was dying. He had just months to live. Cancer."

I felt my mouth drop open. Of everything I might have thought June would tell me, I never would have guessed that in a million years.

The corner of her mouth twitched, despite her pain. "You're shocked. I understand. When I first found out, I couldn't believe it. But hang on for what I have to say next." Her smile grew, although she was still crying. "It was a mixed blessing. Because of his illness, he finally decided to go to church. He committed his life to the Lord. That's why he moved back here. He had a lot of things here he felt he'd left undone. People he'd hurt. And he wanted to make everything right."

I felt like the floor had dropped out from under me. Philip Grenville? He'd *moved* back here? And he was in a relationship with God?

"I'm sorry," I said. "I don't know what to say."

"I understand. It took me awhile to believe it. While he was sick, I went to see him. I wasn't sure I believed him. He was always such a good manipulator, even though Mary assured me it was true. I have to tell you, I was still skeptical when he walked in here two weeks ago with a suitcase in one hand and a Bible in the other." She clasped her hands tightly. "I feel terrible, really. Here he was dying, and I was suspicious that he was just being the same old Philip. Somehow being manipulative because he wanted something. Or poking fun at my religion. His own mother didn't believe him. Then he started to talk to me about what had happened." She smiled despite teary eyes. "Can you imagine?"

"No. I can't." Something shifted in my head, making me think beyond my shock of Philip's transformation. "He came here two weeks ago?"

June reached for a tissue from a box on her coffee table and wiped her cheeks and nose. "Yes. He'd spent brutal months in treatment. Then the cancer returned, so he came here to die. He didn't go to a doctor again, except once to Dr. Starling for an unrelated illness."

June picked up a pillow and hugged it. "His sister, Mary, was with him for his last few weeks of treatment. I had to work and couldn't get the time off."

"I'm glad he had someone there with him," I mumbled. I was still trying to wrap my mind around everything June had said.

She nodded. "I was, too. And I think you'll need to talk to Mary, as well, after she's had a couple of days to settle in. She recently experienced a bad real estate deal in Atlanta and lost some money, so she needs to get financially stable again. At least that's her excuse for moving in with me. I know she really wants to make sure I'm okay.

"Anyway, she was as shocked as I was at his change. When the treatments were over, she went back home. Then we got the news that the cancer had returned. The doctors told him he should get his affairs in order."

"But. . .how. . ."

"How did he have such a change of heart?" she asked.

I nodded.

"He had a fellow officer who had been witnessing to him for years." She paused and wiped her eyes. "When a person comes face-to-face with their own mortality and sees imminent death, it changes their perspective."

I nodded.

"I've prayed for him and the people he hurt for years," June said. "He was a manipulative, selfish man. I still loved him as a son, but I saw the trail of misery he left behind him. That was difficult. His change of heart was certainly an answer to my prayers, but I had to work through a surprising evolution of feelings before I could believe him and accept what had happened. Then when he was shot, I once again had to sort through mixed emotions."

I waited for her to explain.

"The cancer diagnosis was tragic," she said, "but it led to his salvation. His murder was tragic, but it did save him from the suffering he would have eventually endured from his illness. I wish I'd had the extra month or two with him, but the little time we did have was perfect. . .so you can see why I feel the way I do."

"Yes." The tangled spaghetti that was my brain was having trouble taking all of this in. "So. . .that's why he was pursuing Abbie."

June squeezed the pillow. "Yes. He wanted to make things right. He knew what he had done to her. He told me that she wouldn't talk to him. Not that I blame her, mind you. He probably came on too strong." She smiled briefly. "Just because someone gets saved doesn't mean they have a personality transplant. But I was going to intervene and call her that night and ask her to see him."

"Were you aware of a letter he sent to her?"

"Yes," June said. "He wrote that right before he left New York City. He wanted to get together with her once he'd settled in here. But she returned it without opening it." I watched June's face for any anger, but there didn't seem to be any. She noticed my perusal. "I can't blame Abbie for her reaction. And he didn't, either." Anger suddenly flashed in her eyes. "That detective took the letter away. I was stupid. I was in such a state of shock after I was told he'd been shot that I just gave them blanket permission to go through his belongings. I should have insisted on a warrant and taken the time to get what I wanted. Now they're using it against Abbie, I'm sure."

"You didn't know," I said. "How could you?"

June took a deep breath. "Yes, you're right, of course, but I still blame myself."

"Abbie is going to blame herself, too," I murmured, "for not giving him a chance."

"He understood." When June leaned back and her body seemed to collapse in on itself, I realized our talk had worn her out. I had three final things to ask.

"Did you go with Philip to the fall festival?"

June shook her head. "No. I had to work that day, so he dropped me off at my job and then he went out there to see if he could talk to Abbie."

"Did he say anything about being there? Anything unusual? Like maybe about someone he'd seen besides Abbie?"

June pursed her lips and frowned. "You know what? He was acting funny. He didn't say anything—that I remember. But he was a bit late picking me up. And he was distracted. I thought at first he and Abbie had quarreled, but he said no."

"Well, if you think of anything else about that, let me know, okay?"

She agreed.

I sat forward and put my arms on my legs. "Did Philip have any signs of having been in a fight with someone?"

She sighed. "You mean that black eye?"

I nodded.

"He got that last Sunday. We ate lunch after church, and then he took the car out for a while. When he got back, he had that shiner, but he refused to tell me what happened."

"Do you know Jaylene and Henry Adler?" I asked.

June frowned. "Vaguely. I've heard the name. Pet store?"

"Yes."

"Why?" she asked.

"Because they hated Philip for some reason." I stared at my hands before looking up at her. "I really appreciate your time. You've been more help than you realize."

"You're welcome. I want to make things as right as they can possibly be for Abbie." June smiled again. "Philip would have wanted it that way."

I stood. "I'll leave you now. If you think of anything else, would you call me?"

She stood up, as well. "Yes. And I'll tell Mary that she needs to speak with you." We walked to the front door. "Trish?"

I faced her.

"Will you tell Abbie what I told you? I think it might be better coming from you. Well, at least easier right now. I—I think this will take some adjustment for her. And it will be easier if she doesn't have to see me while she's figuring things out."

"Yes, I'll tell her."

June touched my arm. "When she's ready to hear it, please tell her this. Philip was happy she was successful. He wanted to tell her that he couldn't think of anybody better than Eric Scott to take care of her."

**12**

I walked to my SUV feeling overwhelmed by the information I'd just learned. Philip had not died the bad man I thought he was. Although I was relieved, now I wondered how to deal with all the anger and resentment I felt toward him. At first glance it might seem simple. He'd changed. He was trying to make things right. God had forgiven him; therefore, I should. But feelings can't be eradicated that easily.

I thought about the song "Amazing Grace" and realized that though I'd sung it in church all my life, I'd never grasped the depth of the simple truth. God can walk into someone's life and so totally transform them that they aren't the same person they were before. Even someone who has hurt other people so badly.

The Bible says that God leaves the past behind. I couldn't do that so easily. How odd to be in the position of having to forgive a dead man. That might take some time. But I did feel an odd sense of relief. If a tragic death can have a good side, Philip's did.

And now I had to prepare myself to tell Abbie what I'd found out—why Philip had been so insistent about talking to her. And I would have to watch her go through the same emotional processes I was going through, only magnified hundreds of times.

Given her already fragile emotional state, I had a feeling she would take her response to what I told her and add it to the heaps of guilt she was already carrying. But I hoped that gradually she would be able to come to peace with his death. And take the gift God offered her through Philip's change of heart— freedom from the past. And his wish that she would be happy with Eric.

*Lord, please give me the right words.*

I shivered from the cold, stuck my keys in the ignition, and turned on my SUV, but I didn't go anywhere. Instead, I blindly stared at June's house, trying to think of the best way to handle this. Maybe I should ask Abbie to meet me somewhere for lunch so I could tell her in a neutral place. If she was in public, she might not retreat so quickly into herself.

I dug through all the junk in my purse for my cell phone. As I called her, I made a mental note to clean the mess.

"How are you?" I asked when she answered.

"Hanging in there." She sounded livelier than she had that last time I spoke with her.

"Anything new?" I asked.

"No. I spent some good time with Eric. He just left."

"I'm glad," I said. "Listen, can you meet me for lunch?"

I heard her inhale. "Today? I don't really want to go out in public right now. I hate it when people stare at me."

"Let's go somewhere out of town. Where no one will notice us." I thought about it. "You know that really great Italian place near Angelica's? It'll be my treat."

"I don't know. . . ."

"Abbie, you need to get out." How could I convince her? "But more than that, there's something I have to tell you."

"Something you *have* to tell me?"

"Yes. About Philip. Please."

"About Philip." She paused. "You just talked to June, didn't you?"

"Yes."

Abbie didn't say anything for a moment, and I flicked my keys with my finger, making them jingle.

"I won't be able to convince you to tell me on the phone, will I?" she asked. "Or to come over here?"

"No," I said.

She sighed. "Okay. I know you wouldn't ask me if you didn't think it was important."

"Oh, Abs?" I said quickly before she hung up. "Would you please bring a blank bookplate with you? I need an autograph for someone."

❦

I arrived at the restaurant before Abbie and got a table right away. After I slipped into my chair and put my sunglasses on the table, I pulled my steno pad from my purse to make notes. I hadn't felt right making notes while I was talking to June, but I needed to do so now before I forgot anything.

I wrote a small paragraph about Philip's transformation—something I was still having trouble wrapping my mind around. Then I began adding specific clues.

> *Philip making amends. Had he approached someone with a real grudge? A grudge big enough to kill him?*

To my last notation about Philip leaving the fall festival abruptly, I added:

> *He was distracted—maybe disturbed by someone or something. What?*

*And he'd been in town for a couple of weeks.*
*He got the black eye the Sunday after the fall festival. He went*
*somewhere alone after church.*

Then I tapped my pen against my lip. After talking to Gail, I had another potential suspect for my list. Linda Faye King.

I wrote:

*Linda. Possibly slept with Philip long ago. She was trying to avoid*
*him now. Was she angry enough about the past to kill him now? Or*
*possibly afraid of him for some reason?*

Something niggled in my mind. The fall festival seemed to be the one place where all my suspects and Philip had been at the same time.

*Clark, Linda, the Adlers. . .Hayley and Leighton.* I paused my mental rundown of suspects and bit the end of my pen. What about Gail and her daughter? Though I hated to think about it, there was definitely some hostility there. Just to be thorough, I jotted down "Gail."

My quest for information would continue that afternoon. I'd drop by Clark's mother's after lunch with the bookplate.

And maybe it was time to look for houses—a good excuse to see Linda. I yanked out my cell and gave her a quick call at her office. She was in, and we agreed to a meeting on Saturday afternoon when we could discuss what I had in mind.

I put away my phone. And looked at the names on my list. I needed to find out more about Hayley and Leighton. Sammie and I would go visit the kitten again. But I'd give Angelica a call a bit later and try to pry some information out of her.

I was concentrating so hard, I didn't notice Abbie until she joined me at the table. I shut my notebook and put it away. She kissed my cheek then slipped into her seat and pulled a bookplate out of her purse. "Who is this for?"

"Clark Matthews's mother, Eunice."

She wrote on the plate and then handed it to me. "So is there a reason for this?"

I tucked the plate into my purse and met her gaze. "Yes. I'm trying to find a killer."

"Still hard at work on my behalf," she said.

"Yes."

"Thank you." She clasped her hands on the table. "I don't deserve the kind of friend you are to me. And I don't deserve Eric, either. Not after the way I've kept things from him."

"Don't be silly." I reached across the table and squeezed her hands. "You've put up with so many of my faults."

"No more than you put up with mine." She smiled. "Hey, how many people have a best friend—a true best friend? And you've been mine since before kindergarten."

We touched the tips of our index fingers, something that had been a sign of our friendship for years. When we were little, we decided we wanted to be blood sisters. We'd pricked the ends of our fingers to make them bleed and then held them together. Strangely enough, that childish action meant more today than it had then. It represented the covenant of our friendship.

We were both silent for a few minutes after that. My mind was filled with a montage of memories. Finally, Abbie broke the silence.

"Eric suspects that Nick Fletcher is investigating Philip's murder on his own time."

I tried hard to look innocent, but she'd caught me off guard, and I was sure my face gave me away.

"You knew, didn't you?" she asked.

I stared at the tablecloth. "I can't say."

The corners of her mouth twitched. "I understand. Eric says he can't officially know what Nick is doing because he'd have to order him to stop, so he hasn't told Nick he knows. However, during one of their conversations, Eric mentioned offhand to him the name of someone at the state police who might be able to feed him a bit of information, and vice versa."

I glanced down at the table to cover up my surprise. While I was glad for what Eric was doing, I was pretty sure Abbie didn't understand the implications. Eric was a letter-of-the-law kind of guy. Black-and-white. For him to be encouraging Corporal Fletcher to step outside the system, even in such a subtle way, told me just how frightened Eric really was for Abbie.

"So what did you want to talk to me about?" Abbie asked.

No getting around it. Things were getting more complicated by the minute.

"Why don't we order," I said. "Then I'll tell you everything."

We didn't have to wait long for our server. I ordered the Tuscan chicken; Abbie ordered lasagna.

"Are you really going to eat?" I asked.

"I'm going to try," she said. "Talking to Eric helped." She smiled softly. "He understands why I kept things from him. All in all, I'm feeling a bit more upbeat."

"I'm so glad." I wished with all my heart that I wasn't about to shatter her good feelings into a million pieces.

I began by telling her how June had looked. How well she was doing despite everything. How pretty the house was. How nicely June had kept things up.

Abbie put a finger in the air in front of my mouth. "You're avoiding telling me something, aren't you?"

I sighed. "Yes."

The muscles in her face tightened. "That means I should brace myself." She sat up and straightened her shoulders.

I took a deep breath. Then I blurted out everything. As I spoke, a gamut of emotions washed over her face. Several times, I could tell she was on the verge of tears.

"That's it," I said when I was finished.

"That's it?" She swallowed hard.

"Yes, that's it." I'd done the right thing by bringing her here. Abbie would not fall apart in public, and I needed time to get through to her.

I watched her jaw clench and relax and clench and relax, as if she were chewing gum. I knew the signs. She was about to let loose.

"So because I was afraid of Philip and angry at him, he wasn't allowed the satisfaction of asking my forgiveness. That's selfish of me, isn't it?"

I was right about her blaming herself. "It's not that simple," I said. "You can't—"

"But it's worse than that. Not only did I *not* allow him to talk to me but I'm still terribly angry at him. How's that for ironic? I'm angry at a dead man. That's really selfish."

"I understand. That's how I—"

"And now"—she slapped her hands on the table—"even dead, he's making my life miserable. He had the nerve to die in the middle of my wedding plans. And I'm mad about that. How's that for selfish?"

"Well, you—"

"And to top it all off, I'm a suspect. Is this right? Is this fair? He makes everyone's lives miserable for years, then he comes riding into town like some kind of heroic, dying, movie-hero cowboy, ready to fix everything. And he wants the woman he left behind *plus* all the townspeople to forgive him. Just like that." She snapped her finger.

"I'm not sure he was expecting—"

"Then he ups and gets shot by a bad guy and doesn't even have to follow through on his plans. And he dies and goes to heaven, leaving the rest of us here to pick up all the pieces and try to put things back together."

"That's probably—"

"And the worst thing is that I'm a Christian. I'm supposed to be rejoicing that he turned to the Lord at the end of his life. Rejoicing that he was delivered from the fires of hell." She glared at me. "I'm glad he didn't go to hell, but I am not rejoicing. I'm just plain mad."

Abbie had a way with words. Considering she was a writer, that was to be expected. She'd managed to express some of what I'd been thinking, only better. And she summed it up quite nicely.

I waited to see if she was done. She appeared to be. She was breathing hard, and her face was flushed. Truthfully, I was glad to see her feisty and angry instead of morose and depressed.

"Well. . ." I paused long enough to give her a chance to interrupt me. She didn't. That meant her tirade was over. "You've probably just expressed some of what I was feeling, too."

Abbie finally noticed I was speaking and stared at me with wide eyes. "You mean you don't think I'm horrible for thinking all of that?"

I shook my head. "Absolutely not. I'm having some pretty deep issues of my own about this."

"Really?"

"You'd better believe it." I leaned toward her. "So did June at first, and she's his mother. I think she suspected you'd feel all of this, which is why she didn't want to tell you herself."

Abbie blinked as tears filled her eyes again. "I'm a wreck. A total emotional basket case. I go from one emotion to the other in a matter of seconds."

"I know," I said. "Do you want me to tell Eric?"

"No. I'll tell him." She pulled another tissue from her purse.

Our food arrived, and Abbie turned her head so the server wouldn't notice her tears. After the server left, I reached over and patted Abbie's arm.

"I'm so sorry. I knew this would be hard. Will you be able to eat?"

She blew her nose and smiled valiantly. "How could I waste the best lasagna on the East Coast? I'm going to try."

She managed to eat half her meal, and I did the same. To give her time to recover, I did most of the talking—about the kids and Max. I told her I wanted to go back to work.

"That doesn't surprise me," she said. "You've never been able to be at home and settle. Even when you were a kid."

We chatted about a few more things and avoided the topic of Philip altogether. When we were done, I paid our bill and we both stood. I pulled her into a tight hug.

"I love you. This will work out. You wait and see."

"I want to believe that," she said.

So did I.

"Oh," said Abbie, reaching into her purse. "I forgot to give you this." She pulled the smashed button I'd found in the parking lot from her pocket. "This isn't mine."

I took it from her and dropped it into my purse. Perhaps it just belonged to a church member.

We exchanged good-byes, and I watched her leave, shoulders slumped. I ached for her.

I went to the bathroom before I left. That's when I realized I'd left my sunglasses on the table. I went back to get them and noticed a couple walking into another room of the restaurant. I would recognize Linda anywhere. I also recognized the man with her. Leighton Whitmore. Hayley's husband! Why were they together?

And that's when I remembered there were two other people who'd had gold buttons on their clothing on the day of Philip's murder.

Linda Faye King and Hayley Whitmore.

—

I'd brought my headset with me that day, so I was free to make all the calls I needed to as I drove.

First, I called Clark's mother, Eunice Matthews, to ask if I could come by and deliver her bookplate. She seemed eager for the visit and explained how to get to her house. Then I called April to see if she wanted to come with me to visit Eunice, but April informed me that she was, like, *way* over Clark and that Linda could have him. But did Linda want Clark? Or did she have her sights on a wealthier man—Leighton Whitmore?

As I drove to Eunice's house, I called Corporal Fletcher. I needed to update him while everything was fresh in my mind.

"Fletcher," he snapped into the receiver.

"This is Trish Cunningham. Is this a good time to talk?"

"Mrs. C." His tone lightened. "I'm on the road, so yeah. You have news for me?"

"I don't know. Maybe."

"Well, just shoot. I'll ask questions if I have them."

I told him everything I'd learned so far. Several times, he grunted. I even mentioned Leighton and Linda. Then I told him about my visit with June and everything we'd talked about, including Philip's change of heart.

"You gotta be kidding me," Fletcher said.

"Kidding?" I asked. "Kidding about what?"

"Philip got religion?"

I could hear the derision in his voice, and I felt defensive for June's sake. "Well, that's what his mother said. And she would know. She *is* his mother."

Fletcher snorted.

"Hey, why so cynical?" I asked. "Why don't you believe it?"

"His mommy said so?" After a bark of laughter, Fletcher sighed. "Sorry, Mrs. C., but you wouldn't believe how many people's mothers cover for them. And how many people claim religious conversion. Or lie to get something. Now, granted, he probably didn't have anything to gain from this, so it's possible. But. . ."

"I'm sorry, too," I said.

"Sorry for what?"

"I'm sorry that you're so cynical. Really, Corporal Fletcher. What a horrible way to live."

He laughed again, and this time it sounded genuine. "That's what I like about you. You tell me exactly what you're thinking." He sighed again. "You're right. About the cynicism. It's my job that does it. I see the bad side of people all the time. You wouldn't believe the stupid stuff people lie about."

"I can imagine." And I really could understand, given my brief foray into crime. Especially since I'd lied one time, too.

"I'll tell you what." He chuckled. "Since Philip is so tragically dead, I'll believe his mommy and give him the benefit of the doubt."

"That's just slightly insensitive," I said primly. "I think it must be a form of cop humor. A lot of people wouldn't find that very funny, you know. Still, I'm glad you can make an exception to the way you usually think and believe a dead man, but don't strain yourself."

That just made him laugh harder, and I joined him.

"You, Mrs. C., are exactly what I needed at the moment. And while we're at it—how about you call me Nick? Seeing as how we're working together and are going to be related by friendship."

I felt warm inside. "That is probably one of the nicest things you've ever said to me. And I'd be honored. You can call me Trish."

"I can try, but I think Mrs. C. suits you better."

I heard his car radio in the background. "Listen, gotta go. And the other things you told me today? Good stuff. Keep me posted, okay? Anything you hear. It might not seem like much, but you never know."

"You got it," I said and clicked my phone off.

How true a statement was that? Sometimes it was the smallest detail, the quirkiest turn of events that led to a killer.

---

Shortly after, bookplate in hand, I showed up at Eunice Matthews's double-wide.

She must have been waiting for me, because she opened the door before I could knock.

"Trish Cunningham?"

"Yes."

"I'm Eunice. You made it here quickly. Please come in."

The tiny birdlike woman stepped back for me to walk by. Her dark hair was tightly permed and curled close to her scalp. I could see a very faint resemblance to her son in her nose and mouth, but they both looked a lot better on him than they did on her. And she didn't look sick to me, but what did I know?

Inside, I was immediately overwhelmed by the smell of floral air freshener. She pointed to a small living area just next to the foyer. I looked around and felt like I had stepped into a peach-orchard explosion. The couch was a floral peach pattern, the carpet a darker shade of the color. Even the flowers in the large print hanging above the sofa were peach. The only relief came in the little bits of brown and green accent colors and the wood of the other furniture, including a glass case standing in a prominent corner of the room. That was filled with a collection of angels, mostly fat little winged babies—with peach-tinted skin.

I dropped onto the sofa and took the bookplate from my purse. As Eunice passed me and headed for a peach-colored lounge chair, I handed it to her with Abbie's regards.

She took it from my hand and sat with a smile.

"Oh my," she said. "How exciting! This is very thoughtful. Clark told me that he'd asked you for it. He's such a good boy. Always thinking of his mama."

So Clark had told her it was his idea? I eyed my hostess. Her blue cotton pants had a knife-edge crease in them, and the sleeves on her matching blue-checked shirt had the same. She wore white socks and black loafers. Everything about her screamed "neat and tidy."

"He went to that book signing to get me an autographed copy of the book, but he said there was a line and then he had to leave because someone he knew needed help changing a tire." She smiled. "He's such a thoughtful boy. He bought me all this when he was working in New York, you know." She lifted her hand and pointed at everything in the room.

I wondered which of them was the interior designer. Still, I had to admit the decor somehow suited her.

"Well now, look at me. Look at my manners. Let me get you some coffee." She stood and walked to the tidy kitchen where the peach decor was continued in the accents and wall color.

My mind had gone totally blank. I wondered if it was shock, perhaps as a result of the color detonation surrounding me.

"Clark loves my coffee. He thinks it's better than anything, including the coffee at Doris's Doughnuts, and you know everyone loves hers, me included."

I remembered how Clark had complimented my mother's coffee, and I wondered if Eunice knew that I was Doris's daughter. I wasn't sure, and I didn't ask.

She asked me how I wanted my coffee, fixed it for me, and brought it to me. The peach-colored mug said TOMORROW IS ANOTHER DAY on the side.

"Clark gave me these mugs."

I made the appropriate complimentary noises and took a sip of the coffee. It was bad. Like dishwater.

"Good, isn't it?" she asked.

"Mmm," I said so I wouldn't have to lie outright. "So I understand that Clark only recently moved here?"

A smile lit her face. "Yes. I was never so glad in my life. I wanted him to get away from the city. Now he's here to be near me."

She seemed fine to me. "So Clark lived in New York City, then?"

"Oh yes." She took a deep breath and clasped her hands together. "I suppose you've heard what he was doing there."

"You mean. . .modeling work?" I wasn't sure exactly how to say what I'd heard his job was.

"Yes." She beamed. "He was a successful model. Always sending me money."

"Did you, um, see his work?"

She waved a hand. "I've seen some pictures in his portfolio. He said those were the best."

I thought about what Angelica had said a few days ago. Something about how long it takes mothers to see the truth about their children.

"He's settling in nicely," Eunice said. "Making nice friends. Better than some of the people he knew in the city." Her mouth pursed in disapproval. "I know he always adopts people and tries to take care of them. He'd bring them with him to visit me, but I didn't like them."

I murmured something sympathetic to encourage her to talk. Not that she needed much encouragement.

She hopped up from her chair, once again reminding me of a little bird. She snatched a framed picture from a shelf in the corner and held it out to me. Somehow I must have missed it in the peach overload.

"That's one of his best shots."

"Very nice." At last, I was telling the truth, because Clark *did* look good. Classic movie-star kind of looks. In the image of Cary Grant and Clark Gable. I handed the picture to her, and she put it back on the shelf. Then she perched on the edge of her chair again.

"I was so glad he moved here to get away from the city and be near me."

I put my cup on the end table after several brave attempts to drink the coffee. "Well, I'm glad he's living here, too."

"Yes, but I'm worried about him. He's having problems with complaints at work."

"Complaints? What kind of complaints?"

Her chin wiggled in indignation. "He told me about how that nasty woman at the pet store called his boss and complained that he was breaking open bags of cat litter. She probably did it and just blamed him, but he got in trouble."

"Well, I'm sorry to hear that," I said. I thought about how charming Clark had been to Jaylene. It had all been an act.

She shook her head. "I'm sure it couldn't have been as bad as she said, although I did pick cat litter out of the carpet in his bedroom for five minutes."

Cat litter. Again.

Eunice clasped her hands together. "Clark is getting involved quickly in the community. He's taking some classes at the junior college to improve himself. He's gone out hunting with some of the men he met on the job. He's also involved with some activities at the YMCA now. Helping underprivileged youth."

That surprised me. He hadn't hit me as a philanthropic kind of guy. But the thing I was most interested in was the hunting. "Does he have his own guns?"

"Oh my, well, they're his father's. He and his father used to go hunting, so this is like a return to his childhood."

Clark just moved up on my suspect list.

"He also has a very nice girlfriend," his mother said.

I stared at her. "He does?" I waited for what I knew was coming.

"Yes. Very pretty and successful. Her name is Linda."

On Friday morning, I was at loose ends after updating my clue notebook with a few notations about Clark. Like the fact that he hunted and was taking classes. I also noted that he was an actor. Saying whatever the person he was talking to wanted to hear. That wasn't really a clue. Most people do that to a degree.

Sherry called me between classes.

"Hey," I said.

"Dad isn't telling me very much." She sounded so down that I wished she were with me so I could hug her.

"There's not a lot to tell, but things are progressing." I tried to sound cheery.

After a moment of silence, she sighed. "You don't have to fib to make me feel better."

"I'm sorry," I said. "I wish I had more to tell you."

"Can we go over your clues one more time?" she asked.

I obliged her.

"Mrs. C., I know you're trying hard, but this wedding has to happen. My dad hasn't been this happy in a long time. And neither have I. We both need Abbie." Her voice broke.

I felt tears in my eyes along with the weight of my failure so far.

I agreed. We both hung up feeling worse than we had when we started. I looked at my suspect list again. I had to find out more about Hayley and Leighton. I picked up the cell phone and did something I rarely do. I called my mother-in-law.

"Patricia." I could tell by the tone of her voice that she was as surprised to hear from me as I was that I actually called her. "Is something wrong?"

Guilt slapped me. If I needed another indication that she wasn't the only problem in our relationship, that was it.

"Yes, everyone is fine. I have a couple of questions for you."

"Questions?" she asked quickly. "What about?"

"I'm just curious. What do you know about Leighton and Hayley?"

She paused before she answered. "Enough. Hayley is a good friend of mine."

"Well, how long have you known them?"

"For nine months. Since they moved here."

"So you know nothing about them before that?"

"Well, certainly I do. Hayley and I are friends. Patricia, what is this about?"

"I was just wondering."

She didn't say anything, and I knew the wheels in her head were turning. But before I could figure out a good way to distract her, I heard her quick intake of breath. "You're trying to solve the mystery of who killed Philip Grenville, aren't you? Because your friend was arrested."

I had to hand it to her. My mother-in-law might be a snob, but she's a smart one. She is, after all, the mother of the smartest man I know.

"You can't think that Hayley or Leighton had anything to do with this," she said. "They don't even *know* Abbie."

"Yes, well, I saw Leighton with someone who does know Abbie. And Philip. I have to follow up on all the leads."

"Well, I'm sure you're wrong. You're wasting your time."

The frost in Angelica's voice would have discouraged most anyone else, but not me. I had to find out more information. I felt a little prick of conscience and made an impulsive decision.

"Would you like to go with me and Sammie to look at her kitten? Maybe tomorrow, if Hayley is available?"

In the silence after my question, I realized I'd surprised her. That's when I knew I needed to make some changes. It was time to be an adult and try to cross the bridge of hostility and reach out to my mother-in-law. Then it would be her choice to accept me or not.

My offer distracted her from my questions about Leighton. We agreed on a time, and she said she'd check with Hayley and let me know if it wouldn't work. After I hung up, I went to the kitchen and dropped into a chair. My overly stuffed purse sat on the table. I needed a distraction, and a good one was sitting right in front of me.

I dumped the contents on the table, pulled the trash can next to me, and began sorting. Pens from coins. Important receipts from old grocery lists. I was about to drop what looked like an old list into the trash when I realized it wasn't my writing. And I didn't recognize the torn paper.

I laid it on the table in front of me and smoothed it out. The scrawl was strong and looked masculine. And it was only partial:

> . . .*to meet with you. We have to talk. It's important. Can you meet me Sunday afternoon at the store?*

It was the signature that made my heart flip over. *Philip Grenville.*

Sunday afternoon. When Philip got his black eye. Where had this come from? I banged my fist softly against my forehead. Not from Sammie. She never added her collections to my purse, just kept them in her pockets. Store? Then I remembered how Chris had knocked my purse over in Adler's Pet Emporium.

Jaylene had scooped up stuff off the floor at her feet. After Henry had riffled through the drawer under the cash register. I'd seen some of the papers from that drawer fall to the floor. Could this letter have come from the Adlers' store?

I didn't have time to think about it because my cell phone rang. I actually remembered to check the caller ID and wished I hadn't because suddenly I wanted to throw up.

"Hello?"

"Mrs. Cunningham, this is Detective Reid."

"Yes?" I asked.

"I wonder if you could come talk to me at the state police barracks, say, in an hour?"

"All right," I said, dread tightening my stomach.

She explained where the barracks were.

I pushed the END button on the phone and picked up the scrap of paper I'd found in my purse. I knew a responsible citizen would give this to Detective Reid. But I didn't like her; therefore, I didn't want to help her. I punched Nick Fletcher's number into my phone.

"Hey, Mrs. C.," he said as a greeting. "I'm in the middle of something. Is this important?"

"Yes." In a rush, I told him about the scrap of paper and going to see the detective.

"Give it to her," he said without hesitation. "It could help Abbie."

His words were like a slap. I was so busy not liking Detective Reid that I'd failed to think of the bigger picture. "Okay. I'll do that."

"Listen, anything could help right now." He took a deep breath. "I gotta tell ya, Mrs. C., things aren't lookin' so good for Abbie right now."

I dropped Chris off at Gladys's house. Corporal Fletcher's last words kept rolling through my mind as I pulled up to the state police barracks. I felt a tremor of nerves as I approached the door.

Inside, I was immediately escorted to a plain white interview room. Unlike the sheriff's office, this room had seen much better days. I was surprised that Detective Reid didn't keep me waiting long. She bustled in, carrying a folder, a pen, and a bottle of water.

"Can I get you anything before we begin?" she asked. "Like some water or a cup of coffee?"

"No, thanks. I just had lunch. But before we begin, I have something to give you." I pulled the scrap of paper from a pocket in my purse and handed it to her.

She glanced at it, her eyes widening as she read it. Then she looked back at me. "Where did you get this?"

I explained everything while she watched me with emotionless eyes.

When I was finished, I said, "I'd just found it when you called me."

"Mmm." She sounded like she didn't believe me, but it was hard to tell, given she always sounded like that. "I'd just like to cover a few additional points today."

"Okay." I sat back to wait for the conversational hail to begin.

She opened the file, slipped the scrap of paper I'd given her inside, and turned to another page. Then she looked up at me.

She tapped a stubby-nailed finger on her notes. "Your mother was overheard to have said something about shooting Philip."

Of all the things I thought Detective Reid would say, that wasn't one of them. My surprise must have been evident on my face. Her eyes narrowed. I wanted to kick myself. One point for her. Zero for me.

"When was that?" I asked, even though I remembered very clearly because it had bothered me at the time.

She glanced at her notes again and back at me. "The day before Philip was shot."

"My mother says a lot of things, including that one day *I'm* going to kill *her*. You can't take what she says seriously."

"Does your father own a rifle?"

Another zinger. And she got me again.

"Doesn't everyone around here?" I volleyed.

"That doesn't answer my question." She slapped her pen down on the table.

If she thought she was going to intimidate me, she was wrong. However, I couldn't lie to her. "Yes, my father owns several guns. So do a lot of men in this county, some of whom would have loved to see Philip dead."

"Answer my question," she snapped. "Does he own a rifle?"

"Yes," I said.

"What kind?"

"Two." I took a deep breath. "A regular shotgun and a 30-06."

She eyed me with her flat glance. "Don't make things rough for yourself, Mrs. Cunningham. And remember what I told you. Don't interfere with my investigation."

I stood and slung my purse over my shoulder. "I've done nothing to prevent you from doing your job. I gave you something I found. I've answered any question you've asked me. Am I free to go?"

She stood, too. "Yes. You may go."

I walked from the barracks to my car, shaking. I'd always had a deep regard for law enforcement officers, despite what I'd said to Eric about their attitudes, but Detective Reid was pushing my limits.

❦

Back at home, I was standing in front of the clothes dryer folding socks, wondering if I would like doing laundry any better if I had a large laundry room like Hayley's. With lots of storage and a top-of-the-line washer and dryer. With a family our size, laundry is one chore that is never done in our house. I don't particularly enjoy it, but at the moment, I was glad for the seemingly insurmountable pile of clothes waiting to be sorted then washed, dried, and put away.

I turned my attention to a basket of dirty clothes and began checking pockets. As usual, I found stuff in Sammie's pockets. A screw, a stone, and an empty Tootsie Roll wrapper. I shook Angelica's words from my mind. This was normal behavior for a kid.

My interview with Detective Reid had left me with a feeling of foreboding that I couldn't shake, like I was waiting for the other shoe to drop. So when my mother called me an hour later in a frenzy, I wasn't surprised.

"Trish, your father just called me. The police have a search warrant, and they're taking his hunting rifles from the barn. I had trouble understanding him on the phone. He said something about Buddy, but he was so upset, I couldn't understand him. I can't be there. I have to go down to the state police barracks for an interview." Her words were breathless, not like her normal harsh tone.

"I was just there myself. Watch out for Detective Reid—"

She interrupted me with a string of words about the detective that were surprisingly uncomplimentary, even from my acerbic mother. Under normal circumstances, I might have been shocked and amused. However, my concern right now was my father. He was such a calm man. That Ma said he was unintelligible on the phone meant he was very upset. Things were bad.

"I should stop by the farm first," my mother said.

"You don't want to keep the detective waiting," I said. "It'll just make her nastier. How about I go over to the farm and see what's going on with Daddy."

"Good." I heard the relief in her voice. "Thank you."

When I arrived at the farm, the last state trooper was pulling from the driveway. I pulled up next to the house and hopped from the car, wondering if Daddy was in the house or the barn. His truck was next to the barn, but that meant nothing. I headed to the house first. Then I heard the squeal of the barn door and turned to see Daddy walking from the barn with Buddy lying limp in his arms. He didn't see me.

"Daddy?" I dropped my purse to the ground and ran to meet him.

He glanced in my direction and stopped.

When I reached him, he had tears on his cheeks. I didn't need to be told. Buddy was dead.

"What happened?"

He swallowed. "The stress was too much, sugar bug. If I'd known they were coming, I would have put him in the house." He laid Buddy in the back of his truck with such gentleness that I began to cry. Then he turned to me. "I'm going to bury him in the field. Will you come with me? Your mother wouldn't be able to do it."

"Yes. You know I will." I threw my arms around his neck, and even while I tried to comfort him, anger filled my gut, so red and hot that I shook. The old Trish, the redneck who never used to think twice about taking on anyone in a fight for right, warred inside me with the new Trish. The good Christian mommy who was trying hard to be a nice person.

At the moment, old Trish was winning. I wished with all my heart that I could grab Detective Reid by the hair and beat her up.

Daddy stepped back and saw my face and shook his head. "I see that flash in your eyes."

"They had no right." I gulped and took a deep breath to control my temper. "They murdered our dog."

"No." Daddy pushed aside the hair hanging over my eyes. "It was his time. I knew when I woke up this morning that he was going to go soon. He didn't eat, just stuck close by me, and you know how he liked his kibble."

"Still. He didn't need to go like this."

"That's what I thought at first, too." Daddy's eyes bored deep into mine. "But I've got to tell you, I'm not so sure about it anymore. For just a couple of minutes after the police got here, Buddy woke up. Like his old self. Got all protective." Daddy's mouth quirked into a trembly smile. "When I told him to back down, he looked at me with that little doggy grin of his." ____

I smiled at the memory even while I blinked back tears. Throughout his life, when Buddy knew he was out of line, he used to roll back his upper lip, like he was laughing at us.

Daddy turned and shut the tailgate, then glanced at me over his shoulder. "Maybe this was a good way for him to go. With honor." He waved at the pasture. "I'm going to bury him in his favorite place."

I knew exactly where he meant. "I'll go get two shovels while you open the gate."

He nodded.

Shortly, I joined Daddy in the truck. He stared straight ahead, lips pressed firmly together. As the truck bounced down the hill to the creek at the bottom of the pasture, I wondered if Philip's last choices before he died meant that he died an honorable death, too.

When we reached a small peninsula jutting into the water, Daddy stopped and turned off the engine. Then he stared out the windshield with an unfocused gaze.

"Remember how Buddy always came down here when I mowed the field in the summer? How he used to run through the water?"

"Yep, I do." I smiled as I recalled the little black-and-white bundle of irrepressible energy Buddy had been when Daddy brought him home.

Daddy turned to me and returned my smile. "I thought I'd lost him that first day I brought him out here. He was running so hard that he ran straight off those rocks, right into the creek."

"Yeah. And then you couldn't keep him out of the water after that."

Daddy still smiled, but his eyes had filled with tears. Mine did the same.

"Guess we should get it done," he said gruffly.

"Yep."

We buried Buddy on a piece of high ground, next to the rocks overlooking the creek. When we'd finished, Daddy leaned against his shovel. I put my arm around his waist, and we stood quietly together, both of us lost in our own thoughts.

Then Daddy sighed. "I'm worried."

"Why?"

"The deputy in charge asked me if anyone else had used my guns." He turned to face me. "I had to say yes. The last time I used that 30-06 was when I brought Abbie out here in this field to shoot it."

The panic I'd been fighting since Ma found Philip's body returned, gnawing my insides.

"I didn't want to have to tell them, but I had no choice. Her fingerprints will be on it, anyway. I hope she won't think I'm a traitor." A small tic appeared at the corner of his mouth. "She's like a daughter to me, you know."

His expression was so pained, I rushed to assure him. "She won't think that. She knows you have to tell the truth. She had to tell the truth, as well."

"I just hope it doesn't make things worse," Daddy said.

"Me, too." But even as I tried to sound assuring, I knew things *had* just gotten worse for Abbie. And I needed to work harder to solve this mystery before she ended up in jail.

---

I bounced against Max as the hay wagon bringing us back from the corn maze jostled to a stop in front of a big red barn. The owners had placed thermal containers of hot chocolate and Styrofoam cups on tables for guests, along with supplies for s'mores. Chris babbled in my arms, pointing with a chubby finger at two roaring bonfires where visitors could roast marshmallows. For once, he wasn't grumpy.

Charlie and Sammie leaped off the wagon and headed for the hot chocolate.

Max kissed me. "You haven't said a word about Abbie or the investigation."

We'd left the house immediately after he'd gotten home from work. The only thing I'd had time to tell him about was Buddy.

"I'm trying to be normal for a few hours." I smiled at him.

He hopped off the wagon and turned to take Chris from me. I slipped to the ground and swiped hay from my jeans.

We followed slowly behind Charlie and Sammie. She was giggling at something he'd whispered in her ear. Chris grinned at me from Max's shoulder. He always seemed happier when we were all together. Was it possible that my dissatisfaction with life was affecting my children? Could that be the reason for Sammie's insecurities and Chris's fussiness?

I reached for Max's spare hand, but before I could grasp it, I heard a familiar voice behind me. I whirled around in time to see Jaylene Adler holding the hand of a young girl, walking toward the pasture where guests were parking their cars.

Jaylene must have sensed my stare. She glanced over her shoulder, saw me, and glared. Then she pulled the girl in front of her, as though shielding her, and kept walking.

"Max." I yanked at his arm. "I have to talk to Jaylene."

"Honey—"

"I'm sorry." I ran after her. "Jaylene! Please wait. I want to talk to you."

She picked up her pace, and the girl had trouble keeping up. I called to her again. When she reached her car, she whirled around and heaved a sigh. "What?"

"I just want to talk to you for a minute."

"Fine." She unlocked the car then leaned down and whispered something in the child's ear. She obediently got inside.

Suddenly Jaylene turned on me so quickly that I thought she was going to hit me.

I felt a hand on my shoulder and realized that Max had followed me. I leaned back against him, grateful for his presence.

Jaylene looked from me to him. Chris babbled, and from the corner of my eye, I saw him reach an arm out to her. Her mouth twisted into a grimace.

She met my gaze. "We've known you all of our lives, but that doesn't give you the right to pry."

Max tightened his grip on my shoulder.

"All I'm interested in is keeping my best friend out of jail," I said. "And finding the truth about who killed Philip. If you didn't do it, why should you worry?"

"I know you're trying to pin it on Henry," she said. "He might be a louse sometimes with a bad temper, but he's not a killer."

I shook my head. "You don't understand. Like you said, I've known you all my life. I care for you and Henry. I'm not out to pin it on him."

She tapped her foot. "Then why don't you leave us alone?"

"Because I think you have some answers I need."

She crossed her arms. "There's nothing I know that will help you. Nothing."

I took a deep breath. "I found a piece of a letter from Philip that I believe came from your store."

Jaylene's eyes widened. I felt Max stiffen behind me. I felt bad. I hadn't had the time to tell him about it.

"What are you going to do with it?" Jaylene whispered.

"I had no choice," I said. "I've already given it to the police."

Anger suffused her face with red. Her lips trembled. "I might have known. Just remember this. I won't let you or anyone else hurt my family."

With those words, she whirled around and got into her car. I didn't try to stop her.

Max and I watched her pull from the parking lot.

I felt like a horrible traitor to a family friend.

## 14

On Saturday morning, I prepared to go talk to Linda and then take Sammie to see her kitten. Max took the rest of the kids out for their regular weekend outing with him. He left me with a stern "Be careful today, and call me to let me know exactly where you are." I didn't blame him. I was disturbed, too. But for more reason than that. I was making no headway with the mystery.

As I pulled my keys from my now neat purse, I noticed something gold sparkling on the bottom. The smashed gold button. There was a clue I hadn't pursued yet, and today was the perfect opportunity.

An hour later, I stood in Hayley's kitchen with her and Angelica, fingering the button in my pants pocket. Sammie was playing with the kittens in the laundry room. Hayley's face looked drawn and tense.

When something soft brushed my leg, I jumped. Then I looked down. Mr. Chang Lee was perched next to my right foot. He met my gaze and yowled. I crossed my arms, looked away, and hoped for the best. I still didn't trust him.

Angelica's eyes widened as she stared down at him. "I've never seen him accept anyone else but Hayley."

I relaxed a fraction. That was good news from an objective source.

"From the first time Trish showed up, he acted that way," Hayley said.

Angelica shook her head. "That's amazing."

"I'm so glad you both came over," Hayley said, but she was focused on Angelica. I was surprised they didn't make little kissy sounds at each other.

"Would you like iced tea?" Hayley turned to me. "Coffee? Lemonade?"

"Do you have Mountain Dew?" I asked.

"I don't have that, but I have other sodas," Hayley said.

"It's fine. I'll take coffee." The time was drawing near to break my addiction.

"I'll take the same." Angelica took some mugs out of the cupboard.

Angelica had no idea where the coffee mugs were in my cupboards.

"So, Trish," Hayley said after she ground coffee beans and began preparing the coffee in a professional-style, stainless steel coffeemaker. "Angelica tells me you like to solve mysteries. You've been involved in two, and you're looking into the death of this Philip fellow?"

I glanced at my mother-in-law, surprised she'd said anything. "I do it only when I need to—to protect someone. At first I thought it was intriguing, like solving a puzzle, but then I started counting the cost for my family. It can be dangerous."

422

"I told Leighton what you were doing. He said he'd never allow me to do anything like that. He says it could be too dangerous." Hayley shuddered and rubbed her arms.

I felt a stab of resentment at her insinuation that Max didn't care enough for me, and I wanted to say, *At least my husband isn't seeing another woman.* Not that I knew for certain that Leighton *was* seeing Linda.

"Murder is so terrible," Hayley said. "And so awful for your friend. He was her husband, right?"

I shook my head. "Ex."

I wasn't real happy that Leighton Whitmore knew about my sleuthing. He was still a suspect in my book, no matter what. For that matter, so was Hayley.

Well, now was as good a time as any to pursue my latest line of questioning. I pulled the button from my pocket.

"Is this yours?" I asked Hayley.

She leaned over to stare at it. "No. I don't recognize it. Why?"

"I just found it and wondered."

My question hadn't made an impression on Hayley at all, but Angelica was studying me with narrowed eyes. She knew what I was doing.

The coffeemaker burbled on the counter, and the smell of coffee began to permeate the air.

"It's just hard to believe something like that could happen around here," Hayley said.

"Too unpleasant to think about," Angelica added.

I took that as a cue to change the subject. What I needed to know could be learned without talking about Philip. "So is Leighton retired?" I asked.

"Not exactly. He was supposed to be, but. . .anyway, he's happier working." Hayley didn't look at me; she just watched the coffee drip into the pot.

"What did he do when he worked full-time?"

She crossed her arms. "Real estate. . .construction. A long time ago he had a law degree." She finally looked at me. "What do you take in your coffee?"

"Just cream." Her answer was rather unrevealing. I'd try a blunt question. "Do you know Linda King?"

Hayley's gaze slid to the wall. "Linda King?"

"She's a real estate agent. She works part-time for my mother. I just thought you might know her. She acted like she knew you. Talked about your cats."

"Oh, *that* Linda King. Yes." Hayley swallowed and straightened her shoulders. "I know *of* her."

Angelica met my gaze over Hayley's shoulder and shook her head slightly.

Hayley sniffed, and I realized she was almost in tears.

Was Leighton having an affair with Linda? Did Hayley suspect?

"I'm sorry," I said, although I wasn't sure what I was apologizing about.

"No, it's not you," she said.

Angelica put a hand on Hayley's shoulder. "Why don't you go sit down? I'll get the coffee."

Hayley nodded and went to the family room.

"They might be moving," Angelica whispered as she walked by me to the counter. "That woman is their real estate agent. Hayley doesn't want to leave, and she's upset."

So Leighton's meeting with Linda could be totally innocent. She was going to sell their house.

Angelica handed me my cup of coffee and then carried hers and Hayley's to the family room. They sat on the couch. I settled in a comfy chair facing the french doors that led to the pool. Why were Leighton and Hayley moving now? After all the trouble and expense of the pool?

Mr. Chang Lee jumped up in my chair and settled next to me, his body resting against my thigh. For once, I welcomed his attention. He was communicating happiness with his purrs—at least I assumed it was happiness. That was better than the stilted attempts at conversation between me, Angelica, and Hayley. I felt like the proverbial third wheel and wondered if I was the cause of the awkwardness. Perhaps Hayley wanted to talk about her troubles, and I was preventing her from doing so.

I had already decided to leave when Sammie came running into the room. Angelica's face lit up.

"When can I take my kitten home?" Sammie asked Hayley.

"Tuesday," Hayley said.

Sammie clapped her hands. Angelica continued to gaze at her with bright eyes. I'd never watched her face around the children before. I felt my heart constrict. My bad attitude had prevented me from seeing anything good about my mother-in-law.

Hayley smiled. "Angelica has a class Wednesday night."

"A class?" I asked.

"She's taking a citizen police academy class," Hayley said.

"What did you say?" I was positive I hadn't heard Hayley correctly. I glanced at Angelica, and she was blushing.

Hayley smiled. "I told Angelica it would be the perfect way for her to understand more about what Tommy's going to do." Her smile faded. "We were both going to do it, but Leighton said it wasn't a good idea for me right now."

"It's fine. I can do it alone." Angelica patted Hayley's arm then turned to me. "If Tommy insists upon pursuing law enforcement, I've decided to support him. Max assured me that it was Tommy's choice and not something"—she glanced at me—"not something he was talked into."

I understood what she was saying. She thought I was just as controlling as I thought *she* was. This was her way of explaining. Maybe even trying to apologize. To say I was amazed at what she was doing would be an understatement.

I did the only thing I could.

"Angelica, the kitten is a gift from you. It would be special if you're here with us when Sammie picks up her cat. Then maybe you and Andrew can come to our house for dinner that night to celebrate." I glanced down at my lap then back up at her. "And if you do want company at that class, I'll go with you."

Angelica's surprised smile told me everything I needed to know.

---

Linda's office was in downtown Four Oaks, just one block down from Abbie's apartment. The windows of the real estate business were plastered with pictures of houses for sale.

"Don't pick anything up," I whispered to Sammie as we walked through the door.

"Mommy. . ."

Inside, I smelled coffee and some kind of cinnamon air freshener. Several agents sat at their desks. Linda was perched on the edge of hers, chatting on the phone. She saw me, smiled, and held up one finger.

I settled Sammie on a chair with a book to read. I didn't have to wait long. When Linda was done talking, she slid off her desk and reached into a bowl on her desk. Then she walked over to us and handed Sammie a Tootsie Roll. Sammie grinned, unwrapped the candy, and stuffed it in her mouth.

"Come and tell me what you're looking for."

I explained our criteria. "I don't want to look today. I'd just like some listings to show Max."

She rested her elbows on the desk. "So what area are you interested in?"

I needed to find a way to bring up the Whitmores. "Do you have anything out Brownsville way?"

Her eyes lit up. The houses out there were expensive. "Yes, I do."

"My in-laws live out there," I said. "And we're also getting a Siamese kitten from Hayley Whitmore."

"Yes, your mother told me that." Her brown eyes reminded me of the button eyes on Sammie's stuffed bear. No expression at all. "So how many bedrooms do you want?"

I told her and wondered if my trip here was going to be wasted.

She turned her gaze to her computer screen and tap-tapped on her keyboard. As she sifted through listings on her computer, sending some to a printer across the room, I studied her desk. Lots of pink stuff, including several pink ceramic picture frames. Most of the pictures featured Linda. Two were taken in the same place, in front of a fountain. It looked familiar to me, but I couldn't place it.

I pointed at it. "Is this a vacation you took? Looks like fun."

She nodded. "Yes, I went to a real estate convention last year in Atlanta. I stayed an extra week with some friends and toured everything. I met some interesting people there." The printer hummed in the background. She continued to chat about everything and nothing.

I decided to interrupt her. "I met Clark Matthews's mother the other day. Eunice?"

"Oh?" Linda asked.

"I took her an autographed bookplate from Abbie. She thinks very highly of you."

"She's a nice lady," Linda said.

"She's happy that Clark is living with her and doing so well. Like taking classes at the junior college and volunteering at the YMCA. She says he's not happy at his job, though."

Linda shot me a gaze. "Sometimes she exaggerates." Then she stood. "I think that's about all the listings I can find right now."

I was desperate. I stood, too, and yanked the button from my pocket. "Is this yours?"

For a moment, her eyes narrowed. She took the button from my hand then dropped it back into my palm. "I don't think so, but even if it was, it's too damaged to do me any good." She stepped around her chair. "Now I'll go get the listings."

While she was doing that, I stared at the pictures. I suddenly remembered where I had seen a similar fountain. In the picture on Hayley's mantel. But Hayley had said it was her wedding photograph. I had assumed they'd gotten married in New York City. Did they get married in Atlanta? And was this even significant?

When Linda returned with the papers, she covered the main points about each property. I pretended to pay attention, but I didn't hear a word she said. I had one more doubt in my head about Leighton and Hayley Whitmore. And I knew in my heart that time was running out for Abbie.

15

I was so discouraged on Sunday that all I wanted to do was go back to bed after church. Knowing that Philip was being buried added to my blues. Abbie felt similarly. I'd talked to her earlier when we confirmed that she and Eric were joining me, Max, and the kids at my mother's for Sunday supper.

At the moment, Karen was on the phone in her room. Charlie and Sammie were in the family room watching an old Sherlock Holmes movie on television. Max was in the living room with his nose buried in the newspaper, and I'd just put Chris down for a nap.

Only one thing would help my mental state. Solving Philip's murder. I grabbed my notebook from my purse and joined Max. I needed to write down the clue about the picture on the Whitmores' mantel.

He saw what I had in my hands, sighed, and put the paper on the coffee table. I thought he might be about to lecture me about my sleuthing and opened my mouth to protest.

"Maybe I can help," he said. "I know you're discouraged. You want to talk it all through with me?"

"Really?" I grinned.

"Really," he said.

"Do you realize this is the first time you've offered to help me with an investigation?"

"I guess it is. What is it that your mother says? If you can't beat 'em, join 'em?"

"Yep, among a million other clichés."

He stood and pointed at the couch. "Let's sit."

I snuggled next to him. "So why are you helping me?"

"I want this solved. I want it over."

I shared his sentiments. Despite the comfort of his solid body next to mine, I felt uneasy. Like a storm cloud was rushing toward me and I needed to find shelter.

He tapped my notebook. "Well, tell me what you have so far. Maybe I'll see a connection you've missed."

One by one, we went through the clues. When we were done, I looked up at him. His eyes were narrowed.

"I have to agree with you. Philip was so determined to make things right with everyone he'd wronged, that seems the most likely reason he was killed. Jaylene was awfully hostile on Friday night." His brows were drawn into a deep V.

427

Jaylene's hostility had frightened both of us.

"That leads me to my suspects." I flipped to another page. "What do you think?"

Max read down the list then pointed at Leighton's name. "Why are Leighton and Hayley on here?"

I felt defensive. "I know they're your family's friends, but I have my reasons. More him than her, though."

"Go on." Max's face was unusually blank.

"Well, like all the others, I know he was at the fall festival. Hayley told me. And Philip saw something there that made him leave in a hurry."

"Anything else?" Max asked.

"Well, he's from New York. And. . ." I hesitated.

"And?"

I told Max about the picture on the mantel.

"Are you sure you're remembering right?" he asked.

"I'm sure," I said. "And then I saw him at a restaurant with Linda King. Now he and Hayley might be moving. Something just isn't right. I'm not sure what."

Max blinked. "They're moving?"

"I found out yesterday when Sammie was visiting her kitten."

"I hadn't heard that yet," Max said. "I'll be honest with you, though. Despite the way my mother champions Leighton, I've never felt right about him."

"What about your father?" I asked.

"He agrees with me." Max grimaced. "I think my mother felt sorry for Hayley and just wanted her to be happy."

The doorbell rang. "I'll get it!" Charlie yelled, sliding down the hall to the front door.

"Can you explain what you mean about Leighton?" I asked Max.

"Not really," he said.

"Mom! It's for you," Charlie yelled. "It's a lady."

"Go on," Max said. "There's nothing else I can tell you. Really."

Charlie was regaling our visitor with chatter about the movie he was watching. I walked from the living room and felt the cold November breeze sweep down the hall, the perfect prelude for the entrance of the woman with the grief-lined face who stood on my front porch. Mary Grenville, Philip's sister. She wore a black wool coat over a simple black dress that emphasized her pale skin, red-rimmed eyes, and drawn face that looked like a wax mask.

"Thank you, Charlie," I said. He scampered away to continue watching his movie.

"Come in." I opened the door wide.

She brushed past me then stood in the foyer with her arms crossed. "My mother said you wanted to talk to me, so I stopped by. I hope it's okay."

"It's fine. I have a few hours before I have to get ready to go out."

I took her coat and draped it over the coatrack.

Max walked into the hallway, and I introduced them.

"I'm so sorry about your brother," he said.

"Thank you."

Max turned to me. "Why don't you two go into the living room? I'll make sure the kids leave you alone."

"Thank you," I whispered as we walked past him.

He squeezed my hand then walked away.

Mary and I settled on the couch in the living room, then tears began to fall down her cheeks. She swiped at them with the back of her hands. "I'm sorry. I made it through the burial without crying."

"I'm so sorry," I said. "I can't even imagine how hard this has been for you."

"It's not like this was unexpected. His death, I mean. I just didn't expect the emotions to hit me so hard." She took a deep breath then pulled herself together, gathering her emotions and covering them with a shell of self-control, almost like putting on a coat.

Her lips were now set in a firm line. Her eyes weren't hostile, but her gaze was steady. "You've been asking my mother questions about Philip."

"Yes." I wondered if she was going to ream me out for being a pest.

"She says you're trying to solve his murder?" She eyed me with wariness. "You're not just curious about him, are you? Or trying to make him look bad? Because of Abbie?"

I liked the fact that she was blunt. It would make our conversation easier. "Yes, I'm trying to solve his murder. To clear Abbie, not to make him look bad. But if he ends up looking bad because of what my investigation reveals, that's out of my control. I'm sorry."

She met my gaze with her unblinking one. "That's honest, and I appreciate it. There are some things you should know. I'd rather tell you than that detective. She left my mother in tears." Mary's nostrils flared. "There is no excuse for leaving a grieving mother in that state."

"The detective isn't on anyone's most popular list right now," I said.

Her hands clenched into fists in her lap. "That's an understatement. I'm going to make sure I'm there the next time Reid talks to my mother."

I wished I could be there for that.

"I'm going to start back over a year ago," she said. "I think what I say will help you."

"Do you mind if I take notes?" I hesitated to without her permission.

She waved her hand. "Fine with me."

I pulled my notebook from the coffee table where Max had put it. When I was settled, she began.

"When Philip got sick, I went and stayed with him while he went through chemo. We hadn't been close since we were kids, but he begged me to come." She pulled at the fabric of her dress. "I'm ashamed to say it now, but I didn't want to do it. He'd been such an awful person, and I hated being around him, even if he was my brother."

"I can understand that," I murmured.

"I finally did after Mom begged me to. She couldn't because she had to work." She paused. "Mom told you about his conversion, right?"

I nodded.

A tiny smile played on her lips. "I don't share my mother's strong faith, but I recognize true change when I see it. I knew he was different as soon as I walked through the door to his apartment. He hugged me."

"That must have made you happy."

"Yes, but I didn't understand at first. Only that he was somehow different. Unfortunately, that wasn't the only change." The light in her eyes died. "His face was haggard. He looked like a scarecrow that had lost its stuffing. It's funny, but when someone is dying of an illness like cancer, it seems to permeate everything. At least that's the way it seemed with him." She paused. "It was odd, but even before chemo, he seemed to know he was going to die. Going for treatment was just going through the motions."

"I can't imagine what that was like for you," I said again.

She acknowledged my comment with a nod. "Not unless you've watched a friend or relative go through it. And to make it worse, I'd just lost a lot of money in a real estate scam, so I was feeling really low anyway."

She glanced at me. "Now things weren't perfect. Philip had changed, but he still had secrets."

"What kinds of secrets?" I asked.

She shrugged. "Probably a lot more than I will ever know. But I wanted to know what really happened with Abbie. He refused to talk about it. Said he needed to make that right with her before he'd say anything to anyone." Mary picked at a fingernail. "I like Abbie. We were never close, but I felt like she got a bad deal when she married my brother. The old Philip was a brutal man."

"Yes," I said.

She clasped her hands together. "I don't want Abbie accused of this murder. I know for certain it wasn't her. I'm convinced this had something to do with Philip's past. Or something that he knew about someone."

"That's what I think, too," I said. "Why do you say that?"

"Because he returned home to make amends and probably talked to someone who didn't want to make things right."

"Do you have any thoughts about that? Any ideas?"

"Two." She shifted on the couch and dropped her gaze to the carpet. "This

430

is hard to say. I feel like I'm giving away his secrets, even though he's dead." She looked up at me. "I didn't tell the police about this. I just couldn't. Because it doesn't just affect Philip." After a deep breath, she met my gaze. "You must promise me that no one will know unless it's necessary."

"But if it's necessary to keep Abbie from prison, I can tell?"

After the briefest hesitation, she nodded. "I know that sooner or later it will come out. I just need a couple of days to tell my mother. I don't want her hurt any more than she already is right now."

"All right. You have my word. But why are you trusting me with something so important to you?"

"For Abbie. Because it was so important to Philip that he make amends with her. I don't want to see her accused of something she didn't do." Mary took a deep breath. "Philip had a weak moment during his hospital stay. He saw a little girl pass by his door, and he started to cry. I asked him why. He said it was because he had a daughter, but he wasn't allowed to see her."

I felt the shock of her words physically. "A daughter? Where?"

"Here," Mary said. "Seems that was part of the reason he left town. He and Abbie weren't doing well. And he was being threatened by the father of the girl he got pregnant." Mary's lips twisted into a grimace. "I suspect she was underage."

"That could have ruined his career." I stated the obvious.

"Yeah. Whoever it was had mercy on him, I guess. Or maybe they just didn't want their daughter involved in a scandal like that." Mary bit one of her nails. "After that day in the hospital, he never said another word about it. I asked him about it again—once—and he told me to forget it. But I think he wanted to see his daughter. To meet her before he died."

Something of that magnitude certainly could lead to hostility. My mind immediately flitted to Jaylene's daughter, Peggy. I had a vague memory of her leaving town and returning later on, married and with a baby. The child we saw her with at the corn maze looked to be the right age.

I looked at Mary. "I assume Abbie doesn't know this. She never said anything. I think she should know. It would be horrible if it came out in the investigation." Even coming from me, the news could push an already emotionally battered Abbie over the edge.

Mary frowned, and I hastened to make my case. "Think about how humiliating it would be for her to find out from Detective Reid."

Mary's eyes flashed at the mention of Detective Reid's name. "That woman! Okay. I agree with you. In fact, I could see Detective Reid uncovering that and using it to try to make Abbie confess something." She paused for just a heartbeat. "And if you have to, tell Eric. It might help the investigation. I'll tell my mother as soon as possible." Mary smiled sadly. "With Philip dead, it's just me, and I'm not particularly the marrying kind. I know Mom would love to know she had a grandchild, but what if the woman's family doesn't want my mother involved at all? The possible complications are too much to think about right now."

I agreed, and I didn't want June hurt more, either. Still, she had a core of strength I wasn't sure Mary saw. Perhaps living with her mother would help Mary see that.

"You said you had two ideas. Do you know anything else that might help?" I asked. "Do you think there's a possibility that his murder had anything to do with work? Like a case he was investigating?"

Mary shook her head. "I can't answer that. The last job he'd had was in Narcotics, but he'd been out of work for almost six months. Would it take that long for something to catch up with him?"

Probably not. "Is there anything else you can think of that was bothering him?"

"Yeah." She grimaced. "Me. Well, I mean, what had happened to me. I lost money in a real estate scam. It was quite the scandal. I couldn't believe I'd been sucked in. Two men were jailed, but the ones at the top got away scot-free. Philip wanted to fix that for me before he died. Get my money back."

My mind veered right to Leighton Whitmore. He was into real estate. He had been in Atlanta—presumably to get married. But he was from New York.

I met Mary's gaze. "Those are two really powerful motivations for murder."

⟿

After Mary left, I immediately called Nick Fletcher and told him everything she'd told me about Philip's daughter and added my suspicions about the Adlers. Finally, I reiterated my misgivings about Leighton Whitmore. I told him about the real estate scam in Atlanta. He didn't say much, but I could tell he was listening.

"And worst of all," I said, "I don't know what to do about Abbie. This daughter of Philip's could push her over the edge."

"Tell Eric, Mrs. C.," he said. "Let him tell her."

The idea was perfect. And Corporal Fletcher sounded more upbeat than he had the last few times we'd talked, so when we finally hung up, I felt encouraged.

After that, Max and I got the kids ready and we headed to my folks' house. Karen had gone to visit a friend, so we just had the three youngest. We hadn't found the time to discuss my visit with Mary.

"You're quiet," Max said as we drove.

I didn't want to say much in front of Charlie and Sammie. I motioned with my eyes toward the backseat.

He nodded and reached for my hand.

I took his and squeezed. "Max, I've been thinking recently about how selfish I am. I think if I were facing the end of my life, I wouldn't want to frantically try to make things right with people."

"Oh?" Max asked.

"I have a couple of things I need to do now. And I need to start with your mother."

His surprise was obvious by his upraised brows. "My mother?"

"Yes." I glanced at the backseat. "I'll tell you more later. Just know that things are going to change for the better. At least on my side."

"Really?" The tiny smile on his face cut me to the core. I suddenly realized how hard my hostility had been on him, despite his humor and understanding.

"I'm so sorry," I whispered.

When we got to the farm, I asked him to wait after the kids hopped from the car. Max reached to get Chris from his car seat, and briefly I told him what Mary had said.

"Whew!" he said. "Things just seem to keep getting worse. Are you going to tell Abbie?"

I fingered my coat zipper. "I'm going to let Eric do it. But first, I need to talk to Ma about the Adlers without telling her why I'm asking."

———

Getting my mother to talk about Jaylene and Henry wasn't hard. Ma was angry that Jaylene wasn't speaking to her. Ma confirmed that Jaylene's daughter, Peggy, had a child out of wedlock. Nine years ago. No one ever knew who the father was. Everyone assumed it was one of two boys she was dating at the time. Jaylene and Henry had sent Peggy to a private school that allowed her to raise her daughter and graduate at the same time. Despite the fact that unwed mothers were relatively common at the time, Jaylene and Henry wanted to avoid the stigma Peggy would have lived under in Four Oaks.

We sat down to eat shortly after Abbie and Eric arrived. Dinner was subdued, despite the chattering of the children and Chris's constant babbling. Ma kept offering everyone food. Max and Eric tried valiantly to keep the conversation flowing. I made an effort to eat, even though I felt sick to my stomach holding the secrets Mary had spilled to me.

Charlie kept eyeing Eric. Finally, he put his fork down. "Uncle Eric, Mike says his brother might have to go to juvie jail."

Eric met Charlie's gaze. "Really?"

Sammie squirmed in her chair.

"Yup. Drugs." Charlie looked at me. "What was it called?"

"Ecstasy," I said, staring at the Mountain Dew in my glass.

"Big problem right now," Eric said. "Especially with the under-twenty-five crowd."

"I read about that in the paper," Max said. "How they hide tablets in candy and—"

"Aunt Abbie, are you going to jail?" Sammie blurted out.

Ma gasped. Abbie blanched.

"No, she's not," I snapped. "We told you that already."

"But—"

Eric smiled, but it was strained. "We aren't going to let your aunt Abbie go to jail, honey. People go to jail when they do very bad things. Aunt Abbie didn't do anything bad."

"Mom won't let her go to jail, either," Charlie said. "She's investigating. Things will be fine."

"Mommy is good at that," Sammie said.

My children were my biggest supporters. Unlike Eric Scott. I picked at my nails to avoid his eyes.

"Well, I should say so." Ma waved her fork to emphasize her words. "I don't want to be critical of the police, Eric, but I don't understand how that Detective Reid person can begin to solve the crime if she's focused on only one person. We all know it wasn't Abbie. Right, Simon?"

"Yes, we know Abbie isn't guilty," Daddy said. "But we don't know for sure who the police are looking at."

"Well," Ma huffed. "They're looking at Abbie."

This conversation wasn't making things better. I glanced at my friend, who was studiously avoiding everyone's eyes.

Daddy had been quiet most of the meal. He kept glancing surreptitiously at Abbie, and I knew he felt guilty about the gun, even though it wasn't his fault.

My mother launched into a discussion about Daddy's search for a new dog. A friend of a friend had a litter of border collies. Then Sammie began jabbering about her new kitten.

With the change of topic, Abbie relaxed. When dinner was about over, she took Eric's hand and looked at my father.

"Simon," she said.

He blinked and looked at her.

"I. . .we. . .have something to ask you."

Daddy clenched his jaw.

"If things work out—"

"*When* things work out," Eric corrected.

Abbie swallowed. "*When* things work out, we want to know if you'll walk me down the aisle. Since I don't have a father to ask and you've been like a dad to me."

Daddy's mouth opened and shut like a goldfish. Then a big tear rolled down his cheek.

"Yes," he said.

Ma's grin couldn't have been bigger.

—

After dinner, Abbie was helping Ma clear the table. I pulled Eric into the hallway near the stairs under the pretense of a secret wedding surprise for Abbie.

"What is it?" he asked.

"I talked to Philip's sister today," I said. "I have something to tell you. Well, Corporal Fletcher suggested I tell you. He said you'd be the best one to tell Abbie."

Eric's expression was like that of a man who had been hit too many times. "Okay. Go on."

I told him in as few words as possible about Philip's confession and his child.

"Oh man." He rubbed his face with his hand. "Can things get worse?"

"Yes, they can," I said. "Abbie can go to jail."

I glanced at the door to the kitchen through which we could hear the low murmurs of Ma's and Abbie's voices. "I'm worried that Detective Reid will find out and try to use it somehow against her. And I think Henry and Jaylene Adler's grandchild is Philip's daughter."

He reached out and tapped his finger on the banister. Then he looked at me. "I can't speculate with you."

"I know." I had to be satisfied with that answer.

## 16

I woke to the phone ringing. I snatched it from the bedside table and held it to my ear. But I didn't need to in order to hear my mother. She was yelling.

"Jaylene just called me. Said Henry was taken in by the state police for hours yesterday evening, thanks to you."

"At least they're looking at someone else and not just Abbie," I said.

"Well, she's threatening to sue you and us," Ma said.

Great. Just what I needed. Something else to worry about.

"She said we would pay one way or another."

Apprehension wiggled on the back of my neck. "Did she say it like that?" I asked.

Ma hesitated. "Well, not exactly, but that was the gist of it."

"All right. I've gotta go. The kids will be getting up soon."

I hung up then turned to Max, who was lying next to me with his arms behind his head. "Your mother," he stated. "I heard her voice through the receiver."

"Hard to miss." I lay on my side, head cradled in my hand.

"So what's up?"

I relayed the context of the conversation.

His face tightened. "Maybe I should talk to one of my friends, have someone go by the Adlers' store. These threats are going to stop right now."

I stared at Max in admiration. As long as I didn't have to personally deal with his lawyer friends and he wasn't getting bossy with *me*, I loved it when he took control.

He rolled on his side and ran his hand down my arm. "I have some good news for you. I think it will make you happy." He touched the end of my nose. "I was going to wait until Abbie's situation cleared up, but this might be a good distraction for you."

"I'm not sure I need a distraction," I said. "I need to solve this murder."

"Yes, but maybe giving it a rest will allow your brain a chance to regroup, so to speak, maybe see things in a different way."

"What is it?"

"A job," he said.

I jerked my gaze to meet his. "A job? At Cunningham and Son?"

"Yes and no." He grinned. "We're about to put up the trailer at the construction site for the new housing development. Someone needs to run the office."

I sat up and felt a quiver of excitement in my stomach. "That's perfect. It uses all my skills."

He leaned back against the headboard. "Yes, I know. And, honey, I want you to know you have my blessing whether you decide to go full-time or part-time. Hire someone else to help you if you need to."

"It sounds wonderful," I murmured, and tears started to burn in my eyes.

"You can go out there today, if you'd like. Start to figure out what you need in terms of equipment and things." He frowned. "Baby?"

I buried my head in his shoulder and the tears flowed.

"Hey," he said, stroking my back. "Aren't you happy?"

"Yes," I mumbled into his shoulder. "You're so sweet. And I'm so blessed. But then I think about Abbie and everything, and I feel bad for being happy about anything."

He wrapped his arms around me and pulled me tight to his warm, muscular chest. "I understand."

A bit later, I was pulling on my slippers and Max was walking to the bathroom to take a shower.

"I'm going to the construction site today. I think you're right. A break will help." Despite everything I'd learned, I was beginning to think I would never solve this crime. I just hoped everything I'd told Corporal Fletcher would aid the investigation.

"I think that's good," Max said.

I grabbed my bathrobe from a chair. "Honey, you don't think Leighton Whitmore killed Philip?"

"I don't see how. Since they're moving, I haven't done any more checking into his background. If I were a betting guy, my money would be on Henry Adler."

Mine, too. And that was my biggest problem. I didn't want it to be Henry.

17

I woke on Tuesday feeling guilty that I'd spent all the previous day at the construction job site trailer, figuring out how I was going to set up my new office. I spent the morning going over my clues between catching up on bookkeeping for Max and pacing my kitchen. The break hadn't helped my investigation at all. I was no closer to figuring out who killed Philip than I had been two days previous. I was panicked that Abbie would end up in jail.

With my mind still turning, I dropped Chris off at Gladys's; then Sammie and I were headed to the Whitmores' to pick up her kitten.

I'd asked Max if he thought we'd be safe going there, and he'd said yes. Then Angelica had called me at the last minute to say we needed to get there thirty minutes earlier than planned. Leighton had come home early and wanted to take Hayley out to dinner.

That meant Sammie hadn't had a snack. She was complaining that she was hungry, so I decided to make a pit stop at the Gas 'n' Go. I was once again in an inner struggle, salivating for a Mountain Dew. I vowed to break my habit—but not today. Inside the store, I overheard three teens in line ahead of me order hot dogs. That sounded so good that I ordered hot dogs for me and Sammie.

While we waited for Pat, the clerk, to fix them, I got my Mountain Dew and some juice for Sammie, then we went to the rack of chips. I waited for her to pick out the one she wanted. Through the front window of the store, I saw Clark pull his blue WWPS truck into a space next to my SUV.

Sammie tugged on my arm. "Mommy, I want these."

I glanced down at the bag of Doritos she held. "Okay, that's fine." I grabbed one for myself. Then it occurred to me that I was giving in to the power of suggestion an awful lot lately. First Mountain Dew, then hot dogs, and now chips.

Our food was ready by the time we got back to the counter. The teens had already paid for theirs and were headed out the door. A rack holding the latest weekly edition of our local paper was next to the counter. The headline was Philip's death. It was now officially a murder investigation, surprise, surprise. Abbie's picture was featured in the article, next to a picture of Philip. I felt sick and glanced away to calm myself. Clark was on the sidewalk, holding a box and talking to the kids.

"He's really built, isn't he?" Pat said as she rang up my order.

I swiveled my head to look at her. "What?"

"That WWPS delivery guy." She grinned like a wolf. "This is my daily eye candy break. He comes in every day at this time to get a drink and a snack."

"Oh." That was one way to put it. But I couldn't have cared less about Clark. Like a magnet, my attention was drawn back to the article. I finally picked up the paper and put it on the counter. "Add this, please."

Pat shook her head. "Isn't that tragic? Seems they're about to arrest that guy's ex-wife. And her being an author and all."

Whatever being an author had to do with anything.

Pat leaned toward me and pointed at Philip's picture in the paper. "You know this Philip guy? He was in here. With her." Pat jabbed at Abbie's picture. "Cops asked me about that. Fact, he and Eye Candy talked once, too."

Clark and Philip had talked? As she continued to chat, I paid for my purchases, took the bag, and handed the paper to Sammie to carry. Then I headed for the car.

The teens had left, and Clark was standing next to his truck. He seemed to be waiting for us. "I wanted to thank you for taking that autograph to my mother."

"She's very proud of you," I said. "Told me you were taking classes and helping kids at the Y."

"Charlie goes to the Y," Sammie said. "His friend's brother was arrested."

Clark glanced down at her then looked up at me.

"Sammie, honey, I don't think Mr. Clark cares about all of that." I smiled at him.

"Charlie is your son, right? I've heard your mother talking about him."

"Yes," I said. I wished my mother would zip her big mouth.

"And I'm getting a kitten today," Sammie informed him. "My grandma bought it for me. It's Siamese and lives in a big house right now."

Clark raised an eyebrow.

I glanced at my watch. "And we're going to be late if we don't get moving."

He smiled at me then told us both good-bye and went into the Gas 'n' Go. A cold breeze whipped my hair in my eyes, and for a moment, I couldn't see. I shoved it aside and dug in my purse for my keys.

As I unlocked the SUV, Sammie dropped the paper on the ground. It fell apart. Perhaps it was just as well. Reading it would just upset me.

"I'm sorry, Mommy." Sammie bent over to pick it up.

"It's okay." I put her food in the back where she could reach it.

The paper was a mess. She handed it to me section by section, and I stuffed it on the floor. After I buckled her into her seat, I shut the door and glanced into the store as I walked around to the driver's side door. Clark was standing at the counter, staring out the window at us. For some reason, he made me uneasy. I decided to review my clues when I got home. If Clark had had contact with Philip, maybe he was the killer. Once again, he moved to the top of my list. I just needed to figure out why.

Although Sammie had claimed hunger, she hardly touched her hot dog. When we arrived at the Whitmores', she undid her belt and exploded from the SUV. I followed behind her as quickly as possible. She pressed the doorbell and looked up at me with sparkling eyes.

"The kitty can sleep with me, right?"

"Sure," I said. I hadn't even thought about where the cat would sleep.

Leighton answered the door. "Hello, Trish. We were expecting you. Angelica is already here."

"Can I go on back, Mommy?" Sammie looked from me to Leighton. She was ready to burst. "I know the way."

Leighton nodded. "Certainly."

She scampered down the hall. We followed more slowly.

The family room was empty when we got there. Leighton paused. "I guess everybody's with the kittens. Come in and make yourself at home. I'm sure Hayley and Angelica will be back out in a minute."

He walked to one of the french doors and stared out over the pool and backyard. I felt awkward and realized it was because in my mind he was a suspect. Not that he could read my mind, but it was strange being in a room with someone about whom I'd had such bad thoughts.

I went to the mantel to look again at the picture of Hayley and Leighton at their wedding. The fountain *was* the same as the one in Linda's picture. So they'd been married in Atlanta. I didn't have time to think about it. I heard footsteps behind me and turned. Hayley walked through the kitchen and into the family room looking very upper-class suburban in nice slacks and a sweater set.

Leighton turned and their gazes met for a moment, then he stuck his hands in his pockets and returned to staring morosely at the pool.

Hayley looked at me. "Sammie and Angelica will be out in a minute. Sammie is just letting her kitten say good-bye to his siblings. She's sad that he has to leave his family."

That was so much like Sammie. Sometimes her sensitivity overwhelmed her.

The doorbell gonged.

"I'll go get that," Hayley said.

I turned back to the photo on the mantel, then my cell phone chirped, telling me I had a text message. I glanced at the screen. It was from Max. *Don't go to Whitmores'. I talked to Fletcher. Will explain when I can talk. And call my mother.* I squinted and read it again.

"You've figured it out, haven't you?"

I hadn't realized that Leighton had crossed the room and was standing behind me.

What had I figured out? And what was Max's message about? Had Leighton killed Philip? And had he seen my text message? I slapped my phone shut and slowly turned around. "I don't know what you mean." Not a lie. I really didn't know for sure.

"I thought we'd be safe here," he said. "Who would have thought that a drunken one-night dalliance with a stranger at a real estate convention would come back and bite me? Alcohol gives a person loose lips."

"Linda?" Her name slipped from my mouth before I could stop myself.

His head snapped toward me. "You *do* know. Your husband said you were sharp."

"I don't really know anything." I glanced at the phone in my hand. "Max is on his way." An outright lie, but it was all I could think of in the fear of the moment.

Leighton shrugged. "And if that wasn't bad enough, Philip Grenville figures out who I am. I have no idea how he did that. The company scammed his sister, not him. And him a cop. I should have moved us to Europe. Or Costa Rica."

Leighton had been part of the scam in which Mary had lost money? "Who are you?" I was trying to distract him so I could push buttons on my phone. I wished they didn't beep.

"A corporate real estate lawyer. A wanted man." He fisted his right hand and banged it into his left palm. "The people I worked for in Atlanta set up real estate deals and scammed people. They had connections, if you get my drift. When they hired me, I didn't know who they were. By the time I figured it all out, I was in too deep. They were scamming people right and left.

"They forced me to clean up the mess and point the finger at the hapless agents they'd set up to take the fall. Then they paid me to keep quiet and disappear." He paused and inhaled. "I was lucky they didn't just kill me and bury pieces of my body in some landfill."

"But what about Philip?" I asked.

"He saw me at the doctor's office one day and thought he recognized me. Only thing I could figure is he must have seen pictures of me from the investigation. He was a cop. He could have had access to that. He kept pursuing me, asking me questions. I knew if it got out, my old employers might kill me. And Hayley. I had to protect her. I married her after I changed my name, you know."

"You changed—" I was interrupted by something I saw out of the corner of my eye. I turned. So did Leighton.

"Leighton. . .honey?" Hayley had come into the room, followed closely by Clark Matthews.

Leighton frowned, then he gasped when he saw what I saw.

Clark had a gun pointed at Hayley's head.

W hat—who. . ." Leighton looked as astonished as I felt.

"Your friendly neighborhood WWPS man at your service." Clark's usual model smile had been replaced by a sneer.

Leighton took a step toward Clark. "Put your gun away and let my wife go."

"Don't move again, Mr. Leighton Whitmore," Clark said. "Of course, that's not your real name, is it?"

I began wildly pushing buttons on my cell.

"Drop that phone," Clark said to me, then jabbed the gun into Hayley's head.

I dropped it on the floor. I had one thought: Keep Sammie safe.

Leighton took a step toward Clark and Hayley.

Angelica walked into the kitchen, holding Sammie's coat in one hand and a plastic bag in the other. I heard Clark swear.

"Patricia, Samantha has been collecting things again." She finally noticed Clark. "What is going on?"

"I wondered where that bag went. Might have known the kid picked it up." Clark kept his gun pointed at Hayley's head. "Trish and Leighton, go sit on the couch."

He watched us as we obeyed. My mind was frozen. All I could think about was Sammie. What if she walked into the room?

Leighton began to clench and unclench his hands. That brought me out of my stupor. Who was the worst bad guy here? The man next to me on the couch? Or Mr. Model Perfect, Clark? Obviously Clark had a gun, but why? And who had killed Philip?

I noticed a shadow slip into the room behind Clark. Mr. Chang Lee had finally made an appearance.

Clark paid no mind to the feline. He pointed at Angelica. "Bring me what you have in your hand."

Angelica just stood there, her mouth hanging open.

"Lady!" Clark yelled. "Do what I say, or I'm going to kill her." He shoved the gun hard into Hayley's head, and Hayley whimpered.

Leighton jumped up from the sofa, hopping across the coffee table. In one fast blur, Clark aimed his gun. The deafening shot echoed through the room. Leighton dropped to the floor next to the fireplace. A red spot bloomed near his collar on his shirt.

442

"No!" Hayley screamed. She raced to his side, oblivious of Clark's gun. He didn't try to stop her.

"You." Clark pointed at Angelica. "Give me what's in your hand."

She tilted her chin in the air as she walked over to him. "Whatever do you want with a bag of Tootsie Rolls and little candies?"

Clark laughed and snatched the bag from her hand. "Little candies? Lady, you live in a fantasy world. Now go sit down next to Trish."

The couch shifted slightly as Angelica sat next to me. "Where's Sammie?" I whispered.

"Where's the kid?" Clark asked at the same time.

I felt the couch shift as Angelica glanced at the doorway to the laundry room.

Clark's sharp gaze followed hers. He smiled. "We'll take care of her in a minute."

Fear made my chest burn.

"I told her to stay with the cats for a couple of minutes while I talked to you," Angelica whispered.

"Shut up!" Clark waved the gun at us.

I begged God to keep Sammie in the laundry room. I'd lost sight of Mr. Lee, but I heard his familiar yowl.

Clark swore. "What was that?"

"Mr. Chang Lee," I said.

"Who?"

Mr. Lee strolled into the middle of the room from behind a chair, yowled again, and sat hard on his haunches, staring at Clark.

"Oh, a cat." Clark dismissed Mr. Lee with three words.

I was pretty sure he had no idea what Mr. Lee was capable of. Well, truth be told, *I* had no idea what Mr. Lee was capable of, either.

Hayley was murmuring to Leighton. She'd taken off her sweater and pressed it against his wound. It looked to me like the bullet had gone through his shoulder, but I couldn't tell for sure.

Clark turned to me. "You ask way too many questions. I should have known when you offered to take that autograph thing to my mother."

I frowned. "You should have known what?"

"I should have known you'd figure it all out. Your mother always bragged on you. And idiot Linda, all panicked because you asked her about a button. I just couldn't believe you'd be that smart. Or stupid. . .depending on how you look at it now."

*That stupid.* If I'd been a little smarter, I might have figured things out by now. In fact, I might have known what was actually going on.

"So Linda helped you kill Philip?"

"Linda does anything I ask her to do," he said. "She's like a puppet. All I have to do is pull the strings."

Leighton hadn't killed Philip. Clark had. With Linda's help. Somehow. I thought of my earlier impression of Linda—that her eyes were like those of a stuffed animal. Maybe she really wasn't that bright.

"So what's in the bag?" I asked.

Clark glanced at the bag in his hand then stuffed it in his pocket. "Ecstasy. My bread and butter. And that cop was trying to catch me."

"But there are Tootsie Rolls in there," Angelica said.

Clark sneered at her. "The kids put the ecstasy in the Tootsie Rolls. This was for one of my customers."

Drugs. He sold drugs. I almost stopped breathing when I realized how easily Sammie could have ingested the ecstasy, thinking it was candy. I wanted to leap across the room and tear into Clark for endangering her life like that.

And that explained everything. Philip had somehow stumbled upon Clark's little business. As a narcotics cop, Philip would notice things like that. Ironically, his death had nothing to do with making amends and everything to do with his job. Like our dog, Buddy—Philip had died doing what he did best.

Now I just wanted to know how it all happened.

Angelica shifted on the couch next to me. I glanced at her. For the first time since I'd met her, I saw true fear etched across her nearly wrinkle-free brow. However, I also saw a glimpse of her haughty fury. I could relate, and it made me feel good. I reached for her hand and squeezed it. She squeezed back.

A cell phone rang in Clark's pocket. He pulled it out with his left hand and flipped it open. "Yeah, babe. Come on in. We've got some complications."

In the distance, I heard the front door open, followed by the tapping of heels coming down the wood-floored hallway.

Clark was looking around. "Where's the cat?"

I shrugged. Mr. Lee had dematerialized. The cat seemed to have almost supernatural powers to appear and reappear.

I wasn't at all surprised when Linda Faye King walked into the room. She glanced around with wide eyes. "What's going on here?"

Clark's gaze on her was disdainful, but she didn't seem to notice.

"Did you shoot someone else?" Linda asked.

Leighton groaned from the floor. "He's going to bleed to death," Hayley screamed, her eyes blazing with anger.

Clark shrugged. "He'll die no matter what. It doesn't matter."

Mr. Lee hopped up on the sofa behind me.

"I thought you said this would be easy. We'd get the money then just disappear." The pitch of Linda's voice rose. "You said no one else would have to die."

"Things happen," Clark said.

"Well, you've got the plane tickets, right?" Linda was beginning to hyperventilate. "We've got to get out of here. Let's just tie them up and leave. No one will find us."

Clark snorted. "You are naive, babe. You have been all along."

"You cannot possibly get away with this," Angelica said.

Clark smiled. "Of course I can. I have a flight out of the country tonight. Money courtesy of Mr. Idiot Real Estate Scammer there who paid Linda to keep quiet so he wouldn't have to tell his adored wifey who he really was." Clark motioned with his head at Leighton. "Too bad he's gonna shoot all of you, set a fire, and then shoot himself."

"I knew. He told me all about it. He told me last Friday." Hayley began crying and murmuring to Leighton that it was okay.

Mr. Lee rubbed his head against mine. Not a pleasant picture, any way I looked at it. Such irony. Dying with an attack cat on one side and my mother-in-law on the other.

"What should I do now?" Linda asked Clark. "I'm not going to touch another dead body. Never again. You said I wouldn't have to."

"You touched Philip?" I asked. "You helped kill him?"

Linda shrugged. "I hated him, so it wasn't *that* bad. I had to put a receipt in his pocket. I also left that book on the counter. Our original plans didn't work out, so we pointed the finger at Abbie Grenville. Easier to do than I thought it would be."

Original plans? "Did you move his car?"

Clark smiled. "Yeah, she did." He pointed at the couch. "Linda, go sit next to Trish."

She frowned. "What?"

He aimed the gun at her. "Go sit next to Trish."

"Wait. You mean. . ." Tears filled her eyes. "But I thought—"

"You thought I loved you?" Clark laughed. "Never. I was just using you. Just like you used other people. And just like Philip used you so long ago."

Talk about what goes around comes around.

Mr. Lee jumped off the back of the couch. I heard him hit the floor with a thud. Angelica shifted next to me and took a breath as if she was going to speak. I elbowed her in the ribs to keep her quiet.

While Clark's attention was on Linda, I was trying to figure out how we could escape. The magazines on the table were thick and heavy. We could throw some, but it was risky. He might shoot one of us. The decoration book and the glass vase looked like better alternatives, but I had to have the right opportunity.

"Book," I whispered to Angelica.

Her face squished into a frown that reminded me of Charlie. I'd never noticed before the resemblance between the two. I'd never taken the time.

Linda was sobbing quietly next to me. I ignored her. She didn't deserve any sympathy. I wished I could help Hayley, who was crying over Leighton. He was bleeding profusely.

Mr. Lee appeared by my feet and butted his head against my ankles.

"I did everything for you," Linda whined at Clark. "I gave you most of the money Leighton paid me. I can't believe you're doing this. I planned it all out for you."

I turned to face her. "You planned Philip's murder?"

Clark snorted. "Hardly. That would take brains."

She pouted. Definitely lacking in the brains department. "Well, I helped." She seemed proud, and that made me want to rip out her hair by the roots. "Clark and I needed to get rid of him, because he knew about the drugs. I pretended to be nice to Philip, and then I made sure he knew Abbie would be at the church hall. See, he was all hot to make all these amends to people, including me. And he was desperate to get to Abbie alone. I'd overheard her tell your mother she'd be at the fellowship hall early that afternoon."

"I'm tired of your voice, Linda," Clark said. He was looking around the room. I imagined he was trying to figure out how best to kill us all.

She glared at him. "Well, it doesn't matter, does it?" She turned to me again like she was possessed with the need to tell me everything. "At first we were going to kill them both. I was going to lure Philip and Abbie to the back of the church. Clark was going to shoot Philip. Then we would shoot Abbie with a handgun and put her in the woods. Make it look like she shot Philip then shot herself. But then she left early in a snit. She almost ruined everything. We had to rethink fast. Killing him and making it look like Abbie had done it was *my* idea. The receipt. The book. All of it. I lured him to the back of the fellowship hall so Clark could shoot him. He had his rifle and a pistol in his truck."

She sounded so proud. I wanted to slap her. "You didn't stop to think maybe he'd already told someone else about the drugs?" I asked.

Clark and Linda both frowned. Neither one of them was too bright.

"He had no proof. And I'm tired of the talking." Clark waved the gun. "Everyone shut up."

Mr. Lee was still rubbing my ankle, but his tail was switching against Linda's leg. She kicked at him. He growled. I didn't know that cats could growl.

"Call your daughter out here," Clark ordered.

"You're no better than Philip was," Linda said, still crying. "Philip promised to leave his wife for me, but he never did. You're a traitor, too."

She kicked Mr. Lee again. His tail twitched, and he hissed and puffed up.

Clark strode over to the couch and slapped Linda. She gasped and pulled back, holding her mouth.

He pointed the gun at her head. "You're going first."

Clark took another step forward and stepped on Mr. Lee's tail. The cat yowled—the loudest I'd ever heard. I met Hayley's gaze, and one side of her mouth lifted. That's when I knew we were going to get a miracle. Mr. Lee grabbed Clark's leg with his paws and sank his front teeth into Clark's calf.

The man yelled, sounding amazingly like the cat. His gun arm flew up, and a bullet discharged into the ceiling. In one quick movement, I grabbed the vase and slammed it against his temple. As Mr. Lee bounded from the room, Clark dropped to the floor and rolled to his stomach. He was out.

"Oh, hurry," Hayley moaned. "Leighton is still bleeding, and I can't stop it, but he's alive."

I leaped from behind the table. Linda, who had been frozen in place, suddenly came alive. She jumped up and pushed me. I stumbled over the coffee table, falling against Angelica. Suddenly I was in a race for the gun. Linda won, snatching it from the floor. Then she pointed it at me.

"No way. I can't let you get away. I'm going to finish this here and now."

Linda was not the criminal that Clark was. She didn't have the same kind of nerve. The gun in her hand was shaking, and she eyed me and Angelica nervously.

"Oh, for heaven's sake, not again," Angelica said behind me. "Will these people never stop?" I agreed with her sentiments exactly.

"Shut up," Linda said.

"Mommy?"

Angelica inhaled, breath hissing through her teeth. My stomach clenched. I felt Angelica's hand on my arm.

"Go back to the laundry room, Sammie," I said, keeping my eye on the gun in Linda's hand. It was still pointed in my direction.

"No," Linda said, gun wobbling in her hand.

"But, Mommy, the lady has a gun. It's like something Charlie—"

"Go now!" I yelled.

"Don't go." Since the gun in Linda's hand still pointed at me, I knew she wouldn't shoot Sammie, but I was poised to launch myself between my daughter and a gunshot.

I heard Sammie's feet patter down the hallway.

Linda's eyes wavered between me and the hall where Sammie had disappeared. "Call her back out here."

I said nothing. I wouldn't. I would never call Sammie back into the room without a fight. I hadn't given up hope that we would find a way out of this.

Clark groaned. Linda's eyes widened with fear. If he woke up, we were all in trouble. I exchanged glances with Angelica, and she narrowed her eyes and gave me a slight smile. That's when I knew our second miracle was coming.

She gasped suddenly and pointed at the doorway behind Linda. "Oh no—

watch out! Here comes that cat! He's vicious."

The cat wasn't even in sight, but the distraction was exactly what we needed. Linda turned, long enough for me to grab a magazine, lunge at her, and slap her hand away from us. The gun clattered to the floor.

Angelica hopped to her feet, snatched up the decorating book, and walloped Linda across the head with it. That stunned her and allowed me to push her into a chair and grab the gun.

Hayley reached over and snatched my cell phone from the floor where I'd dropped it. "I'm calling 911."

"Good," I said. I stared at my mother-in-law with amazement. "Wow. Way to go, Angelica." I had never been prouder of anyone in my life.

For the first time since I'd met her, we shared grins. I hadn't known she *could* grin.

"The curtain ties will do well to contain those two, don't you think?" she asked as she glided over to the windows.

"Yes, I believe they will."

Hayley's voice was hysterical on the phone. Linda was crying and babbling as we tied her up. She didn't fight us. She was a wimp. Too bad. I was ready to take someone on.

Clark, on the other hand, was not a wimp. And he probably lifted weights to keep his model shape. He began to come to as Angelica finished wrapping maroon ties around his wrists. As soon as he figured out what was going on, he swore and tried to get up on his knees. I used my foot to shove him off balance, then I sat hard on his legs while Angelica tied his feet. When she was done, I bounced for good measure, making Clark groan. Not hard for me to do. I kept thinking what would have happened if Sammie had eaten some of the ecstasy. I was furious.

"Please go take care of Sammie," I said to Angelica.

But she didn't have to. Sammie walked into the room holding a phone.

"I called the police," she said proudly. "They're here."

I heard banging at the front door. Then I heard a voice I thought I'd never be glad to hear.

"State police!" Detective Reid bellowed down the hall. "Put your weapons down."

## 19

Later that evening, I was perched on a chair in my mother's kitchen holding Sammie, who cuddled her kitten in her lap. Abbie was sitting across the table from me. She still had circles under her eyes, but the tension that had lined her face for days was gone. Ma had just hung up the phone and dropped into a chair at the end of the table. Eric and Daddy leaned against the counter. A little black-and-white border collie puppy scampered on the floor between their legs.

"Well, Trish, you helped nail a killer," Ma said, glancing at Eric.

He winked at me.

"Did you know that Nick Fletcher and I were working together?" I asked him.

He nodded. "I did. And I have to say, I was relieved. He was feeding information to someone at the state police. They were already closing in on Clark. And Leighton."

"So Detective Reid isn't all bad?" I asked the question reluctantly.

Eric shook his head. "Personality challenged and stubborn. Perhaps too eager at first to believe that Abbie did it. But she did look into the other information when she got the information. I can't fault her for that."

"So the cops were already on to Clark, weren't they?" I asked. "He was an idiot to think he could get away."

He nodded. "Clark would have been arrested shortly."

I bit my lip as I thought. "Do you think that's what Philip was calling you about the day he was murdered? Had he learned what Clark was doing?"

"I think so," Eric said. "I think he had suspicions, anyway."

"I think Clark is a sociopath," I said. "And he certainly had his mother fooled." I rummaged through my purse and pulled out my steno pad and a pen. "I've dubbed him the Kitty Litter Killer for the litter next to Philip's body."

I wrote "Kitty Litter Killer" across the cardboard front of the notebook and stared at it. This would be my last mystery. No more.

I glanced across the table and met Abbie's gaze. My best friend.

"So what about the kitty litter?" Abbie asked. "How did it get next to Philip's body?"

"From Clark's shoes, right?" I glanced at Eric.

"That's what Detective Reid thinks," he said.

"When the police roared into the Whitmores', Linda started babbling. One of the things she said was that Clark used the containers or packages of things he was delivering to hide drugs sometimes. Twice he used bags of kitty litter destined for the Adlers' store. One of those times was right before he killed Philip.

"They happened to be at the Gas 'n' Go at the same time. Clark panicked and shoved his handgun into a bag of litter. The litter fell all over the truck, and he stepped in it." I looked at Abbie. "That was the gun they were going to use to make it look like you killed yourself after you shot Philip."

"Well, all's well that ends well," Ma said, patting Abbie's hand.

Abbie smiled at me, and for the first time in almost a week, her eyes smiled, too. "Thank you. You've saved my wedding day."

"It wasn't all me," I said.

We touched index fingers.

Sammie wiggled in my lap.

"I'm so proud of you, honey," I whispered in her ear.

"I did what Charlie would have done," she said. "Mommy, you're squeezing me too tight—I can hardly breathe. Can I go watch TV?"

"Sure." I didn't want to let her go, but I did.

"I thought for sure Henry had done it," Ma said. "Their granddaughter is Philip's daughter, right?"

Eric nodded. "And Henry gave Philip the black eye at the store that Sunday afternoon. Philip wanted to see his daughter. Peggy, the Adlers' daughter, was seventeen when Philip got her pregnant. The Adlers agreed not to report him to the authorities if he signed an agreement giving away his parental rights. That was the deal. Henry was furious when Philip came back. But he wanted to see his daughter before he died."

"It's like a soap opera," Ma said.

Daddy nodded. "That's the truth."

"Well, there might be a happy ending," Abbie said. "The Adlers have contacted June. They're still having trouble with this, but they have promised that at some point, June will meet her granddaughter. June says she's going to be patient."

"Are you okay about it all?" I asked her.

Abbie and Eric exchanged a glance, then she looked at me. "It's hard. Especially when I look back and realize how all the choices I made keep reverberating through the years." She smiled, but her expression held an edge of sadness. "It will take me awhile to take it all in, I think, but I get to start over." Suddenly she grinned. "And I have a fine man to start over with."

She stood and walked over to Eric. He wrapped his arm around her shoulders.

Max strolled into the room and kissed my forehead.

"Chris is finally asleep."

"Good."

"Honey, I'm sorry," he said. "I should have paid attention to your suspicions about Leighton. This afternoon never would have happened. You wouldn't have even been there to confront Clark. Nick Fletcher called me to ask a few more questions about what I knew about Leighton Whitmore. He explained why he was asking. That's why I warned you not to go over there. And when I realized you and Mom and Sammie were already at the Whitmores', I called Nick back. They were already on their way over there when Sammie called them."

I grasped his hand, and he pulled me to my feet. "Well, if it hadn't worked out the way it did, we might never have known exactly what Clark and Linda had planned. That they were going to kill Leighton and Hayley then burn down the house. Make it look like a murder-suicide. As if Leighton just got tired of running from his past."

"I certainly hope Whitmore is going to jail," Ma said.

Eric shook his head. "I'm not sure. He may testify against his former employers and then go into witness protection."

I heard the sound of the back door opening. Angelica and Andrew walked in from the mudroom. I'd never been so surprised to see anyone in my life.

Ma, bless her heart, hurried across the room and greeted them as if they dropped by every day.

"Did you know they were coming?" I asked Max.

He nodded, and humor sparkled in his eyes.

After Angelica said hello to my mother, she crossed the room and pulled me into a hug. The hush that fell over the kitchen told me everyone else was as shocked as I was. If she hadn't had her arms around me, I would have fallen to the floor.

She stepped back, hands still on my arms. "You made me so proud today."

"Thank you," I said.

Apparently no one expected this from her, me included. I was at a loss for words.

Daddy cleared his throat. "Hey, how about the whole story. I wanna know what happened."

Angelica and I took turns telling everyone about the chilling scene at the Whitmores'.

"So how did Linda get the money to run away with Clark?" my mother asked.

"She recognized Leighton when he moved here and approached him," I said. "She'd met him at a real estate convention in Atlanta and had a one-night fling. In his drunken state, he told her things he didn't even remember telling her." I paused. "She's someone who takes advantage of a situation when it arises."

"Gail was right, you know," Ma said. "I'll never forgive myself."

I smiled at her then continued my story. "Linda started dating Clark. And after Philip caught on to Clark's dealings, she told Clark she had a way to get money to help them move to a safe place. Being what he was, he decided to take her up on that. Leighton was frightened of his former employers and wanted to protect Hayley. He offered Linda a million dollars to leave him alone."

"What about Leighton and Philip?" Ma asked.

I glanced at Eric.

"I can only speculate at this point," he said. He explained about Mary losing money in a real estate deal. "I think Philip figured out who Leighton was and wanted to talk to him. That scared Leighton, which was why he began making plans to move."

"He had me and Angelica snowed," Max's father said. "His resumé was faked. The folks he had worked for were organized. They knew if Leighton went to jail that he'd blow the whistle on the organization, so they arranged to protect him and give him a new identity. He thought they'd be safe in a small town like this. Hayley had no idea."

"She's the one I feel sorriest for." I glanced at Angelica. "She did nothing wrong except love her husband."

"It's all about choices," Abbie said.

The back door opened again. Gail walked into the kitchen.

"My lands. Looks like a used-car lot out there." Ma's longtime employee smiled, looking like the Gail I used to know. She rubbed her hands together to warm them. She stared at me then at Eric. "You should hire Trish, you know. You need her to help you solve crimes and keep this town safe." She glanced at Ma and they nodded.

"I agree," Ma said.

I smiled. The town was safe once again. Gossip central was back in business. Ma and Gail were friends again.

"Well, we hope Tommy inherited Trish's good sense by osmosis," Angelica said. "If he handles a law enforcement job the way she handled the situation today, he'll do fine."

I glanced at her to make sure she wasn't being sarcastic. She was smiling at me—really smiling. The Lord had used a bad situation to bring about a miracle. I was sure things wouldn't be perfect, but we had a good start. And a chance at a real relationship.

# Epilogue

I stood at the front of the church in my green dress, holding a bouquet of ivy, a red rose, and a white rose with red tints. Abbie said they were like me and her. I was the red rose. All heat and outright emotion. She was the white rose with hidden passions.

White Christmas lights, ivy, and evergreen adorned the pews and the platforms.

I glanced over the crowd of people, recognizing so many faces, thankful they had come out to help two special people celebrate their second chance at love. My mother clutched a tissue. On her right side sat Gail. On her left, Sammie and Charlie sat remarkably still. I smiled when I realized I no longer had to worry that Sammie might slip items in her pockets during the reception. She'd stopped doing that as soon as she brought the kitten home.

Max sat next to Charlie. I caught his eye. He smiled, a slow and very personal smile. I felt it down to my toes.

Eric stood tall and handsome in a black tux. Next to him stood Nick Fletcher and Tommy.

The sanctuary doors opened. Sherry walked down the aisle, and the handkerchief hem of her green dress whirled around her ankles. She held a bouquet of ivy and three roses that represented her new family—Eric, Abbie, and Sherry.

When Sherry reached the front of the church, she handed me her bouquet then walked over to Eric and gave him a big hug and kiss—the unrehearsed, impulsive moment perfect. He pulled her tight and whispered something in her ear. Then she walked over to join me with a smile.

The music stopped. We waited for my very best friend to come through the doors on the arm of my father. I slid my gaze to Eric watching the door at the back of the church with a boyish eagerness that belied his age. Nick met my gaze and winked.

When the "Wedding March" began, Abbie appeared in her silky ivory dress with rich lace on the sleeves. Slowly she made her way down the aisle on my grinning father's arm.

When Abbie reached the front, Daddy placed her hand in Eric's. Abbie looked over at me and extended her index finger. I returned the gesture as a precious reminder of a friendship that would never end.

As Eric and Abbie turned to the pastor, I remembered a sermon I'd heard once about heaven. Only people enter into eternity, not possessions or money. I was glad Philip had learned that before he died.

Love was all about choices. I wished Linda had understood that before she hooked up with Clark. True love isn't demanding or grasping. True love is unselfish and gives. A healthy love—God's love—always hopes for the best, and it sometimes means sacrificing for another.

And that's what we were celebrating today with Abbie and Eric. True love that stands the test of time and lasts forever.

Candice Speare lives in Maryland with Winston the African Gray Parrot and Jack Pup the dog. Please visit her Web site at www.candicemillerspeare.com.

# ALIBIS IN ARKANSAS

THREE ROMANCE MYSTERIES

CHRISTINE LYNXWILER
JAN REYNOLDS
SANDY GASKIN

Two sisters find mystery and love in small-town Arkansas. No matter where southern sisters Jenna and Carly go, murder turns up like a bad penny. When the local newspaper editor is killed and Carly's son is a suspect, Jenna decides to go undercover to get the scoop on the murder. A vacation in Branson, Missouri, sounds like fun, but Jenna and Carly are surprised to find that the glittering lights and twanging tunes make a perfect backdrop for. . .murder! Back home in Lakeview, Carly's new diner is really cooking. But last time she looked, murder was not on the menu.

ISBN 978-1-60260-229-8
$7.97

# COZY IN KANSAS

## THREE ROMANCE MYSTERIES

### NANCY MEHL

Mystery, love, and inspiration in a small town bookstore. College student Ivy Towers has definite plans for her future. But when her great-aunt Betty is found dead inside her rare bookstore, Ivy must travel back to a place and a past she thought she'd left behind. She discovers that Betty's supposed fall from her library ladder seems quite suspicious. Ivy's decision to poke her nose into things changes her destiny and propels her into uncovering carefully hidden secrets buried deep below the surface in the small town of Winter Break, Kansas. Along the way, she will discover that love can be found where you least expect it—and in the most mysterious of circumstances.

ISBN 978-1-60260-228-1
$7.97

Available wherever books are sold.